Dark Times

Michael Gerhartz

"This is a fantastic book, really well written with some great characters in it. It is properly paced, with plenty of action and suspense that leave you guessing right to the very end. There's a whole range of emotions in this story and you will struggle to put it down. Highly recommended for fans of thrillers or those who just want a really good story to lose themselves in." Reader's Favorite

"This is certainly a well-constructed novel with a brilliantly executed plot. I honestly didn't want to put it down. If you enjoy watching plots and schemes unravel in a character and event-driven plot filled with dark happenings, mystery, and danger, then you will love this." K.J.Simmil, British bestseller author

"The writing style of the author is truly riveting and deserves the fame it got internationally. Dark Times makes you root for the characters, enjoy the plot, live in a world created by Gerhartz and make you curl your toes. It's the kind of book that you literally want to read in a sitting. This gritty, fast-paced, intelligent thriller is worth every single moment." Blue Book Review

"What I liked about the book was the fact that I couldn't predict what was coming next; I found this very refreshing. If you like an action-packed story to really get your teeth into, Dark Times is the one for you." Reader's Favorite

Books in this series by Michael Gerhartz

Thin Ice
Dark Times

Dark Times

Special thanks to my friend
Sandra for her eyes
and, most importantly,
to Laurén Hardy for all her work and support.

The following story is a work of fiction. All characters, organisations and events portrayed in this novel are either products of the author's imagination or are used fictitiously.

Cast of principal characters

Nick Rehfeld (EuroSec Corporation Team A)
Natascha Rehfeld (marine biologist and secretary at EuroSec Corporation)

EuroSec Corporation
Retired Admiral Brian Whittaker (former British Navy)
Retired General Klaus Schwartze (former German Bundeswehr)

Operation Control and team leaders EuroSec Corporation
Ariel Rashid (Member of Operation Control and team leader EuroSec Corporation)
Sean MacLeod (former Scotland Yard Inspector)
Jack MacDonald (former British SAS team leader)
Gunnar Eriksson (former instructor of the Norwegian Navy Special Operations Commando)

EuroSec Corporation Team A
Shira Hadad (EuroSec Corporation Team A)
Olaf Magnusson (former Norwegian Navy Special Operations Commando)
Ole-Einar Alsgaard (former Norwegian Navy Special Operations Commando)
Rolf Brengmann (former German Kampfschwimmer)

American Business Tycoons
Victor Gates (American patient on board the *Asklepios*)
Walter Leroy "L.J." Jackson (American oil tycoon)
Samantha Elisabeth Jackson ("L.J." Jackson's wife)

British Business Tycoons
Sir Samuel Archibald Cunningham (British aristocrat and business tycoon)
Rowan Dean Harrison (heir of British business empire)
Victor Dalton (head of Cunningham's security, former SAS)
Robert Black (Cunningham's security, former S014 Royalty Protection Group)
Wayne Shea (Cunningham's security, former S014 Royalty Protection Group)
Paul Ferguson (Cunningham's security, former S014 Royalty Protection Group)

Asklepios
Dr Sheridan Evans
Dr William Edwards
Lamar Hatcher (male nurse)
Kevin Wilson (male nurse)
Leo Swan (male nurse)
Melissa O'Brian (nurse)
Kurt Morrison (guard)

Whitmore Abbey
Abbot Augustinus Hetley
Prior Clemens Finnigan

Friends of Natascha Rehfeld
Erika (scientific diver)
Andreas (scientific diver)
Mario (scientific diver)
Mark (forensic scientist)
Nicole (forensic scientist)

Supporting characters
Cathy Sheppard
Gordon Ferguson
Jean-Pierre (Canadian scientist)
Kyle McRae (Reporter)
Adriana Gabor (*A-14*)
Lawrence Whittaker (brother of retired Admiral Brian Whittaker)
Charles MacLean (friend of Lawrence Whittaker)
George Davis (Barber)
Alba "Saphir" Casillas (independent escort)
Elena Romanov (Romanian woman)
Monique (French woman)
Freja (Swedish student)
Dragan Jankovic (Slovenian border patrol)
David (teenager at Whitmore Abbey)
Peggy (teenager at Whitmore Abbey)
Iain Walker (Hollywood movie star and owner of *Cloud Dancer*)
General Rashid (Israeli Mossad)
Chief Inspector William Conolly (Scotland Yard)
Giulio Cardinal Baldacci (President of Governatorate of Vatican City)
Jake (patient on *Asklepios)*
Amber (young Western European woman)
Colonel George Harris (Regimental Head Quarters Royal Engineers)
Colonel Edward Thompson (Regimental Head Quarters SAS)
Gregor Powell (Intelligence Manager MI5)

EuroSec Corporation Team B
Noah Cohen (former Israeli military)
Tamar Peretz (former Israeli military)

EuroSec Corporation Team C
Talia Levi (former Israeli military)
Maya Azulay (former Israeli military)

British SAS unit
Captain Callum Finlay (British SAS)
Major Alastair Brooks (British SAS)
Sergeant Fergus MacRory (British SAS)

British MERT (Medical Emergency Response Team)
Major William McCoy
Captain Kent Wallace

***HMS Montrose*, British Duke class frigate**
Dr Crawford
Dr Pitt
Commander Hardy

Syrian Fanatics
Moonif Nasser (Elder)
Nizar Algafari
Sami Alnasseri
Tarek Homsi
M,shakour Ahmadi

Shadow of the Orient
Prince Tarek bin Mohammed (Arabian playboy and owner of the *Shadow of the Orient*)
Djamal (captain of the *Shadow of the Orient*)
Hilal (first mate of the *Shadow of the Orient*)
Nabil (crew member of the *Shadow of the Orient*)
Sameh (crew member of the *Shadow of the Orient*)
Kamal (crew member of the *Shadow of the Orient*)
Hamit (crew member of the *Shadow of the Orient*)
Alim (crew member of the *Shadow of the Orient*)

Prologue

Whitmore Abbey, Western England, Great Britain, April 1942

It was just past midnight when seventeen-year-old Gordon and Cathy ran through the cold night as fast as they could. Although not obscured by any clouds, the shine of the moon provided little light, but it did not matter to Gordon. He firmly locked his hand around Cathy's as he led them along the outside walls of Whitmore Abbey.

He could feel her hand tremble under his grasp, their desperation gliding their steps through the dimly lit trail they followed. They had waited for their chance, Gordon using the time to memorise the route to each detail. The opportunity seemed like it would never arise, but tonight they finally got their chance.

The young couple instinctively ducked as the German fighter bombers flew overhead to raid the nearby mine. The first bombs hit close by, and Gordon's head snapped back quickly as the abbey began ringing the bells in alert. The two young orphan teenagers knew that this distraction would allow them to sneak out of the abbey unseen, for whatever future may lay ahead of them.

Reaching one of the corners of the wall, Gordon and Cathy pressed themselves against the stones just as another grenade exploded with a thunderous roar in the distance. They could hear the fighter planes up in the sky, but their attack was not matched by any anti-aircraft defences. Gordon remembered that it would take the Royal Air Force at least ten to fifteen minutes before they could pursue the intruders.

Gasping for air, Gordon looked back the way they had come. The teenager's eyes scanned the wall as far as the darkness would allow, but he did not see any signs that they were followed. Somewhat relieved, he looked at his panting girlfriend. Cathy had her eyes closed and struggled to catch her breath.

"How are you doing?" Gordon whispered as another detonation ripped through the night.

"I'm okay", Cathy gasped, her hand bracing her belly. "I just need another minute."

Gordon placed his hand next to hers, and for the first time that night they both smiled at each other. Cathy was carrying their child, and, being four months pregnant, it would be impossible to hide her condition any longer from the monks and sisters in the abbey. Having spent most of their life behind those walls, they knew that they would never have a chance to be a family and care for their child.

With another bomb hitting close to the mine, Gordon focussed on the next section of the trail. He was suddenly unable to hide his concern as he squeezed Cathy's hand for reassurance. They would have to cross a couple of hundred yards of open field before they would reach the safety of the old forest. He knew that the darkness of the night would hide them from being seen, but he never considered the greater threat.

Gordon and Cathy instinctively ducked as another bomb detonated in the field, sending a shower of shrapnel in the air the moment it hit the ground. Gordon glanced back to Cathy. She swallowed hard, then offered a weak smile. Gordon decided that it would be better to stay closer to the mine's old abandoned maintenance sheds. It would mean a slightly longer route, but they could take cover behind the wooden structures if they had to. Gordon knew the miners no longer used those buildings, and he took comfort that they would be of little interest to the German fighter pilots. He surveyed the area to plan another route quickly, and his jaw tightened when he reached the resolve. This was the only way. He waited until the next bomb detonated with a deafening sound before he took Cathy's hand again.

"Okay, let's go", *he said, and they both sprinted into the open field.*

Inside the nearby mine was chaos. The war had created a high demand for the precious resource, and the men worked around the clock to meet the orders. They knew that their mine was a strategic target, and they all feared nights like this. The moment they heard the detonation of the first grenade, they rang the alarm bells. They tried to get above ground as fast as they could. With the carriages overfilled, some older miners hung on to them, while many of the younger workers sprinted for the exit.

The miners knew the first wave of attack from the German fighter pilots was to dial in on their target. While the first wave of grenades hit the surrounding area without causing too much damage to the mine entrance, they knew the second wave of attack would be more precise. Praying to whatever power they believed in, and hoping to see their families again, the men dashed to the open field.

The last of the men were just a few hundred yards away, when another series of loud detonations shook the whole mine. With a loud thunder, the cribwork in front of them collapsed, sealing their small group inside the mountain. The miners slowly got back on their feet, holding up their lanterns.

"What a bloody mess", *one miner moaned and looked at the survivors. Nobody seemed to be seriously wounded. Although muffled by the caved-in mine, they could hear that all the detonations of the third and final wave of attack were in the immediate area.*

Unaware of what had happened inside the mine, Gordon and Cathy ran through the open field. Gordon knew they would soon come upon the remaining structure of an old well. Just seconds later he could see the silhouette of its old stones rising from the ground. With desperate energy, Gordon tugged Cathy behind the old well, as the third wave of attack sent another shower of shrapnel around them. Cathy pressed herself against her boyfriend, her whole body shivering in fear.

Gordon peeked over the little wall to determine the safest route to the nearby forest. For a brief moment he even glimpsed inside the well. He knew that this well was fed from the same underground river as the wells inside the abbey. One was in the gardens and the other deep inside the catacombs. Gordon and his friends had discovered it during one of their night time strolls inside the abbey. He could still feel the pain of the severe punishment that had led to. Back then he had wondered if they could have used the wells to escape, but it proved to be impossible.

Another loud detonation ripped him out of his thoughts, and Gordon quickly looked around before he checked on Cathy.

"How are you doing, love?" *he asked with concern in his voice.*

"I'm good, let's do this!" *she replied courageously, peeking over the well.*

Gordon nodded and they both started running again. They were about two hundred yards away when they heard the whistling sound of a dropping bomb.

"Over there!" *Gordon yelled as he pulled Cathy towards one of the old derelict maintenance sheds. Cathy crouched to the ground, and Gordon covered her with his thin frame as best as he could. With a deafening roar the bomb hit the same well they had just been hiding behind barely a minute ago. The impact of the detonation propelled most of the old stones up in the sky before they rained down again. The teenagers flinched as some of them hit the little shed they were hiding behind. Its old wooden walls and rotten roof crumbled under the force of the falling stones, sending a myriad of splinters through the air.*

A loud scream reverberated from deep within Gordon as a sharp pain rose from his leg. Like a fire, the pain burned up through his hips as he rolled on to his back in agony. He cradled his leg and fought against the tears that stung his eyes as a wave of nausea overcame him.

"Oh my God! Let me see!" *Cathy yelled at him as he writhed under the torturous pain. Looking at Gordon's leg she realised that he had caught the shrapnel that would have otherwise wounded her.*

"Let me look at it", *the young woman demanded again as her boyfriend twisted in agony. Cathy saw a large amount of blood already staining Gordon's pants. She pushed Gordon's shoulder back, forcing him to lie still long enough that she could look underneath his hands. The blood froze in her veins as she recognised a large piece of wood sticking out of Gordon's thigh. Her hands shook with helplessness, she knew there was nothing she could do except leave it there.*

"How bad is it?" *Gordon moaned.*

"I...I don't know", *Cathy stammered as she frantically looked for something to use as a dressing, but with no success.* "You will be fine."

Cathy pressed her hands on Gordon's in her attempt to stop the bleeding. She motioned for Gordon to move, but the moment he did, the blood started to flow again. Almost ten minutes had passed since the shrapnel had showered around them. Cathy frightfully applied more pressure on his leg, fearing they were running out of time. They could hear one of the abbey's bells ringing, signalling that the air raid was over. Soon enough volunteers would swarm the area, looking for wounded and assisting those trapped inside the mine. The young couple knew that someone would discover them within minutes if they wouldn't move.

"Dammit!" *Cathy cursed after another failed attempt to move her boyfriend. Tears streamed down her face as Gordon placed his hand on Cathy's shoulder,*

"Go, Cathy! You have to run! I will find a way, but you have to run! I cannot make it today, but you can! I will come later, and I will find you, okay?"

"No!" *Cathy cried, shaking her head in protest.*

"Yes, you have to! Do it for us! Do it for our baby! Please!" *Gordon begged her. Cathy's voice caught in her throat as tears burned against her cheek. She knew that he was right. If they would catch her, there would be no chance for her and her baby to escape those walls again. Gordon would have a much better chance to flee once he was healed up again.*

Gordon and Cathy both looked to the abbey. They could see a small number of people with lanterns heading towards the mine, towards them.

"I love you, Cathy! I will find you! But please, run!" *Gordon whispered in a commanding tone that prohibited any further discussion. His thumb rubbed against her cheek. Gordon was uncertain when he would see her again.* "Promise me that you will *not* stop!"

Cathy kissed him passionately, her heart fluttering with fear. She looked deep into his eyes and nodded, her tears striking against her cheek. She kissed him one last time before she rose to her feet and ran towards the forest. Gordon's eyes trailed after her as she disappeared into the tree line. He stared blankly to the forest as the voices neared him.

"Over here! I found one", *one of the miners yelled, shining his light at Gordon.*

"Don't worry, mate, you'll be fine!" *the miner reassured as he opened a first aid kit and tended to the teenager's wound. Gordon groaned under the sharp pain as the miner continued.* "What were you doing out here during a raid? You must be mental! We'll get you to the abbey. They can take care of you."

Less than one hundred yards away, Cathy hid behind a large uprooted tree to catch her breath. She watched closely as three lanterns illuminated four men placing Gordon on a stretcher.

"Oh God, please don't", *her cracked voice stammered as she watched them carry him back to the abbey. Her heart beat erratically as she watched the gates of the abbey close behind them, confining Gordon behind the old stone walls again. Tears ran down her cheeks as her stomach heaved with fear and anguish. Gordon was locked behind walls that were built to keep evil out of the abbey for centuries, the same walls that had kept Cathy, Gordon, and dozens of other children from freedom.*

Cathy forcefully turned around and ran through the forest, determined to get as far away from the abbey as possible.

- 1 -

Present Day

London Aquarium, London, England, Monday, May 5
It was just before 8.00 a.m. when Natascha steered her Mini into the employees' parking lot at the London Aquarium. Like any other morning during the week, she had just dropped her daughter Shira-Sarah off at her playgroup, and the young German scientist had to promise to pick her up again in the afternoon. Just as Natascha parked her car, a smile spread across her lips from her reverie. Like clockwork, Shira-Sarah had asked again today why her parents' had named her with a traditional Hebrew name and an English name. Time and time again, Natascha explained that she liked that the Hebrew name *Shira* meant *poetry*. While most people were reasonably satisfied with that explanation, those who knew Nick and Natascha knew better.

Natascha cut the engine and decided to stay in the car to listen to one of her favourite songs playing on the radio. She absentmindedly stared at the dashboard as her thoughts instinctively drifted back to her living nightmare on board the research vessel *Northern Explorer*. Natascha was astounded that it had happened so long ago, yet the memories remained so vivid like it had happened yesterday. She could remember the smell of him, the American politician she had taken on a little sightseeing tour in a research submersible. She never dreamed it would escalate to a life-threatening situation. To cover up their heinous criminal activities, the Americans had framed Natascha and her friends with a crime that she did not commit. While Natascha had been held hostage, her then-fiancé Nick had tried to rescue her with the help of two of his teammates, Shira Hadad, a young Israeli woman, and her brother Ariel Rashid. Natascha recalled that despite how much she had disliked Nick's boss, Ariel, they were now best friends. The experience on board the *Northern Explorer* warranted Ariel and Shira to be their daughter's godparents. Within the same five minutes, Shira had saved both Nick and Natascha's lives, so naturally they decided that their daughter's first name would be Shira. Following their successful escape from the research vessel, their ordeal had been far from over. For a short while, Natascha had not only been identified as a terrorist but also as one of the ten most-wanted people in the United States.

For several months, Nick and Natascha had lived in hiding before her name had officially been cleared. With her past hopefully behind them, the young family had finally moved to the outskirts of London, where Nick continued to work for EuroSec Corporation, the very security company that had protected Natascha back on board the *Northern Explorer*. Prof. Dr Richard Weber, Natascha's father and a well respected scientist in Europe, had arranged for Natascha to work part time at the new London Aquarium.

"Well, one of us was totally off", Natascha barked at the radio, after she noticed her lyrics and melody didn't match the radio version of the song. Natascha shook her head, freeing herself from the lyrical uncertainty and *those* memories. Although she no longer felt threatened, she maintained the habit to look around before exiting her car. Walking to the entrance, the twenty-nine year old felt a spark of excitement at the thought that her husband would be returning from a ten-day shift tomorrow. Her thoughts then veered to their special guest at the aquarium.

It was a little over a year now since the aquarium was home to two juvenile polar bears. The aquarium had successfully raised enough money to build a rather luxurious outdoor enclosure. Like all the other employees, Natascha immediately grew attached to the white fur balls. To guarantee the best care for their new attraction, they had contacted several different experts. One of them was a Canadian by the name of Jean-Pierre. The energetic Canadian scientist was on vacation in England and took the time to visit the aquarium while his wife was shopping. Not only was Jean-Pierre the head of a large Canadian aquarium, he was also considered one of the leading experts on polar bears.

The timing of his visit was not perfect due to the short notice, but Natascha volunteered right away to give their guest a private tour. Natascha believed the tour to be an excellent opportunity to ask him as many questions as possible.

Just minutes after 9.00 a.m. Natascha got called to the entrance where her guest waited patiently.

"Good Morning! I am Natascha. We exchanged some e-mails", she greeted with a hand shake.

"Good Morning! I just arrived. Man oh man, this is a very nice building you have here", the energetic Canadian replied.

"Well, we luckily received some healthy, private donations. Without those, things would definitely look different. You know how it is."

"Yes, I know. It's a shame. It's the same everywhere, no money."

Although Natascha had just met the guy, she already liked him. After exchanging the typical pleasantries, Natascha did not waste any time and started the tour. About two hours later she led their guest towards the polar bear enclosure.

"We only got them last spring. The enclosure is not much older. As you can see, everything is still in pretty good shape. They have enough space to swim a couple laps, and we make sure that the water is as clean as possible", the young scientist explained and leaned over the fence to look down to the two polar bears. "We are trying to let them catch some of their own food, but we haven't figured it out quite yet. We believe it's because they are still so young."

"Could be", Jean-Pierre replied and looked at his most favourite animals. "Did you ever see a polar bear in the wild?"

Natascha hesitated for a moment, the terrifying encounter was a particular memory she did not want to reminisce.

"I did, once. I was snorkelling in the North West Passage, watching orcas, when a polar bear got pretty close to me." Natascha finally explained, agreeing with herself that it was one of the happier days she had experienced on board the *Northern Explorer*, despite the fright.

"Ah, yes, that's right. You were on that expedition", Jean-Pierre stated finally, assuming that Natascha did not want to discuss the subject any further. He recalled her picture had been all over the western news, and she hated that some people still recognised her. Since her father had been the expedition leader, their name was now well known among the scientists who worked the same field. They could have used the money, but Natascha had never accepted any of the invitations to talk to magazines or TV Shows. She had been publicly cleared of all charges, but everybody, including Jean-Pierre, knew that some of her emotional wounds would not heal for a long time, if ever. Natascha and Nick's goal was to live as normal as possible.

Natascha appreciated Jean-Pierre's gesture and smiled at him. She turned her attention back to the two polar bears, who dipped under the surface.

"Yes, I was. I am glad that it's over", she finally said quietly, more to herself than to Jean-Pierre, before she focussed on her guest again.

They continued to monitor the cubs and stayed during the feeding session. Natascha explained in great detail the daily routine with the two carnivores and how the aquarium planned to make their habitat natural.

Just as they walked down to another enclosure, the rain started to pour down on them.

"Let's go inside and get a coffee. It will rain for the rest of the day", Natascha suggested and hurried to one of the doors. The young woman unlocked it and let her guest in. "My apology. This is the storage room for the dive gear, if you want to have a look at that."

Knowing that Jean-Pierre had been significantly involved in dry-suits and scientific diving throughout his career, she figured right that he was interested in their gear. While Natascha disappeared into the little staff kitchen, Jean-Pierre took a closer look at the gear.

"I am sorry", Natascha said after a few minutes, coming out of the kitchen empty handed. "Our fridge is full of glue and other items, but I can't find anything edible, there's not even coffee in there. Let me invite you to our canteen."

On their way to the canteen they visited the medical station and the food kitchen, where two volunteers prepared a variety of foods for the different animals. After a few minutes at each station, they finally sat down in the public cafeteria, and Natascha brought a little tray with coffee, mugs, milk, sugar, and even some cake.

"Here, be my guest, please", she said placing the tray in front of Jean-Pierre. Proud of herself for not tumbling and covering her guest in all the food, Natascha sat opposite to him. She looked him over quickly and determined that she enjoyed his enthusiasm and energy, especially when it came to the polar wild life.

"So, what else are you planning to do here in London? Are you visiting any of the sites?" Natascha asked just as she had finished her cake.

"Well, we did most of those. It was nice, but I like spending time here at the aquarium more", the Canadian replied. "I am sure you have heard about that big fundraising concert this weekend. We are going there. One of my favourite artists is playing. Carlos Santana! You should come, I can get you tickets!" Jean-Pierre exclaimed and looked at her hopefully.

"I really appreciate that, but I have to decline. It's possible that my husband is going, which means that I will be with our daughter at home", Natascha laughed.

"He's going to the concert without you?" Jean-Pierre asked in disbelief.

"Yes, he is. But that's okay. He is actually working there. I believe it'll end up being a sixteen hour day for him. I wouldn't be of any use to him there", Natascha smiled playfully before she continued, "I would just stop him from flirting with other women, and that's no fun for him."

"He doesn't know how to treat a fine lady", Jean-Pierre laughed with a grin.

"He is trying", the young scientist laughed as she acknowledged some passing co-workers with a wave. "Speaking of my daughter", she suddenly stated, looking at her watch. "I have to get that little pumpkin. Feel free to stay as long as you like." Natascha explained and apologised for her sudden departure.

"No problem. I might take another stroll around. Maybe I will come back again later this week."

"Sure, I'm always in from eight to twelve. Just let the cashier know you are here to see me. They can find me."

"I might do that", Jean-Pierre smiled and accepted Natascha's handshake before she hurried away.

Asklepios, Aegean Sea, Monday, May 5

It was not yet summer, but the temperatures in the Aegean Sea had already reached thirty degrees Celsius. The mild year-round climate was perfect for this state of the art medical facility. This modern facility only catered to the very rich and famous, who could afford treatment from some of the best physicians and specialists globally.

Named after the ancient Greek God of medicine, *Asklepios* was so well-equipped that there was not a medical case they could not handle. As long as the patients were wealthy, they would receive the best medical care money could buy. Only the best physicians were contacted and gladly accepted attractive and lucrative contracts promising much higher earnings than any other private hospital would offer. But *Asklepios* was more. *Asklepios* also served as a spa and retreat, addressing those for whom the best was only good enough.

Privacy and an excellent ratio between patients and medical staff was a key factor in the facility's enormous success. Victor Gates was lucky enough to be one of those patients, although he would definitely argue the definition of "lucky." The American had spent the last year at *Asklepios*, and he was disgruntled that he would most likely have to stay for another one or two. Dr Sheridan Evans had just finished her daily visit with him and had, as so many times before, reassured him that a donor lung should soon be available.

With most of his body severely burnt, his lungs were damaged beyond the point of recovery. His medical condition did not allow Victor to talk any more, but he could communicate over the little monitor beside his bed with a throat microphone. The fifty-six year old American always made a gargling sound when using it. Dr Evans patiently looked at the monitor and saw a smile face. She returned the smile and read his next question.

"Once we get the new lung, we can try to repair the vocal cords. This will allow you to talk relatively normal again", the physician explained patiently, reading his next question. "Yes, Mr Gates, we are still looking for a liver and kidney donor as well. They are more commonly available than lungs."

Victor Gates gave another gargling sound while the computer translated his message to a text.

"Yes, of course. I will send one of the nurses later. They can bring you outside in the sun after your oxygen therapy. I also heard that you will receive a more sophisticated and much smaller computer by the end of the week that will also process the text into speech."

The monitors showing his pulse indicated that her patient was really excited about this news. She checked the settings on the several machines again and updated the electronic database.

"I am around, Mr Gates. You know how to reach me if you need something, okay?" she finally said, announcing her departure.

Walking down towards her next patient, Dr Sheridan Evans shook her head. From a medical point of view it was a complete miracle that Mr Gates was even alive. She smiled briefly at the very thought that cases like his was exactly why this facility existed.

One hour later, male nurse Lamar Hatcher opened the doors of the elevator and pushed Victor Gates out under the blue sky. He guided Victor into the shade right beside the pool.

"Here you go, Mr Gates, your usual spot." Lamar enthused and rearranged the oxygen tank again. Although his lung had lost most of its function, with the aid of a nasal cannula delivering extra oxygen, he could still breathe on his own.

Thank you! Lamar read the message on the monitor.

"You are very welcome."

Once Lamar left, Victor Gates rearranged the monitor a little bit to have a better view of it. He could also use it to browse the internet or watch TV. He loved to absorb the beauty of the horizon, but he always made sure that he kept up to date with the world news.

A young boy, not older than six, walked towards the pool. Like every day, the young kid respectfully greeted Mr Gates when he saw him. With loud laughter he threw his towel on one of the chairs and jumped into the water.

Victor watched him for a few seconds before searching for his parents. They usually walked together with their son, but today they came a few minutes later. Like their son, they usually greeted and chatted with him, but this time only the father nodded absentmindedly towards him. Victor looked to the mother, who wiped her eyes again, attempting to stifle her tears. The American didn't know their names, but he knew they were from somewhere in Scandinavia.

He watched further as the father got into the pool to play with their child, while the young mother tried to make herself comfortable in one of the chairs. Her shoulders buckled as she began crying again. The update on the medical condition of their child must have been devastating, Victor surmised. He watched them for a few more minutes, until the mother joined them in the pool. Even the best doctors couldn't perform miracles, no matter how much money was involved.

Victor shifted his attention back to his monitor and tried to find a football game. While he switched through the sports channels, he counted about thirty other patients around the pool, some of them even getting massages or other medical treatment that did not require them to be in their rooms. Victor finally found the game he was looking for, and he turned up the volume just enough so that he could hear the commentary over the music playing from the hidden speakers somewhere behind him.

***EuroSecCorporation*, London, Tuesday, May 6**
Natascha lay helplessly on her back. With both her arms stretched above her head, her assailant bound them tighter with his hands. Natascha panted heavily and threw her head from side to side, trying to escape the hold. The weight of her attacker pressed her to the ground, and his head was moving as he leaned forward. His face was now only centimetres away from hers.

"Well, I would say Mommy is screwed", Shira Hadad commented calmly, as she glanced up from the puzzle she was working on with her godchild in the corner of the combat room.

"Oh...I can get....this is...shoot!" Natascha cursed as the grip around her wrists slowly tightened. She found it difficult to admit defeat, but knew this moment signalled just that.

"Use your hips. Get some momentum going and then head-butt him", the Israeli woman explained, still working on the puzzle with Shira-Sarah. Shira was clever enough to keep Sarah's back turned towards her mother. "That should free your hands. As soon as you have them free, ram your fingers in his eyes and tear his head back. It should give you enough space to roll out from underneath. Hit him in the throat or kick him in the groin, and then run away. Simple! But don't stay like that! The moment his hand is around your throat it's over." Shira suggested and gave her godchild another piece for the puzzle, but Shira-Sarah finally turned around and looked at her mother.

"Mommy, what are you doing?"

"Oh, Mommy is fine, pumpkin. We're just playing here", Natascha quickly explained and looked at her daughter. Ariel immediately released her from his hold, making sure Natascha could show her daughter that everything was fine.

"Looks like you and Daddy", Shira-Sarah commented seriously and turned back to her puzzle. Natascha glanced to Ariel with embarrassment, but soon after found herself laughing with the Israelis.

"So, that's what it looks like? You like it rough?" Ariel teased his friend and sat back on the training mats.

Natascha blushed and threw him a killing glance, but she still struggled to hold back another laugh herself.

"I admit we get carried away sometimes, but this is definitely not what it looks like. Forget about me, you seemed to be rather comfortable on top", she commented fixing her long black hair.

"Just trying to help you", Ariel replied with a mischievous grin, but Natascha only raised her eyebrows, indicating she did not believe a word he said.

"Can we do that again later? I wasted way too much time", Natascha admitted and rushed over to catch her daughter and roll around with her.

"Yes, we can do that. The meeting is at fourteen-hundred, and I expect we will be finished within an hour. So we'll have at least ninety minutes left for practice", Shira explained.

"Perfect. I'll just get my little pumpkin to the playgroup downstairs, and I'll be right back."

Although Natascha worked five days a week at the aquarium, she could only work there for half a day. With Nick working full-time at EuroSec, they were relatively financially stable, but would certainly be better off with Natascha being able to work full-time as well. It was no surprise that Natascha gladly accepted the opportunity when EuroSec asked Natascha to work a couple hours a week to help their secretary. It allowed them a little more financial freedom, which they usually spent to spoil their daughter.

Natascha appreciated the opportunity, and she had also noticed that both Brian Whittaker and Klaus Schwartze, the owners of EuroSec Corporation, were extremely supportive to her and Nick. Ariel admitted earlier to Natascha that EuroSec Corporation had technically failed in protecting her onboard the *Northern Explorer,* and that both Brian and Klaus continued to bear the guilt. The German scientist refused to see it that way. She didn't think twice about accepting the position, especially considering many of her closest friends worked for EuroSec.

The security company owned a three-storey building outside London and occupied the two upper floors for its day-to-day business and to offer special training. The ground floor was rented out to a fitness centre, which also offered a daycare and playgroup for children. Employees of EuroSec Corporation could not only work out for free, but also take advantage of the daycare for their children, if need be.

"So, you're going to play with Amelia again?" Natascha asked her daughter as they stepped through the door leading to the play group.

Shira-Sarah nodded with excitement, already looking for her friend.

"Can you paint me something, darling?" Natascha called after her daughter, but Shira-Sarah was already too occupied with Amelia. Natascha watched her for a few minutes before turning towards one of the caregivers.

"Hi, how are you today?"

"Good, how are you, Natascha?"

"Fine. I'll pick her up around five, if that's okay. She was pretty active all morning, so I expect her to nap within the next few minutes. I will be upstairs. You can either reach me at my desk or at my cell." Natascha handed her Shira-Sarah's bag. The two women updated each other on the latest gossip before Natascha had to leave. She quickly waved to Shira-Sarah, who ran over for her usual kiss Goodbye.

With ten minutes to spare, Natascha prepared the big conference room on the third floor for the upcoming meeting. Usually it was Brigitte, Klaus Schwartze's wife, who would prepare all the notes and set up the PowerPoint presentations for those weekly meetings, but today Natascha was left alone to prepare everything by herself. Slowly the room started to fill.

"Hey, how's my sunshine doing today?" Rolf Brengmann teased and clapped her on her shoulders as he walked by her.

"Your sunshine is doing fine. When you get over there, turn the projector on, will you, sweet-cheeks?" Natascha asked him without looking up from her laptop.

"Yes, Ma'am!" the former German Kampfschwimmer stated enthusiastically with his boyish grin. He flicked on the projector within a moment. Together with the

Norwegians Ole-Einar Alsgaard and Olaf Magnusson, Rolf took his seat at the long horse-shoe shaped table. Natascha glanced and smiled at them. Besides Nick and Shira, the three of them were the only remaining members of Team A, and it had been those very people who had spent months with Natascha on board the *Northern Explorer*. Rolf had actually caught a bullet in his shoulder to save Natascha one night in Berlin, and she still pondered how she could properly thank him. It certainly did not help that Rolf continuously teased her about still suffering from the pain of being shot, although everyone knew that he was back to full duty and doing quite well. Natascha stopped fighting the smile that pervaded her features every time she saw them; they were the most loyal friends she could ever ask for. Nor could Natascha forget to think of Oliver Schneider, who had also been on board the research vessel to protect her, but he had fallen victim to the Americans.

"So, this is your big moment! Your first full meeting you are in charge of. You think you can handle it?" Rolf continued to tease her, just as Shira Hadad sat in the chair beside him.

"Shira, will you please slap him for me? Really hard, if you don't mind", Natascha asked her Israeli friend without even looking up.

"My pleasure", the Israeli combat specialist replied and hit Rolf rather hard on the back of his head not a second later.

"Geez Shira! That hurts!"

"That's the point, Rolf." Natascha explained dryly. Shira just smiled at him.

"You know I'll get you back for that", he playfully threatened.

"I can hardly wait", Natascha replied. She looked up from her laptop and noticed with satisfaction that all the remaining members of EuroSec Corporation had taken their seats. The company employed a little over two hundred guards for more simple jobs like loss-prevention programs, or to provide security at smaller events. Teams A, B and C, as well as Operation Control only employed members of former government Special Forces, and they concentrated on more advanced and demanding tasks. The heightened terror alert kept them all on their toes, and Teams A to C were also the only ones taking part in these meetings. Just before 2.00 p.m., Ariel Rashid, Sean MacLeod, Jack MacDonald, and Gunnar Eriksson walked into the conference room, representing Operation Control. With their arrival the chit-chat ended, as both retired Admiral Brian Whittaker and retired General Klaus Schwartze entered the room immediately after them. As usual, they both walked to their seats at the top of the table between the members of Operation Control. Before they sat down, they took the time to look at each of their employees.

Standing 1,95m, retired General Klaus Schwartze exuded an aura of authority that prohibited anyone from questioning his judgment. During his former military career he had been a leader of multiple task forces and an advisor on many peacekeeping missions. His blue eyes were in constant motion, and he barely missed a detail. With his great experience came an analytical mind that allowed him within seconds to evaluate a new situation and readjust the plan of action.

To his left stood his long time friend and now business partner, retired Admiral Brian Whittaker. Measuring only 1,72 m he was shorter than everyone else in the room, including their new female personnel, but the retired admiral's tactical mind and his experience made him the perfect match for retired General Klaus Schwartze to lead this corporation.

Brian still maintained his military-style crew-cut, his grey hair complimenting his weathered face. His face's contours seemed like it was chiselled out of stone, making it nearly impossible to read any emotions in it.

"Good afternoon", the former British admiral finally said and sat down.

Without wasting time, he flipped through his papers and reminded everyone about their first aid certification. "Natascha, we have three First Aid Instructors in this room. Maybe you can create a schedule for everyone so that it can be done within the next four weeks?"

Natascha nodded and made a note.

Brian continued without missing a beat, "Another thing is our break room. We now have six women permanently working with us, so I suggest that you lads turn that bloody man-cave into something that is a little bit more appealing to our ladies. Am I clear on that? I'm not going to assign anyone specific to this task. Just make it happen, okay?" Brian snarled at the guys and gave the message a few seconds to sink in.

"No problem, sir. Add a feminine touch. We'll take care of that", Rolf promised.

"Why doesn't that make me feel any better?" Brian growled back at him.

"Sir, please! I'm deeply hurt!" Rolf pretended to be upset.

"Yeah, right. Well, we will see. Where were we? Right, our security guys on the oil rig. They are ahead of schedule. We got confirmation that our crew is already off the rig. They are scheduled to touch down in London in a couple of hours instead of late tonight."

"Yes!" Natascha enthusiastically cheered a little too loud. She failed at hiding her excitement. Nick was on that flight. She earned a couple chuckles in return.

"Keep laughing", she defended, "he was gone for ten days."

"Oh, the romance!" Rolf teased, earning a very rude hand gesture from Natascha in return.

"If the two of you are done, I would like to continue", Brian Whittaker interrupted. Natascha turned her attention back to her notepad as he continued.

"There are a couple things that I want to mention. First, there is a message from our friends at Scotland Yard. Chief Inspector Conolly mentioned that they received several reports of missing homeless people during the last couple weeks. It seems to be mostly the younger crew that disappears. They have no idea what's going on or where they are. With the warmer weather it could be nothing, but he asked us to keep our ears and eyes open. Natascha, maybe you can prepare a little memo for our Loss Prevention Guards, they are more likely to get in contact with them, unfortunately", Brian's voice trailed as his thoughts drifted over his notes.

"It will go out tomorrow afternoon, sir." Natascha made another note, not without noticing how serious the retired admiral was with this subject. Curious about it, she looked up and noticed that Klaus and the rest from Operation Control also seeming to be unusually focussed.

"London is still under a heightened terror alert. That means we really have to be on our toes with all of our assignments. I trust that I do not have to emphasise the importance of this. There is also a minor issue for this weekend. You are all aware that we will be working the benefit concert and the following fundraiser gala. The concert itself is covered, but we might be one person short for the gala. Talia, how is your ankle coming?" Brian asked and looked at one of their latest recruits.

Like Shira, Talia Levi was Israeli, working in team C. She and three other women, Maya Azulay, Tamar Peretz, and Noah Cohen had all been handpicked by Ariel and Shira back in Israel from the military academy.

"It is much better, sir. It shouldn't be a problem." The young woman enthused, not wanting to disappoint.

"What's the doctor saying?" Klaus asked.

"Not to do active duty until next Friday", Talia grimaced, knowing very well this prohibited her from working this weekend.

"Your enthusiasm is well noted, but we'll go with the doctor's recommendation. The bloke is an old friend of mine, and he'll give me hell if he finds out that I let you work against his advice, okay? So, that means we are officially one person short."

"Can I suggest something?" Shira asked.

"By all means."

"Talia was scheduled to work with Ole-Einar, Nick, and I as personal protection detail for Rowan Harrison. We all know there is no threat level for him. He is just showing off in front of everybody else. Why else does he request two female bodyguards for him?" Shira explained and did not hide her annoyance for this particular client. "We all know he'll be extremely disappointed and very vocal during the event if we show up one woman short, especially once he's drunk", she continued, her frustration evident in her raised voice.

Brian and Klaus both looked at Ariel, who had also dealt with this Rowan Harrison character a couple of times in the past.

"My sister is right. There is absolutely no logical reason why Mr Harrison needs any protection detail in the first place. He likes to show off, especially in front of others during such events."

"Come on, Ariel. The guy is a drunk and an idiot." Shira continued with the same tone, not being as polite as her older brother.

"Okay, so the guy likes to party and show off. That fits the bill for about eighty per cent of these guests. The issue is that he has already paid us, so unless he makes any improper advances against anyone of you, I tend to grant him his wish, whatever his threat level is. Did he make any improper advances in the past?" Brian asked to be sure.

"No, he did not. At least not any more than any other drunk clients have", Shira stated reluctantly.

"So, back to square one. You said that you have a suggestion?"

"Yes, if we have to show up with two women in the team, I suggest we give Natascha a chance."

"Natascha?" Brian wondered out loud.

"*Me?*"

"Yes, Natascha, you. For crying out loud, we will meet the guy for the gala at twenty-one-hundred. By then he will most likely be drunk as a porcupine...."

"It is *drunk as a skunk*", Rolf corrected her, holding back a snigger.

"Whatever", Shira hissed with annoyance. "All we do is drive him to the event, walk with him through the entrance, and that's it. He's only going to be there for the fundraiser dinner. The actual concert will be over by then. All the artists only play three or four songs each, and people paid for a seat at their table. That's what he's after. Once he's at the dinner, we'll be sitting somewhere backstage. By two-thirty we escort him back to his limo and that will be the end of it. We don't even leave with him. The biggest threat will be someone asking you for your phone number."

Natascha was taken aback by Shira's suggestion and looked at Brian, who seemed hesitant to accept the idea.

"What other choice do we have? Maya, Noah, and Tamar are already working that night at more demanding venues. We all know this job is for show purpose only, not because he's in any danger."

Brian looked at Klaus before turning to Natascha.

"What do you think, Natascha? Is that something you would be comfortable with?"

"Well, I don't know..." Natascha hadn't a moment to think about it and was actually lost for words, something that rarely happened.

"For heaven's sake, Natascha, seriously?" Ole-Einar reassured her, questioning her hesitation. "Of course you will; you'll be fine",

"Well, I guess I can do it. I mean, nothing is going to happen there, right?" She still wasn't completely convinced.

"Natascha, we are talking about a benefit gala, not about a visit from the royal family in Afghanistan", Shira reminded her.

"Okay, why not? I'll give it a try." Natascha's resolve quickly dwindled upon her next thought. "Wait, I don't have to wear a dress or a gun?"

"No, you just wear plain clothes. And we'll most definitely not give you a gun. We all know what happened the last time you used one!" Shira reassured her friend with a smile.

"True. I don't want to be the centre of another international incident and declared a terrorist again. Okay, I can pull that off. Oh, wait a second! What about Sarah? I'm not sure if I can get a babysitter on such short notice."

"I'll be at home", Talia entered the conversation, raising her shoulders with sudden disappointment.

Natascha looked at her and had completely forgotten the obvious solution. Talia lived with Shira on the lower floor of their rented three-storey house.

"I'll take care of the little turnip", Talia proclaimed proudly, earning some chuckles.

"She's a pumpkin, not a turnip, Talia, and thanks for the offer", Natascha explained, laughing. Like Shira a couple of years ago, the four new Israeli women still battled certain English phrases, causing quite a few laughs during conversations.

"So we're all set?" Brian asked, approving the solution.

"Yes, sir, if it's all right with you, we are all set."

"Okay, I'm not sure if we can get a licence for you, for obvious reasons, and I don't want to waste time or money trying to find out. Talia, you and Natascha don't look too different. Make sure you give her your licence on Saturday. And Natascha, by all means, don't bring any other ID for that evening. Okay, any questions? Anything else?"

"I will be with the women in the combat room, and we need four volunteers for the next hour and half." Shira explained calmly and looked around.

"The angels of death are on a mission again!" Rolf commented beside her and laughed with Ole-Einar.

"You now have two of your volunteers", Klaus declared, pointing to Rolf and Ole-Einar.

"I'll do it. And Olaf." Ariel added.

"And *me*? Why me?" Olaf asked surprised.

"Oh, are you scared to take me?" Tamar teased him, immediately realising her wrong choice of words. "That's not what I meant to say", she blushed and quickly defended herself against the laughter.

"Maybe this will be fun after all!" Ole-Einar mentioned to his Norwegian friend.

Asklepios, Aegean Sea, Tuesday, May 6
A breeze carried fresh air over the medical facility. Victor Gates inhaled and enjoyed the smell of the saltwater. He rested at his usual spot again, his attention shifting between some boats on the turquoise water, and back to the young boy in the pool. Both his parents played with him in the water today. Unsurprisingly, his mother never left the facility, always staying with her son, while his father usually left for a couple of days before returning. Victor sipped some ice-cold liquid through a drinking tube and noticed that the mother was a little bit more composed today than she had been yesterday.

Since the replay of yesterday's game was at the halftime break, his concentration shifted to a new patient, whose bed was just rolled out from the elevator. One of the nurses had told him that the new arrival was a distant member of the Spanish royal family, who had suffered severe, but non-life-threatening injuries during a private car race. Victor looked at the heavily bandaged person and watched the same procedure he had seen so many times during his time at *Asklepios*.

During the first week or two, most of the family would stay with the patient, and there were usually lots of tears. After a couple of weeks, it was usually just the spouse or maybe one or two other direct relatives who stayed, keeping the patient company. Victor thought this was quite sad, but on the other hand, accessibility to *Asklepios* was not as standard as just taking a cab or the subway in downtown New York. Located in the Aegean Sea, it usually involved a couple of hours on a shuttle boat.

Victor looked up again. Just by the sheer number of people standing around the new patient's bed, the American could tell that he had not been here for more than a couple of days. But even with such a large and even famous crowd, total anonymity was guaranteed. Watching them for a few more minutes, Victor almost didn't recognise his own visitor. His long-time friend and former business partner, Walter Leroy "L.J." Jackson, walked towards him, his arms gesturing a hug.

"Hey, Victor, ol' buddy. It's nice to see you! God bless you!" L.J. announced his arrival and carefully shook Victor's hand.

Hi LJ. Nice to see you, too.

"Oh my Lord almighty, you finally have a speech computer. I'll be damned! When did you get that?"

Just this morning. Listen to this.

Victor demonstrated to his old friend that the computer could imitate many different celebrities, but he set it back to one of his most favourite actors, John Wayne.

"I bet the nurses are already complaining about it, aren't they?" the Texan oil tycoon laughed.

Yes, I tried to whistle after one this morning. Almost choked to death.

"Ah, what the hell buddy, you don't deserve this. That goddamn accident!" L.J. shook his head, then started with a new beat, "Listen, I want to thank you for putting in a good word for me and for making the connections. The doctors here looked at Sam, and they promised her a transplant within a few weeks. Back home she would've had to wait years to get a new kidney. I'm wondering why the Lord allowed our country to be ruined like that", the three hundred pound Texan complained and shook his head as he played with his Stetson. "Can you believe that back home they're not able to treat her immediately? They said they can put her on a waiting list. Can you believe that? A goddamn waiting list! And the doctor barely spoke English. What the hell are they thinking? Thank God they don't have waiting lists here. They're doing some more tests with her right now. May the Lord bless them." L.J. paused a moment, then considered, "Did the doctors give you any news?"

Not much longer for lung. Liver and kidney also within weeks. Maybe I will be able to speak again. Maybe skin transplantation. Hopefully only one more year here.

"Jesus, Vic, I hope it all works out. How's your pain?"

New medication. Much better now.

"That is good, buddy. That is really good!"

How is business?

"Ah, damn. You read the news. Business is bad. The oil price is down. Once we clean up that mess over there, things will get back to normal", L.J. growled and looked with disgust at the eastern horizon. "How the hell can you look at that direction all day long?" he asked his friend, wiping his forehead with an expensive handkerchief.

It's east. Beautiful sun rise. What else do I have to look at?

"Yeah, you're right. Can you believe that? Just couple hundred miles from here those goddamn camel jockeys do whatever they want. They're even threatening us. And what's our government doing? Those damn morons are sitting there with their dicks in their hands and do nothing, while a bunch of idiots with kitchen towels wrapped around their heads are trying to create a new world order. We should send our boys in and level that whole goddamn country. That would show them who's on top of the real world order."

Yes, but don't panic. We will get them. We will get them where it really hurts.

"I'll pray to the Lord that you're right. Have you heard from our British friend? Anything new there?" L.J. lowered his voice.

No, he's in London. Hosting an event. Couldn't come.

"Did he say anything? Are they still cool?"

Yes. Everything is fine.

"Good! The last thing we need is someone getting cold feet!"

That's why small group. The smaller the better. Only right people.

"Yeah, you're right, like always." L.J. straightened up as he continued, "We better change the subject. My wife is coming." L.J. waved to Samantha Elisabeth Jackson.

"Over here darling! Tell us the good news!"

- 2 -

Paris, Tuesday, May 6

"Oh my God! He is so cute! Have you ever seen such blue eyes before? They're almost as blue as yours! What do you think?" twenty-one-year old Monique exclaimed as she and her new friend Freja pressed themselves out through the café's side door.

"Monique, they're both from the middle-east. They're wearing coloured contact lenses. But they are cute", Freja laughed with a strong Swedish accent.

"Whoo", Freja sang and spun around, her arms stretched out to her sides. "This is so cool!" she yelled and started laughing again. The Swede was the same age as Monique and had arranged to take the next year of university off. She had enough of all the studying and simply wanted to party her way through Europe. Against the protests of her parents, she had taken off with nothing else but two credit cards and a backpack, and what better place to start her journey than in Paris? She and Monique had met on the social network, and the French girl had promised her bestie to show her Paris' best places to have a great time. Monique described herself as a drifter. She was a certified paramedic, but had realised the hard way that she wasn't cut out for the job. Like Freja, she wanted to have as much fun as possible before she would have to settle down and decide how to continue with her life. Freja quickly glanced around in the side alley and reached for her pocket.

"Here, take one!" Freja opened a little box with two pills in it and offered them to Monique.

"Oh! Yes, please! I like those. They're really good", Monique laughed, and, savouring the moment, placed it on her tongue and swallowed. "What do you say? Should we go back inside and see if we can find a better place to sleep tonight than at my cousins?" the young French woman asked with a devious smile.

"Well, we could, but maybe we should see how his friend is. Maybe he has a better place", Freja laughed and welcomed the idea of how their adventure could end.

"I'm pretty sure either of their places is better than ours. They don't look like they're cheap. They keep the drinks coming. Oh my God!" Monique laughed, covering her mouth with her hand.

"What?

"What if they are some Arab princes? Super-billionaires, or something like that?" Monique burst out laughing at the very thought.

"That would be too cool. Can you imagine? A billionaire in general would be fine with me. Ah, what the heck, we're only young once." Freja motivated herself and straightened up. "Let's go back inside. How do I look?" the Swede asked and turned towards Monique.

"Like the typical Swedish supermodel."

"Good! Come on, let's make this happen!"

Freja opened the door to the café again, and it wasn't too long before they found their two friends at a corner table.

"Ah, you're both back. We were concerned about you", one of the guys mentioned in a strong foreign accent.

"Just had to catch some fresh air. It's so hot in here", Freja waved her hand to cool her skin. She reached for his drink with the other, emptying it in one gulp.

"Ah, come on, you can't just take my drink like that. What if your parents found out? I'd be in trouble", the young man theatrically complained.

"My parents don't even know where I am!" Freja enthused, throwing an arm around his neck.

"Don't worry, I don't even know my parents", Monique laughed as she took the drink from the other guy. Freja burst out with laughter, while the two young men exchanged promising looks.

Just one hour later, the four drove through Paris with the young man's Citroen, listening to the latest club music as loud as the speakers managed.

Freja flipped her sun visor down to work the mirror, noticing Monique had made herself comfortable with the other young man in the back seat. She jealously watched them kissing ferociously.

"Where are we going?" the young Swede asked with anticipation, dancing her fingers up the driver's thigh. She had absolutely no idea what part of Paris they were in.

"Two more minutes, be patient", the driver promised with a smile.

While Freja rearranged her long blonde hair, the driver parked the little Citroen on the side of the road.

"Oh, this is cool", the Swede commented, looking up at a typical old architectural French building. The driver opened the door and invited them in.

"Uhuuu, let's get this party *really* started", cheered Monique, her arms tight around her new friend as they walked through the door. They followed a little hallway to the back of the building before entering a staircase through another side door. Just a minute later, they were in the living room, and this time it was Freja who feverishly kissed her newest friend, both of them landing on the couch. Monique watched them for a minute and started the stereo, where she picked her favourite radio station. Dancing to the music, she turned around to see her friend carrying in some drinks.

"So, ladies, shall we?" He dared, handing them the drinks. "To a wonderful night without regrets!"

"Whooo, damn right! To a wonderful night without regrets! Skoal!" Freja enthused, accepting the drink that was offered to her. As soon as they had emptied their glasses, the two women started dancing with each other, teasing their hosts as they laughed out loud.

Monique turned with Freja and noticed one of their new friends talking on his cell phone for about a minute. "Who are you talking to?" Monique asked quickly.

"Just a friend, don't worry."

"Whooo, what happened to you?" Monique laughed as Freja stumbled and fell on the couch.

"Don't know, I'm just a bit dizzy", Freja admitted, but she was far worse than dizzy. She could no longer hear the music; everything was just a blur. She felt the room spin upwards, then around and back. She couldn't determine if she was standing or lying down. She tried to concentrate, but she had never experienced anything like this before. Slowly, she leaned back into the couch and tried to get Monique's attention. Something felt horribly wrong, and all her alarm bells were ringing. Despite her lack of conscious thought, she knew the best thing was to get out of here, but she couldn't even move. Finally, Monique leaned over her to help her, but Freja couldn't hear what her French friend said. She tried to say something but was unable to produce a single sound. The music now sounded like screams, and it took Freja a few seconds before she realised that it was actually Monique screaming. She saw two, no, three shadows forcefully pulling Monique away from her, slamming her to the ground. Helplessly Freja watched as three guys got on her French friend. One pressed her head down to the floor by her hair, while a second, much larger man kneeled on her back. The third person hit Monique, pulled her arm out from underneath her body, stretched it, and inserted a syringe. Monique struggled for almost a minute, but it was only another moment before her body went limp. The guys turned her on her back and handcuffed her hands in front of her body. Two of them carelessly lifted her unconscious body up and carried the young French woman out of the room. Freja tried to fight against the drug from the laced drink, but she was still unable to move. She knew she would be next, and her helplessness intensified her fear.

"No!" the young Swede begged, tears streaming down her cheeks. She was terrified of the horror that would come. She cried her objection again, but the three assailing figures maintained their purpose as they approached her. Freja screamed with pain as one of the guys pulled her forward by her long blonde hair. The two other men held her up by her arms, but despite how much Freja tried to squirm, it was no use. Her attacker felt her blonde hair slip through his thick fingers, and he turned to his friends, saying something with a devilish grin. A ripple of fear overcame Freja as his friends replied. She couldn't understand a single word.

"No… please!" Freja begged as best she could, but the men suddenly pulled her to her feet and dragged her out of the room and down a corridor.

Freja tried to watch where they were taking her as her feet dragged behind her. Her fear rose further as they went downstairs into the basement. Another man, this one armed with a gun, stood there and laughed. Freja tried to avert her eyes, but they were fixed on him.

The armed man pulled the Swede's head up by her hair. Freja groaned in pain, but her capturer just nodded his satisfaction and gave a harsh command. The two guys kept dragging her helpless body through another corridor before opening a door to another room. A single naked bulb provided dim light, and Freja could hear something else. Crying! She was convinced that it was Monique, but she didn't see her. There was a mattress on the floor, and the two men just dropped her helpless body on it. Without resisting, Freja could do nothing but just watch as one of the guys handcuffed one of her hands to a steel ring in the wall beside her. Her capturers left the room and closed the heavy, sound-insulated door behind them without a word. The young Swedish woman heard the key engaging the lock.

She still lacked any function over her body, and her senses were still blurred, but she somehow realised that it would be useless to scream. She was convinced her capturers would be back immediately if she did, and she somehow knew they would resort to other forms of violence. With tears streaming down her face, Freja turned to her side and looked at the ceiling. She noticed two cameras were transmitting their every move. Still crying, Freja continued to look around. She saw two more mattresses, but she did not see Monique. Another young woman about Freja's age sat on one of the mattresses, handcuffed to a steel ring, and her knees pulled up.

Freja looked at the girl, her hair dyed in multiple colours and her clothes torn and dirty. The Swedish woman tried to talk to her, but she still could not manage to form a sentence. The other captive just looked at her, crying and speechless.

"Where...are...we?" Freja finally managed to stutter, her voice barely audible. "Monique? Where...my friend?" Freja stammered, but still no answer.

"Hell...We are in hell!" the other woman cried and rolled to her side.

EuroSecCorporation, London, Tuesday, May 6

With the arrival of the four new female colleagues, Shira had designed a specific close combat training for them. Nursing her injury, Talia was not allowed to participate in the training, but she still joined her friends in the combat room to watch them practise.

Considering the traumatic events on the *Northern Explorer*, Ariel and Shira had no issues to convince Natascha to participate in the training on a regular basis. They figured it would also help her regain her self-confidence. After an intense warm-up and basic techniques, Natascha and her friends took a break to drink some water and wipe their exhaustion off with a towel.

"Okay, we can partner up for the next part. What do you want to work on?" Shira asked and sipped from her bottle.

"If it's okay with everyone, I'd like to work on what you and Ariel showed me earlier today", Natascha finally suggested, after everyone else glanced around blankly at each other. "I mean, if that's okay with you." She added and stretched her arms.

"Yeah, why not? What was it?" one of her friends piped up curiously.

"Defendant on the ground, attacker on top. We need the guys", Shira explained and turned around, fixing her ponytail. "Guys, can you please come over here? We need your help."

Ole-Einar, Olaf, Ariel, and Rolf, who worked out in the corner of the combat room, strolled over almost immediately.

"Careful, brother. She fixed her ponytail."

"Ah, Shira. Remember the conference room about an hour ago? Time for some payback. I am going to lay you out!" Rolf playfully challenged and walked straight towards her.

"You couldn't lay a carpet", Shira shot back dryly. If she was scared, she didn't show it. Usually, just the sight of 1,93 m tall and over 100 kg heavy Rolf walking like that towards anyone would make them take at least a couple of steps back to assume a defensive stance.

"Are you ready?" Rolf offered his last warning. Natascha chuckled as she watched his large stature approach Shira, who appeared less than tiny in comparison. She hid her grin under her towel, wiping her face one last time.

"I was born ready", Shira whispered to Rolf and winked at him as she shifted her balance.

A split second later, she controlled his head and swiped him from his feet. Another fraction of a second later, and Rolf landed hard on his back as Shira controlled her forward motion with a roll and stood back up again about three metres away. Rolf stared at the ceiling, wondering how he had landed with that view.

"What is one of the rules of close combat, ladies?" Shira asked and offered Rolf a hand to get up.

"Shit is about to get real once you fix your ponytail?" Rolf asked.

"That too, but seriously, what is one of the rules?"

"Size doesn't always matter", they all answered in unison.

"Can I see that again, please? I didn't quite catch that", Natascha smirked at Rolf, who replied with an obscene hand gesture in return.

"Okay, ladies, get on the ground, attacker is on top. Ariel!" Shira ordered, asking for her brother as she lay down on her back.

Shira slowly showed the different sequences of the escape technique with her brother trying to hold her down and lock her arms. Natascha paid close attention, knowing she had struggled with this before.

"Any questions?" Shira asked after she was back on her feet. Everyone shook their head. "Okay, let's go."

Natascha tactfully looked for Ariel for the simple reason that he was the lightest of the four guys. After all, she naturally didn't feel *that* comfortable being in such a vulnerable position. Before she got on the ground, she quickly glanced at her three friends, who were already in the middle of the exercise.

"Okay, let me see if I can remember this..." Natascha said more to herself than to Ariel, but she eventually managed to execute the proper techniques in the correct sequence.

"Not bad, now do it much faster and in one controlled movement", Ariel suggested after a couple more successful attempts.

"Okay. Any questions?" Shira asked and looked around.

"Yes, what if the guy is much bigger and stronger?" Natascha asked curiously, then quickly added with an apologetic wave of her hand, "No offence, Ariel. I know you say that size doesn't matter, but I'm not as strong or trained as you are, so is there anything different?"

As if someone had given a silent command, everyone looked at Ole-Einar. Their Norwegian friend was literally a powerhouse, and, standing 2.02 m and weighing in at just over 130 kg, he even made Rolf look small.

"Do you want me to demonstrate with Ole, or do you want to give it a try, and I talk you through it?" Shira asked.

"Well, if you can show me first, that may be better."

"Okay, big guy. Gear up", the Israeli told Ole. While the Norwegian put a head mask, a neck guard and his cup on, Shira took Ariel and discussed something with him in Hebrew. Natascha didn't pay too much attention to their conversation, she didn't understand them anyway, but she also didn't notice the other four women looking at her during their debate.

With Shira having the last argument, she turned back to the group and looked at Ole-Einar. Ariel walked over to him and checked his protective gear.

"Don't hold back. She asked for this", Ariel clapped his friend's shoulder. Ariel knew very well that Ole-Einar would never harm Shira with any uncontrolled actions during the training.

Shira assumed position and waited until the Norwegian had control over her.

"This is the problem, Natascha. Your best defence is to make sure that you never end up in this position. In a position like this, size and weight do matter. As you can see, there is not much I can do. So, in order to get out, you really have to mean it. Normally you could..." Shira had closely watched Ole-Einar, and she had just waited for the moment where he relaxed just a little bit during her explanation. Shira literally exploded underneath him, and seconds later she was free.

"That's what I mean", Shira explained, bending over and panting. "You really have to mean it, and you need to create an element of surprise. Are you okay, Ole?"

"Yes, I'm fine. You do throw a mean elbow, missy."

"Remember, if you're going up against someone like Ole-Einar, you can hit him in his muscles as much as you want, but you will never get away with it", Ariel interjected as Shira caught her breath. "You have to go to the soft tissues and control his head, his senses." Ariel turned to Natascha. "Do you want to give it a try?"

"Yes, I do", Natascha complied as she got in position. "Come on, Ole. Let's do this", she laughed and looked at her Viking friend, who couldn't help but chuckle.

"I thought you'd never ask", he laughed and got in position.

But as Natascha had feared, she could not create the momentum she needed to start the first sequence of her counter.

"Come on; you have to try harder. You have to mean it", Shira encouraged her.

Suddenly she saw Ariel kneeling beside her.

"You can hit harder than this, Natascha", the Israeli whispered. "Think back to your time on the ship. This guy is Chuck Hogan. He's the guy who killed Oliver, he's the guy who took you hostage, he's the guy who made you believe that you killed Nick, he's the guy who wanted to..." but Ariel couldn't finish.

Natascha felt a wave of anger rise deep within, the kind of anger she had only felt once before. The memories swarmed her entire being, sending her back on the *Northern Explorer,* when she had taken matters and the cold steel of a gun into her own hands. Natascha was unaware how often or how hard she had elbowed Ole-Einar in his face mask, but she suddenly realised she was standing.

"What the hell was that for?" Natascha yelled at Ariel, attacking him with a forceful push, not noticing that Shira yelled at her brother in Hebrew.

"I'm sorry for pushing your feelings, but you needed an ignition to harness the strength and energy that you otherwise wouldn't have had. You said yourself; you're not as trained as the others here, so I had to use something to trigger that response. I'm afraid that trigger was hatred in your case."

"That's bull! You know damn well how I react when someone brings that asshole up." Natascha yelled furiously again. Ariel only raised his arms in defeat, but she did not take it as a sign of apology. She slowly realised that she had just confirmed what he had told her.

"That wasn't fair, Ariel, you know that..." Natascha calmly whispered as she swallowed back the emotion.

"I am sorry", Ariel apologised and embraced Natascha. "Like I said, I didn't want to hurt your feelings. I just wanted you to know that you can do it with the right trigger. Now you know you can. We just have to find a different trigger. I'm sorry, it will never happen again", Ariel promised and placed a soft kiss on Natascha's forehead.

Natascha knew that he really meant it. She slightly nodded and walked over to wipe her face off with her towel. The anger was subsiding as embarrassment quickly grew. She almost forgot everyone else was in the room. Natascha swallowed hard to reach resolve before turning around to face her friends.

"Look, I know I'm not as good as you all are. So can you please stop pitying me like that?"

"We don't pity you, Natascha. We're sad for what you had to go through. We can only imagine the kind of pain you're feeling. No one should have to experience that." Tamar answered, offering her sympathy.

"Thanks", Natascha smiled weakly and was relieved. To know her friends knew what she had gone through made her feel a stronger connection.

"Um, Natascha..." Noah tried to get her attention.

"Yes?"

"You might want to check on Ole-Einar. I think you hit him pretty good."

"What?" Natascha stared at her Israeli friend in disbelief.

"Our Viking. He's bleeding!" Tamar explained.

"He is what? Oh my God!" Natascha spun around, and it was only now that Ole-Einar caught her attention. Still kneeling, the Norwegian had his face mask off and a towel pressed against his nose.

"Here, keep pressure on it. That should stop the bleeding soon", Rolf assisted his friend.

"Ole, are you okay?" Natascha wanted to know, rushing to his side.

"Well, I don't know. Why don't you tell me?" The Norwegian removed the towel, and Natascha flinched at the sight of the blood streaming out of a large gash on his nose.

"Oh, my God!" Natascha placed her hand on his solid shoulder. "Was that me?"

"Don't worry, I've been hit harder than this." Ole-Einar rose to his feet and pressed his towel again on his face before adding softly, "Just not by a woman."

Covering her face behind her hands, Natascha watched closely as her friend retreated back to the corner. Natascha could see he was going to collect his bag, but not before kicking the punching bag with such a force that it kept swinging. As the huge Norwegian left, a smile finally appeared on Natascha's face.

It worked. It really worked. I did it! Natascha could feel the pride swirling deep within her. She returned to her friends with new motivation.

"If I could only remember what I actually did, I might be able to do it again." Natascha joked with them.

"You did everything the way you were supposed to. It was—"

"Dear Lord IN HEAVEN! What happened to you Ole-Einar?" they heard Brian Whittaker yelling outside in the corridor. They couldn't decipher the Norwegian's answer, but they could still hear Brian's voice loud and clear.

"Was that Shira again?...What do you mean *not her*?...*Who* was it?... Seriously?... But *how*?" Brian continued as the girls were eavesdropping. They grinned as Natascha smiled weakly, guilt-stricken.

"Okay, let's get back to training. We wasted enough time." Shira finally demanded before they continued their workout.

They finished just before 5.00 p.m., and Natascha sat down for a minute to catch her breath.

"Talia, can you please do me a favour and pick up the little pumpkin downstairs? I have to hit the shower." Natascha asked her Israeli friend. Talia nodded her comply before gathering her things.

On her way to the showers Natascha quickly called the daycare to let them know the arrangement. Knowing that Shira-Sarah was in good hands, she took her time under the shower and joked together with the other women.

"Anyone interested in a sauna?" Tamar asked, "I think the guys are heating it up."

"I would love to, but I have to run. Maybe next time. Nick is coming home early, and I have to do some laundry and get the place back in shape. Are you coming with me, Shira?" Natascha asked.

"Yes, I'll be ready in a few minutes."

Shortly after, Natascha stood in some comfortable gym clothes, tackling her long black hair with a hair dryer. She worked her brush as she looked at herself in front of the mirror, promising herself to lose another few pounds.

"I'm just going to find Sarah", Natascha informed Shira before leaving the dressing room.

Usually Talia would wait with her daughter upstairs in the kitchenette. As expected, the young Israeli stood outside in the hall, talking in Hebrew on her cell phone. She was gesturing elaborately with her free hand.

"Hey Talia, thanks for picking her up", Natascha whispered as she sneaked by her, but her daughter was obviously not in the kitchen.

"Um, Talia, I don't want to interrupt, but did you pick Sarah up?" Talia looked at Natascha with confusion. "Because she's not in the kitchen!"

"What?" Talia asked, taken by surprise. She peaked into the kitchen. It took them just one moment to conclude the turnip was not there. Talia quickly ended the phone call and turned towards Natascha.

"We just came back ten minutes ago. She was fast asleep, and we couldn't wake her up. She was just here", the young Israeli panicked and started to look in all the cupboards.

"Well, if she was here, then she'll be somewhere on this floor. She can't open the door to the staircase, and she doesn't have a key for the elevator."

"But she was just in the kitchen, I don't understand?" the Israeli almost cried.

"Those little buggers never stay where you put them. She has two healthy legs, Talia. You will be surprised how far they can get. Don't worry, we'll find her", Natascha tried to calm Talia down, and, after she was convinced that her daughter was not in the kitchen, turned towards the hall.

"Where did you go, sweetheart?" Natascha asked herself and looked into two rooms. She finally stood in front of Brian's office and heard some voices.

Well, for her this just looks like any other door, I might as well ask him. The young German knocked at the door.

"Come in!"

"Excuse me, sir, but I'm looking for my daughter. Have you seen her?" Natascha asked and peeked inside Brian Whittaker's office. Her eyes widened in disbelief when she saw Shira-Sarah sitting in Brian's office chair. The retired admiral stood behind her and showed her some cartoons on the internet.

"I believe your mommy has found you. There's no more hiding now", Brian laughed and asked Natascha to come in.

"I'm so sorry, sir. You know I don't usually let her walk around like that. I promise that it..."

"Stop it, Natascha, it's okay!" Brian interrupted her, still laughing. "She walked in just a couple minutes ago. When she saw the computer, she told me she wanted to watch a cartoon. She's such a little angel." Brian said as Natascha picked her exhausted daughter up and kissed her.

"That she is indeed! Thank you for keeping an eye on her, sir."

"No problem, Natascha." Brian smiled, then continued, "Oh, and I would have to ask you for a favour."

"Anything, sir."

"Can I ask you to stop calling me *sir*? Brian will do just fine." The retired admiral requested in his fatherly tone.

"Mm...well....of course, sir...I mean...Brian. Thank you, sir...ah, Brian...Sorry, this is just confusing. Nick and the others...." Natascha stammered uncomfortably, understanding that only the members from Operation Control were on first name basis with the retired admiral. He did not mind them calling him *boss*, but the first name basis was reserved for only close friends.

"Oh, Natascha", Brian called her back just as she was at the door.

"Yes?"

"Nice job on the Viking", he winked.

Natascha blushed. "Thanks!"

About thirty minutes later, Natascha fought the usual rush hour, steering her yellow Mini in the right lane just before the traffic lights turned red.

"I had an awkward moment with the boss there", she confided in Shira and glanced at her in the passenger seat.

"Really? What happened?"

"Sarah wandered off and ended up in Brian's office. He turned her favourite cartoon on for her on the computer. When I found her, he asked me to stop calling him *sir*, but *Brian* instead. Isn't that weird?"

"Don't read too much into it. He and Klaus are still feeling guilty about the whole thing. They probably just want to make you feel more at home. As long as you deliver, you have nothing to worry about."

"Home sweet home", Natascha said and pulled into their driveway. Shira helped her godchild out of her booster seat and held her hand going inside.

"Okay, pumpkin. We're going upstairs. You might see aunt Shira later this evening. Say goodbye", Natascha told her daughter and watched as she kissed her godmother.

With her daughter spreading her toys all over the floor, Natascha capitulated rather quickly in her efforts to clean their place up. Exchanging text messages with Nick, she hurried downstairs to the basement to complete their laundry. A whistling sound had just announced Nick's latest message.

At the office. Debriefing and taking a shower. Home in 30. Natascha grinned and opened the door to the laundry room. With a quick flip of her hand, she turned the light on and walked over to the machine. They had all decided to use the same appliance and split the cost. Natascha placed her bin on the washing machine and sorted her laundry. She perked when she heard the main door open. *Maybe Shira or Talia.* Natascha thought, but then she heard rather heavy footsteps coming down the basement stairs. She turned around and saw Nick walking through the door.

"Hey, you're early! I didn't even start cooking..." but Nick had already pressed his lips on hers, holding her tight. Natascha succumbed to his embrace, his solid arms securing her against his sturdy frame. Her heart flipped as his hands released to the small of her back.

"Surprise! Talia gave me a ride. She was still at the office. How are you? I missed you", he asked quickly, kissing her again.

"I missed you, too. I'm fine. How was it?"

"Boring. How's the pumpkin?"

"She just had enough energy to spread all her toys on the floor before falling asleep", Natascha informed as she ran her hand along his shoulder. She patted it with purpose as she continued, "That'll change as soon as she hears you."

"Sleeping?" Nick sounded surprised, but then a sly smile crossed his lips. "So we're alone?"

"Yes, sleeping, but we're not alone; we're in the basement. The door is open, and Shira and Talia are ... Nick! ... What are you doing?" Natascha giggled as Nick pulled her closer once again and ran his hands over her body.

"This isn't the right place...they can walk in on us...Nick!"

"You want me to stop?" Nick whispered into her neck.

"No, that's not what I said", Natascha admitted, letting Nick unclasp her bra, "I just don't think that..." but Nick didn't let his wife finish and pulled her towards him again. Natascha passionately found herself submitting to him, her self-defence lessons quickly forgotten. Nick's hands danced along her soft skin as he started to undress her.

"Nick!...Not here...I'm not...I don't even...No, you're not going to do that! Those are my favourite!" Natascha pretended to protest, fearing that Nick would rip the fine fabric as he pulled her slip down. Despite her feeble opposition, Nick didn't slow down. Without any effort, he lifted her on top of the washing machine.

"Oh no, you're so not going to take me on the washing machine", Natascha objected half-heartedly, trying not to raise her voice too loud and hoping her husband would do precisely that.

"Either that or on the floor", Nick grinned mischievously, giving her the choice.

Natascha glanced at the floor. "Okay, the washing machine is fine", she concluded with a naughty smile as they both gave in to their desires.

Time slowed, a feeling Natascha only ever shared with Nick. The moment energetically danced through their minds. They shared another passionate kiss before Nick released his firm grasp.

"Gosh, this thing is not comfortable at all", Natascha commented when she finally slid from the appliance. Nick just smiled.

"Great! One more thing I can scratch off the bucket list. *Getting nailed in the basement on the washing machine.* My parents would be so proud of me", Natascha laughed as she collected her clothes.

"I hope we didn't break it", she stated her concern, kneeling beside the appliance to pick up her underwear.

"Ah, it'll be fine", Nick laughed, slipping his shirt back on. He buckled his jeans as Natascha stood in front of him.

"You're a pig! You still have to please me later tonight. But with a little more romance and effort! And I want a massage", she playfully demanded, slapping him with her shirt.

"Oh, you bet!" Nick promised as Natascha quickly dressed.

"Now leave, my husband will be home any moment", Natascha teased with the most serious voice she could manage as she pulled her T-Shirt down.

For a moment Nick debated his reply, but then he simply took out his wallet and opened it.

"Twenty-pounds, like always, right?" he asked seriously, turning the game back to Natascha. Her eyes narrowed to tiny slits.

"Yes, twenty as usual", she smiled and immediately took the twenty pound bill out of Nick's hand with a devilish grin. She placed a soft kiss on his cheek before she swiftly moved towards the door and ran upstairs.

"I'll put the pizza in the oven and wake up Sarah. Don't forget the laundry. Love you!" Natascha called from the stairs.

Nick looked into his now empty wallet and sighed before picking up their laundry.

A little later that evening Nick sat on their couch, with Sarah sleeping in his arms and Natascha telling him about her week. She told him about the incident during the self-defence session earlier, and updated him that they would be working together the coming weekend.

"So, you seriously broke Ole-Einar's nose? For real?"

"Well, I'm not sure if it's broken or not, but he was bleeding pretty good", Natascha laughed as she stroked Nick's short hair.

"Again?" Nick chuckled. Natascha watched as Nick glanced down at their daughter and then back at her.

"Just a little FYI, I wasn't finished in the basement", Natascha whispered. A smile crossed Nick's lips. "I wonder if Talia and Shira are going to say something." Natascha laughed.

"Ah, who cares", Nick stretched and yawned. "I'm tired", Nick admitted and leaned back, closing his eyes for a moment.

"Don't you even think about it!" Natascha told him.

- 3 -

Whitmore Abbey, Western England, Great Britain, Wednesday, May 7
Abbot Augustinus Hetley sat in his study behind his antique oak desk. With all his correspondence finished for the day, the sixty-five-year old cleric had a couple of hours left before the service in the evening. He would leave for London the very next morning for a couple of days. A benefit concert followed by a gala requested his presence. Abbot Hetley hoped that he could talk some business people or celebrities to provide a generous donation to Whitmore Abbey during the event. After all, this summer would be the first time that the centuries old abbey would be host to the International Catholic Bishops' Conference. Clerics from all over the world would visit the abbey during the conference, hosting several seminars and clinics during that week. Abbot Hetley's hopes rested on the variety of the programs and the performances of their famous choir to attract as many young families to this event as possible. He prayed that, with a little bit of luck, he could even draw the one or the other member of the Royal Family to visit them during that time. But it cost a lot of money to organise the conference, and these days it got harder and harder to receive financial contributions. The abbot rubbed his eyes and decided to worry about that later. He leaned in his chair, attempting to settle his thoughts.

His study was located on the top floor of the south-east tower, which housed all the administrative offices. The abbey was over one thousand years old, and most rooms were now unoccupied. The functions of Whitmore Abbey had decreased, but it still served as a home and spiritual refuge for a large number of monks. The orphanage also no longer existed. Until the mid-nineties, the abbey had been home to an undisclosed number of orphans for over three centuries, but those days were long gone. These days, the old stone building was the destination for many pilgrims and school trips. There was also very few people following their call to the Lord and devoting their life to the church. The abbot hoped he could change that trend.

With no sound disturbing the peaceful silence in his study, the abbot looked out of the window. His eyes travelled over the landscape, watching the fog rising from the old forest just a couple hundred yards away. Minutes later, his eyes rested on the remains of the old abandoned mine. The abbot remembered the history of the mine's final days, which he had read in the abbey's chronicle. During an airstrike in the Second World War, the then active mine had been hit. More than a dozen miners had been trapped inside the mountain. Only with all the villagers' combined effort could they all be rescued. It seemed like a miracle that there were no casualties. Unfortunately, they could never reopen the mine, since one of the bombs directly landed in one of the wells. The large explosion inside the well shaft had rerouted the underground water stream into the mine, eventually flooding the whole system. For decades, the locals had celebrated and thanked the Lord that no lives had been lost. This praise and celebration passed with the rise of the younger generation.

The abbot silently shook his head, thinking about how few people attended the daily services in Whitmore Abbey these days. Determined, the abbot had not given up in his efforts to get the younger people away from the computer and back into the house of the Lord. He knew he was fighting an uphill battle, but he was convinced it could still be done. With all the destruction going on in the world, the constant reporting of bad news, the young people would not only need the safe haven of the church; no, he was sure they would need someone to guide them there. How would they survive without spiritual guidance? The biggest problem for Abbot Augustinus Hetley was the constant threat in the Middle East; radical Muslims reaching for global power, installing caliphates and spreading terror wherever they could. For reasons beyond his understanding, the number of supporters for those radical groups grew by the day, while the Catholic Church struggled to keep its members. Abbot Hetley was a conservative, fascinated by the stories and history of the Knights Templar and their crusades during his youth. During the last couple of years, his frustration had grown the more he had thought about what was going on globally. Even worse, the influence of the Catholic Church and the Vatican in the worlds politic was almost non-existent. He knew many people turned their backs on the church over the scandals about paedophile priests in the news. Nevertheless, Abbot Hetley was still determined to help the Catholic Church rise back to old glory and political power.

When he had been approached three years ago, he had immediately recognised the opportunity as a sign of the Lord. With little hesitation at the beginning, a high ranking official at the Vatican had reassured him in his mission to grant his new allies access to what they were looking for. If their mission would succeed, and the abbot had no doubt about it, millions of people would come back and join the church again. Abbot Augustinus Hetley was still convinced that he was acting in the church's name and interest, but he knew his actions could no longer be considered in the name of the Lord.

"I have sold my soul to the devil! Forgive me, Jesus, for I have sinned", he whispered, looking at the crucifix on his table.

Austrian - Slovenian border crossing, Wednesday, May 7

Thirty-six year old Dragan Jankovic's enthusiasm for today's late shift at the Austrian-Slovenian border was a little higher than usual, but still very limited. With all the new regulations, they usually just checked for proper documentation on those travelling from Austria, but they rarely inspected vehicles. Years ago, young Dragan had been highly motivated, especially when some rich Slovenians came back from an expensive shopping trip north of the border. But as the years had gone by, the father of four had quickly learned that it would benefit his family more to accept a cash bribe from travellers and look the other way instead of writing them an expensive ticket.

Only a few cars crossed the border at his checkpoint today. He checked the passports, asked the usual questions, and wished them a good journey. Watching the car slowly moving ahead, he felt the familiar vibration of the cell phone in his pocket. He quickly glanced around, making sure that he was out of view of his supervisor before checking the message. It took him only a few seconds to send his reply. With newly found motivation, he attended to the next car, his eyes carefully watching the vehicles approaching from the distance. Minutes passed by before he turned his concentration on another vehicle, an ambulance. Not the newest model, but still in excellent mechanical condition and clearly identifiable as part of the United Nations peacekeeping fleet due to its markings and paint. Those vehicles were a no brainer.

Dragan waved the older Iveco 4 x 4 to the stop line. The driver in blue uniform cranked down the window and, without saying a word, handed him a clipboard with the necessary documents. The Slovenian took the clipboard, reading and flipping the pages as he walked around the windowless transporter. With the paperwork complete and the vehicle in safe condition, he just nodded to the driver and handed him the clipboard back. Wishing them a good journey, Dragan watched them drive off south, before he turned towards the next car. The envelope with money hidden under the sheets of paper on the clipboard was now securely stashed in his pocket. He just had pay day.

By late Thursday evening, the ambulance was on the last leg of its three-thousand-eight-hundred kilometre long journey to the Mediterranean harbour of Icel, located in the Mersin province in southern Turkey. After crossing the Austrian-Slovenian border, the vehicle continued south-east through Bosnia and Herzegovina, Serbia, and finally Bulgaria, where they crossed the border into Turkey. An extra diesel tank allowed the crew to drive longer distances and stop only when it was absolutely necessary.

Under the cover of darkness, the ambulance finally arrived at the Mediterranean coast in Icel in the early morning hours. With their engine and lights turned off, they waited in the shadows just outside the harbour area. The driver sent a text to their Turkish contact and waited for further instructions. Just minutes later, some of the street lights in the harbour went dark under the security cameras. Their contact was ready. The driver slowly drove the UN ambulance to meet their contact.

Asklepios, Aegean Sea, Friday, May 9
It was late in the afternoon, and Victor Gates arranged for his bed to be turned around. He simply loved seeing the sun set on the western horizon over the Aegean Sea. The sky shifted into a beautiful array of colours as Victor realised the young family with the sick boy had not been out all day. Their son rarely missed an opportunity to play in the pool, but Victor concluded he may had undergone treatment or surgery today. It was not that Victor really cared about the fate of the child; he simply preferred to know what was going on around him.

The top of the sun was burning the edge of the horizon, and the only sound was the automatic dispenser for Victor's pain medication. Victor watched as it administered another high dose of morphine into his veins. He closed his eyes for a few moments and waited for the drug to affect his nervous system. He hated drugs, but he knew only too well that he would have passed out without it. The pain that would have burned through his body within the next twenty minutes was not worth crossing his boundaries.

When he opened his eyes again, the sun dipped below the horizon, turning the sky into a dark red. As always, once the sun set, darkness came rather quickly. Using his communication system, Victor informed the medical personnel that he would stay outside a little longer. He had spent enough time in the confines of his room, so he took every chance he could to be under the open sky.

For about an hour, he watched the reflection of the moon dancing along the soft ripples of the Aegean Sea. He shivered as the moon grew brighter.

He sipped from his drinking tube and used his computer to notify the medical personnel that he was ready to return indoors. Maybe he would listen to the band this evening. They regularly had famous orchestras or select musicians playing for entertainment. It was one of the amenities that were considered a welcomed change for those who were stable enough to enjoy them. It was also an added pleasure for their loved ones who stayed with their relatives or friends.

Almost instinctively, Victor scanned the horizon again, searching for the small dot of the shuttle boat, but he knew it would not be arriving until later this evening. Resolving that it was still under the guise of the night, Victor listened carefully to the soft music as he waited patiently for the medical personnel.

It didn't take much longer before one of the male nurses, a young American by the name of Kevin Wilson, walked over to Mr Gates. "Good evening, Mr Gates. How was your day today?"

Boring! John Wayne's voice bolstered from the speech computer as Victor unenthusiastically typed each letter.

"My apology, Mr Gates."

It's okay. Not your fault.

Kevin nodded as he prepared the bed and began towards the elevator. They were just by the ramp that led to the BBQ pit when Victor spotted the enlarging shape of the shuttle boat approaching at a relatively high speed.

Wait! I want to watch!

Kevin stopped immediately and rearranged the bed for a better view.

Both Americans silently watched the shuttle boat coming closer. The sixteen-metre long boat operated under complete darkness except the illuminated position lights,

It is early.

"Yes, sir. They had to push the schedule ahead an hour. I believe it had something to do with the harbour patrol."

Did they find out anything?

"No, sir. Everything is fine."

Victor watched silently as the shuttle boat disappeared from his field of vision. For a brief moment he thought back to the day when he had arrived at Asklepios by a private helicopter, barely alive.

"If you don't mind, sir, we should go. They might need me downstairs."

Yes! Victor answered through the speech computer. By now, the shuttle boat would use its thrusters for the final approach. Victor thought it comforting that no one could see what would soon be happening.

How many? Victor asked curiously as they waited for the elevator.

"I don't know exactly. I was told about eight to ten." Kevin whispered, wary of the possibility of a lone patient or family member wandering around.

You think there will finally be one?

"The doctors will let you know once they have the results." Kevin reassured as the elevator doors opened.

Several metres below, two large steel doors sealed the hangar shut, keeping the shuttle boat secured and out of sight. A hydraulic platform adjusted itself to meet the height of the shuttle boat's deck to make the transfer easier.

Dr William Edwards stood on the platform, preparing to give a quick medical check-up for each person leaving the shuttle boat, before male nurses Lamar Hatcher and Leo Swan would direct them to their quarters.

As the British physician checked his watch, one of the crew members escorted the first person off the shuttle boat. She was a young Eastern European woman, maybe even a teenager. Her short black hair was a mess, and her clothes were dirty and torn. Dr Edwards could see she was still fighting the drugs they had given her; she could barely walk.

"Another one from the street", Dr Edwards remarked condescendingly as he snapped a pair of latex gloves, a very familiar sound. He pulled his face mask over his mouth and nose and shone his medical penlight into her eyes to check her reflexes. Like the rest of the human cargo, she was heavily sedated by drugs. Dr Edwards clicked his pen, satisfied.

"I am sorry I'm late, Mr Gates stayed out longer tonight", Kevin apologised, his coat tail following behind his swift footsteps.

"Don't worry, Kev. We just started. This one here is fine. Let's hope we can put her in group A." The British doctor diagnosed after his quick examination and turned his attention to the next young woman. They estimated her to be in her early twenties, short blonde hair, definitely of Western European heritage. The young woman groaned as Lamar and Leo dragged her towards the doctor, her feet trailing behind her, almost lifeless. Dr Edwards pulled her head up by the hair for a better inspection.

"Leo, hold her head up will you?" he asked impatiently and started his examination. "Should also be group A. Let's go, next one", he determined after a short while, and Leo and Lamar dragged the young woman away.

"Dear Lord, he's definitely group C", Kevin dismissively stated as he saw the next arrival. It took two crew members to drag the man off the shuttle boat.

"Yes, I would say mid-to-late forties, definitely homeless", Dr Edwards paused, using his pen to lift up the sleeve of his clothes, his tongue clicked as he continued, "Ah, a war veteran, look at the tattoos. Once we detoxify him, he'll be very useful."

The procedure continued in a similar manner before they were finally done.

"Six for group A or B and three for group C. Could have been worse", Dr Edwards calculated in such a tone that one could be mistaken that he was calling a race between two turtles.

"Ok, guys, you all know the drill. Let's get them all cleaned up, burn their clothes and get them to their quarters. We start testing tomorrow. Start flushing the drugs out of their system and hook up the IV. Once testing is complete, they have to eat and drink. Some of them have been without food for almost forty-eight hours."

"I'll take group A." Leo volunteered.

"Forget it, we clean them all one after the other, like always. There's no fooling around."

"Goddamn it, where is the fun in that?"

"You know the rules."

- 4 -

***EuroSecCorporation*, London, Saturday, May 10**

"For heaven's sake, Natascha, can you please stop looking at your cell phone? You literally checked it thirty seconds ago. It's not Talia's first time babysitting your daughter", Ole-Einar insisted as he steered one of the Land Rovers through London to pick up their client.

"I know, but I think my pumpkin is coming down with something. She was a little bit cranky today", Natascha replied from the passenger seat, concern trailing in her voice. Ole-Einar exchanged brief eye contact with her, and she finally tucked her cell phone into her pocket. She diverted her gaze to the other Land Rover, knowing it was Shira and Nick in front of them.

"I'm really sorry about your nose, Ole. That honestly wasn't my intention", Natascha apologised for what seemed to be the one-millionth time.

"That better be your intention if you're in a situation like that", Ole-Einar interjected. "And if you apologise one more time, I swear I'll beat Nick to a pulp."

"Nick? What does he have to do with this?" Natascha laughed and looked at her Norwegian friend.

"Simple. You know I would never hurt you, so he's the next best thing."

"But he's only half your size", Natascha protested with a lame attempt to protect her husband.

"That's his problem, not mine", the Norwegian stated coldly with a shrug of his shoulders.

"You touch him and I'll break your nose again", Natascha threatened her teammate, imitating a stern voice.

"Now I'm really scared", Ole-Einar laughed and followed the other Land Rover to one of the more notable addresses in London."Okay, we will be there any minute now. I wonder if he's already drunk."

"I can't stand drunk people", Natascha complained, pressing her back into her seat.

"Oh, you're going to love him. I bet you five pounds it will take him less than one hour before he starts hitting on you."

"He really does that?"

"Are you kidding? You heard Shira. The only reason we're here today is for him to show off."

"Did he hit on one of the others before?"

"Of course he did, that's the reason Shira doesn't like him."

"What did she do? I'm not going to listen to some stupid remarks from that guy all night long, and I don't care how much money he pays."

"Ah, it might not be that bad. Shira told him to piss off the last time, after that he behaved much better."

"Shira said that?" Natascha asked surprised.

"Yes, but not in such words. I guess that was the only time his life was in real danger. If it wasn't for Ariel, I believe she would have punched him." Ole-Einar corrected the wheel as he began again, "It's that building over there, the one with the cast iron gate and the black Bentley in front of the main door. We're just going to drive around the block to check the perimeter, standard procedure. You never know, maybe there's someone out there who really wants to punch this guy on the nose. Wouldn't surprise me at all."

They slowly drove around the block before turning into the driveway. The gate opened automatically once Nick identified them. The two British SUVs rolled over the short driveway's fine gravel to the mansion's main entrance.

Natascha watched as Nick and Shira stopped in front of them.

"What is this guy's name again?"

"Rowan Dean Harrison. He's the heir to the Harrison Empire. As far as I'm concerned, he's a total loser, but his family still believes he'll come around one day."

"Wait a second. You mean *the* Harrison family?"

"Yes, that's the one."

"But didn't he study at a university to take over the business?"

"He did. Went to Oxford. I wouldn't be surprised if his parents paid for a new building so that junior would get his degree", Ole-Einar shifted in his seat, his eyes peeled to the door. "I believe he's coming out any moment."

They both watched as Nick and Shira exited their Land Rover.

"There he is", Ole-Einar noted and nodded towards the stairs leading down from the main door.

Natascha tried to get a closer look. After all the delightful stories of her first client, Natascha was very curious what he looked like. She recalled reading about him in the tabloids, but could not recall what he looked like. Rowan Dean Harrison was in his mid-thirties, about 1,74m tall, and definitely not in any physical shape. He was sporting a British hair cut from the sixties, but not even the tuxedo could add any class to his appearance. Natascha knew the man was not stupid, but quickly concluded he was simply too lazy and too preoccupied enjoying his playboy lifestyle than tending to the priorities of the family business. As he walked towards the first Land Rover, Natascha further concluded that he must have indeed already enjoyed one or two expensive bottles of port.

"Yep, he's a keeper", Natascha commented under her breath.

"Oh, just wait until he talks to you!" Ole-Einar laughed.

"Yeah, that's going to be a life-changing moment for me!" Natascha shared his tone, her eyes widening as she watched. "What's he doing now?"

They could both see Rowan Harrison gesticulating wildly, his arms waving at the Land Rover. He was clearly arguing with Shira, who shared the same contempt.

"What's that about? Do we have to get out?" Natascha inquired quickly.

"No, we stay in. I assume he's complaining that we're not here with the Range Rovers. Obviously he's not too enthusiastic about our Land Rovers. After all, they are much cheaper than the Range Rovers. He probably thinks that they are not good enough for him."

After a minute of the heated argument, Rowan Dean Harrison stormed back to the house.

"Wow, what's going on Shira?" Ole-Einar asked his friend over the radio.

"Nothing. The idiot is just getting his company. We are ready to go", the Israeli replied aggressively.

"Relax, take a deep breath."

"One day I will shoot the guy." Shira cursed looking at them, but turned back towards the door once she noticed some movement in her peripherals.

"Okay, who is *that*?" Natascha burst inquisitively as the Harrison heir walked towards the Land Rover again, this time with his escort.

Both Natascha and Ole-Einar leaned forward to take a closer look.

"Who is it this time?" Ole-Einar asked himself, his fingers drumming on the steering wheel with recollection. "Ah, the man has taste. This one is *Saphir*. Well, her real name is ... you know what? I forgot her real name, not that it matters. I think we only know her as *Saphir*."

"You *all* know her?" asked Natascha, her voice much louder than it should have been. Natascha's cheeks burned with jealousy.

"Yes, she's often escorting him to such events. I think she's from Spain. Shira knows her."

Natascha seemed unusually upset about the fact that their client was accompanied by an expensive call girl. She had been informed on various occasions that this could happen, yet Natascha's eyes burned as she inspected the woman further. Her eyes rested on Saphir's three inch stiletto heels. A strange sound escaped Natascha's lips once she realised the Spaniard was an elite escort. Those three inch heels were undeniably Louis Vuitton, Dolce and Gabbana, Manolo Blahnik, or some other prestigious designer. No matter, just her shoes alone were worth far more than what Natascha made in a month. Her elegance radiated from the plunging neckline of her gorgeous red Versace evening gown. Saphir glided down the stairs, her clutch grasped delicately within her hand. She was notably taller than Rowan, who rested his hand on her seemingly perfect waist as Nick opened the SUV door for them.

"She's something else!" Ole-Einar whistled his attraction, then blissfully continued, "And she's not stupid. Really easy to talk to."

"Oh, really?" Natascha sarcastically asked, but Ole-Einar didn't even hear her. His eyes trailed along Saphir's gown, the soft skin of her breasts curving under the plunging neckline. His eyes trailed further down as she turned, the plunging back collecting at her hips.

"Ah, look at that ass!"

Natascha punched her friend on the thigh, snapping Ole-Einar from his fantasy. He collected himself quickly, suddenly realising it was Natascha beside him and not one of the guys. Natascha returned her attention to the pair, watching as Rowan balanced her curved fingers on his own. Natascha's eyes narrowed with disquieting interest as she watched Nick boldly placing his hand on the small of her back. She could see his fingers accidentally slide under the thin red fabric. Natascha's jaw dropped slowly as Nick shared an intimate smile, Saphir's eyes glowing hesitantly. Rowan Dean Harrison was oblivious to Nick and Saphir's exchange as they

approached the Land Rover, but Saphir's subtle wink was unmistakable.

"Excuse me, wait a second!" Natascha blurted as a wave of jealousy came over her. "Did she just wink at Nick?"

"Natascha, calm down! She knows him from work", Ole-Einar explained easily.

"*What?* She knows Nick from *work*? Excuse me?" Natascha snapped at the Norwegian.

"*Our* work, Natascha. Not *hers*. For heaven's sake, don't make a scene, especially not at the gala. You knew damn well there might be an escort with Harrison. And like all the escorts of her price range, she's not only attractive and well educated, but also knows how to behave in public with Rowan. She has been with him before, that's how she knows about us. She knows who we are and what we do. All she does is giving us the same courtesy as we are showing towards her. So relax, for God's sake."

Natascha's grip tightened on her seatbelt, the tension releasing as she thought for a moment, considering she may have overreacted.

"I suppose I should come to such events more often. Here I thought I would support my hard-working husband, and what's he doing? Driving in a fancy SUV with a young Cindy Crawford", Natascha brusquely stated with finality as Ole-Einar put the Land Rover into motion.

"Like I said, don't worry about her." Ole-Einar reassured. "She's making more money tonight than Nick does in a month. She has no interest in him."

"How do you know how much money she makes?" Natascha asked curiously, wondering if Ole-Einar heard her previous thoughts.

"We might have asked her", the Norwegian mumbled to his defence, knowing the argument was far from over.

"Ah, you've already asked her about her rates. Interesting! This is getting better and better! So does Nick, I mean...do you guys always talk to her?"

"Natascha, I told you to relax. We spoke to her couple of times in the past. Besides, we had to check her out for the assignment. She's really not such a bad person."

"Hm, okay..." Natascha considered half-heartedly, "Nick has just never mentioned her."

"Should he?"

Natascha turned her lips, Ole-Einar had a point. Natascha thought about an answer.

"No, I guess not. I just didn't realise this could be part of the job."

"Sometimes it is. But you should know she has way more integrity than most of the other people we protect."

"Maybe, but she is also much better looking than most of the other people, and she is totally Nick's type."

"You can relax. Nick can't afford someone like her anyway", Ole-Einar explained, immediately regretting his choice of words as he watched Natascha's jaw drop.

"Are you calling me *cheap*? Do I look *cheap* to you?"

"No! Absolutely not", the Norwegian defended immediately, then mumbled, "Oh dear Lord, I'm screwed." Ole-Einar shifted uncomfortably in his seat, exchanging a quick glance with Natascha before he continued. "You don't look cheap, Natascha.

You look as expensive as she does." Despite his confident glance, his nervousness was evident. He could feel the sweat on his palms.

"So back then, when we first met, you guys were thinking of me as an *escort* rather than a scientist?"

"No, that's not what I meant! I never thought you could work as an escort", the Norwegian explained further, convinced he had won the argument with that.

"Oh, so you're calling me *ugly* and *stupid* now?"

"Oh for heaven's sake, Natascha..." Ole-Einar was still searching for the right words but could not see the sky from the hole he dug himself in to.

"I'm just kidding, Ole-Einar", Natascha laughed freely, her hands meeting with one loud clap. "You guys are so predictable! And you are such a sexist! And a pig! But I do remember that back then, when we first met in Norway, you guys all graded my bum", Natascha accused her friend.

The Norwegian flushed several shades of red, his gaze retreating from hers.

"Yes, we did. And before you ask, we gave her a higher score than we gave you", the Norwegian calmly added with a renewed confidence.

"Shush", Natascha retorted. "Nick told me the scores you gave me. Back then I had the body of a Greek Goddess", Natascha dramatised with a face.

"Buddha was not a Greek Goddess", Ole-Einar shook his head with a serious expression. Natascha's jaw fell open again, his insult leaving her literally speechless. Before she could recover, Ole-Einar announced they would soon arrive at the concert hall.

"Okay, so when we stop, you and Shira will get out. Shira will open their door and you just wait for them to exit the Land Rover. After that, you just stay beside Shira and walk behind them through the entrance. There are about four or five invited reporters. They will have their credentials around their neck. Make sure you are not in the pictures once they start shooting. That's basically it. Once Nick and I have parked the vehicles, we'll meet you inside. Okay?"

"Okeydokey", Natascha confirmed enthusiastically and unfastened her seat belt.

"Oh, Natascha!"

"Yes?"

"No hair pulling!"

"I can't promise that!" Natascha winked and walked over to Shira, who had just opened the door for the fawn.

Ole-Einar shook his head, already working on an explanation for Brian and Klaus for the impending top news story and tabloid cover pictures of a cat fight between one of their employees and a client's escort.

To his surprise, the small group made it without incident to the entrance. He turned his attention to the SUV in front of him and followed Nick to the valet parking lot. Entering the concert hall through the side entrance, they reunited with the group just minutes later.

Judging by the expression on Natascha's face, Ole-Einar figured she already had the pleasure of talking to Mr Harrison.

"Okay, it's about bloody time to see if we can find something to drink", Rowan suggested and looked around. "Ay-up, ladies, please follow me", he commanded as he aimed for the nearest bar.

"We'll all be following you", Shira explained to him before he took his first step.

"That's fine with me, Miss *One-Thousand-And-One-Nights*, as long as the ladies stay close to me."

"First of all, my name is *Hadad* and I'm not from an oriental fairy tale. And second, we're not here for your pleasure, we're here for your safety", the Israeli explained, not without giving Saphir a quick look. "We had that discussion before, didn't we?" she added coldly.

"Ah, bloody hell. Whatever", the young British heir snickered and laid his arm tight around Saphir's waist. "Let's go darling, you're much better looking anyway", he complimented his escort. Although Saphir flashed him her beautiful smile, everyone other than Rowan noticed she slightly rolled her eyes and shook her head at his behaviour.

With Shira in the lead, the little group escorted Rowan towards the large bar, not without stopping several times to allow the young heir to meet some of his equally drunk and obnoxious friends. Natascha was fascinated by the number of celebrities she recognised, but this fascination quickly turned to disgust upon witnessing their behaviour.

After Rowan had generously helped himself through a couple more drinks, a voice announced that it was time to take their seats.

"Shall we, my love?" Rowan offered Saphir his arm. She gave him her best smile in return and they slowly walked over to a table, closely followed by his protection detail.

"Hey, Dean, my mate! Nice to see you made it", one of his friends, a renowned athlete, greeted him. He assumed a seat next to Rowan as he shook his hand. After a few words and another glass of expensive scotch, Rowan turned his attention to his friend. Saphir discreetly clenched her fist with frustration standing beside him.

"Here, let me help you", Nick offered instinctively, pulling her chair out.

"Thank you, Nick. At least there's one gentleman at this table", she graciously thanked him, not without throwing an accusing glance at Rowan.

"You're welcome", Nick replied softly as he looked up. He attempted to hide his alarm when he met Natascha's jealous eyes.

What? He formed with his lips and shrugged his shoulders. Nick wished that would be the end of it, but knew better.

"We'll be in the back. You know how to reach us", Shira told Rowan in a low voice. The young British playboy stopped in his conversation and looked at them.

"That's right. Unfortunately there's no more room at the table. You can go for now. I'll summon you if I need anything", he smirked at the scowl on Shira's face. Saphir retreated her hands to her lap and looked away, obviously ashamed.

Without a word, Shira turned around and hurried away. Just a minute later they walked through the door to the lounge they shared with other drivers and security detail.

"If there was ever a guy that I really hate!" She growled in Hebrew the moment she closed the door behind her. "Natascha, what did he say to you outside, just before we started walking towards the entrance?" the Israeli demanded to know.

"Nothing", Natascha replied, offering a brief shrug after she noticed Nick's concern. "He just asked me to call him *Dean* or *Rowan.* I told him that I would prefer to call him *Mr Harrison,* and that he would have to address me as *Miss Levi.* You know, I'm supposed to be Talia."

"He's such a drunk idiot!" Shira continued as they stepped over to a table for some free coffee.

"I have to admit, he's really obnoxious", Natascha attested, pouring herself a cup before joining them at the table. Natascha shifted her hot coffee to her other hand, "You're not going to offer me a chair, Nick?"

Nick shifted more comfortably in his seat as the others laughed. "No, why would I? We're already married", Nick replied seriously, but offered a quick wink. Natascha had never been known for her subtlety; her disapproval of his chivalry just minutes ago was very apparent.

"I don't know how much money she's getting for this, but I can tell you it's not enough", Natascha commented before taking a sip. "So, what's going to happen next?"

"Hopefully not much. We wait here for the most part and peek out the door a couple times. After the dinner, the paying guests have a meet and greet with the celebrities and artists. Once that happens, we'll be outside floating on the floor again. Natascha, we'll take the first round." Shira informed, then continued with a shrug, "There's really not much else to it."

"Sounds easy enough", Natascha yawned and stretched.

As Shira had estimated, it was just over an hour before the last part of the social event took place. The two ladies returned to the main hall to their client just in time.

"Ah, here you are again. Listen, there's a bishop who wants to talk to me briefly, it's about a donation my family made to his abbey." Rowan informed Shira with a serious tone. "I hope that's okay?"

"A bishop wants to talk to you? *Really?*"

"Yes", Rowan nodded, shifting his weight from one foot to the other as he continued. "Is that okay, or do you have to check him out first?"

First Shira thought that Rowan Harrison was joking with her, but she now realised he was actually serious.

"Well, considering he's a bishop, I believe we can loosen our standard procedures just this once", Shira assured her client, not without a note of sarcasm in her voice.

"Okay, let's go then", he said and walked surprisingly balanced. Shira questioned how he could handle such large amounts of alcohol. He seemed surprisingly sober after the dinner.

"I'll handle this. You can stay here", Shira whispered to Natascha with a slight nod, before she caught up to their client. To Natascha's surprise, Saphir also stayed back with her, sipping on a non-alcoholic drink.

"You're not going with him?" Natascha asked, unable to hide her surprise.

"No, for some reason the bishop does not approve of me", Saphir stated disdainfully.

"Geeze, what might be the reason for *that",* Natascha whispered, but just loud enough to be certain that Saphir heard her.

"I don't know. Maybe he doesn't like my work. Or maybe he's afraid I might open my little black book. You'll be surprised how many names are in there that the church really doesn't want to see published."

"Yeah, that might be it", Natascha replied with some sarcasm, but she silently had to admit that the Spanish woman had a valid point.

"Or it could be because I got raped by a priest when I was a child, and when I finally came forward about it when I was twenty, I lost my job and couldn't find a new one. At least not what's considered an *honourable* job", Saphir shot back at Natascha.

"I'm sorry", Natascha finally apologised, uncertain how to react. "I didn't know that. I...I don't know you and I shouldn't have said it", she added.

"Forget it, I made the story up. I'm used to other women not liking me, especially when I'm around their spouses."

"How do you know?" Natascha was taken aback, surprise lilting in her voice.

"When you introduced yourself to Rowan earlier this evening, you spoke with a German accent, same as Nick. You also mispronounced your name, which makes me believe that it's not your real name. You and Nick also wear the same style wedding ring. And you wanted to kill him when he offered me a chair. Just because I do what I do doesn't mean I'm stupid. Please respect that." Saphir stated flatly as she watched Rowan and Shira approaching the bishop. A flare of embarrassment rose in Natascha's cheeks as Saphir continued. "The reason I'm not going with him to talk to the bishop is because we mutually disapprove of each other. I don't approve of him and the church."

"At least we got that in common", Natascha noted, establishing a common ground. Saphir was right. Natascha had no right to judge her, so she decided to give her the same courtesy as anyone else.

During the whole conversation, Natascha had not taken her eyes off Shira, who a young man now approached. Judging by the camera equipment he carried and the badge around his neck, Natascha identified him as a reporter. The young guy briefly spoke to Shira, obviously seeking her approval.

"You know that guy?" Natascha asked Saphir, her eyes locked on the reporter.

"No, never seen him before." Saphir answered, but Natascha was already approaching Shira.

"Just a reporter, Natascha. He's fine." Shira explained and told the reporter that he had to wait until Rowan Harrison had finished his conversation with the bishop.

"Why in the world does a reporter want to talk to this idiot?" Natascha whispered in Shira's ear.

"He doesn't. He wants to talk to the bishop", the Israeli explained in a lowered voice just as Rowan Harrison turned towards them again.

"Okay, let's see if we can find something to drink here. Where's the next bar?" Rowan demanded as he moved through the crowd again. His steps slowed as one of his friends stopped him after a few metres. Rowan reached up to the tray a waiter carried, collecting himself and his friend a glass of Scottish whiskey.

Natascha removed her attention from Rowan and surveyed the room again. Her eyes found the young reporter and the bishop. *There are a million celebrities here, and that guy talks to a bishop.* Natascha debated sharing her thoughts with Shira, but quickly decided against it. After all, this was her first security job and the last thing she wanted to do was to make an idiot out of herself. She decided to keep watching. What looked like a harmless conversation from the distance seemed to turn into a heated argument between the bishop and the reporter. The young reporter wildly gestured with his arms, while the bishop simply frowned, shaking his head.

"Shira, I think there's something wrong with the reporter and the bishop", Natascha cautiously alerted her friend, not sure what else she should have done.

"What?" asked the young Israeli and turned around. "For heaven's sake, seriously? Nick, Ole, can you come out please? We have a minor situation here between what looks like a bishop and a reporter. Not our client. Out the door at your two o'clock. Ten metres", Shira calmly spoke into her PTT microphone, her eyes locked on the door to the lounge. Not even five seconds later, Ole-Einar and Nick walked out and approached Shira and Natascha. So far, no one else had noticed the heated dispute.

"Ole, you stay with Rowan, we'll see what's going on", Shira explained and looked at Natascha. "If you want to come, by all means", she invited her and walked over to the discussion.

"Excuse me, sir. Is there something we can help you with?" Shira politely intervened, announcing their presence.

"Yes, maybe you can tell this gentleman to stop bothering me. I'm already late and don't have time for this", the bishop explained sternly.

"And you are, sir?" Shira asked the reporter, who immediately calmed down.

"My name is McRae. Kyle McRae. I'm a freelance reporter. I'm working on a story about an abbey, and I wanted to ask the bishop here some questions", the young reporter explained, gesturing to the bishop.

Shira guessed that Kyle was in his mid-twenties. A rented suit ensured he was properly dressed for this occasion. A quick check on his credentials confirmed that he had indeed been assigned as an official reporter for tonight's event.

"It seemed as though you were getting a little emotional with your questions. May I suggest you request an official appointment for your interview? I'm certain here and now is neither the right place nor the right time for this", Shira explained to Natascha's surprise. She had never seen or heard such a polite side from her Israeli friend.

"Yeah, thanks for the tip. Whitmore Abbey has stonewalled me for two years! And now I don't even get an answer from the bishop", the Reporter explained angrily before turning towards the cleric. "Yes, you know I'm right. Why don't you explain to them why you haven't answered any of my e-mails or phone calls?"

"Like I said before", Shira interrupted him, stepping between him and the bishop. "This is neither the right place nor the right time. I have to ask you to calm down or security will escort you off the premises. If that happens, it'll be very difficult for you to be admitted to such events ever again."

His Scottish temperament urged him to argue, but Kyle knew this lady from the security service was right. He took a couple deep breaths and stepped back.

"Okay, you're right, I will leave. But I just want to tell you that I will go ahead with the story. Here's another copy of what I've already sent you", Kyle explained as he handed a manila envelope to the bishop. "I will publish it, both online and in magazines. No more cover-ups and no more hiding!" the emotional reporter threatened before he turned around and headed for the exit.

"Are you all right, sir?" Shira asked the bishop, but Abbot Augustinus Hetley's eyes trailed the reporter, nervously turning the envelope in his hands.

"Excuse me?" he asked as Shira repeated her question. "Yes, I'm fine. Thank you. I don't know what got into this young man", the abbot lied, attempting to mitigate the situation.

"Well, he seemed very eager to speak with you."

"Hm, yes...indeed. Well, I don't know what he was talking about. If he wants to talk to me, he only has to contact the abbey", the bishop concluded, then turned on his feet. "Now, if you'll excuse me, I really have to go now. God bless you", the abbot looked down at the Israeli and turned around towards the exit.

Shira exchanged a quick glance with both Nick and Natascha with raised eyebrows.

"Well, one of them was clearly lying", Nick commented on their short way back to Rowan.

"What was that about?" asked Ole-Einar who couldn't hear the argument, but stole quick glances.

"We're still not sure, but it's not our concern", Shira explained matter-of-factly.

"Well, whatever was in the envelope, he didn't like it. He just tore it up and threw it in the garbage", the Norwegian noted before turning his attention towards Rowan again.

"I'll be right back", Natascha whispered the moment she located the garbage bin next to the door. She was grateful she wasn't wearing heels tonight as she hurried over to the bin. With a quick look she recognised what was left of the envelope and glanced around. No one seemed to pay any attention to her, and she quickly recovered all six pieces of the envelope and tucked them into her front pocket. With the remains concealed, she slowly walked back to her group.

"Everything all right?" asked Nick, who, like the rest of her friends, had not noticed she had rummaged through the garbage.

"Yes, I'm fine."

"Okay, I think two of us can return to the security room. No need for all four of us hanging around here", Shira noted, then looked to Natascha, "Natascha, you want to come?"

Shira and Natascha returned to the lounge, fixing themselves another cup of coffee.

"No one said this would be exciting", Shira remarked as Natascha stretched and yawned again after another two boring hours in the lounge.

"Yes, but this is *really* boring", Natascha replied and laughed at a text she just received.

"What?"

"It's from Talia. She wrote that Sarah claimed to get really sick as soon as Nick and I were gone. Talia just told her that this is really sad, because she could not have any chocolate cookies if she's sick. Needless to say, that triggered the fastest recovery ever", Natascha laughed again as she explained. Her laugh softened as the lounge door opened and Saphir entered.

"What's going on?" Shira raised her head, still lying in her comfortable chair.

"Ah, nothing", answered the Spanish escort before she sighed with relief. She poured herself a cup of coffee. "Do you mind if I sit with you?"

"Why not? Come over", Shira offered while Natascha frowned at her.

"Are you okay?" Shira asked once Saphir sat down. Shira could not help but notice that Saphir looked depressed. The Spanish woman took her time and continued to stir her coffee.

"Yes, I'm fine, thanks. Rowan is just so annoying when he's drunk. He's actually relatively nice and polite when he's sober, but he turns into a real idiot once he picks up a bottle."

"Yes, we know. Unfortunately he's not the only one like that. Is he not treating you well?" the Israeli asked with a note of sympathy.

Saphir laughed, but it almost sounded like a groan.

"Shira, you know what I do for a living. How do you think he's treating me?" the Spanish escort returned with a lowered, sad voice.

Natascha didn't take part in their conversation. She just listened to them and almost felt sorry for Saphir.

"Believe it or not, tonight is actually one of the better jobs", Saphir continued with a laugh.

"Excuse me?" Natascha asked, certain she misunderstood the Spaniard.

"It's simple. Rowan is so drunk right now that he'll pass out the moment he sets foot through his door. Nothing is going to happen tonight. I just have to endure him for the next two hours."

"Well, Alba, you can stay here with us as long as you want, if that's an option for you. I can tell him you got sick." Shira offered.

Alba? Natascha frowned, but then remembered that *Saphir* was her working name.

"That's okay, Shira. I'll manage. It's all part of the job, and I can walk away from it at any time. He's just one of the better paying clients, so I will just play along. I've been escorting him for over a year now", Saphir reflected. "You know, if he just wouldn't hit the bottle so heavy he could succeed in taking over the family business. But I have to give him credit. His family just got involved in a big business deal a couple of months ago, and he slowed down during that time", Saphir exchanged a glance with Shira, who seemed surprised, then continued, "except for tonight."

"Aren't you supposed to keep those things to yourself?"

"Shira, I didn't tell you anything that you wouldn't read in the tabloids or online. Everybody knows he's a genius when he is sober. We just have the misfortune of watching him drink himself to death with this playboy aspiration. You have no idea how crazy he gets when he parties. I'm very grateful you're here tonight, it means he'll stick solely to the booze."

"Glad we can help", Natascha smiled weakly.

While Saphir and Shira continued to talk about more casual matters, Nick and

Ole-Einar had the pleasure to stay with Rowan Harrison. Within the last hour, he and his friend, a very famous British rock star, emptied an entire bottle of old Scottish whiskey. Even an experienced playboy like Rowan Dean Harrison had reached his limits with that. With the British rock star heading for the men's room, Rowan turned towards Nick and Ole-Einar.

"I think I should go home now. That whiskey made me really tired", he slurred.

"Well, you definitely had enough", Nick stated matter-of-factly.

Rowan looked at him for several seconds, trying to coordinate his thoughts.

"You know...you're okay", he pointed with a shake of his finger, "Nick? Right?"

"Yes, that's me", Nick played along.

"I know what you think of me", the British heir continued. "And I'm not saying that you're wrong...But, hey, what's the purpose of life when you can't party once in a while...I admit, I love sex, drugs and rock'n roll...so what?"

"As long as you're happy", Nick decided that it was best to simply agree.

"You two seem to be nice blokes", Rowan gestured at Nick and his Norwegian friend. "You should both come with me... We can have a great party! It's better than here", he gestured elaborately. "You won't believe the places I can get you in to, Venice, Monaco, great places! Great parties! You know what you should do?" Rowan continued to slur on their way to the exit.

"What should we do?" Ole-Einar entertained his thought.

"You should come and party with me on the Shadow!"

"Party with you in the shadow? Really?" Nick asked with a slump of his shoulders.

"Yes, yes, yes!" Rowan enthusiastically nodded. "You should both come and party on the Shadow. Best music...endless booze...and they only get the best girls."

"Sounds like a party to me", Ole-Einar commented, just as they stepped through the door.

"It is the best. Just let me know and I can arrange everything...Remember! The best parties are always on the Shadow...in the orient", Rowan mumbled as he felt the fresh air burn deep through him. He stood between Nick and Ole-Einar waiting for his limousine to pick him up. He glanced to his right again and noticed Shira, Natascha, and Saphir walking towards them.

"Oh...there they are! I almost forgot about her", he laughed wildly, turning to Nick with sudden thought. "What was her name again? Diamond, Rubin...or something else expensive...oh, wait! It was Saphir. I remember!"

Nick and Ole-Einar exchanged looks and shook their heads.

Just before the women caught up to them, Rowan turned towards Nick and the Norwegian, "Guys, don't tell anyone...but the girl and I aren't really dating", the Briton snickered as he revealed his seemingly unknown secret.

"You got to be kidding me?" Ole-Einar gasped at his revelation, continuing his facade. "Really?"

Rowan just closed his eyes and nodded heavily. Before another word was spoken, the black Bentley pulled up beside them. The driver got out of the limousine and quickly opened the door, first for Saphir, then for Rowan.

"Here, he's all yours!" Shira announced to the driver as he closed the door behind Rowan.

"Yeah, thank you very much", the driver replied with a roll of his eyes. Inside the Bentley, Rowan pressed the button to lower the window.

"Hey...Miss *Thousand-and-One-Nights*. You should really come with me...You don't know what you're missing..."

"I'm sure I'll survive", Shira replied.

"Ah, come on...I can make you breakfast!" He attempted to use his charm and convince her. He slightly hung out the window as he continued, "How do you like your eggs?"

"Unfertilised", Shira snapped at him coldly just as the limousine took off.

Shira looked back at her friends and colleagues, their bewildered expressions fixed on the limousine as it turned the corner.

"I almost feel sorry for him", Natascha commented freely as they walked towards their SUVs. "Can you imagine living like that?"

"Driving home with a beautiful woman?" Nick chided. "No idea how that feels."

"You know you'll regret this, right?" Natascha returned, while Ole-Einar and Shira couldn't help but laugh.

"Okay, let's go home", Shira interrupted with a yawn, taking a backseat in one of the Land Rovers. "It's really late."

Natascha pondered the events of the night, satisfied her first security detail experience had been uneventful. It was just five minutes into the drive when she turned to speak with Shira, who was already fast asleep.

"How does she do it?" Natascha asked with some curiosity. "She can fall asleep anywhere."

"Yeah, it comes in handy", Nick replied, courteously turning the music down. He turned his attention back to his wife. "So, how did you like it?"

"It was interesting. First time I have ever been so close to so many celebrities. They all seem to love their liquor."

"Yes, I guess it comes with the lifestyle", Nick tried to explain. "So what do you think about Mr Harrison?"

"Nick, you know what I think of him. What you really want to know is if I'm mad about that escort."

Nick quickly glanced at her, attempting to look surprised. Natascha knew exactly what bothered him.

"You're not seriously mad about Alba, are you?"

"I shouldn't...I can't....I have no right to be mad at her", Natascha answered and looked out of the window, searching for an explanation she didn't have. "I don't know...it's just stupid. I just didn't like how friendly she was towards you and Ole-Einar. Especially knowing the kind of work she does."

"Natascha, you do..." Nick tried to defend himself.

"I know, I know! Like I said, it's just stupid." Natascha interrupted him. "Maybe I'm a bit confused – she makes so much money doing what she does", she shook her head as she changed the direction of the conversation. "I only took twenty pounds from you for the ride on the washing machine. I think I should've charged you more."

"Hey, look at it this way: for Rowan, Alba is just pocket change, while I literally spent all my money on you that evening", Nick laughed with the soft smile Natascha loved so much.

"Aw, that's so sweet! You always know how to build me back up. You're such a gentleman", Natascha returned his soft smile with her own as she laughed.

"Talking about that money", Nick changed his beat, "you think I can have ten pounds back?"

"Absolutely not", Natascha kept laughing, slapping her hand on his thigh as they drove by the Ritz Hotel.

The couple was so focussed on their conversation that they didn't notice the curtain on the fourth floor open and close several times as they passed. Unbeknownst to Nick and Natascha, another former guest from the benefit gala was not so carefree. Up on the fourth floor of the Ritz Hotel, the person nervously paced through his room, opening the curtain again as he passed by it. Anxiously, he pulled the curtain aside just enough to glance at the road. It was well past midnight, and there was very little traffic. He looked twice as he saw the two black Land Rovers driving by, but didn't think much about it.

Why is he not calling back? The man asked himself again, hopeful to find the answer by looking at his watch again for the third time that minute. He knew he had made a crucial mistake before the benefit gala, and it came back to bite him. He was not sure what the consequences of his mishap could be, but there was too much at stake and he simply couldn't take the risk. As soon as he checked into his hotel room, he used his cell phone. He made sure not to use his official business phone, yet he was so nervous that he looked at it again just to be sure. He confirmed once again that it was the non-traceable prepaid phone. Tonight was only the second time he used it, both times calling the same number in the Vatican.

His call was answered almost immediately, but his contact had to cut him short, promising that he would call back once it was safe. That was little over three hours ago, and the man in the hotel room waited anxiously for his prepaid to ring. He was so focussed that he had not even unpacked his suitcase yet, which was still lying on the bed the same way he had put it there. Just as he stepped towards it, his phone finally rang.

"Yes?" he answered immediately, even before the second ring. "Yes, I'm alone...then I will answer *In Hoc Signo Vinces*", the man replied, confirming his true identity towards his contact, before listening to what his caller had to say.

"Yes, I met him tonight. I had no idea he would be there....of course he was not on the guest list...No, based on the information he gave me, he doesn't know what is really going on. But I don't know what they can find if they dig deeper...Yes, I do have the restraining order against him, but it would've only attracted more attention." The man paced his floor again as he spoke, his temper rising each passing minute. "You have to do something about him! Something has to happen, but under no circumstances can I be involved in it! He is high risk...You have a solution?...Great! But whatever happens, it has to happen fast... No, I don't believe anyone is suspicious about this...Yes, I will. Call me once it's done."

With his hands shaking, Abbot Augustinus Hetley flipped the prepaid phone shut and glanced around the room. He walked every square inch of the room, searched every drawer and closet, but still did not feel alone. He clasped his hands together, attempting to steady himself. His attempt was feeble as his legs started to shake. He tiredly walked over to the bed and sat down.

The abbot drank a glass of water and wiped the beads of sweat from his face with his sleeve. He ought to go to the bathroom, but decided against it. He could not bear seeing his face in the mirror.

"Oh God, what have I done?"

Asklepios, Aegean Sea, Friday, May 16

"Bingo, C57 is a match for Mr Gates. We can get some liver and his kidney. That will improve his recovery significantly. How is C57's detoxification coming along?" Dr Edwards asked enthusiastically.

Dr Sheridan Evans and Dr William Edwards looked at a monitor in one of the labs on C-Level. They were well isolated from the patients on the upper floors and the unfortunate ones one level below. This was crucial for the successful function of the medical facility. The decisions were made here, decisions that would not only determine the fate of their involuntarily donors, but would also determine who of their wealthy patients would survive and who not.

"Wait a second", Dr Evans replied and picked up a clipboard. "He only had some minor traces of marijuana, but nothing serious. Could even be for medical treatment. The hardest drug he ever dealt with was the one we gave him. We should be able to do the transplant within the next week or so, depending on how fast we can prep Mr Gates. He's also Mr Gates' age, so that works in our favour. Is there anything else we can use from him?"

"We can't use his lungs, C57 was a heavy smoker. Considering all the tissue damage Mr Gates sustained in the fire, he needs a young and healthy lung. We should be able to use most of the organs, some tissue and his blood. His heart is in good enough condition. We should double check on his thymus and pancreas. We will make a fortune out of him."

"Perfect. Do we have another match for other patients?"

"Doesn't look like it at the moment. We can get blood from both groups, but since group A is now basically off limits for organs, we have to scramble a little bit."

"I was under the impression that we could still take the kidney and liver cells for regenerative medicine, correct?"

"Generally yes, but they may want us to speed things up, so I don't think that's entirely possible. I suggest that we will still take what we need if we get a direct match. We make more money selling one kidney than selling the whole person. Personally, I consider it a huge waste of resources, but it's not my call. What are the test results for group A anyway?"

"They're good", Dr Evans explained with satisfaction, looking at the clip board again.

"Everyone up to A18 has already received their first series of injections and will receive the second series this weekend. B36 to B49 only received their medical check-up, and they're all cleared to leave."

"When's the pick up? Tonight?" Dr Edwards asked and leaned back in his chair, rubbing his eyes.

"Yes, that's what the schedule says. I already notified the rest of the medical staff."

"Sounds good to me. I don't want them here any longer than necessary. We can't risk our medical personnel getting attached to one of them. Are you going to tell Gates about his new liver and kidney?"

"Yes, I'll send in Melissa. She's his favourite. Considering what he's gone through, he deserves all the pleasantries he can get."

Dr Edwards just nodded his agreement while Dr Evans paged Melissa O'Brian over the intercom system.

Couple floors above, Mr Gates spent the afternoon beside the pool watching the other patients. He could never tire from people watching. As he had seen it so many times before, the entourage around the Spanish patient was reduced to who he believed was his wife and another man, maybe a brother. Other than that, it seemed not much had changed, other than his observations the other day. It had been two days since he had seen the little boy and his family. Mr Gates sipped some cold liquid through the drinking tube and decided to ask one of the nurses about the young patient.

Just as he zapped through the latest news on the internet again, his favourite nurse walked towards his general direction.

Melissa O'Brian was in her mid-twenties and always had her long red hair tamed in a pony tail. Victor Gates couldn't quite place her, but each time she spoke, he could detect a faint Irish accent. As she walked by him, Victor quickly typed something in his keyboard, and a whistling sound chirped from his speech computer.

"Ah, there's where you're hiding. I should have known that could only be you", Melissa smiled, changing her direction towards him. "I was actually looking for you, sir."

Did you miss me? Victor asked, trying to get some fun out of this.

"But of course I did! You will never guess what I have to tell you!"

You want to take me to the dance tomorrow night?

"Well, you know I want to do that, but I have some excellent news."

What is it?

Melissa looked around to make sure the other patients were out of ear shot.

"We do have a liver and a kidney for you", she enthusiastically whispered to him, holding his hand. Victor Gates was speechless. He just looked at the nurse, certain she was an angel descended from the Heavens. It took him over a minute before he realised what she had said. He held her hand tighter and looked at the horizon with a renewed flare in his eyes as he realised the possibilities of his future now seemed endless.

Thank you!

"You're very welcome, Mr Gates. I am really happy for you. Once you have a new kidney and a new liver, we can take a few of those machines off", Melissa smiled candidly, then added, "It's only a matter of time now."

Victor nodded. A large weight lifted from his shoulders as he released a deep breath; finally there was a glimmer of hope that he could hang on to.

Is it from the last group? Victor Gates asked curiously after he turned down the speech computer's volume significantly.

"Yes, sir. The test results came back this morning", confirmed Melissa. She was aware that the American was the only patient who actually knew where the donor organs came from and the procedures that occurred below.

Who? asked the speech computer in the voice of John Wayne. Mr Gates found solace in knowing his supplier.

"I only know him as C57, sir. He's a little bit younger than you. That's all I know. I explained to you before that I prefer not to know their names. If you really want to know, you have to ask Dr Edwards or Dr Evans. If anyone knows their name, they do."

Victor Gates released her hand, returning his gaze to the horizon.

What about the other women?

"They have all been thoroughly checked and they will...leave tonight", Melissa's voice broke off at the end. She knew the fate that awaited the young women.

How many?

"Thir...Thirteen altogether, sir."

Are they all healthy?

"Yes, sir, they are. We flushed some drugs out of their system, but other than that, they are completely fine."

Good! What about the rest? The first group? Victor asked excitedly, but his John Wayne computer voice lacked the expression. It became quite obvious that Melissa wasn't too comfortable talking about their current subject as she shifted her weight from one foot to the other. Victor assumed it had something to do with the fact that the other women were all the same age as her. While Melissa nervously glanced around again, the American took another sip from his drinking tube.

"The rest received their first series of injections and are due for the second series this weekend. It really helped that they concentrated on Western European women. If everything goes well, we will monitor them for a couple weeks before..." Melissa couldn't finish. She clasped her hands together behind her back, attempting to hide her discomfort.

Before it's their turn. Melissa, you're not having second thoughts about this, are you?

The nurse tensed up. "No, sir, I'm not having second thoughts. I will never forget what they did to my brother! You can trust me on that!" she hissed and walked away.

I will have to check that, Victor told himself, his eyes trailing after Melissa. He realised he had totally forgotten to ask her about the boy, but decided to inquire about him later.

EuroSecCorporation, **London, Thursday, May 22**

"I hope we're going to make it. She will be so disappointed if we're late", Natascha worried as she exited the parking lot.

"We should be fine", Nick replied from the passenger seat. "When's the police officer going to be there?"

"One-thirty. I want to be there before he is."

Nick decided not to distract Natascha while she rushed through the dense traffic. A police officer would visit their daughter's playgroup today. The whole idea of the program was designed to teach the children that there was no reason to be afraid of a police officer. Something that proved to be very useful whenever the police had to deal with children. For some reason, Shira-Sarah had shown reserved feelings towards them. Nick and Natascha weren't sure why, but had some theories. During her pregnancy and the first year after Shira-Sarah was born, Natascha had been hiding from said police forces. Their theory held that these events must have had some influence on their daughter.

"How was your morning?" Nick finally asked, hoping that some relaxing conversation would slow Natascha down a little bit. She was very close to triggering the stationary radar-speed-traps.

"I got an e-mail from Dad's institute this morning. My old dive crew. I haven't read it yet. It just came in when I had to leave", Natascha informed nonchalantly. "Other than that it was boring, just the same old stuff", she continued, showing no sign of slowing down as she changed lanes again. "How was yours? Did you guys do the first aid training?"

"Yeah, I just skipped the last five minutes after you messaged me. Brigitte will be in for the afternoon, so we have some time."

"Ah, shoot. I could have used the hours."

Nick silently nodded his agreement. He knew Natascha worried too much about their finances.

"It's all fine. Your hours at the office are just extra."

"I know, but I have to get new tires for this", Natascha reminded him, tapping her hand on the dash.

"We'll manage. We have enough in the account."

"We should. If not, I could sell my shoes", Natascha joked, throwing a quick smile at Nick.

"That would definitely help pay some bills", Nick encouraged her with a laugh, but Natascha punched him.

"You wish!"

"Hey, it was your idea. And there will always be bills to pay, you know. So you should seriously consider that", Nick continued to tease her, a tender smile dancing around his lips.

"Yeah, I should. But not my lace-up knee high leathers. I might need those if the bills keep coming", Natascha made a face.

"Oh, you mean those slutty ones you wear in the bedroom? No, you definitely have to keep those. You look great in them."

"Oh, you're so generous...and you're a pig!" Natascha shot at him and quickly steered her little car in a parking spot not too far from the playground.

"Okay, let's go", Natascha pushed after Nick paid for the parking ticket.

They arrived just in time with a few minutes to spare. Nick glanced around and noticed most other parents were also there. While their daughter was occupied playing with her friends, Nick and Natascha took the opportunity to catch up with some of the parents they knew.

"Mommy...arm", demanded Shira-Sarah as two police officers entered the room and introduced themselves. With both her parents close by, their daughter listened to what the police officer had to say. After a few minutes, Shira-Sarah relaxed enough that her curiosity pushed her a little closer when the two police officers answered questions about their gear. They were demonstrating how their radio worked and showed their handcuffs. To both Nick's and Natascha's surprise, their daughter's curiosity was getting the best of her, and she wanted to get even closer. Natascha decided to approach the younger police officer, who was about her own age. Judging the way he was talking to the children, she figured he had some of his own.

"Hi", she greeted him with a smile. "See, he's not that bad", Natascha encouraged her daughter, who stared at the man in the uniform. He was still showing his handcuffs to some other kids.

Shira-Sarah watched in great detail and shook her head with determination.

"What is it, honey?" Natascha asked her daughter, who was now pointing at the handcuffs.

"They are wrong!" insisted Shira-Sarah as the police officer showed her the handcuffs up close.

"Oh, they are? What's wrong with them?" the young man asked with a friendly smile.

"Mommy has some with fur!" explained Shira-Sarah as loud as she could, or at least loud enough for all the other parents to hear. Natascha's cheeks flushed several shades of red and words escaped her.

"Oh, she has some with fur?" the police officer laughed lightly.

"Yes! In the bedroom", Shira-Sarah continued her explanation and nodded enthusiastically. Natascha noticed her daughter seemed blissfully happy to shed some light on this mystery. Natascha's cheeks burned brighter, and her only way out seemed to be if the earth opened up and swallowed her.

"Okay, honey. That's enough information", she whispered with complete embarrassment, her face still blushing in a deep red. Too embarrassed to talk to the police officer, Natascha turned around and searched for Nick, who stood a couple metres away with his face hidden behind his hand. He was embarrassed for his wife, but also shook his head with laughter.

"Ah, so this is the walk of shame. You got to love kids", Natascha encouraged herself to keep walking towards her husband. She felt her embarrassment burn down her neck, sensing the eyes of the other parents following her. While some of them pretended not to have heard anything, those who knew them were unable to hide their devious smiles. Somehow the embarrassment seemed worse in front of strangers.

"How does she..." Nick started whispering.

"I have no idea", Natascha whispered back as she handed him their daughter who seemed to be very satisfied with herself. "Here, hold our daughter for a second so I can have the chance to bury my own face", Natascha instructed Nick, her hand wiping across her face.

- 5 -

Asklepios, Aegean Sea, Thursday, May 22
The captive who was simply known as C-57 stood in the corner of his private room, at least that was what one of the male nurses had called it. To him it was nothing more than a prison cell. The British war veteran had no idea where he was or how he got there, but something told him he was no longer in London Hyde Park, the last place he remembered being.

During the last few days, he had slowly regained control over his senses and his body again, but he had never gained enough strength to defend himself. His capturers had already taken blood samples and a CAT-Scan when he was still heavily sedated the first day. C-57 looked around the room quietly, uncertain where his clothes were. He wore a light hospital gown after they had cleaned him up. C-57 scratched the back of his head. His stomach growled in protest, the sound echoing from the steel walls. He had not received anything to eat in the last eighteen hours and couldn't help but wonder why. Even when he asked one of the male nurses, he never received a single word to serve as an answer.

Hungry and frustrated, he slowly paced his little cell. With nothing else in it but a bunk and an open concept bathroom in the corner, he found himself turning to pace the room again. He looked at the surveillance camera mounted in one corner in the ceiling and watched as it followed his every move. The British war veteran assumed he was not the only captive here. He had no idea what the *C* stood for, but the *57* gave him a pretty good idea that he was not the first and most likely not the last.

He sat back on his bed, rummaging his thoughts in an attempt to figure out what his options were. *You don't have that many options, do you, mate?* He asked himself after a while. Rising to his feet again, he realised that no one had demanded anything from him. At least not yet. He thought of his history, his time served for the British Crown in Iraq, and if anyone could seek vengeance. Thinking hard, he pondered that it may have something to do with him being a British soldier, but nothing came of it. All he could remember was when he and several other soldiers of his unit had been under friendly fire by the Americans. The Americans believed they were an Iraqi convoy, and before they realised their mistake, they peppered them with everything they had.

He shook his head at the recollection, uncertain if his survival was a blessing or a curse. He and a few others survived the attack, but not without catastrophic health consequences. They received a small amount of compensation and were sworn to secrecy. Although he hated the Army and the war, C-57 honoured his oath. He rubbed his hand over the curve of his face, what else could it possibly be about? Could this all be just a misunderstanding?

C-57 slowly turned around as he heard the door to his cell being unlocked. Two male nurses walked in, closing the door behind them. C-57's eyes flashed quickly, the gurney at the foot of his door was unmistakeable.

What the hell? C-57 thought. He didn't need a gurney.

"You seem to be rather active today."

C-57 blinked a few times. These were the first words spoken to him since he had regained consciousness. C-57 was uncertain if he should reply.

"Where am I?" he whispered, too weak to put a more demanding tone behind his question.

"Lay down in your bed, now!" the second man ordered in English, his voice loud and clear.

C-57 flinched. He still knew a trick or two from his old days, but living on the street for the last twelve years had not improved his physical condition. He knew he would not have a fighting chance against these two men, and they obviously meant business.

"Lay down in your bed now, or we'll shock you", the male nurse pointed his taser towards him threateningly before he continued, "we know from your tattoos that you can understand us."

C-57 still didn't move, but his lack of compliance wasn't from the stun gun pointed at him. He had more than a taser pointed at him before. The British veteran still considered his options, but he waited too long. It almost happened too quickly. The yellow blast covers exploded from the taser as two probes shot toward him, hitting him square in the chest. Several thousand volts of electricity burning through his body forced his muscles to contract involuntarily. His thoughts volleyed as his knees contracted to his chest. The remnants of the pain sparked through him again as he lay paralysed. Unable to move or even scream, the two men stepped closer, roughly pushing him on his bed.

"We warned you", the one male nurse reminded him coldly and opened the door to retrieve the gurney. The electric shock and pain ceased, but his energy did not recuperate as quickly. He was unable to resist them strapping him onto the gurney and wheeling him down a corridor to an elevator.

He felt soft tears descending his cheek with disbelief that this was his end. He tried to occupy his mind by surveying each room and hall they passed through, but all he could see were white walls. He still had no idea where he was. They pushed him through a double-wing door, and the sudden bright lights blinded him. When he opened his eyes again, he found himself surrounded by four people wearing surgical gowns, latex gloves, and face masks.

Still strapped to the gurney, he could do nothing but watch as they cut his gown off. They were careful not to cut him.

"What are you doing?" A whisper was all he could manage, but no one answered him. As soon as all his clothes were removed, he smelled the characteristic odour of povidone-iodine as they cleaned his chest.

"What are you doing?" C-57 asked again weakly, panic slowly starting to rise inside him. His attention darted to his right arm as a sudden sharp prick of a syringe broke through his skin, the contents slowly entering his bloodstream. He tried to wriggle his arm, but his attempts were feeble. He panicked as they injected the remainder of the anaesthetic cocktail into his arm. His head fell back again under the wave of nausea that overcame him, the fear gripping him tightly as a red-haired nurse hooked him up to some monitors. Just seconds later his eyes fluttered as he slowly slipped into unconsciousness. He noticed the pitying smile surface in the woman's eyes as his last fight rolled from his lips, "No..."

Before he dipped further, he heard the faint sound of small containers being arranged on the table beside him.

"Okay, he should be out in a few seconds. We are retrieving the kidney, liver, part of the intestine, all the blood, heart, thymus, pancreas, and skin tissue", one of the surgeons said from under his face mask, accepting the scalpel as it was passed to him. "This shouldn't take too long."

The homeless British war veteran wanted to plead for his life, but darkness surrounded him as he finally fell unconscious one last time. He couldn't feel the churning knots in his stomach, but he knew he would never wake up again, and no one would ever miss him.

Nick's and Natascha's house, just outside London, Thursday, May 22
With the humiliating events earlier that day behind them, Nick was in bed early, still reading a novel when Natascha entered. She carried some papers in her hand, and Nick noticed they were fixed with clear tape. His lips moved as he was about to ask her, but instead he decided to watch his wife. She didn't realise it, but the way her bathrobe slipped from her shoulders and down the curve of her back was irresistibly sexy.

"I forgot to tell you what Dad's e-mail was about this morning. Are you still awake enough for that?" Natascha asked and glanced at her husband, hanging her bathrobe over a chair.

"Yeah, still awake", Nick smiled as his eyes met hers. He slapped his book shut. "What was it about?"

"You remember my old dive crew from the institute, right? The one you met in Norway?" Natascha crawled into her turned down sheets and cuddled into the blanket.

"Yes, of course I remember them."

"Well, there's a new project, and they're wondering if I could join them", Natascha explained easily, but there was hesitation in her voice.

"You mean like an expedition again?" Nick specified. "For how long?"

"Oh no, not like that. Just for ten days, and I would be home for the weekend. It's right here in England", Natascha explained, an excited smile dancing across her lips. "Just a couple hours from here", she quickly added.

"Okay. And I'm guessing you want to participate, correct?"

"Well, you know me. It would be a nice change for a while, and I would be doing some real diving and serious scientific work again, not what I'm doing at the aquarium", Natascha's tone seemed different, and Nick turned to face her more squarely as she continued, "And I could spend some time with my old friends again."

"For someone who's really looking forward to this, you really don't sound too enthusiastic about it. What's the catch?"

"Well...", Natascha tried to find the right words, but knew there was no point in withholding the truth from Nick. "The research will take place in an old mine."

Nick stared blankly at her for a few moments, uncertain if he had understood her correctly.

"Excuse me? I think I heard you say *an old mine?*"

"Yes, Nick, that's what I said", Natascha confirmed and continued quickly; she knew this was the part he wouldn't like. "But it's not one of those tiny holes in the ground, like a natural cave. This one is a man made mine, with large shafts and passage ways. They had carts in there. It's extremely well documented."

"You didn't forget the last time you did that kind of diving was in the North-West Passage, right?"

"I know, but this isn't going to be that deep. And all we're doing is searching for new organisms. We're just taking some samples, lots of video, and pictures. Our maximum operational depth is about twenty metres", Natascha continued to explain and slid closer towards Nick.

"Well, twenty metres is not that deep. How deep is the penetration?"

"According to Dad it's going to be no further than four-hundred metres. But it's all shallow. We won't even reach fifteen metres until we're three hundred metres in."

"And that's the limit? Four-hundred metres in and no more than twenty metres deep?"

"That's the limit", Natascha smiled brightly now, confident he was about to agree. "Nick, you know I would never do anything stupid under water."

"You mean something like squeezing underneath the hull of a shipwreck in eighty-five metres of freezing water; against the rules outlined in the briefing, might I add, just to get a video of a little crab?" Nick had not forgotten Natascha's little escapade during one of the dives in the Arctic.

"Come on Nick, that wasn't *that* dangerous. Besides, I'm a mother now. You know very well that my priorities have shifted significantly since then", Natascha snapped back, her tone getting colder.

Nick had to admit she had a point and thought for a few moments. His wife was right. It would be nice for her to have some change of scenery with her long time friends.

"Well, what do we do with Sarah? I can stay here in London for that time. Worst case scenario, we can ask Shira or Talia for a day", Nick tried to work with her, knowing this was something she was excited about, but was clearly hesitant to show it. He thought harder, "Oh, another question. What about the dive gear?"

"I can use the gear from the institute. Dad said he can bring it with him the next time they visit. I can do some dives with it in the aquarium, too. It's all disinfected", Natascha's smile slanted at that fact.

"Sounds like you already made plans to go..." Nick smiled sweetly.

"So, you approve?" Natascha asked enthusiastically, sitting up abruptly in the bed.

"Under several conditions!"

"Name it!"

"You promise me twenty metres maximum depth and four-hundred metres maximum penetration. And I want to see the plans of the mine." Her smile widened, "I'm serious Natascha."

"Your terms are steep", Natascha teased, her finger dancing along his chest. "You don't trust me?"

"Of course not! I know you too damn well. It doesn't help that your boobs are bouncing; you're distracting me and I can't concentrate", Nick complained with a laugh.

"They were not bouncing, you pig!" Natascha slapped his chest, covering her breasts with her hands.

"What are you doing?" Nick asked curiously.

"Trying not to distract you, you Neanderthal!" She turned her face shyly as she continued, "So, what's your answer? Can I go?"

"You didn't make your promise yet."

"Okay, I promise."

"You promise what?"

"Four-hundred metres maximum penetration and twenty metres maximum depth."

"And?" Nick demanded to hear more.

"And what?...Oh right, I'll let you have a look at the plans."

"And you have to promise me that you'll be a nice girl."

Natascha pulled the blanket back up to cover herself, her eyes turning into tiny slits, "I'll pretend I didn't hear that. Of course I will be a nice girl."

Nick raised his brows, picked up his book again and opened it. "Do I have another choice?"

"Not really, if you want to have sex again this year", Natascha teased him and crawled back to her side of the bed.

"I m going to hide all your toys", Nick threatened. "And I will ask Saphir for a date", he continued to mutter, but this time more to himself.

"Good luck, you can't afford her." Natascha replied dryly as she collected the three pages again from her nightstand.

"Good point. Talia looks cute, and she's just living downstairs. That would be convenient", Nick continued to explore his imaginary options.

"Of course she is cute, she looks like me. But you better keep dreaming. So, what's your official answer?" Natascha asked in return, without the slightest concern in her voice about her husband's adulterous fantasies.

"Of course you can go."

"Yes! Thank you!" Natascha quickly leaned over and pressed a kiss on Nick's cheek. "Oh, you do remember what I told you should I ever catch you cheating? Or do you need me to remind you of that?" She whispered in a more threatening voice.

"Oh, no, no. I'll never forget *that*", Nick winced, remembering her very graphic speech about his testicles, a rusty pair of scissors, and a meat grinder.

"Such a good boy!" Natascha added satisfied and pressed another kiss on his cheek before retreating to her side of the bed again.

She sorted the papers until they seemed to flow into each other. She had spent some time earlier repairing the secrets that lied beneath the words, piecing groups of letters together to complete words and matching the rips to the tears. She flipped through each page, intensely focussed as she read. It was about twenty minutes later that Nick finally put his book on his nightstand and switched off his light.

"What do you got there?"

"Ah, remember that reporter at the benefit gala who had that argument with the bishop? These are the papers he gave to the bishop."

"You *stole* a letter from a bishop?" Nick was suddenly awake again.

"Nope, not at all. The bishop ripped it up and threw it in the garbage. I *retrieved* it. I did not *steal* it. *Huge* difference!" Natascha explained with determination.

"You do know you'll end up in hell for this. Stealing from a priest..." Nick protested with reprimanding clicks of his tongue.

"You know I won't go to hell", Natascha stated with confidence.

"Sure about that?"

"Yep, absolutely. The devil has a restraining order against me." She said and turned one of the pages around.

"I wouldn't doubt that. What's the letter about?"

"It's quite interesting", Natascha enthused and rearranged her pillow to straighten up again. "This is more of a chronological list of events and, as far as the reporter believes, facts. The reporters name is Kyle McRae. I'm not sure of the validity of all this, but it would explain why the bishop didn't want to talk to him."

"Okay, so what's it about?"

"According to McRae's research, he's interested in some events that took place at Whitmore Abbey, which is just a few hours from here. The events he is referring to go back to April nineteen-hundred-forty-two, when Whitmore Abbey was also an orphanage. His grandmother, Cathy Sheppard was raised there. But there was also a guy by the name of Gordon Ferguson. It seems as though Gordon and Cathy fell in love when they were teenagers at the orphanage. But any kind of relationship between orphans was strictly forbidden. Cathy got pregnant at the age of sixteen. Sort of reminds me of what you did to me, remember?" Natascha reflected suddenly, her eyes trailing off to the side of the room. "There I was, a young, innocent scientist, out on a mission to make the world a better place, putting my life in your hands. And what did you do? Against company policies you knocked me up in the middle of the Arctic."

"Well, first of all, it takes two. Second, young is a bit of an exaggeration, you were most definitely of age. And third, you were anything but innocent; in fact, you were well practised", Nick smiled his defence, then continued, "not to mention, we were on a ship, lonely for several weeks, those things can happen."

Natascha returned his smile with a raised eyebrow before she continued.

"Anyway, since there was no future for the two of them and their unborn child to be together as a family, they decided to... *break out*", Natascha paused and double checked the papers.

"What do you mean *break out?*"

"Well, according to some stories from Cathy Sheppard, the place was more like a prison than an orphanage. So she referred to it as *breaking out*. Anyway, they were waiting for the right moment, which presented itself during a German fighter bomber air raid in the late evening hours in April nineteen-hundred-forty-two."

"The Germans attacked an abbey? Why the hell would they do that?"

"No, not really. They attacked a nearby mine, which was beside the abbey. So they waited for the alarm bells and used the general confusion to break out of Whitmore Abbey. Together they ran during the actual attack towards a nearby forest. It turns out that Gordon shielded Cathy during one detonation and got hit with shrapnel in his leg. They couldn't stop the bleeding. Gordon insisted on Cathy to keep going, which she finally did when the search parties were getting closer. Some people from the village found Gordon and brought him back to the abbey for medical treatment." Natascha paused again and flipped the page for some additional information.

"Still a better love story than that vampire series", Nick commented dryly. "What happened next?"

"Not much. Cathy was able to hide in a village not too far away. Couple months later, she gave birth to a boy. Unfortunately for her, there was no one who really supported her. After all, they were still in the middle of the war. Being an underage single mother didn't help either back then."

"No, probably not", Nick muttered as he listened carefully.

"Looks like Cathy got in conflict with the law", Natascha went on, trying to fit the pieces into the right timeline.

"For what?"

"Doesn't say. Probably not much. I assume stealing some clothes or food."

"Hm", Nick acknowledged. He knew that Natascha sympathised with Cathy, and he certainly would have done the same.

"Anyway, Cathy got charged and convicted, and that is when...", Natascha stopped to make sure to get the next part right. "Holy cow!"

"What?"

"It says here that she was sent back to Whitmore Abbey, which also served as some type of penitentiary. Going back there would allow her to keep her child, who would stay in the orphanage at the abbey."

"A penitentiary? In an abbey?"

"Yes, just give me a second here. Want to make sure that I got this right", Natascha mumbled. "Yes, a penitentiary", she continued after a few moments. "Back then, some of the larger abbeys also served as penitentiaries, where women did basic labour, mostly laundry for the abbey and the nearby villages."

"So did she meet Gordon again?"

"No", Natascha shook her head. "Never saw him again. She tried to get transferred to their small medical ward, but it was denied. Looks like she tried really hard to find him, but he had just vanished."

"Hm, that is strange. What about her son?"

"According to this, she was allowed to see him...oh my God, that is horrible", Natascha's voice broke.

"What?"

"She was only allowed to see him one hour a day."

"Only one hour a day?" Nick was appalled. His eyes immediately looked at the little monitor on his nightstand, showing him his daughter sleeping peacefully in her room next door.

"Yes. So Cathy was horrified that someone would adopt her son, and she—"

"Wait a second. How can he be adopted against her will?"

"Don't know", Natascha shook her head and searched for more information. "It says here that this was the time when the church literally *sold* children to families in Australia, Canada, and the US. Mostly orphans or children from women like Cathy.

Young single moms with no income to raise their children."

"Didn't she get paid at least a little bit for her work?"

"Yes, they did pay her, but according to the abbey it wasn't enough to cover their costs for raising her son."

"But she must have officially given him up for adoption, right?"

"Don't know. All it says here is that she felt pressured into signing the adoption papers when he was three years old. She still wasn't able to care for him properly, and she was told that this was the only way for her to make sure that her son would receive basic medical care and food, so she finally caved in."

"Wasn't there any financial assistance back then for women like her? I know it was at the end of the war, but there must have been something."

"Oh, there was. The abbey just forgot to mention that to her. Unfortunately, she had no choice and finally signed the papers. Her son was adopted only days before she was released."

"Jesus...", Nick shook his head in disbelief.

"Yes, Cathy was furious when she found out what had happened to her child. Now that she was a free woman, she was determined to find both Gordon and her son, but wasn't successful. This is so sad", Natascha concluded as she lowered the papers to her lap.

"So she never saw either of them again?" Nick's interest in the story grew bigger with each fact Natascha revealed.

"Apparently not. She even persuaded other people to officially contact Whitmore Abbey, both for finding Gordon as well as her son, but even the sheer existence of a person by the name of Gordon Ferguson was denied, and her son had officially been adopted. Cathy didn't back down and requested to have access to the adoption files."

"How did that go?" Nick wanted to know, but he could already see the answer in Natascha's face.

"Take a guess! She was told that all the files were destroyed in a fire, but there has never been a record about a fire at Whitmore Abbey." Natascha shook her head in disbelief.

"Go figure. What happened next?"

"Cathy spent almost ten years searching for Gordon, but eventually married someone else and had another child, a daughter. But she never stopped looking for her son. Even after the orphanage closed in the sixties, she still searched, but never found him."

"Can't even imagine what she had to go through." Nick shook his head.

Natascha checked the other pages and shivered.

"What is it?"

"Here, listen to this. It's getting even better!" Nick could hear from Natascha's voice how disgusted she was. "According to Cathy, there was more. The reason that the orphanage was closed in the sixties was not only because of the adoption scandal, but also because of former orphans' accusations towards the priests and staff", Natascha continued and shook her head in disgust.

"Uh-oh, is it what I think it is?"

"What else could it be? Those bastards!" hissed Natascha, her mouth twisting in distaste. "The accusations cover everything from physical to sexual child abuse, rape and molestation through all the age groups."

They exchanged a serious look, both their faces showing their disgust towards the accusations. Natascha's mind spun about her daughter, and imagined Nick was thinking the same thing.

"Here we go again. I'm not even surprised. Did this Cathy contact the police?"

"Wait a second, let me check...Yes, she did contact the police, but nothing happened. There were still no records of a Gordon Ferguson or her child, and although she pressed charges against several members of the abbey, the police didn't do anything. Cathy eventually got in contact with other former orphans, and they approached the authorities together, all telling a similar story."

"So what happened next?"

"According to this, the police did start an inquiry, which subsequently resulted in the closure of the orphanage, but no official charges were ever laid, and no one got prosecuted."

"How can that be?" Nick asked and allowed Natascha to gather some more information from the papers. Just by watching the expressions in her face, Nick already knew there was more to the story.

"You're not going to believe this. The abbey was very quick in demolishing the building that housed the former penitentiary and orphanage. They literally destroyed all the evidence and all the files over night." Natascha explained and shuddered.

"That would explain why all those accusations never led to any arrests or official charges", Nick pointed, then continued, "Unfortunately there were several reports like that all over England during that time period."

"Wait, it gets even better!" Natascha continued, her voice steaming with rage.

"What else can there be?"

"Cathy mentioned several teenage girls got pregnant, some of them even as young as thirteen years old. Their babies were taken away from them right after birth, and they never saw them again!"

"What do you mean *they never saw them again?*"

"That's all she said, they simply never saw them again. In some cases they were told they died during infancy, which was not uncommon during that time. Sometimes they just *disappeared.*"

"Why would they disappear? Could they not have been adopted like the others?"

"Looks like this Kyle guy, the reporter, did some serious digging on that. According to former orphans and eye witnesses, there were many more children in the orphanage than the official records made everyone believe. Whitmore Abbey gave an official statement, claiming there was a fire that destroyed most of the records. Funny thing is that the fire only destroyed the records and nothing else."

"Ah, yes, one of those very *convenient* fires. What else did he find?"

"Some of the children were legally adopted, but he also checked the abbey's cemetery, where he found some of the graves. But that didn't account for all the missing children."

Nick paused, considering the information before he continued, "Hm, as disgusting as this is, it all makes sense. If there is no body and no evidence of the child to have ever existed, no one can build a case on that. And it's well known that some of those abbeys were connected to highly ranked members of the society, so it would be easy to cover things up back then. That would explain why the bishop didn't want to talk to the reporter."

"I just hate those bastards. Oh, don't even get me started on them!" Natascha raged and threw the paper on the ground. The disturbing nature of the information removed whatever fatigue Natascha had when she first crawled into bed; she just couldn't bring herself to read any more of it.

"Yes, you know I feel the same."

Natascha pulled up the duvet as the silence amplified within the room. She looked at Nick, before she checked the monitor to watch their daughter peacefully sleeping in the next room.

"Great, I won't be able to sleep for hours now because of those perverted bastards", Natascha barked suddenly, her eyes turning up to the ceiling with despair.

"You should stick to your romance novels for bedtime lecture. At least they make you horny", Nick suggested nonchalantly, trying to ease the tension.

"I should, but I didn't expect *that!*"

"No, no one could've expected something like that", Nick replied with a shake of his head. Nick took a moment before changing the conversation, "So you have self-defence lessons tomorrow?"

"Hm", Natascha muttered and nodded.

"Let it all out tomorrow. Don't try to hold it in. Break Ole's nose again", Nick suggested. After his wife had been wrongfully accused of plotting a nerve gas attack on some indigenous people in the Arctic and being declared one of the most wanted terrorists in the world by the United States of America, Nick was not surprised Natascha reacted so sensitively to such injustice, especially when it involved children. Natascha wiped a tear from her face as Nick pulled her in close.

"Come here, angel. I love you", he whispered, kissing her on the back of her head. She found comfort by resting her head on his arm as she spooned into his embrace.

"Ah, I hate such injustice. I'm just so damn emotional. They remind me of that damn Jonathan Brown: all nice and friendly in public, but just plain criminal behind that facade."

Natascha shivered thinking back at the former White House Chief of Staff. Jonathan Brown had been the mastermind behind the criminal events in the Arctic, and who had personally declared Natascha and her friends as terrorists on international TV. Jonathan Brown and his criminal partners had a habit of taking matters into their own hands, and it shouldn't have been surprising they committed suicide after the truth came out. Natascha recalled the news clipping stating that the FBI found their remains in his torched hunting lodge. She felt no satisfaction. To Natascha, their suicide was their easy way out of receiving justice. There was something so convenient about all the criminal minds being found in the same location, dead. The entire incident seemed suspicious to Natascha; she even was convinced of Ariel having something to do with it. Little did she know he did, but he would never reveal this to her.

"Would it help if you could empty another magazine into one of those bastards?" Nick asked, knowing very well what his wife was thinking. Most of the accusations had been nothing but a well fabricated web of lies created by the CIA, but it was true that Natascha had emptied a magazine of 9 mm rounds into Brown's henchman, a mercenary by the name of Chuck Hogan. What the CIA and the media had called a cold-blooded murder, Natascha considered nothing more than *justice* and self-defence.

"He deserved it. I wouldn't hesitate a second if I had to do it again. And yes, it would make me feel better. There's no difference between them", Natascha bit with a cold voice, thinking back to those horrible events onboard the *Northern Explorer.*

"No, there's not", Nick agreed, then squeezed her tighter as he suggested, "Just try to think about your upcoming research project. And maybe we should find a better place for the handcuffs, okay?"

"I have no idea how she knows about them", Natascha finally chuckled, thinking about the embarrassing moment with their daughter earlier that day.

"God, do you think she saw you in those heeled boots and your black leather underwear?" Nick laughed, his chuckle vibrating up his spine.

"Oh my God. She'd probably think I'm some sort of super hero", Natascha chuckled.

"Considering the alternative, that wouldn't be too bad."

"No, it wouldn't...Thanks Nick. I love you." Natascha whispered and snuggled closer to him.

"Love you, too, angel." Nick gently kissed the back of Natascha's head again, his hand ceased rubbing her chilled bum.

"Hey, who said you can stop? It's still cold." Natascha complained and pushed herself against him.

It was only moments later that Natascha heard Nick's faint snore, the strength of his arm relaxing on her hip. She tried to focus on his shallow breaths with hopes to ease herself to sleep, but she couldn't cease her racing mind. Despite the fact she had stumbled upon the dispute between the bishop and the reporter, she could not deny the accusations had caught her interest. The entire discovery seemed to be quite a coincidence, and Natascha couldn't shake it from her mind. She may have a bit of a problem.

Would it be wrong if I didn't tell Nick the mine I'm going to dive is the mine beside Whitmore Abbey?

- *6* -

Asklepios, Aegean Sea, Friday, June 6
Victor Gates slowly opened his eyes, the white ceiling unfamiliar. It took him a moment before he realised he was in a recovery room and not in his normal suite. His eyes followed the ceiling to the lights, and it was another moment before he noticed the nurse behind his bed.

Melissa had just changed the IV's and updated Victor's file in the computer when she noticed that Mr Gates was just waking up.

"Good afternoon, sir. How are you feeling?" She smiled at him and stepped beside his bed. It took Victor a few seconds, but the speech computer finally said *tired.*

"And you should be. That was a really big surgery." Melissa explained as she adjusted the flow of oxygen for the assisted breathing, now that he was awake.

How did it go?

"Everything went well, no complications. Just give me a second, I'll call Dr Evans; she can tell you more." Melissa turned around and used the computer to contact the physician. "She will be here in a few moments. Do you have any pain?" Melissa asked, but she knew that Mr Gates had so many anaesthetics in him that a horse wouldn't feel any pain.

No. Just tired.

The American closed his eyes again and Melissa decided not to bother him any further.

"Mr Gates! How are you doing?" Dr Sheridan Evans asked just minutes later with a soft voice.

For the second time that day Victor Gates slowly opened his eyes again.

Just tired, he answered and looked at the British doctor who closely checked the monitors.

"Well, it was quite the surgery and everything went perfectly fine. There were no complications and the organs are a perfect match. Do you notice something?" Dr Evans asked curiously.

Victor slowly turned his head, but couldn't figure out what she meant.

"There are two machines missing. You no longer need them. From now on, it's just the oxygen and the IV for the painkillers." For the first time Victor Gates noticed Dr Evans smile was different, there was a certain note of accomplishment within the smile.

"What do you say? Isn't that great?"

Victor closed his eyes again. If his body would have been able to, he would have shed a tear, but he just slowly nodded. Victor knew this surgery was pivotal towards his survival. He knew he could use an electric wheelchair from now on, once he would recover. He slowly typed that question into his keyboard.

"Yes, Mr Gates, that's correct. The guys are preparing one for you. All you need are a couple more days of rest. It was a stressful surgery to the body, patience is key.

We also have a match for some skin tissue, but we have to wait until your body is ready for it."

Lung?

"No, Mr Gates. Unfortunately we couldn't use the donor's lung. Your body has sustained so much damage that only a healthy lung can supply you with enough oxygen, unless you want to rely on assisted breathing for the rest of your life. We checked your donor's lung. We first thought he was a heavy smoker, but it turned out he had severe scarring in his lung tissues. There was unfortunately no way this specific lung would have worked for you." Dr Sheridan Evans knew this was not the news he wanted to hear, but there was no point in withholding the truth from him.

The American always appreciated his medical crew talking to him using direct terms that he could understand, not their medical mumbo-jumbo. Nevertheless, he didn't like the news. He had hoped there would be a light at the end of the tunnel at one point. He agreed that he had just taken a huge step in his road to recovery, but waiting for a donor lung got increasingly frustrating by the day.

"You mustn't worry about the lung right now, your name is on the top of the list. I'm certain it won't take that much longer", the British physician promised and smiled at him.

Victor nodded, his frustration still clearly visible.

"So, Mr Gates, if you promise to behave, I'll have Melissa bring you back to your suite. How does that sound? If everything goes well with the recovery, you should be able to enjoy the sun in a couple days."

Today?

"Your ambition is noted, but no, sir, we cannot let you outside today", Dr Evans laughed. "You just woke up from a very complicated surgery. You really have to stay inside a little bit longer."

EuroSecCorporation, London, Monday, June 9

"So *this* is the feminine touch you added?" Shira stood in the break room and refused to believe her eyes.

"Yes, what do you think? It has *feminine* written all over it and it fits perfectly between the couch and our little counter. Not only that, but us guys won't even get near it, and it will help you ladies to stay in physical shape." Rolf proudly explained, Ole-Einar and Olaf nodding their agreement.

"You can't be serious, Rolf. Please tell me that you do not plan to ask the company to pay for this?" the Israeli asked, still shocked by what her friends had installed.

"Well...actually..." Rolf hesitated and looked up to the taller Norwegian beside him for support.

"Actually we asked the boys, and they all really liked the idea. So...we kind of...well...all the boys threw in some money", Ole-Einar explained further.

"*All the boys?* Seriously? Would that include my brother, Brian and Klaus as well?" Shira demanded, her arms crossing with distaste.

"Well...we didn't ask the guys from Operation Control or the owners. We...we just assumed they would agree, rule of majority, *and* it doesn't cost them anything."

Olaf pleaded their case, attempting to sound convincing.

"Did any of you actually bother to ask us what we wanted? Something like a new fridge, maybe? As it was discussed!" Shira asked with a rise of her shoulders.

The expression on her friends faces told her that the complicated process of simply asking them had never crossed their minds. By now, Shira had received physical back-up in form of her four Israeli countrywomen and Natascha, who had also overheard the conversation.

"*All the boys?* Does this mean that Nick also paid for this?" Natascha asked curiously.

"Ten pounds, like everyone else", Rolf answered quickly with a big grin, hoping to collect some points with Natascha by throwing Nick under the bus.

"Come on ladies. You have to admit it adds to the decor", Ole-Einar added enthusiastically in an attempt to change the mood.

"It's a strip pole!" Shira complained, pointing to the shiny bar. "The place already looks like some bachelor man-cave with all the pin-ups and now this!"

"Oh come on, Shira. You never complained about the pin-ups before. And look over there! You see that? We even took Miss December down."

Shira gave Rolf a stern look, her brow furrowing under the anger.

"Ladies, what do you think?" Shira asked, gesturing to the pole.

"I like it", Natascha laughed and walked toward the stainless steel pole. She trusted it was securely mounted and jumped up, grabbing the pole just below the ceiling. She used the momentum to spin around and down, looking at her friends. She did a double-take as she noticed former Admiral Brian Whittaker and Nick just entered the break room. Nick's mouth dropped open as Brian glanced around the room. His attention turned back to Natascha as she slowly stepped away from the stainless steel pole. Natascha's eyes darted across each face in the room, everyone except Nick and the former admiral were struggling to restrain their laughs.

"Oh Gosh, it's not what it looks like", Natascha stammered, not sure what to say next.

"Her idea", Rolf assured as he and the two Norwegians simultaneously pointed at her. Natascha threw them an angry glare, but quickly looked back at her boss with a weak smile. Both the former admiral and Nick had not moved at all.

"Can someone please say something?" Natascha whispered shyly and looked for support. She suddenly wondered why such things were always happening to her.

"Oh! You almost had it! But you didn't take any of your clothes off", Rolf commented seriously and took a five-pound bill out of his pocket, waving it to Natascha.

Natascha scowled at him before returning her attention to her boss and Nick.

"Hi, sir. This is an exercise pole. We just set it up." Rolf explained, putting the five-pound bill back in his pocket.

"I can see that!" Brian snarled at him.

"How do you like it?" Ole-Einar chimed in, uncertain if he wanted the answer.

The former admiral's jaw clenched, his eyes fixed on the Norwegian.

"Whose bloody idea was that?" he whispered in a threatening tone to Ole-Einar.

"Actually, for the record, it was our idea, sir", young Talia Levi interrupted quickly. At twenty-four years of age, she was the youngest of the four new Israeli employees, and she knew Brian had a soft spot for her. "The guys asked us what we wanted and this is what we came up with. We thought it would be fun and help to strangle our friendship as colleagues", she continued.

"*Strengthen* our friendship, Talia. Not *strangle!*" Natascha whispered the correction.

"Oh, yes. Strengthen our friendship... Thanks."

"A strip pole? To *strengthen* your friendship? I thought you agreed on new appliances and to get rid of those damn pin-ups?" the retired admiral asked, his voice rising with each word he spoke.

"Ah, yes, but the old ones we have are still working fine. We thought this here is more fun. We're all adults. And the guys threatened us with severe bodily harm if we ever touched the pictures, especially Miss October, so they're fine." Talia added as innocent as she could and looked at the pole. "Besides, it's great for the upper body and the core."

"Is that the official version for the record or do you want some more time to work on a better story?" the admiral asked. He did not believe a word.

Talia and the other women nodded enthusiastically. Natascha sensed a little spark of hope on the horizon, but wasn't certain yet if she should put too much faith in it. Shira fought to hold back some laughter.

"I want to see that bloody pole and those pictures gone. Don't let me say it again!" Brian's eyes focussed on each of his employees for a few seconds before he turned around. "You will never be bored with her", the former British admiral apologetically looked at Nick and left the break room.

"*A strip club!....That's what they are turning this place into!*" they heard him complaining from the corridor as he walked to his office.

"So, boys, I assume you didn't expect his reaction to be *that* serious, did you?" Shira teased her friends.

"Uh...no. It was supposed to be a joke. We did order the appliances, but it will be a couple days before they deliver them. We got this from a scrap yard. I mean we knew he wouldn't be too enthusiastic about it, but he seemed to be really mad. I think we owe you, Talia." Rolf admitted.

"You bet you do! It really helped he saw Natascha at it", the young Israeli explained with a wide grin.

"I'm glad I could help", Natascha said, but then continued with exasperation. "Oh my God, why does this always happen to me? For heaven's sake, Nick, will you please stop staring at me like that and just say something? Preferably something nice?"

"I'm just shocked you know how to move on one of those. Is there something you want to tell me?" he teased, pretending to be upset.

"For crying out loud! I don't know how to move on a stripper pole. I just did half a spin. Everyone can do that." Natascha defended herself, while Shira glanced down the corridor.

"I don't know. I don't think I can do that", Shira questioned herself.

"Seriously, Shira? Look, it's really easy", Natascha ensured and stepped closer to the strip pole. She jumped up, grabbed the pole just below the ceiling and, just as five minutes before, used her momentum to swing around and down again, her eyes resting on former General Klaus Schwartze. He stood squarely in the doorframe.

"Oh God! This is not happening....Shira...you set me up!" Natascha stammered again while her Israeli friend roared with laughter.

The former general just shook his head in disbelief and retreated to his office.

"You're right, Brian. She is doing it again. They are turning this place into a strip joint", he confirmed as he walked down the corridor, his voice trailing behind him.

"You saw him coming and you set me up. Now both of them think I'm some kind of a stripper!" Natascha accused Shira, who laughed so hard she had to sit on the floor. Her back leaned against the wall as she wiped a tear from her eye.

"She is all yours, brother." Rolf clapped Nick on his shoulder as he left, the two Norwegians following behind him.

"Ah, another proud moment in our family history", Nick finally commented while Natascha's face blushed another shade of red. "You think you'd get used to this, but no, my wife always knows how to throw a surprise", he complained theatrically and started to make some coffee for them.

"Oh come on, Nick. It wasn't *that* bad. We both know I can do worse", Natascha finally chuckled and glanced at Shira, who still sat on the floor gasping for air.

"Yeah, keep laughing. You know you will pay dearly for this. This is on like Donkey-Kong!" Natascha promised her friend with a determined grin.

Paris, Monday, June 9
Elena slowly regained consciousness and tried to sit up, but her spinning head sent her back down again. The young Romanian opened her eyes, and it took her a while before she recognised her surroundings. She found herself lying on an old stained mattress in a windowless room. She surveyed her surroundings again, attempting to blink away her present reality. There was nothing but a few more mattresses along the wall, a naked bulb hanging from the ceiling, and two surveillance cameras with their red LEDs blinking. Panic started to rise in her, and Elena quickly sat up, completely ignoring her headache. It was only now that she realised with horror that her left hand was handcuffed to a steel ring in the wall. With a loud cry, she tried to free herself, but she could neither slip her hand out nor move the steel ring, which was solidly embedded in the massive concrete wall. Failing to free herself, the young Romanian woman started to cry and sat with her back against the wall.

Elena didn't know how long she had been sitting there when she noticed several sealed water bottles and some bread on the floor beside her mattress. Her first reaction was to kick them away, but her mind told her it would be a terrible idea. She reached for the food and cracked open a bottle, downing it at once. Feeling a little bit better, she leaned back and tried to remember how she had ended up like this.

Everything had been so great the last two years! She had been able to get out of Romania and go to school in France while staying with some relatives. After last summer, she had been scheduled to return to Romania but instead moved to Paris, where she worked as an au-pair in a rather wealthy household. It was the first time she had been able to afford new clothes, and she had even sent some money back to her parents in Romania. Last Friday had been her eighteenth birthday, and Elena had decided to dye her hair blonde and go out and party with one of her new social media friends. That was as far as she could remember. Her memory of the last forty-eight hours was simply wiped clean. She had absolutely no idea where she was or what time or day it was. She was fully aware this situation could only have a few different outcomes, and she certainly didn't like any of them. Taking another sip from the water bottle, she suddenly got an idea. Without moving her head, she glanced at both security cameras. They were installed in opposite corners and gave anybody watching them a complete view of the cell without any blind spots. Knowing she couldn't hide, the young woman went straight to action. Elena used some water to moisten the handcuffed hand and tried to free herself. Tears filled her eyes quickly, streaming down her face with pain. She bit on her lip so she wouldn't scream. Her hand felt as if it was on fire, but it finally glided out of the steel ring.

She cursed and gripped her hand tightly to ease the pain. She forced herself to the next step of her plan and focussed on the door. Although she was no longer handcuffed to the wall, she was still far away from escaping this place. Besides, she was also convinced that whoever was watching her on the two video cameras would have notified someone already. For a short moment, she thought to use the plastic bottles as a weapon, but she heard the door unlock before she could figure something out. Elena stood up and retreated to a corner as three men entered the cell. She looked at them and immediately knew she had absolutely no chance of escape. One of the goons closed and guarded the door from the inside, while the other two just stared at her, dumbfounded.

The shorter of those two said something in a language she couldn't understand and pointed at the handcuffs, which dangled empty from the steel ring. He quickly got into an argument with the other guy and repeatedly pointed at her aggressively. Elena didn't know what he was yelling, but it was very obvious he wasn't too thrilled that she had been able to free herself.

The other guy seemed to try to calm his friend down. She guessed they were in their mid-forties, maybe of Middle Eastern heritage, and they all had beards. With no other option than to just listen and watch, Elena followed their discussion, which got more heated by the minute. The mad guy suddenly stormed towards her, his hand raised as if he wanted to slap her.

"No!" Elena cried, panic rising through her body as she tried to cover her head with her hands. Elena looked up when she realised the strike didn't reach her. She could see the other guy gripping his raised arm tightly, preventing the blow. He continued yelling at him in their native language.

It took him a few moments to calm his friend down, but that still didn't improve Elena's situation. They were still between her and the door. Even if she could reach the door, it was not only closed but still guarded by the third goon. Elena was way too scared to think about anything else and just cowered in the corner, her hands still covering her head and tears running down her face.

The two guys finally stopped their argument and turned towards her.

"No! No! NO!" was all that Elena could scream, but none of it stopped her attackers. They brutally grabbed her arm and threw the one-hundred-and-five pound woman to the ground.

Elena cried out and tried to crawl to another corner, but didn't even get one metre before she was pushed over to her side by one of the goon's feet.

"Ah! No! No!" she pleaded again as they turned her on her belly to kneel on her back. Elena could barely breathe as they pulled her arms away from her body. Moments later, she heard the guys laughing and suddenly felt a quick sharp pain in her arm as they inserted the needle of a syringe. Almost immediately Elena noticed her senses slow down. Within seconds, the laughter was reduced to nothing more than a strange sound, and the whole room seemed to be moving in front of her eyes. She noticed how all her muscles relaxed and how all her strength left her body.

Her capturers waited for about another minute before picking her up effortlessly. Elena didn't even realise they dragged her out of the cell and down a corridor. Her eyes flipped from each passing light overhead, but she didn't know where they were taking her. She couldn't think anymore as the final effect of the sedative ensued. The last thing she saw was something that looked like an old ambulance. By the time they lifted her inside the old Iveco 4 x 4 and tied her hands to the steel bar with a zip-tie, she was already unconsciousness.

- 7 -

Whitmore, Western England, Tuesday, June 10

"So, here we are; this looks like it", Natascha said when she finally steered the same Mercedes Sprinter they had used in Norway into the parking lot in front of their bed and breakfast in Whitmore. Being accustomed to driving on the left side of the road, she was quickly volunteered by her three friends to be the designated driver. It was no surprise that most of the long drive to Whitmore was filled with laughter and stories from times past.

"I could never get used to driving on the left side", her friend Erika announced, still shaking her head even after several hours on the road. "I don't know how you can manage it."

"Easy", Natascha replied with a smile as she unbuckled her seat belt. "I keep my eyes closed. You usually get a VIP bumper sticker and a christmas present from your auto-repair shop after the first year, and I'm sure the police have my number on speed dial, but other than that, you actually get used to it."

"Wait! Didn't the security company have your phone number on speed dial back in university?" Erika teased.

"They might have had it for a little while after that one minor and completely insignificant incident, but at least there wasn't a drink named after me", Natascha jabbed back, winking at her friend.

"That night never happened!"

"Erika, just because you can't *remember* it, doesn't mean it never happened. I was the one who had to drag your butt all the way back to your room. I can guarantee you, it happened."

"We should probably leave the skeletons in the closet. Don't want to get you divorced."

"Hell no, *the closets that must not be opened*", Natascha stated theatrically as they walked towards the registration.

It took them about thirty minutes to settle into their rooms before they eventually walked down the street to the local pub. Erika and Natascha hung back a few metres, still exchanging stories when Natascha answered a text from her husband.

"So, how's marriage going?" Erika asked with a quick glance on Natascha's mobile phone. "Is he still the *one and only*? The knight in shining armour to rescue the damsel in distress, or is he turning out to be just another guy wrapped up in tin foil?"

"He's still the one, no regrets yet", Natascha answered and replied to another text.

"Yes, I suppose. What do they say? Opposites attract", Erika kept teasing her friend.

"What do you mean by that?" Natascha laughed.

"Well, you were pregnant and he wasn't."

"Don't be silly, I know he loves me."

"Ah, good for you. I bet he's the romantic type", Erika noted.

"Yeah, right. When he came back home from a ten day business trip, he tracked me down in our basement, undressed me, ripped my favourite panties off and took me on the washing machine. How is *that* for romance?" Natascha asked without sounding too disappointed.

"Aww, that's so cute. I bet you liked it!" Erika teased.

"Of course I did", Natascha laughed and blushed a little bit before she answered another text.

"Come on! You're gone for a couple hours and you already can't stay off that thing", Erika noticed with a roll of her eyes.

"That's not about him, I'm asking him about our daughter", Natascha laughed as they got closer to the pub.

"Ah, your pumpkin, she's so cute. Who would've thought you'd be a mother at that age, if at all!"

"Not me, trust me on that one. She wasn't exactly planned, but she has definitely changed everything. Even more than that other experience. I have no idea how I could ever live without her", Natascha finally said and put her cell phone away, obviously satisfied with Nick's report on their daughter.

Just over two hours later their stomachs were filled and they were back at their little bed and breakfast. Sitting around a table, they studied the plans from the flooded mine.

"Okay, here's the thing. The mine has always been closed for diving, so the only data we can rely on is from a group of scientists who dove there about fifteen years ago. I don't know if their main line is still in the shaft, but there are tracks from the carts. So navigating shouldn't be the biggest problem. We're also not penetrating beyond that point here", Andreas took the lead and pointed at a certain spot on the map.

"How far is that?" Natascha wanted to know. She and Mario were the more experienced divers in their little group, and it would be them who would conduct those dives.

"It's not that far. The plans are pretty accurate, and it shows us around three-hundred-and-eighty metres."

"Okay, I see. How deep is that going to be exactly?" Looking at the map, Natascha was slightly worried about her promise to Nick.

"We're looking at twenty-two metres, so nothing too exciting."

Relieved with the answer, Natascha relaxed a little bit.

"So our first dive is to just go in and have a look, assess the condition of the shaft, check for any hazards, and determine where we want to take the samples. According to the existing data, we're looking at a constant water temperature of four degrees Celsius. The visibility is generally good, but I don't have to tell you how easy it is to ruin that." Andreas pulled a clip from a file.

"Here, I got this video from the scientists who dove the mine fifteen years ago. They went in much deeper, but it also shows us our area of interest." Andreas changed the program on his laptop and for the next ten minutes they silently watched the video, occasionally jotting individual notes.

"Well, the vis will be a bitch if we don't pay attention. Other than that, there don't seem to be too many tight spots in there. Just that one section there, I believe at one-hundred-and-twenty metres, where some of the cribbing came down. But we should be able to squeeze through there. I think we can even take the scooters. There's plenty of room in all directions. What do you think, Natascha?" Mario asked turning his attention to her.

"Natascha's thinking about how to squeeze her ass through that cribbing", Erika quickly stabbed at her friend.

"My gorgeously shaped bum will fit through there perfectly, thank you very much!" Natascha replied coldly and, looking at Mario, shook her head. "Well, maybe we can take the scooters on the second dive. During the first one we should concentrate on getting as much info about this place as possible. We're on rebreathers, so we got plenty of time. With that profile we also don't need that much bail out gas. Once we know where we are, then we can start thinking about the following dives", Natascha slowed her old dive partner down.

"You *are* getting old. Couple of years ago I would've been the one slowing *you* down", Mario laughed.

"What can I say?" Natascha raised her shoulders with a smile before pointing on the map again. "Andreas, let's have a look at the video again when they pass this section here. What is this?"

"This is where most of the water rushed in when that one bomb hit the well during the war. Some of the miners had been locked in during the air raid, and they marked this location as the main point of entry for the water. Back then they said that the water was slowly seeping through the wall there before it washed away so much of the material that it actually started to rush in rather rapidly." Andreas explained and pulled up the video again. "There it is", the young scientist pointed out and paused the recording.

"Hm, that doesn't look too promising. It seems to be rather tight. Has anyone been in there at all?"

"I think the expedition fifteen years ago might have peeked into it, but they didn't follow it. I was told that about three years ago a company came in to disarm an unexploded ordnance inside the abbey grounds. Rumour has it that they had to detonate it. I wasn't able to confirm that, but if that's true then there is a chance that the detonation messed with the underwater stream. Don't forget the actual mine is closed for divers."

"Hm, interesting", Natascha murmured more to herself. "You said that some of the miners had been locked in. I read the files you sent me, and they say they were all rescued within days, right?"

"Yes, luckily there were no casualties."

"Good, I don't need a creepy dive." Natascha smiled, then continued, "Okay, so what's our schedule?"

"Yes, we have a ten day permit. We can drive our van all the way up right to the mine's entrance and just walk in. We can pick up the keys to the gate tomorrow morning… Are you yawning, Natascha?"

"Excuse me. Yes, I'm yawning. So we can assemble all the gear up there and we don't have to carry it too far. I really like that. It'll also save us lots of time."

"Yes, we just set up the tent right beside the van and that should be it."

"Cool. That sounds like a plan to me", Natascha yawned again and stretched.

Asklepios, Aegean Sea, Tuesday, June 17

For most people it was just the beginning of another day, but for Victor Gates it was more than that. It was another day closer to living a normal life. His medical condition didn't allow him to leave his suite since he was still recovering from the transplant surgery. It was one of those days he had to work hard to remain positive.

"Everything looks fine, Victor. The doctor said things will take time. I'm praying to the Lord every day for your recovery", his old friend and former business partner Walter Leroy Jackson promised him, sitting beside his bed.

I know! I'm just so fed up with nothing but lying around.

"A couple more days and you can use the wheelchair. That'll be a complete game changer."

I hope! How's your wife doing? Can they help her?

"Liz? Oh, well, the doctors are saying they can help her. They actually scheduled the surgery for tomorrow morning. She's talking to them right now. God bless them!"

Before Victor could reply, someone knocked at the cabin door.

Come in!

"Good Morning. How are you doing?" a strong aristocratically British accent asked.

Still suffering, but better. How are you, Samuel?

"I'm very well, thank you", Sir Samuel Archibald Cunningham stiffly replied and steered his wheelchair a little inside the room before shaking Victor's and Walter Jackson's hand. Neither one of them had expected a different answer. Despite sitting in the wheelchair, Sir Samuel Cunningham's custom tailored suit underlined the hardened lines in his over seventy years old face. His medical condition forced the British aristocrat into the dependence of his wheelchair from time to time, but even when he walked, he had to rely on his custom made cane. Despite his fragile body, just the expression on his face was enough to create a certain aura of ruthlessness. Sir Cunningham's face rarely showed any emotion other than that of a serious business tycoon. Walter waited and watched as their guest made himself as comfortable as he could. They updated him on the latest events while listening to some music, but they didn't have to wait much longer before the fourth person for this meeting knocked at the door.

"Come in", Walter Jackson said and pulled another chair out from the table.

Dr William Edwards walked into the room and greeted everybody personally by hand shake before turning his attention to Mr Gates' monitor.

"I'll just be a few seconds", he said and checked some data. "All looking good", he nodded with satisfaction and unplugged the webcam that allowed permanent video contact with Mr Gates.

"Okay, Gentlemen. You all requested this meeting. What can I do for you?" the doctor asked and sat down.

Whitmore, Western England, Tuesday, June 17
With just little movement of her fins, Natascha slowly made her way through the mine shaft. Despite their best efforts not to disturb any silt, their last twenty dives had definitely taken a toll on the visibility. Looking underneath and behind her, she could see Mario following closely. Natascha focussed the beam of her light to a bright spot and shone it in a circular motion underneath her, the international sign for asking if everything was okay. Satisfied that Mario confirmed with the same signal, Natascha slowly continued to follow the white line marking their way to the exit. This was their last scheduled dive, and Natascha could feel a mild sense of disappointment that this whole project was almost over.

Everything had worked out well, and it took Natascha only two dives to get back into her underwater routine. She became quickly familiar with the shaft and decided to take advantage of the last dive by bringing the larger video camera with her. Although the visibility was not as clear as it had been at the beginning, she decided to take a closer video of the small side tunnel that had caused the mine to flood in the first place.

When she reached the tunnel's entrance, she tied a separate cave line and checked that it was secured and safe. Satisfied with the result, the young scientist turned around and looked at her dive buddy. Mario just nodded and shrugged his shoulders as if he was saying *why not?* Natascha turned the video camera lights on and pressed record. She softly flicked her fins to slowly push forward. Contrary to what they expected, the side tunnel was suitably wide, with enough room for her to comfortably swim through it with her camera gear. She was satisfied to see that the visibility was about three metres. Natascha dimmed the video lights and carefully pushed forward, trying to stay an equal distance from the bottom and the ceiling. With less than twenty centimetres to spare above and below her, she continued their exploration into the tunnel, carefully securing her cave line every now and then.

With more than enough breathing gas available, Natascha pushed further and further into the side tunnel, making sure to keep her cave line tight and safe. Just as the tunnel widened up in front of her, she felt Mario pulling at her fins. The tunnel was too tight for her to turn around, so she simply looked back between her legs. Mario signalled that their scheduled dive time was coming to an end, which meant that Erika and Andreas awaited their return within the next few minutes. Natascha signalled back and looked up again. She knew they had to turn around and reluctantly started her way out of the side tunnel.

The visibility was now reduced to about two metres, and it took them a couple minutes before reaching the main shaft. Mario waited for her to take the lead again before he removed the marker showing any potential rescue party where they had gone. Although they were both already over the agreed dive time, Mario and Natascha took it slow. Natascha had the strong video lights on and knew that Erika and Andreas, who were waiting for them at the surface, would see the lights by now.

The mine's bottom started to gently slope up, and it was only a few more metres before they would break the surface. Natascha closed her drysuit valve and slowly raised her head through the surface. The water was now only chest deep. Natascha and Mario looked at each other and nodded, signalling they were fine before turning their attention to their friends. With their own suits on, they waited for them to take some of their gear.

"Here, take the camera first", Natascha told Erika and unclipped the expensive housing and video light combination from her harness. While Erika carefully placed the camera on a rubber mat on the ground, Natascha clipped off her dive light and removed her mask.

"I can take your bail out tanks", Erika offered.

"Yes, that would be great. Thanks!" Natascha appreciated the offer and unclipped the two tanks she carried on her side for emergencies. With all her extra gear gone, Natascha removed her fins and watched as Erika secured the tanks on a little cart at the water edge.

"Well, that was fun", Natascha finally said, noticing Erika's anticipation as they walked out of the water. "The visibility was not that bad. As long as we stayed close to the ceiling we were fine. Since the rebreathers eliminate all the bubbles, nothing got stirred up that way", she explained and placed her mask, neoprene hood, and fins into her bin on the cart.

"Did you get cold this time?"

"Not really", Natascha replied and added some more air to her drysuit as she walked out of the mine and into the little pop-up tent they had erected in front of their van.

"Ah, this is nice", she said and rested her rebreather on a table behind her. Erika held the unit as Natascha methodically got out of it. Together they secured her gear back in the Sprinter.

"So, what do you think, Natascha? That wasn't too bad." Mario commented, removing his remaining diving gear.

"No, I actually expected this whole expedition to be much more challenging. We did how many? Around twenty dives here already? The conditions are still good. Even that little side tunnel wasn't as tight as we expected. The tunnel actually got wider where we turned around. What do you think, Mario? Are you up for it?" Natascha suggested, her enthusiasm clearly evident.

"I don't know. We have no idea what to expect. I mean, we have exact plans and plenty of room for the main mine shaft, but we have nothing for the side tunnel. Did you have any issues tying the line?"

"No, and as far as I could see, the tunnel doesn't seem to be in bad condition. What if we use the ROV to take a closer look? How long is the fibre optic? Five-hundred metres?"

"I don't know, it's a pretty expensive toy to lose in there. What would your father say if we lose it?"

"*I told you not to let my daughter operate it.*" Natascha imitated her father and earned some laughter.

"Well, to be honest, he made that a condition before we left. But since you're bringing it up, does that mean you take full responsibility for it?"
Natascha had to think for a second and dried her hair with a towel.

"Hell yeah, why not? If we don't do it, we will always regret it. Besides, I'm his favourite daughter. How mad can he get?" Natascha smiled innocently.

"Hm, you do remember you're his *only* daughter? Makes that *favourite* part almost mandatory, doesn't it?" Erika reminded her.

"Well, it sounded better the way I said it", Natascha winked at her and turned around to exit the little pop-up tent. She felt her hands instinctively extend forward as she suddenly toppled to the ground. "Ouch!" Natascha yelled as she fell, landing hard on her hip, her toes curled under the pain. She noticed the culprit and frowned at the tent peg.

"Natascha! Did you just fall?" Erika asked with a curious smile dancing on her lips.

"No, I didn't. I just hugged the ground." Natascha replied sarcastically and wiped the dirt from her drysuit.

"Then why do you have a tear in your eye?" Erika teased her friend, knowing that Natascha was fine.

"It was very emotional!" Natascha laughed back.

After disassembling and stowing their gear, it took them only two hours to set up everything at the water edge. The heavy duty moulded plastic case with the monitor and controls for the ROV rested on a folding table. The team gathered around the monitor.

"Okay, that's as good as it gets!" Natascha commented after they had successfully finished the pre-dive safety check for the ROV. "Put it in the water, Mario, and let's hope my father loves me as much as he always tells me." With her eyes glued to the monitor and controls, Natascha prayed that none of the alarms would go off.

"So far so good. If anyone wants to stop me from doing something that can get me disinherited, now would be a good time", Natascha said nervously. Despite her enthusiasm, she knew very well her father would be anything but pleased if something would happen to the ROV. Her problem was that her three friends were as enthusiastic as she was, and none of them had any desire to stop her, especially since she had assumed all responsibility.

"Nobody? Thanks guys! I knew I could rely on you", Natascha's sarcasm grew stronger as she spoke. Her elbows relaxed as she became more comfortable with the controls.

"Anytime, Natascha. Anytime!" Erika clapped her on the shoulder, exchanging a look of encouragement as Natascha glanced over to her.

"Okay, here we go!" She finally exhaled and used the joystick to activate the thrusters on the ROV. It took Natascha only a few minutes to figure out how the small vehicle reacted on her commands. Erika adjusted a slide control on her control station to dim the ROV's lights. With the slight shift in the lighting they were quite satisfied with the visibility on the monitor.

"As long as we pay attention to that fibre optic we should be fine", Mario encouraged her friend.

"Okay, here's the entrance to the side tunnel. So far it was easy. Anyone who wants to talk some sense into me, now is your last chance." Natascha pleaded half-heartedly one last time.

"Tried that so many times, I've given up on that a long time ago", Erika shrugged her shoulders with a bored voice.

"Nah, never worked before", Mario agreed, also sounding disappointed.

"As if you would listen to us now", Andreas finally concluded.

"Thanks guys. You really are my friends."

"Okay! Natascha, you're out of your mind! Turn the ROV around or I'll call your father immediately!" Erika shouted with played authority, knowing very well that her theatrical plea would fall on deaf ears.

"Are you nuts? Forget it! I'm not turning around now!" Natascha replied firmly and held her breath as she sent the ROV into the side tunnel. She slowly steered the little vehicle further and further into the tunnel. Since it was much smaller than a diver, Natascha realised rather quickly that there was plenty of room to navigate the ROV relatively easily.

"This is where we turned around, isn't it?" Natascha asked Mario without taking her eyes from the monitor.

"Yes, I believe so. Look, there's your reel on the ground. How far is that?"

"It's one-hundred-thirty-eight metres from the water edge to the side tunnel, and now we're another one-hundred-and-eight metres inside the side tunnel, so about two-hundred-and-forty-six metres all together. Which means about half of the fibre optic is out."

"Ok. Let's go a little bit further", Natascha whispered and moved the joystick again. The tunnel widened further.

"Wow, what's that up there?" Andreas asked and pointed at the monitor.

"Looks like a shoe or a boot?" Erika said.

"It's an old shoe. How did that get there?" Natascha asked and steered the ROV in front of it.

"I don't know, but I think there are other objects on the ground there. How deep are we?"

"About sixteen metres. Erika, make sure we are recording all of this, please. Let's see what's going on there."

While Natascha held the ROV in position, Erika checked the controls again before Natascha moved in closer.

"Okay, any ideas what that could be?" Natascha asked and looked at some smaller, almost square objects.

"Alien eggs?" Mario suggested with laughter.

"You know what? Look at the direction we're going. I bet that's from the well up there on the hill. You know the one that got hit?" Erika suggested. Natascha frowned as she carefully navigated the ROV closer to the objects.

"What? Why do you look so surprised? You don't believe me?" Erika asked her friend.

"Oh, I believe you. I'm just surprised it was you who came to that conclusion", Natascha stabbed at her friend with a laugh.

"You didn't even tell me you're pregnant again. How far are you now? Eight months?" Erika insulted her in return. Natascha briefly glanced at her, but navigating the ROV required all her attention.

"That discussion will be continued later, missy!" Natascha promised threateningly.

"Wow, look at the top of the screen!" Andreas yelled and pointed his finger. Natascha stopped the ROV and tilted its camera upwards.

"That looks like bricks. Wait a second, let's see what's above us." Natascha tilted the camera a little bit further and they could look straight up the well shaft.

"Ah, that looks pretty tight to me." Mario commented on all the wood and debris blocking the route to the surface.

"Yeah, you're right. I'm not going to risk this. I mean we can clearly see we're in the well."

Erika cleared her throat.

"What's it now? You need a cough drop?" Natascha commented without even looking at Erika, denying her friend any form of recognition. Erika punched her thigh.

"Okay, that explains the shoe. It's simply garbage someone had thrown in the well and it got carried downstream."

"Yes, but where did all the wood come from?"

"Maybe there was a little roof built over the well as a shelter? Or maybe they just threw stuff in there after the war? Who knows?"

"Okay, I think we should slowly get the unit back. I mean, we can clearly dive this tunnel. It's wide enough, we can easily run a line, and there are no narrow passages that are cause for any concern. What do you think, Mario?" Natascha asked.

"Well, we might as well take a look. But we're not taking scooters or cameras with us."

"No, just the GoPro with the two small lights", Natascha suggested as she flipped the camera another ninety degrees. Keeping the ROV in mid-water, she pressed a button to wind up the fibre optic again as the ROV slowly started its way back to the mine entrance.

Asklepios, Aegean Sea, Tuesday, June 17
"I believe we are reaching a stage in our combined interest and effort that we would like to know if the proposed timeline is still accurate", the British aristocrat continued stiffly.

Both Victor and Walter just looked at Dr Edwards with anticipation.

"I understand", the physician opened. "As you are all well aware, we are dealing with some incredible medical challenges here. But the short answer would be yes. We are still operating within the proposed timeline."

Can you give us some details? Victor asked over his voice computer.

"We currently have eighteen young women in group A. Their ages range from sixteen to twenty-five or twenty-six, I would say. The fact that you insisted on the *biblical reference* made the project a little more difficult, but since your laboratories", Dr Edwards glanced at Sir Cunningham, "provided us with the genetically altered bug, we are actually ahead of schedule. They will soon be transported to their final destination. Once they are there, we can expect first casualties sooner rather than later." Dr Edwards explained.

"Is there any risk to the rest of us here?"

"No, there's not. They're all in isolation. Our isolation station rivals the most modern biological weapons research laboratories. Besides, each subject is closely monitored twenty-four hours a day. There is absolutely nothing that can happen", the British doctor reassured them.

What about group B?

"We currently have thirteen women in group B. Not all of them qualified as organ donors, but we got some organs here and there. With the project reaching its final stage, we move them reasonably fast. This current group of thirteen women will leave by the end of the week. Our main task is to ensure they're healthy enough so that there are no complaints. We cannot afford any rejections."

"How many were there all together?" L.J. Jackson whispered, staring at the floor.

"Trust me, you don't want to know", Dr Edwards simply answered.

"May the Lord have mercy on our souls", the Texan muttered.

"It might be too late for that." Dr Edwards said and rose from his chair, indicating he had not much more time to spare.

William, I have one more question.

"Yes, Victor, what is it?" the British doctor asked, his hand already on the door knob.

One of the nurses...Melissa...Is she okay? I have the feeling this might be too much for her.

Both the British aristocrat and the Texan oil tycoon worriedly looked at the physician.

"Everybody working as medical staff underwent strict psychological screening. She passed with flying colours", Dr Edwards explained, his hand tightened on the door knob. "Why? Did she say something?" his eye brows rose.

No, no... It's just a feeling I had. Victor Gates was obviously satisfied with the answer.

"Gentlemen", Dr Edwards finally nodded before leaving the room.

Whitmore, Western England, Wednesday, June 18
With the ROV's recorded video footage still fresh in her mind, Natascha knew how much further the vertical shaft from the former well was ahead. She quickly checked her dive computer and signalled with her light back to Mario to see if everything was all right. Satisfied with his response, Natascha gently flicked her fins to avoid stirring up any sediment. She just passed by the old shoe and took a closer look at it. Since it was covered in fine sediment, it was impossible to determine what kind of shoe it was, and Natascha decided it was best to leave it be. If she would touch the half-buried object, it would only stir up a lot of sediment. Instead, she slowly moved ahead, not without securing her cave line every few metres.

She dimmed the settings on her own light and used the two small video lights to illuminate her surroundings. As expected, the visibility inside the well was worse than in the tunnel itself. Natascha determined it was mostly due to rainwater and dirt washing in from the surface. Natascha took a close-up video of the bricks she found on the bottom. She couldn't date them, but they looked rather old to her, and she decided to take one with her on the way back out. Maybe she could retrieve some data from it.

Looking up, she could not see the surface. Too much debris blocked it off. With a quick flick of her hand she could see her powerful light penetrating the old shaft and tried to get some video footage of it. Natascha carefully studied the debris above her and noticed some old wooden beams that were now wedged between the sides of the well. It was undoubtedly the remains of a former structure that had provided a roof over the well many decades ago. Natascha wasn't too sure how safe her position was and decided not to stay there much longer.

After a quick exchange of signals with Mario she kept looking around and noticed that the tunnel continued beyond the actual well. She slowly moved closer to the dark entrance and carefully shone her light into it. It looked identical to the first section of the tunnel, maybe with a little less vertical height. She fought with herself whether she should push into this new tunnel or not, but she also knew that it was now or never. A quick glance to Mario revealed that he simply shrugged his shoulders and nodded his agreement.

They both checked their air supply and calculated they had a good ten minutes before they would have to start their return. Mario signalled Natascha that he was ready. Inspecting her reel, Natascha noticed she was almost out of her cave line. She looked around and decided to tie the line to a wooden beam. Reaching behind her, Natascha located another reel and unclipped the bolt snap from the D-Ring on her harness. After connecting the line with the previous one, she double checked that it was secured to the wooden beam before studying the new tunnel again. She gently flicked her fins to glide forward, following the new section of the cave that gently led them up a slight incline. They closely monitored their computers and gauges, and by now they had penetrated the new tunnel for almost eight minutes. With their agreed exploration time coming to an end, they started to look for a spot allowing them to turn around. A quick glance on her LED wrist computer informed Natascha that they were technically only six metres deep, and she frowned as she noticed something on the bottom several metres ahead. Several objects were illuminated by her strong primary light, but Natascha could not quite identify them yet.

You got to be kidding me! That can't be! Are those really...? Natascha asked herself as she got closer. She didn't even bother trying to get some video image of them, since she was still too far away for that. Another couple flicks from her ankles cut that distance down to merely five metres, and she was now convinced about what she was looking at.

Yes, that's what they are. But how the hell do they get here? Natascha wondered and decided to take some close-up video and maybe a few samples, although she wasn't exactly sure what to do with them. Before she could flick her ankles again, Mario signalled with his light that he had an emergency. Natascha looked back between her legs to make eye contact with her friend and dive buddy. She couldn't determine what his emergency was, but she could clearly see that Mario had closed his breathing loop and switched to his open circuit bailout stage tanks. Natascha immediately tied her reel off to a secure place and placed the little camera right beside it to make sure her hands were not occupied should Mario need her assistance. It took

Natascha a few seconds, but she eventually managed to turn around inside the tight tunnel to finally face her dive partner. Mario took a couple breaths from the regulator and signalled Natascha that everything was okay. Natascha signalled back and they immediately followed the dive protocol with Mario leading their way towards the exit.

Since he was no longer breathing a closed circuit rebreather, the bubbles from his exhaled air rose to the cave's ceiling, causing a constant rain of fine sediment. With the visibility getting worse, they both safely reached the old well and stopped for a moment. Natascha was satisfied Mario was in control of his dive, his temperament calm and relaxed. He waited for her to catch up before continuing down the side tunnel to the main mine shaft and finally to the exit.

"Well, that was exciting", Mario commented the moment his head popped through the surface.

"What happened?" asked Erika as she and Andreas waded into the water in their dry suits. The moment they saw Mario breathing from his bailout, they knew he was in some sort of trouble. Looking for an answer, Erika looked at Natascha, but Natascha was preoccupied with her own gear. She closed her breathing loop and removed her mask.

"I'm fine, don't worry", Mario calmly announced, trying not to create too much excitement. "I don't know exactly what happened to my rebreather, but somehow my breathing loop flooded. I tried to locate the issue for a few moments but couldn't find it. That's when I decided to bail-out. Sorry, Natascha."

"Don't apologise to me. I'm just glad you're fine. How much gas do you have left?"

"Plenty, more than enough. We didn't rush, and we weren't deep, so I didn't use much."

"Okay, let's get out of the gear and check what went wrong with your unit", Natascha suggested and handed her fins to Erika who gave her a puzzled look.

"What is it? You want me to get the whip again?" Natascha jokingly threatened her friend, who had still not moved but simply stared at her.

"I beg your pardon, Your Highness, but, silly me, I thought to remember that you started the dive with a video camera. Your Clumsiness didn't, by any chance, manage to lose that precious and rather expensive piece of gear?"

"Let it be known that I appreciate the effort my servants put into their thought process. Let it also be known that I decided to leave the camera in the tunnel, once Mario signalled to me that he had an emergency. I wanted to have both my hands free just in case he needed some assistance. Once I remembered that I left the camera, we were already too far gone, and I couldn't leave Mario to go back to get the camera." Natascha explained as they exited the mine.

"Forgive me if I may sound rude, but your Stupidity is well aware that I signed for said camera right in front of the eyes of our ruler, better known to you as *daddy*. I should probably consider following his orders and report this little mishap at once." Erika stated theatrically.

"Let it be known that my servant should get the twist out of her panties, and that I hope she gives natural birth to an enormous baby, should she try to blackmail me. Let it also be known that we'll go back either later this afternoon or early tomorrow morning and recover the camera either personally or with the ROV." Natascha threatened her further as she got out of the gear.

"I'll spread the words of wisdom from our fearless leader. With your permission I will retreat back into the cave to retrieve the rest of the gear." Erika mimicked some bows and walked away to help Andreas and Mario. Natascha laughed and shook her head as she took her drysuit off. She had to admit to herself that it was only after Erika had brought the subject up, that she realised she had forgotten the camera in the mine. Natascha wasn't too concerned about the camera. She knew they could recover it during another dive or with the ROV. There was still plenty of time left. Her thoughts were preoccupied by what she had seen in the tunnel, and for some reason she could not help but think about the papers the young reporter had handed to the bishop during that gala event.

Asklepios, Aegean Sea, Wednesday, June 18
Although Lamar Hatcher was already a few hours into his late shift, he had not found the time yet to relax. He sat in the control room and closely watched the row of monitors in front of him. All patients from group A were under constant video surveillance. For the moment, most of them faded in and out of consciousness, moving in their beds as far as their restraints would allow them. Every now and then Lamar checked the computer for the vital data of each patient. Despite his attentive nature, he still felt on edge. He decided to lean back and eat the sandwich he had brought with him for lunch.

The American exhaled deeply as he finally took the first bite. As much as he loved all the amenities and the international cuisine they had access to, as far as he was concerned, nothing could beat an old fashioned tuna sandwich. He took a second bite and even closed his eyes for a second, allowing his thoughts to drift back to his small home town. His pleasures were short lived and ceased the moment he heard the warning signal from the computer.

"Oh, shit!" Lamar spluttered, tossing the sandwich as he pulled the video on the main monitor. The woman they had labelled A-14 seemed to have a medical reaction.

"Oh, damn!" he cursed recognising the young girl. Lamar always managed to keep an emotional distance between him and any of the labelled patients, but A-14 was different. She reminded him of a girl he had once dated in high school. Virginia was her name and while he would never forget her, he didn't even know the real name of A-14. They only knew she was originally from somewhere in Eastern Europe, something they had established from all the questions she had asked them in the beginning. They had never answered her questions or replied to her desperate pleas. Based on the examination they estimated she was barely eighteen years old.

Watching the monitor, he could see how she violently threw herself from one side to the other, fighting against the restraints that held her in the bed. It was obvious to Lamar that young A-14 didn't realise what she was doing, despite her elaborate gestures to escape. She didn't have much control over her body. Looking at her vital signs he shook his head and paged Dr Sheridan Evans over the Intercom.

"Yes, Lamar, what is it?" the British doctor immediately responded, her face popping up in the top corner of the monitor. It looked like she was at one of the communication stations outside.

"It's A-14, Dr Evans. She's not looking too good", Lamar explained and shook his head. The British doctor didn't waste a second and immediately ran down to the control room. Within two minutes she swiped her security card and punched in her code to open the door.

"What monitor am I looking at?" she panted, staring at several computer monitors in front of her.

"Her vitals are on the main screen. You can see her on monitor two", Lamar said and pointed at the monitor on the top left. Dr Evans glanced quickly at the teenage girl's video feed as she shook violently, but her eyes soon focussed on her vitals.

"Goddamn it! She's burning up. When did it start?"

"About ten minutes ago, Dr Evans." Lamar answered.

"Did she start coughing yet?"

"No, not that I've noticed."

"When did we get her last blood work?" Dr Evans asked but found the answer herself on the computer. "This morning. Okay, we should know something rather soon then", she said and used their intercom to call their lab.

"Hello?...Bill? Sheridan here", the British doctor said, satisfied she reached Dr William Edwards on the other end.

"Bill, we have a problem here. A-14 has a severe medical reaction. How far is her blood work from this morning?...Yes, you can call me back here. I'll be on this number for a while", she said and pressed a button to disconnect the call.

"Is there anything we can do for her? You want us to dress up?" Lamar asked as they both watched the girl, who was now much calmer. She simply had no energy left and only tossed her head from side to side.

"No, not yet. If this is what I think it is, then it won't matter. There's nothing we can do for her then. Can I sit down for a moment, please?"

"Sure." Lamar got up and quickly took his tuna sandwich before letting Dr Sheridan Evans take his place.

"Okay, where are we at?" the forty-two year-old British doctor said more to herself and scrolled to A-14's medical history. She ran her hand through her hair.

"Hm, I don't understand that. She was borderline for group A or B, but we did find some antibodies in her. So, what's your problem?" Dr Evans asked the monitor without receiving an answer.

"Doctor! Look at this. Her temperature went up another tenth of a degree."

"Yeah, that doesn't look good. Her temperature is rising really fast. For now we can only wait to hear back from Bill, but I'm afraid there's not really that much we can do. How are the other patients doing?"

Guinea pigs came to Lamar's mind, but he didn't say anything.

"They're fine. Just as we expected. Everything seems to be working according to the protocol with them."

"Okay, that's good. The parameters for the audible alarm are in fact quite good, so we don't have to change them." Dr Evans commented as the intercom rang.

"Yes, Bill. Talk to me", she quickly answered without taking her eyes from the monitor with A-14's vitals.

"We checked her blood sample. I don't have the full analysis yet, that will be a couple more hours, but it looks like there's something wrong with her antibodies. Maybe she didn't get her vaccination during the recommended timeframe when she was a child. Or maybe there was something wrong with the serum back then. I'll know for certain in a few hours, but this is what it looks like at the moment. We looked at her vitals and I assume she just doesn't have the right antibodies for this...It's a shame! She was a cute one. She could have really helped us."

"Damn! Thanks, Bill." Dr Sheridan Evans ended the call without replying to his comment. She and Lamar understood what this meant for the young woman.

"What are we doing now?" Lamar asked in a low voice.

"Well, there's nothing we can do. We have to follow procedure. You can go and dress up. Take Leo or Kevin with you. You know the drill. Use two bags. Make sure that everything is disinfected accordingly once you cremated her. I'll get Melissa to cover here for you."

Lamar just nodded and left the room as Dr Evans called the Irish nurse over the intercom system.

It took Lamar and Kevin about one hour before they were both dressed up in medical biohazard suits and entered the isolation station through the airlock. Their eyes were already locked on A-14, who noticed their arrival as they slowly walked over to her bed. Once at her side, she tiredly looked at both of them, but she was now too weak to move. Lamar saw her lips moving, but he couldn't hear what she said. He didn't have to understand her language or hear her words, he knew she pleaded for them to help her, but that would not happen. Not getting an answer and too weak to fight, the girl they had labelled A-14 looked at the ceiling. Her last hope of help had just vanished. The two men watched as a spasm of coughing shook her fragile body, blood running now from her nose and her mouth. She tried to sit up, but her head fell back again into her pillow. Desperate tears ran down A-14's angelic face as she realised the two men would not help her. The young woman didn't even notice the needle they inserted into her arm.

A second spasm of coughing shook her body one last time, with more blood flowing from her nose and mouth. A-14's body convulsed one more time before resting still. Seconds later, seventeen year-old Adriana Gabor was relieved from her misery. Her heart finally stopped, and a last breath escaped her lungs. Her now empty eyes stared at the ceiling as Lamar let his hand glide over her face to gently close them.

"Sorry, Virginia. But trust me, this was much more merciful than what would've happened to you in a couple weeks", he whispered as he swallowed the lump in his throat, "rest in peace."

- 8 -

Whitmore, Western England, Wednesday, June 18

"And you're certain you saw *bones* in that tunnel?" Andreas asked Natascha as they sat in their bed and breakfast.

"Yes, I'm sure they were bones. All different sizes and they looked...I don't know, but they looked *human* to me." Natascha explained for what she thought was the one-thousandth time. She understood her friends scepticism, since she knew there wasn't much of an explanation on how or why those bones could have ended up there.

"Look, I know what you're thinking and I agree. If the bones were downstream from the well, towards the main mine shaft, we could all agree they might have been leftovers from a feast that were thrown into the well decades ago, or maybe even an animal that fell into the well. But these bones are quite a distance upstream and also uphill from the well. The well bottoms out at fifteen metres and the bones were in about six metres of depth. There's no physical way they could have come from the well. And besides that, they do look like human bones. You know I've seen human bones before", Natascha added silently, remembering the moments on the research submarine when her friends had been forced to work on a lost Russian submarine in the Arctic.

Erika and the rest of the group silently studied the plans from the mine. They knew Natascha well enough to know she wouldn't take such a stance unless she was certain about it. Although, it was still clear that all three of them remained sceptical of the bones being human.

"Okay, that leaves us with the question where they came from. Any ideas?" Erika asked, glancing at her friends.

"I don't know", Natascha replied frustratedly and shrugged her shoulders.

"We don't even know where that water is coming from."

"Well, we do know that the stream feeding the well has a rather large water flow. After all, it filled up the entire mine eventually. Maybe there's a second surface connection to the water stream somewhere. What direction did you go?"

"The tunnel more or less leads toward the outskirts of the abbey, I would say." Mario explained and pointed on the screen of his laptop, where he pulled up a satellite image.

"It really looks like it. Thinking of it, it would only make sense if there is a well inside the abbey. Do we know anything about that?"

"We don't have any layout from the abbey, but from what I know, the abbey is open to visitors. We could ask if there is a well up there. If that's the case, it could explain where those bones came from", Andreas noted.

"I'm going to ask the owner here if she knows if there's a well in the abbey or somewhere else", Erika offered and rose from her chair.

Natascha couldn't help but think about Andreas' casual comment and a cold shiver ran down her spine. *Could those bones have any connection to what the reporter described in his paper?* She wondered but kept her thoughts to herself. She looked at the monitor showing the aerial view, her mind spinning around her suspicion.

"Ms. Boyle said there used to be another well inside the abbey, close to the outer walls, but it has not been used in decades. She doesn't even know if it's still an active well or if it's filled in. Other than that, there's no other well in the area that she knows about."

"Why don't we go and take a tour of the abbey? Maybe we can find some information there?" Natascha suggested absentmindedly, still staring at the map. "What?" she asked after no one commented on her suggestion and looked at her friends. They stared back at her almost as puzzled as she looked at them.

"What happened to her?" Erika asked in a scary tone.

"Maybe Nick has domesticated her! You never know." Andreas suggested, but didn't sound too convinced.

"Domesticating? *That one*? He won't be able to do that, it's impossible. Aliens must have abducted the real Natascha and we're looking at an extraterrestrial disguised as her!" Mario stated convincingly with a shocked expression on his face, while Erika carefully slapped Natascha with her flip-flop.

"Are you out of your mind? What the hell was that for?" Natascha barked, uncertain what her friends were up to.

"It does feel pain", Erika commented, but totally ignored her friend.

"It does sound like her too", Mario added freely.

"Can someone please tell me what this is about? Preferably without hitting me!" Natascha quickly added as Erika raised her flip-flop again.

"The Natascha we know never went into a church! She always had very strong feelings against the clerics. Who are you and what did you do with our friend?" Erika asked and threatened Natascha with her flip-flop again.

"Will you stop it! I didn't say we should go up there to listen to a sermon or to donate money. I just said we should go up there and take a tour of the abbey to gather some information. Huge difference!" Natascha emphasised, still looking at Erika, who only raised her eyebrows, but still held her flip-flop up like a weapon.

"Natascha! Church! Inside! Not happening! Are you happy now?" Natascha told her friend, who slowly lowered her flip-flop.

"We will trust you for now, but the moment you start crossing yourself I'll beat you silly with my flip-flop!" Erika threatened and got up to change for their little excursion.

About forty minutes later they walked through the huge gates and inside the stone walls of the abbey. Immediately behind the entrance was an information board with the general layout of the different buildings and info paths. It also contained information about upcoming events. They studied the board but could not find any information about a well.

"Oh, look Natascha! They are hosting the next International Catholic Bishops' conference here this summer. Look at all those different seminars and clinics. Wouldn't that be the perfect getaway for you and your hubby?" Erika teased, pointing to the notification with a crooked grin.

"Let's not be silly, okay?" Natascha commented seriously as she turned her friend down.

"I should just register you and have them perform an exorcism on you", Erika commented and studied the map of the abbey for any information about the well.

"Well, if it is or was outside, it can only be here by the gardens and green houses", Erika suggested, and they all agreed to try their luck there. It was already late in the afternoon, but there were still visitors from three different tour busses in the abbey. Most of the visitors were elderly people strolling around and visiting the different sites before they would attend the mass later that evening. Natascha noticed a school bus outside and figured there was at least one school class there as well.

The four followed the path, walked by a cafe and came upon the souvenir shop.

"How about it Natascha? Want to go inside and buy something for Nick?" Erika nudged her, knowing very well what her reaction would be.

"I'd rather give him some money for a stripper", she replied swiftly with a wave of her hand.

"And the scary part is that I actually believe this", Erika noted with mocked frustration.

"But if you want to go in there I'll gladly wait outside, Erika." Natascha added in a much softer tone. She knew Erika's parents were very religious, and she didn't want to keep Erika from buying something for them.

"Maybe later. It's pretty crowded in there now. We should see if we can find that well."

They followed the path leading them to the gardens, but instead of an open field they saw a couple of green houses and a pond. There was no sign of a well.

Natascha didn't feel comfortable, but she knew it was because of the notes from the young reporter. Thinking about Cathy Sheppard's accusations, another shiver ran down her spine.

"Relax, Natascha. You made it this far. You won't burst into flames." Mario whispered teasingly once he noticed her tension.

"Maybe she *should* burst into flames!" Erika poked. "How can you be so strongly against the church?"

"I don't know what you're talking about. I did get married, didn't I?"

"It was a *Celtic druid* who performed the ceremony!" Erika whispered and looked around, as if she was afraid to say that out loud inside the abbey.

"It was so romantic. We sacrificed a goat, drank some blood and danced naked around the fire at midnight during the full moon", Natascha proudly announced. Erika couldn't help but shiver.

"You are a demon!" she hissed at her friend.

"Oh come on, Erika. You know damn well why I don't like the church."

"Don't curse in here!" Erika punched Natascha's upper arm. "What's wrong with you? We'll all end up in hell just for walking beside you!" Erika whispered harshly and noticed a monk not too far away. Giving Natascha a stern look she walked over and asked him about the well.

Natascha didn't exactly understand what he said, but the monk clearly pointed to one of the green houses. With disappointment, Erika came back to her friends and shrugged her shoulders.

"He said there used to be a well where the green house is now, but it was filled in about thirty years ago when they built them. There's nothing left from it, but he said they have a little pond in there. You think it might be worth checking it out?"

"No, I don't think we'll find anything here then. Damned, I would've loved to figure out if their well was connected to the tunnel and how", Natascha sounded disappointed and looked around. She knew that this must have been the former location of the penitentiary and orphanage. Her thoughts lost in the events described by Cathy, she simply stared at the green house.

"Will you stop cursing in here!" Erika hissed at her friend again, but Natascha was so concentrated that she didn't hear her. "Okay, what are we going to do next?" Erika continued, unaware of what was bothering Natascha. "Actually Andreas and I wouldn't mind going back to the souvenir shop and attending mass afterwards. Don't say anything, Natascha!" Erika warned with a stern voice, but it was Andreas who responded first.

"What? Why do I want to attend the mass?"

"Because you love me!" Erika stated matter-of-factly, the tone of her voice not leaving any room for discussion. "If you want to drive back to the village, we can walk back. It's not that far and you don't have to wait for us. I don't want you to disintegrate into ashes for being inside these walls", Erika winked at Natascha.

"That's okay. I actually might hang around a little bit", Natascha answered, her attention caught by a teenage couple sneaking out through an old door.

"Okay, see you at the van by seven then?" Erika asked and began walking back towards the souvenir shop, pulling the reluctant Andreas by his hand.

"Yes, seven is fine with me. I'll text you if I go back before." Natascha answered absentmindedly. "How about you, Mario? Are you up for some exploration?" She asked her friend in a much lower voice, her eyes still focussed on the young couple that hastily walked back towards one of the other buildings.

"Exploration? I thought we already established that the well is gone?"

"Just follow me, my friend, just follow me", Natascha smiled at him and quickly walked towards the couple.

"If I end up in hell, I'll blame you for it!" Mario complained.

"You do that. I get credit down there anyway. It works like reward points on a credit card", Natascha quickly shot back. Mario just shook his head and laughed, but still didn't know what his friend was up to.

"Excuse me!" Natascha called and intercepted the young couple.

"We didn't do anything!" the young girl quickly stammered, clearly afraid of being caught. She quickly let go off her boyfriend's hand.

"Relax, I just want to ask you something", Natascha reassured them with a friendly smile.

"Oh, so you're not reporting us to our teacher?"

"Should I?" Natascha laughed at them, amused at their fear.

"No, we didn't do anything. It's just that, well, you look like you work here, so..."

"I look like *what*?" Natascha cut him off with a stern look, not laughing anymore. Mario fought his laughter. "Never mind. I can assure you I don't work here. I just have a few questions, and I believe you two might be able to help me answering them", Natascha said to the young man. The two teenagers just looked at each other. It was quite obvious they still didn't trust Natascha, and she quickly decided to take advantage of their discomfort.

"So, how long have you been here at the abbey?"

"Since Monday. We're on a school trip", the guy answered.

"What are your names?"

"David."

"Peggy."

"How old are you, David and Peggy?"

"Seventeen."

"How do you like it?" Natascha just shot one question after the other at them, preventing them from thinking about their answers.

"I don't know...kind of boring", David finally admitted.

"Did you get a tour of the whole facility?"

David and Peggy exchanged looks again before he answered. "Most of it, but some of the parts are restricted to visitors."

"And that's when you and Peggy decided to take a private tour? To take in some more *culture*?"

"No, we were just...going for...a walk", David stuttered, while Peggy started to blush.

"So, during one of your *walks*", Natascha winked at them, indicating she knew what they were really up to, "did you happen to find the catacombs or some other structure, that might have water flowing through it?"

It was only now that Mario realised what Natascha was up to.

"Well, we didn't go...actually no." David answered after he exchanged looks with his girlfriend again.

"Well, I can't blame you. The catacombs are not the most romantic places to have a little rendezvous. But do you know where we can find them?"

"The only building that has stairs leading below the ground levels and where the doors are locked is the one over there", David explained and pointed to the door that he and Peggy had just came through.

"Okay, how do I find them?"

"Once you're through the door, you just keep to the right. There's an old door that leads to the stairs, but it's not locked. The second door is locked. We didn't go through that one, I swear!"

"Hm, okay." Natascha replied and looked at the door.

"Ahem, we do have to go now", David said after Peggy looked at her watch. "We *will* be in trouble if we don't show up for the mass."

"What? Yeah, absolutely. Thank you!" Natascha nonchalantly replied, her thoughts racing to the next step of her plan.

"Natascha! Are you out of your mind? You can't break into an abbey!" Mario whispered as soon as the two teenagers were gone. "You don't honestly believe there's another water source down there? That doesn't make sense!" Mario tried to talk some sense into his friend, but he knew how stubborn Natascha could be once she was determined.

"Why not? If we find any water source it will be at the lowest point. That's usually in the catacombs. Are you coming?" Natascha asked and began walking towards the door.

"Natascha, we're not breaking into the abbey's catacombs!"

"They have to catch us first. Not sure if you have noticed, but there aren't any surveillance cameras. This isn't Fort Knox."

"For heaven's sake, you can't be serious. Are you telling me you've already checked this place out?"

"You were with us on that damn ship in the Arctic. You know damn well what happened just after you left. Yes, since then I do pay attention to such things. I can't help it! Look, if you don't want to come with me, fine, then just wait here for me", Natascha offered, knowing only too well that Mario would not let her go alone.

"You don't have to play that card, Natascha. That's not fair." Mario commented, straightening his shirt with a breath. "Oh, you do know I really hate you for this."

"Come on Mario, we both know that you don't hate me." Natascha laughed as she reached the door. She put her hand on the massive cast iron door handle and quickly glanced around.

"So, what is it? Are you in or are you out?" She smiled at her friend.

"Go, before someone else thinks we're both working here. And don't give me that same look you gave that poor kid. It won't work on me." Mario quickly answered and pushed Natascha through the door.

He carefully closed the door behind him and turned around. They both stood in a long hallway, its walls showing several Stations of the Cross.

"Okay, so far so good", Natascha commented, "but I don't see a door on the right or the left."

She took a couple steps and tried to see where the other end of the corridor would lead them, but it was simply not bright enough in there despite the lights on the ceiling.

"We should walk down there and see if there's a door around the corner. I don't imagine the kid lied to us."

"Agreed", Natascha nodded and started walking. While her eyes were focussed on the end of the hallway, Mario took the time to look at each sculpture of the Stations of the Cross. As he expected, each individual station was a masterpiece of art.

"Would it actually be too painful for you to slow down and have a look at these?" Mario asked his friend, gesturing to the sculpture he stopped to look at.

"Ah, can't take the risk. You never know", Natascha replied, still walking with determination.

"Can you at least see the artwork in it? Some of them are rather new." Mario tried to convince her.

"All I see is how much food and medication this could have bought for those in need." Natascha ended the conversation, staring down the hallway. It took them almost a minute before they reached the corner at the other end.

"That's why you should wear sneakers", Natascha commented on Mario's steps echoing from the walls.

"My mistake, but two hours ago I didn't expect we'd be breaking into an abbey."

"We're not breaking in, this is still part of the public section and the door wasn't locked. We're doing nothing wrong." Natascha reassured as they both looked into the chapel. There were a few other visitors inside, admiring the artwork and sculptures around the altar and along the walls.

"Over there!" Mario said and pointed to another large antique double-wing door on the right wall.

"Looks like it. Or is there another one?" Natascha asked, already moving again.

"Not that I can see. There's only the main entrance over there. You know, that's where the *normal* visitors are coming through!"

"Now where's the fun in that? But this looks like a really old part of the abbey. We might be at the right place. I just don't understand why the kid wasn't more precise with this."

"I assume neither the building's architecture nor the blueprints are on the top of his list when he's going for a stroll with Peggy", Mario answered as they both looked at another heavy cast iron door handle.

"Let's hope the door doesn't squeak", Natascha muttered as she quickly glanced around, but no one seemed to pay any attention to them. She slowly pressed the door handle and opened just the left side of the century old wooden door. Luck was still on their side as the hinges did not make a sound. They quickly squeezed through the gap and carefully closed the door behind them.

"Okay, what do we got here?" Natascha asked and looked down several steps carved into the stone, but this corridor was not lit and was slightly wider than the double doors they had just walked through. Natascha took her cell phone out and used it as a flash light. They exchanged quick looks and carefully walked down the hallway. After a couple metres they saw the rear wall with another double door.

Natascha carefully tried to open that door, but as David had mentioned, this time the door was looked.

"Damn!" Natascha murmured and examined the door lock.

"Stop cursing in here", Mario imitated Erika.

"*That* is not cursing. You should know what my cursing sounds like. Here, hold that", Natascha told Mario and gave him her cell phone.

"Yeah, I remember the time we were doing research together at the university. You cursed like a sailor. You also almost blew up the lab." Mario recalled with a laugh holding Natascha's cell phone. "What are you doing now?" he asked curiously as Natascha took the belt off her jeans.

"Relax, don't get your hopes up." Natascha laughed and handed him the belt as well. "You remember Shira, right?"

"Of course I remember her. Who could ever forget that crazy chick?" Mario laughed with a shake of his head.

"She insists that I always prepare for something really stupid", Natascha began to explain, as she fidgeted on the waistband of her jeans behind her back.

"Okay, I assume we can agree that this is really stupid, but whatever you're doing, it looks really cute in those tight jeans." Mario smiled and shone the light at her hands.

"Stop staring at my butt, you're almost as bad as Nick! Gosh, you guys are all the same!" Natascha complained as she presented a little universal key.

"Shira told me they hide these little universal keys in hidden pouches in their waistbands. She insisted that I have them as well."

"Okay, you're now officially creeping me out. You're more like a spy than a marine biologist." Mario admitted, then a frown furrowed his brow with thought, "But why are those pouches on your back?"

"She said your hands will most likely be handcuffed behind your back. And this little universal key also has a sharp edge. So even if they take away your belt and your hands are tied together with a rope or tape, you can still escape."

"That seems carefully thought out. Did you ever have to use that key?" Mario asked as they both looked at the little tool.

"Not really. Since I got married our lives became wonderfully ordinary. Well, we had to use it once. We couldn't find the keys to our handcuffs and Nick had to...", Natascha suddenly stopped once she realised she was sharing a bedroom story. "Well, as I said, not really. And stop smirking like that!" Natascha added and punched her friend on his arm.

"Okay, Lara Croft, what's next? Your shoe laces are some sort of detonation cord and we blow our way through that door? I don't want to rain on your parade, but that key there is rather small and it's not designed to open such a lock."

Natascha gave him a look and took her belt back from his arm.

"How is the battery on the cell phone?" she asked as she started to fidget with the belt buckle.

"About an hour left, but I got mine as well. What are you doing now?" Mario asked as Natascha concentrated to connect the small universal key to the hinged pin of her belt buckle.

"Once we're through that door we can use my other flashlight. There's one on the key ring for the van. Okay, this is it. If I attach the small universal key to this larger pin, I can open those locks as well", Natascha proudly explained and showed him the modified belt buckle.

"Okay, Indiana Jane, how long does it take for you to open a door with this?"

"Hm, Shira does it faster than you could do it with the original key. Talia, Tamar, Maya and Noah can most likely also do it in under a minute. Shira handpicked them from Israel. So I can maybe do it in thirty minutes, if I don't break the key." Natascha explained and started to work.

"Wait a second! Are you telling me there are four more ninja-chicks working with you now? How do they look?" Mario asked excitedly as he shone the light to the lock.

"Ah, you wouldn't like them. They're all in their mid-twenties, totally athletic, well-educated, long luscious hair, exotic looks...stop drooling on my cell phone and shine the light a little bit higher, will you?"

"I would've forgiven you for making me an accessory to a break and enter, but I'll never forgive you for not telling me about them." Mario complained with sad pout.

"Oh for Pete's sake, there are some pictures of them on my cell phone. I'll let you have a look at them later."

"Really?" Mario straightened up with excitement and looked at Natascha's cell phone in anticipation.

"Yes, I promise. Now, can I please have some light here?"

"Oh, sorry."

"Guys! You're all the same!" Natascha shook her head as she continued her work.

"Are any of them mar–" Mario asked hopefully, but he was cut off by the sound of the opening lock. "What happened?" he whispered instead.

"I believe the door is open!" Natascha answered, sounding as surprised as her friend.

"No way!" Mario stammered as Natascha slowly opened the door.

"Thank you for the confidence", she chimed sarcastically as she rose to her feet. Keeping the modified belt in one hand, she took the keys for the van out of her pocket and turned the LED flashlight on. They both stared at a flight of stairs carved out of the stone leading them underground.

"They're definitely old", Natascha commented as she carefully walked down the carved stone steps.

"Thank God they're not wood", Mario added, preferring solid stone rather than rotten wood. "There are no electrical lights in here either", Mario noticed as he shone the light of Natascha's cell phone over the stone walls.

Following the steps deeper and deeper underground, they noticed they changed directions a couple times. "Do you think we're still inside the main walls?" Natascha asked after a while, walking down a little hallway before reaching even more steps.

"I guess so. We were basically in the middle of the abbey. This is all solid rock, no limestone or any other material that would suggest any significant flow of water. But did you notice all the moss on the walls and on the side of the steps? There is only a little on the centre. That could indicate that people have been down here not too long ago."

"Yeah, you're right. Look, there's another door!" Natascha pointed ahead with her light.

This time they looked at a single door. Like the previous door, this one was also at least one hundred years old and rested on sturdy cast iron hinges in the wall.

"Locked!" Natascha quickly announced after she tried the handle. "Why would they close this door? What are the chances of some visitors actually getting lost down here?"

"I don't know. You want to open that one as well?" Mario asked, his tone making it obvious that he would prefer not to break through another door.

"I'll give it a few minutes. It looks like the same lock." Natascha replied and crouched down to pick the door with her belt buckle again.

This time neither of them spoke, but it took Natascha almost ten minutes before she heard the mechanism inside the lock opening up. Disappointed with her performance she sighed before opening the door.

"Okay, we're in", she whispered, her frustration clear in her voice.

The next tunnel was low and narrow, and they both had to duck before they entered it. "You smell that? It's moist down here, more than it was before. There might be some water after all." Natascha commented with newly found enthusiasm.

"Jesus, this place is creepy", Natascha said after a short while.
They walked around a bend in the tunnel and both stopped.

"Okay, this is not what I expected." Natascha said with disappointment. They both looked at a small room that must have been chiselled out of the rock. It was about five metres wide, and they guessed it to be eight metres long. All four walls were reinforced with century old bricks, but there was nothing else. Whatever they had expected, this wasn't it. There was absolutely nothing in there.

"Maybe it was a storage room a couple centuries back. The temperature must be just above freezing." Mario suggested, shining his light around the space.

"Could be, but why all the effort to dig that deep and that far? And why would the entrance be through the chapel and not through the kitchen?"

"Good point!" Mario admitted and examined the room without any success. "Looks like there's some water at the end", he said and they both walked to the end of the room to investigate. There was indeed some water on the ground, but it seemed that it was not deeper than forty or fifty centimetres. It looked more like a puddle, and it covered the last quarter of the floor, reaching the rear brick wall.

"Looks pretty murky. I assume it's the water seeping in through the rocks, maybe even some ground water."

"Yeah, it's pretty murky. You wouldn't see your hands in front of your eyes in that one. If we were smart, we could have brought a little bottle and take a water sample."

"Sorry, I don't have anything with me, Natascha." Mario admitted and already turned around, shining his light at the ceiling. "Here are some water drops. They are pretty dirty as well", he said after picking one from the ceiling with his finger tip. "I think we should go now. Are you coming?" Mario asked, leading the way through the door.

"Yeah, I'm coming. Just a second." Natascha commented. Mario looked around and saw Natascha crouching on the floor at the edge of the water. He decided to take some pictures with Natascha's cell phone while she was still occupied with whatever she was doing.

Let's see if this is really all there is! Natascha thought as she stood up again, quickly sliding the object in her right hand into the pocket of her light jacket.

"Okay, let's go. Erika and Andreas will be waiting for us by now", Natascha hurried and closed the door behind her. Now that she knew how the mechanism worked, it only took her about a minute to close both doors.

Just minutes later they walked along the cloister that lead them back to the main entrance of the abbey. As they expected, Andreas and Erika were already waiting for them.

"Where were you? I was worried about you! We almost started to think that you converted", Erika joked the moment she recognised her friends.

"Ah, long story."

"I sent you a couple messages. Didn't you get them?"

"No, we didn't have reception." Natascha informed, putting her belt back on.

"And exactly *what* were you doing in there? Wait! Do I even want to know?" Erika asked, her curiosity growing as Natascha secured her belt.

"Relax. We just broke into the abbey's catacombs. Nothing spectacular." Natascha defended herself calmly as she sat behind the steering wheel.

"Oh, thank God, I thought you had done something....*Wait!* You did *what?*" Erika exclaimed as she climbed into the old van.

Asklepios, Aegean Sea, Wednesday, June 18

How's your wife doing? The voice computer articulated Victor Gates' question.

"Beth is recovering fine. She'll stay here in convalescent care for at least another four weeks. They said that everything went well. Didn't they?" Walter Leroy Jackson asked, looking at Melissa now, who just unclipped an infusion from Victor's arm.

"Yes, Mr Jackson. The surgery went very well. There were no complications. Your wife will be up and running again in no time", the young Irish nurse assured him with a smile.

"And nagging! God, I already miss her nagging", L.J. admitted in a low voice, looking at the floor while playing with his Stetson.

"Oh, don't worry. She'll be fully conscious later this evening", Melissa laughed, placing a hand on his shoulder, reassuringly.

"Yes, thank God. I'll go up to her as soon as I'm done here. Thank you, sweetheart."

Melissa! I have a question! Victor asked, just as the young Irish nurse was about to leave the room.

"Yes, sir, what is it?"

Will you go to the dance with me? Victor laughed, but it was more like a gurgling sound.

"But of course I will. This Saturday?" Melissa winked at him and closed the door behind her.

Can you imagine? Making stupid jokes to a nurse is the only fun I got left. I remember the times when I could have any woman I wanted.

L.J. didn't comment.

Talking about having women...Did Samuel bring that damn idiot with him this time?

"Yes", L.J. grunted annoyed. The American oil tycoon sat up straight and drank from his water bottle.

"Samuel is in for his regular check-up. Only God knows what else he is up to." L.J. cursed, shaking his head.

I assume he has his reasons. So what is that idiot doing here? Victor didn't even attempt to hide his feelings.

"He sat with Samuel by the pool and BBQ all afternoon. I had lunch with him just a couple hours ago."

Just him?

"Just him!"

What does he know?

"Hard to tell. I know that we didn't tell him much. No idea what Cunningham might have told him. I might be wrong, but from what I know, he believes we're just dealing human organs for money. Granted, that is where the money is. The rest is in fact very expensive."

What did he want? Victor interrupted his friend before he got carried away.

"Ah, yes. Well, he asked me if he could buy one of the girls. One of the healthy ones, of course. What do they call them? *Group B?* He wants to give her as a present to one of his friends. He mumbled something about smoothing a business deal."

Victor didn't reply right away, but carefully thought for a few moments instead. *Did you ask for whom?*

"Of course I did. I even know the guy. Member of the Saudi Royal family. Met him not too long ago in Monaco."

Do you think there's a risk?

"I don't know", L.J. Jackson shrugged his shoulders. "He's the typical playboy, but kind of a wacko. It might not be bad if he owes us a favour. They're no stranger to human trafficking, and the secrets are usually safe with them. Who knows, maybe he can be useful in the future."

Victor Gates thought about what his friend had just told him. Technically less one woman would not make a difference. Besides, it was not the first time they met similar demands of certain wealthy clients from the Middle East. If they could get a reasonable price for her, it would definitely help them finance the real purpose of their mission.

I agree. Let's talk to one of the doctors.

Later that evening, Sir Samuel Cunningham sat in a comfortable chair under a clear, beautiful sky. His wheelchair was where he preferred it: out of sight. He hated how much he depended on that damned thing, but he had no choice. With a bitter expression on his face, his mind wandered back down memory lane to his childhood. Most of his memories were from watching other children playing in the streets and fields, while his body fought with poliomyelitis. The illness had never allowed him to experience many of the joys most of the kids his age had enjoyed. His whole life was determined by it, but he had managed to accept all the challenges his central nervous system threw at him. But he could not deny that at his age most of his energy was gone and replaced by new found bitterness, especially after he had lost his wife of over forty years just this last year. He exhaled deeply as he reflected on her futile fight against cancer.

The laughter of a child brought Samuel back to reality, and he decided it was time to let the past be, at least for today. While Samuel had some tea and picked up the latest edition of the London Times, his middle-aged business partner looked at the expensive chronograph around his wrist. As if he had been waiting for his signal, one of the male nurses walked towards him. The young Briton thought to remember the male nurse's name was Lamar, but he wasn't certain about it.

"I'll be back in about one hour", he said and got up.

"I will be back in my suite by then. Will you join me for dinner later?"

"Yes, of course. I will see you then", he waved as he walked with Lamar.

Sir Cunningham didn't know exactly what his friend was up to, but he expected it not to be any good.

"How many are there?"

"Thirteen", Lamar answered shortly.

"Only thirteen?"

"Yes, but that's a rather large number, considering the circumstances."

The Briton didn't say anything further and just followed Lamar as the elevator doors opened.

"Where are we going?" he impatiently asked.

"We have to go to the security room. You can see them on the monitors there."

"On the monitors?" The disappointment was clear in his voice.

"Yes, here we are." Lamar commented, using a card key and a security code to open the door.

"Hi, Dr Evans. This is the British gentleman."

"Oh, hi! I'm Dr Sheridan Evans. How are you doing?" the British doctor politely asked and got out of her chair to shake her countryman's hand, but she did not ask for his name. They both waited for Lamar to leave them alone. Once the door was closed behind him, Dr Evans stepped forward and greeted her friend with a hug.

"Doing good, thanks. How are you doing, Sheridan?"

"I'm fine. It is so nice to see you again!" the British doctor said.

"Do they know?"

"What? That we know each other? No, they have no idea."

"Good, let's keep it that way."

"Of course. So, I was told that you are interested in our *merchandise*?"

"Yes, I am. I hope that's not an issue?"

"No, it's not. You're not the first client who has shown particular interest, but I have to admit you are the first one who will see them inside the facility."

The Briton nodded and looked at the monitors.

"Okay, there are thirteen available. They're all scheduled to leave on Friday."

"How can I see them? It looks like most of them are in bed."

"That's correct, and we can't just have them all line up here. You have to know they're all from one group, we call them group B. They're together during the day, but sleep in separate rooms. However, no matter where they are during the day, we see everything. Since we didn't exactly know how to do this, we simply...." Dr Sheridan Evans stopped, not knowing how to explain. "We simply shot some video of them", she eventually finished and shrugged her shoulders. "Do you have a preference?" Sheridan wanted to know.

"Oh, she's not for me. She's for a friend of mine. He is actually more of a business partner. I don't know, do you have someone blonde?"

"Their hair is coloured, but we do have four blondes."

"Are any of them...?"

"Healthy? They are all healthy."

"No, I mean, are any of them...still..." despite being friends, the Briton didn't finish the sentence. He didn't know why, but he certainly felt embarrassed.

"You mean to ask if we have virgins? Two of them are ." Dr Sheridan Evans told him matter-of-factly.

"Hm...okay...how old...how old are they?" he asked uncomfortably, shifting his weight from one foot to the other.

"We don't know that either, but I would estimate between seventeen and twenty-five. Look, it's quite obvious you're having second thoughts about this. It's none of my business what you or your friend are going to do with her, but I think I do have a pretty good idea. I can guarantee you it will still not be as horrible as what the rest of them will be expecting in about ten days from now. So, you might think about this as doing her a favour", Dr Evans explained to him freely, waving her hand with indifference. He didn't know if Dr Evans was sharing the truth or not, but for now he believed he could offer the lesser evil.

"Okay, let's see them", he said and looked at the monitor she indicated to him. Dr Evans pressed a button and they silently watched the video together.

"Maybe the young one with the almost white hair? How old is she? She's one of the..."

"Yes. I'd say she's not older than nineteen." Dr Evans explained and played her video again.

"Yes, I'm definitely interested in her. I have to make some arrangements to get her back to my friend. Would it be possible for her to stay here for another ten to fourteen days?"

"Yes, that is not a problem. As I said, the rest of the group is scheduled to leave by the end of this week. There will also be a new arrival by next week."

"How many?"

"We don't know yet. We typically receive around eight to ten. If you want, you can have a look at them as well."

"Yes, I will certainly do that. Is there a chance I can meet her in person? Where is she from? Do you have a name?"

"She speaks Romanian and French, even a little bit of English. We don't ask for their names", Dr Evans explained to him with a smile as she stood up and walked to the door.

"Trust me, it is much easier for us if they are just a number", she added as she closed the door behind her on her way out.

One floor below, the young woman with the blonde hair lay in her bed, her sleep disrupted by the frequent nightmares. As eighteen year old Elena turned around in her drug induced sleep, she didn't know that someone had just thrown her a life ring.

- *9* -

Whitmore, Western England, Thursday, June 19
"Breaking into an abbey! At least we know now you're not an alien. It'd be only you who'd not only think but actually do something like that." Erika commented dumbfounded. She was still shocked about Natascha's and Mario's excursion. While Erika slowly stirred her tea to help it cool down, Natascha enthusiastically filled her bowl with the last of the cereal that she had brought with her.

"You should've come with us, Erika! It was a great tour! You would've liked it", Natascha teased her friend as she cut some fruit and put them in the bowl.

"What if they would have caught you?"

"So? It's not Fort Knox. It's an abbey. Or do you expect they're hiding something down there in those dark, cold places?" Natascha scoffed at her with a wink.

They knew they had little to agree about on such topic, so Erika let it rest as she placed her spoon on the saucer. Natascha knew it wasn't the last of it.

Instead, they switched the subject and discussed their last day in the mine. Their focus was clearly on recovering the video camera Natascha had left in the tunnel behind the well.

"So, Mario, do you have any idea what happened to your rebreather?"

"Yes, it looks like the corrugated hose of my breathing loop has a hole in it. That would explain the flooding."

"How would you get such a hole?" Natascha made a face when she couldn't help but think about the consequences.

"Beats me", Mario answered and ate another sandwich.

"Maybe in the well? Could it be that you nicked the breathing loop with an old nail? After all, there are many old wooden beams in there. I bet some of them have some nails sticking out", Erika suggested while pulling the tea bag out of her mug.

"Yes, that's most likely the case. There aren't any sharp edges down there, and I don't think I bumped into anything, but it was tight getting through the well." Mario said and looked at his dive buddy.

"No, I think we were pretty good down there", Natascha confirmed and added some milk to her cereal before she stirred it. "Do you have a spare breathing loop with you?"

"No, I don't. But we still have the double tanks should we go back in. What's your plan anyway?"

"I think we can try to recover the camera with the ROV. The fibre optic should be long enough for that?" Natascha asked and looked at Erika and Andreas for confirmation.

"Yes, it should be."

"Okay, so we can all agree on the ROV." Natascha stated as she scooped her first spoon full of cereal.

About two hours later they all sat around the mobile control station for the ROV inside the tunnel again. With the water edge just two metres away, Natascha and Erika both watched carefully as Andreas and Mario gently placed the remote operated vehicle in the water.

"Okay, all tests are positive and all systems are a go. It's all yours, you pagan", Erika informed her friend with enthusiasm.

"A little prayer actually wouldn't hurt", Natascha replied, returning the smile.

"Seriously?" Erika's shoulders dropped in surprise.

"Yes, I told you before I'm very open to the beliefs of a higher being; I'm just disgusted about the way some of his representatives behave down here on earth."

"Oh, right. I do remember. You're just against the church", Erika reflected, both waiting for the ROV's video camera to adjust.

"But you do pray, right?" Erika tried to remember.

"Well, actually just two weeks ago, Nick and I..."

"Hold it! Screaming *Oh my God* during coitus does not count as praying", Erika quickly reminded her friend with a sharp breath.

"Oh...okay, well, then I didn't. At least not lately", Natascha admitted disappointedly before taking control of the joystick.

"So in what or whom do you actually believe in?" Erika asked seriously while watching the ROV's self diagnostic software on the monitor.

"Odin!" Natascha quickly shot back.

"In *Odin*? As in the Viking's god?" Erika couldn't believe what she had just heard.

"Yes, Odin."

"But why him?"

"Simple. The church promised to free us from the liars and thieves. And? How did that work? Look around! Odin, on the other hand, promised to free us from the ice giants. And?" Natascha asked and theatrically looked around. "Have you seen any ice giants lately?"

"You are so stupid! I hate you so much!" Erika said with a serious face and punched her friend on her thigh.

"You two aren't arguing about your beliefs again, are you?" Andreas joined them, not hiding his annoyance over their discussion.

"No, no, we're all clear. Natascha's a pagan and I'm a nun, but we're still friends." Erika convinced her partner as Natascha steered the ROV away.

Although everything went flawlessly, it still took over forty minutes before the unit reached the old well. Natascha let the ROV hover neutrally buoyant in mid-water and carefully handed Erika the controls. Natascha slipped out of her chair and stretched.

"You can run it for a while if you want", Natascha offered her friend before eating an apple and drinking some water.

"Oh no, I don't want my fingerprints near those controls, missy. I am just holding it in place for you. This is all on you! Your father is biologically programmed to love you. I'm not certain why, but that's a fact. So, if someone is going to damage the ROV, it should be you!" Erika respectfully declined her offer. It was only then

Natascha noticed the gloves on her hands.

"You're so supportive! Gosh, no wonder I didn't miss you. Move over now", Natascha stabbed back and hip-checked her friend to squeeze beside her to manoeuvre the ROV the rest of the distance.

"See, that's sort of still leading straight to the abbey. Those wells must have been fed by the same water source at some point", Erika noted and pointed at the digital compass on the monitor.

"Yes, but it's too bad we couldn't find anything. Okay, we should be there any moment. I remember that formation there. Based on that and the markings on my cave line, we should be about ten metres from where we turned around." Natascha carefully steered the ROV through the tunnel, staying clear of any obstructions. Just as she came around another bend, the video footage blacked out for a second.

"Whoa! Not cool! What just happened?" Natascha asked and immediately stopped the ROV in mid-water. "Erika! I need to know what's going on!" Natascha could not hide the concern in her voice as the monitor flickered again.

"I am on it", Erika reassured her, but she had to admit this was the first time she experienced such a problem. While Natascha tried to keep the ROV distanced from the ceiling and the ground, Erika pressed a few buttons to check its systems.

"So far everything is looking good. I have to..." was all Erika managed to say before the monitor showed nothing but snow.

"Oh boy! That's not good. Did we just lose the camera, or did we lose all the controls, too?" Natascha asked, hoping for the lesser of two evils.

"If you ever considered praying, now would be a good time, Natascha", Erika commented, working the emergency check-list as fast as she could.

"I already sacrificed a chicken this morning, but I might give it another try", Natascha replied nervously, still hoping they had only lost the video.

For a second, the monitor showed the video footage again. It wasn't much, just long enough for them to realise that the ROV was now hovering against the tunnel's ceiling. Just as everybody sighed with relief, the monitor went black again, and most of the green lights on the control station turned red.

"Oops!" was all Natascha managed. Her matter-of-fact response left the rest of her team confused, considering she had just lost her father's pride and joy inside the flooded side tunnel.

Just sixty minutes later, the white walls of the Whitmore mine reflected Natascha's strong dive light. It seemed the mine was darker this time around, but Natascha realised only a moment later it was her fear the ROV could be seriously damaged. Their lights being the only source of illumination, Natascha and Mario followed the mine shaft, orienting themselves by the rail system on the ground and their cave line. Determined to recover the ROV without wasting any time, they only slowed when they reached the entrance to the side tunnel. Natascha carefully inspected her cave line leading away from the main shaft and towards the well. Satisfied that it was still secure and tight, she looked back at Mario; and after his okay sign, she gently flicked her fins to glide into the tunnel.

Her eyes on her cave line, Natascha ran the fibre optic cable from the ROV through her free hand, making sure she wouldn't get entangled in it, while Mario did the same behind her. The wide-angle beam of her light illuminated the mine differently, but neither Natascha nor Mario had any time to be captivated by it. Before the dive they had elaborately debated about how to proceed, but finally agreed on restarting the ROV on site first. Although it required them to pay extra attention to the fibre optic cable, which looked almost invisible under water, it would make recovering the ROV much easier.

With Mario using his double steel tanks and several stage tanks, Natascha checked on him more often. Looking back up, she noticed they were almost at the well and slowed down. She tried to remember which way she had sent the ROV through the maze of wooden debris. She paused another moment to take a quick look at the LEDs of her heads-up display. It showed that her rebreather was functioning flawlessly.

Okay, you little bugger. Which way did I send you? She asked herself and followed the fibre optic through the tight maze of beams. She recalled this was the area where Mario had punctured his breathing loop. Satisfied she could not spot any immediate hazard for herself or her gear, Natascha opted for a safer route and picked the fragile fibre optic cable back up just before the entrance to the next tunnel. Once more she checked on her cave line, communicated quickly with Mario and slowly entered the next tunnel, running the fibre optic through her free hand again.

Deeper and deeper they pushed into the tunnel, knowing they had to continue for about roughly one-hundred-and-twenty metres before they would reach the ROV.

Natascha checked her gas supply and they finally spotted the ROV floating at the ceiling just a few metres ahead. With a quick glance to Mario, she released the fibre optic and positioned herself behind the ROV. They both checked the unit, but none of the LEDs were illuminated. Shrugging her shoulders, Natascha watched as Mario took his wet notes from his leg pocket.

Before the dive, Mario had written down the instructions for the manual restart of the ROV, and he signalled Natascha that it would most likely take fifteen to twenty minutes to check the unit. After another quick check of their breathing gas, they agreed to continue with the plan.

While Mario started the check list on the ROV, Natascha decided to go ahead and recover both her reel and the little video camera, which were just ten metres away. She noticed she was no longer obstructed by the fibre optic and swam a little quicker, her curiosity growing by the second. As she reached her items, she picked them up and looked back. They could clearly see and signal each other, but it was obvious to Natascha that Mario was rather occupied with the ROV. Knowing that her dive buddy would still see the shine of her dive light, Natascha decided to take a closer look at the bones she had found during the previous dive. Natascha was by no means an expert on the human skeleton, but she could clearly identify the lower jawbone with some teeth as human. She quickly took a zip-lock bag from one of her leg pockets and bagged the bone. A quick glance back showed her that Mario was still working on the ROV, and an exchange of dive signals assured Natascha that everything was still okay. Satisfied with their progress she started to look for more bones and noticed something else.

You got to be kidding me! Natascha couldn't help but smile as she noticed a slight stream of bright orange dye in the water, which immediately sparked her curiosity again. She followed the tunnel with her dive light and noticed that it ascended aggressively. Another thing she noticed immediately was the presence of more orange dye, which slowly started to find its way towards her. Natascha quickly looked back to Mario, uncertain of what to do next. She decided on pushing down the tunnel further, but to stay within sight of Mario's dive light, so that he, in return, would also still see her. If he would lose sight of her, he would immediately come after her, and that was the last thing she wanted.

Signalling that everything was okay, Natascha waited for Mario's confirmation before letting some more line from her reel. Her depth was less than five metres, but she noticed she got shallower rather fast. The tunnel now pointed uphill almost at a forty-five degree angle. She glanced back and could still see Mario's dive light through the orange dye. Looking up, Natascha could already see the surface, but, more importantly, she found more bones below her. A cold shiver ran down her spine as she identified the human jawbone of a little child. Natascha's jaw clenched with shock and she was unable to move.

Only Mario's dive light, who signalled to her from the ROV, caught her attention again. Natascha quickly descended again and signalled back that everything was okay. Satisfied that Mario turned his attention back to the ROV, Natascha quickly turned around and added two more jawbones to her bag. Natascha felt a wave of disgust flowing through her, but she could not resist examining this place further.

Her eyes followed her dive light over the walls, where she noticed some distinct marks, but she couldn't make sense of them. She quickly shot some video of it and decided to surface. As she looked up, she noticed the first thirty to fifty centimetres below the surface were bright orange. Slowly her head emerged from the water. Her dive light immediately lit up her surroundings as Natascha looked at the insides of a room that seemed very familiar to her.

You lying bastard! She thought as she looked at the brick wall. It was the same brick wall she and Mario had looked at from the other side during their excursion into the catacombs. Natascha didn't know exactly what to make of all of this, but she knew she had absolutely no time to waste and decided to take a quick video of what she saw. To her left, she was only a few metres away from the brick wall, but the cave opened up to her right and was so deep that she could barely see the other end. She estimated this part of the cave to be the size of a school gym. It took her less than ten seconds to capture what she needed. She knew it was time for her to get back to Mario before he would start looking for her. She quickly descended again and reeled her line back in. Just as she looked up, she already saw Mario's light shining at her, but from a much closer distance than before.

Natascha quickly signalled him that everything was okay, but she could tell by his expression that he was extremely upset. Instead of swimming back to the ROV, he signalled Natascha to lead and took the reel from her. Natascha knew she had screwed up by leaving his direct sight and breaking protocol, but her deviance was important. Despite it all, she knew her reaction would have been similar. She didn't argue and decided to follow his instructions.

Back at the ROV, Mario harshly handed her the reel and made it very clear to her that she had to stay right beside him while he finished the last steps of the restart. With nothing else to do but watch, Natascha noticed his focus shifting regularly from the ROV back to her. Natascha decided to take some video footage of him. Just as she adjusted the dive lights to the right angle, some of the LED lights on the ROV illuminated. The little camera on the ROV moved up and down, the agreed signal that Erika and Andreas had a video link. Mario waited a moment to ensure every light would turn back on. With all the LEDs now shining green, Mario signalled that everything was okay, and together they listened to the humming sound of the little thrusters as their friends propelled the ROV slowly back to the entrance.

Natascha and Mario checked their gas supply and signalled their status to begin their return. Mario took the reel away from her and told her once more to lead. Natascha was not surprised he was still upset and decided to do as she was told. After all, he had every right to be upset. Natascha knew he was a more experienced diver, and thought to use that to her advantage. Her relative inexperience may serve as the excuse she needed, but she wouldn't bet on it.

They both followed the ROV closely and kept their communication to a minimum. Despite the ROV's successful recovery, neither Natascha nor Mario were very happy at the moment. Natascha could feel the dread increasing as they continued. She knew Mario would talk to her at some point after the dive, and she could not blame him. She tried to focus on avoiding stirring up any sediment as she patiently waited for Mario to untie her reel from the wooden structure once they reached the well. He handed her the reel and picked up the next one. Natascha clipped the reel to her D-Ring and continued to lead their way out of the tunnel. Once they reached the main tunnel, she waited for him again to untie her reel and clip it to his gear, following the railways back to the entrance.

While the ROV reached the surface, Natascha stayed with Mario for a short decompression. Just minutes after the ROV they both emerged from the dark water to be cheerfully greeted by Erika and Andreas.

"YES! That was great! Oh my God! I'm so glad this turned out well!" Erika squealed, clapping her hands as Andreas walked into the water to pick up Mario's stage tanks.

"How did it go?" he asked Mario and walked out with the two tanks.

"Good. No problems. Just took some time", Mario replied. Natascha was surprised there was no trace of anger in his voice.

"How did it go with you, Natascha? Did you get your camera back?" Erika asked as she approached to help her with her gear. Natascha closed her breathing loop and waved to her with the little camera.

"Found it right where I left it", Natascha answered, not quite as enthusiastically as Erika.

"Perfect! That means we can go home now!"

Later that afternoon, after all their gear and mobile dive station was stowed away in the old van, Natascha stepped towards her laptop in her little room. Just coming from the shower, she tucked the tail of her towel behind her head and tightened her robe as she sat at her small table. She had about thirty minutes to spare before they would go for a bite to eat. Natascha felt the pit return to her stomach as she looked at the plastic bag holding the three fragments of human jawbones. She was not an expert but judging by the size of the one fragment, she knew it had to be the jawbone from a child. The other two fragments were either from teenagers or young adults.

Is this really the answer to everything? Natascha wondered, thinking about Cathy Sheppard's story and her grandson, reporter Kyle McRae. Before she had left for the research project, she had spoken with Nick again about Kyle's accusation and the proximity from their research site to Whitmore Abbey, which was sheer coincidence. Natascha was horrified and disgusted by the potential evidence in front of her. She rotated the sealed jawbones in her hand and decided to contact Kyle McRae upon her return to London. He would have the determination to link the bones to the horrific crimes that had taken place behind those mighty walls. Frustrated about the abbey's history, she took the bag with the remains and put them into her backpack. With the bones out of her sight, she focussed on the next issue.

Okay, what am I going to tell Mario? She asked herself, pacing through her little room. Natascha appreciated his silence in front of Erika and Andreas, but she knew Mario long enough to realise that the last word about her unforgivable action had not yet been spoken. With her mood sinking further, she decided to shake her mind by calling her husband.

Combing through her hair, she initiated the familiar sounds of an outgoing Skype call on her computer and waited for Nick to answer.

"Hi Nick! How are you?"

"Good! How are you, angel?"

Like always, Natascha smiled at the nickname.

"Good", she lied. "We're done here and will be driving out tomorrow morning. I should be back in the early afternoon. How's pumpkin?"

"She's downstairs with Shira and Talia. They'll bring her up soon. Did you get the ROV back?"

"Yes, we did", Natascha said, immediately feeling guilty again for breaking protocol. Just as she thought about it, she heard a gentle knock at her door.

"Can I come in?" she heard Mario's voice.

"Just one second, Mario, I got to get dressed." Natascha answered and dropped her robe. She darted to the bed and collected her underwear. She turned again to the desk chair and pulled her shirt over her head, flipping her still wet hair from her face. She paused a moment, glanced around the room and found her jeans. It was when she buttoned her jeans that she noticed Nick grinning from the computer screen. She loved the way his smile still made her heart flip fervently.

"Pervert!" She blurted once she realised, "I'll call you later, got to go. Love you!"

Natascha ended their conversation and asked Mario to enter.

"Are you decent?" Mario asked, the door open just a crack.

"Yes, you can come in. I just took a shower", Natascha smiled weakly.

"We got to talk, Natascha", Mario said with determination and closed the door behind him.

"Yeah, I know I screwed up. I shouldn't have..." Natascha started, but Mario cut her off.

"We both know you screwed up, and I don't want to hear your apology. You know better than pulling such a stupid stunt. You left my sight while I was already occupied fixing the ROV. You haven't done that kind of diving for a while, and I had to promise your father to look out for you. You know very well your father is more than worried about you, and frankly that's another conversation. What you did down there today didn't only put us both at risk, it was outright stupid and completely irresponsible.

Look, we go way back and we definitely have some skeletons in the same closet when it comes to diving, but we could always rely on each other underwater. I don't care where you went and what you did there. I noticed the orange dye too, and I guess it came from the abbey; but that doesn't mean I'm going to disappear from my diving buddy and break all procedures. I'm officially in charge of the diving operation here, and you know I have to report that."

He noticed Natascha's eyes drop to the ground and her shoulders slump. He shifted from one foot to the other, frustrated. "But I'm not going to say anything to your father or to Erika and Andreas." Natascha looked up as Mario continued, "the reason is because you are one of the best active divers we currently have at the institute. But if you even think about pulling such a stunt again, I'll personally make sure you never put fins on for the institute again", Mario finished sternly.

Natascha knew Mario had every right to be upset with her, and she appreciated the fact that he informed her in private. She felt the familiar burn in her cheeks and tried to control it. She turned her head away as tears filled her eyes.

"Oh for heaven's sake, Natascha, don't do that to me", Mario winced and walked over to give her a hug and a kiss on the cheek. Natascha sobbed in Mario's shoulder.

A few moments passed as Mario rubbed her arm. "Well, I think I'd feel better if you would say something."

"No point", Natascha whispered and stepped back to wipe off her tears. "You don't want to hear an apology, and you don't want to know why I did that stupid stunt down there. So, thank you!"

"*Thank you*?" Now it was Mario who was surprised.

"Yes, you're spot on. You know how hard it is for me to admit when I'm wrong, but you're right about everything you said", Natascha shrugged. "And I appreciate you for not saying anything in front of the others. So I do have to thank you."

Mario still wasn't convinced this was really happening. He knew Natascha for many years, and she never agreed to her mistakes so fast, if at all.

"What did Nick do to you?" He stated sincerely. Her reaction had totally caught him by surprise.

"Oh shush! Don't you ever tell Nick I surrendered that quickly." Natascha ordered, wiping her eyes dry.

"That will cost you", Mario smiled at her.

"Fine! Dinner is on me!" Natascha hissed as she grabbed her jacket on her way out.

Just thirty minutes later, the four friends walked down the street, hoping to spend their last evening together with some good laughs over old stories. For that occasion they decided to eat at the Italian restaurant, then visit the pub later. There was absolutely no tension between Mario and Natascha, and she knew him long enough to know he had forgiven her. Natascha also knew he would never forget what she had done, and that his threat would stand. But all that was forgiven now, and they picked at each other as usual.

For a Thursday evening the place was relatively busy. It seemed that most of the customers were tourists, many of them visiting Whitmore Abbey. Natascha and her friends all glanced as the door opened and another group entered the restaurant. Natascha was in the middle of telling Erika the embarrassing story about her daughter's meet and greet with the police officer in her playgroup, when Natascha's eyes locked on the newcomers. There were two older gentlemen and four older women. It looked to Natascha like it was a semi-formal meeting rather than a gathering of friends. Natascha couldn't help herself, but she was convinced that she had seen the one gentleman before. Just as the waitress brought them their bill Natascha recognised the man, but she decided not to say anything to her friends.

"I'm getting yours", Natascha reminded and pinched Mario's bill from his hand. "I can't risk having you talk to my husband", she winked at him and put some money in the little folder.

"What did she do now?" Erika wanted to know, the surprise in her voice nonexistent.

"Just the usual", Mario laughed at his friends as they got up, ready to leave.

"Why is it always you who causes trouble?" Erika rhetorically asked her friend, not really expecting an answer.

"Ah, I don't know, must've been hanging out with the wrong crowd during my time at the university. Some things never change", Natascha replied as they walked out of the restaurant. She glanced to the other table and noticed the older gentleman excused himself and also headed for the door, looking at his cell phone. While her three friends already walked towards the pub, Natascha hung back a little bit. She used the moment to zip up her jacket, watching the man answering the call.

Are you sure you want to do this? Natascha asked herself as the man ended his call and put his cell phone back into his pocket. She walked towards him.

"Good evening", Natascha greeted, just as he reached for the door again.

"Good evening. What can I do for you?" Abbot Augustinus Hetley asked.

"Not much, thank you", Natascha replied rather coldly. Abbot Hetley's eyes immediately narrowed.

"I just recognised you inside, and I debated with myself whether to say something or not, but I decided to give you the heads up. I'm aware of the accusations against Whitmore Abbey, and I just want to let you know that I found some rather interesting evidence today, which I'll make sure they get examined and made public."

"I don't know what you're talking about, my child, but..." replied Abbot Hetley hard faced, but Natascha cut him off.

"I am *not* your child." Natascha's disapproval was evident in her voice, her eyes still locked on his. "I read the reports, I know about the accusations. I know what happened behind those walls, and I found some of the children's skeletons that you tried to bury in the mud. Your cover ups won't work much longer because I found some evidence to prove all of it", Natascha whispered, rage releasing her tongue.

"Natascha! Are you all right? Are you coming?" Erika called her from a distance, not knowing what was going on.

"You have a nice evening, *Your Excellency*", Natascha hissed at the abbot, who just scowled at her as she turned around to catch up with her friends.

Whitmore Abbey, Western England, Great Britain, Friday, June 20
Augustinus Hetley had spent the last couple hours staring at the horizon, sitting behind his desk and lost in thoughts. It was already late in the afternoon, but his daily correspondence was still untouched on his antique oak desk. Even the letter bearing the crest of the Royal Family could not spark his interest. The abbot could not get the words out of his head that the young woman had thrown at him last night in front of the restaurant. He was outraged at first, but after a while he considered himself lucky that no one else had witnessed their conversation.

Actually it was more of a monologue. Abbot Hetley sighed, recollecting how she had confronted him with such lack of respect.

What does she know and how did she get that information? This question kept spinning through the cleric's mind, leaving no room for anything else. At first, he thought she had read some of the accusations the reporter had spread on the internet, but there was something different with her. She sounded much more resolute, much more confident. She was almost as persistent as the young reporter himself. The reporter had legally been pressured to take his accusations off-line again, but the abbot knew very well there were still copies of that article out there. Somehow Abbot Hetley knew this woman understood more of the dark secrets of Whitmore Abbey. Earlier that day he had tried to remember exactly what she had told him, but he was only able to write down some key words. For the first time in over an hour, the abbot moved and picked up the note from his desk.

She said she found skeletons from children buried in mud. How can she know about that? Where did she find them? The abbot put the note down and stared at the horizon again. The only accessible place where she could have found human remains was the cemetery. And he would have definitely been informed if someone had been grave robbing there. The sixty-five year old shook his head. All those graves were legit and well documented with certificates of death. The only other places inside Whitmore Abbey where someone could find human remains were either in the crypt or the catacombs. The crypt was inaccessible without several keys, and Abbot Hetley held one of them. The catacombs were also locked. Granted, the doors were old, but they were hidden on any official maps.

His thoughts went back three years ago when his partners had accessed the catacombs. Only his own persistence had made that part of their deal necessary in the first place, but Abbot Hetley still stood by his and his superior's decision. In order to get to the area inside the catacombs that was of interest to them, they had to tear down an old brick wall. After they were finished, they had simply rebuilt the same wall, but a couple metres closer to the entrance. If someone wasn't familiar with the previous layout of the catacombs, that person would never see the difference. They had literally erased all signs that they had even been there.

There is no way she was in the catacombs. And even if, she would have had to be behind the wall to find something. It was only now that Abbot Augustinus Hetley thought about the diving operation that was going on at the mine during the last week. The abbot had no idea about the underground water systems and eventual connections between the mine and one of the wells. His hand tensed on the desk, his thoughts working diligently to understand her confidence.

"Could it really be?" he murmured to himself, thinking about the impossible. He was ignorant of modern technology when it came to exploratory and scientific cave diving, but he somehow felt this woman posed a serious threat, and not only to him.

"But how can I be sure?" he asked himself, but before he got an answer someone knocked at this door. The sound startled him.

"Yes, come in, please", he finally said and turned towards to door.

"Your Excellency, I see you have not finished your daily correspondence yet. Is everything all right?" Prior Clemens Finnigan asked him with a concerned look on his face.

"Yes, yes. Everything is fine, Clemens. I'll look after that tomorrow."

"Of course", the Prior answered and bowed, already on his way back out.

"Clemens? Can you please bring me the keys to the catacombs? Do you know if someone accessed them during the last couple weeks?"

"The catacombs? Why would someone want to access the catacombs? I believe the last time someone had been behind those doors was three years ago."

"So you haven't heard anything?"

"No, Your Excellency. Do you still want me to get the keys?"

Abbot Hetley hesitated for a few seconds. He didn't know what he could expect to find down there, but he had to check it out himself.

"Yes, Clemens. Please go and get the keys and a flashlight. I will meet you at the door."

"Right away, Your Excellency." Prior Clemens Finnigan bowed again and left the abbot's study, not without carefully closing the door behind him.

The abbot remained seated behind his desk for a few more moments before finally getting up. There was something else about that woman that made him nervous. He thought hard about it on his way to the catacombs. Since he had to walk through most of the abbey, it gave him enough time to think about her again.

Let's assume she and her three friends are actually the divers. That means that she is not from here; but she said that she had recognised me at the restaurant. How does she know who I am? The abbot knew everyone in the little village recognised him, but he was sure she was a stranger to this area. He remembered her accent was not British, but European. Last night was one of the few moments where he had been out in normal clothes instead of his formal attire, and yet she had recognised him.

Taking a shortcut through a cloister, the abbot decided to call his contact later. It would be no problem for them to find out who those divers were. The more he thought about the woman, the more he was convinced he had seen her before as well, but he couldn't quite place her just yet. Just as he entered the chapel that lead to the catacombs, he remembered her.

I met her at the gala a couple of weeks ago. She was with Rowan Harrison and walked over when that reporter confronted me again. That's her! That's how she recognised me! He slowed down for a moment, realising his instincts that evening had been right.

The question now is where did she get her information? From that reporter? The abbot stopped suddenly, his eyes closed with anger as he remembered how he had angrily thrown away the notes the reporter had handed him that night. What if the woman had simply picked them up from the garbage bin? All she had to do was watch him leave the gala, and she would have seen him throwing the paper away. Cursing himself over his own stupidity, the abbot decided to revisit that thought later this evening. He had just arrived at the antique double door, where Prior Clemens was already waiting for him with two flashlights.

"You're certain you want to go down there, Your Excellency?" The Prior was obviously still uncertain what the issue was.

"Yes, Clemens. There is a chance we had an intruder here. I just want to check something", the abbot reassured his friend with a fatherly voice.

"An intruder? But how?" Prior Finnigan asked and handed the abbot a flashlight as he opened the double-door's left side. With the shine of their powerful LED flashlights, they quickly walked down the corridor and reached the second door. Prior Finnigan checked the lock, but didn't find anything unusual and opened it with the old key. The lock was well maintained and opened without a problem. The Prior looked at the abbot, who simply nodded his approval. Slowly the Prior opened the door and they both shone their lights on the ancient stone steps, which they were soon following deeper and deeper underneath the abbey. Neither of them said a word.

It was so cold that their breath condensed in front of their faces. The closer they got to the catacombs, the more nervous the abbot became. They finally reached the last door standing between them and the actual catacombs. Prior Clemens Finnigan finally opened the door, but not without glancing to the abbot. Abbot Hetley briskly took a couple steps into the chamber. He froze in his steps and, holding his breath, a cold shiver ran down his spine as his flashlight reflected from the bright orange water.

"Salvum me fac Deus!" Prior Finnigan groaned crossing himself, while the abbot remained silent.

- *10* -

Nick's and Natascha's house, just outside London, Saturday, June 21
Natascha's whole body was tense as she carefully read the page again. The same page she had read at least a dozen times. Her mind was so focussed that she didn't even hear Nick coming up behind her.

"Summoning another demon, are we?" Nick whispered in her ear as he gently clapped Natascha on her bum. Unfortunately he had totally underestimated how focussed his wife had been. Natascha jumped with a shriek and the cook book went flying over the kitchen table.

"Jesus, Nick! What was that for?" she gasped, her hand reaching her own cheek with embarrassment. "I didn't hear you coming."

"Sorry, I was talking to you from the hallway", Nick smiled sweetly and continued. "Since you didn't answer I thought to check on you. What demon are you calling this time?" Nick asked curiously, looking at all the ingredients that were strewn over the kitchen table. He could not help but tease his wife the moment it came to her baking and cooking skills. His attempts to domesticate her to do anything beyond basic recipes had failed as miserable as the several courses Natascha had taken. Nick found it even more astonishing how she could make such a mess with so few ingredients.

"I'm not summoning a demon!" Natascha defended herself. He could hear a sense of defeat in her voice but he ignored it. "I am baking!"

"You call this baking? We can't even clean this up any more. You're making such a mess I'm seriously considering new tiles!" Nick protested. "Look at all the flour!"

"I'm baking and it's not *that* messy!" Natascha insisted and made a face.

"Okay, then, what are you baking?"

"Waffles. Our daughter wants to have some waffles." Natascha forlornly admitted and looked at the mess on the table.

Nick noticed rather quickly that his wife was really disappointed with herself again, and he quickly hugged her. Natascha usually didn't mind the teasing at all, but she felt horrible when she struggled to prepare something as easy as waffles for her daughter. She knew Sarah was patiently waiting for them.

"Okay, come here, angel. I'll help you before we have a nuclear meltdown with our daughter", Nick kissed her on her forehead.

"Thanks", Natascha whispered, returning the kiss. "Tell me those three magic words that I need to hear from you", she added and looked hopefully in his eyes.

"*Dinner is ready*?" Nick teased, but Natascha's eyes narrowed as she gave him a threatening look. He loved it when she pretended to be upset and gave her a quick kiss.

"*You are right*?" Nick continued with a smile, getting the same response. Her eyes were barely open now. She received another kiss.

"*I got chocolate*?" Nick shrugged, preparing to hold Natascha's arms to prevent her from physically attacking him.

"You will regret those comments later tonight, *lover*", Natascha scowled at him and turned around to retrieve her cook book.

"Oh, talking about those waffles. How much dough did you eat while our daughter was starving?" Nick interrogated with a smile.

"None! Why?" Natascha lied, but she knew she was busted. She quickly licked her lips, hoping to destroy some evidence, but had a hard time keeping a straight face. Nick just stared her down.

"Okay, I might have had half a spoon just to taste it", she finally admitted, but Nick didn't break his gaze. "Okay, fine! I had a couple spoons. There, I confess. Are you happy now?" Natascha laughed with her drama face. Nick raised his eye brows and took inventory of the ingredients already on the counter top. Not talking to her was his way of punishing his wife for not sharing.

"Can you at least tell me what gave it away?" Natascha asked innocently, hoping to figure out how to get away with it the next time.

"You should have wiped your lips before kissing me", Nick winked at her.

"Oh, darn, yeah, I should have known about that! That's a rookie mistake!" Natascha was obviously disappointed with her own carelessness.

"Or you could have shared!"

"Don't be ridiculous. Can we please focus on the waffles now?" Natascha turned to the counter and sorted the ingredients again. "When did you get home anyway?"

"Just five minutes ago with Talia. I worked out at the office and watched the game with the guys during the sauna. I just said hello to pumpkin."

"Where is she?"

"I was with her in her room. She is playing. Why?"

"Because she's so quiet", Natascha noticed and they looked at each other in horror. "I better check on her", Natascha added hurrying out of the kitchen. It was usually rather expensive or rather messy when their daughter was so quiet.

"And make more waffles, she already invited Shira and Talia", Natascha called from the other room.

Nick rolled his eyes but he couldn't help smiling. Trying to gain control over the situation in their little kitchen, Nick started to arrange the bowls with all the different ingredients and opened the cook book again in search for the right recipe.

Whitmore Abbey, Western England, Great Britain, Wednesday, June 25
Neither the abbot nor his guest spoke as one of the monks placed a tray with coffee, tea and some biscuits on the table in the corner of the study.

"Do you want some?" Abbot Hetley politely asked his guest. Despite the seriousness of the situation, he still made sure to follow the proper etiquette. After the discovery of the bright orange water in the abbey's catacombs, the abbot had immediately returned to his study to use his prepaid cell phone. As before, his contact had returned his call upon verification of his identity at once. With the urgency and potential threat of this certain situation to their operation, his contact insisted on meeting him personally.

"I'll have some tea, please", his guest replied without taking his eyes from his notes. Abbot Augustinus Hetley nervously watched as the young man arranged the cups and plates before asking if there was anything else he could do.

"No, thank you. That will be all", the abbot quickly told him. The young monk bowed and carefully closed the door behind him on his way out.

"And you're absolutely certain this woman was with Rowan Harrison during the gala on May tenth?" Sir Samuel Archibald Cunningham, patriarch of the Cunningham family and business empire, asked. His voice was a mix of both suspicion and concern.

"Yes, Samuel, I am certain. That was the only place and time that I've seen her. She came over during the argument I had with that reporter; just after I spoke to Mr Harrison." Abbot Hetley waved his arms. He couldn't hide his nervousness. Back then, he had feared this evening would come back to haunt him. He couldn't stop his hands from shaking. The last couple of days of waiting had been excruciating, but the abbot mysteriously found it both fascinating and scary how fast Sir Cunningham had been able to gather specific information.

The aristocrat drank some tea before picking up his notes again. "I spoke to Rowan Harrison, and he told me the name of the company that provided the security for him. A friend of mine at the Ministry of Justice sent me some information about the registered security guards for that evening. According to their records, and they are usually correct, the two women who worked for Mr Harrison that night were Shira Hadad and Talia Levi. Mr Harrison confirmed those names as well. Both women are *Israeli*", Samuel closed and raised his eyebrows, as if their heritage made them something special. He looked at their faces on enlarged copies of their security cards and handed them to the abbot. Augustinus took both pages with still shaking hands. He quickly put Shira's copy down and stared at the face of Talia Levi.

"That's not her!" Augustinus Hetley shook his head.

"Are you sure?" Samuel asked. For the first time he sounded surprised.

"Yes, I'm sure. They look alike, but the woman that I spoke to was older. Not much, but definitely older. This one here could be her younger sister, but she's definitely not the one I met at the gala and who spoke to me outside the restaurant."

"Hm, okay. That means someone there lied to the Ministry of Justice. Interesting!" Sir Samuel Cunningham made a note and went through his information before continuing. "I also managed to get some information about the diving company performing the scientific diving in the mine. The company in question is actually a well known research institute, working together with a local university. They registered two female divers for this project. Natascha Rehfeld and Erika Schmitt. One of them looks like the Israeli." Samuel explained and handed another sheet of paper to the abbot. This one showed the enlarged copy of Natascha's diving certification, which was attached to the diving permit for the mine.

"That's her!" the abbot quickly identified Natascha. "That's definitely her. I also remember that this other woman had called her Natascha that evening in front of the restaurant." Abbot Hetley was convinced and kept staring at the picture.

"Ah, okay. That makes sense. Let me see what we know about her", Samuel calmly said and helped himself to a biscuit before going through his notes again. Augustinus Hetley had no idea whom or how many of his friends Samuel had called to gain all this information, but it turned out that Sir Samuel Cunningham was extremely well connected.

"Natascha Rehfeld. She works part time at the same security company that provided the security detail for the gala and for Mr Harrison. I don't know what she does there yet, but I'll make some calls. Fact is she's not registered with the Ministry of Justice as a certified security guard, so I assume she works there as a secretary or something else. She's also a very experienced diver, I might add."

"If she's an experienced diver she could have accessed the catacombs underground." The abbot quickly concluded.

"You said that you don't know how she entered the catacombs, am I correct? If she came through the doors, then she would have found nothing?"

"No, the only place she could have found something would have been behind the wall your team rebuilt three years ago. Fact is that someone was down there. She dove the mine and claimed she had some hard evidence against me. She sounded very convincing."

"There's no video surveillance in place at the entrance of the catacombs? Or did you see any other signs of forced entry?" Sir Samuel Cunningham knew the answer, but he did not want to leave a single detail untouched.

"Samuel, this *is* a house of the Lord. There are no surveillance cameras anywhere. You know the doors that lead to the catacombs. They are centuries old and so are the locks. They work, but they're not high tech."

"Well, we do know there might be a connection between the catacombs to the well and the mine. If that connection is large enough, she might have used it. The question is how well she has documented it and what she has found."

"You have to do something about her. She could risk everything."

"You're right. She poses a serious threat." The business tycoon drank some tea and helped himself to another biscuit. "But let us think here for a second before we hasten into action too soon. We first have to know more about her, and what kind of evidence she claims to possess. We don't know if her friends know anything. Now that I know her name it'll be easier for me to find out more information about her and what her motives might be. If she poses a threat to our operation, we *will* certainly take action against her, but only then. If her actions are connected with the history of this abbey, then we will not get involved", Samuel stated and drove his wheelchair to the door.

"May the Lord have mercy on our souls", the abbot whispered, crossing himself.

"It might be too late for that, my dear friend", Sir Cunningham said on his way out.

London Aquarium, London, Monday, June 30
Eating an apple, Natascha watched the video she had recorded in the catacombs of Whitmore Abbey now for at least the sixth or seventh time. She paused the footage now and then to take screen shots for further examination. With her daily routine at the aquarium behind her, she simply enjoyed her lunch break and planned to stop at EuroSec later that afternoon after picking up her daughter. For now she closed the video program and opened all the still images in a graphic program.

"Okay, let's see what we got." Natascha enthusiastically said and started nibbling on a carrot. She looked at the first image and zoomed in on a point of interest. Although she had used the small camera, the quality of the image was still very good.

"Bingo!" She said and leaned forward as she recognised what she was looking for. "There is no way that anyone would have ever found this by accident." Natascha concluded to a non-existing audience, which she didn't mind at all.

Knowing that her work day was officially over, she took all the time she needed to examine those pictures. Her investigation was only interrupted occasionally by one or two co-worker sharing their surprise that she was still at the aquarium. After about one hour of tedious work, she was convinced she figured out what she had seen back in the catacombs. Thinking back, she only wished that she would have spent more time down there, but she knew she had already strained Mario's trust.

"Maybe I can do something like a mosaic picture?" she asked herself, but decided against it rather quickly. Leaning back in her chair, she looked at what was left in her lunch box.

"Come to Mommy!" She said and picked up the piece of chocolate she had left for dessert. Natascha glanced around as a small wave of guilt came over her. Her feeling of guilt was quickly overpowered by the taste of the German milk chocolate melting in her mouth.

"Ah, this is so good", she whispered with her eyes closed. With her guilty pleasures satisfied, she closed her laptop and turned to the official computer she shared with her co-workers. She signed in with her username and password and opened the program for the video conference. Natascha nervously played with her fingers, waiting for the other person to answer her call.

"Hi Mark. Long time no see. How are you doing?" Natascha finally greeted her old friend as his face appeared on her screen.

"Natascha? I didn't know it was you. Haven't heard from you in ages. How are you?"

"Oh, I'm doing fine. Things have settled."

"Yes, I heard all about that. I'm sorry about everything. Is that the reason for the fake name I see on the screen?"

"Yep, that's still the reason. I decided not to take part in that whole social media thing."

"That explains why I couldn't find you anywhere", Mark laughed. "So I heard you were diving with the old crew. How was it?"

"Good, it was really interesting. How was your vacation?"

"It was really nice. Our first vacation with the little one. It was awesome. Today is actually my first day back at work."

"Yeah, I know", Natascha laughed and smiled at him over the webcam.

"Uh-oh, I remember that tone." Mark laughed. He remembered how she had been in university, at a time when they were dating. It was that same tone of voice she would have used when she had tried to sway her way into asking for something. He shifted in his seat as he continued, "What do you want?"

"Hey, that's not fair! I did ask how you are doing, remember?" Natascha laughed, but couldn't help feeling guilty. "Did Erika send you that parcel from me?" Natascha finally asked.

"Wait a second...let me see. I believe there is something here...yes, I got it", Mark said and held up a well-wrapped parcel in the size of a shoe box.

"What's in it?" Mark curiously asked and weighed it in his hands.

"Mark, can I ask you for a favour?" Natascha eventually caved, this time with a more serious tone.

"Are you in trouble again?" Mark asked in the same serious tone as he placed the parcel back on his table.

"No, no. I'm not in trouble. I just need to know something, and you're the only forensic scientist that I know, so...."

"Okay, what's in the box?"

Natascha nervously glanced around to make sure she was alone before she answered. "Listen, during the expedition I found human remains underwater in the cave system. I picked up three jawbones, but there are more buried in the mud. I would like to know how old they are."

"Are you insane?" Mark reached the height of his voice, almost sliding from his office chair. "You picked up human remains from at least two different people? Did it ever occur to you that there's a law out there that demands both of us to report such finds?"

"Mark! I know!" Natascha tried to calm her old friend down and closed her eyes for a second. "I know that I'm legally obliged to report those findings, and I promise you that I will do that. But here's the thing. I found those bones during our expedition in that mine shaft. They were underwater in a natural cave leading from the catacombs of an old abbey. I have proof on video that the catacombs have been tampered with, most likely to cover up all those bones that are behind a man-made brick wall now, but I'm not sure. The only way to access those bones now is from underwater. There are many accusations involving the abbey, a whole range of sexual crimes against children back when the abbey was still an orphanage. I have some proof from a reporter whose grand-parents grew up there. Wait, I'll show you!" Natascha quickly held up the sheets of paper in front of the webcam. "Look, if you want, I can take some images from this and send them to you", she offered and hoped that Mark would at least take a look.

"Wait, hold them up again, I'm just taking a screen shot", he finally said, but Natascha noticed the lack of enthusiasm in his voice.

"Mark, I really appreciate it, you know? Someone has spent a lot of time and effort in those catacombs to hide those bones. If you can date those bones back to a certain time period, then that could help to prove what was going on behind those walls. As soon as that's the case, I'll hand over the video of the catacombs to the police and I will tell them what I've seen down there. Those bones won't be allowed as evidence any more anyway, so I'll leave you completely out of this, okay?"

"For heaven's sake Natascha, you can't be serious. I've read about those accusations against Whitmore Abbey online. You know as well as I do that some very powerful people were accused in that whole story. Considering there has never been a proper investigation, I naturally tend to believe the accusations are true. And you're outrageously naive if you believe you can change all this by digging up some old bone fragments in some catacombs." Mark's tone made it very clear that he was less than impressed about her idea. Natascha knew that it had been a long shot, but she wasn't ready to quit yet.

"I'm not that naive, Mark, and I'm not sure if you're aware of how familiar I am with government cover-ups and false accusation", Natascha calmly explained, knowing very well that Mark had no argument to counter her. They had always remained friends after their break-up, and he had always believed Natascha was not a terrorist. "Do I believe something happened behind those walls based on what I know? Absolutely! Otherwise they wouldn't go through all that trouble to make sure that no one can access those remains. Do I believe that I can make a difference? Hell, I have no idea", Natascha said rising her voice. "But I am damn certain that I'll do everything that I am capable of to make sure that children like my daughter or your son won't have to go through such horrors as the ones behind those walls. So, Mark, we go all the way back to kindergarten, and we certainly had our time together. You know how much I respect you and I'm asking you as a friend. Are you going to help me?" Natascha asked with determination and watched Mark on the monitor. For a while neither of them said anything. Arguing with each other brought back some unpleasant memories. Natascha anxiously waited for Mark to make up his mind. Natascha eliminated the risk of him being held accountable in hopes it would make his decision easier, but he still took his time.

He finally shook his head.

"And there's that damn stubbornness again that'll keep getting you in trouble, Natascha, you know that? I'll look at the information from the screen shots I just took. *If*, and only *if* I believe you are on to something, I *might* look at the fragments. Until then I won't even open that damn parcel. That's all I can promise you."

Natascha sighed. This was certainly not what she wanted to hear, but at least he didn't say *no* right from the beginning.

"That's all I ask, Mark. I appreciate it."

"You know, Natascha, it would've been easier to persuade me if you would have contacted me once in a while to tell me how you were doing after all that trouble you had, not just when you need to ask me such a favour. You owe me that much."

The wave of guilt running through Natascha was more significant this time than when she had eaten the chocolate five minutes ago, but she knew Mark was right. She simply nodded.

"You're right, Mark. I'm sorry." Natascha whispered apologetically, her voice honest and soft this time.

"Like I said, I can't promise anything. Now that I finally have a contact for you, I'll let you know what I think after I take a closer look at those notes. Take care."

"Take care, Mark. Next time I'm in Germany we'll go out, okay?"

"Careful with those promises, I might hold you to them." Mark smiled and ended their video conference.

***EuroSecCorporation*, London, Friday, July 4**

Natascha barely dodged Nick's punch, but it was just enough for Nick to miss her. Instead of retreating, Natascha closed the distance with some palm strikes and landed two elbows to his head. Nick reeled back as Ariel attacked Natascha from behind, pulling her back by her hair before putting her into a chokehold.

"You bugger!" Natascha panted, but she remembered the right technique and was able to counter her Israeli friend. Just as Nick grabbed her around her waist and lifted her up, Shira blew the whistle to end the drill.

"Time is up. You hit like a vegetarian, Nick", Shira commented on Nick's efforts to attack his wife. It had been quite obvious that Nick had been extremely easy on Natascha.

"You do know I love my wife?" Nick asked in return, still holding Natascha like a rag doll in the air.

"That thought might have crossed my mind in the past, yes. But you can let her down now, we're finished for today", Shira said and watched as the others picked up their towels to wipe their faces.

"Oh, yes", Nick noted and put the now struggling Natascha back on her feet, not without giving her a kiss.

"I told you not to hold back!" Natascha complained, looking at her husband.

"Yes, I remember that", Nick shrugged and picked up a towel. He knew Natascha would not let this go, but he decided not to say anything.

"You didn't hold back like that with the other women", Natascha continued, but Nick just shrugged again and noticed Talia walking over to them.

"Next time you can take me hard!" Talia offered Nick with a serious expression on her face. The attractive Israeli had clearly misunderstood their conversation.

"Oh, really? I can?" Nick asked, smiling with anticipation as Talia reconsidered her choice of words. She suddenly realised she might had offered more than she actually wanted to.

"No, no, no, no! Definitely not, missy!" Natascha quickly stepped in to Nick's disappointment. "I'm the only one here he's taking hard", Natascha continued to explain in a serious tone to everyone's amusement. "In fact, I'm the only one he's taking period. Whether that'll be gentle or hard totally depends on the mood I'm in. But as long as we're married, he's not going to take anyone else. Isn't that right, *Nick*?" Natascha confirmed with a question, emphasising his name over the laughter.

"Yes, that's right", Nick acknowledged with a disappointed tone in his voice.

"Your enthusiasm is well noted, *husband*! And you, Talia, yes you! Don't pretend you don't hear me or that you don't understand English all of a sudden. You stay away from my husband! Gosh, with the competition these days you can't lose focus for one second", Natascha finished her rant, joining the laughter. Just as she looked up, Nick gestured to Talia to call him. The young Israeli laughed and played along by winking back.

"Will you two stop it now!" Natascha hollered and threw her towel at Nick. "Not only does she look like me, she's living downstairs", Natascha protested, still pretending to be the jealous wife.

"You want me to set him straight again?" Ariel offered flatly from the far corner of the combat room. Every muscle in Nick's body tensed up as he heard the former close combat instructor for the Israeli special forces. Ariel had joined the self-defence session relatively late, and he was nowhere near exhaustion.

"Natascha, don't!" Nick pleaded.

"Sure, why not? That'll teach him a lesson on flirting with younger women when I'm standing right beside him. But no bruises in the face. I somehow like it. And we have to do the laundry later today, so he has to be able to walk the stairs", Natascha joked, not knowing what Ariel would do to Nick. She could not remember the last time she had seen them going at each other; and Natascha was quite interested in how it would turn out. It was only now she realised that her husband gave her a look that meant he was dreading this sparring session; but Natascha assumed that because of Nick's and Ariel's similar size and weight, it would be an even fight. It turned out quite the contrary. About six minutes later Natascha had her face buried behind her hands as Nick laid on the floor gasping for air.

"You didn't have to hit him that hard!" Natascha snapped at Ariel and punched him on his arm on her way over to her husband.

"My pleasure", Ariel winked at her.

"Nick! Are you okay?" Natascha kneeled, the pain and concern clear in her voice.

"Oh boy. For a moment I saw grandma and Elvis at the end of a bright tunnel", Nick replied and winced sitting up.

"I'm sorry, I didn't think he'd hit you *that* hard", Natascha apologised as she took Nick's head gear off.

"Never mind. I promise not to talk to young women again when you are around..."

"*When I am around?*" Natascha asked back, appalled. "Pfff....", she added and walked away, pretending to be upset, while Nick, without her holding him anymore, sank back to the floor with another wincing sound.

About a half hour later Natascha sat freshly showered behind her desk and looked over her work from this morning, but there was nothing left to do. Her official day was over, so she waited another two hours for Nick. They would then pick up their daughter from the playgroup downstairs and drive home.

Since she had not heard back from Mark yet, she decided to make good use of her spare time and investigated the case a little bit on her own. Ever since her return from Whitmore Abbey she had tried to contact Kyle McRae to tell him about what she had found, but so far she had been unsuccessful finding him. She logged into the closed loop computer at EuroSec and pulled up the gala event's guest list.

"Okay, where are you hiding?" Natascha asked herself as she skimmed through the names. It took her only a few minutes before she located him, and she wrote his name down on a piece of paper.

"Let's see if I can find you on social media", she enthusiastically said and used her private laptop to enter his name in several social media platforms, but it always ended with the same result. All his social media accounts were linked to his blog, which ended about one week after the gala.

"Something is wrong here!" Natascha stated and leaned back in her chair. She couldn't quite point it out yet, but there was something odd with his blog. Taking another bite from her apple, she leaned forward again.

"So he says here that he's looking forward to meeting the abbot at the gala, and three days later he's posting that he's feeling depressed and needs a time out. Hm... He didn't look that depressed to me", Natascha concluded, realising she was talking to herself. Just as she made a few more notes on her computer about her findings, Talia walked in.

"Natascha?"

"Hm? Yes, Talia. What is it?"

"You wanted to know when Shira is done with the sauna?" Talia was puzzled.

"Oh, yes! I do! Is she out yet?" Natascha enthusiastically asked back.

"Yes, she's about to take a shower. Why are you asking?"

"Revenge, my young friend. Revenge!" Natascha jumped to her feet and quickly ran out of her office. She had not forgotten how Shira had set her up by talking her into demonstrating a dance move on the strip pole just as Klaus had walked in on her. Natascha had sworn her Israeli friend revenge and had patiently waited for her time to come. She quietly opened the door to the women's dressing room, satisfied to still hear the shower running. Natascha carefully peeked around the corner and saw Shira's towel and open locker. An evil grin appeared on Natascha's face noticing Shira was still under the shower in the next room. Her grin widened as she realised that Shira's key was also still inside the locker.

As quietly as she could, she walked over to the locker, stuffed the towel and all the other clothes except for the underwear into it, locked it up and took the key. She quickly got out of the dressing room and ran to the nearby break room, where Nick and the remaining members of team A and B were having a loose debriefing from one of their jobs on an oil rig.

"Don't mind me", Natascha quickly apologised on her way to the strip pole. She climbed up and taped the locker key at its top, just underneath the ceiling. Seconds later, she was down again, finally noticing how everybody stared at her.

"If Shira asks, I wasn't here and don't help her", she quickly added on her way out, ignoring them otherwise. Just seconds later Natascha sat behind her desk again, staring at her computer as if nothing had happened. It didn't take much longer before she heard Shira yelling her name, followed by some Hebrew curses. Natascha chuckled and picked up her apple again as Shira's curses turned into threats. Not understanding Hebrew, Natascha didn't know the difference and pretended she didn't hear a thing.

About a minute later she heard the roar of laughter and whistles from the guys in the break room, indicating that Shira had not only found, but also successfully recovered her locker key. Satisfied with the success of her revenge, Natascha concentrated on her research again. With the reporter being a dead end for now, she tried to find out who might have worked at Whitmore Abbey for the bomb disposal.

But Natascha's efforts to start a new search were brought to a halt when Shira slowly walked towards her desk. The young Israeli was now fully dressed, only her hair still wet. Natascha pretended not to see her, which was literally impossible, since she stood right in front of her. Like a cat on the prowl, Shira stalked around Natascha's desk, her eyes not leaving her friend for a second. Natascha still tried to pretend Shira wasn't in the room, but it became more difficult and she bit her lip to prevent her laugh.

The Israeli came close enough to smell Natascha's hair. Natascha's ignorance turned to puzzlement as she tried to concentrate on her online search. Shira turned on her heel and paced in front of her again, nodding her head knowingly.

"I got several whistles, two marriage proposals and pocket change for the next two weeks", Shira finally whispered in a threatening tone.

Natascha couldn't control herself any longer and had to laugh.

"Two marriage proposals? That's so nice! I'm really happy for you! From whom?" Natascha tried to sound serious, looking at her friend for the first time.

"Doesn't matter, but your husband was one of them."

"Hm", was Natascha's only comment as she made a face.

"Do you want to know *how* I got those marriage proposals?"

"Not really." Natascha shook her head.

"Glad you asked", ignored Shira. "Can you imagine that, after the shower, I found my locker closed and locked, my key missing, and only my underwear available? I had to climb that stupid strip pole, half naked to get my locker key back. That's when two of our co-workers proposed to me. Anything you want to say to your defence?"

"That is some story, but why do you think I had something to do with it?" Natascha still tried to sound serious, but she knew she failed miserably.

"Let's see. When I was desperately searching for my towel or anything else that I could have used to cover up myself, I noticed the hint of a rather expensive perfume in the air. Interestingly you're the only one who uses that fragrance. Next, my locker key was taped to the top of that stupid strip pole, forcing me to climb up there to get it. Finally, having the boys chant *Natascha got you back good* and *Natascha doesn't want us to help you* as I was literally begging for help was actually a dead giveaway. So, since you're sitting here, I came to ask you how many women work at our company who go by the name *Natascha*?" Shira whispered and leaned forward over the table, not without demonstratively sniffing at her perfume again.

"Oh, Gosh, I honestly don't know. We have some Israeli women working for us now. Very secretive and shady. They might be using an alias. I would have to check the personnel files. That could take some time." Natascha tried to win some time, biting her lip again.

"No need. You're so busted."

"Oh come on, Shira. You have to admit I got you pretty good."

"Enjoy your moment of glory, trust me, it will pass. This is not finished! You are dead meat!"

"Is that a threat?"

"No, my love, it's a promise", Shira winked and left the office.

Natascha laughed, knowing she had not seen the end of this, although she had to admit she seriously considered checking her car before leaving. Natascha took some comfort in knowing Shira would take her time before she would seek revenge; so

Natascha assumed she could spend the next couple days relaxed.

She focussed again on her research, trying to find out more about who could have been responsible for the bomb disposal at Whitmore Abbey. A quick internet search didn't help her much and she sat back to think.

Who could I ask for this? We should have someone in this building who should know something about that. Natascha wondered and felt silly for not thinking about it any sooner. She quickly checked former Admiral Whittaker's schedule, noticing that he had nothing important scheduled for today. Natascha had confirmed confidence knowing he was always willing to help. She raised her fist to rap on his door.

"Come in, if you're one of us", the admiral hollered from behind the closed door.

"Can I bother you for a second, sir?"

"Only if you call me Brian, Natascha." The retired admiral said and waved her to come in.

"Thank you, Brian...Sir. I have a question, and I'm certain you can help me with it."

"I'll try my best, but I can't protect you from Shira. You have to deal with her yourself, preferably without demolishing this building", retired Admiral Whittaker said in his usual fatherly tone.

"Oh, good news travels fast. No, I should have her under control." Natascha had a weak smile, but it dimmed as she continued, "I'm wondering who would be responsible for the disposal of an unexploded bomb from the Second World War?"

"The unexploded ordnance, is it under water or on land?"

"Excuse me, sir?"

"The bomb? Where is it?"

"Oh, it's on land, just outside an abbey, a couple hours from London."

"It'd most likely be the Explosive Ordnance Disposal Unit from the British Army. Why?"

"Oh, I'm just curious. I heard about a story when I was diving for my father's institute a couple weeks back. It caught my interest, since it might have affected the water flow inside the underground tunnels. Is there a chance I can find out details, like who exactly did it?" Natascha was happy that she didn't have to lie to her boss.

"Hm, if they worked on an explosive device planted by domestic or foreign terrorists, it could be considered a matter of national security and therefore argued to be confidential. But if it's an unexploded ordnance from the war, it's most likely considered public information. I assume you can file a request for information with the British Army. They'll answer it, but I can guarantee you'll be waiting quite some time. Those are first class pencil pushers."

"Couldn't they just give me some information over the phone?"

Whittaker laughed so loud that Natascha startled.

"My dear, we're talking about the bureaucracy of the British Army. It'll take you about three weeks to get someone on the phone who'll tell you they have no idea what you're talking about. The best part is, he won't even be lying. No, your best bet is to simply send an official letter of request and then wait for the information. That way you'll have something in writing as well as a name or two that goes with it."

This was certainly not the answer Natascha had hoped for. She considered for a second to ask her boss if he could make a call, but she quickly remembered he had retired from the Royal Navy, and not the British Army.

"Okay, thank you very much, sir. I guess I'll try my luck with the pencil pushers then. I think it could be really helpful for our research to know when and where exactly they worked." Natascha concluded and rose from her chair. She half-heartedly hoped that the retired admiral would offer to call one of his many friends, but that didn't happen.

"Good luck with them!" Brian encouraged her and focussed on his computer again as Natascha made her way out of his office.

"Oh, Natascha?"

"Yes?" Natascha answered and enthusiastically turned around, hoping Brian might have changed his mind.

"Can you please send Ariel or Shira in, when you see them? Thank you!"

"Yes, Brian...sir."

Already thinking about what her next move would be, Natascha slowly walked back to her desk, from where she sent a quick message to her two Israeli friends. She would go and find them if they wouldn't reply within in the next two minutes.

"I could probably ask around in the village outside Whitmore Abbey." Natascha told herself and thought about it for a while. But she quickly realised her chances of success were very slim. An internet search revealed almost twenty registered restaurants, and she doubted any of the employers would recall guests from several years ago, let alone know if they were from the Explosive Ordnance Disposal Unit.

"That would also require they actually had something to eat there in the first place." Natascha noticed the next flaw in her plan. She pushed back in her seat with some frustration. She didn't know anyone who could know about the bomb. She jotted this unproductive note down just to keep it out of her thought process.

Just as she opened the document on her computer, someone gently blew into her ear. Natascha shrieked and jumped to her feet, toppling her chair.

"You're dead!" Shira coldly whispered as Ariel laughed out loud. Natascha had been so focussed on her work, she had not noticed them approaching.

"For heaven's sake Shira! Are you insane?"

"Insane? No, I'm just testing your situational awareness. You'll be an easy prey, very easy", the young Israeli played her mind game, whispering in a lethal tone.

"Well, you scared me pretty good. We should call it even now." Natascha offered, but Shira just laughed, clearly refusing her offer. To make matters worse, Brian walked over from his office.

"What happened? I heard a scream. Is someone hurt?" the retired admiral wanted to know as he saw the toppled chair.

"No, sir. No one's hurt. This...this *terrorist* here just scared me to death while I innocently sat here performing my duties." Natascha explained, trying to win the admiral to her side.

"You deserved it! You sent me up that strip pole in my underwear in front of all the guys", the Israeli hissed back.

"Okay, so we're even now." Natascha tried again, being cautiously optimistic that Brian's presence would cause Shira to cave in, but that did certainly not happen.

"Oh no, Natascha. You're not getting out that easy! This was just a test." Shira told her with an impish grin before turning towards her boss.

"You wanted to see us?" the Israeli asked and followed Brian to his office.

"Stop laughing!" Natascha warned and punched Ariel as he walked by, shaking his head.

- 11 -

Asklepios, Aegean Sea, Sunday, July 6

"How's Victor doing today?" After his late night arrival by helicopter the previous day, Sir Samuel Archibald Cunningham took the time to update his Texan partner on his latest finding. They sat at one of the many private tables, secluded from everyone else by some palm trees. He watched as the Texan cut a piece of steak, the red myoglobin juice spreading into his potatoes. The British aristocrat forked spinach leaves and a slice of orange, immediately preferring his healthier diet. Chewing on his salad, Samuel looked at his cane beside the table and was satisfied that his aching body did not rely on the wheelchair today.

"Victor is doing fine." The Texan replied before placing the meat in his mouth, the patriarch appreciated his suddenly eloquent manners. "He's finally in a wheelchair, thank the Lord. They're just performing a minor follow-up surgery on him today. He should be up again tomorrow. I'm praying to the Lord he'll recover quickly. We need him", L.J. said as he cut another generous piece from his steak.

"Hm, yes", was all that Samuel replied. Instead, he carefully looked around, but he could not see any potential eavesdropper.

"So, I assume you got my message that our valued abbot is concerned about certain activities?"

"Yes", L.J. confirmed, just before he shoved another large piece of steak into his mouth. "I was under the impression this issue was resolved once that reporter had been taken care of?" he asked in return, the slop of meat sloshing to the other side of the mouth. His etiquette was short lived.

"So did I, but it turns out there might be another issue. Couple of weeks ago, our friend was confronted in front of a restaurant by an unknown woman. She briskly told him she knew what he was hiding, and that she found evidence to prove it. She also threatened to take that evidence public." Sir Samuel Cunningham paused for a second to allow his words to sink in. L.J. drank from his beer and carefully glanced around before he replied. Samuel noticed he drank with food still in his mouth.

"Do we know if she referred to our current operation or to that goddamn paedophile scandal decades ago?" he whispered, dabbing the corner of his lips.

"We're not certain, but all the evidence points to her referring to the scandal. Our friend told me he met the woman during a benefit gala, where she was working for a security company, just moments before this reporter confronted him again. I assume she overheard them. There's simply no way she could have found out about our mission."

Neither of them spoke as a waiter stopped by to offer more drinks and to ask if everything was to their satisfaction. It was only when they were alone again that the Texan spoke. "Were there any witnesses to their discussion?"

"No, she approached him when he was outside the restaurant alone."

"That's a bonus. Didn't your government do a great job covering up that scandal? When we looked into that matter years ago, we found out that every investigation into the paedophile ring had been stopped before it took off. We were promised nothing from that direction could hurt us."

"I'm very much aware about the activities and involvement of my government in this case, Walter. I also don't expect anything to happen in that regard. However, we do have to be cautious. I believe I do not have to remind you of the consequences if what she found can be traced to our project. Nowadays someone can raise a lot of attention and ask a lot of unpleasant questions just by using social media. It turns out this woman has done nothing of that kind yet."

"Good. How's the reporter's social media? Anything unusual there?"

"Well, I believe Victor would know more details there. So far I've heard nothing concerning."

"Okay, I'll make sure to ask Victor tomorrow. So, what do we know about his woman? Do we know what kind of evidence she has?"

"No, we don't. With the abbot's help and some of my contacts, we were able to identify her. She was one of four divers who performed some scientific research in a flooded mine just outside the abbey. We believe that it must have been during that project that she found whatever evidence she claims to have. Once I knew her identity, I could do some digging. I made some calls and we monitored her usual communication channels. Her cell phone, e-mail and social media accounts. She's more or less non-existent on social media, but all her other communication didn't reveal anything to us either. She has not once mentioned anything online. However, she did try to find that reporter, but all her search ended at his blog. It turns out she did a really thorough search for him, but we can say with confidence that she didn't find anything."

"How could she?" Walter chuckled and drank some more beer. "Do we know if her friends, those other divers, know something?"

"Unless she's communicating with them by using smoke signals or carrier pigeons, she has never mentioned anything to them. Besides, when she approached the abbot at the restaurant, she did it alone, without her friends; so based on that I would rule them out."

The Texan thought about what his British friend had just told him. That woman was certainly a cause for concern, but they had to be extremely careful not to raise too much attention.

"So, we can agree she poses a certain risk to us. Question is how credible is she and how dangerous can she actually get?"

"That's the thing, Walter. She works part time at the London Aquarium as the dive supervisor and also as a secretary at this security company. It took us a while to set up all the surveillance, so there's a relatively large time period during which she could have communicated in any form that we don't know about. Yes, we looked at her e-mails, but we didn't find anything there. Not only does she use an alias name when she's on the internet, but she also worked under a third name as a security guard during that gala. So there's a certain risk that she might have mentioned something under a different name, but again, so far we didn't find anything. We also checked the conversation from the other divers, but everything was negative."

The Texan cut his baked potato, digesting the information he had just received.

"What does your gut tell you?" he bluntly asked his British friend.

"That's the thing. The facts are telling me not to worry too much about it for now and to keep monitoring her further. If we find something, we get active. But my instinct is ringing several alarm bells. With the information I just told you, what would you say?"

The Texan shrugged and had some more beer, weighing the information.

"I would agree with monitoring her, but that's not my decision. We should present all the information to the others and then take a vote."

The British aristocrat agreed and they both watched as the waiter cleaned their table.

"That's what I would do." Samuel stated. His gaze told his Texan friend that there was something else.

"So? What is it? There seems to be another issue."

"Yes, Walter. There is another issue. The woman I'm talking about is Natascha Rehfeld, her maiden name is..."

"I know her maiden name, Sam", Walter interrupted his friend and threw his napkin on the table. "Goddamn it", he cursed through clinched teeth. Walter's anger rose suddenly. He diverted his eyes from Cunningham, searching for an answer.

"If *she* goes public, someone *will* listen to her." Samuel said what they both knew and rose from his chair. "I have to go now. I trust you'll present all the information to Victor?"

"Yes, definitely." The Texan got up and shook his friends' hand before waving at the waiter for another beer. He watched as the British aristocrat walked towards the entrance of the elevators. His gaze shifted to the horizon. "Some vote that's going to be", he chuckled at the thought, shaking his head.

EuroSecCorporation, London, Monday, July 7

"So, if I should summarise this, Mrs. Boyle, then I can say that a couple years back there was a group of about six to ten uniformed men who worked at Whitmore Abbey, correct?" Natascha nodded her head with Mrs. Boyle's response, jotting notes as the conversation continued. "Yes, and they all stayed at the abbey during the time they were up there. Do you remember how many days they stayed?...No, that's okay, but we can say that it was for three or four days?....Yes, you mentioned that you saw them there every day when you went to mass...But their vehicles didn't look like they were from the British Army?...Okay, so they were just white vans...Well, thank you very much, Mrs. Boyle. I really appreciate your help...Yes, the next time we're up there we'll definitely stay at your place again", Natascha promised and ended the call on her cell-phone. Sitting in the break room, Natascha finally managed to uncover some additional information about the Explosive Ordnance Device Unit. As Natascha expected, Mrs. Boyle, the elderly landlady from the bed and breakfast in Whitmore, knew pretty much everything that happened in and around Whitmore and the abbey.

Drinking some tea and taking a bite from her apple, Natascha looked at the information after she had entered some more notes on her computer. It didn't really tell her much, in fact it didn't tell her anything that she had not known before, but she decided to file this confirmation as a success. She just went through her notes again as

Shira and Brigitte walked in.

"Oh, there you are! I'm going home now, Natascha. Would you mind finishing the work sheets this afternoon, including the overtime for the last week? I want to make sure the payment records are up to date." Brigitte Schwartze requested politely.

"Yes, no problem. I'll go over there right now." Natascha replied and rose from her chair, collecting her items. Putting her lunch back into the fridge, she glanced over to Shira. "I would've paid to see you on that pole. You're sure none of the guys recorded it with their phones?" Natascha kept teasing her Israeli friend.

"I did get money, remember? And yes, I'm certain no one recorded it. They knew what was best for them. I am afraid you missed your chance, it will be removed shortly." Shira laughed back and accompanied Natascha on her way to her office.

"Okay, where are we at?" Natascha asked herself and flipped through a stag of folders on her desk after she made herself comfortable. "Ah, shoot, this'll take me all afternoon! I might have to cut my walk with the pumpkin short", Natascha complained as she put the last folder away. Not wanting to waste any time, she logged into the computer and opened the program.

"Are you still planning your revenge?" Natascha finally asked Shira, who still stood at the window, looking outside.

"No, my revenge is already planned. You'll stand no chance." Shira promised matter-of-factly, her arms crossed. "It'll be so embarrassing for you. I can't wait to see that", she added with a laugh.

"Great, why doesn't that make me feel better?" Natascha asked with a weak laugh.

"It's not supposed to make you feel better. But you can relax for now, the time is not right."

"Thanks, I really appreciate that." Natascha looked up from her files. "What are you looking at anyway?"

"There's a car in the parking lot that looks weird. A blue Ford. I can't see the licence plate. Did any of our employees get a new car lately? I've seen it regularly for almost three weeks now. It's either this blue Ford or a grey Ford. But they always use the same parking spot."

"Not that I know of. I can check if you want." Natascha offered and frowned. "Why are you so interested in the car? Maybe they're just new clients for the gym?"

"Maybe. But something is odd. Yes, please check the files, if you don't mind. It seems to me there is always someone sitting in it." Shira noted, her voice changing with new thought, "Where are my girls?"

"Give me a second here. No one has registered a new car with us, so that's negative." Natascha looked up as she continued, "Talia and Maya are on the road with Team C to deliver a client and some documents to the airport. Noah and Tamar should be in the gym with the rest of Team B, but they'll most likely be back any minute now. You want me to call them?"

"No, that's okay. Where's Ariel?"

"He had a meeting with the police this morning about some clinics, but he should be in for the afternoon."

Shira just nodded, her eyes fixed on the vehicle. The Israeli took a quick moment to retrieve a pair of binoculars from the gear room before returning to her observation post in Natascha's office. With the help of the binoculars she had a much better view and estimated that the lone occupant behind the steering wheel was in his mid-forties. Just as she put the binoculars down, she noticed Ariel revving his motorcycle in the parking before he parked.

"My brother's back. And on second thought, maybe you could call Noah and Tamar up, please. Tell them not to change."

"Is there something wrong, Shira?" Natascha asked, her concern beginning to peak. She rose from her chair and walked over to her Israeli friend to have a look at the vehicle, but didn't find anything suspicious. "Maybe he's just waiting for his wife or kids?"

"Maybe, but I want to make sure."

"Okay, no problem." Natascha went back to her desk and called the gym downstairs.

It took a few moments before she had one of the Israeli women on the phone, but they promised to come up immediately. Natascha concentrated back on her work while Shira still watched the vehicle through the binoculars. It was just minutes later they heard Ariel and the two women laughing as they exited the elevator and came down the corridor.

"What is it?" Ariel asked his sister, looking out the window.

"You haven't noticed?" Shira asked her brother in return.

"The blue Ford? Yes, always parking in the same spot. Sometimes it's a grey Ford, but always the same two guys in it. I assume the second guy is at the gym. Why? What's wrong with it?"

"I don't know, it just feels odd."

"Can we get a better view of it?"

"I don't know. Maybe from Brian's office", Shira suggested and turned around.

"What are you doing, Shira?" Natascha asked as her friend briskly walked over to Brian Whittaker's office.

"Getting a better look. He's not in a meeting, is he?"

"No, but I think Klaus is with him."

"Good", Shira replied, already knocking on Brian's door.

"Come in, if you're on our side!" Brian hollered from his desk.

He and Klaus were surprised as they saw Shira, Ariel, Noah, Tamar and Natascha entering his office.

"Can we help you?" he offered as he and his friend watched them taking position around his much larger window.

"No, thank you. We're fine. We're just checking something out. Here, Ariel, what do you think?" Shira said not even looking at the retired admiral or the retired general as she handed Ariel the binoculars.

"Glad to hear that. If there's anything we can do, just let us know. Maybe we can get you some coffee or tea?" Klaus offered from his chair, drinking a cup of coffee himself, while his five employees completely ignored them. He and Brian exchanged looks, shrugged their shoulders, and kept drinking their coffee as they watched the four Israelis and Natascha passing the binoculars around to take a quick look. For almost five minutes the two owners of EuroSec Corporation watched in silence as their employees used Brian's office as a stake out.

Shira finally turned around and looked at both Noah and Tamar, who were still in their gym clothes.

"Noah, Tamar. Take your cell phones and go get some close-up pictures of the driver and the licence plate. Once that's done, I want you to check the security footage for the building's main entrance, going back...How long does it go back?" Shira asked and looked around.

"Five days", Klaus helped her.

"Five days? Thank you! So, Noah and Tamar, once you're back, check the surveillance video for the last five days and see if it is always the same guys and what vehicles they used. The footage should give you a good enough view of the entire parking lot. Maybe we can get a close-up when one of the guys is going to the gym. Once we have a face, check the gym if we can get a name to it. Understood?"

The two Israelis nodded and turned around to leave the office, while Ariel, Shira and Natascha still stood at the window.

"We can watch them from your office, Natascha." Shira eventually said, and they finally decided to leave Brian's office without explanation.

"I'll give five pounds if someone tells me what they're up to." Brian commented as he and Klaus watched them close the door behind them.

"I'll make that ten, and you know I'm cheap", Klaus offered, but none of them turned around.

"I'm not sure if I want to know, but maybe we should have a look." Brian finally sighed and got out of his chair. He took his cup of coffee and joined Klaus at the large window overlooking the parking lot. Since they had absolutely no idea what to look for, they just waited for Noah and Tamar to show up in the parking lot.

It was only a short moment before they saw the two blondes strolling along, aiming for a vehicle in the rear quarter of the parking lot.

"When did they dye their hair again?" Brian noticed suddenly, but Klaus only shrugged. "What are they up to..." Brian whispered in anticipation. He and his friend watched as Noah purposely dropped a set of car keys on the ground. She bent down to pick them up, taking full advantage of her Capri cropped compression pants to attract the undivided attention of the male driver sitting inside a blue Ford.

"The good old honey trap. Some things will always work", Klaus commented.

"Jesus Christ, look at her. Can you blame him?" Brian asked regretfully and emptied his cup.

"Would work on me", Klaus admitted, not taking his eyes from the scene in the parking lot. By now Noah and Tamar had reached their car, rummaged through its trunk and quickly returned to the building.

"So this was all about that blue Ford and its driver? Did they tell you anything?" Klaus asked as he returned to his chair.

"Hell, Klaus. You were sitting right there when they invaded my office. They didn't say a word. Sometimes I wonder if they even need us anymore."

"Hm, yeah, you're right. I trust they'll tell us if it's something we should be concerned about."

Outside the office, Shira and Ariel still watched the car while Natascha continued her work. It didn't take long before Noah and Tamar stepped out of the elevator and into the office.

"We sent the picture to your phone, Shira. Can we go and shower now? It was rather cold outside and we're still sweaty from the gym. We'll take a look at the video footage once we're done."

"Yes, of course. Just make sure you lock up all your belongings, including your towels. Wouldn't want to see you having to climb that strip pole half naked." Shira warned her co-workers with a stern look at Natascha.

"I don't know what you're talking about!" Natascha replied, not taking her eyes from her monitor. Shira's eyes narrowed as she closely watched her friend. Ariel excused himself and left the two rivals to themselves.

"Shira, can I ask you a question?" Natascha eventually asked after a few minutes, while her friend still watched the vehicle.

"Sure. What is it?"

"Do you remember that reporter during the gala in May? The one who confronted the abbot? His name is Kyle McRae."

"Yes, of course I remember him. What about him?"

"Do you have the impression he was depressed that night?"

"Why? What are you up to?" Shira asked in return, denying a clear answer. Natascha rolled her eyes. She should have known better than to think Shira would just give her an answer. Her Israeli friend was and always had been extremely suspicious about everything. Nevertheless, Shira was also Natascha's best friend, and there was literally nothing she wouldn't confide in her.

"It's just that I might have some information for him about Whitmore Abbey, and I'm trying to reach him."

"Whitmore Abbey? Isn't that the abbey he mentioned in his conversation with the abbot?"

"Yes, that's the one. When we dove up there, I might have found something that could be of interest to him, but I'm not certain. So I'm trying to find him, but it seems he has fallen from the face of the earth."

"You tried social media? He's a reporter and should have a strong presence", Shira suggested the obvious.

"Been there, done that. All his social media accounts are linking back to his personal blog. Last entry there was just after the gala, telling everybody that he's depressed and that he's taking a time out. Just days before that he was very motivated to see the abbot at the gala. So, I didn't get the impression he was depressed during that gala. What about you?"

For the first time in their conversation Shira turned around to face her friend. The Israeli searched her memory before she answered. "We only saw him for a minute or two, so it's difficult to base a judgement just on that. He was certainly up to the dress code and looked very neat. He seemed to be very anxious, but that might have been during the heat of the moment. But overall I wouldn't say he seemed to be depressed. If anything, I would say he was even more motivated when he left. After all, he had himself under control."

"That's what I'm thinking."

"Who knows? Maybe something else happened afterwards? We don't know."

"No, we don't", Natascha concluded and thought about that possibility. It seemed like a realistic alternative, but she somehow didn't believe it. She quickly opened the file on her laptop and made a note to check the missing person files with the police. She knew there was a way of directly accessing that list from the main computer on her desk, but she didn't know how and wanted to ask Brigitte the next time she would see her.

"Okay, here we are", Noah and Tamar said as they returned from the shower.

"Where do you want us to watch the video footage?"

"You can use my office." Shira told them and led the way to the little office she shared with her brother.

- *12* -

Vatican City, Sunday, July 13
The sun shone unusually strong on this summer day as Abbot Augustinus Hetley walked through the garden of Vatican City. His last visit had been years ago, but he had always wanted to come back with more time to pray and meditate in this beautiful garden.

Now that he was finally here again, he was so nervous about his upcoming meeting that he didn't even look at the well-maintained area. Lost in thought, he slowly walked down Viale Centro del Bosco, which would lead him directly to the most northern area of the park and Vatican City.

Earlier that day the Abbot of Whitmore Abbey had enjoyed both the mass at St. Peter's Basilika at noon and a tour of the museum. During these few hours, he realised he had forgotten the real reason why he had come to Vatican City. Preparing for his meeting with the President of Governatorate, he continued to follow the Viale Centro del Bosco. The abbot briefly looked up as he noticed he was nearing the large trees, indicating that he was almost there. For a moment he even looked at some birds, but then he concentrated on the task ahead and kept going. As he turned right towards the little pond, he had to admit that he was nervous to meet the second highest official in the Vatican, His Eminence Giulio Cardinal Baldacci, but recent events had made this visit necessary. It was up to Cardinal Baldacci to cast the final vote in their important matter. The abbot would then report to his British friend, Sir Samuel Archibald Cunningham and present Cardinal Baldacci's decision.

It was as Augustinus Hetley approached the pond when he couldn't resist any longer and paused for a few moments to take a look around. He checked his watch and gladly realised he was almost ten minutes early. Enjoying the view, he decided to rest on one of the benches, and he finally relaxed a little bit as took in the scenery. As always, tourists could only visit the garden on a guided tour, which was already over for the day. As a result, the abbot noticed there were only a handful of people enjoying the sun. His smile quickly vanished as he remembered the real reason for his visit again. It was up to him now to present Cardinal Baldacci all the facts and to ask him for his decision.

With the minutes ticking by, he finally got up again and walked further down the path when he saw the silhouette of His Eminence emerging out of the trees at the other side of the pond.

"Your Eminence", Abbot Hetley greeted him in accordance to the statutes of the Holy Roman Catholic Church. Giulio Cardinal Baldacci walked with his guest around the pond and through the older part of the garden with the tall trees. Safe from being overheard by anyone, Abbot Augustinus Hetley updated the Cardinal on the latest development.

"I agree, she can pose a serious threat to our cause." The Cardinal calmly stated. "The project is still on schedule?"

"Yes, Your Eminence. According to the leading physician, everything is on schedule.”

Cardinal Baldacci quietly thought about what he had just heard as he kept walking along the path through the trees. Neither of them spoke for the next twenty minutes. The British abbot walked a short distance behind the Cardinal, trying not to distract him. Abbot Hetley had nothing more to say on the matter, and he patiently waited for Baldacci to come to a decision.

“These are troubling times for our church. We are threatened in many ways, and it is important for us to rise to our old strength. We once again have to be the beacon for humanity, to follow the path shown to us. What will happen will be seen as a punishment from God. Our Lord will guide us on our path, we must not lose faith now and must do what has to be done”, the Cardinal announced and stopped to face Hetley. He looked deeply into Hetley’s eyes.

“I made my decision”, Giulio Baldacci eventually announced and filled the abbot in.

“Your Eminence!” Abbot Hetley said as he parted ways with the Cardinal, the decision weighing heavy on his conscience.

“May our Lord Jesus Christ bless you!” Cardinal Baldacci said more to himself, watching as the abbot slowly disappeared behind the trees.

Nick’s and Natascha’s house, just outside London, Wednesday, July 16
Natascha’s assessment of her current situation ranged anywhere from total embarrassment to funny mishap. Nevertheless, her situation did not improve. She was still handcuffed to their bed, and it didn’t look as if that would change any moment soon.

“Where are the keys? This looks like Sarah was at it. Everything is out of order”, Nick wondered as he rummaged through the nightstand.

“I have no idea, Nick. There must be something else we can do? Body lotion, maybe?” Natascha shook her head and blushed. “Ah, why is it always me?” she grimaced as she tried to squeeze her hand through the handcuff.

“Why didn’t we use the scarf again?” Nick laughed.

“Used that to blindfold me, remember? But seriously, Nick, what are we going to do now? Don’t you have keys for handcuffs? Aren’t they universal?”

“They are, but they’re at the office. What about your little universal key you hide in your belt? Wouldn’t that one work?”

“It would, except that Shira wanted...” Natascha stopped mid-sentence and closed her eyes. “I’m going to kill her!” She finally gasped and couldn’t help but laugh.

“What?” Nick also had to laugh. He actually found the situation much more amusing, but that was mostly because he was not the one who was handcuffed naked to the bed.

“Shira! This is her revenge. I told her earlier this morning that...well, that tonight could get a little bit louder, since Sarah-Shira wanted to sleep at her and Talia’s place downstairs. She asked me later this afternoon for my universal key, so she could upgrade it. Stupid me thought nothing of it and I gave it to her. And now I’m handcuffed to the bed and need her help to get out.” Natascha closed her eyes, desperately thinking for another solution. "That will teach me to never trust that demon again!" Natascha mumbled under her breath.

"Well, if that's the case, I'd say she played you very well", Nick commented with another chuckle.

"Yes, she did. Next time she's in the sauna I'm pulling the fire alarm and have that terrorist run naked to the parking lot. I swear!" Natascha promised and shook her head.

"But how did she get the key to the handcuffs? You think she asked Sarah to steal it? I don't think our daughter can do that."

"No, she can't do that. I assume Sarah just found the key and proudly told Shira about it. Maybe she's hidden it somewhere in her room."

"Well, I guess I better call Shira and ask for the universal key then."

"You've only used them once, remember? It takes practise."

"Hm, that actually did take some time. I remember." Nick laughed.

"Or you can go to the office and get the keys from your handcuffs", Natascha suggested, certain there must be another way.

"Can't do that for various reasons, and you never know if our daughter will walk in the door. We can't have her seeing you like that, not to mention Shira is just downstairs."

"Okay, let's make this fast and painless. Call her up so she can bask in her glory. Besides, I got to pee, so we should hurry before this gets really embarrassing."

Nick got up and quickly put his pants on.

"Nick! Wait!" Natascha hissed as her husband was already on his way to the door.

"What?"

"For crying out loud, will you please cover me up!"

Nick shrugged his shoulders as he looked at his wife again. Never before had he ever seen anyone so beautiful. His eyes rested on her dolphin tattoo, but he finally looked into her eyes before he became overwhelmed with unquenchable urges.

"She has seen you naked before..."

"Nick! That was in the sauna or under the shower, not when I'm handcuffed to our bed after having sex. Cover me up!" Natascha pleaded despairingly, tears of embarrassment rising in her eyes.

Nick covered her with her blanket. "There, is that better?"

"No, cover my face, too. I don't want her to see me", Natascha insisted.

"This is getting too funny. Can I at least take one picture of this?" Nick reached for his phone.

"Nick! Don't you dare!" Natascha hissed from underneath the blanket, but Nick was already on his way downstairs.

"There's no way this is a coincidence", Natascha mumbled underneath the blanket and shook her head. "Well, at least this humiliation is not public", she sighed, knowing this offered little comfort. That comfort vanished the moment Natascha heard the door opening again, followed by a gentle knock at the bedroom door.

"Natascha? Are you decent?" Shira asked, not entering the bedroom. To her surprise, Shira sounded relatively sincere.

"As decent as it gets when you're handcuffed to the bed."

"You want me to give the key to Nick?"

"No, I really got to pee. Can you just come in here, glow a little bit and release me?" Natascha begged, a nervous laugh of embarrassment escaping her lips. "Don't tell me that you didn't plan this?"

"Well, this might sound strange to you, but I honestly didn't." Shira answered convincingly and walked over to the bed.

"Seriously? You didn't?" Natascha sounded puzzled and struggled to free her head. With just her eyes peeking out from underneath the sheet, Natascha looked at her Israeli friend.

"No, I didn't. I promise", Shira replied honestly.

"Oh, great, this is even more embarrassing!" Natascha sighed.

"Well, I think this is really funny", Shira finally burst out with laughter. "By the way, those are nice boots!" she added with a wink at Natascha.

Natascha winced and pulled her legs up in an unsuccessful attempt to hide them under the blanket, but she just rearranged her whole sheet and was less covered than before.

"You want me to cover you again?" Shira laughed and pulled down the blanket from Natascha's face.

"No, I'm fine, thank you. Just get me out of those handcuffs", Natascha scowled.

"I'm wondering what the guys at work will say when I tell them about this", Shira wondered aloud as she started to work on the handcuffs.

"Shira! You must be joking!" Natascha begged, her eyes pleading.

"Just kidding! Here you go", the Israeli said as one side of the handcuffs finally opened.

"Found the key!" Nick enthusiastically shouted and held the little key up with a bright smile. Natascha just threw him a killing glance as she covered herself with her blanket and stalked out of the bedroom, the handcuff still dangling from her wrist. The loud echo of her high heels on the wooden floor barely covered the complaints she uttered through clinched teeth. She had difficulty keeping balance and slammed the bathroom door behind her. Shira sat on the edge of the bed and bit her lip to prevent breaking into another fit of laughter.

"Just for the record, the key was in her nightstand, not mine. She put it there!" Nick defended himself, but Shira only raised her arms as she got up.

"That's none of my business. I'm so not getting involved in this!" She finally laughed on her way out.

"Bye Natascha!" their Israeli friend shouted from the hallway.

"Not a word!" Natascha hissed back from the bathroom. "And thank you!" She quickly added. With Shira gone, the sound of Natascha's high heels announced to Nick that his wife was on her way back to the bedroom. Natascha stalked in, the sound of her leather boots now covered by the thick carpet, and sat on the bed.

"Where was the key?" she asked as she started untying the boots. He knew it would take her about five minutes.

"It was in your nightstand, not mine. It was in the lockable drawer. Remember we said we would put the key in there so Sarah wouldn't find it?" Nick revealed, not certain how he should feel. After all, Natascha had just experienced a very embarrassing and totally avoidable situation.

"Yes, now I remember. Would've been nice if we would have remembered that ten minutes ago", Natascha finally laughed and shook her head. "Well, we just forgot rule number one. Always make sure where the keys are before you use the handcuffs."

"How do you feel?" Nick asked, not sure how he could comfort his wife.

"Well, it was embarrassing, but it could've been worse."

"Yes, that it could. Are you okay?"

"Of course I'm okay Nick", Natascha laughed and finally flicked the second boot away. "It would have been much more hilarious if it would have been you instead of me, but hey, maybe next time."

"Oh dear Lord, that would've been so embarrassing", Nick commented, imagining it.

"Oh, really? Tell me about it", Natascha laughed and threw herself on the bed, where she finally took the time to unlock the handcuff from her wrist. Nick watched her and started to slowly massage her back. "Oh, yes! That feels really good! I so deserve that!" Natascha whispered. She quickly made herself more comfortable and closed her eyes as she enjoyed Nick's hands on her bare skin. Nick repositioned himself and kept caressing his wife's back with his hands and lips. Her eyes closed, Natascha moaned and bit her lip as Nick continued to please her. She quickly turned around and helped Nick out of his clothes, before they finally sunk back on the bed together, her lips now meeting his.

***EuroSecCorporation*, London, Thursday, July 17**
Natascha stretched in her office chair and exhaled sharply. After her morning routine at the aquarium, the young scientist had been enthusiastic to do a little bit more research on her own in the afternoon, but so far she hit a dead end. She had sent the request for information to the British Army ten days ago, and she didn't even know if her e-mail had reached the right contact. A message sent to Mark earlier this week had also not been answered yet, and Natascha started to think that it might not have been the best idea to ask her ex-boyfriend for help. She thought about their conversation many times, and she had to agree with him that she had only contacted him when she needed his help. Still hoping to hear back from him, her last chance rested on the missing person database from the police.

Unfortunately for Natascha, Brigitte had already left for the day, and Natascha simply didn't know where to find the program. Leaning back in her chair, she stared at the ceiling, yawned, closed her eyes and stretched again.

"Oh my God! You're going to kill me one day", she shrieked as she opened her eyes again, seeing Shira's face right in front of hers.

"Well, considering that I caught a bullet for you, I have every right to do so, besides, you're so easy to scare. It's so much fun and I simply can't resist", Shira admitted with a laugh and sat on Natascha's desk.

"Glad you're having so much fun", Natascha replied and leaned forward again, not without yawning another time. "Excuse me", she apologised and shook her head.

"Long night?" Shira smiled knowingly.

"Oh God, don't even start. Yesterday was so embarrassing", Natascha whispered, not without a chuckle as she blushed.

"Again, I found it rather amusing."

"Well, if I remember correctly, it was your idea that we try this. Associating my feelings of being helpless and not in control with pleasure was the right idea, but I didn't know that you had *that* in mind when you suggested it."

"Would you rather I sent you to a psychologist?" Shira asked, knowing the answer.

"Don't be silly, Shira. We both know I can never talk to anyone else about what had happened in that engine room. And besides, I'm not complaining. I enjoy *that* therapy much more than talking to a shrink", Natascha laughed mischievously.

"You're really seeing it as therapy?" Shira was curious now.

"No, of course not. We just see and enjoy it as what it is." Natascha shared, then thought to change the subject, "But on a completely different subject, do you have access to the missing persons file from the police?"

"Everybody has access to it. You never used the program before?" Shira asked curiously.

"No. I didn't know everyone has access to it. I thought only Brigitte has access. I don't even know where the program is." Natascha admitted and was more awake now as she looked at her computer monitor again.

"Well, it's not exactly a program, you go through their website and log in as EuroSec", Shira explained and showed Natascha where to find the website.

"Check your folder with passwords. The information should be in there."

Natascha opened a drawer and pulled out a little binder, in which all the different log-in information and passwords were written down. It only took her a few minutes before she found the correct information, and just moments later she had access to the online data.

"There you go", Shira commented and clapped her friend on her shoulder and got up from the desk to head to her own office.

"Thank you, Shira", Natascha called after her, her mind already focussed on the database, but the Israeli just waved her off. Natascha shook her head and oriented herself on the monitor. Her first attempt was to simply search for Kyle's name, but that search did not produce any results. Disappointed, Natascha made a face and rearranged the search parameters, checking the missing persons file starting from the date of the gala. Natascha was shocked as the new search produced little over thirty names.

"Wow, that's scary", she said to herself as she started to read them. Natascha half-heartily hoped she might have misspelled Kyle's name, but there was no person listed in there whose name came even close. Disappointed, she closed her eyes, sat back again and sighed as she felt two hands starting to massage her neck.

"Not now, my husband is somewhere in the building", she whispered, not without enjoying Nick's caressing touch.

"Why did I marry you again?" Nick asked and kissed her on the head.

"Because I'm an amazing wife!" Natascha proudly proclaimed and opened her eyes.

"Yeah, right! What are you doing?" Nick pretended not to sound too convinced on the *amazing wife* part.

"Just checked the missing persons file. I wondered if the reporter, Kyle, is listed in it, but he isn't."

"Well, he'd only be listed in it if someone did actually report him missing. If he's just taking a time out, then he's technically not missing."

"I know", Natascha admitted and exited the database. "I just thought I would give it a try." Natascha tilted her head back to look at her husband, who kissed her on her forehead again.

"I love you, angel!" Nick whispered. Natascha returned his smile.

"Are you looking down my shirt?" Natascha frowned as she noticed his eyes weren't meeting hers.

"Of course I am." Nick admitted freely.

"Pervert!" Natascha complained and leaned forward again just in time as Brian and Klaus walked around the corner.

"We saw that. You want to file an official complaint, Natascha?" Klaus offered jokingly.

"I'll let it slide for now, sir. That wasn't too bad. I could tell you what he did to me on that ship back then. *That* would've been a slam-dunk complaint." Natascha explained. After all, it was against company policies for personal protection detail to date their clients. The fact that Natascha had gotten pregnant onboard the research vessel while under Nick's official protection could be called a clear violation of company policies. Brian and Klaus never got tired of teasing Nick about it.

"Way too much information, Natascha. Way too much!" Brian waved her off and closed his office door behind him.

"You almost make it look like it's my fault. If I remember correctly, you were the one seducing me." Nick complained to his wife.

"Maybe, but it's so much more fun if the bosses believe that I was little Miss Innocent." Natascha laughed and got up.

"Where are you going?"

"I think I'll go for a little run. Nothing big, just about forty-five minutes. Have to clear my head. Around the block and through the park, the same route like always. Want to come?"

"I should be able to squeeze that in. It has been a long time since we ran together."

"Well, let's go now then, so we're back in time for the pumpkin", Natascha said. While she went straight to the dressing room, Nick informed Shira and Ariel to expect them back in about one hour. He quickly changed into his running clothes and waited for his wife, who took a little bit longer to prepare.

"I believe we might get wet", Natascha noted as she looked out of the window, noticing the typical dark grey clouds hanging over London.

"Yeah, let's not waste any more time", Nick cheered her on and stretched as they waited for the elevator.

"Oh, gosh, I would've so preferred a *'you're right, let's go to the cafe and have some ice cream"* Natascha joked and stretched her arm over her head.

"Wimp!" Nick teased and smiled at her as the elevator door finally opened.

"Nick! Wait!" Olaf Magnusson, Nick's teammate, called from the other side of the corridor.

"Yes, Olaf?" Nick turned around.

"Can you fill in? We're short one guy and have to leave in twenty minutes."

"What is it?" Nick asked and made a face, disappointed he had to change plans.

"Nothing big. Document transportation. We just have to escort a client to the airport. Ole-Einar can't make it. Are you up for it?"

"All the routes are planned?" Nick asked the obvious.

"No, we thought we'd take public transit and ask for directions on Facebook, you moron! Of course the routes are planned."

Nick looked at Natascha, who just shrugged her shoulders. She was clearly as disappointed as Nick, but tried to hide it.

"Well, look at it this way, it'll be a couple extra hours. The boys can give you a ride back home?" Natascha encouraged him.

"Sure. See if you can find someone else to run with. Love you."

"Will do. Be careful. Love you, too", Natascha whispered back and placed a quick kiss on his lips.

Nick went to the dressing room to change as quickly as possible as Natascha pondered who was available on such short notice. It was only a moment later her mind quickly wandered again as she looked out of the window.

The rain had already started and Natascha wondered how the two homeless people were doing. They used an old wooden playhouse in the park as a shelter, but she knew it must be cold. Since the weather was getting warmer, she regularly saw them there, greeting her on her run. Absent-minded, Natascha pressed the button to the elevator again.

Ninety minutes later Shira and Ariel both got ready to call it a day. They just finished a Skype call with their family in Israel as the phone rang.

"Yes, Ariel Rashid here...Really?...Of course...Shira or Talia will be right there...Thank you", Ariel frowned and hung up the phone.

"Where will I be?" his sister asked him as she reached for her jacket.

"Strange. That was the daycare downstairs. They told me no one has picked up Sarah yet, and they're getting ready to close for the day. Didn't Nick say he and Natascha would be back in forty-five minutes?"

"Yes, they did. That is strange. They would never be late to pick up their daughter." Shira shared his concern. She and Ariel left their office, only to find Natascha's desk empty. Shira took her cell phone and dialled Natascha's number, but the call went straight to her voice mail.

"This is weird. Maybe we should look for them", the Israeli suggested, but they only found a few members from Team B in the combat room.

"Does anyone here know if Nick or Natascha are back from their run yet? Or where they are?" Shira asked looking around the room.

"Nick didn't go. He had to fill in for Ole-Einar on a last minute change. Ole-Einar had to leave early. Nick and them are not back yet from the airport. We haven't seen Natascha." Jack Connory answered as he lowered the dumbbell to the floor. Shira didn't like the answer at all. She quickly exchanged looks with Ariel, and for some reason a chilling feeling ran down her spine.

"Did someone else run with Natascha?" Ariel asked quickly, but the three guys only raised the shoulders.

"We don't know. She never asked us."

Shira felt the familiar knot form in her stomach and spun around.

"Talia! Where are you?" She yelled as she and Ariel ran back to Natascha's office. Realising the urgency in Shira's voice, Talia almost immediately stuck her head out from another room.

"Yes? What is it?" she asked. Alarmed by Shira's reaction, the members of Team B, consisting of Jack Connory, Peter Clark, John Davis, Noah and Tamar also joined them in the hallway, wondering what exactly was going on.

"Talia, take Jack and Peter and get immediately downstairs to the daycare to pick up Sarah. Call us as soon as you got her. Natascha is well overdue from her run. Has she spoken with anyone before she left?" Shira yelled as Talia, Jack and Peter already ran to the fire escape stairs, which were faster than the elevator. Shira and Ariel stared at everyone who stood in the hallway, but they all shook their heads.

"What's going on?" Brian Whittaker asked resolutely as he and Klaus came out of their offices, alarmed by the loud voices.

"Natascha and Nick wanted to go for a forty-five minute run about ninety minutes ago. On a last minute decision, Nick filled in for Ole-Einar for a little trip to the airport. The daycare just called five minutes ago telling us to pick up Sarah. Looks like Natascha went by herself, and now she's forty-five minutes overdue", Shira quickly summarised checking the parking lot through Natascha's office window.

"I'll check if I can see her from here", Ariel quickly walked into Brian's office, closely followed by his two superiors.

"I assume she never did that before?" Brian wondered, his voice carrying his concerns for Natascha's safety.

"Well, we didn't tell her, but we always made sure she never ran alone. Besides, she always wanted to run with company. Not sure what happened", Ariel explained to Brian and Klaus, his eyes also scanning the parking lot and surrounding streets.

"Ariel? Remember the grey and blue Ford? Do you see them? The grey one was here this morning, but I can't see it anymore. Usual spot." Shira yelled.

"No, I can't see it either", Ariel yelled back and abruptly turned around.

"Okay, everybody listen up!" Klaus took the command with his calm voice. "Noah and Tamar, you both check each room in the building that she has access to. You also know the surveillance system. Go there and check if you can see something on the video feed, starting from the time you see Natascha leaving the building. Find out if and when the blue or grey Ford was there and when they left. We don't know exactly what has happened yet. Maybe all this is for nothing, but we have to make sure we cover every angle. Do we know where she wanted to run?"

"Nick told us they would take the usual route down the street through the loop in the park." Shira informed.

"That's the route she always takes?" Klaus confirmed.

"As far as we know, yes."

"John, you and Maya take a car and follow her route to the park. Shira, you and Ariel take another car and concentrate on the park alone. Make sure you get there as fast as possible." Klaus explained just as Shira's cell phones rang.

"Yes...You got Sarah?...Everything is okay with her? Perfect. Come up right away", Shira ended the call, knowing everybody else heard the news as well.

"Okay Ariel, let's go!"

Brian and Klaus looked on as their employees hurried down the corridor towards the elevator. As the doors opened, Talia was carrying Sarah with Jack and Peter behind her. They curiously watched the others entering.

"Peter, Jack, you got the keys for one of the cars?" Shira asked, already inside the elevator now, holding the doors open.

"Yes!" Peter Clarke answered as he and Jack quickly joined their colleagues.

"How is Sarah?" Brian wanted to know as Talia walked over to him.

"She's fine, but she's wondering what's going on." Talia explained, trying to laugh with Natascha's daughter.

"Did they say anything downstairs?" Brian asked with a smile. He didn't want to make Sarah feel more uncomfortable than she already was.

"No, just that she came in by herself, but since Sarah took her nap at that time, she quickly left again. That was all."

"Okay. You can keep an eye on her? She's fine with you?" Brian asked placing his hand on Talia's shoulder with a fatherly gesture.

"Oh, yes, we're fine. We're best bunnies!" Talia laughed with Sarah.

"We're best buddies", Shira-Sarah laughed, pointing out her error, "Bunnies are baby rabbits."

"Oh! Silly me!" Talia laughed. "We are best buddies, that's right."

"Okay, Klaus, what are we doing for communication?" Brian was suddenly businesslike again as he turned around, but his friend was already in the conference room, starting a rough timeline on the board.

"Brian, project the street map from the satellite feed on the white board. I want to see where our guys are and what areas they cover. We don't have much for communication at the moment, but we should be able to get away with cell phones and group calls."

"Yes, sir!" Brian acknowledged his friend and looked at the computer. His hands moved various ways, stalling before he touched the machine. "Might take a while here", Brian apologised as he fidgeted with the program, uncertain how to start it.

"No time, sailor. Show me the map! How could you ever win a war?" Klaus demanded.

"Back in my day I used to work from a chart table to plot my course." Brian defended himself.

"Back in your day, Moses parted the Red Sea and you all just walked across on dry ground." Klaus stabbed back.

"Talia, would you please be so kind and give me a hand here?" Brian eventually asked.

"Of course, sir", the young Israeli offered and started the right programs. Sarah watched as the wall lit up.

"Map is coming up in five seconds, sir. Anything else you need?"

"I think we can handle it, Talia. Thank you. I want you to make sure that our little guest here is doing fine."

"Very well, sir. Hm, can I ask a question, sir?"

"Of course. Go ahead."

"Shouldn't we contact Nick, sir?"

Brian and Klaus looked at each other for a moment, but decided against it.

"As far as I know, he's already on his way back. If we call him now he'll only start to run some red lights and maybe cause an accident. Right now, we don't even know what's going on."

"Yes sir, of course." Talia obliged and led Sarah by her hand out of the room.

"Okay, where are we at?" asked Brian and took a couple steps back to get a bigger picture of the map. Klaus looked at the GPS markers from their cars overlaying a street map.

"This isn't a live satellite feed?" the retired German general wondered aloud as he looked at the projected map.

"Of course not, Klaus. We don't have access to live satellite feed other than the GPS trackers."

"Oh, right, I forgot."

"Do you know how we can get a conference call to all three of our teams?" Brian asked and looked at the phone.

"I think we can use them as two way radios. Bloody hell, I can't remember how it works." It took both of the veterans a frustrating amount of time, and they both shook their heads when they finally managed to establish the connection.

"This is Brian here. Our building is negative, so far no visual or audio contact. Sit-Rep, please."

"Team one, covering the streets from parking lot to the east and south to the park are negative", Jack Connory replied.

"Team two, park area negative", Shira answered, her concern clear in her voice.

"Team three, covering the streets south, east and north of the park are negative."

"Roger that, keep looking until further instructions", Brian ordered while Klaus marked the search areas.

"How certain are we that she actually took that route, Brian?" Klaus wondered.

"I don't know. We should maybe cover the other side as well", Brian shook his head and activated the conference call again.

"Team three, expand search area to the north, west, and south of our building. Acknowledge."

"Team three confirms."

Brian shook his head and walked over to the window to take a look at the parking lot himself.

"Hm, her car is still there", he mentioned as he recognised the little Mini parked in Natascha's favourite spot. He was certain one of his teams would have reported it if the Mini was missing, but he just wanted to make sure it was actually there. "Nick is coming back", Brian added as he saw one of their black Range Rovers turning into the parking lot. He was already thinking about the best way to tell Nick without him going berserk.

"This is going to get interesting", Klaus noted, his voice sharing the same concern as Brian.

"Yes, it will be. Let's get Shira and Ariel back. Shira seems to have a good relationship with him."

"Agree, and it's not bad to have Ariel here as well."

It was around twenty minutes later that Nick sat in the conference room, shaking his head in disbelief. His first wave of emotions was sporadic and powerful. Within seconds, he turned from disbelief to wildly pacing the room, overwhelmed with guilt and rage. His lack of control ebbed off, and he was much more reasonable now, but that was primarily due to the support the others showed him.

"Do you think they got her, sir?" Nick finally broke the silence and sat down again, asking Brian and Klaus what everyone feared.

"We don't know that, Nick. But I honestly don't believe the Americans are behind it. You know that we have some friends in very important positions, and someone would have heard something. No, Nick, I don't believe that. I don't *want* to believe that. Besides, we don't even know if something has happened to her at all. Did Natascha mention anything to you before she left?"

"No, sir, she didn't. We just talked about the route we wanted to take, but that was all."

"So she did take the route through the park?"

"I suppose. That's what she said. But wait a second, maybe we can find her!" Nick suddenly said and rose from his chair. Filled with new hope, he ran to Natascha's desk. "She never runs without her cell phone. She uses it to listen to music, and she also has an app on it to track her running. If the phone is on, shouldn't we be able to localise her?" Nick asked and rummaged through the drawers of her desk, searching for the phone. "Good, it's not here. Talia, can you check her locker, please? I don't think she locked it." Nick sensed some hope and, taking Natascha's laptop with him, followed Shira and Ariel back to the conference room, where they activated a program to track their employees' cell phones.

"Her cell phone is not in her locker either. Has anyone tried to call her number, by the way?" Talia asked as she also joined the conference room.

"Yes, we called her a couple times, but it went straight to voicemail. Nick, can you check her laptop to see her latest running data? Maybe there's another route on it that we don't know about. Did she ever run alone?" Shira asked a general question, but all she got in return was a room full of shaking heads.

"I usually ran with her, but we always took the route through the park", Talia confirmed.

"Same with me. She's not at the aquarium either", Ariel added and ended a call on his own cell phone. In the meantime Nick started Natascha's laptop and entered her password. He quickly found the file showing the detailed data of her running activity. As they had all assumed, the only route she ever took was through the park.

"Okay, I guess we can all assume that this is the route she took today. Nick, what do we know about her daily routine for today? Did she say anything, or did she want to meet someone? Was there something different?" Brian asked Nick, but also looked at Shira and Talia, knowing they were living in the same house with them.

"Not that I know of, everything was normal. We briefly spoke about her morning at the aquarium, but there was also nothing new there." Nick shook his head and looked at Shira and Talia, but they also confirmed they had not noticed anything unusual.

"Nick, do you have access to Natascha's e-mails and other social media accounts? Can you check if there's anything there that could give us cause for concern?" Klaus asked.

"Sure, sir. She doesn't use social media that often, but I will check. I just hope she hasn't changed her password since the last time."

"Nick, do you know if there was something that bothered Natascha? Something she might have been working at on her own?" Klaus asked, vaguely remembering that Brian had told him about Natascha's interest in the Explosive Ordnance Disposal Unit. Nick thought for a few moments, not sure if there really was something that had bothered his wife, but then he remembered it.

"Well, she went up to the diving expedition in that old mine. She mentioned that quite often because of the old abbey that is right beside it. Whitmore Abbey is the name as far as I know. We met a reporter during our assignment on the gala back in May. I believe Natascha overheard an argument between him and the Abbot of Whitmore Abbey. The reporter claimed to have found evidence linking the abbey to the paedophile scandal a couple decades back. But that's all as far as I know."

"How did that bother her?" Klaus interrogated.

"Well, we do have a little child of our own", Nick replied and looked at Sarah, who sat on a blanket in the corner playing with some toys. "As far as I know, she looked for that reporter on the internet, but to my knowledge she hasn't had any luck yet." Nick explained and looked back at their laptop.

"Okay, I'll just be in my office for a few minutes, in case someone needs me. I will be back as soon as I can", Brian said after a few seconds and left the conference room, leaving everyone else behind. Nick just checked Natascha's latest e-mails.

"Nothing!" he said and shook his head. Next he pulled up the computer's history trying to find out which files and programs his wife had used most recently.

"Wait, what's this?" he wondered as he noticed Natascha's file about Whitmore Abbey. With everybody else assembling behind his back, he clicked through the different folders, noticing several hours of underwater video footage and a couple dozen images from above as well as below water, but nothing unusual.

"There is a text file", Rolf pointed to an icon he spotted in the folder.

"Let's see what it is", Nick said and opened Natascha's notes. "Okay, seems like Natascha made some notes about the abbey. It will take me a while to read all that, maybe there is something in here", Nick started as the others gave him some privacy. After all, they were looking at Natascha's private file.

"Keep looking, Nick, I'll check on Noah and Tamar. They should be finished with the surveillance video by now", Shira said and left the conference room.

"Will do, maybe I can find something on Skype", Nick said absent mindedly. He could not deny the concern for his wife growing stronger by the minute, but actively trying to find her was the best he could do for now. While Nick continued to search for any clues that would help him find her, Shira walked into Brian's office.

"You wanted to see me, Brian?" Shira asked and waved her cell phone with Brian's message on it. The retired admiral stood at the window and stared outside.

"Are you alone, Shira?" he asked, his voice barely more than a whisper, as he looked back over his left shoulder.

"Yes." Shira responded and closed the office door behind her as she stepped closer.

"Good." The retired admiral still stared out of the window, his concern for Natascha carrying in his voice. "How good do you know Natascha, Shira?"

"I'd say we can be considered best friends. Our friendship grew stronger once she realised that I was still alive, after I had caught that bullet for her."

The admiral nodded, but still didn't turn around to face his Israeli employee.

"Would she confide in you with something that she wouldn't share with Nick? Something like another man or an affair?" Brian asked directly. He didn't want to leave any option out, but those were certainly not the kind of questions he could have asked Shira in Nick's presence at this certain moment.

"She probably would, Brian, but I'm absolutely convinced there is no other man in Natascha's life. Yes, she has her little secrets and she certainly still has contact with her old friends back in Germany, but there was absolutely nothing in her recent behaviour that would indicate she is having an affair or had an affair. Besides, there is no way she would leave her daughter."

"What about a disgruntled admirer? After all, she's sort of famous, although she always followed our advice to never go public."

"No, I'd say she and Nick are living their lives as normal as possible. They're very happy. I'm also very confident that she could handle herself if a secret admirer would stalk her. She trained under Ariel and myself four times a week for the last three years now. She's no longer the easy prey she used to be. She can kick some ass now. You've seen what she did to Ole-Einar the other day." Shira reminded her boss.

"Okay. What about that expedition? When she came back, she asked me how to contact the Explosive Ordnance Disposal Unit. She claimed the work they might have done at that abbey could have affected the results of their findings. Was that true or did she lie to me?"

"I think that was true. But I also believe she might have found something up there that could be of interest to that reporter. Kyle McRae is his name, I believe. I don't know what and even if she found something, but she tried very hard to find him lately. Just this afternoon I showed her how to access Scotland Yard's missing persons database."

"You did?" Brian asked surprised and turned around, making eye contact for the first time.

"Should I have not?"

"Hm, you're right", the retired admiral grumbled and turned around to stare out of the window again. "How determined is she about finding that reporter?" he wanted to know. He didn't know why, but he somehow felt that there was more to Natascha's absence.

"She was determined, but it wasn't like she spent every minute of her spare time on it. She just tried the normal things that every normal citizen can try, mostly through social media."

"Do you think there's a chance that she's meeting with him right now? That it simply took longer?"

"I doubt that. Natascha originally wanted to run with Nick, and he only filled in for Ole-Einar as a last minute replacement. They were literally out the door when they asked Nick to come back. If that's the case, she must have contacted the reporter after leaving the building. That would have been on very short notice."

"But not entirely impossible. You think she would've told you if she would've done that?"

For the first time during their conversation Shira had to think for a while before she could answer. Brian certainly had a point there.

"I believe she would've told me if she had scheduled a meeting with him, yes. But a meeting out of the spur of the moment...him contacting her...I honestly don't know, Brian." Shira had to admit that she believed Natascha could have arranged a spontaneous meeting with Kyle without telling her.

"Here's the thing, Shira. You know how it is. With every minute we lose valuable time. Once I pick up the phone to make a call, we are all in. Klaus and I will use all our resources and friends, including your friends in Israel, to find Natascha and to bring her back safe. After her name was cleared, we got a lot of very important contracts with some very important government agencies. The moment we pick up that phone, some very important people in some very high places will ask us some very uncomfortable questions. The answers and speculations around those questions can cause a lot of trouble. International trouble. You know as well as I do that some fingers will automatically point westwards, and that's the last thing we need."

"I understand, Brian." Shira nodded.

"Don't get me wrong, Shira. If I seriously believe for even one second that she really is missing and that her life is in actual danger, I couldn't care less about international diplomacy and everything else. But before I pick up that phone, I have to make sure that she's not sitting with someone in a cafe, if you know what I mean."

"I certainly do."

"So, Shira, let me ask you directly", Brian started and spun around, facing Shira for the second time during this conversation. "Do you want me to pick up that phone and unleash hell?"

- *13* -

On board a Sikorsky S-76 over the English Channel, heading south-east, Thursday, July 17

Natascha slowly regained consciousness. Her headache was so intense she feared her head would explode. The piercing pain behind her temples was rhythmic with the noise created by the Sikorsky's four rotor blades, but Natascha could not figure out where it was coming from. She choked on her breath as her whole body tightened under the constant vibration of the floor she was lying on. Her teeth clenched with pain as she rolled onto her back, bending her wrists under the pressure. She turned her head but still couldn't see anything. It was only now that she realised she was blindfolded. Natascha rolled back on her side, alleviating the pressure of the zip ties around her wrists.

Forcing herself to concentrate, she tried to figure out what had happened, but her headache was too strong. Slowly moving her head against her shoulder, she was able to reposition her blindfold a little bit, and she eventually risked opening her eyes. She was uncertain what she hoped to see, but she quickly learned she was in a dark moving vehicle, with maybe two other people lying on the floor right beside her, who seemed to be unconscious.

"Hey, she's awake!" She suddenly heard a male voice. It was apparent someone noticed her waking up.

"Want me to hold her?" Another male voice shouted over the sound of the helicopter.

"No, that's okay. She's just waking up. We'll fix that right away." Natascha heard a third male voice respond.

She didn't know what to expect, but quickly realised she was not in any condition to put up any resistance. Before she could think any further, she felt the sudden sharp pain of a needle stabbing into her arm. Just seconds later, Natascha noticed her pain numbing and the sound of the helicopter fading away as the anaesthetic spread through her veins.

Only thirty minutes after their take-off from a private airport outside London, Natascha lost consciousness again. The Sikorsky was now minutes away from reaching France. The four men in the back smiled as they watched Natascha slipping into unconsciousness again.

"She never saw it coming", one guy laughed and gently kicked against Natascha's bum with his combat boots to see if she would react, but she didn't.

"What about the two other guys? What are we doing with them?"

"They can have them, too. They wanted her; we got her. That's five grand extra for each of us!"

***EuroSecCorporation*, London, Thursday, July 17**

"So, what do we got from our surveillance video? Noah? Tamar?" Brian asked, hoping there was something they could add to the little information they had so far.

"We first checked the whole building for her, so it took a little bit longer. When we looked at the surveillance video, we noticed that the grey Ford entered the parking lot about thirty minutes before Natascha arrived from the aquarium. So if someone was following her, they worked with at least two cars. We don't believe the car's occupants in the parking lot realised they were within range of our surveillance video. We checked the footage from the last couple of weeks, and this is definitely the same grey Ford, but we also noticed it's using up to three different licence plates. Natascha left the building alone for her run, there was no one else leaving or entering the building for three minutes before and eight minutes afterwards", Noah explained and took a deep breath before she continued. "Unfortunately, two minutes after Natascha is out of view from the surveillance cameras, the grey Ford also left."

"Damn, that's bad. Okay, I'll notify the authorities right away. Klaus you finish here. Noah, I need stills of both Fords as well as all the licence plates they used. I also need an exact timetable and I need it now!" Brian barked as he was already on his way to his office.

"Already sent it to your computer, sir." Tamar shouted after him.

"Okay, Noah, Tamar, I need another still of Natascha when she left the building. We should have a pretty decent image of her. We need that for her description. Put it together with her personal data, height, weight, you know the drill. You can find it in her file. Nick, was there anything else you could find on her computer?" Klaus asked and turned towards Nick, but Nick just stared outside the window and shook his head. With each second that passed, the pressure around him grew bigger and bigger.

"Nick!" Klaus addressed him again, much louder now, knowing he had to keep Nick's mind occupied.

"Yes, sir?" Nick finally turned around.

"Was there anything else on the laptop?" his boss repeated his question.

"No, not really. She made some notes about that reporter, but nothing that indicates she actually contacted him. Nothing in her e-mails or social media. The only account I couldn't access was her Skype account. I know she usually talks a couple times a week with her family in Germany, sometimes with a friend, but I can't log in. We have a little notebook at home with all the passwords. I'll get it later today", Nick explained, his voice breaking. Everybody felt sympathy for him, his attention turning back to the window. Shira walked over and took him in her arms.

"We'll find her, Nick. I promise you that."

Nick couldn't speak as a tear ran down his face. "If someone hurts her...", he whispered, slowly shaking his head.

"I know..."

"Okay! I got something! Her cell is back on!" Ariel interrupted with a shout. "It just came on at the bus station in the park, but it went to her voice mail. That's right at the jogging route", Ariel explained as he and the rest ran down the hallway, leaving only Klaus and Talia behind in the conference room. Klaus immediately marked the bus station on the board and noted the time beside it.

"Talia, keep an eye on the monitor and update the guys as soon as anything changes with her location. See if you can find out what the bus schedule is, just in case it becomes mobile. I'll let Brian know. I'll be back in a minute", Klaus said and rushed out of the conference room as five SUVs were already leaving the parking lot.

With Tamar and Noah gone, Talia used a second computer to create Natascha's current description. She sent the file to Klaus' and Brian's e-mail. Next, she checked the website to pull up the schedule for the bus stop at the park. As she expected, buses were leaving there almost every ten minutes at this time of the day.

Ariel steered the black Land Rover through the park. Although not entirely legal, it was much faster route since rush hour had almost reached its peak by now.

"We need an update on the cell phone", Shira shouted into her cell phone.

"Still at the bus stop. Do you have a visual yet?" Talia asked back.

"Damn!" Shira said once the bus stop came in sight. "What are they? Hooligans?" Shira wondered as she saw the group of eight intoxicated men. Ariel slowed down to see if he could see Natascha somewhere, but there was no sign of her.

"They look more like a local gang. They're rather young", Ariel assumed as they got closer. As he brought the Land Rover to a standstill, he estimated the men to be between seventeen and twenty-two years old.

"There's no sign of Natascha, but we'll see if we can locate the cell phone. For your information, there are eight drunk guys here who might have seen something. We will ask them", Shira informed Talia.

"Confirmed. Do you need me to send back-up or the police?"

"No, we're fine. The others will keep looking in the area. We'll have another look at that wooden playhouse here as well." Shira responded, spotting the old shelter. "Nick? How are you doing?" Shira checked in, but Nick had already left the SUV.

The arrival of the black Land Rover speeding through the park and coming to a sudden stop right in front of them had not been unnoticed by the drunks, but so far they did nothing but shout and drink beer.

"Nick, we don't know if they're involved in it or not. They were not here when Ariel and I searched the area about a half hour ago. Maybe they just found the phone", Shira tried to calm Nick down.

"That's okay, Shira, I just want to know where the phone is", Nick replied, pressing the redial number on his own phone. The three patiently watched the display until Nick heard the familiar sound of Natascha's cell phone. As he expected, the sound came from one of the drunken guys, who now looked at Natascha's phone again. But since it was locked, that was all he could do with it.

"Let me, Nick!" Shira quickly intercepted him and held him back.

Reluctantly, Nick stayed back with Ariel as the Israeli walked over to the intoxicated man holding their friend's phone. He appeared to be the oldest in the group, and Shira expected him to be the leader of this little gang.

"Don't worry, Nick. Shira might have better luck getting the phone than you", Ariel tried to calm his friend down, but the expression on Nick's face showed Ariel he disagreed. "Or not", Ariel corrected himself after they both heard the drunk guy laughing loudly and shouting some obscenities at Shira. "Wait! Let her handle it. If we get in a full blown fight we'll lose valuable time explaining everything to the police afterwards. They might even confiscate her cell phone. My sister will be fine", Ariel explained in his typically calm voice. He didn't seem to be too concerned about Shira's safety. However, Nick's concern grew and he looked at Ariel shaking his head as a loud scream caught his attention again. The Israeli quickly spun around and saw the big guy crouching on the ground holding his groin. A second guy joined him just seconds later.

"I told you my sister will be fine", Ariel smiled as he and Nick finally walked over before the situation could escalate. "I advise against that", Ariel's voice rose sharply, looking at the remaining six drunks who came dangerously close to Shira. The level of intoxication had clearly impaired their judgement, and Ariel noticed they were weighing their odds. They were obviously humiliated, getting their asses kicked by a woman. They glanced around nervously and backed off.

"I told you before that I just want my friend's cell phone; and that I want you to tell me where you found it", Shira calmly repeated her request and held her hand out expectantly. The guy reluctantly turned Natascha's cell phone over to the Israeli. Shira briefly looked at it before handing it to Nick. "Now, where were we? Right! You wanted to tell me how you got the cell phone." Shira stated and watched as the bully slowly got back to his feet.

"I found it. I didn't steal it", he insisted with a groan as he finally returned to his feet.

"How and where did you find it?" the Israeli continued.

"Over there", the guy said and pointed to the old wooden playhouse.

"You found it inside the shed?" Shira asked and turned towards the playhouse.

"No, it was outside in those brushes, I swear. We just heard it ringing, that was all."

"When was that?"

"About ten minutes ago. What the hell is your problem anyway?"

"Nick?" Shira looked at her friend, ignoring the bully who suddenly felt powerful again now that he was back on his feet.

"He could be right. All incoming calls are from us, and her outgoing calls are to our numbers." Nick shook his head and frantically searched the brushes around the shed for any signs of his wife.

"Nick, be careful, the police might have to look there as well." Ariel reminded him, but he couldn't blame Nick for not caring about it.

"I really don't care about the police right now, Ariel. We only have a few hours of daylight left, and I'm not going home until I know what happened to my wife", Nick insisted. Ariel didn't say anything, but he had to agree. While Shira took the moment to call in to update Talia, Ariel entered the shed. He stopped almost immediately behind the opening and looked around. After all, he had to be conscious of tampering with any potential evidence.

Like all the other equipment in the park, the wood from the shed was in an advanced deteriorated state. While it had been deemed unsafe for the children to play inside, the old playhouse was still regularly used by two homeless men as a shelter. Ariel's eyes scanned the floor and the walls, but all he could see were indications that the homeless people had been there recently. Two older-style military sleeping bags, a jacket and some other personal clothes were spread out on the floor or hung on the walls to dry. Ariel took all this in within a second, but the homeless men were not there.

"Shira, come here for a second, please." Ariel asked his sister. "Have a look around, what do you see?"

His sister looked around for a couple seconds and slowly shook her head.

"Looks like they spread their belongings out to let them dry from the rain. They have some newspaper there and some old wood, most likely what they found on the ground here in the park. I assume they wanted to make a fire to dry out their belongings. Seems like something disturbed or prevented them from doing so. A couple plastic bags full of empty bottles, looks to me like they were collecting them for the refund. A couple tin cans with food, but I don't see any booze. Or any signs of a fight."

"That's what I noticed. Do you think they could've done anything to Natascha?" Ariel whispered. Nick was still searching the area around the shed, and Ariel did not want him to overhear.

"I don't know, Ariel", Shira whispered, shaking her head. "This is definitely the stuff from the guys that are always here. We've seen them so many times when we were running here, but I've never seen them drunk or shouting any stupid comments. They were always very nice, to be honest. I also cannot believe Natascha wouldn't be able to defend herself against them, to tell you the truth."

"That's how I remember them. So what about the opposite?"

"You mean they might have tried to help her?"

"Well, your friend claims he found Natascha's cell phone right beside the shed. I tend to believe him. The place is perfect for an ambush. Concealed from the main street, no surveillance cameras, easy access back to the street by car and less than two minutes to the highway. What if someone waited here to abduct Natascha and the two homeless intervened?"

"That would make sense, but what happened to them after? There's no sign of a struggle."

"Go ask your friend if they've seen them", Ariel suggested.

"He's *not* my friend", Shira scowled back at her brother.

"Nick? Did you find anything?" Ariel asked as Nick finally came around the shed.

"No, absolutely nothing. No foot prints, no signs of a struggle, no broken branches, nothing", Nick shook his head and struggled to keep his emotions under control.

"Come over here, I want to show you something", Ariel tried to keep Nick's mind going as he showed him the inside of the shed, while Shira walked back to ask the group about the two homeless people.

"Why would we pay attention to some homeless bumps? We're not members of the neighbourhood watch program!" The gang leader laughed, masking that he was still uncomfortable in Shira's presence. She simply took another step towards him and locked her eyes on his.

"Look, tough guy. The woman who owns the cell phone you found is my best friend, and she's missing. There's a chance the two homeless people who stayed in that shed over there, might have seen something. So, every minute you waste being a bully reduces the chances of my friend coming back alive. I'm going to ask you nicely one more time before I let my friend over there ask you. By the way, he's her husband and his patience is running thin. Have you seen the two homeless guys or anything else that could help us find my friend?"

The thug looked at Shira as if she had kicked him in the groin again, but like all bullies, he was totally out of his element because Shira didn't express any fear towards him or his friends. He briefly looked at Ariel and Nick, who both glanced at them now, carefully calculating his response. Somehow he knew a confrontation would end up very badly for them.

"No", he finally said and shook his head. "We arrived with the bus about twenty minutes ago. The moment we got here I heard the cell phone ringing, but there was no one in the shed. We haven't seen them or anything else that looked unusual, but we didn't pay too much attention either. What are you anyway? Some sort of cops?"

"No, we're not. You see, that wasn't too difficult", Shira said and turned around to meet Nick and Ariel. She shook her head with frustration. "They haven't seen anything."

"I suggest we drive back to the office to meet with the police. I assume they're there by now. Let's call Rolf and Tamar and keep this site here secure. Nick, did you find any tire tracks?" Ariel wanted to know.

"There is maybe something here, but with all the rain and the people walking around, I just don't know if it's anything valid." Nick said and showed his friends what he believed to be signs of a tire track, but Ariel also wasn't too convinced if that could help them. He noticed Nick was getting more nervous by the minute as he continuously looked at the street gang.

"You think I should talk to them?" Nick asked seriously.

"Well, most definitely not. I can guarantee you it will make you feel better for the moment, but you're no help to your wife sitting in a holding cell. Let's go, we're driving back!" Ariel persuaded his friend, just as Rolf and Tamar stopped behind them. Ariel quickly filled them in on the situation, and just minutes later he steered the black Land Rover back into EuroSecCorporation's parking lot. As he had suspected, two police cars were already there.

"Nick, it's good you're back. You remember Chief Inspector Conolly from Scotland Yard? I've already briefed him about everything we know. Maybe you can help with the detailed personal description?" Brian asked minutes later. Chief Inspector Conolly was one of the few officials who had believed and fought with them years ago when Natascha had been declared a terrorist.

"Hi Nick, I'm sorry to hear about all this. I can promise you that we'll do everything we can to find her", he promised as he shook Nick's hand. The chief inspector could feel the tension in the room growing thicker. Nick was silent. Their chances of finding Natascha were getting smaller with every minute that was ticking by.

Talia walked over to him to hand him his daughter. Nick took Sarah on his arm and stared outside the window, hoping to see his wife somewhere, but all he saw was her car in the parking lot. He sighed, fighting the tear that ran silently down his face. Shira's hand pressed on his shoulder,

"We'll find her, Nick. There's no sense in projecting the worst into this, you know that", she tried to comfort him.

"I know, but you know damn well what I'm afraid of."

Shira knew perfectly well what Nick was referring to. There were still enough disgruntled and very powerful people in the United States who wanted to see Natascha dead.

"Nick, I've already contacted all our agencies. They assured me that none of them have any knowledge about anything that could've predicted this." Conolly tried to calm Nick down. Like everyone else in the room, he had also overheard Shira's and Nick's conversation.

"What difference does it make?" Nick shot hotly and turned around, the anger deeply furrowing his brow. "Why does it matter who snatched her?" he snapped and handed his daughter to Shira. "Look at the board! Look at what we got! We got nothing! Whatever happened was a well-planned and well-executed operation in broad daylight in the middle of a public park. I don't give a damn who's behind it! Whoever it is knows what he's doing, and that scares me. Back then on the ship we were with her, we were right there! Right now we don't even know if she's even in the country anymore. No one in this room is an idiot. So please do me a favour and do *not* tell me not to worry and do *not* promise me anything. We all know better than that!" Nick finally shouted and stormed out of the room. Shira moved to follow him, but Brian held her back.

"Let him, Shira. He'll most likely go to the combat room to blow off some steam. Give him a couple minutes", Brian suggested knowingly. The silence in the conference room weighed heavily on everyone, even as Rolf and Tamar returned.

"The police secured the scene and are working on gathering some evidence. The others are still out there taking another look around and helping the police canvas the area. We ended up with nothing so far", Rolf shrugged his shoulders as he gave the latest update.

"Bloody hell!" Brian cursed through his clinched teeth and looked at the board again. "Come on, guys, we're missing something! There has to be something we can use! Shira, once Nick calms down I want you and him to go through Natascha's cell phone. Maybe she saw something and took a picture of her attackers before throwing it away. If someone snatched her in broad daylight they wouldn't have had time to stay in the area and search for her phone once she tossed it. Ariel, you have to get on the phone with Israel. Find out if they picked up something. See if they can position someone on the major airports, get Natascha's picture out there. Have them check into flight plans filed on short notice. Private jets, cargo, medical transport, everything! Rolf and Tamar, get back out there. Check the streets and all the businesses around the park. We're looking for traffic cameras and business surveillance cameras that might have caught something. Bill, I assume your guys are looking into traffic cameras to see if someone was speeding from the scene or running a red light?" Brian asked and turned to Chief Inspector Conolly.

"Already on it. Look, I know your guys are good at what they do, but please keep us in the loop as soon as you find something, okay? We're actually pretty good at what we do, too."

"Don't worry, they will. Okay, Shira and Talia, my office now", Brian instructed and led the way. "Close the door", he asked the two Israelis just seconds later as the three were in his office. "Okay, we can only imagine how hard this is going to be on Nick. He had a valid point with what he said just minutes ago. We have to make sure he's not going to run off the reservation. So I need you two to stay close to him, really close. If he's hiding something from us, we have to know. We cannot afford him running around out there trying to find her by himself."

"I wouldn't worry about that too much, Brian", Shira defended her friend. "Nick was actually much more reasonable in the park than I would've been. If it weren't for his daughter, I'd agree, but at the moment I don't believe he'd do anything rash. I'll make sure Ariel stays at our place tonight as well, you never know. Since we're talking about it, what's the plan with Sarah?"

"I'm working on that one. We do have a sort of safe house that not even the police know about. We can place her there with one of our teams if need be. For now we have to make sure we find Natascha. Shira, see how Nick's doing and if there's something on Natascha's cell phone. Talia, you seem to get along very well with Sarah. Make sure she stays happy, okay?"

"Okay", Talia promised and left the office.

"Brian?" Shira stopped on her way out and closed the door again.

"Yes?"

"What if we find her before the police do? How do you plan to stop Nick from going after them? I can tell you from personal experience that he'll do whatever it takes to get her back."

"You think his mates would help him?" Brian asked, staring out of the window.

"Of course they would."

"Would you go, if he asks you?" Brian wanted to know and sat behind his desk.

"You really have to ask me that? I caught a bullet for her!" Shira replied as calmly as she could, but her voice made it clear that she felt insulted.

"Good! I'd be very disappointed in my crew if they wouldn't!" explained Brian, their eyes locking in on each other. Shira hesitated for a second, not sure what to say. The Israeli finally nodded before she turned around to leave the office.

"Shira!" Brian called her just as she was about to open the door.

"Yes?"

"Who said Klaus or I would stop Nick or anyone else from going after her?"

A devilish smile crossed Shira's lips as she closed the door behind her. She turned on her heel, following the loud thuds to the combat room. Shira slowed her steps and leaned against the door frame, from where she continued to watch her friend working the punching bag. It was only a minute before Nick finally noticed her. He eventually slowed down, just throwing some sporadic punches and kicks, but most of his energy was gone now.

"What is it?" he panted, throwing another jab.

"Ariel is talking to the Mossad to see if they heard something. We're currently looking at all angles. Brian and Klaus are doing what they can. Ariel will stay at our place tonight, just in case", Shira calmly explained. Nick listened, but tears filled his eyes again.

"Thank you, Shira. I really mean it", he sobbed and looked at the floor.

"Don't mention it, Nick. That's what we're here for." Shira replied and wrapped her arms around Nick to offer him some comfort. He didn't say anything, but Shira noticed his tears were flowing uncontrollably now. All the energy had left his body, replaced by sorrow and pain as he sank to his knees, but Shira didn't let go.

"It's okay, Nick", she comforted him.

"I can't lose her! I love her too much!" he sobbed.

"We all do, Nick. We all do", Shira whispered softly as a single tear burned a trail down her angelic face.

On board the shuttle boat, Aegean Sea, 120 nautical miles south of Icel, Turkey, heading south south-west, Friday, July 18

Natascha had no idea how long she had been unconscious as she slowly started to wake up again. She was no longer blindfolded, but she still had difficulty determining where she was. There was a deep humming sound pounding her head, but it was only a moment before she realised it was coming from an engine.

Natascha looked around, but her eyes had difficulty adjusting to the darkness. Whatever drugs they had given her, they still maintained their paralytic function. She was too weak to sit up, and her sense of balance was wavering. Natascha lowered her head to the floor, closing her eyes tightly to stop the swaying. She could feel the engine rumbling and the boat's rocking nature. Natascha closed her eyes again, fighting hard not to throw up.

Where the hell am I? She asked herself, but she didn't know the answer. She focussed again on the rocking boat, and to her dismay confirmed the validity. *I could be anywhere!* She seethed as she slowly opened her eyes again, concentrating on a dark area in a corner to adapt to the darkness.

It didn't matter how hard she tried; everything was still clouded, her senses working slowly under the prevailing drugs. It was only now that she realised the pain in her wrists caused by the zip ties binding her hands behind her back. Another swoop of nausea overcame her as she weakly tried to wriggle her hands free. The concentration alone was exhausting, depleting whatever energy and strength she had left.

She coughed feebly during her attempts to salivate her dry mouth as she lifted her head to study her surroundings. As expected, this simple task took all her energy. Her body wreathed under the burning pain that soared through her. She worked to find a more comfortable position on the hard floor. She rolled over with a deep groan and finally noticed several other people were lying on the floor around her.

Okay, at least it's not just about me. Natascha took whatever comfort she could find in that thought. It was too dark for her to see how many shared her fate, but she believed to see at least three more women. With the effects of the drugs wearing off to a level to allow her to form a cognitive thought, Natascha looked around the room again, realising there were no guards present. Whoever had kidnapped them had to be confident they couldn't escape from where they were, which further convinced Natascha that she was on a boat.

Now that she could think more clearly, Natascha pushed herself further, lifting her head high for a few seconds to gather more information about the dark room. She felt another swoop of nausea overwhelm her, forcing her to lay her head back on the floor with familiar exhaustion. She closed her eyes for a few moments, settling her mind and stomach. She didn't know how much time had passed, but when she opened them again, she realised that the sound of the engine was more subtle.

Maybe we have arrived? But there was another sound that was new to her. It took Natascha a lot of energy to concentrate, but she finally heard people crying. Right beside her were maybe one or two women crying.

If they're crying, it means they're awake! Natascha told herself and lifted her head again to see if she could locate the women. It turned out that both women were lying right beside her.

"Hey! Can you hear me?" Natascha whispered and immediately closed her eyes again as a wave of nausea overcame her. Each word she spoke sent a surge of pain piercing through her head, but Natascha was not willing to go down without a fight.

"Hey! Can you hear me?" Natascha repeated, this time louder. Since there was no guard present, she assumed that no one outside this room could hear her over the sound of the engine. The other women did not answer her, but their sobbing stopped, and they both turned around to face Natascha.

"Hey! Are you awake? Can you talk?" Natascha wanted to know.

"Yes...who are you?" one of the women responded with a strong French accent.

"My name is...Talia", Natascha lied, thinking about one of the many lessons Shira had told her so many times: to not trust anyone in a situation like this.

"I'm Monique", the first woman answered between sobs.

"Freja", the other woman introduced herself, also with a strong accent.

"Are you both okay? Are you injured?" Natascha voiced her concern. Her plan was to build up a level of trust first.

"Everything hurts, but we're not injured", the French woman answered for both.

"Do you have any idea where we are?" Natascha continued.

"No", they both replied in unison.

"I believe we're on a ship, but I'm not sure", Natascha shared some obvious information, and watched as both women tried to raise their heads to confirm her observation. Natascha gave them the time they needed to realise that she had spoken the truth.

"How do you know?" One of them asked.

"The sound of the engine, the bouncing up and down on the waves, typical for a ship", Natascha explained patiently as she noticed that whatever ship they were on had just come to a complete stand still. She wasn't sure, but she had a feeling she would only have minutes before someone would come and get them.

"Where are you from?" Natascha continued her questions.

"Stockholm", Freja answered.

"Paris", added Monique.

"I'm from London", Natascha shared some more information to further bond with them. "How did you get here?"

"We got kidnapped in Paris...couple guys drugged us...we were so stupid...they kept us in a basement, handcuffed to a wall....they...they..." Monique cried, trying to find the word that could reflect the horrors she and her friend had been through.

Natascha was shocked. She knew that she was in deep trouble, but listening to Monique just showed her how hopeless her situation was, and what she could expect. Her mind started to spin, trying to find a solution, an escape plan, just something to help, but before she could think of anything, the door opened. Instinctively her attention darted to the door, her eyes closing against the suddenly bright lights illuminating the room.

"Welcome to Asklepios! Rise and shine", a man laughed devilishly as he walked in.

- 14 -

Asklepios, Aegean Sea, Friday, July 18

"Okay, you know the drill!" Natascha heard someone shouting outside. Still groggy, she managed to keep her head high to look outside the door. She didn't see much, except for some sort of ramp which someone secured to their deck. Considering what she could see, Natascha had the feeling they were inside a closed structure somewhere. Natascha still tried desperately to develop a plan on how to escape, but there was no opportunity.

Monique's story revealing their horrible experience set a particular fear within Natascha, and she could feel the panic rising inside her. Despite all her training with Ariel and Shira the last few years, she still had a strong sense of helplessness. There was simply nothing she could do with her hands tied behind her back and remaining subject under the influence of whatever drugs they had given her. Nevertheless, Natascha had promised herself not to go down without a fight; she just had to gather some more information to be ready for the right opportunity should it present itself.

Natascha stared through the open door, but all she could see from her angle were the legs of four people, most likely men, who walked down the ramp and onto the shuttle boat. The echo of their shoes on the steel floor grew louder as they walked over to their cabin and through the door. Natascha guessed that they were of Eastern European heritage. They spoke to each other, but Natascha couldn't understand what they were saying. The way they spoke and how they acted made Natascha believe they were having a rather casual conversation.

Trying not to attract too much attention, Natascha lowered her head and closed her eyes enough that she could still see. Monique and Freja started to scream as two of the four guys carelessly picked up the person closest to the door and literally dragged her out of the cabin. Natascha was shocked by the brutality she had just witnessed and clenched her teeth, knowing she would receive the same treatment. While the two men dragged the unconscious women over the ramp and off the boat, the other two men stood guard at the door. The fluidity of their actions convinced Natascha this was not their first time. It only took about five minutes before the two guys came back to pick up the next person. Natascha didn't know who it was, but she noticed how they hesitated for a moment, before they started laughing and shaking their heads, all the time gesticulating wildly with their hands. They finally picked the person up, and Natascha frowned as she realised that this person was an older man. *So this is not only about young women?* As with the first thought, Natascha took some comfort in this fact.

While they dragged the unconscious man out, Natascha felt a twinge in her stomach at the familiarity of the man, but she couldn't quite place him yet. The drugs in her system seemed to have erased all her memory. The last thing she could remember was sitting at her desk at EuroSec, laughing with Shira. Natascha's search for where she knew this man from was cut short when the two men returned to pick up the next person. This time, the person moaned as they forcefully lifted him up, but that was the only reaction the older guy showed as they dragged him out and over the ramp. Again, Natascha felt the same twinge of familiarity.

"NO!" screamed Freja as they eventually came back to pick her up next. The two guys laughed at her and tossed her long blonde hair back. Overwhelmed with memories from her torture in the basement in Paris, Freja screamed even louder, but there was nothing she could do to stop them from picking her up. It seemed to Natascha that the more Freja tried to resist, the more they enjoyed it. Rage and disgust overwhelmed her, but Natascha eventually realised that her life was not in immediate danger and that her chances of a successful escape were literally non-existent.

"Don't resist them!" Natascha tried to whisper to Monique, who realised she would be next, but the young woman didn't listen to Natascha and started to scream frantically the moment the two men stepped through the door again. As Natascha had feared, they both looked at Monique and started laughing at her before aggressively pulling her to her feet. Like the other victims, Monique was too weak to offer any serious resistance. Her screams grew softer as they dragged her off the boat.

Okay, you're next! Natascha prepared herself mentally. She decided not to give her kidnappers the satisfaction of treating her like the others. Natascha rolled around to land on her knees. She quickly closed her eyes, swallowing hard as stomach acid burned deep in her throat. With her eyes closed, Natascha took a couple of deep breaths, trying to calm her stomach down and control her unbearable headache.

Natascha opened her eyes, took another deep breath and got up to her feet. She leaned her shoulder against the wall and had to repeat the breathing exercise to regain control over her body. After a few seconds, she felt comfortable enough to open her eyes again, but she still struggled to keep her balance when she pushed herself from the wall. She could hear by the chatter that the two men were on their way back to get their last victim.

Just as she looked at the door, the men walked in, their conversation stopping as quickly as their feet. Natascha recognised their surprise to see her standing on her feet. Natascha tried to say something, but she was too weak and just shook her head. It was now that she realised she had made a mistake. After what seemed to be an eternity, one guy started shouting at her, still in a language she couldn't understand.

"NO! I do not resist!" Natascha exhaustingly reassured and shook her head even more, but it turned out that the guy didn't care what she said. He kept shouting at her, his alarm causing the two other men to arrive as back-up. Natascha quickly realised her situation was getting worse, but there was nothing she could do further except plea her compliance.

The four men positioned themselves in a semi-circle around her, obviously uncertain what to do. Natascha had not forgotten how brutally they had treated the others, and she almost panicked at the thought of what they might do to her. Just as she looked up again, she realised that the guy who kept shouting at her was now pointing something at her as well. Natascha first didn't recognised what it was, but then realised he was pointing a stun gun.

"NO! NO!" Natascha begged now, horrified about the pain that this device could inflict on her. Her panic increased her capturers' confidence, and they started laughing.

"What the hell is going on here?" a man dressed in medical scrubs finally asked. Alarmed by the commotion, male nurse Lamar Hatcher had come down the ramp to check what was happening. Natascha was relieved to hear English, and the commanding voice deterred the guy with the stun gun. He lowered the taser and started to talk to Lamar. Natascha didn't know who the guy was, and she definitely didn't trust or regarded him as her saviour, but for now she was happy he had showed up. He was obviously in a position of authority over the other four men, who now gesticulated at Natascha several times trying to explain themselves. Since they still spoke their native language, Natascha had yet to understand what they were discussing, but she was somehow satisfied to see that the English speaking person waved them off and simply shook his head.

"For heaven's sake, she's just standing there. Her hands are still tied behind her back. Just bring her out", he yelled at them in English as he turned around and walked away without paying any attention to Natascha.

Two guys finally found enough courage and walked over to grab Natascha by her elbows before roughly pushing her towards the ramp. Natascha had difficulty keeping her balance, her legs and feet having trouble following her. Despite her efforts to rise to her feet and walk off the boat, she sensed she was still being dragged. She closed her eyes tightly from the bright lights. Her stomach churned as they dragged her over the ramp. The drugs were much stronger than she had thought.

Natascha opened her eyes again and looked around. To her right she saw the two familiar looking men getting dragged away through another door. She looked to her left and saw Freja and the other women they had taken first. She noticed they were sitting on chairs. Natascha expected all the women to be in their early twenties.

Natascha looked up again and saw Monique, in front of her were five people wearing medical scrubs. Four of them were men, and she recognised the one who had saved her from the stun gun, but there was also a young female nurse with flaming red hair.

"I'll take her from here", male nurse Kevin Wilson announced and grabbed Natascha's elbow roughly. He pushed her closer to Monique. The boat's crew were already on their way back and started to remove the ramp.

Natascha had no idea where she was, but the air quality was refreshing compared to the stench she had breathed inside the little shuttle boat. Natascha felt the adrenaline she had had moments earlier drain from her veins, leaving her struggling to keep her eyes open. She weakly looked to the man holding her up by her elbow. Natascha knew that if he would let go of her, she would collapse to the ground.

"Where...", Natascha whispered, incapable to string a sentence. She noticed he completely ignored her anyway.

Desperate, Natascha turned her head and watched how one of the men quickly examined Monique right in front of her. As it had happened to Natascha, everyone else was also affected by the fresher air and brighter light. Two people supported Monique to prevent her from collapsing. While she had been screaming desperately when they dragged her out of the shuttle boat, she was now barely conscious.

"Cute little thing. Reflexes are normal, given the circumstances. Other than that she seems to be fine. No obvious needle marks, so that's promising", the man who examined her said and watched as the redheaded woman helped Monique over to the chairs.

Natascha slowly determined that the man who had just examined Monique was obviously in charge. Not only was he clearly older than the rest, there was a certain stature that identified him as a doctor, separating himself from the nurses.

"Sorry, Doc, we didn't quite catch that. How are those categorised?" the third male nurse, Leo Swan, asked.

"Clean those three up and test them. The one with the long blonde hair is definitely group A if she tests positive. If she tests negative, we put her in group B. Same with that one over there. She still goes as a blonde", the doctor said looking at Monique. "We test if any of those three are a direct match to one of the organs that we need. If that's the case, we take what we need, if not, we just draw some blood and they go out right away. The two guys are obviously group C. Standard procedure for them as well", Dr Edwards ordered as the female nurse helped Monique over to the other two women.

"Whose idea was it to bring those two bumps anyway? I thought we weren't expecting any of them during this delivery?" Dr Edwards demanded to know, pointing his medical penlight daringly.

Natascha had to concentrate hard to understand what they were saying, but the way they talked about other human beings made her blood turn to ice. Just listening to them spent all her energy, and her eyes closed as her head dipped forward.

"I don't know", Kevin Wilson answered and shrugged his shoulders. "From what I was told, those two witnessed the guys snatching that one here. Apparently they came out of the nowhere from a park. There was no time, so they neutralised them with the taser and brought them here. They couldn't leave any witnesses behind, I suppose."

"Yeah, I suppose they couldn't. Well, if they're remotely healthy, we can make a couple hundred grand out of their organs. It will most likely be their largest favour to society lately", Dr Edwards spat coldly as he started to examine Natascha. By now, Natascha was so weak that a second person had to come over to help Kevin to keep her in an upright position.

"Just make sure she doesn't collapse on my feet, please", Dr Edwards asked as he pulled Natascha's head back by her hair. Natascha barely felt the pain and she struggled to open her eyes. Dr Edwards lifted her eyelids with his fingers, shining his bright medical penlight into her eyes to determine her pupillary response.

"She was awake when they tried to take her out from the shuttle?"

"Yes, she stood in the middle of the cabin. Scared the shit out of Mehmet and his gang. They didn't know what to do and almost shocked her. Mehmet already aimed his taser when I got there", Lamar explained. He was now supporting Natascha by her other elbow.

"Such idiots!" the doctor cursed the Turkish crew. "I'm more impressed she was able to stand. They gave her enough anaesthetics to put a horse down", the doctor commented as he quickly examined Natascha.

"So that's really her?" Dr William Edwards marvelled, concluding his examination.

"Considering the description, the tattoo and her age, yes, I'm positive. We will check her closer to be sure." Kevin assumed from the information he had.

"Well, Natascha, welcome to hell!" the British doctor smiled coldly, before he turned away.

It had been over three years since she had heard that malevolent tone. The words were simple, but their serrated edges cut deeply. Any comfort she had gathered since she had regained consciousness left her with an increased fear rippling through her veins. After her persistence to regain confidence, strength, and hope for a future, it was unbeknownst to her that the nightmare of the *Northern Explorer* expedition was still haunting her. The tormenting apprehension she tried desperately to wane became a terrifying reality. Not only had someone persistently hunted her, they had also found her.

- *15* -

***EuroSecCorporation*, London, Friday, July 18**
Brian Whittaker was soaked from the rain, but he even didn't notice it. His mind was too focussed to be disturbed by such a triviality. While his friend Klaus walked around the old wooden shed in the park, Brian stood at its door frame and looked inside. The rain was falling harder now as his eyes scanned the inside of what used to be a children's playhouse, but its only remaining purpose was to provide shelter for some homeless people now and then.

Brian knew about the two homeless men from his crew, but there was no sign of them, not to mention Natascha. Brian swallowed hard as he watched a young police officer collect the few items the homeless had carefully hung up to dry. For many people those items looked like garbage, but they were priceless and essential possessions for the two missing men. The retired admiral was uncertain what to look for, but whatever answer he was hoping to find in here, it remained hidden. With one last glance, he slowly retreated back into the heavy rain where he was soon joined by Klaus and Chief Inspector Conolly.

"Nothing", the retired general shook his head.

"My men have combed the entire area, but we found no sign of either Natascha or the two homeless." Chief Inspector Conolly added as he wiped the rain from his brow. "We brought in some dogs, but all the tracks end right here, so for the moment we believe this is the place where they put them in a getaway vehicle. My guys confirmed what your men found yesterday. There is no surveillance footage from any of the stores from across the street that covers this area. There are also no street view cameras, so we have nothing there", Conolly continued explaining and looked as frustrated as Klaus and Brian.

There was a lengthy pause as they considered the information, searching for the missing pieces of the puzzle, anything that would provide them a direction. Brian looked at Klaus, knowing he had nothing either. As the rain continued to pour, the retired admiral watched a young police officer carrying several clear plastic bags containing the few possessions the homeless had to a police van.

"We don't know their names yet. We didn't find any identification among those items. We'll pull some DNA from the sleeping bags and see if we can find something in our database. If they're registered somewhere, we should know their names shortly", the chief inspector explained what both Klaus and Brian already knew.

"How is Nick holding up?" Conolly turned to Brian after a few seconds. Brian knew his friend from Scotland Yard was sincerely concerned. They would never forget Conolly's loyalty and trust when Natascha had an international arrest warrant. Without him, it would have been more difficult to clear her name.

"Not very good", Brian answered with a sigh. "He's back at the office with their daughter and his closest friends. They're keeping an eye on him. I told him to go through their computer again. He and Natascha used the same, and he knows her passwords for her different online communication accounts. They already skimmed over her files yesterday, but they're going to take a closer look at them today. Maybe we can find something there that will point us in the right direction."

"Well, it would certainly be helpful. I still find it hard to believe that someone can pull this off in broad daylight in the middle of a park." Conolly shared his thoughts, surveying the area again as if he expected to see something new. Neither Klaus nor Brian said anything for a few moments. They all knew what they were thinking.

"Yes, this was a professional job." Brian agreed with a click of his tongue. "Damn well executed."

"Between the three of us", Conolly started and quickly looked around for any potential eavesdroppers. "Do you think an American agency sent a wet team to take her out?" the chief inspector asked, undeniably bringing up the worst case scenario.

"I honestly don't know, Bill. I can't see why? Everybody who was involved in orchestrating that ploy back then is dead. The former Chief of Staff, his personal aid, the head of his security detail, even the Canadian! They all committed suicide when the authorities came to pick them up. There is no one left. You've seen the reports and the pictures. You were there when the American ambassador gave Natascha the letter. You know the Intel yourself, they were happy this was all over. Besides, our friends from Israel haven't heard *any* chatter about someone being after Natascha. For heaven's sake, she didn't even have to change her name." Brian shook his head. All of this didn't make any sense.

"So what are the alternatives? You said someone had surveillance on her?"

"Yes, that's true. You got all the information about that already. Did you get anything from the licence plates?"

"They were all stolen, we're looking into that."

"Hm. That doesn't sound like a black op. Let me call the office for a moment", Brian excused himself and dialled Ariel's number from speed dial. The Israeli picked up after the third ring. "Ariel! Whittaker here. How's Nick doing? ...Well, stay close to him, will you?...How's his daughter?...Okay, that's at least a little bit better news. Ariel, I have a question. Do you know if the blue or grey Ford have been in the parking lot after Natascha disappeared?...No? Neither of them?...Okay, thank you. Is there anything else new?....No, we didn't find anything either. Klaus and I will walk back Natascha's jogging route, maybe we missed something...Any word from Israel yet?... Okay, you let us know as soon as they have something." Brian ended the call and shook his head looking at his friends.

"No sighting of either the blue or the grey Ford after Natascha disappeared, so that means they have been keeping an eye on Natascha as we suspected. Goddamn it!" Brian cursed and stormed towards the wooden shed again. His eyes scanned the now empty shed, but he still didn't find the missing clue. "Klaus, let's walk back to the office. Ariel said the rest of Operation Control will be back shortly. Maybe three new sets of eyes will help when we have a closer look at when they started to trail Natascha. If we have a detailed timeline, we should be able to draw some conclusions", Brian suggested looking at his long time friend who nodded his agreement.

"Okay, Brian, we'll keep each other informed", Chief Inspector Conolly said and quickly walked over to his car.

Brian still looked inside the shed as Klaus stepped up behind him. "Do you think it was him?" Klaus asked his friend, also scanning the inside of the shed.

"I don't know. It could be. Some of the stuff looks like his", Brian muttered shaking his head as he walked out into the rain again. Just as they started walking back the same route Natascha had taken, his eyes caught some movement on the other side of the street where several small storefronts were lined up. Brian stopped and took a closer look as an older gentleman closed his barber shop.

"What is it?" Klaus asked, looking the same direction.

"Remind me to get my hair cut tomorrow, okay?" Brian requested and continued walking.

"You want to get your hair cut? For what?" Klaus asked perplexed as he inspected Brian's fresh crew cut, not entirely sure what Brian was thinking.

Asklepios, Aegean Sea, Saturday, July 19

Natascha lay in her bed. Her eyes were closed and she could feel the tenderness of her cheeks from the tears that were pouring down her face. She still knew nothing; not the time or the day, and most definitely not where she was. She guessed she must have been crying for hours. Most of her memory was still a blur, but she could feel some relief that she was starting to regain control of herself. Her hands were cut loose from behind her back, and the effects of the drugs almost completely subsided.

The young woman had no idea how long it had been since that doctor had called her by her name, and she couldn't exactly remember what had happened afterwards. She had been so horrified she had simply stopped functioning. It was almost like everything after that moment had never happened. Natascha felt the deep bruise in her shoulder and remembered getting pushed into her room, where she finally picked herself up to crawl into the bunk. Under all the distress, she fell unconscious shortly after. It had probably been for hours now that she tried putting the pieces together, but there were still parts missing. It didn't help that her thoughts quickly staggered to self-pity and helplessness, not to mention the fear of her final outcome.

Shaking under another wave of tears, Natascha thought about her daughter. The thought of her child seemed distant like it was a part of another life. Even though Natascha had no idea where she was, she felt an unusual solace that Shira-Sarah was safe with Nick and her friends.

My daughter, my sweet baby girl! Natascha crumbled again, weeping harder under the anguish. She was not sure if she would ever see her again. *I have to see her again!* Natascha told herself in desperation. *I have to see her again!* Natascha repeated again after a few minutes, but this time it was more like a promise, a vow that she made not only to herself, but also to Nick.

Looking at the cold white ceiling, Natascha stopped crying and saw a third face in her mind. Shira! Her best friend and loyal confidant. She had selflessly taken a bullet for her without any hesitation or regret.

I'd be rather pissed if you give up now, just after I took that bullet for you! She could hear her Israeli friend talking to her. *Are you done crying? Because now would be the perfect time to get your ass out of that bunk and see what you can do. What information do you have and what are your resources?*

Underneath the emotional distress, Natascha was shocked about how well Shira and Ariel had trained her mentally. She pressed against her temples, knowing her Israeli friends were right. She wouldn't get out of this by lying in bed crying all day and night. *I have to do everything I can to get back home to my daughter. I have to pick myself up and come up with a plan.* Natascha told herself and swallowed hard. She wiped the tears from her face and sat up. Thinking about her daughter and Nick had given her new motivation, the much needed purpose. She slowly shook her head.

"This is not over yet!" Natascha eventually whispered and tried to remember what Shira and Ariel had taught her about such a situation. First she concentrated on her body, trying to find out if she was injured or if something was hurting. Besides the dull headache she felt relatively fine. She noticed she was still dressed in her running clothes, the black sweat pants and hoodie. Almost instinctively she removed a piece of lint from her pants, glad to see she was not stripped of them, especially considering the horror story that Monique had told her. The only things she was missing were her cell phone and wrist watch.

Natascha's thumb rolled over her wedding ring. Despite her situation, she could feel the faint butterflies as she thought of Nick. Natascha looked up from her ring, her hands falling to her lap. *I have to get out of here.*

With her body relatively intact and her mind functioning again, Natascha looked around for the first time. The bunk she used was barely one metre wide, and she could feel the support bars under the thin mattress. The steel walls and ceiling were painted in a cold white colour, and there was no window or any other furniture. She estimated the room to be around three by three metres square. She couldn't deny her *room* felt more like a cell. The floor consisted of green linoleum, and the whole cell was lit by one naked bulb hanging from the ceiling. Even the bulb was protected by a steel frame.

Opposite her bunk was a steel door, but Natascha didn't waste a second believing it was unlocked. Her eyes fell on the other opening, a door frame without door. Without even rising from her bed, Natascha could see a sink, a toilet, and even a shower. Her eyes concentrated on the ceiling, where she soon spotted metal covers for some air ventilation shafts and a typical surveillance camera lens protected behind a steel frame.

So whoever is watching you now knows that you're awake. Natascha told herself and pretended that she had not seen the camera. Slowly she rose to her feet and walked into the tiny bathroom where she immediately spotted a second camera. *So much for taking a shower!* Natascha thought and took another look around, but the only item she found was a cheap towel lying in the sink.

Natascha turned from her non-private bathroom and slowly paced her small cell trying to get the blood circulating in her body. Just as she turned around, she noticed a plastic water bottle beside her bed. She quickly picked it up and twisted the cap with desperation.

Wait! What if there's something mixed in it? She asked herself just as her lips made contact with the bottle. She did not recall hearing the distinct cracking sound of the seal breaking when she had hurriedly opened it. Resisting the urge to drink the whole bottle, Natascha sniffed at the water first, but didn't find that it smelled odd. Fighting the temptation, she decided to take a little sip and made sure she kept it against her lower lip. The water felt so refreshing that she fought swallowing it. She could almost hear Shira yelling at her, and she decided to walk to the bathroom and spit the little bit of water into the sink. The water tasted normal, and even after a few minutes she didn't feel anything different on her lips and tongue. She rolled the bottle in her hand before carefully taking another sip. Looking at it again, Natascha didn't feel as if she had drunk anything. She lowered the bottle with defeat, promising herself to drink more if she felt fine in an hour.

With the dry feeling in her mouth satisfied, Natascha returned to her previous objective. She searched for details in her attempt to remember how she had gotten in this mess in the first place. Instead of lying down, Natascha decided to keep pacing her small space to keep her circulation going.

Okay, what happened to me? How did I get here? After I visited Sarah, I walked out the door and started the music on my cell phone. Natascha pushed her daughter's face from her mind as a sharp pain tightened her chest. She then remembered that Nick had been unable to go with her. *Well, that would've changed things for sure.* Natascha decided not to waste any more energy on 'what ifs.' *There's nothing you can do to change what happened. All you can do is try to change what* will *happen. So concentrate! I got out of the building, started the music and ran the usual route down to the park. Think! Did someone follow you? Maybe that grey or blue car from the parking lot? What was it? A Ford?* Shira had taught her that she was more likely to remember important details when she interrogated herself, rather than just trying to remember them. That way she could use older, confirmed memories to link to new facts.

No, I have not seen them following me, but I also didn't pay any attention, to be honest. Okay, so I turned into the park. There were only a few people there since it started to rain. So whatever happened to me had to happen soon after because my clothes are completely dry. Wait a second! I came close to that old shed, and wondered if the two homeless men would be there. I saw them standing at the door, and they waved at me like always. I waved back as I passed them. That's all I can remember! Natascha stopped for a second and took another sip from the bottle. She was confused, but it didn't matter how hard she tried to remember; her memory was blotted out from the moment she had seen the two homeless men standing inside that shed. Yet, for some unknown reason, she didn't believe they had anything to do with her abduction. Taking another sip, she paced her tiny cell once more. *The memory will come back eventually. Just keep asking yourself what happened;* Natascha remembered another one of Ariel's lectures. Her efforts to reconstruct her memory ceased when she heard the lock of the steel door opening. Not sure what to expect and fully aware that she couldn't escape, Natascha simply turned around to face the door as it opened. To her surprise, the first thing she noticed was the ambitious expression on the redheaded woman's face. A male nurse accompanied her. Natascha soon recognised him as the one who had prevented her from being neutralised by the taser. As far as she remembered, his name was Lamar. For the first time she was able to get a closer look at him. Natascha guessed him to be in his early thirties, about as tall as herself, but clearly overweight.

"Why is she awake?" the redhead nurse bellowed, her disgust of Natascha's condition clearly evident in her voice. Natascha quickly scanned her. She didn't know why, but just from looking at her, she knew that they would never be friends. Natascha guessed she was in her late twenties, and she was slightly shorter than herself, but definitely athletic.

"Relax, Melissa. Dr Evans ordered not to sedate her", the man explained.

"But why? We sedate everybody else." Melissa demanded to know. She was still very upset that Natascha just stood there watching them and drinking some water.

"Orders from the highest place, I suppose. I don't know why, and I'm not going to ask, and neither should you. We have to go, we already wasted enough time. The doctor wants to see her."

Natascha followed their conversation with great interest and realised that Melissa was obviously nervous about Natascha's condition. Lamar seemed to be in charge between the two of them, and Natascha was glad he was much calmer. Natascha noticed they did not address her directly, which she assumed was to maintain an emotional distance to prevent bonding. That was something Natascha was concerned about, so she decided to wait for them to talk to her.

"Put the water down now and you can keep it for later. Turn around and place your hands behind your back. You got three seconds, or you'll experience a new level of pain", Lamar instructed and pointed a stun gun at her. Melissa smiled devilishly as she held up the handcuffs.

Realising there was nothing she could do at the moment, Natascha obeyed. Besides, the guy had mentioned that a doctor wanted to see her and that she would be back in the cell later. Considering that, Natascha determined that her life wasn't in any immediate danger. She took one last sip of water and obliged by throwing the closed bottle onto her bunk before turning around with her hands behind her back. It didn't take two seconds before she felt Melissa roughly securing the handcuffs. The Irish woman pinched Natascha with the cuffs as she tightened them more than necessary. The sudden pain forced Natascha to bite her lip. She did not want to give the redhead the pleasure of showing any signs of pain if she could help it.

"Can you please tell me where we are going?" Natascha asked, looking at Lamar. She hoped to be regarded as a human being by addressing the guy personally, rather than asking a general question, but he didn't answer her and just guided her along the corridor by her elbow. Natascha decided that it would be best not to push him and remained silent, taking mental notes about where they were going.

No windows...staircase to the right...all the other doors look like mine, so they're dead ends...emergency staircase to the left...no signs for communication.

Before she could gather any more information, Melissa opened a double-wing door and Natascha's surprise was evident. Right in front of her was a large medical treatment room that would rival most modern hospitals in Europe. Overwhelmed by the unexpected sight, Natascha slowed down, only to be pushed forward again by both Melissa and Lamar. She clenched her teeth again under the tightened handcuffs. A woman in a white lab coat briefly looked up from her computer before she gestured to an empty chair right beside her.

"Take her handcuffs off, but stay right here", she said apathetically.

Before this is over I'm going to punch that bitch on the nose! Natascha swore herself as Melissa unlocked the restraints and unnecessarily pushed her towards the chair.

"Take your sweatshirt off", Dr Evans ordered. Natascha hesitated for a moment, not certain where this would lead, but then she noticed that the doctor was reaching for her stethoscope and the cuff for the sphygmomanometer to read her blood pressure. Natascha knew this wasn't because the doctor was concerned about her well being. Taking in some details of the room, Natascha knew the guy behind her still had the taser, and he would not hesitate to use it. Reluctantly, Natascha took her hooded sweatshirt off, and she could smell her sweat.

Well, it sure won't hurt if I smell bad, Natascha told herself but tried not to show any other reaction. While the doctor measured her blood pressure, Natascha checked out all the monitors on her desk. It was the monitor on the left that caught her attention. Every few seconds it switched to a different surveillance camera, and Natascha recognised the water bottle she had thrown on her bunk in one of the images. Trying to win some more time, Natascha simulated a coughing fit.

"I'm sorry", she apologised, earning a stern look from Dr Evans. She had to start the reading for the blood pressure again. The extra time was all that Natascha needed to check out the additional images of the surveillance camera before recognising her own cell again. She had lost count of the individual cells, but they were all empty anyway. The one image she was interested in was of a much larger room, which showed at least ten or twelve people in it. But before Natascha could concentrate more on the image, the doctor started to rummage through a drawer.

"Wow, wow, wow! No thank you!" Natascha disapproved as she realised that Dr Evans prepared some vials for drawing her blood.

"You want me to strain her arm?" Lamar immediately offered. He moved so quickly that Natascha could almost feel his breath on her neck as he spoke.

"No, that won't be necessary. She won't resist. She has too much self-preservation to be that stupid. Isn't that right?" the doctor asked and, for the first time, looked directly into Natascha's eyes. Natascha couldn't help making a face, but she certainly didn't want to argue with the female doctor and held her arm out. Although she knew what to expect, Natascha still winced as Dr Evans injected the needle into her arm.

I'll definitely punch that bitch in the face! Natascha promised herself as she heard Melissa laughing at her reaction.

"Okay, that's it. Melissa, can you please bring those to the lab when we're done here?" Dr Evans said as she pulled the needle out of Natascha's arm. "I'm just going to check your pupillary response. I heard you were active rather quickly?" she asked Natascha with a note of surprise. Natascha didn't know what to answer and just shrugged as the doctor shone her medical penlight into her eyes. Satisfied with what she had seen, the doctor made some notes in the computer and allowed Natascha to put her sweater back on.

"What are we going to do with her?" Lamar asked.

"We can put her in the common room with the others for now, but until we receive further instructions, we separate her for the night and lock her up in her room."

"Should we sedate her?"

"No, we don't. We were told not to", the doctor eventually explained.

Natascha noticed that Lamar frowned at this answer, but he certainly didn't want to argue with Dr Evans and simply stepped towards Natascha. Not trying to show any form of resistance, Natascha rose from her chair and followed his instruction as he and Melissa led her out of the examination room and down the corridor again. Before they reached her cell, Lamar used his magnetic key card and a punch code to open the door to the stair case, which they followed to the floor below. Using his magnetic card and a punch code again, Lamar opened the door to another corridor and led Natascha to a double-winged door. She was now directly underneath the large examination room, but the double-wing doors here could only be opened with the magnetic card and the code. Natascha couldn't see the exact combination, but she observed enough to know that he had used a different four-digit combination for each door so far. Not only did this door require the magnetic card and the punch code, it also had two guards in front of it. Each man was equipped with a stun gun, a baton, and several sets of flex-cuffs.

"Lamar", the one guard nodded while he and his friend carefully watched Natascha. It seemed to be unusual for them to see someone not heavily sedated in this part of the facility. Natascha pretended she didn't notice them staring at her and waited for the door to open. When it finally did, the blood in her veins rushed cold as ice.

EuroSecCorporation, London, Saturday, July 19

I would unleash hell, Brian's thoughts drifted down to the private conversation he and Shira had had in his office not too long ago. *Forget unleashing hell. What we got is not even enough heat for a bloody barbecue*, the retired admiral thought, hiding his frustration as he watched the remaining five members of their Operation Control taking their seats in the control room.

"Okay, where are we at?" Klaus asked his employees.

"I've sent out notification to all our security staff at the malls and the airports, but so far we've not heard back from anyone."

"They all received a current picture?" Brian asked their secretary.

"Yes, I sent them one to their cell phones, so they have permanent access to it."

"Okay. Let's hope they pick something up. Sean, do you have anything else?" the retired admiral continued without missing a beat. Sean MacLeod had been Chief Inspector Conolly's predecessor at Scotland Yard and was still very well connected with his former colleagues.

"Not that much at the moment, Brian. They've agreed to use me as an unofficial liaison, but we know about the legal implications that our own *investigation* can bring", the former chief inspector started.

"Yes, we all know about the legal implications and we don't give a damn about them", Brian cut him off. "Continue!"

"They didn't find much since you and Klaus talked to Bill yesterday. They're processing the belongings from the two homeless men. No identification yet, but they're convinced the items are from two male adults, as we all assumed."

Brian slammed his empty hand on the table, obviously disappointed with that result.

"My apologies! Continue!"

"The tire tracks, if they're connected to the actual crime, can be from any commercial van on the market built in the last four years. They're looking at tens of thousands of vehicles that are using those tires, but they're trying to narrow it down. They're also looking into those two Fords from your parking lot, but they haven't much to go on there either."

"Bloody hell! What else?"

"No surveillance, no witnesses, not even that useless street gang has seen anything!"

"So Scotland Yard has nothing?" Brian summed it up, his frustration clearly evident in his voice.

"No, they don't, but Conolly is pushing them really hard. Both Interpol as well as Europol are also informed, but I haven't heard back anything. Their cyber crime unit is also monitoring the internet to see if her name or some references to her person are popping up somewhere, but that's also negative so far. There hasn't been any statements or demands posted on the internet yet. I'll drive over to Scotland Yard as soon as we're done here."

"Thank you, Sean", Brian said and watched as Brigitte added the additional information on the timeline. Right beside the timeline was a large picture of Natascha. Her beautiful smile in the photo seemed different now. The purpose of the photo was to constantly remind everyone why they were here, and Brian knew it was working.

"Jack, what did you find out?" Klaus addressed Jack MacDonald, the former British SAS Team Leader.

"Unfortunately, not much. I spent all morning with Team C in the park. You all know they're former SAS, and some of the lads are pretty good trackers. We looked at everything, but we didn't find any additional evidence that the police might have overlooked. We watched for people who visit the park on a regular basis and asked them, but they didn't notice anything unusual. The only information we got was about the two homeless men", Jack explained as Brian got more anxious. "We had two joggers confirm the two were back at the shed for about a week. I'll take my lads again this afternoon and see if we can find some more people who might have been in that area during the actual time of abduction. Maybe we'll get lucky", the former SAS Team Leader closed with some optimism.

"Yes, you do that. Gunnar, what's your status?" Brian continued immediately.

"Three guys from Team A are on their way to Germany to pick up Natascha's parents. We first considered preparing the safe house, but Shira persuaded us to move Natascha's parents into Nick's house. That way Sarah won't be forced out of her trusted environment and Shira and Talia are right there. That was the plan Shira, correct?" Gunnar asked his Israeli friend for confirmation.

"Yes, that's correct. Sarah is very comfortable around Talia and me. We'll both move up to Nick's unit to keep her company. Natascha's parents will stay in our unit downstairs. We'll also make sure that at least three people are around Sarah at all times. It's important to Nick that she continues with her daily routine as much as possible."

"Hm, okay. I agree. How's Sarah doing anyway?" Brian asked out of courtesy.

"For now she's doing fine, considering the circumstances. She's highly influenced by Nick's emotions, which is why we're trying hard to keep her distracted, but I'm not sure how long we can keep that going."

"And how's Nick doing?" Brian continued, but this time he knew he didn't want to know the answer. As he had expected, both Shira and Ariel just looked at him. They didn't have to say what the retired admiral already knew.

"That's what I thought", Brian whispered and nodded before looking at Gunnar Eriksson again. "Was there anything else, Gunnar?"

"No, not for the moment", the former instructor for the Norwegian Navy Special Operations Commando replied.

"Ariel, Shira, what about Israel? Did they hear anything?" Brian wanted to know further. He almost sounded desperate, but he knew about the vast net of *sayanim*, the secret worldwide brotherhood, who would go great lengths for information to help protect Israel.

"I visited the embassy yesterday morning and briefed them over a secure video conference", Ariel started. "They promised us to immediately spread the word and to keep us informed. Shira or I will be the official contact. We agreed to call in once a day for updates, unless something important comes up. When I mentioned what has happened, they were very surprised. According to them, there was absolutely no indication that something like this would happen. They keep looking everywhere."

"How long until we'll hear back from the sayanim?" Brian asked the impossible.

"Could be hours, could be days, could be never. You know the answer to that question, Brian." Shira answered.

"Yeah, I know." Brian mumbled as they all looked at Natascha's gigantic picture on the wall. "Your people have her latest photo?" Brian wanted to make sure, but he knew that neither Shira nor Ariel would make such a crucial mistake as forgetting that.

"Of course they do, Brian. We sent it with all the other information." Shira answered nevertheless.

No one spoke for the next few minutes as they all stared at the board, trying to think if they might have forgotten something that could help them find her.

"Shira, do you know if Nick has found anything important on their laptop?" Klaus finally asked, breaking the silence.

"No, we haven't found anything yet. Nothing in her e-mails indicates anything different from what we know already. She made some extensive notes about that abbey where they went for a dive, but nothing that is concerning."

"I don't know, maybe she did stumble upon something up there. Might be worth looking at. Do you know the people she was there with?" Klaus asked, desperate for a lead.

"No, I only met them once at their wedding. Nick might know them a little bit better."

"Tell him to contact them, maybe they know something. Ariel, have you been at the aquarium?" Klaus asked hopefully.

"Yes, and everyone there was genuinely shocked when they heard about it. I spoke to her co-workers, but the aquarium is a dead end."

Klaus shook his head. He shared Brian's opinion that they were simply overlooking one important piece of information.

"Come on, all we need is a break. One tiny, little break. Is that too much to ask for?" Brian muttered under his breath before he looked at Shira. "Shira, I know I've asked you before, but you are certain that Natascha didn't just leave with another guy to wipe the slate clean and start a new life somewhere else? We all know that she seemed happy and all that, but we also know that she had gone through a very stressful time, and she couldn't just go to a shrink and tell him what happened."

"I've been living downstairs for two years, and I find it highly unlikely that Natascha was capable of living a secret life without me noticing it. Yes, they had their arguments, but certainly nothing that would make her run away like that. She cares about her daughter too much. That's not the Natascha we know." Shira vowed for her friend.

"No, it's not", Brian agreed. "I just want to make sure we covered every avenue. Does anyone else have anything to add? Anyone believe there's another angle we have to look at this from?" Brian asked and stood up, looking around the room hopefully. "Okay, we'll meet again this evening at twenty-hundred hours. If someone is looking for me, I'm going to get a haircut", the retired admiral announced and briskly walked out of the conference room. While everybody looked at Klaus for an explanation, Brian was already in the elevator and on his way down. Just minutes later he steered one of the companies Land Rovers out of the parking lot and towards the park. Once there, he circled around and looked for a parking spot close to the barber shop he had watched from the park the previous day. The retired admiral parked the large SUV on the side of the road before he walked over to the shop.

"Hi George, how are you doing today?" Brian greeted as he walked through the door.

"Brian! Good to see you again. I was wondering when you would walk in", the barber greeted his long time friend.

"Yeah, I figured you'd be expecting me", Brian said and sat down in a chair, where he picked up the latest newspaper and started reading.

George Davis was a traditional barber and operated this very location for over thirty years. Not only did he and Brian know each other for decades, they had also been close friends back in school.

Brian waited the few minutes for his friend to finish with his current customer. Once the gentleman had left the business, George invited Brian over to sit in the barber's chair.

"What do you want me to do? Just polish it?" George joked about Brian's military style crew cut.

"Might as well", Brian replied half-heartedly. During any other occasion, he would have laughed, but he was certainly not in the mood. Natascha was like a daughter to him, and her disappearance weighed heavily on his mind.

"I've seen you and Klaus in the park yesterday with all those cops. I assume something important happened, since you stood there in the pouring rain."

"Yes, George, something very important happened", Brian replied and quickly filled his friend in. George was so shocked he had to sit down for a few minutes.

"My God! That's horrible. I'm sorry to hear that, my friend", he stuttered, but it took him a while before he regained his thoughts. He got up and quickly disappeared through a door to the back of his small shop, from where he returned just a minute later carrying a bottle and two glasses.

"Here, you might as well", he offered and generously poured Brian a drink.

"Bloody hell, why not?" Brian reasoned, accepting the glass from his friend, "Cheers, mate."

"So, how can I help you?" George started a new beat and raised his hands in a helpless gesture. He was not entirely sure what he could do for his friend, except listen to him.

"George, you've been running this barber shop from this location for over thirty years now. I just want to ask you two things."

"I'm afraid you'd say that", George nodded and sat down again.

"Have you seen anything that could help me get her back?" Brian asked from his chair, all the time staring through the window at the back of the wooden shed across the road in the park. George got up and walked over to the window. He had to see the shed for himself, trying to remember if he had seen something unusual. He couldn't recall anything in particular, definitely nothing that looked like an abduction. But then something occurred to him.

"Actually there was something. There was a black transport van parked there during the time you mentioned. Three or four guys, all wearing ball caps, were in and out of the van, working on that old box from the phone company. I found that odd, since that box has been out of service for a couple of years now. They weren't there for long, just a few minutes."

"Do you remember anything about the transporter?" Brian's interest peaked, and he turned his attention to his friend, searching his face for more information.

"Black Mercedes Sprinter, not that old."

"Did you see any markings on it? A logo maybe?"

"It had some advertising from a cable company on it, but I really don't know what it was. But it was just writing, no logo. It was dark, maybe black or grey", George shook his head. He was obviously disappointed that he couldn't be of any more help.

"Don't worry, that's already a huge help. What about the guys. You said there were three or four of them?"

"Yes, three or four, plus the driver. The driver never got out, at least not that I saw. They were all dressed the same, dark coveralls and ball caps. That's all I saw."

"Do you remember if there was anyone else around who could've witnessed this?"

George looked at Brian, a sad expression on his face.

"No, I don't think there are any witnesses", George was unable to conceal the disappointment in his voice. Slowly the barber sat down again.

"What do you mean, George? You're telling me they can abduct a woman in broad daylight and no one sees anything?"

"Brian, you know this area. This isn't the finest part of London. This is the outskirts of the industrial park. The people who live here are poor, they're used to crime. Even if they've seen something, they'll never come out as a witness. Look around you!" George said and gestured out through the window. Brian knew his old friend was right, but he just refused to give up, especially with this valuable information.

"Yes, I know the area. I grew up here, too", Brian admitted, much calmer now. "There's another question I want to ask you. I told you that we believe there were two homeless men in the shelter during the time of the abduction. All their belongings were still in there, but they're missing, too. We know they're not the perpetrators, which makes them important witnesses. Do you know what happened to them?"

"No, I don't." George answered honestly and shook his head.

"Given the circumstances and what we know so far, we actually believe, and the police shares our opinion, that they either might have seen something while it happened, or that they might have even tried to help Natascha. For either reason, the perpetrators had to kidnap them as well. Does this sound reasonable to you?"

"Well, I suppose. They were enough to do that, besides they all looked rather tall, so they might have had the muscle as well."

"That's what I'm afraid of", Brian commented and shook his head, still looking at the area that was taped off with police tape. Brian felt the heat from the question that was burning him deepest, the question that had brought him here in the first place. He swallowed hard, afraid to hear the answer.

"George, the two homeless men..."

"Yes, Brian. It was them. It was Charles and Lawrence."

"So it was my brother..." Brian's face paled as his fear became reality.

- 16 -

Asklepios, Aegean Sea, Sunday, July 20
Holy Shit! This is a hell hole! Natascha shook her head and stared at the ceiling. After what she had witnessed yesterday, her confidence had simply vanished.

I must look like hell. She had no mirror, but she knew there were dark rings around her red eyes. Although she had basically passed out with exhaustion last night, the recurring nightmares of her time on board the *Northern Explorer* had immediately returned and had kept her awake for most of the night.

She could feel the exhaustion in her bones; her fear of getting captured had materialised. It was the second time that she found herself being locked up in a tiny cell, but this time she had little hope for survival. Back then, her friends, who had been hired to protect her, had been on the ship with her, allowing her to escape physically unharmed. She had them to rely on, but now it was that much more frightening. Worse still, she had no idea why she was here in the first place.

This time she was all alone, and, as far as she knew, her friends had no idea where to look for her. After what she had seen yesterday behind those double doors, she wasn't even sure how long she would still be alive. It had taken her two years to get rid of the nightmares, but now they bombarded her in just one night.

I'm not getting out of this! The young scientist thought and shook her head. Natascha crouched in her bunk, her nose was rubbed raw and her face traced with tears. She looked at the little water left in the bottle. Slowly, she picked it up, emptied it and tossed the bottle on the floor, staring at the corner of her little cell. It didn't matter where she looked, everything inside this cell was too familiar. Her worst memories resurfaced, flashing back in sequences. She could suddenly even smell the same stale air, the paralysing sense of fear and the loss of control.

Pull yourself together! You managed to escape once, you can do it again! Natascha told herself, taking a deep breath.

No! You didn't escape! You sat in the cabin crying all day and night, and your friends had to drag your ass out of there! You didn't do anything! She immediately argued with herself. Natascha closed her eyes and punched her mattress. She hated herself for being so negative.

Come on! You can do better than this! You're not the only one held hostage here, but you are the only one who's not drugged out of your mind. Use that to your advantage! Natascha told herself and tried to push her negative experiences aside.

For heaven's sake, fight! This is not what they taught you! You have to get back! You can do this! Use memories! Use positive memories! My daughter! Nick! My parents! My friends! Natascha forced herself to think of something positive, and she noticed her energy slowly coming back. She continued to think of a successful self-defence class, always followed by a memory of her daughter and Nick. Ariel's lecture came back to her mind. She *knew* she could defend herself against much stronger people; she just had to find the right motivation. Her memories flew by, each one growing more intense, until she thought of one of her latest classes when she had fought back two guys.

Flip the switch! She could hear Ariel telling her as she remembered how she had gotten out from underneath Ole-Einar, even breaking his nose during the exercise. Natascha clenched her teeth and finally punched her mattress again, this time with much more power than before. Her determination to survive was finally back.

Okay, let's try this again! You managed to escape once, you can do it again. Yes, I had help from my friends, but I didn't know what I know now. I can do this! I will do this! I will find a way to get out of this! Think! Go back to the park when you were kidnapped. What happened? Natascha asked herself and immediately hit a road block again. She still couldn't remember what had happened.

I remember I ran past that wooden shed and the two homeless guys waved at me. Why can't I remember what happened next? What else did I see? Something was different! The van! There was a black van parked beside the track just behind the shed. It had some sort of advertising on it. What was it? I'm not sure, but there were two guys working on something in the bushes. What were they working on? I think there is a box from a phone or cable company. That's it! That's what they were working on. Okay! What happened next? I kept running and the door from the van opened. There was another person inside the van...He called me...I looked...what happened next? Natascha raised from her bed, starting to pace back and forth in her little cell as her memory slowly came back. The next thing she remembered was excruciating pain.

That idiot shocked me with a taser! That's how it was. He shocked me with a taser and I fell down...No! I didn't! The other two guys working on that box in the bushes caught me. They were right behind me! They threw me into the van, but the door didn't close immediately. Why not? The two homeless guys! They came to help me! They shocked them as well! And then they threw them into the van! Those were the two guys on that boat, that's how I recognised them! They're here! So the door closed and we immediately took off. Natascha finally remembered, but she had to admit that everything else from then on was just a blur, most likely because she had been shocked. *Maybe not only because of the taser! They injected me with some drugs and that's when I passed out!*

Natascha was satisfied that she finally remembered the last moments before she had been drugged. She didn't try to dig any deeper, she knew the drugs had literally wiped her memory clean of details.

Maybe it will come back later, she told herself and sat down on her bunk again.

So I do have at least two allies here in this godforsaken whatever it is. Natascha tried desperately to remember if she had seen the two homeless people yesterday in the large recovery room behind the double doors, but she was convinced she had seen neither of them or the other two young women from the ambulance shuttle.

What were their names? Monique and Freja, I believe. Natascha recalled her memory, but she was certain she had not seen them either.

So technically I have more than just two allies on my side. I don't even have to convince them to help me. I just have to gain their trust. The issue is getting them off the drugs.

Natascha was so deeply caught in her thoughts that she shrieked when Melissa opened the steel door again. *Show time!* Natascha encouraged herself under her sudden fright.

"Turn around, hands behind your back, no questions, no talking!" Lamar ordered and showed her the handcuffs. Natascha hesitated for a second to weigh her options, but quickly decided to obey as Melissa pointed the taser at her with purpose. Like the day before, they led Natascha by her elbow through the corridor and down the stairs before stopping in front of the double-wing doors.

Natascha watched closely as Lamar used his electronic key card, and it seemed as if he used the same combination as yesterday, but Natascha couldn't read all the numbers. Two different men guarded the double-wing doors this time, and Natascha quickly caught a glimpse at one of their wrist watches. She only noticed that it was around eleven o'clock, but she had no idea if that was in the morning or in the evening. Without sunlight and with her interrupted sleep she had no idea if it was day or night.

Natascha took a deep breath as the door opened. As rude as usual, Melissa punched Natascha's back, propelling her through the doorway. *She's so going to lose some teeth!* Natascha promised herself, fighting to resist the urge to turn around and head-butt the redhead. Instead, she exhaled sharply to keep as calm and level-headed as she could. She focussed on scanning the room and the patients again.

No! They're not patients! They're prisoners! Natascha corrected herself as she glanced at the beds. There were even more beds there today than yesterday. Natascha counted a total of eighteen beds, each of them occupied with a patient who was either strapped to the frame or so heavily sedated that they could barely move. Some of them were only able to move their head from one side to the other, while some cried and others sobbed silently. Four men stood guard at the two doors leading out of the room, and Natascha saw the same two male nurses working here today as yesterday.

"Make yourself useful before we change our mind and drag your ass back to your cell!" Melissa ordered and pushed Natascha forward again. Natascha grit her teeth, holding her tongue. She could feel her nails digging into the palms of her hands as they balled into tight fists at her sides. She swallowed hard, evaluating her odds again. Yes, she was no longer handcuffed, but she was still outnumbered. She paused momentarily and knew that it would have been very stupid to react. Instead, she massaged her wrists and slowly walked to a cabinet in the corner where she picked up a pair of latex gloves and a surgical mask.

"Guys, keep an eye on her. If she does anything stupid, taser and handcuff her", Melissa instructed the guards with a tone of satisfaction in her voice. Natascha chose to ignore her and walked towards the first bed.

Assuming that the two male nurses would do the actual medical treatment on the prisoners, Natascha couldn't do much more than hold their hands and try to comfort them. As she got closer, Natascha immediately recognised Monique. Natascha hastened over and checked on the young French, but she was barely conscious.

"No! Don't...", was all that Monique could manage, shaking her head the moment Natascha took her hand.

"It's okay! It's me! Talia! Remember me? We came in on the same boat", Natascha softly reminded her, rubbing the back of her hand.

"Yes..." Monique groaned and nodded with recollection. "Freja?...Where is...?" she whispered with exhaustion. Natascha quickly looked around and found the Swedish woman lying in the next bed.

"She's right here beside you. Wait, I'll just check how she's doing", Natascha promised and quickly turned around to look at her. Like Monique, she was just waking up and barely recognised Natascha.

"She's just waking up, but seems to be doing fine", Natascha tried to convince Monique, holding her hand again.

"Why are you...? You one of them?" Monique whispered, being more suspicious now as she realised Natascha walked around freely.

"No, no, I'm not. You remember I was with you on that boat. I don't know what they want from me, but you can trust me, okay? I will help you!" Natascha promised with a smile. Only time would tell if Monique would believe her or not, but at least she returned her smile as best as she could for now. Natascha's care for her two friends got interrupted when one of the male nurses walked over towards them.

"We'll serve something to drink and some food in about thirty minutes. You can help us wake them up", he instructed Natascha before he turned around and ignored her again.

Natascha turned her attention back to Monique and carefully stroked her hair.

"Go and help Freja. She's in bad shape", Monique pleaded, shifting her weight in her bed.

"I will be back soon", Natascha promised and turned around. There was a spark in Freja's eye when she saw Natascha. She knew she recognised her from the boat. Natascha fought hard to keep her tears back as she scanned the room again. Natascha knew what had happened to Monique and Freja, and seeing the other thirteen young women in this room, she assumed they might have met the same fate. She felt her gut clench.

Since the two male nurses worked on the other patients beside her, Natascha decided to step across the aisle to check on the other prisoners. Natascha noticed three new faces and to her surprise, they were all men. Stepping between two beds, she finally recognised the two homeless people from the park. The fact they were now dressed in green hospital gowns made it more difficult for Natascha to recognise them.

"Hey, here you are!" Natascha finally smiled and took the hand of the person closest to her. The man slowly opened his eyes. His restraints were relatively loose, allowing them some movement.

"Here, let me help you. That's the least I can do", Natascha offered and assisted the man as he tried to sit in a more comfortable position. "I know both of you tried to help me in the park. I want to thank you for that!" Natascha quickly told them.

"Never mind, it didn't work out that well", the one guy groaned. "Do you know where we are?"

"No, sorry, I just know this is some sort of a hospital. Looks like a relatively modern medical facility to me, but that's all I know. I have yet to see a window", Natascha shared all the info she had. She knew she could at least trust these two.

"Yeah, we figured that much. They ran some tests on us for hours yesterday, but no one said a word."

Natascha carefully listened and was surprised. Natascha recalled the female doctor had only checked her vitals and drawn some blood.

"What's your name anyway?"

"Talia", Natascha lied. Although she trusted them in one way, she wasn't planning to reveal her real name. This was another one of Ariel's and Shira's lessons that she followed.

"I'm Lawrence. My friend's name is Charles."

Natascha turned around and helped Charles to get into a more comfortable position.

"Did you say *Talia*?" Lawrence reconfirmed.

"Yes", Natascha answered and immediately felt uneasy. *Do they know my real name?* She wondered.

"You're one of the Israeli's my brother hired?"

"What?" Natascha asked, the shock evident in her voice.

"Talia! That's an Israeli name. My brother hired four more Israeli women. You must be one of them?"

"Your brother? Brian Whittaker is your brother?" Natascha was stunned.

"Yes, he's the one."

Natascha was so taken by surprise that she was lost for words.

"But if he's your brother, why are you...how...", Natascha stammered, unable to find the right words.

"Why am I living on the street, you wonder?" Lawrence laughed with a cough.

"Yes", Natascha admitted and looked apologetically. She felt like she had crossed a line with her question, but somehow it didn't seem to matter now.

"It's a long story, but it's my choice. The government doesn't do much for veterans, so I have no place to go." Lawrence's voice was filled with bitterness, and Natascha decided to drop the subject. After all, it was none of her business.

"Do you have any idea what's going on and what they're going to do with us?" Natascha asked after a while. Charles and Lawrence just exchanged looks.

"No, we don't know what they want to do, but I can guarantee you it won't be pretty", Lawrence answered matter-of-factly.

"No, most definitely not", Natascha replied in frustration.

"Did they do anything to you?" Lawrence asked. His concern was sincere.

"No", Natascha quickly shook her head and glanced around, wondering if anyone would say something about them talking too much. "There was a female doctor who just took some blood and did a general check-up, but that was about it. Some of the other girls here have not been so lucky. They're in rough shape." Natascha whispered and swallowed hard. All her mental training aside, Natascha had to admit she feared for her life. "I'd open your restraints, but all the guards have tasers and orders to shock us if we do something. I'm trying to find out a little bit more", Natascha whispered as she leaned over Lawrence to wipe his forehead.

"Just don't get caught, we can't help you like this", he whispered back. Knowing she had found her first two allies, Natascha immediately felt a little bit better, but that feeling was short lived as one of the male nurses approached her.

"Hey, you can help the other two with the food." Kevin Wilson instructed her.

Natascha looked at Kevin, who gestured to one of the doors at the other side of the room. Natascha walked over as the double-wing doors opened. A younger guy and a very young woman pushed a hospital trolley through the door.

"Kyle?" Natascha didn't believe her eyes as the young man turned around. It was indeed Kyle McRae, the young reporter she had so desperately tried to contact. Kyle's attention turned to her, but he only gave her a puzzled look. Natascha flinched as she saw his face. There were several dark bruises that covered his face, evidence their capturers had beaten him. The young reporter also seemed to be suffering from sleep deprivation; and it looked like he could barely stay awake. A gleam crossed his eyes when he recognised Natascha's face from somewhere; but he didn't quite make the connection yet.

"We briefly met in London at that fundraiser gala when you talked to that bishop!" Natascha quickly explained in a whisper as they neared the first bed. She briefly glanced up to see if the male nurses or guards were suspicious, but their attention was elsewhere. Bringing the trolley to a stop in front of the bed, Kyle looked at Natascha again.

"Right. You...you're one of them! You were with the bishop", he stammered as he finally seemed to recognise her face. He took a step backwards.

"No! I'm not! I wasn't there with the bishop, remember? I actually tried to contact you. I..." Natascha stopped as one of the guards looked at her, the rise of her voice attracting their attention. "I picked up that letter you gave to the bishop, and I think I found some evidence to prove your grandmother's story", Natascha hastily whispered. Kyle just stared at her and shook his head. It was clear he did not believe her. Natascha decided that it was better not to say anything further for the moment. Thinking about it, Natascha eventually understood his reaction. After all, she had sort of taken the bishop's side. It was obvious why he didn't trust her. Hoping that she would get a chance to talk to him later, Natascha simply continued with her task and handed out trays with food. She noticed they were serving sandwiches, and realised there were no utensils she could steal for future use. Natascha felt a shiver descend her spine as this reminded her of the nightmare she had endured on board the *Northern Explorer*.

Trying not to pay too much attention to Kyle, Natascha handed both Charles and Lawrence a tray.

"Hello! They can't eat with the restraints. Can I open them?" Natascha asked and looked around for permission. One of the male nurses, Leo Swan, walked over and loosened one of the wrist restraints enough so that they could eat the sandwich without assistance.

"Can you try to convince Kyle he can trust me?" Natascha whispered to Lawrence when the nurse was out of earshot.

"Who's Kyle?" Lawrence asked puzzled as he took a large bite out of the sandwich.

"He's the guy pushing the trolley. Long story, but he might be able to help us." Natascha quickly filled Lawrence in about Kyle and what she had found at Whitmore Abbey.

"Well, we can try. Is that why they were after you as well?"

"Honestly I have no idea", Natascha admitted. She was almost certain that she had been kidnapped because of who she was, and not because of what she had found at Whitmore Abbey. But until someone would tell her the exact reason, she had no way to be sure. For that reason, Natascha decided not to reveal her real name to anyone yet.

Since she didn't want to draw even more attention to herself, Natascha picked two sandwiches for herself and searched for a quiet spot to eat. Looking around, she noticed that Kyle and the young woman sat on the floor by themselves, their backs against the wall. While Kyle slowly ate his sandwich, the young blonde woman just crouched and buried her face in her hands. It was quite obvious to Natascha that she was crying. Natascha knew only too well how the blonde woman felt, and she sat beside her on the floor, trying to offer her some encouragement. She wrapped her arm around the young woman's shoulder and she seemed to melt into her. After a few minutes she offered her half of her own sandwich, which the girl hesitantly accepted and ate.

Natascha estimated the girl with the almost white hair not to be older than twenty. The young woman was scared first, but after Natascha smiled at her, she relaxed a little bit. Natascha couldn't help her own tears from welling up as she noticed how helpless the woman was. She said something to Natascha, but she couldn't understand her language. Natascha shook her head apologetically as the young woman repeated herself. It was barely a whisper, but Natascha was convinced the poor woman was from somewhere in Eastern Europe, maybe Romania.

"I'm sorry, but I can't understand you", Natascha explained with a soft voice, hoping she could understand some English.

"Not speak English very good", the Romanian woman answered.

"You're doing just fine. My name is Talia", Natascha encouraged her.

"Elena. My name is Elena", the young woman replied with a faint smile before resting her head on Natascha's shoulder. Natascha choked back some tears as she realised how vulnerable Elena was.

"Elena, do you understand me if I speak slowly?" Natascha whispered after a few moments. Elena nodded.

"How long have you been here?" Natascha wanted to know, but Elena just shrugged her shoulders.

"Three or four weeks. Many come and many go. I stayed", she sobbed and shook her head. Natascha was worried that she would draw the guard's or the two male nurses' attention. Natascha surveyed the room quickly and noticed they still went about their business.

"Do you know where they take them? What's happening to them?" Natascha asked, but Elena just shook her head. "What happened to you? How did you get here?"

Elena told Natascha what had happened to her since she had been kidnapped in Paris. It was almost the identical story that Monique and Freja had told her.

This is a high profile human trafficking ring! Natascha thought as a shiver ran down her spine. After she had noticed that most of the women in the beds were relatively young and rather attractive, this possibility had already crossed her mind.

However it did not explain why they also kidnapped men.

"Elena, how many men have you seen here during the last couple weeks?" Maybe this young blonde girl knew some of the answers she was looking for.

"Not many. Maybe ten."

Natascha glanced around, still not certain what to make of all of this.

"This other guy over there", Natascha said and pointed at Kyle.

"Kyle?"

"Yes, that's his name. How long has he been here?"

"Don't know. Longer than I am."

"Has he always been around?"

"No", Elena shook her head again. "Was in his room for long time. Doctor cut him open. I took care of him."

"Surgery?" Natascha asked. She had no idea how that piece of information would fit into the greater picture, but Elena nodded. Natascha just pulled the tiny woman closer to herself as one of the guards looked over. Once Natascha noticed him, she decided to get up and sit somewhere else to avoid suspicion, but Elena reached out to her.

"Please! Stay with me." Elena begged with more tears in her eyes.

"Sure! I will stay with you", Natascha promised and put her arm around the Romanian girl again.

"Elena, how old are you?" Natascha asked, not exactly sure why.

"Eighteen."

"The guy, Kyle, do you talk to him much?"

"No, trusts no one", Elena shook her head as she picked at her sandwich.

"Yes, I noticed that", Natascha commented, and allowed Elena to rest her head on her shoulder again. Natascha watched as the young Romanian woman nibbled at the rest of her sandwich.

"Last week, man came to me with two nurses. He looked at me. Said, that he bought me. Said, that he will pick me up soon", Elena confessed with a tight voice.

"He did *what?*" Natascha asked. Although she knew she shouldn't be surprised, Elena's confession did just that.

"Yes", Elena nodded before she continued. "Sat down on bed beside me. Said that he bought me. Said that I would be gift for friend. Said that I should be happy."

Natascha felt her stomach twist up in knots. She closed her eyes and leaned her head back, but the horror didn't go away. She tried to think of a way to protect Elena, but Natascha quickly realised that there was nothing she could do.

Natascha's thoughts dispersed at the sound of the door opening. Her attention darted up, and she quickly recognised the female doctor, Lamar Hatcher, and the redhead. There was another man with the group, and Natascha assumed he was also a physician.

"Okay, let's see what we got", Dr William Edwards said as they approached the first bed. Natascha got ready to stand up, but Elena grabbed her arm.

"Don't!" the young Romanian woman warned her with a sharp whisper and shook her head. Natascha felt a rush of panic swell from deep within and sat back down. Her attention followed the group.

"She tested negative for antibodies, but we did find traces of drugs in her system, so we cannot use her", Dr Sheridan Evans commented and pointed at Monique, who looked at them horrified. "She's group B and we can send her off with the other group tomorrow evening. We need the space", Dr Evans continued coldly as they moved on to the next bed. Freja almost panicked as they looked at her.

"Ah, yes, this one has antibodies. Definitely group A. She'll be a ringer if she pulls through. Lamar, you can bring her down so that we can start the treatment immediately. We cannot afford to lose much more time with them."

Natascha kept watching as the assessment went on.

"Do you know the difference between group A and B?" Natascha whispered to Elena, but Elena just shook her head.

"No, don't know. I was group B. Girls in A taken somewhere downstairs. Not see them again. Men are all C. They cut them open. I sometimes have to care of them. Girls in B, they sometimes cut them open, but then they disappear", Elena quickly explained. Together they kept watching the doctors and nurses as they spent several minutes categorising the individual patients until they reached Charles and Lawrence.

"Ah, the two heroes", Dr William Edwards sarcastically proclaimed as he looked at them.

Dr Sheridan Evans smiled at his humour and handed her friend the clipboard. "They're not in bad shape, considering. The blood results are surprisingly normal. Some issues caused by malnutrition, but no signs of any drug or alcohol abuse. Just a little bit of marijuana", she commented as Dr Edwards looked at the clipboard.

"Is that right?" he asked with surprise, flipping through the lab results with disbelief.

"Yes, there's hope in this world after all", she laughed, clapping his back.

"Well, gentlemen, your heroic efforts are much appreciated. You're not a direct match to anyone high on the list, but we'll still make a fortune out of you. Your service to society will be much appreciated."

"What the bloody hell are you talking about?" Lawrence hissed from his bed, but they completely ignored him.

"How is our capacity?" Dr William Edwards asked his staff.

"We may be cramped up a little bit, but I think we can put two in one room", Lamar Hatcher suggested.

"Yeah, that might be an idea. Can you take care of that?" Dr Sheridan Evans asked him in return.

"Sure, no problem", he answered as they stopped in front of Natascha and Elena.

"What are we going to do with that one?" the redhead asked and pointed at Natascha, not even trying to hide her dislike for the young German. Natascha seriously considered saying something back, but decided against it. Her chances of learning more information regarding her own fate were much higher by just listening, rather than provoking her capturers. Besides, Natascha already felt somehow responsible for young Elena, who grasped her arm now with both hands. Natascha noticed how the young Romanian woman started to shiver the moment they looked at her.

"We're not sure yet. I believe they'll be talking about her this evening. What are they doing here anyway? Aren't they finished for today?" the female doctor wanted to know and looked around. "If they're finished, you can bring them both up to her room, we need the space. Lamar, Melissa, take care of that, please."

And with that, the two doctors simply turned around and ignored Natascha and Elena again.

"Get up", Lamar told Natascha and picked a pair of handcuffs from his belt. Staring into Melissa's taser, Natascha slowly rose to her feet, turned around and put her hands behind her back. With her hands securely cuffed, Lamar gestured to Elena to stand up as well, but the young blonde hesitated a little bit too long.

"Have it your way", Lamar said and used his foot to push her over. Although it had not been a very hard kick, Elena immediately screamed as she fell to her side.

Lamar kneeled on her back and cuffed her as two guards immediately walked over.

"Is that really necessary?" Natascha asked as they roughly pulled Elena back on her feet. Natascha didn't even see the hand coming; she only felt the sting of Melissa's strike across her face.

"Bitch!" the Irish yelled at Natascha. "No one asked you for your opinion, so you keep your stupid mouth shut!"

Natascha's eyes closed again as the pain slowly diminished. Biting her lip, she immediately tasted the blood in her mouth. Melissa grasped Natascha's hair and pulled her head back.

"Unless we ask you a direct question, you have no reason to open your mouth. Do I make myself clear?" Melissa reprimanded and pulled Natascha's hair tighter.

"Yes", Natascha whispered, resisting the urge to fight her aggressor.

"Great! Now move your worthless ass", Melissa snarled at her and pushed Natascha hard in the back. Just as Natascha started to walk, Melissa grasped her hair again and used her firm grip to lead Natascha all the way back to her cell. It was only when they were inside the cell that Lamar unshackled Elena first before taking the handcuffs off Natascha.

"You better do what she says, I have the feeling she doesn't like you", he suggested to Natascha with a laugh before closing the door behind him on his way out.

"Oh, I'm going to kick her flabby ass!" Natascha growled and stared at the closed door, massaging her wrists. Natascha swirled her tongue around her mouth and noticed she didn't taste any more blood. She knew Melissa had not hit her that hard, but Natascha promised herself not to forget it. She slowly turned around to see Elena crouching on the bunk again. The young Romanian hung on to a fresh bottle of water.

"Where did those come from?" Natascha asked and pointed at four more water bottles on the floor in front of the bunk.

"Kyle and I, before we came down with sandwiches", Elena sobbed.

Natascha sat beside Elena.

"Come here", Natascha comforted her and put her arm around Elena's shoulder. Elena leaned over, and her tears started to flow almost immediately.

"I'm so afraid of what will happen to me", she sobbed barely inaudible.

"Yes, I am too", Natascha whispered and kissed her friend on her head.

Walter Leroy Jackson and his wife Samantha arrived at the reserved table close to the open BBQ pit in the early evening. A quick glance at his expensive gold watch showed the American oil tycoon that he would have a few minutes with his wife before his friends would join them.

"Here you go, sweetheart!" L.J. said as he offered his wife a chair.

"Thank you, darling. It's so nice to sit outside again!" Samantha commented as she watched the sun setting on the horizon. She took in a deep breath, exhaling slowly.

"Yes, it is. I'm glad you managed that surgery so well. God bless you!" the Texan praised his wife and the doctors on board.

It didn't take long before Victor Gates drove over with his electric wheelchair. *Can I join you?* the voice of John Wayne asked.

"But of course you can, old friend. We just got here. Wait, I'll make some room for you." L.J. hurried to his feet and moved another chair out of his friend's way, allowing him easier access to the table. Only when he was satisfied that Victor was okay, L.J. sat down again. It took only seconds before a waiter came over, guiding Sir Samuel Archibald Cunningham and their other guest to their table. With the party complete, the waiter quickly took the order for the first round of drinks and discretely disappeared.

Walter covered the few minutes it took for the waiter to bring the aperitifs. He didn't skip a detail when he updated everybody on his wife's amazing recovery. He also made sure that everyone knew how grateful he was to the hospital staff and the Lord. His monologue was only interrupted when the waiter arrived with their order. They silently watched him serve the drinks before he opened an exorbitantly expensive bottle of champagne.

Walter turned his attention back to the group when the waiter left the table and began, "Gentlemen, let's raise our glasses to celebrate the success of our mission. The first group has successfully been delivered. From now it'll only be a matter of time until those goddamn towel-wearing camel-jockeys and their ridiculous claim for world power will be history. To the victory of our civilised Western World!" Walter cheered exuberantly.

"Hear, hear!" They replied and emptied their glasses as Walter sat down again.

"So, how many women in total were in that, what did they call it, Group A?" the young Briton asked as they waited for their dinner.

"I don't care what they call that group, but the doctor told me there were eighteen in it. So they arrived at their *final destination* two days ago." Walter explained and chuckled at what he thought was funny.

"May God have mercy on their souls!" Sir Cunningham said forlornly, more to himself, as he looked east.

"They were nothing but bumps in the road, Sam. This is probably the biggest favour they will ever do for society. We are better off without them", the Texan stated emotionlessly and watched as two waiters served their dinner.

"What about that other group? Group B? How much money did we make there?" the younger of the two Britons wanted to know as he cut a piece of his filet.

"Difficult to say at the moment. I don't have the final numbers, but the demand for young organs is definitely much larger than the supply. We have also sold a few girls directly to clients, but that's only profitable when they're still virgins. Didn't you buy one for your buddy there?" Walter asked curiously.

"Yes, for a friend and business partner of mine. I picked her out not too long ago. It'll help us smooth an unrelated business deal I have with him", the young man explained after a quick glance toward Sir Cunningham. Everybody noticed how Samuel did not show any reaction at all. For them it was a clear indication that the business tycoon most likely didn't approve of his partner's methods of negotiation.

"We arrived with a private helicopter and I'll take her with me later tonight after everybody is in bed. I just wanted to wait to see the new delivery", he added as if they were talking about some cheap items in a thrift store. He didn't seem to be bothered by the fact that Sir Cunningham didn't support his decision.

"Hm, makes sense", Walter nodded and chewed on his steak. He pretended that he had not noticed Samuel's disapproval.

"Those...women", Samantha naively asked, "they're not under age, are they?"

"No, I don't think so", Walter shook his head, not really caring if they were or not. He looked at them purely as merchandise and nothing else. Victor Gates didn't take part in the conversation. He mostly listened and shook his head slightly. He also didn't care if the women were of age or not. For him, their whole purpose was to make money. Their future lives were nothing but hell for them, leading to a certain death. What difference would it make if they were of age or not. He could never understand Samantha's concern or way of thinking on several matters, despite the fact that he and Walter had been business partners long before his accident.

"Do we know the timeframe when we can expect to hear something?" Samuel asked curiously. L.J. shook his head as he swallowed a piece of his baked potato.

"If I understood Dr Evans right, first casualties should occur within the next two weeks. How did they say it in the bible? *They had breakfast with their family and ate lunch with their ancestors.*" L.J. quoted with a chuckle as he looked at the sky. "We just don't know how fast the outside world will get reports of this. You know yourself how difficult it is to get any confirmed and reliable insider information. Once the word is out, it shouldn't take much longer before the first video appears somewhere. Worst case scenario would be if they run out of bodies before our friends in Rome had time to start their campaign", Walter explained. "They made it clear how important the right timing is for them."

"I am aware of their position, but that really is not our concern any more at this point, isn't it?" Sir Cunningham replied in his typical aristocratic way.

"No, it isn't. Can't really have any connection to them, can we? As far as I know, all they can and will do is use the news to their advantage."

None of them argued the Texan. He and Victor Gates were still unconvinced that Samuel had made the right decision by informing their young British business partner about everything that went on. Without discussing their operation any further, they changed the subject for the next couple hours and enjoyed some expensive cognac.

By eleven in the evening they were the only ones still sitting outside. The temperature was just right, and they enjoyed every minute of it, especially since the band played exclusively for them.

"Samantha! Gentlemen! I'm afraid I have to go now", the young Briton mentioned with a quick look at his chronograph and rose from his chair. "I have to conduct some other business now", the young man explained with a crooked smile as he fixed his jacket.

"Don't forget to transfer the money", L.J. winked at him and toasted in his direction.

"Please, of course I'll pay", he replied, not realising how serious L.J. was.

"I think I'll retreat downstairs. I'm rather tired now", Samantha Jackson took the opportunity. L.J. immediately rose from his chair to help his wife.

"I'll be down there shortly, sweetheart. Just a few more minutes", the heavy Texan promised her as she walked away. "The doctors here really did a miracle on her. May the Lord bless them", he said and poured himself another generous cognac. "That friend of his?" L.J. began suspiciously, looking at the dark golden liquid in his glass, "Can we trust him?"

"Of course. I reluctantly have to admit that I wasn't aware of his business practice in this particular case, but it seems to have worked in our favour. We've been in business with his client's family for over two decades. His client's father and I go back a long time."

"Good. Talking about gifts, Victor", L.J. said and leaned back in his chair as he toasted his friend.

What? You got me a new lung? Victor asked over the computer in John Wayne's voice. The electronic voice made it impossible to determine in what kind of emotional mood Victor was at the moment, but his long time friend L.J. was usually very good at reading it.

"No, sir, unfortunately not. But I have the second best thing to a new lung. You will see it in a few days. You will love it, trust me!" L.J. promised with a laugh.

Now I'm curious.

"Just a few more days. It's not quite ready yet." L.J. winked and looked up as Melissa slowly approached their table. She waited in the distance to allow herself to be seen, giving them time to change the subject. It was a common courtesy they showed towards their patients and clients. Samuel just nodded and waved her to the table.

"Good evening, gentlemen. How is everyone?" Melissa laughed as she came closer.

Lovely. Why don't you sit with us? Victor asked her.

"I'd love to, but I'm afraid it'd get me in trouble if I do that. Besides, I have to kidnap you for about twenty minutes. We have to change your oxygen tank and you need some medication as well. It's much faster if we do that in your room", Melissa told the American.

If you insist. Victor commented and activated the controls of his electric wheelchair. This time, the frustration was clearly visible on his face. Both Walter Jackson as well as Sir Cunningham watched closely as Victor followed Melissa to the elevator.

"Goddamn it! Can you imagine living your life like he does?"

"No, certainly not. I don't think any of us can imagine that", Samuel replied pitiably. "Just shows you how fast your life can change. So he doesn't know yet?"

"No, he doesn't. It'll lift his spirit until he gets a new lung. I think it's the least I can do for him."

"Agreed. How is she doing anyway?" Samuel asked curiously and looked at Walter.

"She's tough. Much tougher than I thought. When you first mentioned her name, I hired a couple specialists to create her psychological profile. Very interesting stuff they found out about her. I had them meet with Dr Evans and Dr Edwards to fill them in. They're currently treating her outside the normal program and according to the recommendations of the specialists. They said she'll break relatively fast if we use her psychological profile against her."

"What did the doctors say?"

"They're not too enthusiastic about it. They're concerned she'll interfere with the treatment of the other patients, but they agreed to follow the recommendations. The plan is to prey on her emotional vulnerabilities. We expect she will break in a couple of days."

"And that's why you want to wait so long?" Samuel concluded for him.

"Yes, that's the exact reason why", the Texan said coldly.

"Interesting", Samuel replied, unimpressed, and had another cognac.

A few floors below, Natascha and Elena shared the tiny bunk. Mentally and physically exhausted, the sleep deprivation started to take its toll on them. Elena's sobbing finally silenced just before she fell in an unsteady sleep. Natascha didn't know why, but she felt obligated to protect her new friend from whatever would happen to her, even though she had no idea how to achieve that. Uncertain about her own fate, Natascha closed her eyes to encourage some much needed sleep. It didn't take long before she dozed off, but her recurring nightmares made sure she never slept for more than a few minutes.

"How long has she been sleeping now?" Dr William Edwards asked, watching them on a monitor in the control room.

"They laid down about two hours ago, but I don't think she is sleeping for more than an hour", Leo Swan answered from behind the control desk. "At least the taller one was very restless."

"Okay, that's perfect timing. You can send Kevin and Lamar. Tell them to take two guards as well."

Leo acknowledged and paged his buddies with the new instructions.

In her room, Natascha was finally sleeping for almost twenty minutes when she heard the loud noise. She first thought that it was part of her dream, but the sound seemed out of place. It was only when the door burst open that she realised it wasn't a dream. Both Natascha and Elena shrieked as four men rushed into the cell. Elena immediately screamed as they pulled her away from Natascha and forced her onto the floor, where they kneeled on her back to cuff her. Before Natascha even realised what had happened, the other two men pinned her down on the bunk.

"Time to go!" One of the guys laughed as he rose to his feet from Elena's back.

The young Romanian screamed out in pain as they roughly pulled her back to her feet and out of the cell. The other two men waited a moment longer before they released Natascha and retreated quickly. The door was locked before Natascha was even able to get up from the bunk.

"Open up!" She yelled, hammering her fists against the steel door, but she knew that this was a futile attempt. Furiously she turned around and paced the length of her little room as far as the limited space allowed it.

"Dammit!" She yelled and kicked one of the water bottles against the wall, but it didn't help her rage. They had taken Elena away from her, and there was nothing she could have done to prevent it. The horror of the thought of what would happen to her new friend fuelled her rage even more.

"Well, that went better than I thought", Dr William Edwards commented as he watched Natascha on the monitor. "They can bring the Romanian to the examination room on C-Level. We'll meet the client there in thirty minutes. We can sedate her there for the transport. As for her", Dr Edwards nodded at Natascha on the monitor as she was still pacing her cabin, "continue as instructed", the physician ordered and turned around to leave the control room.

When Dr William Edwards stepped out of the elevator on C-Level about thirty minutes later, he was accompanied by Dr Sheridan Evans and their British customer. Dr Evans led their way to the examination room.

"Here we are", she commented and ran her magnetic key card through the reader. With the green LED blinking, she opened the door and invited their guest in.

"Thank you", the Briton said enthusiastically in anticipation as he entered. His smile brightened as he immediately recognised Elena, who crouched on one of the examination tables. Kevin Wilson kept an eye on her, but the young Romanian woman was so frightened, she didn't dare to move.

"So, those are the new ones. They arrived within the last couple days", Dr Evans said and gestured at Monique and six other women who stood in one row at the other side of the examination room. Like the rest of them, Monique was shaking with fear when she saw the young man and the two physicians walk in. The young, strawberry-blonde French woman quickly looked around, and noticed that the two male nurses and the four guards paid close attention to them. She hoped to see Freja again, but two of the guards had taken her friend away earlier that evening. Monique didn't know that she would never see Freja again.

"I see", the Briton said and approached them to take a closer look. He already knew these women were of no interest to him without spending too much time. "Are any of them...?" he hesitated, as he turned around to face Dr Evans.

"No, none of them", the British doctor answered.

"I understand", he said and turned his attention towards Elena. It was only the second time that he saw her in person, but he was still stunned by her innocent beauty. He thought her tear struck eyes added to it. "I really appreciate the offer, but I guess I'll stick with her", the young man eventually said and thanked the two doctors.

"Of course", Dr Evans nodded and gave order to bring the women back to their rooms. "Except that one", she stopped the group, just as they reached the door, and pointed at Monique. "That one will leave tomorrow evening with the others. You can lock her up with them. Make sure you don't overdose them."

The young man turned his attention to Dr Evans as the seven women were escorted out of the examination room.

"Did you examine her any further? I remember you said she's healthy and free of drugs?"

"Yes, that's correct", the doctor answered approaching them.

"That is good. So, what's the procedure from now on?" he asked curiously. He had to admit this was the first time he was actively involved in human trafficking. His inexperience in these matters showed.

"Usually all our regular patients are in their rooms by midnight, and most of them are fast asleep not long after that. So it won't be much longer now. The nurses are doing their last round as we speak. She can stay here for now. We'll sedate her in a few minutes and bring her up to your helicopter. How long do you want her unconscious for?"

The Briton had to admit the doctor caught him off guard with this question. He had never thought about that before.

"Well, let me see", he started and took a couple steps away from the doctor, calculating the hours until their arrival at their final destination. "I would say...maybe seven to eight hours? I mean, she doesn't have to be out cold, just enough that she doesn't struggle."

"Yes, that shouldn't be a problem." Dr Edwards reassured and made a note.

"As a general question", he started curiously. "She's not aggressive when she's not sedated, is she?"

"No, more like the opposite, to be honest. She's not a trouble-maker at all. Isn't that right?" Dr Edwards asked expectantly as they all looked to the young Romanian woman for an answer. Elena followed their conversation as good as her limited English allowed her. She certainly didn't want any attention or trouble and just nodded.

"You see, there you go. She will not cause you any problems."

The young man seemed relieved and smiled at the doctors, when their attention was suddenly drawn to one of the phones ringing on the control desk.

"Melissa, can you put it on speaker, please?" Dr Evans asked the redhead who sat behind the desk.

"Certainly, Dr Evans", she obliged and pressed a button.

"Dr Evans here. What is it?"

"Sorry to interrupt, but I just want to know how we're proceeding with our other guest?" Leo Swan asked them over the speaker.

"Good question. How is she doing?" Dr Evans answered in return and looked at the monitors. Melissa already selected the video camera showing Natascha's cabin, and they all watched Natascha on the large high definition monitor. She was still pacing her cabin, her frustration and rage clearly visible.

"She's feisty, you have to give her that!" Dr Evans acknowledged and stepped a little closer to the monitor.

"She is. I thought she'd be a bit exhausted by now." Dr Edwards agreed.

"Leo? Can you hear me?" Dr Evans called and slightly turned her head towards the phone.

"Yes, I can hear you loud and clear."

"She has to be dead-tired. I cannot see her going much longer. Just keep watching her closely and follow the instructions, okay?"

"Yes, understood." Leo answered and ended the call.

They all kept watching silently for a few more minutes as Natascha aggressively paced her cabin. It was only now that their British guest attentively looked at the huge monitor they were all drawn to.

"This is not possible!" he commented as he finally recognised Natascha. He walked over to the monitor to take a closer look. It took him only a second, but there was no doubt in his mind. He simply shook his head.

"I'm sorry, but she's not for sale. She's also rather old compared to the other women." Dr Evans commented the moment she noticed his interest in Natascha.

"No, no, no! I know her!" the Briton couldn't hide his surprise as he pointed at the monitor. "But how can it be? I wasn't told anything about it."

"Well, you would have to ask them, I suppose. All I can tell you is that she's not for sale." Dr Edwards answered and nodded towards Melissa as the phone rang again. The Irish picked up the receiver, but the conversation didn't last very long.

"Leo said the nurses have completed their rounds. We're all clear. Sir Cunningham is also waiting with the helicopter pilot. They're ready whenever we are", Melissa smiled at them.

"Okay, very well. Might as well not wait any longer. We got a long trip ahead of us", the young Briton said and held his hand out towards Elena. The young Romanian woman didn't know what to do and just stared at him, the confusion and fear reflecting in her face. "Do you really have to sedate her? I mean, she does look rather calm. How much trouble can she be?"

"Unfortunately we cannot take the risk. If we don't sedate her, there's a realistic chance she'll tell someone about our location. I presume you agree we cannot risk that."

"Certainly not, my apology!" the young man agreed and shook his head. He did not notice the two physicians exchanging a stern look. They were obviously not too impressed about his carelessness.

"Well, let's get started", Dr Evans announced and walked over to a cabinet to collect a syringe and a little flask from a drawer. With a quick look at Elena, she drew some of the sedative with the syringe. Dr Evans collected a couple sterile gauze pads and a disinfectant spray bottle before walking over to Elena.

The Romanian's eyes grew bigger and Elena straightened up, her back butting against the wall behind her. Dr Edwards cornered her from the other side and grasped her arm. Elena tried to voice her protest but it came out as a wavering pant.

"Don't be silly now", Dr Edwards said and stretched her arm so she could pull back the sleeve of the hospital gown. Elena didn't know what to do, but there was no strength left in her body to resist anyway. She couldn't see what Dr Evans was doing, but she felt the moisture as the doctor sprayed the disinfectant on her skin. Just after she had cleaned the area, she noticed the sharp pain of the needle piercing through her skin. She flinched, but Dr Edwards held her arm so tight she couldn't move much. She anxiously looked at the Briton, who tried to comfort her by holding her other hand, but she didn't know what his intention was and pulled her hand away from his. Only seconds later, Dr Edwards released her.

While the two physicians watched her from a few metres away, the Briton sat beside the young woman and attempted to put his arm around her shoulder. Still not knowing his intentions, Elena moved away from him, but she already noticed that her reaction time was much slower now.

With her senses dwindling, Elena looked helplessly from one person to another, but they just watched as she got weaker and weaker. Her eyes finally met his, but Elena didn't hear what the Briton said. It looked like he tried to comfort her, but her instincts told her not to trust him. Her body didn't function any more, and Elena felt her extremities fall limp as she finally sank down, barely able to keep her eyes open. She didn't realise who helped her, but someone pulled her back on her feet. She would have fallen, but they were holding her up by her arms, and someone even threw a blanket over her shoulder. Elena could hear how they talked to each other, but the voices were so distant, she couldn't understand a word they were saying. She barely noticed how they strapped her into a wheelchair before they pushed her down the hallway to one of the elevators. Elena's head fell forward, and it took all her strength to open her eyes for just one second, but all she could see was the inside of the elevator.

It didn't take long before its doors opened again, and the fresh cool night air hit Elena's face. As they pushed her past the pool, the young Romanian woman opened her eyes again. She had never been outside before, but she noticed a helicopter waiting for them, the rotor blades already starting to swirl. Without being able to put up any resistance, they lifted her into the helicopter and placed her into one of the rear leather seats. Elena opened her eyes again, petrified of what would happen next as someone fastened her seat belt. She looked to her left, where she saw an older man in the next leather seat beside her, but as soon as her eyes met his, Sir Samuel Archibald Cunningham looked away, not hiding his distaste for the young woman.

The last thing she remembered was the black blindfold someone placed over her head. Outside the helicopter, Dr William Edwards and Melissa watched as the helicopter increased the rotor speed before it finally took off. They looked after it until they could only see the position lights. The rotor sound faded away soon after, and Melissa couldn't help but shiver.

"Don't worry, Melissa. Her hell will not be as bad as the one the other girls are facing", Dr Edwards tried to comfort the Irish nurse.

"Oh, no, that's not it. I'm fine."

"You're sure?"

"Yes, I was just getting a chill."

"Okay, if you say so", Dr Edwards commented as they both walked back to the elevator. The helicopter was already out of sight.

Deep inside the facility, Natascha eventually accepted the fact that Elena would not come back. She was still furious, but the sleep deprivation finally took its toll, and she noticed how tired she really was. Not knowing how long she had been awake for or what time or even day it was didn't help either. When she finally laid down in her bunk again, she stared at the light on the ceiling. It was always shining with the same brightness, and she had no control over it. Ready to sleep, Natascha turned to her side and pulled the blanket over her head. She was completely exhausted, but too many thoughts raced through her mind. Eventually, she drifted into another nightmare.

Natascha slept for about two hours when the door to her cabin opened again. It took her a few seconds to realise what was happening, but Natascha finally woke up and turned around. Her hopes that they would bring Elena back were shattered the moment she saw the two guards brutally pushing another man into her cell. Before Natascha was even fully awake, they had already closed the door again.

Natascha didn't say anything first and just watched as the man struggled to get to his feet. She could hear his groans and knew that he had been severely beaten.

"Oh my God!" Natascha scowled and pushed herself from the bunk to help him. "Here, let me help you!" she offered and assisted the guy to sit on the bunk. "Give me a second; I'll get some water", Natascha said and hurried into the tiny bathroom to soak the towel with water.

She reached forward to wash his wounds, but his hand snapped up quickly when she reached for his face. The shock of his aggression caught her voice in her throat.

"Wait, let me clean you up", Natascha told him, and he struggled to see her as his left eye was swollen shut. His breath was short and laboured, and Natascha could feel him searching her with his right eye.

"Look, I'm trying to help you, okay? I'm not going to hurt you!" Natascha reassured him softly. He finally let go of Natascha's wrist and allowed her to clean the blood from his face. He winced and refused to relax under her care.

"Well, I can't blame you for not trusting me. I certainly wouldn't trust anyone here. What's your name?" Natascha looked into his eyes, waiting for an answer. "I am Talia. I am also one of the *special guests* here. Not certain what they want to do with me, but their hospitality suggests it won't be nice."

"Jake...", the guy finally said after a brief silence. His breath was much calmer now.

"Jake? Nice to meet you, Jake. Can I ask what happened to you? I haven't seen you before", Natascha pointed, but Jake still didn't know if he should trust her. "That's okay, Jake. Like I said, I don't trust anyone here either, but there might be some hope." Natascha went on as she studied the young man. She guessed he was around her age and, judging by his accent, British.

Once she had all the blood washed off from his face, she recognised a clear resemblance to Mark, her ex-boyfriend to whom she had sent the bone fragments from Whitmore Abbey.

"Great, that's the last thing I need now", Natascha commented and made a face. Jake had no idea what she meant, but he gladly accepted the water bottle she offered him.

"So, a little bit of luck and your face will be as good as new. It will take a couple days for the bruising and swelling to go back down, but other than that you should be just like new. You look like they gave you a warm welcome. How are you feeling? Do you think you have serious injuries?" Natascha wanted to know. Based on the condition of his face, she was seriously concerned about internal injuries.

"No!" Jake quickly said and shook his head."They just beat me up. I'll manage!" He tried to sound convincing, but he still winced as he repositioned himself on the bunk. The young man looked around. Natascha could see that he still had no idea where he was.

"This is not my old cell. Where am I?" he asked with a wavering voice.

"Look, Jake, you can clearly see that I'm not residing in the luxury suite here either. This is where they kept me since I got here couple of days ago, I guess. You can tell me what happened to you." Natascha explained and sat beside the young man. She pulled up the blanket and placed it over both of them. "Here! I know it isn't cold, but it will help." Jake just nodded and leaned his back against the wall. His hands shaking, he almost drank the entire bottle of water.

"I'm a freelance reporter. I was in the States doing some work for an article about human trafficking for a magazine. During my research I overheard two guys in a nightclub one day. They were kind of rich. Totally loaded with money", Jake started and emptied the water bottle. "The more they drank, the more they talked. So I just stayed at the next table and listened in. Turned out they were talking about human trafficking. I hung around and waited until they were completely pissed. One of them mentioned a name. At first I didn't know what it was, but then I did some research. I knew it was Greek, so that's where I looked."

"Wait! You're saying you know where we are?" Natascha cut him off.

"Oh, yes, we are on *Asklepios*." Jake answered and looked at Natascha.

"*Asklepios*..." she whispered and shook her head. It was only now that she vaguely remembered someone mentioning that name when she had arrived.

"You don't know who it is?" Jake asked.

"No, not really. Sounds Greek to me, too."

"I didn't know it either, so I did some digging. Turns out that *Asklepios* is the God of medicine in the ancient Greek mythology. Once I knew that, I did some more research. It took me a while, but I finally found some chatter on the internet. It turns out that it is one of the thousands of little islands that Greece put up for sale during their financial crisis. I guess someone bought it and built this facility. The chatter on the internet has it that this is the medical facility for the rich and famous."

"What do you mean?" Natascha asked perplexed. She had a pretty good idea about what direction the story would go, but she wanted to hear it from Jake.

"Well, for all those who are willing to pay top dollar to jump ahead a few numbers on the organ transplant list or for top of the line treatment by leading experts in their medical field. Many patients are also coming here just for rehabilitation. The facility is quite famous in certain circles." Jake reached down to pick up two more water bottles from the floor. He offered one to Natascha, who accepted the bottle absentmindedly.

"That would make sense", Natascha exhaled and took a sip from the bottle. She stared at the floor thinking about what Elena had told her before. The story connected, but Natascha still had some questions. "That would explain the young people."

"The young women are mostly for human trafficking, but they usually take some non-vital organs from them first. There's more money in human trafficking these days than ever before, unfortunately. For just the organs, they mostly concentrate on homeless people. No one misses them", Jake explained and closed his eyes. He was still suffering from the severe beating he had received.

"Oh my God!" Natascha said with sudden realisation. Brian Whittaker had mentioned an increased number of missing homeless people in the recent staff meeting. She couldn't help but think this was all connected. She would have to tell Brian, should she ever get the chance. "So what happened next? How did you end up here?" she wanted to know instead.

"So I got curious. Turns out that the patients do not have a clue about what is really going on here. Most of them are so happy to receive the necessary treatment that they forget the obvious questions, like where these organs are coming from. Well, who can blame them? I dug deeper and tried to meet with someone who had been a patient here before; and I finally found someone. A young family with a sick child. The mother's parents are big time industrials in the States. Their six year old child was in desperate need of a new lung, but there was no match. The grandparents took matters in their own hand, and within weeks they had an appointment and a new lung. The parents were extremely grateful, that's why they agreed to meet with me."

"So what happened next?"

"Hm...", Jake drank some more water and shook his head. "What happened next? Things went downhill very fast from there. I still don't know if the whole story about the family was bogus or not, but once I started to research this place by its name, I quickly caught the attention of some really powerful people. *Asklepios* must be a key word in the internet that is monitored by someone. I don't know", Jake continued and shrugged. "Fact is they set me up with a fake meeting. I showed up, and before I knew what happened, the *mother* of the young child shocked me with a taser. I got tossed in a van, drugged, and when I woke up, I was here."

"Sounds familiar", Natascha admitted and took Jake's shaking hand in her own.

"Once I was here, I just got a brief glimpse of other people, but not for long. They ran some tests on me, blood samples, x-rays, the yards. After that, they brought me to a room somewhere on the lower floors, but it was more like a holding cell. They asked me what I knew and tried to beat the answers out of me."

"I'm sorry to hear that", Natascha commented sincerely. She didn't need to be a medic to see that they had done a number on him. "Did you tell them?"

"Of course I did. At first I thought that I shouldn't say anything, but what was the point? No one else knew where I was or what exactly I was looking for, so there was no one I had to protect and there is no one looking for me. Besides, someone can only tolerate so much pain. What can I say? I sort of dug my own grave." Jake shook his head, and it was only now he noticed that Natascha was caressing his hand. Natascha felt sad for him.

"Trust me, I know what you're talking about", Natascha whispered.

His story reminded her of her own experience on board the *Northern Explorer*. Although she knew that it was odd to take solace in someone's misfortune, Natascha somehow felt better knowing that Jake could somehow relate to her own past.

Jake picked up the wet towel and wiped some more blood from his lips, which had started bleeding again. "I was convinced that the beating would stop once I told them everything, but no such luck", he continued and shook his head again. "They kept me awake and paid me regular visits, but this time they were just beating me for fun. There is one woman amongst them, a redhead. I think she's a nurse..." Jake was searching for the name.

"Melissa?" Natascha asked, immediately recognising her from his description.

"Yes, I think that's her name. Do you know her?"

"Not really", Natascha explained and shook her head. "She dealt with me a couple times. She was extremely rough, and I think she's a psycho."

"Sounds like her! Anyway, she *is* a bloody maniac. She shocked me with a taser couple times just for fun. She only had pleasure when I suffered. She's a nut case", Jake finished and rested his head against the wall again, closing his eyes. "They visited me tonight, turned me into this and told me they need my room. They had beaten me senseless before they dragged me here."

"God, I'm really sorry!" Natascha noted.

"Thanks, but don't worry. It's not your fault."

"Did they say anything about me?" Natascha asked curiously.

"No, they didn't. They didn't even mention a name."

Natascha thought about it, but remembered that he had not shown any reaction, when she had introduced herself as *Talia* to him.

"How did you end up here?" Jake asked and turned his head to look at her.

"Me? Almost the same story", Natascha answered with a shrug. "Stumbled about some rumours, did some research on the internet, went for a jog, snatch and grab, and voila, here I am", Natascha summarised the events with as minimal details as possible. Natascha knew that staying relatively close to the truth would be easier for her to recall the story, but she decided not to mention Kyle or his letter.

"Sounds familiar. How long have you been here?"

"Not one hundred percent sure. Maybe three days now. I have no idea."

"Are you okay? Did they..." Jake asked and looked at her. The expression in his face clearly showed his concern for her.

"Oh, no, I'm better off than most of the other women. They haven't touched me yet, except for Melissa. She just hates me", Natascha told him.

"She just hates everybody." Jake complained and closed his eyes again.

A shiver ran through Natascha's body as she thought about what she had just said. They had not touched her yet, that was true, but Natascha knew that the worst was yet to come. Trying not to let the panic of the unknown overwhelm her, she closed her eyes and swallowed hard. She fought the lump rising inside her throat and cursed the tears welling in her eyes. It took her a moment to pull her emotions back in check.

"Well, let's try to get some sleep. Tomorrow is another day." Natascha suggested when she finally opened her eyes again.

"Yes, you're right. Who knows what they have planned for us. Let's watch out for each other, okay?" Jake replied exhaustedly and laid down in the bunk. For a second, Natascha considered sleeping on the floor, but she quickly withdrew the thought. This was about survival, and they were both hostages. She needed as much rest as she could get. She kissed her wedding ring before laying down beside him. This time, it didn't take long before she fell asleep.

***EuroSecCorporation*, London, Monday, July 21**

"Any news over the weekend that we have to know about?" Brian opened their briefing. The retired admiral looked at the rather slim timeline, which, at the moment, reminded them more of their defeat rather than progress. This fact was confirmed by the concerned and disappointed expressions on everyone's face.

"We don't have much, but we hope that Scotland Yard has some more details by the end of the day", Sean MacLeod started. "Their cyber crime unit has still not picked up anything on the internet that could even remotely be connected with this. They are looking to track down the black Mercedes Sprinter with the advertising, but without a licence plate it will take more time. So far they haven't been too lucky here in London."

"Hm, okay. Are they looking at traffic cameras now that they know what to look for?"

"I believe so, but there is also a chance they might have switched vehicles. Bill promised to update me the moment they find something."

"Very well. What about the two Fords here in our parking lot? Anything on them?"

"Stolen licence plates from identical models are all we got so far. Nothing else."

"What about Natascha's cell phone?"

"Nothing unusual. No activity within the last three hours before the abduction. She just listened to some music. All the history on the cell phone checks out, nothing unusual and nothing that was erased."

Brian shook his head. His eyes were still focussed on the timeline of events, when he picked up his cup of coffee. They were not getting anywhere like this.

"Shira, you mentioned something about Nick checking into the laptop over the weekend. Was he able to find anything? How is he doing anyway?"

"He had a very rough weekend. Natascha's parents are heartbroken. Nick pulled himself together and is much more focussed now, which is a good thing. We keep an eye on him. Ariel is with him now. I expect them both to be here within the hour. As far as the laptop goes, we went through the material again that we already had access to. Natascha kept detailed information about that diving project at the abbey. There are tons of video files and pictures. We flipped through them, but there is nothing that gives us reason for concern. We have also found nothing that would indicate that she is seeing someone else. However, there was one thing. After Nick finally found the password for her Skype account, we first didn't find anything unusual. Just the history of her normal calls to her parents and some friends in Germany. Mostly Erika who had been with her at the abbey. However, there was one contact that sort of stood out. A guy in Germany, his name is Mark. For whatever reason, Natascha contacted him from the computer at the aquarium. We only saw the conversation in the history."

"Interesting. How long was it?" Klaus asked, while Brian answered a phone call.

"They talked for little over five minutes, but that's all we know."

"Any idea who he is?"

Shira shook her head. "No, neither of us know him. Nick wants to skype with Erika once he gets here. Maybe she knows something about him."

"Okay, I have some news", Brian interrupted the second he ended the phone call. "I was just informed that due to Natascha's past, the British government has called in the American ambassador to brief him. I'm not certain if I agree with that move or not, but that's what they're doing right now. The German ambassador has also been informed. She seemed to be more willing to help and promised all the support. After all, she is still a German citizen", Brian finished and had some more coffee. Klaus just shrugged, he also wasn't sure what to think about that information. They all looked at the door as Nick and Ariel entered.

"Good Morning. My apologies for being late, but we were at the Israeli embassy. They received a piece of information that might be related to this!" Ariel stated enthusiastically and helped himself to a cup of coffee. "One of our informants has seen something at a private airport, just outside London. According to her, a Sikorsky S-Seventy-Six ambulance helicopter was involved in some suspicious activity. It's permanently stationed there and available for medical charters upon request. The helicopter was booked for a solid week, ready for takeoff at minutes notice, but it never left the ground until thirty minutes after the kidnapping. Our informant said that this is not all that unusual, but according to her, the crew dragged three people into the helicopter, all of them blind-folded, none of them on stretchers, but one person with longer, black hair." Ariel paused for a second to let the information sink in. Brigitte was already adding all the information, while Brian and Klaus straightened up like everyone else. Something seemed to shift in the room.

"And? What else?" Brian barked, demanding to know more information.

"Not much. The helicopter left with a total of seven or eight people. Our contact didn't see the vehicle they arrived with, but later confirmed that it was indeed a black Mercedes Sprinter after watching the security footage."

"There's our lead!" Brian slammed his hand on the table, a smile threatening to dance across his lips. "What about Scotland Yard? Did you tell them?"

"Briefed them from the embassy. They're picking up our informant as we speak."

"What else? Could she find something out about the flight plan or who chartered the helicopter?"

"Flight plan was filed for a direct flight to a private airport outside Paris. Urgent medical supplies, human organs. Paperwork was in order, nothing to raise any suspicion. The group provided their own pilots, so Scotland Yard is going to track them down and informed the French authorities to pick up the trail in Paris. For our informant, the trail went cold the moment the helicopter took off British ground."

"Okay. You spoke to Conolly?"

"Yes, called him on his cell phone."

"Your source, how reliable is she?" Brian asked. He knew about the vast network of informants supporting the Israeli government, but he wanted to be sure.

"She is *sayanim*. We have no reason to doubt her. Besides, she can back her facts with the security camera as well as the flight plan. Chief Inspector Conolly should have something for us before noon, I suppose."

"Perfect! Nick, how are you doing?" Brian felt more relieved, knowing that they would get some valuable information soon.

"Could be better, sir. I'm barely hanging in", Nick answered, his voice broken. It was evident that he had not much sleep at all. Even now, his eyes filled with tears as he saw his wife's enlarged picture on the wall.

"How is your daughter, Nick?" Brian continued with his fatherly voice.

Nick shook his head and shrugged, searching for an answer that he couldn't find.

"I think she's okay? She's with her grandparents now. Talia, Scott and Rick are with her."

"They'll make sure nothing happens to her, Nick. You can trust them." Brian reassured him. Nick wanted to say something, but he just nodded.

"Nick, how good do you know Erika?"

"Not that well, to be honest. I'll skype with her once we're done here. Shira, did you already tell everyone what we did on the weekend?" Nick asked and took a deep breath to control himself.

"Yes, I already filled them in", Shira smiled and took Nick's hand.

"Okay! So we'll meet at fourteen-hundred then. Nick, if you can hang around I can fill you in on what we said before, but Ariel's information is certainly much more helpful than anything else we have at the moment."

With nothing else to add, Brian and Klaus rose from their chairs and walked to their offices. Nick stayed behind, and it didn't take long before he and Shira had the conference room for themselves. Nick stared out of the window, waiting for Shira to start Natascha's laptop. It took Erika only a few seconds to answer their Skype call.

"You remember Shira?" Nick finally asked her, after Erika had gone on for minutes about how sorry she felt and how horrible this all was.

"Yes, I do remember you. Natascha spoke of you like a sister", Erika remembered. "Nick, I wish I could help, but I really don't know how."

"Was there anything unusual with Natascha while she was diving with you guys?" Nick's voice fell flat.

"No, not really. Everything went according to plan. The only thing was that she thought to have seen some bones that could have been human. She saw them in a natural side tunnel to the mine. The tunnel has a connection with at least one surface well. She was the only one who had seen them, so the rest of us wouldn't know. We didn't think too much about it. First we thought that it could've been an animal that had fallen into the well decades ago, or leftovers from a party or a feast that someone had thrown in there a while back. But then we noticed that they were upstream and shallower than the well. You know how stubborn Natascha can be once she has her mind set. We went to visit the abbey to see if there was another well, but that search turned up negative. Andreas and I attended the mass and she and Mario kept looking, but I have no idea if they found something or not. You would have to talk to Mario about that. Nick, you remember Mario, right? He was on the *Explorer* with you."

"Yes, we do remember him. Do you know how I can reach him?"

"Yes, sure. I can e-mail you his contact. I believe he's at the institute this week. Just give me a moment here."

"Okay. I'll make sure to contact him as soon as I can."

"Do you have any idea where she is?" Erika finally asked, desperation clearly evident in her voice.

"The police are following some leads. I'm certain we'll know more this afternoon", Shira explained.

"Let's hope so. This is so horrible!"

"Erika, I got one more question", Nick continued and looked at his notes to find the name. "When we checked Natascha's Skype records, we came upon a guy named Mark. Do you know him?" Nick asked, still looking at the paper.

"Mark? Hm, do you have a last name or something else?" Erika asked after a second.

"Yes, I'll send you his Skype address, give me a second." Nick said and typed in the address.

"Got it. Hm, maybe from the institute? I'll check. How can I reach you, Nick? I can see that you're at work?"

"You can either call our direct line or my cell. If you send me a message, we can skype almost right away. I won't be far." Nick explained and texted the phone number over Skype.

"I'll give you my cell number as well", Shira offered and Nick sent that information to her as well.

"Okay, perfect! Please let me know if you find something, okay? And please let us know if we can help."

"We will. Thank you, Erika." Nick ended the connection and leaned back. "Okay, what's next? Shall we try to talk to Mario first, or does it make more sense to give Brian an update?" Nick shifted in his seat, his impatience and lack of direction leaving him guessing.

"Let's see if Mario is online. Maybe he can shed some more light into this." Shira suggested and already established the connection. They were lucky, and Mario basically confirmed what Erika had already told them.

"Erika mentioned something about Natascha seeing human bones during that one dive. Were you not with her at the time?" Nick asked.

"She was under the impression, that's correct. She had the lead during that dive and saw them in the distance. Before she could get to them, I ran into some equipment issues and had to call the dive. We tried to get back there later with the ROV, but lost it a couple metres short. When Natascha and I went in to recover it, she broke protocol for a moment and I assume she went to check on the bones while I fixed the ROV." Mario saw that this was news to Nick, but it didn't matter now. "So if there were any bones, she's the only one who had actually seen them."

"What about the abbey? Erika said that you and Natascha continued searching for another well?" Shira followed the next lead. Despite the seriousness of the situation, Mario had to laugh.

"Yes, she talked me into it. You know how she can be. She asked some school kids for directions to the catacombs. We actually found them, but Natascha had to use her little tool to unlock two old doors. It was kind of stupid, but I honestly didn't think too much about it back then. Once we reached the catacombs, we were kind of disappointed. It was only one tiny room. Technically the whole catacombs are a natural cave, just widened by people centuries ago, but the last room was reinforced with some brick walls. There was a puddle of murky water on the bottom. Took you ten seconds to see that it was a dead end. I think Natascha put some orange dye into the water when I turned around to leave. I am not one-hundred percent certain, but we saw some orange dye the next day when we recovered the ROV, and that was basically the only place she could have done it."

Nick and Shira exchanged puzzled looks.

"That sounds like her", Nick admitted. "Any chance that someone else might have placed the orange dye?" Nick wondered curiously, but he knew his wife well enough.

"Unlikely, Nick. If you saw the place you'd know why."

"We've found some pictures of the catacombs that Natascha took. It does show the orange dye everywhere. It makes sense. We first thought the water just looked like it because of her lights." Shira explained.

"What are you talking about? Natascha never took pictures of the room. I was right there with her. She didn't even have a camera with her", Mario replied. Now it was his turn to look puzzled.

"Wait a second, let me send them to you", Shira told him.

"Yeah, that's the room all right", Mario confirmed after he had taken a quick look at the pictures. "The room looks the same when it comes to the height and width of it. I believe those pictures were taken from the other side of the brick wall. The brick wall you are looking at is the same wall that we stared at from the other side. So it technically divides the cave into two rooms. One side, which is much smaller, is the one we accessed through the abbey. This side here is only accessible from the side tunnel we dove in. It also seems to be larger. Much larger. It's strange that she never mentioned it to me", Mario explained. Neither Nick nor Shira had any reason not to believe him.

"So you've never seen that room yourself?" Nick wanted to clarify.

"No, she must've been there while I fixed the ROV. I saw her wandering off a little bit, but I always saw her primary light, Nick. She really wasn't that far away. That must be less than twenty metres."

"So the bones she claimed to have seen must have literally been in that room?" Shira wanted to further clarify. Mario didn't answer immediately, but took his time again to go through the pictures and his own recollection before he slowly nodded.

"I would say so. I think it's safe to say that the bones were either from that room or not far away from it. Maybe it had been used as a grave site or storage room before it flooded? It's a natural cave system after all."

Nick took some notes. "Mario, would you be able to take a closer look at her pictures and videos? It might help us piece together all the info we have. Maybe she did find something after all."

"Certainly, just send them to my e-mail address and I'll get right at it. Whatever I can do to help", Mario offered without hesitation.

"I really appreciate it, Mario. Thanks!" Nick said before ending the connection. "What the hell did she get herself into?" Nick demanded to know, closing his eyes with frustration. "She promised me she wouldn't do anything stupid!"

"Nick, we don't know if that has anything to do with her disappearance. We're just following this as another lead that might give us some answers. But I highly doubt this has anything to do with her kidnapping", Shira tried to calm him down, then suggested, "We should go and brief Brian and Klaus now."

Both Brian and Klaus listened carefully to what Nick had to say, and they even jotted their own notes. While Nick showed Natascha's pictures from the catacombs, Shira excused herself. It took Nick a few minutes to go through all the pictures with them, but they eventually agreed that it had been a good idea to ask for Mario's opinion on it.

"Okay, so where does this leave us now?" Brian asked at the end.

"I don't know, sir, but do you think she found something up there that could've gotten her into trouble?" Nick asked curiously, providing the other angle they were looking for. Both Brian and Klaus exchanged some looks, and it was Klaus who shook his head first.

"I don't know, Nick. It might have been odd, even with the alleged paedophile accusations around the abbey, but I cannot see a direct connection between it. I mean, even Mario didn't know that she was in there, and we do know for a fact that she hasn't sent any of those pictures to anyone over the internet. What's her name? Erika? Even she had no idea about it. If Natascha had posted them everywhere and started to ring some bells, maybe. But without telling anyone? I can't see the connection to be honest."

Nick pondered Klaus' argument, and he came to the conclusion that his boss was right.

"Yeah, you're right, sir. So, what are we doing next?" Nick asked as Shira returned to the office.

"Well, you should probably update our timeline and get those pictures and videos to Mario. Maybe you can put your notes together on this and leave them in the conference room?"

"Yes, I'll do that." Nick got up and took his laptop with him, glad that he could actively do something.

"I'll be right with you, Nick", Shira told him as he walked by her. She waited until he had closed the office door behind him before turning towards Klaus and Brian, who both looked at her anxiously.

"We got a problem!" Shira announced seriously, showing her cell phone to her superiors.

- 17 -

West of Al-Hasakah, Syria, Monday, July 21
Monique just woke up. Her head felt like it was about to explode, the throbbing headache being fuelled by the loud noise of an old diesel engine. As if the headache itself wasn't enough, the rest of her body felt like it had been put through a meat grinder. It was as they hit another bump and she bounced across the hard floor that she learned where the pain was coming from. To make matters worse, the erratic movement made her feel dizzy, and she fought the urge of throwing up.

Monique didn't know where she was or what had happened to her, but even when she opened her eyes, she didn't see anything. The black hood someone had used to blindfold her made sure of that. The young French woman tried to sit up, but she kept being tossed around and found it difficult to keep her balance. Panic started to rise inside her once she noticed she could no longer move her arms. The pain of the zip-ties cutting into her wrists was hurting more than the first time, digging into the old wounds. Monique listened to the sound of the engine again as it revved. She couldn't hide her shock when she eventually realised she was in the cargo bed of a large truck.

Her arms were tied in front of her body, but she finally managed to sit up. Another bump in the road threw her back against the boards forming the side wall. Monique wanted to scream, but she somehow knew that it wouldn't make a difference. She crouched against the side boards and tried to piece the last twenty-four hours together, but the last thing she could remember were two guards holding her to the ground while another guy stabbed a needle into her arm. It didn't matter how hard she tried, everything else from then on had been wiped clean.

She had been terrified back then at the hospital, but somehow this seemed much worse. The growing panic inside her caused her panting to descend into hyper-ventilation. Monique tried deep-breathing exercises, but the fear was gripping her tightly. She opened her eyes again, but she could only see black shadows. The air was thick, hot and dry, making it more difficult to breathe under the black hood. She could hear the crisp sounds of the canvas flapping overhead, concealing the loud truck's cargo bed.

Her stomach flipped as the truck fell with a dip in the road, causing her head to hit the sideboards, the pain shooting tears to her eyes. She ducked down quickly from the next bump, avoiding the cargo bed's sides. The old engine's dominant sound increased her headache as the old military vehicle moved eastwards over the desert road.

Monique tried very hard to ignore the diesel engine's omnipresent howling, but it was so loud that it was impossible. As her journey to the unknown continued, she noticed another sound. Faint at first, but then it became clearer and clearer, until she identified the distinct sound of people sobbing. She turned her head to the left and suddenly realised that there were other women with her in the back of the truck. Despite the high temperature, a chill ran down Monique's back and she pulled her legs tighter to her body.

To Monique, it seemed that the longer the journey took, the more dominant the crying and sobbing became as more people began to wake up, finally realising where they were. The French woman guessed they were travelling for several hours before the engine sound finally changed.

The old truck slowed down and jerked to a complete stop. Monique waited for something to happen, but aside from the sobbing she could hear men talking in what sounded like Arab. She couldn't understand what they were saying, but she shrieked when someone pounded his fists twice on the sideboards. As if that was the signal, the truck slowly started to move again, away from the checkpoint and further down the road. Monique noticed it drove slowler this time.

It didn't take long before the truck left the main road and turned right onto what was nothing more than a wide path. The old truck protested against driving on the rough terrain, but managed to keep moving forward. The vehicle followed the path leading to an ancient settlement carved deep into the canyon's stone walls just below the top of the hill at the horizon.

Despite the bad conditions, the truck steadily closed the distance to the hill. The old six cylinder diesel engine had to work harder as the truck slowly crawled up the dirt road leading them to their final destination, the plateau on top of a hill. From the air, it looked like a normal plateau, divided by natural canyons. Nobody knew about the old caves, chiseled into the massive stone walls centuries ago, hidden from the sky. Just before the truck reached the top of the plateau, the driver steered the truck into one canyon. With just a few centimetres to spare on each side to the rock walls, the truck kept going.

Monique still didn't know where they were. She could feel the truck veer around a sharp bend revealing another sound: Gunshots! Fearing for her life, Monique and the rest of the women in the truck started screaming as more shots echoed from the walls. It didn't matter that none of the bullets hit the truck, the strangeness of the sound itself shrieked terror in the air. The driver hit the horn repeatedly, announcing their arrival, Monique presumed, and the sound of chanting and shouting echoed through the air followed by more gunshots.

Carefully, the driver steered the old truck into a cavern with some other vehicles. The cavern was so spacious that it could successfully hide several vehicles from the spying eyes of passing satellites. Eventually, the truck came to a complete standstill, and the silence of the engine as the driver turned it off was a welcomed change.

Monique listened intently as she slowly sat up again, fearing what would happen next. The shooting had stopped, but she could hear people approaching the truck shouting and cheering in Arab. Despite the heat, Monique started to shiver. She had no idea what would happen next, but she knew it couldn't be good. She swallowed hard, and it was only now that she realised how dry and thirsty she was. She flinched under the sudden sound of at least a dozen men pounding the truck's side louder and louder. She couldn't see them, but she heard two men climbing on the back of the truck, the suspension shifting under their weight as they opened the gate and whipped the tarp off the top of the steel frame. Although Monique still had the blindfold on, she could now see their silhouettes against the bright background. The men's laughter and shouting turned into a roar when they finally saw the women. With panic rising inside her, Monique started to scream.

EuroSecCorporation, **London, Monday, July 21**

"What is it?" Brian growled, knowing that this couldn't be good.

"When we spoke with Erika, we asked her about this guy, Mark. She evaded a direct answer, just saying that he might be working at the institute, but I saw her reaction after Nick had sent her the Skype address. I'm not sure if Nick noticed it, but it was clear to me that Erika at least recognised the name. Erika promised that she would look into it, and she just texted me", Shira explained and exhaled sharply.

"And?" Brian carefully asked. He didn't like the direction this was going. Shira turned around to make sure that the door was closed before she continued.

"It turns out that Erika knows Mark. She knows him very well actually. She just didn't want to say anything in front of Nick."

"Oh dear Lord", Brian sighed and rolled his eyes. "Please don't tell me..."

"Yes, Brian. Mark is Natascha's ex. They dated for a couple of years. Erika said that they even went on an expedition together, but that's when their relationship ended."

"So Natascha was in contact with her ex-boyfriend just before she was kidnapped?"

"Yes, but according to all her data she only contacted him once, and that was the five minute Skype conversation we noticed."

"Could Erika tell you why she contacted him?" Brian wanted to know.

"She could do even better than that. She said that Natascha had given her a little parcel to give to him, but she didn't know what was in it. Natascha made her promise to hand deliver it only to Mark, which Erika apparently did."

"Did Erika hear back from this fellow after she delivered the parcel?"

"No, she hasn't. Brian, we know that Natascha got kidnapped. Our source at the airport told us that..."

"I know what the source told us, Shira, and unfortunately I believe that Natascha has been kidnapped. It's just going to be the icing on the cake for Nick to hear that. Do *you* want to tell him that?" Brian asked. Shira made a face. She knew that the retired admiral had a valid point. It would also be rather difficult to hide this fact from Nick. "So, this guy, Mark is his name? What do you know about him? Did Natascha ever mention him to you during some girl talk?" Brian asked directly. He was beyond the point of being discreet.

"She only referred to him as her ex. I cannot recall her saying his name, she only mentioned him once or twice. She never talked about him or their time together in a way that would let me think that she still has feelings for him. Like I said, she only mentioned him once or twice."

"You think you can talk to him? Without Nick noticing it?" Klaus asked.

"Already tried, but he didn't pick up his phone. I left him my cell phone number and told him to call me as soon as possible."

"What did you tell him?"

"Only that it was about Natascha and that it's important for him to contact me only."

"This is the last thing we need!" Brian said and shook his head. His mind spun around Nick's possible reaction. He picked up a pen and played with it, trying to find a way to follow the lead without hurting Nick any further. "Okay, Shira, I trust you on this one. Get in contact with him and see what you can find out. Until we know what was in that parcel and what they talked about, I want you to keep Nick out of this. Understood?"

"Absolutely!" Shira confirmed.

Casino de Monte Carlo, Monte Carlo, Monaco, Wednesday, July 23

Alba "Saphir" Casillas was bored. Sitting at one of the large bars in the casino's VIP section, she looked at her watch for the third time within the last five minutes. Her client was already over two hours late, but Rowan had texted her to simply stay put and wait. Considering that he had already paid for her time, she couldn't care less about where he was. She took another sip from her orange juice while watching the rich and famous through the mirrored wall behind the bar. Since her client could show up any moment, she followed her own rules and refused several drinks offered by other gentlemen and sat just by herself. Making sure not to make eye contact with anyone, she waited as patiently as she could and yawned behind her hand hoping that Rowan would take his time.

For the last thirty minutes she had eavesdropped on the conversation between two business managers to her right. They were talking strictly about the latest news on the stock market, but Saphir didn't mind. At least it kept her mind busy. Once they emptied their glasses they got up and left for the tables again. Saphir frowned and smiled at the bartender, signalling him that she wanted another orange juice.

"Here you go, Miss Casillas", the young man offered politely as he placed the glass in front of her. As before, he automatically charged the drink to Mr Harrison. Rowan Harrison had a standing tab in the casino and was well-known. The bartender also knew about Saphir, and he made sure to always treat her with the utmost respect.

"Thank you", the beautiful Spanish woman smiled back.

"My pleasure", the young man replied and stepped over to the computer screen.

The obnoxious fake laugh of a woman caused Saphir to turn her head. The lady had obviously had one or two too many glasses of champagne, but her friends didn't seem to mind. Saphir politely smiled in their direction, just in case they would look at her. Her smile froze as she saw a door opening behind them. Rowan Harrison entered with Prince Tarek and his entourage.

"Oh, hell no!" Saphir cursed the moment she recognised the Saudi prince. He was one of the closer members of the Saudi royal family. Saphir knew Rowan and Prince Tarek were friends, but she had not known she would meet him and his entourage here. Her last meeting with him had ended with her fearing for her life, and she had sworn herself to never have contact with the prince or anyone from his entourage again. She knew Prince Tarek was about the same age as Rowan and noticed he had a similar build as they walked side by side towards her. The prince continued his conversation with Rowan and, based on his hand gestures, Saphir assumed that it was rather important. As the group neared, Saphir took another look at the Prince's entourage. She immediately recognised his usual bodyguards.

While Prince Tarek wore the traditional Saudi garb of a prince, including the smagh and igal, his four rather large bodyguards wore black suits. She knew they were more muscle than brains and didn't have any respect for them. Especially not after her last meeting with the Prince. Behind them were three women. Saphir recognised two of them, but she couldn't remember to have seen the third one. Saphir frowned as she finally saw her face. She estimated her to be not older than twenty. Even the expensive blue dress and the make-up couldn't cover the fact that the young lady was horrified. The rest of their party followed a few steps behind, about ten men and women. It was quite obvious they were already heavily intoxicated.

"You have got to be kidding me", Saphir scowled at Rowan as he finally came over and kissed her. Prince Tarek and his group continued to one of the exclusive VIP lounges, and the Saudi prince had not taken any notice of Saphir yet.

"What are you talking about?" Rowan slurred. He clearly had a couple drinks already, and judging by his dilated pupils, Saphir knew he had taken some drugs as well.

"I told you several times that I will not have any contact with that asshole ever again!" the Spaniard hissed, carefully watching the group through the mirror.

"Relax! Why are you so upset? We just came from the *Shadow*", the British heir tried to calm her down.

"You came from where?" Saphir asked, not hiding her disgust.

"His ship! It's called the *Shadow of the Orient!* We just came from his ship. He'll be leaving in a few hours. We're just here to have some fun at the tables. Besides, you are my date. He has his own. You have nothing to worry about, I promise!"

"The hell I don't! You know damn well what that pig did to me the last time! If he or one of his goons gets close to me, you'll never see me again."

"Okay, okay, relax. I will tell him", Rowan mumbled unnerved and was about to turn around, but Saphir grasped his arm.

"I mean it Rowan! The guy is a psychopath! I did not sign up for this!" Saphir insisted. Rowan just looked at her beautiful face, but even in his intoxicated state he could clearly see that the Spaniard wasn't joking.

"Okay, I told you I'll talk to him!" Rowan said and freed his arm, but he had difficulty keeping his balance.

"You're such a jerk!" Saphir snapped at him, not even trying to hide her disgust.

"Yeah, whatever. Are you coming?" Rowan asked and already aimed for the door to the VIP lounge. Saphir just shook her head and turned to the bar to pick up her purse. The bartender frowned as his eyes met hers. Saphir didn't mind that he had overheard their little argument. After all, she couldn't care less for Rowan on a personal level. Saphir just shrugged and mouthed a goodbye to the bartender before she followed Rowan.

The British playboy was almost at the doors before Saphir caught up to him. Two of Prince Tarek's goons had already taken position at the door to make sure that no unauthorised person would enter the private lounge. Both of them were well over one-metre-ninety tall, but neither of them showed any sign that they recognised

Saphir. They just nodded to Rowan and opened the door without comment. Saphir decided to completely ignore them and walked through the door as fast as she could.

"Why am I doing this? This is so stupid! I should walk out of here right now!" the Spanish escort muttered, more to herself than to Rowan. She knew she couldn't expect any sympathy from Rowan, at least not while he was intoxicated. Being very familiar with the room, Saphir aimed for the bar in the middle.

The guests were evenly spread out. A smaller group including the Saudi prince had gathered around a gambling table. His remaining two goons stood close behind him, keeping their guard up even in here. She could see that they were actively scanning the room. While Saphir glided to the bar, Rowan walked over to the gambling table, finding his place right beside his Saudi business partner. Saphir followed his actions in the mirror. There was still a realistic chance that the prince had not recognised her yet, and, as far as Saphir was concerned, there was no reason for her to change that. There was only one other couple with her at the bar, both of them were relatively sober. The rest of the party had found their places either at one of the three gambling tables or on the leather chesterfields. Saphir was mad at herself for not walking away from Rowan earlier, but the fact that he had easily brushed off what she had told him really did upset her. She fought to conceal her disgust, and she distracted herself by picking up the menu. She wasn't really hungry, but decided to have a small salad. In her experience, eating something healthy was the easiest way to make sure that intoxicated people left her alone.

"Anything to drink, Miss Casillas?" the bartender asked.

"Just the usual, please", Saphir answered with a smile. He looked surprised, but professionally returned the smile. "Wait, whose tab?" Saphir leaned over in a whisper, making sure that only the bartender could hear her. Saphir knew this was a very inappropriate question, but the bartender knew her from earlier visits and, quite honestly, Saphir didn't care.

"His Highness, Prince Tarek, has told me to charge everything to his name", the bartender whispered back, knowing very well that he would lose his job if anyone would have heard him.

"Thank you! In that case, I'll also have a small bottle of nineteen-ninety-eight Krug Clas d'Ambonnay", Saphir whispered with a lascivious smile. The bartender frowned, not exactly sure how to react, but he quickly recovered and just nodded before he forwarded the order. Satisfied to have charged the most expensive bottle of champagne available in Monaco to Prince Tarek's spending account, Saphir watched both him and Rowan in the mirror. Their exchange seemed superficial, though she was glad that neither of them paid any attention to her.

Nibbling on her salad just a few minutes later, Saphir enjoyed a glass of the perfectly chilled champagne when Rowan walked over.

"Is there a reason you're not joining me at the table?" he wanted to know.

"Yes! The reason is standing right beside you. As long as you're standing with him, I won't. And I don't care what you say." Saphir snapped. Her tone made it very clear that she would not change her mind and that this was not up for debate.

"Well, as long as you're enjoying yourself", Rowan said, finally noticing the champagne. He took the bottle out of the cooler and read the label. "Bloody hell, you must really hate him", he mentioned after a few seconds and made a face.

"You have no idea, Rowan!" Saphir replied. She was surprised. It was the first time she had heard any sense of care in Rowan's tone of voice. She almost believed he had some sympathy.

"So there's really no chance for you coming over to the table?"

"No, Rowan. Absolutely no chance. I told you that before."

"Oh, well, he's about to ship out in two hours anyway. I don't think he'll be here that much longer. You don't mind waiting until he's gone?" Rowan asked and looked at Saphir's angelic face.

"No, I don't mind", Saphir replied, this time in a much friendlier tone. She kept watching the other guests through the mirror and couldn't help but notice the young woman in the blue dress again. She sat on a chesterfield with another person, but she was obviously not enjoying herself. While Rowan helped himself to a glass of the ridiculously expensive champagne, Saphir kept her eyes on the young lady.

"How old is she?" she finally asked Rowan, her mouth twisting in distaste.

"Says nineteen-ninety-eight on the label", Rowan slurred and took a closer look at the champagne bottle. He had no idea what Saphir was talking about.

"Not the champagne, I'm talking about the girl. Blue dress."

Rowan turned around to take a look for himself.

"Oh, that one", he mumbled, his voice clearly reflecting the fact that he didn't care at all for the young blonde. "She's with Tarek. Don't know how old she is. Who cares how old she is?" Rowan explained and turned his attention to Saphir's salad.

"For heaven's sake, Rowan. Look at her! She can't be twenty years old!" Rage pushed the words from Saphir's mouth as she watched the young lady who was now sitting by herself again.

"Yeah, well, I didn't see her passport. Are you done with this?" Rowan asked, staring at her remaining salad.

"Sometimes you're such a jerk!" Saphir snapped at him, whatever sympathy she believed he had was certainly nonexistent now. Her southern European temperament fuelled the rage inside her, and she decided to get up before someone else would hear their argument. Rowan just shrugged and sat on her bar stool, his concentration fixed on the leftovers of her salad. Saphir shook her head and walked over to the young blonde, trying her best to stay well out of the way of Prince Tarek and his two bodyguards.

"Hi, how are you doing?" Saphir asked as she approached the young woman. The lady flinched as she heard Saphir, but that was about her only reaction. "Do you mind if I sit with you?" Saphir invited herself and offered a pleasant smile.

The young woman looked at her and shyly shook her head. The Spaniard sat beside her and waved at a waitress.

"Can we please have some juice as well as a small salad for the lady?" Saphir asked. The waitress confirmed the order and disappeared immediately. "There's always time to eat some salad. Besides, as long as you're eating, everybody else leaves you alone. It's sort of an unwritten rule. And you certainly look like you're hungry." Saphir explained and searched the woman's face for an answer. It seemed to Saphir that her smile brightened by the thought that she would be kept alone. The two women didn't speak until the waitress brought the salad and two glasses of fresh orange juice.

"I...I don't have...money", the blonde whispered, barely audible, the moment the waitress had left.

"Don't worry about that. Just eat and relax a little bit", Saphir laughed, successfully hiding her concern. The blonde shyly looked around, but eventually picked up the fork and started eating. Saphir decided to give her some time and waited until she was finished.

"Can I ask how old you are?" Saphir finally asked.

"Eight....Eighteen. I'm eighteen."

"Eighteen?" Saphir was appalled by her answer.

"Yes."

Saphir wasn't sure why she was so frightened; she looked around to see if anyone followed their conversation, but a quick glance showed that everyone else was having a rather good time.

"Rowan said that you're with the Prince. Prince Tarek. Is that correct?"

The young lady didn't answer. She just flinched at his name and nodded. Saphir had a hard time to control her rage.

"Are you with him voluntarily?" she clarified quickly.

The blonde woman first nodded hesitantly, but, after making sure that no one was watching her, she shook her head.

"No, I'm not. I...he....he said that I belong to him now."

It cost Saphir all her willpower not to stand up and walk over to the Prince, but she knew that it would have been an ill-advised action on her part and decided against it.

"Okay, do you have a passport?" She wanted to know instead.

"No."

"Any other ID? Or a credit card?" Saphir continued, but the young woman kept shaking her head. Saphir looked around and didn't say anything for a few minutes as she cycled through her options. "Okay, I got an idea. Just do what I say, okay?"

The young woman's eyes widened. She was obviously too scared to do anything that would upset the Prince. Saphir could only imagine what consequences he had threatened her with.

"Look, I can help you, but you have to trust me, okay? Just give me a minute", She tried to reassure her. The blonde only nodded and watched as Saphir walked over to the bar again.

Rowan had taken his time with Saphir's leftovers and was talking to another couple still sitting at the bar as Saphir walked up to him.

"Oh, there you are. I guess I owe you a salad", he snickered patting the seat beside him, inviting her to sit.

"Don't worry about it. I'll just be a few minutes. I have to freshen up", Saphir explained and turned around again.

"Yes, whatever. I'm not going anywhere", the British heir replied and turned his attention to his friends again.

"Okay, let's go! If someone asks you, I'm showing you the facilities so you can freshen up, understood?" Saphir whispered to the blonde and walked with her to the door. "Just smile, everything will be okay", the Spaniard reassured her. For a moment, Saphir considered fleeing to the suite Rowan had booked for them, but she decided against it.

Heading to the nearest exit, Saphir mentally went through the items that were still in her suitcase. She wasn't too concerned about her clothes and her shoes. She was more concerned if she would leave something behind that would have her address on it, but she couldn't think of anything. Walking through the main hall she remembered she wasn't even registered as a guest, and every time she went shopping the bill got charged to Rowan's name, never hers. As far as she was concerned, it was almost like she didn't exist. Nothing she left would leave too many traces behind. She knew that Rowan would find her eventually, but at least she would have a decent head start. No one had stopped them yet, but it still took them several minutes before they reached one of the exits. Saphir gave her chip to the valet and nervously looked back over her shoulder, but no one had followed them. It seemed to take forever, but only minutes had passed before her black BMW parked in front of her.

"Okay, get in. Time to get out of here", Saphir nervously said and threw her shoes on the back seat. As soon as they buckled their seat belts, Saphir took off and steered her car north-west on Place du Casino.

"Do you have a cell phone with you?" she asked hurriedly as she turned left onto Avenue de la Madone.

"No, I do not", the young lady shook her head.

"Good!" Saphir smiled and searched for her own devise in her purse. As Avenue de la Madone became Boulevard Princesse Charlotte, Saphir had already turned her cell phone off. Her original plan had been to call someone for help, but now that they were actually on their way, she had no idea whom to call. She didn't know why, but she had the feeling that it would be better to not have the cell phone turned on at all.

Just as Boulevard Princesse Charlotte became Pont Sainte-Devote, Saphir looked in her rear mirror again, but this was Monte Carlo, and there was so much traffic that it was impossible for her to figure out if someone was following her. The Spaniard shook her head, but as far as she could remember, not even Rowan knew what car she was driving. She took the first exit in the roundabout and stayed on Boulevard du Jardin Exotique. The French border was now right in front of them.

"Okay, just relax. Put on your best smile and everything will be okay", Saphir advised, but she wasn't sure if she was reassuring her new friend or herself. As she looked into her rear mirror again, Saphir slowed her car down further and picked a lane. She took a deep breath and opened her window, but the young officer just briefly peeked inside the BMW before waving them through without even stopping them.

"Welcome to France!" Saphir laughed euphorically and looked at the passenger seat. Her new friend looked back to the border crossing, and she slowly realised she actually might be safe now. For the first time in many weeks the young woman smiled.

"Okay, that was the hardest part. I don't think they'll follow us. They don't know what car I'm driving. We'll drive to London. I'm living there. You can stay with me for now. Don't worry, Rowan doesn't know where I live. We'll find a place; I have some friends there! We'll find a solution. You can sleep for now if you want." All the tension fell from Saphir as she looked over and smiled at her.

"Thank...Thank you!"

"By the way, I'm Alba."

"I am Elena."

- 18 -

Asklepios, Aegean Sea, Thursday, July 24
The last couple days all followed the same routine. Early in the morning, the guards would burst into their room to wake them. Threateningly pointing their tasers, Natascha and Jake were then separated and guided to their designated work stations. Once back in their cell in the evening, they usually told each other about their day, hoping to find some helpful information.

Natascha was about to start her own chores in the large treatment room, when she heard a scuffle behind the doors. She could hear Jake's objections about something, and, as another guard moved through the door for backup, she watched as he was roughly taken away. Natascha wanted to protest, but one of the guards pointed his taser at her, threatening and daring her to try anything. Natascha just raised her hands in defeat and continued her duties.

It used to be difficult to track the time, but with each passing day, the normal things seemed more noticeable. One of the more helpful details Natascha noticed was that all the guards wore watches. Another quick glance to a wrist-watch of an unaware guard showed Natascha that Jake was gone for a few hours now.

"You missed a spot", Melissa pointed out with an impish grin and spit on the floor. Natascha looked over to the area she had just cleaned, her anger burning up her neck. Natascha's grip tightened around the mop she held in her hand. She was tempted to swing it around and beat Melissa with it. Instead, she shook her head as she pushed the mop across the floor. Both the Irish nurse and Kevin Wilson had their eyes fixed on her every move to ensure she did not take anything she could use as a weapon from the examination room.

Despite Jake's unusual absence, Natascha found her rhythm in her daily routine again. Glancing at the clock beside the monitors, Natascha knew that it was almost time for supper. Instead of hunger, nervousness returned. Jake was still gone, and her concern for her new friend resurfaced. Jake was the person she spent the most time with, but she didn't trust him enough to tell him the truth about her story. She couldn't deny that his presence had helped her tremendously the last couple of days. Just to have someone to talk to during the nights helped her keep her emotions in check. To take care of the majority of the female patients by herself was emotionally exhausting. Against her better knowledge, Natascha developed the urge to help every one of them. She made sure to spend time with each of them, hoping to forget about the one she couldn't. Despite her best efforts, she thought about Elena every day. Natascha considered asking the guards or the nurses about her whereabouts, but she knew they would only use her name to increase her emotional distress. Natascha didn't fool herself about Elena's fate. After all, she knew she was in the midst of a human trafficking ring. Elena herself had told her that someone had bought her not too long ago. Natascha focussed on her own situation and realised that her best chances of survival and escape required the help from other people. Even then, the odds were against her. She didn't even know how many more prisoners were at this facility, but she was realistic enough to know there was no chance for her to save them all, if any. Her escape required her to be selfish, yet the thought of rescuing others weighed heavy on her mind. With the hospital trolley loaded with sandwiches and fruits, Natascha started her rounds.

"For heaven's sake, you'll manage without your new boyfriend." Kevin Wilson yelled as he noticed Natascha was still looking for Jake. "He's occupied otherwise, but don't worry, you'll have him back soon enough", he laughed.

Natascha had to swallow hard as she heard that. Whatever Kevin was referring to couldn't be good. With one of the guards escorting her, Natascha started her rounds on C-Level, where the examination rooms and medical centre were located. She relied on the guard to open the doors with his electronic key card and the four digit code.

During the last four days, Natascha managed to gather little new information. Crucial details of her escape plan were still missing. She knew where the elevator was, but again, an electronic key card and a four digit code were necessary to move above E-Level where the control room was located. Natascha knew that her own cell was on D-Level, but she had never been on any of the other floors, and without windows it was impossible for her to know if she was above or below the ground.

When the elevator door opened again, Natascha and her guard walked out to C-Level, and just minutes later Natascha served the imprisoned patients in the large examination room. Her hopes to see Jake down here didn't materialise, and the disappointment was clear on her face. Only a few of the beds were occupied, but Natascha's hopes rose again when she eventually recognised Lawrence and Charles. They had spent the last couple days in their individual cell, not allowing Natascha to talk to them, but this could be another chance.

"Hi guys! How are you doing?" Natascha greeted them after she made sure the guards were preoccupied with their own duties. A quick glance over their bodies didn't reveal anything concerning for Natascha.

"Could be better. They drew some blood this morning. Not sure how much they took, but it was a lot", Lawrence whispered and closed his eyes. He and Charles were still very dizzy.

"Here, I have lots to drink for you then. That should help you", Natascha offered and placed a couple plastic bottles with juice on their beds.

"How's your plan coming along? I'm not too certain if Charles and I have much time left."

"What do you mean?" Natascha's eyes grew bigger as she heard this.

"Well, we know that they're going to use us as organ donors. They have all the results from the examinations and already drew some blood from us. I assume they're just checking for a match, and we all know how long those lists are. You do the math." Charles explained.

"I didn't make much progress. I know a little bit more about the layout of the facility. Every exit needs a magnetic key card and a four digit code. As far as I know, that code changes almost every day. I overheard a technician this morning in one of the control rooms. I don't know exactly what the issue was, but he complained about the old wiring of the video surveillance system and that it is a closed loop. I also may have an idea about how to get outside."

"So, what's your plan?"

"Still working on that part. Opportunities seem to be rather rare, but there's at least some good news. The doors to the cells just have traditional locks, so I can easily open them to get you two out once I got the keys."

"Yeah, we noticed that too." Lawrence nodded. "Any idea what to do once we are outside? We will still be on the godforsaken island."

"Like I said, working on it. Our options are limited, but we have no way of knowing what kind of resources we will find out there, so we have to wing it."

"Let's hope there is something out there we can use, but we don't have much of a choice."

"I don't want to sound rude or impolite, but what kind of shape are you two in?" Natascha asked. She felt guilty they were both in this mess, but she also knew that it wasn't her fault. Her plan, if it would ever come to execution, would only work if they wouldn't slow her down.

"We were living on the street for years now, we're survivors. Don't worry about us. We still have one last fight left in us. Isn't that right, Lawrence?"

"Bloody hell, yes! How's this new guy? What about him?"

"Jake? He seems to be okay", Natascha answered and told them the short version of his story. "I don't know. He helps me through the nights, and it's nice to have someone to talk to." Natascha explained in a whispering tone and shrugged. A shiver ran down her spine.

"Are you okay?" Lawrence wanted to know. Natascha slowly shook her head, a tear running down her face.

"I'm terrified about the moment they will come for me. I can keep my mind occupied during the day, but as much as I try, the nights are horror for me. Having someone I can talk to really helps."

"You trust him?"

"Haven't decided on that one yet. I assume that he has figured out by now that I don't plan to go down without a fight, but I haven't told him anything." Natascha glanced back to her guards nonchalantly before she continued, "By the way, have you seen him today? They took him away this morning and I haven't seen him since."

"No, not a sign. As we told you before, we have never seen him."

"Yeah, they usually put him to work somewhere else. I guess they want to keep us separated. What about Kyle? I have the feeling he's still avoiding me. Did you get a chance to talk to him?" Natascha wanted to know as she spotted the young reporter on the other end of the examination room for the first time since their previous meeting.

"Today is our first day back in here. He was cleaning the floor when they brought us here. We talked to him a little bit, told him that you're okay. He listened, which was good. Maybe you should give it another try." Lawrence encouraged her.

"Maybe I should." Natascha considered the option and turned around. She pushed the trolley towards him and offered something to eat and drink. Just by the way he looked at her it was rather obvious that he still had his doubts.

"Thank you, I guess", he said as he took the food. "So the two guys over there told me about your story", Kyle mentioned between two sandwiches.

"Yes. Thank you for listening to them", Natascha replied as they both sat on the floor. She decided not to push her luck and waited for Kyle to take the initiative. Natascha took the moment to eat something.

"So, how come you were with that bishop back then?" he eventually asked after making sure that no one paid too much attention to them.

"I wasn't. We were with someone else. Rowan Harrison. He was talking to the bishop when you showed up." Natascha explained. She hoped that by telling him Rowan's name, she could build up a certain level of trust.

"Rowan Harrison? That explains a lot!"

"You know him?"

"I'm a reporter, remember?"

Natascha frowned. Basically every reporter in London knew Rowan Harrison.

"So you said that you have found some evidence?" Kyle prodded. Although they whispered, his anxiety was clear in his voice.

"Not certain, but I might have found something", Natascha answered and quickly filled him in. Their situation didn't allow her to go into all the details, but she had at least enough time to tell him the most important parts.

"That's bloody marvellous. Exactly what I thought!" Kyle enthused, trying to keep his voice to a light whisper. "Not that it matters anymore", he added with a sarcastic laugh.

"Well, we're not dead yet. What are they doing with you anyway? Elena said something about a surgery?"

"Elena?"

"Yes, the young blonde girl. Romanian."

"Ah right, I remember. She's gone now, isn't she?"

Natascha swallowed hard and nodded.

"Bloody bastards!" Kyle cursed through his lips before he continued. "They took some of my blood. Took one of my kidneys, too. Turns out that I'm worth a lot of money to them. If you don't pose a physical threat to them and stay healthy, they keep you alive so that you can do the general labour around here. The moment they think you're a threat or that you're plotting your escape, it's game over."

"What do you mean by that?"

"They take all the spare parts they can from you, including tissue, skin and all the blood. The remains will be cremated. That's with the men. With the women it's different. They only take the organs they can live without, like a kidney. They always take blood. After that, well, you know what they're doing with them."

"They sell them. Elena told me about it." Natascha whispered. Kyle just nodded and ate another sandwich, while Natascha tried to digest the information.

"That's correct. I just haven't found out why."

"What do you mean?"

"If they sell them, they're only worth so much money, but they can make at least ten times the money if they sell all their organs."

Natascha thought about it for a second too, but she knew that her time was running out. Kevin Wilson already checked his watch, and Natascha knew that he would start his usual round shortly. By then they would kick her out and escort her back to her cell again.

"Do you know where all the extra food goes to? When I am done with my rounds, I usually have tons left."

"I don't know, but I assume that there are more people on B-Level. I've never been there. Rumour has it that no one has come back from that floor alive, so I honestly don't know."

Natascha started to feel the frustration growing inside her.

"Do you know most of the male prisoners?"

"I guess I have seen most of them, why?"

"What can you tell me about Jake?"

"Who?"

But before Natascha could ask again, Kevin gave her the order to get up. Not looking for a confrontation, Natascha immediately obeyed. As the previous days, she was instructed to leave the trolley with the remaining food and two of the guards escorted her back to her cell. It didn't take long before they opened the door. She didn't even care about being pushed into the cell, her eyes were already focussed on Jake. Her new friend crouched on their bunk, his face swollen and bleeding.

"Jake!" Natascha shrieked as she kneeled in front of him. Jake looked at her through his swollen eyes, but the only thing Natascha could hear was the guards laughing as they locked the door again.

West of Al-Hasakah, Syria, Thursday, July 24
The last three days had been a complete horror for Monique and the other young women. Since their arrival at the camp a couple of days ago, her worst nightmares had turned into reality. Despite screaming and crying, the men immediately took the still blindfolded women from the truck and gathered them in one of the larger tents, where they kept them prisoners. They took off the blindfolds, but their hands remained tied together. Including herself, Monique counted a total of eleven women, and she recognised all of them from *Asklepios*. However, Freja was not with them, but the young French didn't know how or if that would have changed her own situation. Monique felt hopeless.

The last couple of days had been enough time for all the drugs they had given her to leave her system. Fuelled by dehydration, Monique was facing a serious headache. She was uncertain if her whole body ached from the transport to this desolate place or from the effects of the drugs. Like the other women, she spent most of the last two days crying, but it didn't change anything. She even tried to talk to the other women, but most of them just laid lethargically on the few dirty carpets covering the rock floor, waiting for what horror would come next. Monique didn't try to think too much about it. Although she was young and naive, she wasn't stupid. She pulled her knees back and assumed her crouched position, shaking her head at the sound the chain around her ankle made when she moved. She brushed her dusted hands against her dirty torn scrubs. She could see another tear on the side of her scrub pants from sleeping on the bare rock and the old carpets, but at least she wasn't cold.

Despite their tent being hidden inside the cavern out of the direct sunlight, the temperatures were still blistering hot during the day, just to dip a couple degrees above freezing during the nights. While huddling with the other women during the nights helped maintaining body heat, the putrid stench of being in such close proximity was overwhelming.

Monique had only heard the men talking in Arab during the last couple of days. She didn't understand a word, but she knew they were out there. And there were many of them! They guarded the tent and the rest of the camp, protecting it with lethal force against anyone or anything that got in their way.

The tent flap opened just as Monique went to lie down again, and the same three older women who had cared for them before entered. So far, no men had set foot in their tent yet. Monique glanced to the other prisoners around her. They also noticed the three older women, carrying jugs of water and the usual bread. Monique didn't bother talking to them, knowing it was useless. They wouldn't speak to them, and the little they said was in Arab anyway.

Monique didn't notice it at first, but there was something different. The women didn't leave after providing the rations. They stayed with them, even after they had finished their scarce meal. Something else was different. The Arab women kept watching the entrance and, gesticulating wildly with their hands, started whispering with each other.

It took Monique a while before she realised that they were not talking, but rather arguing with each other. Every few moments they stopped, and it seemed to Monique as if they were listening to something. As Monique concentrated, she could also hear that something was happening outside the tent. Voices! The more Monique concentrated, the more voices she could hear. There were just a few at the beginning, and now more voices were recognisable as they joined the chanting. A shiver ran down Monique's spine.

After a few minutes, Monique estimated by the noise that the crowd outside had grown to at least two hundred people. By now, everyone in the tent knew that something was about to happen. And everyone knew that it wouldn't be good. Breathing heavily, Monique swallowed hard and looked around. Most of the women had stopped crying, and, the fear for their lives clear in their faces, they also looked at the tent flap to see what would happen. It didn't take long before the flap opened and four men walked in.

As if their appearance was the signal, the women started crying again. The men quickly talked to each other. It seemed like they were arguing about which woman to take first. They eventually pointed at the young woman closest to them. The twenty-two year old started to scream, panic mechanically moving her body away from them. Two of the men grabbed her firmly as she tried to kick them off. The third one opened the shackle on her ankle. Free from the chain, they dragged her out of the tent, leaving Monique and the rest of the women behind. The horror was about to begin.

Alba "Saphir" Casillas's apartment, London, Thursday, July 24
"Thank God!" Alba exhaled with relief and closed the door to her apartment behind her. "That was a long drive", the Spaniard commented on the fifteen-hundred kilometre trip they had just finished, only stopping to fill up the BMW and get some snacks. With her keys in her hand, Alba kicked off her shoes before throwing the keys in a little bowl close to the door. Elena followed her.

It had taken her the twenty hours trip to finally trust Alba. After all, the Spanish woman was risking her own safety to help the Romanian escape from Prince Tarek. It was the first time in Elena's young life that someone went so far to protect her. Overwhelmed with the situation, Elena just stood there and watched as Alba disappeared into her bedroom.

"There's not that much space here. I live here by myself, but the couch folds into a bed. I say we should take a nice hot shower first and then have something good to eat. I don't know about you, but I need something healthy. All that fast food on the trip was horrible. After that, we can go out and get you some other clothes. I might have something here that should fit you until then", Alba went on and tossed some sweatpants, a t-shirt, and a sweater on the couch. Elena had still not moved and just watched as Alba threw more clothes on the couch before she disappeared into the bathroom.

"I put some fresh towels out for you if you want to shower first. I'll make something to eat. You do eat fish, do you?" Alba asked enthusiastically and finally looked at her new friend, but Elena just nodded. Facing so much generosity, the young Romanian didn't know what to say, but she liked the thought of a fresh shower and some clean clothes. She couldn't wait to get the dress off that Prince Tarek had given her.

"I can use those?" she asked with excitement, looking at the clothes.

"Si", Alba confirmed, falling back into Spanish, "they won't fit that great, but they're fresh. We'll get you something later tonight or tomorrow morning. And don't worry about the money. It's okay." Alba quickly added before Elena could protest.

Opening the fridge, Alba glanced back at the Romanian as she retrieved the clothes and disappeared into the bathroom. It was only when she took some food out of the fridge that Alba noticed how much she was shaking. Everything seemed to have gone so smoothly, and that unnerved her. The Spaniard realised that it was only a matter of time before Rowan would find her. And if that wasn't enough, she had another problem in her hands. She had promised Elena her friends would protect them, but she had no idea who those friends were. All she had was an idea, nothing more than a hope, but she didn't even know how to contact them. Despite all that, Alba knew she had to remain positive and pretend like she had a plan. She could sense that Elena was still on edge, and if she would find out that Alba did not have an actual plan, she knew Elena could have a hysterical fit or even run away.

With the shower running in the bathroom, Alba started her MacBook and searched for the information she was looking for.

"Come on, that can't be so difficult. Why are there so many?" Alba wondered out loud, a string of Spanish curses following as she worked the keyboard.

"Finalmente!" Alba finally sighed with relief once she found what she was looking for. She instinctively reached for her cell phone, but withdrew her hand.

"No, it's better to call them with a new cell phone and number. Don't take the risk", she ordered herself and wrote down the phone number instead. Satisfied with her decision, Alba closed the laptop and walked to her bedroom where she removed her clothes. She picked them up and walked into the bathroom, where Elena was just drying herself off. Alba smiled at her and threw her worn dress into the laundry basket before she entered the shower.

"I put some food on the kitchen counter. Maybe you can start cooking. I won't take long", Alba instructed with a smile. She closed the sliding door and turned the water back on. The Spaniard closed her eyes and enjoyed the warm water dancing across her skin. It felt like the stress from the last twenty-four hours was just washing away. Alba took her time as she felt the sleep deprivation starting to catch up to her. She couldn't expect less, realising that she was awake for almost forty hours now.

Almost instinctively, a yawn overcame her and she closed her eyes. Enjoying the hot water, she dreamed of sleep. By the time she stepped out of the bathroom in a pair of old sweat pants and a pullover, the smell of fresh cooked fish, rice and vegetables drifted over from the kitchen.

"Oh my God, that smells so good!" Alba complimented the cook and took two plates from a cupboard. The Spaniard turned on some music before they both enjoyed their meal. For Elena, it had been the first real food in weeks. It didn't take them long to clean their plates and they found their place beside each other on the couch.

"Don't worry, Elena. You are safe here", Alba reassured the young Romanian as she stroked her hair. Elena heaved a wobbly sigh and rested her head against Alba's shoulder. The Spaniard absentmindedly stared at her cell phone, wondering how many texts and calls from Rowan she had missed. She reached for the device, but decided against it at the last second.

"You think he called you?" Elena finally whispered, her eyes growing wide. Her voice reflected the fear she felt, and tears welled in her eyes. She was fixed on the phone, which rested silently in front of them on the table.

"No, Tarek does not have my number. Rowan has."

"Rowan?" Elena wanted to know and sat up.

"Yes, he was with that asshole in Monaco. He doesn't know where I live. They can't find us. I won't use the cell phone, and I'll get a new one tomorrow morning. You're safe", she whispered her support, feeling Elena shaking under her tears.

"Thank you, Alba. I'm scared they find me and I have to go back there."

"Don't worry. They won't. I promise. I have some really good friends that will protect us", Alba reassured the young Romanian woman. She couldn't blame her for being scared. Elena just nodded and wiped the tears from her face.

"This Rowan...You know him?" Elena's voice was shaking with fear.

"Sort of, why?" Alba asked curiously, but Elena took her time before she continued.

"Do you...like him?"

"No, he is just a client. What is it? Did he do something to you?" Alba wanted to know, rage pushing her words from her mouth as she prodded Elena for the truth.

"He is person who bought me. He gave me to Prince."

- *19* -

West of Al-Hasakah, Syria, Thursday, July 24
Monique felt the panic rising inside her as the chanting grew louder. Her eyes looked passed the three old Arab women, who were still inside the large tent with them. Her focus was set on escape, and despite her hands still being tied together, she tried as hard as she could to open the shackle on her ankle. The French quickly looked up, but the three old Arab women kept peeking outside the tent. Judging by the expression on their faces, this wasn't the first time something like this was happening. Just as the crowd chanted even louder, Monique and the other women heard something horrific rise above everything else: blood curdling screams! Monique felt a wave of heat flushing through her and a shiver descending her spine. Her stomach churned in knots. The young woman who had just been taken away moments ago screamed from the top of her lungs. Not once or twice, but continuously. Monique and the other women stopped whatever they were doing and just looked at each other, their faces reflecting the horror that was going on outside.

Another scream amidst the laughter and chanting woke Monique from her lethargy, and she shook the shackle on her leg, pulling at it every which way trying to open it. She didn't notice one of the old Arab women approaching her. It was only when she was right in front of her that Monique finally saw her. The young French screamed, not knowing what the old woman was about to do. She watched as the woman rummaged with her hands underneath her hijab before she eventually revealed an old, rusty knife. Monique shrieked at the sight and moved farther back. It took her a few seconds to realise that the old woman did not threaten her. She shook her head, attempting to understand as the woman held the knife flatly on her palm, offering it to her. But what would be the reason for that? Monique didn't know exactly what was going on outside the tent, but she knew that she had a snowball's chance in hell of escaping now with all the people outside. The Arab woman spoke to her, gesturing, encouraging Monique to do something, but Monique didn't understand. Her mind refused to make sense of the situation.

The young woman's heart was pounding violently under the paralysing fear and panic. Monique didn't understand a thing, and it became more complicated when the old woman gestured with the knife, drawing the blade up her wrist. Monique still didn't understand and shook her head, but another loud scream and the rise of nefarious laughter from outside made her swallow hard. One of the old Arab women was still looking out the tent flap and said something, but Monique couldn't understand it.

She shrieked as the Arab woman in front of her pulled on her sleeve to get her attention. Monique looked back at her, panting, horrified, but she finally understood. Monique slowly shook her head in disbelief, but the Arab woman continued to encourage her. Another lump formed in Monique's throat as she realised that the woman tried to persuade her to commit suicide. Monique looked around, searching for an answer she couldn't find, but it eventually became clear to her. Tears filled her eyes again, and she suddenly felt much calmer. There was no more hope for her. She realised that she could not escape from this hell, and the old Arab woman offered her a way out.

Monique didn't know what to do, but she knew that she didn't have much time left. It dawned to her that taking her own life would be much more merciful than what was waiting for her outside. The realisation sunk in, and Monique slowly nodded. The old Arab took her hands, comforting her, encouraging Monique in her decision, but it was not an easy one. Slowly Monique opened her eyes again and looked up. The old woman smiled at her, her face clearly showing the sorrow she felt. Monique reached for the rusty knife, but before she could take it she heard the woman at the tent flap yelling a warning, and immediately the other two women backed off. Monique stared at her, but the woman had already hidden the knife again.

The flap opened and the same four men walked in. Monique started to panic as they pointed at her. She could hear the scream, but didn't realise that it was her own as they pulled her up and unshackled her. She tried to resist much like the previous woman, kicking at her assailants. They aggressively grabbed her legs, dragging her out of the tent. She could feel her nails digging into the sand and gravel, desperately trying to grab something, anything. The men continued to pull her by her legs, their movements seemingly effortless.

The bright sun burned against her face, and Monique couldn't see anything for a few moments. She closed her eyes and kept screaming. She didn't even notice the pain from getting dragged over the rocks. The chanting and laughter grew louder and louder again, but this time she was surrounded by it. Even worse, she was the reason for it. Monique opened her eyes again, but all she could see were men. Men dressed in the layered robes of the desert people, men she had only seen on television before, mostly from the news. Most of them were heavily armed, belts of ammo tied around their waists, looped over the shoulders. Their faces were hidden, and the little exposed skin was weathered by the sun.

Monique turned around and screamed, realising that she was in the middle of a large circle. There was absolutely no way out. The chanting grew to a roar, amplified by the deep rock walls of the canyon. Some of the men even fired shots in the sky. The two assailants pulled her up to her feet and cut her wrists loose before pushing her forward. Monique couldn't balance and fell hard to the ground, a sharp pain shooting through her body as her knees contacted the rocks. She cried out, causing the crowd to laugh harder. Monique didn't know why, but she got back on her feet and desperately looked for any chance, any possibility of escape.

One of the older men pointed at her and started shouting towards the crowd. Even if she could understand Arab, there was so much shouting and chanting that it would have been impossible for Monique to comprehend what they were saying. The older man briskly walked towards her, and before Monique realised it, he had already grasped her blonde hair, pulled her up and lead the young woman in a parading circle. The pain was almost unbearable and Monique could do nothing but scream. Another roar of laughter echoed through the air. The pain caused Monique to close her eyes, which was the reason that she didn't see two more men coming towards her. Before she knew what had happened, they ripped the torn dirty scrubs from her body. The roar grew even louder and more celebratory gun shots burst through the air as Monique tried to cover herself up. She was grabbed by the hair and paraded around the circle again. The bidding had begun.

***EuroSecCorporation*, London, Friday, July 25**
Shira's cell phone finally rang early Friday afternoon. The Israeli quickly looked at the display and was relieved to recognise Mark's number from Germany.

"Finally!" Shira exhaled and answered the call sitting in her little office. "Yes, this is Shira. I am the one who left you the message. Thank you for calling back", Shira replied. "Yes, I called about Natascha. I am her friend and she is working here at our company, EuroSec. The same company Nick is working for." The Israeli hoped to break the ice a little bit sooner by identifying herself immediately. To her relief, Mark had no reason not to believe her. Shira sighed, happy that she didn't have to spend too much time to persuade Mark to trust her. "Mark, what I have to ask you is very important. Can I ask you to just hold on for a few moments? I have to change the office." Shira made a face and looked at Ariel as he sat on the edge of her desk, following his sister's conversation with great interest. They both hoped that Shira's little request would not cause Mark to distrust her, but he seemed to be fine. "Okay, just hold on, we are on our way", Shira confirmed, already on her way out of her office. Just seconds later they sat in Brian's office, together with Brian, Klaus as well as Chief Inspector William Conolly, who had stopped by to attend the briefing in the afternoon.

"Mark, if it is okay with you, we will call you back at your number. That way you can see our number in the caller ID, and it won't cost you an arm and a leg to call my cell phone", Shira suggested and carefully listened as Mark agreed. All eyes were focussed on the Israeli who finally nodded and ended the call before showing the display with Mark's number to Brian. Without a word, the retired admiral dialled the number. Mark picked up almost immediately.

"Yes, this is Mark", the German scientist said in clear English.

"Mark, this is retired Admiral Brian Whittaker, Royal British Navy. I am the owner and CEO of EuroSec Corporation Limited in London and officially Natascha's and Nick's boss. Thank you for getting back to us."

"No problem, what is going on?" Mark replied, his voice shaking now. The German wasn't sure where this was heading and an uneasy feeling started to swell inside him.

"Mark, I want you to know that I have you on speaker", the retired admiral continued without missing a beat, ignoring Mark's inquiry. "There are several other people here listening in. They will introduce themselves now. Are you alone, or is there anyone else listening on your end?" Brian frowned.

"No, it is just me", Mark answered, swallowing against the lump in his throat.

"Very well. We will introduce ourselves now."

"Retired General Klaus Schwartze, former NATO command and United Nations peace keeping troops. I am the other CEO of EuroSec Corporation and I also speak German, should you prefer that."

"Chief Inspector William Conolly, Scotland Yard. I am the lead investigator in this case and I also act as liaison to EuroSec Corporation. It is great talking to you."

"Shira Hadad. Team Leader at EuroSec Corporation and Natascha's best friend."

"Ariel Rashid. Operation Control at EuroSec Corporation and godfather to Natascha's daughter."

"That is bloody marvellous", Mark replied and took a deep breath. "So what kind of trouble is she in now? Did the police arrest her?"

Mark's question caught everyone in Brian's office off guard, but it took the retired admiral only two seconds to refocus.

"Why would the police want to arrest her?" he asked as Shira and Ariel exchanged a concerned look.

"I would like to ask a different question first, if you don't mind. Shira Hadad has left me about twenty messages the last couple of days, and I have to admit that I just listened to them today. All I was told was to call back immediately and that it concerns Natascha. Judging by the way you all introduced yourself, I guess that I'm talking to some sort of task force, am I correct?"

"You are correct, Mark. Something has indeed happened to Natascha. She is missing for eight days now, and it is safe to assume that she has been kidnapped by yet unknown persons. I would tell you the details if there were any, but there are not. We are working in close cooperation with Scotland Yard, and during our own investigation we found a Skype conversation between you and Natascha. We do understand that you have a romantic history with her. Mark, we are also aware about the little parcel that Erika gave you on behalf of Natascha. I want to assure you that we are not interested in any possible legal wrongdoings regarding this parcel, should there even be any. We are just desperately looking for any piece of information that can help us to find her. So, why would the police arrest her and what was in that parcel?"

"Oh my God! She has been kidnapped?" Mark was shocked, and it took a moment before he could focus again. "It is correct. She did contact me over Skype and we spoke for a couple minutes. She told me about the parcel, but I haven't opened it yet."

"But you have it?"

"Yes, Erika gave it to me. I just didn't open it."

"Why not?"

"There is a reason for it. Actually there are two reasons for it. When Natascha contacted me, she asked if I had received the parcel, which I confirmed. She wanted to know if I can date the bone fragments that she had sent me."

"Excuse me? Did you just say that there are bone fragments in that parcel?"

"Yes, she said that there are three jawbones in it. Natascha was convinced that they are human. She wanted to know if I could carbon date them, which would determine the approximate age of the people and how old the bones actually are."

Brian closed his eyes for a second and Klaus shook his head in disbelief.

"Mark, did Natascha tell you where she had found those jaws?" Brian wanted to know. He already knew the answer, but he was curious to know what Natascha had shared with him.

"Yes, she told me that she found them during some scientific dives in an old mine. Something about Whitmore Abbey, I believe. From what I know, she stumbled over some information regarding a former paedophile ring which involved the old orphanage in the abbey. She showed me some screenshots with some info about someone's grandmother."

"Kyle McRae", Shira whispered.

"I saved the images to have a look at them later. I can't believe that she has been kidnapped. Do you have any sign of her?" he wanted to know, his voice shaking with desperation.

"Unfortunately not. We are following a couple leads, but we are still waiting for a breakthrough", Chief Inspector Conolly admitted, not without some frustration in his voice.

"So, what did you find out regarding the bones? Human jaws, you said?" Shira followed up.

"Nothing yet. Natascha assumed that they are human jawbones. I guess she judged them by their shape."

"What do you mean with *nothing yet*?"

"Well, I told you that I haven't opened the parcel yet. There are several reasons for it. First, I just simply didn't have the time to do it. I was out quite a bit. The other reason is just the fact that she had literally sent me human remains from at least two, if not three human beings. There is a legal obligation to report those findings. She didn't exactly follow protocol by removing them. So I was hoping that she would change her mind and tell me to report it in her name. We officially do forensic work here, so I might be able to come up with a decent story. But if you know her as well as I do, you also know that she can be very stubborn. I should have known that she wouldn't change her mind."

"Okay. That is some helpful information. Thank you very much!" Brian commented and looked at Chief Inspector Conolly. "Bill?"

"I have no questions. I just need your contact information in case we have some more questions. I also want you to contact me directly should you remember something else or hear from her."

"No problem. Can I ask you something?" Mark's voice started to shake again.

"Of course, Mark", Brian answered, this time in his fatherly voice.

"Natascha...she is missing for eight days now. Do you...do you think that she is still alive?"

Brian didn't respond immediately. Mark had just asked the very question everybody feared to answer. They all looked at each other, not knowing how to properly answer him.

"We still hope to get her back alive, Mark. We will certainly do our best." Brian whispered in a calm voice. He knew that he didn't sound too convincing, but it was against Brian's principles to promise something he couldn't keep. No one spoke for the next few seconds. Everyone just had a grim reminder of the actual situation.

"Shira?" Mark finally asked, his voice breaking under his emotions.

"Yes, Mark?"

"You said that you are her best friend?"

"Yes, that is right."

"Can you please keep me updated on this? I...I still care a lot about her."

"I promise, Mark", Shira replied, "but do not lose hope yet, okay?"

"Okay, thank you. I appreciate that. Goodbye."

"Thank you very much. You provided us with some crucial information. We will stay in touch. Goodbye." Brian thanked and pressed a button to end the call. For the next few moments they all silently stared at the phone as if it would reveal more clues to them. Brian finally shook his head. "Well, that was certainly interesting. Bill, what do you think?"

Chief Inspector Conolly shrugged and took a sip from his coffee.

"Well, Mark does have a point. It was rather careless of Natascha to take those bones, assuming they are indeed human. Worst case scenario, Whitmore Abbey charges her with grave robbery, should they find out about this."

"Bloody hell, Bill", Brian barked at his friend. "I do not give a rat's ass about eventual legal complications that this might bring with it. I would be more than happy to see her arrested as that means we would have her back. I am more interested if Whitmore Abbey is behind her disappearance. It is a direction we have to look at."

"Based on what, Brian? Illegally obtained evidence?" Bill shot back.

"For heaven's sake!" Brian slammed his hand on the table. "Don't give me that legal crap, Bill. We are not talking about reopening an investigation about that bloody paedophile ring. I know how many high ranking people were involved in it and that the highest authorities covered it up. The only thing I am interested in is how to get Natascha back alive. We are eight days in; we all know what that means. Don't tell me that you don't want her back."

"Of course I want to get her back, Brian. We all know that Natascha didn't mention anything about the abbey. Not to a person and not on the internet. How can they possibly know that she took the bones? They cannot! We all know that. If I have to look at Whitmore Abbey to bring her back, so be it. But do I have to remind you about the shit storm we create if we start investigating in that direction? The moment we start, they will tamper with our investigation. They will slow us down. They will take my men off the case. They will do *everything* to keep that quiet."

"Including sacrificing Natascha, if they have to." Brian concluded what Bill couldn't say.

"Including sacrificing Natascha, yes. Even if it is not connected to her kidnapping. Right now, I believe her disappearance has nothing to do with Whitmore Abbey. No matter the reason, once we start looking at them, certain people will do everything to block us, and we will lose even more valuable time."

"What do you suggest?"

"I don't know yet. I will have one of my men look at the old files, if there are any. I will..."

"What do you mean with *if there are any*?" Shira interrupted the chief inspector in her dangerously low voice.

"Just what I said, *if there are any*. I do not have the time now to brief you about one of the biggest cover ups in Britain's criminal history. I will put one of the guys I trust in charge. Just have him look around to see if anything stands out that could be somehow connected with this. Maybe, just maybe, that place was an ancient storage room for food, and she found nothing more than old animal bones." Chief Inspector Conolly defended his course of action.

It was obvious that no one else in the room agreed with him, but they understood that he was bound by legal issues. Shira just shook her head in frustration and, walking to the window, hissed a curse in Hebrew through her clinched teeth.

"Shira, please!" Ariel tried to calm Shira down. He was obviously relieved that no one else understood what his younger sister had just said.

"This doesn't help us. We have to stay focussed!" Brian reminded everyone before he got up. "Okay, so we now know what the deal is with Mark. Ariel, can you go and update the timeline, please. We will be there shortly for the main briefing. Shira?"

"Yes?" The Israeli was still on edge, staring down to the parking lot through the large office window.

"We have to tell Nick about this. I trust you are the right person to do so?" Brian asked, but everyone knew that his question was more like a suggestion. Shira turned around abruptly, glancing at the retired admiral.

"Of course I am", she replied briskly and slammed the door on her way out.

"I am confused. She does know that I am on your side?" Conolly asked the rest of the group.

"Oh, she does. Shira just has a different understanding of justice than you and I have. If you think that she is pissed now, you haven't seen anything yet, I can tell you that much", Brian reassured his friend. "Okay, we just have enough time to get another cup of coffee before the briefing. Let's go, gentlemen."

Natascha's former Marine Biology Institute, Germany, Friday, July 25
Mario had no idea how many times he had examined the material Shira had sent him. Whatever Natascha had captured in those pictures and videos, it was nothing that he had seen during his dives at Whitmore Abbey.

"Oh, Natascha, what did you get yourself into this time", he muttered and rubbed his eyes. He had spent hours creating a mosaic picture during the last couple of days, trying to edit both the pictures and the videos in a way that they looked natural. The fact that the water had been bright orange from the dye made this task nearly impossible. No matter how many times he looked at them, he didn't find anything concerning.

"There has to be another way", he told himself and stared at the computer screen. "Maybe that will work", he mumbled and started to play with the shadows of the pictures. He immediately saw the difference, and the shadows also gave him a better understanding of the dimensions. "Okay, that looks better. Much better. Now, let's have a look at those walls and the ceiling." Mario concentrated on certain areas of interest to him. "Holy cow!" he said and abruptly sat back. What he had just seen totally shocked him. "That can't be!" he shook his head and checked the picture again, but he came to the same conclusion as before. "But that would mean... but why?" he asked himself, searching for an explanation. Mario reached for his phone and dialled Shira's number.

***EuroSecCorporation*, London, Friday, July 25**

"Okay, so this is what Mark had just told us", Brian finished the first part of the briefing and looked at several concerned faces. Nick just shook his head, but he didn't say anything. Natascha's whereabouts weighed much heavier on his mind than her having contact with Mark. "If there are no more questions we can continue with the helicopter." Brian commented and looked at Chief Inspector Conolly, "Bill?"

"Yes, the helicopter. Unfortunately we do not have much there yet. The flight plan was scheduled and filed according to the regulations. It is not unusual that companies provide their own pilots for such charters. We picked up both pilots listed in the flight plan, but neither of them actually flew the helicopter that day. They have solid alibis and didn't even know that their names were on the list. By the time the helicopter landed at its final destination in France, the two pilots were the only ones on board. They disappeared without a trace from the small airport, but you don't have to be a genius to do that. The flight manifest stated emergency medical supplies, so no one checked it. It is safe to say that they flew under the radar, landed somewhere remote, and everyone but the pilots left the helicopter. The company that chartered the helicopter does not exist either, so we are at a dead end there as well. The French tried to secure some evidence, but as of right now they have not found anything that could help us."

"So it is safe to say that the helicopter doesn't help us much at the moment?"

"That is safe to say. Needless to say that the French are looking pretty hard in every direction, but if you consider the range, flight path and actual flying time, it gives you several hundred square kilometres of potential drop-off zones." Chief Inspector Conolly didn't have to say anything else.

"Jesus Christ!" Jack MacDonald said and shook his head. Like everyone else in the room, he knew that it would be impossible to find a trace of evidence within such a great search area. With everyone lost in their own thoughts, the ringing of Shira's phone almost sounded intruding.

"It's Mario from Germany", the Israeli quickly announced before she answered the call. "Yes, Mario, this is Shira. What can I do for you?" Shira asked, all eyes on her. "Okay, please slow down. Can we talk over Skype? We are just in the middle of our daily briefing here." Shira offered and almost immediately gave Ariel the signal to establish the connection on the computer. It took only a few seconds before they could see Mario on the large high definition screen.

"Mario, this is Brian Whittaker. You remember who I am or shall we introduce each other again?"

"I certainly remember you, sir. Most of the faces look familiar, so if you don't mind I would like to get straight to the point. I think I found something very unusual."

"Of course", Brian agreed and let Mario lead the conversation. Without wasting another second, Mario sent his mosaic image and asked Shira to open it.

"Okay, you are looking at a mosaic image that I created based on the pictures Natascha took during that one dive. Before you ask me too many questions, I have to tell you that I was not with her in that room when she took those images. My position was around twenty metres away where I was busy recovering our little ROV. Anyway, I believe that Natascha actually did find something important in this room. Before I get into details, I want to give you a quick summary about the geology up there. Whitmore Abbey and the mine Natascha and I dove in are just a couple hundred metres apart, but the abbey is at a much higher altitude. Because of the geological features in that certain area, there is a vast reservoir of ground water. During World War Two, there was a well outside the walls of the abbey which was mostly used by the village nearby. Another well was inside the abbey. During an airstrike, one of the bombs landed directly on the outside well and rerouted the underground stream into the mine which consequentially flooded. The well was repaired within days after the air strike, but the mine was lost. I can also tell you from the aerial images that no bomb hit inside the walls of Whitmore Abbey. When we explored this side tunnel, not only did we pass literally through the outside well, we also pushed well beyond the outside walls and inside of Whitmore Abbey. The next picture you see is a map of Whitmore Abbey", Mario explained with excitement and sent another image. "I marked the location of that underground chamber. Natascha and I first explored it from inside the abbey, which I already explained to Shira in our first conversation. The chamber is part of the abbey's catacombs, maybe used as a crypt, but it could also have been used as a simple storage room, but that is unlikely. The tunnel and that very chamber were chiseled out of the rock centuries ago. It was most likely a natural cave, washed out by the water over millennia, that they simply widened, but it is clearly manmade. Based on these pictures, I estimate that the inaccessible part of the cave is about the size of a school gym." Everyone listened closely as Mario spent the next minutes explaining the exact location of the chamber in relation to the abbey and the flooded side tunnel.

"So there is no doubt that Natascha took those pictures in the same chamber the two of you explored from the abbey, just from the other side of the wall. Is that correct?" Brian summarised.

"That is correct. If there are no questions so far, I would like to show you what I believe I have found on those pictures." Mario continued, but no one interrupted him. "The orange dye makes the lighting conditions less than perfect, but I want you to have a look at the side walls. If you zoom in...", Mario waited for Shira to enlarge the picture, "you will notice those markings on the wall. I first thought that they were simple shadows, but I don't think that they are. I believe that we are looking at some marks from modern tools, like a pneumatic drill or chisel."

"From a dive team?" Brian was clearly surprised.

"Yes, sir. Standard tools in the commercial diving world."

"But how do you explain the brick wall? It does look old."

"I'm not certain yet, sir, but if I'd be a betting man, I would say that they carefully took down the old wall. Once they finished whatever they did, they simply rebuilt it and that was it. If you didn't know better, you would never see the difference."

"Understood. So, someone goes down there, obviously with the knowledge and permission of the abbey, carefully tears down an ancient brick wall, sets up a professional diving operation, rebuilds the brick wall afterwards and disappears again. Why? To what end?"

"That is the question." Mario replied with a shrug of his shoulders, "I am still looking for an answer myself."

"Mario, based on the pictures, can you give me a rough estimate when that work could have taken place?"

"It is difficult to make a proper statement just based on the pictures, but I would say within the last five to ten years, maybe. This is also the work of a professional dive team."

"Wait a second. Natascha asked me one day about how to contact the Explosive Ordnance Disposal Unit. She mentioned something that they had worked up there. Is that correct, Mario?"

"Yes, that is correct. I should have that somewhere."

"Hm, okay. That could have been a smoke screen. Shira, get me whatever Natascha had on that, please. I will make some phone calls later on. So, let's think logically. Why would someone go through all those difficulties to execute such an operation and to rebuild the brick wall once they were done? One, they knew what they were looking for, and two, they knew where to find whatever they were looking for, and three, they did all this with the permission and knowledge of Whitmore Abbey", Brian concluded.

"Yes, but that leads us to another question", Klaus added. "Whitmore Abbey would have never agreed to this without great benefit to themselves. Whatever was in there, I don't have the feeling that it was some old roast beef. Why would you go through all the trouble to close the wall behind you, so that whatever is still hidden in there remains hidden?"

"Question is: what were they hiding there in the first place? Back in the day, deep underground, out of sight, and hidden behind a wall?"

"Well, don't forget that this is where Natascha had found those bone fragments. The ones that looked human to her."

"So, do you really believe that this is...where they buried...all those...", Brian asked his long time friend, struggling to phrase his question.

"Can there even be any other conclusion?" Klaus shrugged.

Alba "Saphir" Casillas's apartment, London, Friday, July 25
The young Spaniard and Elena both slept through the night and enjoyed a quick breakfast, after which they went out shopping for a new cell phone. Alba didn't even bother with something fancy; she just bought a cheap prepaid unit. For now that was all she needed. The Spaniard used most of her cash to buy some clothes for her new Romanian friend before stocking up on some groceries and hunkering down again in Alba's apartment. They had been out of the apartment for barely two hours. The stress of the last couple of weeks had clearly taken a toll on Elena's condition and started to catch up. Curled up under a blanket on the couch, the young Romanian slept again. Alba lounged in her easy chair and stared at her new cell phone. She sighed with disappointment as she disconnected her latest call. She had tried calling the number several times over the last couple of hours, and it always ended with the same result. Every time someone answered, which was almost immediately, the young woman didn't know what to say and simply ended the call. Alba knew that this wouldn't get her anywhere, but she realised she had to do something. A quick glance on her watch

showed her that it was late in the afternoon, and she decided that it would be better to just go to the company to meet her friend in person.

How can you call her a friend if you don't even have her phone number? Or know her last name? How can you be certain that she is even there? Not knowing the answers to her own questions, Alba looked over to the couch, which brought her to her next question. *What am I going to do with you?* Alba wasn't sure whether she should wake Elena up and take her along, or if she should let her sleep. She looked to Elena and noticed that her breath was a deep rhythm. It was then that she realised that the young Romanian had finally found some sound sleep without the constant interruption from nightmares. Alba reached for a pen and paper and wrote her a note instead.

She carefully took her jacket and sneaked out of her apartment, not without locking the door behind her. With the door closed, she finally put on her sneakers and rushed downstairs to the underground garage. Alba hoped that the address she had found on the internet was still the current one, especially since it would take her thirty minutes to get there.

She nervously tapped the steering wheel of her BMW as she made her way through the dense traffic. Alba caught herself checking her mirrors more frequently than usual, but the typical London traffic did not give her any indication of any potential followers. It was only when the GPS guided her into the parking lot that she finally sighed with relief. Turning the ignition off, it was only now that Alba noticed how much she was shaking. She cursed in Spanish and shook her head. The young Spaniard had no idea what to do next and examined the three storey building in front of her.

Every minute painfully ticked by, and Alba was still uncertain about her approach. Watching the entrance closely, she noticed that there was a steady flow of people entering and leaving the building, and she guessed that it had something to do with the fitness centre on the lower floor. Alba Casillas hissed another Spanish curse and finally decided to get out of her car and walk towards the entrance. She nervously looked around as she covered the short distance over the parking lot. Although she would never tell Elena, Alba had to admit that she was really scared. The more she thought about her actions, the more she realised that Rowan would be anything but understanding and supportive towards her. Generally she couldn't care less about him and his money, but Alba was smart enough to know that Rowan would most likely not favour her if he would have to choose between her and his friend, Prince Tarek. The young Spaniard was convinced that she could persuade Rowan not to hurt her, but his Saudi friend and business partner would not be so gentle. Still looking nervously over the parking lot, Alba swallowed hard and turned her attention back to the entrance.

"Oh my God! It is you!" Alba almost yelled, the relief clear in her voice as she recognised Shira coming out of the building.

"Alba! What are you doing here? Is everything okay?" the Israeli asked her in return, the surprise clear in her voice. It was the first time that Shira met Alba outside an assignment, and it took the Israeli a second to recognise her. It was also quite obvious to Shira that the young Spanish woman was under a lot of tension.

"Shira, can I ask you for a favour?"

"Generally yes, but I am currently rather busy, Alba. It would have to wait, I am sorry!" Shira tried to comfort her, but the Israeli's mind was still set on Natascha as she continued to walk by Alba and towards her car.

"Shira, I might be in trouble. No, forget that! I *am* in trouble. In big trouble! Can you help me? Please?" Alba pleaded with her, checking over her shoulder again.

"Trouble? What kind of trouble?" Shira finally stopped and turned around.

"Not here. Can we talk somewhere private? Somewhere safe?" Alba insisted, nervously looking at two Middle Eastern men who walked towards them.

"Alba, I don't want to sound rude, but I'm really in a hurry. I don't have much time and I don't know how I can help you", Shira tried to explain. It was not that she didn't like Alba, but the timing was just inconvenient.

"My life is in danger, and so is the life of a friend of mine. I need some help. I need to talk to someone. Shira, you are the only person I know. The only one I can trust. Please!" Alba begged. It was only now that Shira noticed Alba's desperation in her voice. She finally stepped closer to Alba.

"Your life is in danger? Right now?" Shira asked and scanned her surroundings.

"*Si*", Alba whispered, carefully watching the two men who walked by them and towards the entrance door.

"Okay, follow me", Shira offered her friend and escorted her back to the building. Alba didn't say anything and nervously watched as Shira used her keys to activate the elevator that would bring them to the top floor. When the door opened again, Shira showed Alba the break room.

"You want some tea or coffee?" the Israeli asked and helped herself to a cup of tea.

"No, thank you!" Alba replied, curiously looking at the stainless steel pole that was still installed in the room.

"Don't pay attention to that. Boys! It will be removed later today." Shira commented as she noticed Alba's scrutiny.

"I just have to tell my boss why I'm back already, just give me a few seconds." Alba just nodded and waited patiently for Shira to return. The Spaniard wondered for a moment wether Elena would be awake by now and if she would see her note, but before she could think more about it she heard the Israeli return.

"Okay, I spoke to my boss. Here's the thing, Alba. If you are in any kind of legal trouble, then neither I nor this company can really help you, you have to understand that, okay? We are also extremely busy at the moment, and we are sort of in the middle of an emergency, so I cannot promise you anything."

"I understand!" Alba nodded, but immediately got distracted as Brian Whittaker and Sean MacLeod escorted their friend Chief Inspector Conolly to the elevator. The men just wished her a good day, but it was enough for Alba to wince.

"Don't worry, Alba, you are safe here. One of them is actually the owner of this company", Shira smiled, trying to calm the Spaniard down. Alba sighed and felt relieved to have someone to talk to.

"Okay", Shira smiled and shrugged as she sat down beside her. "Tell me about your problem."

- 20 -

Asklepios, Aegean Sea, Friday, July 25

"Take your goddamn hands off me!" Natascha yelled. The moment she had feared most was about to become reality as Kevin and Lamar stormed into her cell. Natascha had absolutely no idea what would happen next, but every scenario that had haunted her during her nightmares was worse than the other. Natascha knew that she couldn't rely on Jake, who was in no physical condition to be of any help, but she had promised herself not to go down without a fight. Now that the moment had come, she couldn't even think any more, she just reacted. Just as Kevin tried to grab her arm, she threw a punch at him, hitting him in the shoulder area. Kevin's only reaction was nothing more than a short laugh before he exchanged looks with Lamar, who also chuckled at Natascha's futile effort to defend herself. Kevin looked back at Natascha, who aimed to punch him again. Determined to show Natascha how helpless she really was, Kevin allowed her to execute the attack. Little did he know that he reacted exactly the way Natascha had planned it. Instead of punching him on the shoulder again, Natascha quickly opened her hand and rotated her hips to throw all her weight behind her open palm strike right underneath Kevin's nose. She immediately felt the blood on her hand as Kevin screamed in pain. Before Kevin could even get his hands up in defence, Natascha had already dug two of her fingers into his eyes, pushing as deep and as hard as she could. As Kevin tried to defend himself, Natascha withdrew her hand back, only to immediately thrust her open hand against his throat. Kevin sank to his knees instantaneously, gasping for air as blood ran down his face.

"What the..." was all Lamar could say totally surprised by the sudden turn of events. He looked at Kevin gasping on the floor, giving Natascha the split second she needed. Just as Lamar looked back at her, he saw Natascha aiming for his face now. Lamar reacted just in time and instinctively raised his hands in front of his face, inhibiting her blow. Natascha continued her attack and kneed Lamar in the groin a split second later. The pain shot through his entire body, and he didn't even realise how loud he screamed as he sank to the floor. His knees had not even touched the ground when Natascha's knee hit him directly in his face. A new level of pain shot through his body, and Lamar fought hard not to lose consciousness. Natascha quickly glanced between the two assailants, knowing very well that this fight was far from over. Her instincts told her to spin around and look at the door. For a split second her eyes locked on Melissa's, whose face was nothing but a grimace of hate. Before Natascha could even react, Melissa pulled the trigger of her powerful taser. Natascha could recognise her own scream as a surge of pain ripped through her, completely paralysing her as she collapsed. Natascha didn't even notice when she hit the floor. Her body convulsed under the painful electrical current running through what felt to be each of her nerves. Natascha begged for mercy, but nothing but screams left her mouth as Melissa repeatedly pulled the trigger until she finally fell unconscious.

"Bitch!" Melissa yelled as she released the trigger. Her eyes were still focussed on the now unconscious Natascha. The Irish nurse placed all her hatred and anger in a strong kick to Natascha's hip, but the young woman showed no reaction. Not taking her eyes off Natascha's motionless body, Melissa stepped over her and helped Lamar up to his feet. His face was just a grimace, blood still flowing from his mouth and nose. With Melissa calling for back-up, the male nurse wiped his face as he threw a hateful look at Natascha.

"She is going to regret that!" he hissed through clenched teeth and spit some blood on Natascha. Another wave of pain shot through his body and he dropped to his knees again with agony.

"How is Kevin doing?" he groaned through his clenched teeth.

"He's not doing well. That bitch got him pretty bad", Melissa complained and threw another hateful look at Natascha, who was still unconscious. It was only when the Irish kneeled beside Kevin, that she realised he had difficulty breathing.

"Shit! I think she hit him in the throat!" Melissa yelled and looked at Lamar.

"What?" Lamar was still disoriented himself. The whole fight had only lasted less than five seconds, and he had no idea in what shape Kevin was. Lamar spit out some more blood before he could finally look at his friend. It only took him a second to notice that Kevin was in serious trouble. His eyes were in a deep red colour, a direct result from Natascha pushing her fingers into them. The even bigger issue was that he couldn't breathe. Kevin had his eyes opened wide, gasping for air as he clasped his throat.

"Damn, you're right. He needs a tracheotomy!" Lamar yelled, just as their back-up arrived.

"What the hell happened?" Leo Swan barked as he took in the scene.

"Kevin needs a tracheotomy, and he needs it now!" Lamar repeated and looked up, relieved to see that they had brought a gurney.

"Quickly, let's get him up there", Lamar ordered as Melissa notified the medical staff about their emergency.

"Dr Evans is on her way. She will be here any moment", the Irish nurse said just as the guards placed her friend on the gurney. Lamar tried to straighten up, but the pain shot through his lower body again, his eyes closing under the pain.

"What happened?" Dr Evans wanted to know. She didn't waste a second and immediately started to work on Kevin, still demanding an answer. "You had one simple job to do. Explain to me what happened, Lamar!" The physician was anything but impressed by the turn of events, and she didn't even try to hide her frustration and anger. While the guards pushed Kevin down the aisle to the medical ward, Dr Evans quickly examined Lamar.

"You still owe me an answer", she coldly stated, as her attention shifted to Natascha's motionless body. She briefly checked her pulse and was obviously satisfied.

"Well, it happened really fast. Kevin and I were about to pick her up as scheduled, when all of a sudden she turned into a freaking ninja-chick", Lamar explained with a grimace as breathing was still very painful.

"What are you talking about? Our profilers have found nothing in her daily routine indicating that she received any training."

"Screw the profilers. She kicked our asses", Lamar defended himself, not caring that the profilers couldn't know that Natascha had received all her training *during* her working hours.

"What happened to her anyway? I don't have to remind you how much money we will lose if something happens to her?"

"Melissa shocked her, that's all. I'm fine, thank you for asking", Lamar returned her frustrated tone. He was tired about the special treatment Natascha had received from everyone. Dr Evans threw him a disapproving glance.

"Just make sure that she has no injuries. Can you and Leo bring her up, or do you want me to call for back-up?" Dr Evans scowled as Natascha slowly regained consciousness.

"We can handle it", Lamar stated coldly and slowly walked to the German.

"What about him?" the physician looked at Jake, but he had not been in a condition to take part in this.

"Hasn't moved. Don't worry about him", Lamar shrugged before returning his attention to their prime prisoner. Natascha just opened her eyes, and it took her a few moments to remember what had just happened. The pain in her body was gone, but everything was numb. She closed her eyes again, trying to control her breathing when she felt the sharp pain on her hip where Melissa had kicked her. Her first thoughts immediately drifted to her daughter, Shira-Sarah; and Natascha couldn't help the tears running down her face. The realisation that she had been defeated quickly kicked in, and she faintly heard the voices around her as her memory came back. She didn't know why, but she started crying as she slowly pulled her legs up to get on her knees. Just as she wanted to get up, she felt the sharp pain as Lamar kicked her legs out from underneath her.

"You damn bitch!" he screamed kicking her, but Natascha didn't hear him. The new wave of pain took the little remaining energy she had left. Her body curled under the pain. Her sobbing did nothing but fuel Lamar's hatred towards her as he violently twisted her arms behind her back to pull her up from the floor roughly. Melissa took the chance to pull Natascha's head back by her hair, causing her to scream again.

"You are going to regret this!" the Irish nurse threatened as they dragged Natascha out of her cell.

"Wait, let me take her", Leo offered, bending Natascha's other arm to her back. Lamar closed the door behind him. It was obvious that he was still fighting with the pain from Natascha's attack. Lamar leaned against the wall, spit more blood and watched as Melissa and Leo dragged Natascha towards the elevator.

"Please! Let...go...of...me", Natascha cried desperately, the pain clear in her voice, but she knew that her pleas would fall on deaf ears. They didn't even bother to slow down, and Natascha had trouble staying on her feet. The pain in her body almost paralysed her, and they regularly pushed her against the steel walls of the corridor, her muscles tightening as she fought to keep balanced and stay on her feet. It was only when they stepped into the elevator that she was able to catch a breath.

When the doors opened again, Leo and Melissa dragged her out and down the corridor before they stopped in front of another steel door. Natascha's mind was hazy, but she was sure that she had not been in this area of the facility before. The little group slowed down to allow Lamar to open the door. Leo and Melissa didn't wait and pushed her inside as hard as they could. Losing her balance, Natascha fell hard to the floor, the impact causing another wave of excruciating pain to run through her already battered body.

The steel door was locked before she even realised what happened. No light shone in the room and Natascha was engulfed in total darkness. The young woman stayed on the ground; the pain in her body made it impossible for her to move. Still fighting the unconsciousness, she rolled to her side, her heavy breathing the only sound.

"Son of a bitch!" she cursed between a couple of deep breaths and rolled on her back. Natascha closed her eyes and could do nothing but wait for the pain to slowly leave her body. It took her a while, but even the pain in her legs and hip was eventually bearable. With her breathing under control, she looked around. It was so dark that no matter how hard she tried, the young woman could not even see the walls, which she assumed couldn't be that far away. Just as she slowly sat up, the lights turned on. The strong flood lights left Natascha with no choice but to close her eyes immediately. She grimaced as she used her hand to cover her eyes. Even after a few minutes, she could barely open them. Glancing around, it took her a second to notice that she was alone in this room. It took her only two more seconds to realise that this room was nothing more than another cell. It had only one steel door and no window. She looked around and noticed there was absolutely nothing in it.

"Damn!" Natascha cursed as she slowly got up on her feet again. She held on to the wall for support, her balance still not fully restored. As she slowly opened her eyes again, she took another look around. It was only now that she realised that one complete wall of her cell was made of glass.

"What the hell?" she muttered and examined the glass further. All she could see was her own reflection, and it didn't take her long to figure out that someone was watching her from the other side.

Less than five metres from her, on the other side of the two centimetre thick privacy glass, Walter Leroy "L.J." Jackson grinned from ear to ear. The Texan knew that Natascha could not see them as he glanced at Victor Gates right beside him. His friend rested as comfortable as he could in his wheelchair. The moment the lights in Natascha's cell had come on, Victor's heartbeat and breathing went up with excitement. He didn't speak, he didn't move, he just stared at the young woman on the other side of the safety glass. The woman, his long promised surprise. The woman, who now pressed her face against the window, determined to see through the glass. Victor Gates had at first been reluctant to come with L.J. when he had promised him earlier that evening that he could finally see the surprise. Now that Victor finally laid eyes on Natascha, he couldn't believe them. His eyes trailed after her as she paced the room. L.J. chuckled beside him. Proudly, L.J. turned around and looked at both Dr Sheridan Evans and Dr William Edwards, his satisfaction clear on his face.

"What can you tell us about her?" L.J. enthusiastically asked them, turning his attention back to Victor to witness his reaction.

"Well, she has been with us for six days now. As instructed, we treated her with the utmost...care." Dr Edwards tried to explain with the most appropriate word. "We ran a general blood test and based on those results and her examination, she is in perfect health.”

“What about her mental state?” the Texan prodded purposefully, his eyes searching Victor’s, trying to read any emotions on his severely scarred face.

“From a psychological standpoint she is much more stable than the experts predicted. We have to give them credit, since they couldn’t talk to her in person. We followed their instructions and she had a couple mental breakdowns. We always put her in a position that triggered her protective instincts, just to take the other person violently away from her. The sleep deprivation certainly didn’t help either. We can break her mental resistance at any moment.”

“What about her physical resistance? How much physical torture will she be able to handle?” L.J. asked, his voice quivering with anticipation.

“Like I said, she is young, perfect physical health. As a matter of fact, she was strong enough to seriously injure two of our male nurses just a few minutes ago. One needed emergency surgery; they are still trying to save his eyes. If you take it easy, she will survive a couple of days.” Dr Evans informed, her voice carrying her own disgust she felt for Natascha. L.J. liked the answer and a wicked smile crossed his lips. Victor had yet to take his eyes off Natascha, but he absorbed every piece of information like a sponge.

“Just to waive any doubts, we are certain that this is her?” L.J. asked again. He knew the answer, but he wanted Victor to hear for himself that there was absolutely no doubt.

“Yes, it is definitely her. We don’t have a DNA sample to test it against, but she has the right blood type, age, eye colour, and tattoo. There is no doubt.”

“I told you that I have a good surprise for you, my friend!” L.J. chuckled as he looked at Victor, but his friend had still not moved. It was like he had turned to stone, impossible to read. L.J. exchanged a glance with the doctors. Victor’s eyes were still fixed on Natascha, who restlessly paced the cell to get her blood circulating again. Victor didn’t even notice as Dr Edwards stepped beside him, quickly checking the monitors. After he was satisfied, he just adjusted the oxygen flow rate and nodded to L.J. that everything was fine. Dr Edwards gestured to Dr Evans and both physicians departed the room in silence.

L.J. made sure that the door was closed before returning to his friend’s side. He didn’t speak when he rested his hand on Victor’s shoulder. This was the moment that had kept his friend alive. It was only now that he noticed that Victor was shaking. L.J. quickly glanced at the monitors, certain the doctors must have missed something, not that he would be able to tell.

“So, my friend, are you ready for the grand finale?” L.J. asked after a few moments, looking at Victor’s face. For the first time in what seemed to be an eternity, Victor moved. Not much, he just nodded. It was barely noticeable, and L.J. would have missed it if he would have blinked.

“Showtime!” the Texan announced as his hand reached for a switch.

On the other side of the privacy glass, Natascha had no way of knowing what was happening. Her instincts told her that the next confrontation would happen sooner rather than later. She turned on her heel as she reached the end of the room and continued her pace to the furthest wall. The more she moved and stretched, the more pain left her body. She grimaced every now and then, but she knew that she couldn't afford to be vulnerable. Natascha knew that someone was monitoring her through the privacy glass, but she had no idea who or how many were watching and what they were waiting for. Moving around, Natascha took her time to take in the details of the cell, but there was nothing more to see than the blank steel walls. No fittings or openings, no other lights or ventilation shaft, just steel walls. She had also noticed that there was no water anywhere. She figured the worst case scenario would be that whoever was on the other side of that glass wall would watch her starve to death over the next couple of days. Natascha shook her head. *No! This is not the way you can think. You have to keep fighting. They want something from you, they will be back!* She reminded herself, turning her attention back to the door. Her mind kept spinning. Natascha realised that she would no longer have the element of surprise in the next encounter. Her captors knew now that she could fight. With them knowing that, she also knew that they would not hesitate to use the taser against her.

Before Natascha could plan her next strategy, she noticed some lights flickering on the other side of the privacy glass. Her pacing stopped instantly as a cold chill ran down her spine. Natascha carefully watched as the light on the other side illuminated the room, finally allowing her to look through. It didn't take long before she acknowledged to herself that these two men were the reason she was here. Stepping closer to the glass, her face was nothing more but a grimace. Natascha focussed on the guy standing beside the wheelchair. She was sure that she had never seen him before, but she promised herself to never forget his face. When she broke eye contact with L.J., she concentrated on the second person. It was obvious to Natascha that he was in extremely poor medical condition. Half of his face as well as his arms were severely scarred from burns, and she could see that he was breathing from an oxygen tank. Natascha didn't recognise the man, but she somehow didn't feel pity for him either. She could see the pure hatred burn through his eyes as they connected with hers. Natascha took another step closer. Her eyes turned to slits, another chill running down her spine. Her instincts warned her about this man, but Natascha still didn't know why. All her alarm bells were ringing. She stepped as close to the glass as she could without touching it, still not breaking eye contact with him. She could feel such hate, but she struggled to understand why. Natascha could see in her peripherals that the other man took a step back, indicating to her that this man in the chair was the only reason why she was here. Natascha still had no idea who it was, but his eyes were different. She had seen those eyes before. *Who the hell is this?* She kept asking herself. All of a sudden it dawned to her. *That can't be. How can it be?* Natascha's lips quivered as a wave of hatred burned through her, filling every cell of her body. *How can it be? How can he still be alive? Ariel killed him! Ariel shot him! He died in the fire!* Natascha tried to explain to herself. She had no idea how he could still be alive, but there couldn't be a mistake, and *Asklepios* was certainly the perfect spot for him. Natascha kept staring at his eyes. The same eyes she had seen back on the *Northern Explorer.* She would *never* forget his eyes. The same eyes that were still staring back at her now. The realisation kicked in within a second, and there was no doubt in

Natascha's mind. All her fear and self-control were pushed away by the rage and anger swelling deep inside her. Her emotions burned through her composure, and she screamed her hatred against the glass.

"You see, Jonathan, that didn't take too long", L.J. laughed as they watched Natascha hammering her fists against the safety glass as hard as she could. He figured her screams were loud, and that she was cursing profanities, but they could not hear them. Jonathan Brown maintained his stone composure, but his breathing increased at the scene. For years he was living under the name of Victor Gates. For years he was suffering excruciating pain. He had lost everything because of this one person who stood before him on the other side of the glass. His career as the White House Chief of Staff, his house, his friends, she had taken everything from him when she had sent that terrorist to kill him. But he didn't die. His survival was a medical miracle. For years he had hoped, he had even prayed that he would die because the pain was so unbearable. Now all of that was forgotten. To see Natascha on the other side of the privacy glass, to know that she was under his control, made up for all those years of suffering. His voice remained silent but his eyes sparkled with such excitement that L.J. couldn't help but laugh.

"I always promised you that you will get your revenge, Jonathan. There she is. She is all yours!" L.J. proclaimed clapping Jonathan's shoulder. It was finally payback time.

- 21 -

***EuroSecCorporation*, London, Friday, July 25**
Alba Casillas nervously tapped her fingers on the table. Her eyes danced between the faces of the four people staring at her. The cup of tea in front of her was untouched and cold by now. After only a few minutes, her story had become so unbelievable that Shira decided it would be best for Brian, Klaus and Ariel to listen to Alba's story themselves.

"Okay, Miss Casillas, let me see if I got this straight", Brian started with a quick glance at his watch. He found himself in the same predicament as Shira had in the parking lot earlier. It was not that he didn't want to help the Spanish woman, the timing just could not be anymore inconvenient. "You were at a casino in Monaco to meet Rowan Harrison."

"Si!" Alba enthusiastically confirmed with a nod.

"When he arrived he was in the company of a Saudi prince, Prince Tarek what-ever-his-full-name-is?"

"Si!" Alba nodded again, grimacing at the memory.

"And Prince Tarek was escorted by several women. And one of them, I believe you said her name is Elena, is only eighteen years old, correct?"

"Si!"

"And Elena confirmed to you in her own words that she is being held against her will as a *slave* by this Saudi Prince?" Brian's mouth twisted in distaste.

"Yes, that is what she told me. First in the casino and again on our way back."

"Okay, and when she told you that in the casino, you just walked out with her and drove all the way back to London. Is that also correct?" Brian just wanted to make sure he had all the facts straight. Unfortunately, Alba had been so nervous when she told them what had happened that she had jumped through the story and even spoke Spanish at some points.

"Si...I mean, yes. That is correct."

"And your friend, Elena, she does not have any identification documents? No passport, driver's licence, student card or anything?"

"No, they have taken everything from her when she was kidnapped." Alba shrugged and shook her head. Brian rubbed his eyebrows and looked at Ariel. The Israeli slightly shook his head. The concern was clear in his face.

"And Elena told you that she was kidnapped in Paris and held prisoner in some sort of a medical facility before Rowan Harrison *bought* her and gave her as a personal gift to this prince?"

"Yes, that is what she told me."

"And there is no doubt in your mind that Elena spoke the truth when it comes to Rowan Harrison?"

"Si, there is no doubt. She told me that it was Rowan who had bought and delivered her personally to that perverted pig." Alba shivered with disgust. She always thought Rowan to be an immoral character, but she felt nauseous thinking he would do anything like this

"Okay, so it is safe to say that by now Rowan and the prince know what has happened", Brian surmised and looked at his friends for their thoughts.

"They might want her back!" Klaus stated his concern, speaking what everyone else was already thinking.

"Alba", Ariel started. "Did Rowan try to call you once you and Elena left Monte Carlo?"

"I believe so, but I had my cell phone turned off. I got a new phone and number this morning and took the card out of the old phone."

"Good. That is very good", Ariel noted, but his main concern remained. "Alba, does Rowan or Tarek know where you live?" Almost everybody held their breath, waiting for an answer.

"No, definitely not. None of my clients do, but he is well connected. He will find out eventually", the Spaniard quickly added.

"Why didn't you go to the police?" Shira wanted to know.

"The police? Seriously? Tell them what? My word against the word of the Harrison family? You know how much money his family donates every year so they look a different way when that idiot is screwing up playing playboy? Do you have any idea what kind of people they are dealing with? Politicians, lawyers, judges, police officers, business tycoons, movie stars, you name it. I learned my lesson the hard way. I do not trust them at all." They all knew that Alba had a valid point there. Her story was nothing that could be called watertight in front of a court. "I am not concerned about prosecution or any of that, Shira. I didn't come to you because I want to press charges against them." Alba continued with frustration as she looked around the room. "I came to you because I am downright scared! I am scared for my life! They want her back, and they will do anything and everything to get her back. You don't just walk out of these circles! I barely escaped with my life when Tarek was a just client of mine. You have no idea how brutal he is. And Elena is his *slave.* She is his *property*! He will do *everything* to get his hands on her. And on me!" Alba concluded with heat. They all looked at each other. This was the last thing they needed now, but they also knew that they couldn't just send her away. After all, they were convinced that both Elena and Alba's life were in immediate danger.

"What are we going to do?" Ariel asked.

"Miss Casillas, do you have any money? I mean cash, not credit cards." Brian asked.

"No, maybe a hundred pounds, that's it. I usually use my credit cards", Alba disappointedly shook her head.

"Have you used your credit cards since you left Monte Carlo?" Klaus wanted to know.

"No, I didn't. I know how easy they can trace them. I only used cash, but now I am out."

"Still, what are our options?" Shira asked again.

"Hotel?"

"No, they require a name and someone will see a face. The Harrison's own a few hotels and we don't know which ones they are involved in. Can't take the risk. It would also take us one team for protection", Brian shook his head.

"They can stay at my place. I got a spare room", Ariel suggested, grasping for options.

"Klaus?" Brian looked at his friend, waiting for his opinion.

"I like the idea, might be the quickest and best option for now", the former German general replied.

"Okay, your place it is, Ariel. Miss Casillas, Ariel and Shira will escort you back to your apartment to pick up Elena. Just pack a few items. The faster we get you out of there, the better it is. Are you comfortable with that?"

"Si! Muchas gracias!"

"Okay, go!" Brian finally ordered. "Shira, you keep us updated, okay? Who is with Nick at the moment?"

"Talia is home. Ole-Einar and Rolf are also there until I'll get back."

"Perfect!" Brian nodded and watched as the three stepped into the elevator. Just as the elevator door closed, he turned around and looked at his long time friend. "We needed that like a root canal."

"I had a different expression in my mind, but yours is pretty close to it. We are not telling Conolly about this, are we?"

"Are you nuts?"

While Brian and Klaus were still at their office thirty minutes later, Ariel steered Alba's BMW into the underground parking garage.

"I have one of the parking spots close to the elevator. They are reserved for women. That one there", Alba pointed out. She had to admit that she was relieved that the Israeli drove her car, she was way too nervous for it. Unfortunately, it had taken her running a red light and almost causing a traffic accident to figure that out, after which Ariel insisted on taking over the wheel to everyone's relief.

"I wonder how she's doing", Alba wondered, more to herself than anyone else as they walked over to the elevator. She had long regretted her decision to leave her young Romanian friend behind.

"I am certain she's fine", Shira tried to calm her down. It was only a few moments later that Alba opened the door to her apartment. With Shira in the lead, the Spaniard quickly walked into the living room, but there was no sign of her new friend.

"Is that the shower?" Ariel asked the obvious as he looked at a closed door, listening to the sound of the running water.

"Si!" Alba sighed with relief and rushed over to peek into the bathroom. "She's fine. Thank God!"

"You might as well tell her right away and start packing. We don't want to lose too much time. On our way back, you can pick up some money from a bank machine. It won't matter anymore." Shira suggested as her brother checked outside the window.

"Do you mind?" Shira asked and wandered into the bedroom.

"No, go ahead", Alba nervously replied and looked for her sport bag. Ariel followed Shira into the bedroom, seeking eye contact with his sister.

"All clear", she whispered and raised an eyebrow.

"Well, even we can get lucky sometimes", Ariel noted and watched as Alba opened her closet and rummaged through some clothes.

"Just take something comfortable and what you really need. We can have someone pick up the rest later", Ariel instructed her.

"Si!" Alba quickly replied and disappeared with an arm load of items to the living room. Ariel couldn't resist and took another step towards the closet to take a closer look at Alba's large selection of lascivious underwear.

"I don't think there is an attacker hiding in there. Her underwear is none of your business", Shira hissed at her brother in Hebrew and closed the door, protecting Alba's privacy. "Make sure that doesn't change!" She reminded him with a stern look before she left the bedroom. Her brother just shrugged and made a face, but eventually followed his sister back into the living room, where Alba finally introduced them to Elena. It was obvious that she didn't trust Ariel or Shira, but they couldn't blame her for it. As planned, Ariel let Shira do all the talking and decided to carry Alba's bag into the bedroom instead, where the Spaniard finished packing her belongings.

"I can't believe this is happening", Alba complained, reaching her head as she tried to figure out what else she would need.

"You'll be fine, don't worry. You are safe now. We just need some time to figure out what we are going to do next." Ariel reassured her.

"I don't know how I can ever thank you. You have no idea how..." Alba continued, but was interrupted as Elena ran into the bedroom, her eyes filled with panic.

"What happened?" Ariel asked and rushed into the living room, Alba trailing behind him.

"Are those friends of yours?" Shira calmly asked Alba, who shrieked at the sight of the two men who entered her apartment. No one had heard them sneaking in, and for some reason Alba found the two intruders much more threatening than Shira did.

"They are Tarek's bodyguards", Alba whispered, fearfully stepping back.

"Is that so?" Shira confirmed with a chilling calmness in her voice.

Ariel stepped beside his sister. "Alba, Elena, stay in the bedroom. Don't worry, everything will be fine", he calmly promised. The two intruders had not yet spoken a word, their eyes shifting between the two Israelis and Alba, their lips quivering with tension. They couldn't quite understand why the man and the woman were not afraid of them, especially since they threateningly pointed two knives at them.

While they studied their opponents, one of the intruders noticed Shira's necklace. He mentioned it to his partner, whose eyes widened as he recognised Shira's Star of David. Their reaction did not go unnoticed by Ariel and Shira, who quickly flipped her necklace under her shirt, but it was already too late. The two intruders spoke to each other in an Arabian dialect that neither Shira nor Ariel quite understood. They could detect the aggressive tone in their voice as they squared their stance against the Israeli's.

"Oh my God! What are they saying?" Alba cried, taking a few more steps back as she noticed the rage building up in them.

"I am not completely sure what they said, but I believe they want to gut me", Shira explained in a serious, but still calm voice. Despite the situation, Ariel found enough time to give her a look for her choice of words, which had caused Alba to freak out even more.

Tarek's bodyguards just came to the realisation that their mission had hit a huge road block, but they would not leave without a fight. For them, failing the mission was equal to losing their honour, and that was not an option. The expression on their faces made this very clear.

"What is going to happen next? Shall I call the police?" Alba nervously asked and looked at the bodyguards as if this would deter their attack.

"There is no need to call the police. That would only complicate things. Besides, we can ask them for some information", Ariel explained, staring at the two much larger men as they started to slowly move in on them. Shira stepped away from her brother and couldn't help but notice the white carpet on the floor.

"Do you have any bleach, Alba?"

Natascha's former Marine Biology Institute, Germany, Saturday, July 26
It was still early in the morning, but Mark didn't care about the time or that it was a weekend. After yesterday's phone conversation with Natascha's friends and employers, he also didn't care about the look his wife had given him just before he had left their house. He had his coffee in the car, glad that he would beat the weekend rush hour by at least thirty minutes. Nevertheless, the drive to the institute seemed to be endless, and he parked his little car as close to the entrance as possible. It was still too early for anyone else to be here, especially during a Saturday morning, but for once he was glad that no one stopped him for the usual chit-chat on his way to his lab.

He fumbled with his key card to open the door, switched on the lights and did not waste a second starting all the machines he would need for the upcoming task. Although he had performed the same examination dozens of times, he could not deny his nervousness this morning. He went for a pair of new gloves while putting on his lab coat and finally took Natascha's parcel from a shelf.

"Oh Natascha, what the hell did you do now? I hope that this is all worth it", he murmured, but couldn't stop his eyes from filling with tears. It took him a few moments to control himself, but he finally looked for a cutter to open the parcel. With the box finally open, he carefully removed three zip-lock bags, each carefully wrapped in newspaper. Each bag contained one of the lower jawbones Natascha had removed from Whitmore Abbey. Without even taking them out of their bags, he closely examined them, flipping them around several times in the process.

"Well, definitely three different people, I can tell you that much... I would say one child... This one here could be a teenager or petit woman, the teeth will tell me... This one might be a guy", he told himself and scribbled some notes on a piece of paper. He also took the letter Natascha had left for him out of the box. It was only just a short description of where she had found the remains. He stopped for a few seconds, staring at the folded piece of paper. To see a letter with her handwriting stirred a wave of memories to flood his mind, and he had to take a couple of deep breaths to concentrate on the facts.

"Okay, let's see....water temperature was around two degree Celsius...just below the surface, but muddy bottom...even some clay...hm, not much oxygen in their water sample. Okay, I better get started", he motivated himself and finally sat down. His forensic work did not leave any room for mistakes to begin with, but Mark made sure to triple check every step of the process. After he inserted the last sample in the machine for radiometrical analysation, he poured himself another cup of coffee and sat down to examine the bone fragments more thoroughly. By now he was relatively certain that one fragment was from a child, while the largest fragment was most likely from a man. His focus switched on the third fragment, which, like the other two fragments, still had some teeth in it.

"Okay, what can you tell me?" He asked as he examined the teeth closer. "Hello! What is this?" Mark commented with surprise. For the first time today he was excited. "I might be able to get some DNA from this", he noted and took a closer look at the other two fragments. "This is interesting", he kept commenting on his own work and decided to try to secure some DNA. Spending most of the day in the lab, his work was only interrupted by some fast food from the canteen and some left-overs he had stored in the fridge. With all his work done, Mark could do nothing but wait. Usually he would spent that time on social media or he would watch a game on the TV, but not today. His mind was lost in his memory, only to be brought back to reality by the sound of the radiometer. It took Mark a few seconds to focus again, but the results of the machine were not what he expected.

"Okay, that's strange..." he murmured as he read the result. "You wouldn't lie to me, would you?" he asked the machine, but knew that everything was fine. He went back to his desk with the results in his hands and searched for Chief Inspector Conolly's phone number in his notes. As agreed, he wanted to share the results with him first. It didn't take long for the Chief Inspector to answer his call.

"Hi, Chief Inspector Conolly? Mark here from Germany....Yes, that is correct...I just finished some tests on the bone fragments that Natascha had sent me. They are indeed parts of the lower jaws from three different people. One child, I assume around ten years old, one female, maybe in her mid twenties, as well as an adult male, most likely over thirty years old. The samples have been under water for quite some time, which makes it more difficult to determine the correct age. I determined the age of the people at the time of their death based on the teeth and general shape of the bones, but the interesting result is the actual age of the bones. According to Natascha, she found the woman's jaw fragment in some deeper sediment. That one is around six-hundred-fifty to six-hundred-seventy years old. The fragments from the adult male and the child are both around three-hundred-and-fifty years old...No, there is no mistake. It is absolutely impossible that those fragments are only fifty years old...That I do not know...I will run the test again, but it will be the same result. I might have been able to pull some DNA from the teeth, not certain if it is enough or not. I can run the DNA if I can get enough material for it, but I honestly don't know if that is going to help you or not...okay, so I won't run the DNA", Mark confirmed and made a face as he looked at the machine that was already processing the samples. "Is there any news on Natascha? I know we only spoke yesterday, but still...No news?" Mark swallowed hard, that was not what he wanted to hear. "Okay, thank you. I appreciate it. Do you want me to inform Shira and them about the results or are you going to do that? Okay, that is fine. I understand that you have the lead in this investigation. I just wanted to make sure...No problem, whatever I can do to help. Thank you!" Mark ended the call and leaned back in his chair. His eyes fell on the DNA samples, which were still being processed. To hear that there was still no progress in finding Natascha heavily impacted his mood. He had hoped to shed some light into her disappearance, to provide something that would help getting her back, but he had the feeling that he had failed. Even worse, he felt that he had failed her. The human bone fragments Natascha had found were from a time period long before any of the scandals at Whitmore Abbey started. Mark knew that they would not bring them one step closer to Natascha. He cursed and started to turn the machines off. For some reason, he didn't want to wait for the DNA results. It would reveal nothing that would help getting Natascha back, and he did not want to waste any more time. Cleaning up his table, he labelled the fragments and samples and locked them all in the designated freezer. Eventually he returned his lab coat to the closet and left the lab, not without wiping a tear from his eye.

Asklepios, Aegean Sea, Saturday, July 26
The oxygen regulator worked harder than normal, keeping up with the elevated heart rate Jonathan Brown felt. Other than that, he showed no emotions. Twenty-four hours after their first meeting, Jonathan and Natascha were staring at each other again through the glass. For over an hour they stared each other down, none of them saying a word. Natascha struggled to control her emotions, but so far she managed not to reveal too much. Only once before in her life had she experienced the same rage as now, and that was only seconds before she executed Chuck Hogan. If she had a gun right now, she knew that she would not hesitate even for a second to kill the man sitting in the wheelchair. But the situation was different. Not only did she lack a weapon, there was also the thick privacy glass protecting Jonathan from any physical harm.

The adrenalin rush of the last twenty-four hours had filled Natascha with new found energy. Energy that fuelled her to pace the room much like she had before, clenching her fists. She circled back again, glancing at the glass that was nearly invisible now with the way the lighting was set in the divided room.

Natascha turned her head again to look at her nemesis. The eyes were the same, but it was obvious to Natascha that most of his body was severely burnt. The medical staff had certainly done a miracle with reconstructive surgery, but Natascha couldn't care less. Natascha thought she would never feel such hatred again, but knowing that this man was still alive, this very man who had caused her so much pain and suffering, it was like this hatred had never left. She did not care that he was in such a state, confined to a chair, severely burned. If anything, she felt sorry that he was still alive.

"At last, we finally meet again!" Jonathan Brown eventually broke the silence, this time using a more neutral voice. Natascha slowed down, threw him a hateful look and mockingly nodded at his way. She knew provoking him was not an advantage in her playbook.

"Things have changed since the last time we met", he continued, his words interrupted by his heavy breathing. Natascha briefly looked at him, but kept pacing the cell, biting her tongue to hold her silence. "I can imagine you're surprised to see me. After you sent your Israeli friend to kill me, I am sure you thought I was dead."

Natascha remained calm.

"Don't be too hard on yourself; I thought that I died, too", he continued, his eyes locked on her. "That evening I sat with my friends in my hunting cabin discussing what our next move would be. All of a sudden he appeared, out of nowhere. It was the second time that he surprised me like that in my own home, but I am sure you know that already. That son of a bitch didn't waste a second. Before we could even move, he started executing us. First was Abigail, followed by Carl and Pierre. By that time I tried to take cover and get away, but he stopped me almost right away. He took the time to show me his face before he gave me your greetings. That was also the second time that bastard did that. I knew he would kill me like the others, and I crouched. The bullet hit me in the head, but for some miracle it didn't kill me. He thought that I was dead, and so did I. He set the place on fire and left. I would have burned to death in my own house if it wouldn't have been for a handful of close friends. They saved me just in time, replaced my body with a homeless John Doe and fixed the autopsy report. I woke up months later. By then I heard what had *officially* happened. My house, my career, my friends, my body, my identity, I had lost everything", Jonathan paused.

Would have served you right to die that night! Natascha thought, but did not dare to speak. His presence harrowed her, but she didn't show it.

"Most of the time I spent here. The medical team is great, the food is excellent, the weather is always sunny and warm, and the entertainment is not half bad. I was barely alive when I arrived. They patched me up and I needed some transplants. Everything took time. Endless, painful time. Not a day went by that they told me that I was making great progress. Not a day went by that I didn't want to die."

Natascha didn't interrupt Jonathan. She didn't care about his misery. She tried to conserve her energy, knowing that the conversation would change shortly.

"As far as the medical support goes, I could not have asked for a better place. The docs are doing miracles with what is left of my body, and I even have a favourite nurse. Melissa is her name", Jonathan continued, but he missed Natascha's reaction.

Go figure, Natascha bit her lip. She wasn't sure if Jonathan knew about her and Melissa's *relationship*, but assumed that he did.

"But it wasn't the medical care or the staff and not even the promises from my friends that kept me going. You know what really kept me going?" Jonathan addressed Natascha directly. It was the first time that he expected her to say something in return.

"Your unconditional love for me?" Natascha asked with a shrug of her shoulders. She regretted it the moment she had said it. The comment had literally slipped her tongue, and she knew from his silence that his reaction wouldn't be good.

"I see your arrogance remains unchanged. But, you're right. The only thought that kept pushing me through those years of excruciating pain and surgeries was you. Knowing that you were out there, somewhere, living a normal life after you had destroyed mine. Knowing that one day I will get my revenge. *That* kept me going." Jonathan explained.

Natascha stopped and looked at his eyes. She fought the urge to yell at him, but knew that she better kept her mouth shut. *Oh, you think that I destroyed your life? You're the one who declared me an international terrorist. You are the one who arranged the bounty on my head. You're the one who hired that monster who killed my friends and made me almost kill my own husband.* Natascha almost lost control.

"It is just like we are back on that ship. You and I have a very different opinion on who destroyed whose life", Natascha hissed, her disgust for Jonathan clear in her voice. "So, what is next? Your goons finally got your hands on me."

"Yes, that's right. We finally meet again. You can't even imagine how much I was looking forward to this." Jonathan replied, his voice getting dangerously low. Natascha tried to hide her fear, but she swallowed hard. "For years I have dreamed about what I'd do to you, and now you're finally here. You know what the best part is?" Jonathan asked, carefully observing Natascha's reaction. But she had her back turned towards Jonathan to make sure that he would not see the tear running down her face.

"That I am alone?" Natascha answered. Jonathan didn't answer right away. He had waited so long for this moment that he enjoyed every second of it.

"You are arrogant, but you're not stupid. You are right. You are alone. You have no friends here. Your private army doesn't even know in which hemisphere you are. Hell, they don't even know if you're still alive. As far as they're concerned, you might already be dead", Jonathan continued in a low, whispering tone. Natascha swallowed hard again, panic starting to rise inside her. He had just pointed something out that she had never even considered.

What if he is right? What if they think that I am already dead, and they stopped looking for me? Natascha's mind started to spin, but she came to the only conclusion that was acceptable to her. *They will not stop looking for me. They will find the trail, and they will find me. I just have to make sure that I live long enough.*

"But, from what I have seen, I don't think you need your private army any more. They showed me the surveillance video from yesterday, when they were about to bring you to our first meeting." Jonathan continued before he continued, not without admiration, "When did you learn all that stuff?"

"The world is full of bad people", Natascha simply shrugged, clenching her emotions into her fist to control them. "How are Kevin's eyes?"

"It looks like he will have permanent damage from what I have been told. They had to do a tracheotomy on him as well. You certainly ruined his day. He might not like you anymore."

"He deserved it", Natascha shrugged with disinterest.

"Maybe he did, but that's not important. The important part is what's going to happen to you", Jonathan paused for a moment to let the words sink in. "I'm sure you can imagine that I had a lot of time to think about this, but unfortunately, my hands are somewhat tied in the greater scheme of things, so I am reduced to only a few options." A cold shiver ran down Natascha's spine as Jonathan continued.

"You know where you are?" he asked, the curiosity carried by his voice.

"Some godforsaken island called *Asklepios*. Officially a hospital for the rich, for the *better* people." Natascha spit. "And, of course, the base of an illegal, international human and organ traffic ring."

"You never cease to amaze me", Jonathan laughed. "You should feel right at home here. This place does so much good. Many people are getting their lives back here."

"Yeah, right. What about all those innocent girls you send into slavery? Or all the homeless people that you literally butcher for parts?"

"Still that ray of sunshine, aren't we? They are nothing but bumps in the road. What happens to them here is most likely the best thing they will ever contribute to society. So spare me your morals. It is the same as it was back then. You are hopelessly naive. The lives of many brilliant minds can be saved here. You have no idea what is going on in the world these days. What happens here has *biblical* proportions." Jonathan emphasised, but Natascha couldn't follow.

"Yeah, whatever. Like I said, we have a different understanding of good and evil."

"True, but let's get to the point. We have wasted enough time. You have three options. Your first option is simple. We offer you on the market and sell you to the highest bidder. Granted, you are not the youngest person any more, but there are enough people out there who really like women who fight back. Once they are done with you, we sell your organs and that will be the end of it."

Natascha couldn't help but shiver. She had expected something like that, but finally hearing someone say it made it so much more of a possible reality. Jonathan enjoyed watching her struggle, and gave her a few seconds before he continued.

"Your second option is my favourite. It turns out that you and I have the same blood type. We are just waiting for some more tests. If the results are positive, I can even use some of your organs for myself. I desperately need a new lung. Wouldn't that be ironic? After all that time, it is actually you who gives your life to save mine? I think that is fantastic. You will be surprised once you learn how long they can keep you alive with machines these days. I could put you on ice for some more spare parts, who knows?"

Natascha blood seemed to run cold. The second option was not much better than the first.

"What about the third option? Quite frankly, I don't like what I have heard so far", she whispered, trying to sound cool, her back still turned towards Jonathan. She had no idea how she remained so calm, but she didn't want to give Jonathan the satisfaction of looking weak.

"The third option? Oh, my dear Natascha. The third option is so horrible that I struggle to find the words to describe it. Your worst nightmares won't even come close to this. Let me put it this way: you will help fight global terrorism."

"What?" Natascha asked puzzled and turned around to face him again, but the lights had changed, and she saw nothing but her reflection in the glass. Their conversation was over.

***EuroSecCorporation*, London, Saturday, July 26**
It was late morning when Ariel arrived with Elena and Alba at the office. He would have preferred an earlier start, but both women had slept in. Considering what they had been through, he decided to let them have the much needed rest. They had skipped breakfast and stopped at a coffee shop on their way in. After parking his car, he escorted them upstairs to their break room.

"Here we are. Over there you will find everything you need to make yourself some coffee or tea. I will go see my boss and we will have proper introductions shortly. Is there anything you need?" Ariel offered, a wide smile lighting his face.

"No, we are fine", Alba replied after exchanging a quick look with Elena. The gratitude she felt was clear in her voice, and she and Elena opened the paper bags from the coffee shop. They both started eating, and even Elena sighed with relief. It was her first smile in a long time.

Their breakfast was only interrupted now and then when several members of *EuroSec* used the break room to get some coffee or their own breakfast. Elena couldn't help but feel nervous the moment someone joined them, but the friendly and reassuring comments and greetings she heard made her feel welcomed. The tension of Natascha's disappearance amongst the EuroSec members went unnoticed by Alba and Elena. While Elena and Alba finished their breakfast, Ariel joined his sister in Brian's office.

"Good Morning, Ariel." Klaus greeted him. "How did your guests sleep?"

"Good Morning. They both told me they slept well. I didn't hear anything that would make me believe otherwise. Do we have anything new on Natascha?"

"Unfortunately not. At least nothing substantial, only bits and pieces here and there. Sean is over at Scotland Yard to meet with Conolly. I made a few calls about the bomb squad, but so far I haven't been very successful. The people in charge will be back by Monday. I have to pull some strings." Brian's frustration was evident in his voice. His eyes wandered over his desk, searching for some clues he wouldn't find. Ariel's aggravation increased with every passing hour. He shook his head and looked out the window.

"How is Nick doing?" he wanted to know from his sister.

"Barely slept last night. Sarah was fine, but I think that Nick is going to lose it sooner than later. I stayed up with him for most of the night. At one point we just fell asleep on the couch", Shira explained tiredly and yawned.

"Did he come here with you?"

"Yes, Sarah is at the daycare with Noah and Tamar. Nick is in the conference room, staring at the facts and the time sheet."

"Not much to stare at", Klaus added absentmindedly.

"Except for Natascha's large picture."

"Okay, let's talk about our new guests. Shira already filled me in. What do you make of this?"

"Well, I do believe that we ruined Miss Casillas's white carpet", Ariel replied with mock laughter before he continued. "Two goons came to her apartment. Alba recognised them as Prince Tarek's bodyguards. We don't know exactly how they found out about her address so soon, but it is safe to say that Rowan had his hands in it. Anyway, their mission was either to kill or to abduct whoever they would find there, but they didn't expect to meet resistance. They were nervous, didn't know what to do, but it looked like they assumed that they could take us and finish their mission."

"Weapons?"

"Each had a tactical knife, but limited skills. Unfortunately, we didn't carry anything. To be brief, one guy ended up with his own knife in his thigh. They both fled the apartment once they realised that they were not going to succeed. We didn't pursue or try to arrest them for obvious reasons, we just made sure we weren't followed when we left there. Alba and Elena were shaken up pretty bad, but they calmed down."

"Okay. We sent Team C to Miss Casillas's place to retrieve the remaining personal items. How are our guests looking for money?"

"She took some cash from a bank machine last night on our way back. It doesn't look like that really matters much anymore."

"No, not really. At some point we have to decide where to go from here with them, but until I am convinced that they're both safe, they will have to stay put. Klaus?"

"Agreed", the retired general eventually said after he had taken a few moments to carefully consider all available options.

"Can I ask something?" Shira eventually broke the silence. Brian didn't say anything and just looked at the Israeli.

"What are the chances that Natascha is actually still alive? I mean realistically." It was the first time that both Klaus and Brian saw tears running down Shira's face. Thinking about her best friend's fate, the young Israeli wiped her sudden and unexpected tears and swallowed hard. She looked from each person in the room and did not receive an answer.

"I'm not going to lie to you, Shira. You know that the chances are minimal", Brian started in his low voice before his eyes met hers. "But I can tell you one thing", he continued, his voice taking a dangerous tone now, "None of us, not even *one* of my employees, friends, or sources, will rest until she is back. Bloody hell, I don't give a damn about the law, Scotland Yard, or diplomatic issues. Right now we don't have the faintest idea where she is, but as soon as I even know so much as a general direction, I will personally go there to get her back."

Shira wiped more tears from her face and looked at Klaus.

"What he said", the German simply added and nodded towards Brian. Shira blew her nose and excused herself. She left the office and went straight to the washroom.

Looking at her reflection in the mirror, she thought about the events of the last couple days. Natascha's abduction and uncertain fate, the endless hours at home, where she not only had to support a heartbroken Nick, but also Natascha's parents and her godchild Sarah. The brutal knife attack on her and her brother last night by Prince Tarek's bodyguards. She felt a swell of helplessness overwhelm her, something she had never felt before. Her lip twitched with a certain fragility as more tears ruptured through her hard exterior. Back then, when she had caught a bullet for Natascha, she had had weeks to cope with the situation, but this time it was different. Too much had happened and there was no time. She knew that Brian and Klaus would do anything to save Natascha, but they didn't even know where she was.

It took the young Israeli a few moments to collect herself. The cold water she splashed in her face revitalised her almost immediately. *Okay, enough of this. Natascha needs you to be strong,* she told herself looking at her reflection in the mirror as Alba opened the door and walked in.

"Oh, here you are. I think they are waiting for us", the Spaniard told her friend and stepped beside her, recognising Shira's reddened eyes. "Are you okay?"

"Yes, Alba, I am fine. Don't worry", Shira smiled back, turning the tap off.

"Shira, I understand that you and your friends have a very important thing going on right now. I just want to thank you for helping us", Alba thoughtfully said.

"Of course we help you. Just make sure you tell Brian and Klaus, okay?" Shira replied and dried her hands off.

"I'm serious, Shira. If it wouldn't have been for you and your brother, Elena and I would be dead by now." Alba's voice cracked. Last night's events had certainly taken a toll on the young Spaniard, showing her clearly the consequences of trying to help Elena.

"Don't say that, Alba", Shira tried to comfort her, but she knew that Alba was right. She wouldn't mind continuing this conversation, but remembered that Brian and Klaus were waiting for them.

"How do you do it?" Alba wanted to know, just as Shira turned to leave.

"How do I do what?" Shira asked puzzled and looked back at her.

"What you did last night. The guy with the knife! I would have died of fear!"

"Who said that I didn't fear for my life?" Shira asked back seriously before she opened the door.

They both went to the conference room, where Brian introduced Alba and Elena to all the members of Team A and C, as well as Jack MacDonald and Gunnar Eriksson from Operation Control. Shira listened as Brian brought everybody up to speed on their new guests, and Alba took a moment to thank Brian, Klaus and everybody else for helping them, especially Ariel for allowing them to stay at his home.

"No need to thank us, Miss Casillas", Brian continued, this time in his fatherly voice. "As I mentioned before, we are currently facing an extremely important and delicate situation, so accept my apologies in case we come over a little bit too harsh. You are free to do whatever you want, but I believe that last night's events proved that both your lives are indeed in danger. At the moment we have limited resources, so I simply recommend that you stay put with us in this building until we figure something out. I am certain that our personnel will introduce themselves to you during the day. If you have any questions, do not hesitate to ask. Can we agree on that?"

"Si!" Alba answered and nodded with understanding. She was totally overwhelmed by Brian's and Klaus' generosity.

"We recovered some of your personal items from your apartment, as it was discussed with Ariel last night. Our team also took the liberty to clean your carpet. We locked the apartment and installed some surveillance in it which will alarm us in case someone tries to gain access", Klaus explained. Alba nodded again and thought for a moment. She wasn't sure whether to ask or not, but finally took the courage to speak again.

"I know that we discussed this before, but are you going to report us to the police?"

"Should we?" Brian asked in return. "From what we know, neither of you have broken any laws, and you are both of age. We understand why you do not trust the police and we accept your position on that issue."

"What about last night? The attack at my place. Are the police not going to investigate this?”

“What attack?” Brian looked puzzled. Alba didn't know how he could have forgotten about the attack already, but she finally understood.

“Never mind”, she smiled. She liked this place better and better by the minute. Shira walked over and led her and Elena back to the break room after giving them a quick tour of the other rooms and offices on this level.

“Shira, I really owe you for this. You have no idea.” Alba thanked the Israeli for the one-thousandths time.

“Careful, I usually collect”, Shira replied before introducing Alba and Elena to Noah and Tamar, who just came up from daycare with Sarah. Elena immediately grew fond of the little girl, much to everyone's relief. It didn't take long before Alba and Elena played with Sarah, allowing the Israelis to head back to the conference room. The mood had changed, as they now all stared at Natascha's large picture. As painful as it was for Nick to see his wife's picture being projected on the wall, it was a stern reminder for everyone about what was at stake. He had paid little attention to Alba and Elena as his mind was somewhere else. With the timeline and Natascha's picture back on the wall, he looked harder than anyone else, trying to find what detail they were missing, the little link that would lead them to his wife. He scanned the timeline again, but there was nothing they had not already discussed in great detail.

“Ariel, anything new from Israel?” Brian barked at the Israeli just seconds after he got off the phone with the embassy.

“No, nothing. Still nothing on the internet. No chatter, no clues, nothing.”

“Sean just texted me from Scotland Yard. They are making minor progress with the licence plates and there is a chance that the French have something for us, but he will not know until later this afternoon.” Klaus informed as he put the phone down.

“Not good enough”, Brian barked at his friend. “Call him right back and tell him that the bloody frogs should stop faffing around.”

“Way ahead of you. I already told him that.” Klaus shot back. He and Brian glanced at each other before they scanned the room. Everybody worked together in small teams, looking at each piece of information again, calling some old contacts or coming up with theories. Their concentration was broken as Sarah came running into the conference room, laughing loud, closely followed by Elena. The Romanian stumbled once she realised where she was, the laugh on her face quickly disappearing as Sarah ran to Nick, who picked her up.

“We are so sorry! We didn't want to interrupt, but Sarah played hide and seek and ran away”, Alba caught up and quickly apologised for Elena, who just stood there silently.

“No need to apologise”, Brian reassured with his fatherly smile. Sarah was still laughing, and even Nick eventually smiled at the sight of his laughing daughter. Everybody looked at him and his daughter, happy for the moment they had.

“Talia!” Elena suddenly said and pointed at Natascha's picture.

- *22* -

Asklepios, Aegean Sea, Saturday, July 26

"Don't!" Natascha told Jake as he went to place his hand on her shoulder to show his support. "I don't want them to see me crying." She added with determination, convinced that someone was watching them from the camera in the ceiling. No matter what would happen, she wouldn't give them the satisfaction to see how bad she felt. Feeling uncomfortable, Jake slowly took his hand back.

Since her return from the meeting with Jonathan, Natascha lay in her bunk and the emotions got the best of her. She just stared at the wall and let her tears flow. Jake didn't have to be a genius to figure out what they had told her.

"I am sorry. I just..." he stopped and just shrugged with lack of words.

"It's not your fault, Jake", Natascha whispered, her eyes still fixed at the same spot as if it could offer her a solution.

"Do you want to talk about it? It might help?"

"Talk about what, Jake? All the different ways they want to torture me to death before they butcher me?"

Jake swallowed hard. He knew that Natascha just needed some time alone, but he couldn't just walk out of their cell. With nothing else to do, he just laid beside her, trying to get some sleep. It wasn't even five minutes later that the door opened.

"Okay, time for the evening rounds. Let's go", Melissa yelled at them, and, as usual, didn't even try to hide her hatred towards them. Natascha and Jake slowly got off their bunk and led their way to the kitchen.

"A little bit faster", Melissa commanded and pushed Natascha hard in the back.

You are so going to lose some teeth over this! Natascha thought to herself, but for now she just added Melissa's behaviour to the ever growing list of her insults.

"Wait! You go with Lamar and dress up. It will take you a while", O'Brian said and pushed Natascha again, this time past the kitchen door. Natascha had no idea what Melissa was talking about, but she also knew that she wouldn't get an answer if she asked. Instead, she simply saved her energy and looked at Lamar, who guided her to the elevator. Once the doors closed, her fear peaked as she noticed that Lamar pressed the button for B-Level. *No one has ever come back from B-Level alive!* Kyle's statement shot through her head as the elevator moved down. Natascha exhaled sharply and fought hard against the rising panic.

"Relax, princess. You're just here to help with dinner. One of our guys is sick", Lamar explained as he noticed Natascha clenching her fists. The door opened again and Lamar ushered her out before Natascha could react. To her surprise, she stared at an airtight lock. With the elevator gone again, Natascha slowly stepped towards the sealed door. Lamar swiped his key card and entered his PIN. As he waited for the door to open, he looked at his prisoner. If Natascha felt any fear, she was at least not showing it. Honestly, she didn't know how to feel, shifting constantly between panicking and attacking Lamar. She startled when the door slowly opened, drawing air inside the air lock.

"Step in", Lamar ordered. Natascha hesitated, her instincts telling her not to set a foot in that lock.

"Listen, I told you before, you are here to help with the lunch. Do as I tell you and nothing will happen to you today, okay?"

For a second Natascha considered her options, but eventually stepped inside.

"See, that wasn't too bad", Lamar commented and stood clear from the door, which slowly sealed them in. With her back against the wall, Natascha didn't take her eyes off him when he used both his magnetic key card and his PIN again. Before the other door opened, Natascha felt the change in the air pressure again. After a few seconds the red light over the second door turned green and the door slowly opened. Natascha reluctantly followed Lamar through the second door, which led them to a changing room. Her eyes scanned the walls. The room was relatively large, allowing several people to change at the same time. Lamar pointed at several yellow biohazard suits lining one of the walls.

"Find one that fits you. You find the size on the label inside the suit", he told her and picked his own personal suit from a hanger. Natascha hesitated for a few seconds, but eventually walked over and picked a suit she thought would fit her just fine. It took her a few minutes to get it on. Just as she was ready to close the airtight zipper, the door opened again and Leo Sawn and Kevin Wilson walked in, pushing a cart with several dishes of soup.

"Wait, we will help you connect the suit", Leo said, showing her how to connect the support hoses to the suit and how to activate the built-in emergency breathing apparatus in case something would go wrong. Lamar already ushered her through the next airtight door before Natascha even knew what to think about this. It took Natascha only two seconds to realise that this shower-like room was the disinfection area. Since there was no need to scrub off on their way in, they just walked through the shower to the next door, where Lamar entered his PIN again.

When the door opened, Natascha had to swallow hard. Her mouth fell open as she slowly stepped into the large treatment room. Following the same layout as one deck above, Natascha counted a total of sixteen beds, eight on each side. Fifteen beds had patients in them. Natascha couldn't know that she had just met Group A. What she did know was that they were in much worse shape than the patients on the floor above. Natascha slowly took a step forward, allowing herself to take in the horror in front of her. The fifteen young women were loosely restraint to their beds, but Natascha doubted that they would even have the energy to sit up.

"Freja!" Natascha noted the Swedish girl in one of the beds, but Freja had not even noticed that someone had entered the room. It wasn't clear to Natascha if she was unconscious or just sleeping, but like the rest, she was wired to several monitors.

"Wakey, wakey!" Natascha startled when she heard Lamar yelling through his speaker phone, and indeed most of the young woman woke up and slowly turned their heads towards them. "Hey, princess!" Lamar shouted and waved at Natascha. "I want you to go to each patient and clean them. You will find what you need in that air lock over there. Once you are done with that, you will bring them some soup, which will also come through that air lock. Once they are finished, you put the dishes and everything else back in the air lock, understood?" Natascha wanted to say something, but noticed that her microphone wasn't activated. They obviously didn't want her to talk to the patients. Not able to speak, she simply nodded and started to work. It didn't take long before she reached Freja. The beautiful Swede stared at her, but even as she recognised Natascha, she didn't show any reaction. Her expression made it clear that she had lost all hope. Natascha continued her routine and cleaned Freja's face from some minor blood sputter around her nose and mouth. A quick look at the monitor showed Natascha that Freja ran a high fever, and even now the Swede coughed violently now and then, the same as all the other women. A tear ran down Natascha's face. Even if Freja could have heard her, Natascha had no words to comfort her. Instead, she just held on to her hand, not knowing what else she could do.

"Where is Monique?" the Swede asked weakly, but Natascha couldn't understand her through the suit. "Where is Monique?" Freja repeated, and this time Natascha was able to read her lips, but she still owed her an answer and simply shook her head and shrugged. She had no idea what had happened to the young French woman, all she knew was that it couldn't be good.

A couple more minutes was all that she could spend with Freja before she continued her work with the other patients. It took a while, but eventually she had finished her routine and placed the empty dishes inside the air lock before she followed Lamar back into the disinfection room.

What is going on here? Natascha asked herself again. She had no idea why they needed the biohazard suits, but assumed there had to be a good reason for it. Her thoughts explored everything she could think of while the shower sprayed her with disinfectant from all different angles for several minutes. Even minutes later, when she took the suit off, her mind still raced about what she had just witnessed. Still not finding an answer, she simply looked at Lamar.

"Can you tell me what is going on here?" Natascha bluntly asked, but the look Lamar threw at her was answer enough.

"No, I cannot", he simply snapped at her. "Let's go. They are waiting for you upstairs", Lamar told her and watched as her body tensed. "For heaven's sake, I told you before that nothing is going to happen to you today. So don't piss me off or I will change my mind", Lamar ordered and pushed her through the airtight door. He didn't say anything else to her until they were in the common room one floor above. "Help finish the rounds and then you can get something to eat yourself", the nurse ordered her. Natascha decided to simply obey and walked over to help Kyle with his duties.

"Where the hell have you been?" Kyle asked. "You are late. I thought they got you."

"I was on B-Level", Natascha whispered back and quickly filled the Briton in as much as possible.

"Bloody hell! Do you got any idea what is going on down there?"

"No clue, but whatever it is, it can't be good. But there is more", Natascha continued and quickly looked around. While she pretended to have some issues with the food cart, she told Kyle about the fate she was expected to face soon. "I'm running out of time, Kyle. I have to make a move soon."

"No argument there, but do you got a plan yet?"

"No, not really. Couple ideas, but I might have to wing it. Are you in?"

"Hell yes!" Kyle whispered back with enthusiasm. "When do you want to do it?"

"Like I said, I got an idea, but I will have to wing most of it. You will be the first to know. You are still in the same cell?"

"Yes."

"Okay", Natascha nodded and pushed the food cart ahead to avoid rising any suspicion. It didn't take her long before she stopped beside Lawrence and Charles. She quickly filled them in about what she had told Kyle.

"Jesus, what is this place?" Lawrence asked in disbelief and shook his head.

"It's not the Four Seasons, I can tell you that." Natascha replied as she handed them their food. "Look, I have a plan, kind of", Natascha continued and glanced around before explaining them her idea. For some reason she trusted them more than Kyle.

"That could actually work", Lawrence mentioned after a while. "It won't be a walk in the park, but it seems like the best available option. So there will be five of us?"

"Yes, Jake, Kyle, the two of you and myself. Can't do it alone, can I?"

"No, won't work alone."

"Did they mention anything about separating you in different cells?"

"No, but that doesn't mean anything. You know them. Last couple nights they locked us in the same cell as always."

"Listen, no disrespect, but what kind of shape are you two in?" Natascha bluntly asked.

"Brian was the smart one. He made a career", Lawrence replied, "while I did some dirty work. I was SAS."

Natascha couldn't hide her surprise. She knew that almost half of EuroSec's Teams B and C were former SAS.

"Well, that might come in handy", she acknowledged with a smile and looked at Charles.

"Special Boat Service of the Royal Marines Commando", Charles replied not without pride. "Retired, of course", he added with a face.

"But of course", Natascha smiled at him, thinking that her plan might actually work.

EuroSecCorporation, London, Saturday, July 26

"Yes?" the Israeli sounded puzzled as she turned around to face Elena. All eyes in the room now rested on the Romanian.

"Talia!" Elena said again and pointed at Natascha's picture. She didn't take her eyes off the projection. The whole room fell silent, confused. Even Brian and Klaus were lost for words.

"I am Talia", the Israeli reassured Elena and slowly stepped closer to her.

"No, no! That is Talia. I met Talia! She prisoner. She and I in same room. She helping me." Those few words of broken English were enough to shock everyone. For a few seconds everyone remained speechless, only Nick walked slowly towards the Romanian, the disbelief clear in his face. It was Brian who first reached clarity at the revelation. He raised his hand, demanding everybody else not to speak as he searched Elena quizzically.

"Elena", he started calmly and paused for a second, trying to find the right words. "This is important. Very important! Take a very close look at the picture. Have you really seen this woman?" Brian pointed at Natascha's projected picture on the wall. He impatiently waited for an answer even though Elena immediately replied.

"Yes! She and I in same room. She prisoner same as me." It didn't matter that Elena's English was far from perfect and with a strong accent, but the tone in her voice left no doubt that she was certain. They all looked at each other in disbelief. Whatever they had expected to find out during this meeting, this had not been it. It was Klaus who broke the silence and suddenly rose from his chair.

"Miss Romanov! Elena! This is an urgent matter and lives are at stake. Can I ask you to come into our office? We have to ask you some very important questions", Klaus told her. Elena first looked scared as Ariel and the rest of Operation Control rose to their feet in unison, ready to leave the conference room, but Alba put her hands on her shoulder.

"It's okay. We have to help them find her", she reassured the young Romanian and looked back at Natascha's picture herself. She had immediately recognised Natascha, but it was only now that she realised what the urgent event was.

"With all due respect, Boss", Ole-Einar came forward, "if she has some crucial information about Natascha's whereabouts, then we all want to hear it. Let's not lose more precious time." Brian and Klaus exchanged a brief look, but it took them only a second before they sat down again.

"You're right, Ole-Einar. My apology", he stated and offered both Alba and Elena a chair. Nick sat right beside them.

"Elena. The woman you know as Talia is one of our employees. Not only is she a good friend, she is also Nick's wife and the mother of little Sarah here", Klaus started, speaking slowly and gesturing at Nick and Sarah. "Her name is Natascha and she is missing since the seventeenth of July, which was a Thursday. Do you understand me so far?" Elena nodded. "Very good. You said that you were with her, correct?"

"Yes!"

"And there is no doubt that this is the woman you saw?" Klaus wanted reconfirmation. Like everyone else, he still had a hard time believing this.

"No! She and I in same room! It is her!" Elena insisted.

"Does she have a tattoo?" Nick asked, with all the eyes in the room locked on Elena as the young Romanian recollected her thoughts for a second.

"Yes! A fish! She has tattoo of...of...dolphin right here!" Elena snapped her fingers and pointed at her hips.

Nick sat back in his chair and gazed at Brian and Klaus. There was no doubt now and Klaus quickly took over. "You said that you and Natascha were in the same room. When was that? When did you leave?"

Elena took a moment to concentrate. "Not sure. They gave me drugs before I left. Four or five days."

Klaus and Brian looked at each other while Gunnar immediately started a second timeline.

"What condition is she in? Is she still alive?" Nick burst out, earning a disapproving look from both Klaus and Brian, but he didn't care. Elena turned her head and nodded encouragingly.

"Yes. When I left, she is alive. She strong. Back then, she is not hurt." It seemed as everybody exhaled a sigh of relief, easing the tension in the room.

"The fact that she was still alive a couple of days ago is a good thing, Nick." Shira encouraged her friend, but Nick just nodded.

"I'm more concerned about the now", he replied, the tone reflecting his concern, but eventually leaned back as Klaus raised his hand, demanding Nick to stop talking.

"Elena, if I remember correctly, you mentioned that someone bought you. Is that right?"

"Yes", Elena nodded.

"And that person, the one who bought and picked you up at that facility was Rowan Harrison, is that correct?" Klaus asked, his voice and hands shaking in anticipation as he showed her a picture of their former client. The conference room was so quiet they could have heard a needle dropping. Everyone waited for her answer.

"Yes! He know her. He saw her on monitor when picking me up. He said that he know her!" Elena enthusiastically answered. Brian and Klaus exchanged a look which could be described as dangerous at best. The retired British admiral rose from his chair, resting both hands on the table as he leaned forward to look at Ariel and Shira.

"Rowan Harrison was at the same place where Natascha is held hostage. He knows exactly where she is. Find him!" he growled at them, but the two Israeli were already on their cell phones.

- 23 -

West of Al-Hasakah, Syria, Saturday, July 26
The hot, stale air inside the tent made the stench almost unbearable. The hygienic conditions made it that much worse. After Nazir Algafari had bought Monique for not much more than a few bucks, her last forty-eight hours had been hell. Curled up on an old dirty rag close to one of the tent walls, both her spirit and body were broken. She didn't have any tears left, the little strength remaining allowed for nothing more than staring at a stain on the ground. She knew that it was the blood of another young woman about the same age as herself. This young woman, whose name Monique had already forgotten, had chosen suicide over this hell by cutting her arteries with a sharp stone she had found outside the tent. The image of the young woman bleeding out right in front of her was still fresh in front of her eyes. It was the only time Monique had seen her smile. When their *owner* had discovered her lifeless body, he had just called for a friend to drag the woman's dead body out of the tent.

Monique stopped thinking about the reasons why she was in this situation. She didn't even know which country she was in, but it didn't matter to her. Her thoughts were interrupted when one of the other women in the tent started to cough and sat up. She had introduced herself as Amber and was obviously from Western European heritage. Monique watched Amber for a few moments before her eyes gazed over to the third woman. She was of African heritage and Monique assumed that she was five or six months pregnant. They didn't understand each other, and Monique knew her name at one point, but had already forgotten.

As Amber's cough got worst, Monique's eyes shifted back to her. It took Amber a couple of minutes before she had herself under control again. It was obvious that Amber was very sick. Her poor physical condition could very well be the reason the middle aged desert warrior had bought Monique to replace her. Their eyes met.

"Are you from that hospital?" Amber asked weakly in English.

Monique nodded.

"Are you also one of the sick ones?" Amber wanted to know, but Monique didn't understand.

"A or B?"

"What?" Monique still didn't understand.

"What group were you in? A or B?"

"I think I was B. I was only there for a couple days", the French explained and watched as Amber turned her head away, this time looking at the tent flap.

"I was A, but it doesn't matter", Amber said, before another painful spasm of coughing shook her battered body. "Oh God!" the ill woman moaned with closed eyes as she wiped some blood from her mouth and face. "Won't make a difference", she continued and shook her head. "We will all die." Another spasmodic cough shook her violently, causing her to lie down again as more blood dripped from her nose. Despite the heat in the tent, Monique couldn't help but notice that Amber shivered uncontrollably. Just as the young French tried to crawl over to help her, the tent flap opened and two men walked in.

Monique immediately startled as she recognised Nazir. Even now he was heavily armed, the assault rifle slung over his shoulder. The second man was obviously an elder, but Monique could not remember if she had seen him before. Amber had no energy left to pay too much attention to them. Monique crawled back to the tent wall, not exactly sure what was about to happen next. Both men argued, with the younger of them repeatedly pointing at each of the women. Monique couldn't understand them, but recognised that the elder tried to calm the warrior down. He didn't succeed. Nazir left his tent agitated. The elder just looked after him for a few seconds and shook his head before turning his attention to Monique.

"Come!" he said with a strong accent. Monique eyes widened with fear, not certain what horror would wait for her next. "Come!" the elder repeated and held his hand out to her.

The French swallowed hard, but for some reason she didn't believe that this man was here to hurt her like the others did. Monique slowly rose to her feet and followed the elder outside. Although the tent was inside the large cavern, Monique had trouble adjusting her eyes. There was no breeze, but the hot air smelled fresh compared to the stench inside the tent. The elder gave her a few moments before he gestured her to follow him to the largest tent on the other side of the cavern. Monique reluctantly followed, but knew that there was no point in trying to escape. Everywhere she looked, she saw dozens of heavily armed warriors, either standing guard or working on one of the many vehicles hidden in the cavern from spying satellites. Monique felt their preying eyes on her, but for some reason their faces didn't reflect it. Something seemed to concern them. Keeping her head down, Monique followed the elder.

"Oh my God!" Monique stammered as they came closer to the large tent. Her eyes caught a pickup truck parked just outside the tent, its cargo bed full with dead bodies. A cloud of flies was buzzing over them. Monique didn't count the bodies, but saw at least five or six corpses, while two armed men carried another dead body from the tent, only to put him on top of the pile. Monique's hand flew to her mouth as she shrieked.

Amongst the corpses she recognised the young woman from her tent, who had just committed suicide less than twenty-four hours ago. The elder briefly looked at her, but otherwise showed no reaction as he stepped inside the tent. Monique's eyes were still glued on the dead bodies. She felt her stomach retch at the sight, imagining how many more would be loaded onto the truck before being disposed in a mass grave. When she looked up again, the elder waited for her at the tent's entrance, ushering her forward. She looked at the large tent once more before stepping through the flap. A swoon of nausea overcame her.

***EuroSecCorporation*, London, Saturday, July 26**
"Elena, before we continue, I want you to try to remember as best as you can. I will first ask you some questions about Natascha, then some more questions about the facility itself and the people working there. This can be exhausting for you, but Natascha's life depends on it. Do you understand me?" Klaus asked. Elena nodded her understanding.

For the next hour, Elena answered Klaus' questions to the best of her memory, but due to the drugs she had certain memory-lapses. At one point the young Romanian simply couldn't concentrate anymore and needed a break.

"It's okay, Elena. You helped us more than you can imagine. Let's take a break and maybe we can talk after you had something to eat, okay?" Brian smiled at her in a fatherly voice. Talia walked over and led Alba and Elena out to the break room.

"Let's go, we ordered some Italian food. It is really good", they could hear the Israeli on her way out.

"Okay, let's see what we got", Brian continued immediately and looked at the new timeline. "So according to our new best friend here, she was with Natascha last Sunday, which is six days ago. At that time Natascha was in good enough physical condition to perform general labour for whoever is behind this. She also tended to approximately ten to twenty other hostages or prisoners, whatever you want to call them. Okay. That makes me believe that she is in better condition than the rest of them. How many guards did she say?"

"She mentioned nine different people, but there are most likely more."

"Okay. Around twenty people being held captive in some kind of a hospital or prison for human and organ trafficking. They do surgeries there as well, obviously." Brian's eyes narrowed as he processed the information. Everybody in the room looked at Klaus and Brian, knowing that they would bark orders any second now.

"Okay guys! Here is what we need to know. First we need everything about Rowan. We have some of his information already on file since he is a customer, but I want everything about him. Most importantly, where he is at the moment, understood? Second, based on the number of prisoners and guards and everything else she told us, we need to find out what facility she is talking about. Most importantly, where the hell it is. Finally, we all know that she has been kidnapped because of who she is. That means that the kidnappers know her real name. I have to know why she is using Talia's name and why she is getting away with it. I know that this is a shot in the dark, but I want all reasonable and unreasonable theories on this."

"Do you plan to tell Conolly that Rowan Harrison is involved in all of this?" Klaus asked his friend. The tone of his voice clearly showed Klaus' hesitance of sharing the information with the authorities.

"Not for now, my friend. Not for now. Let's wait until we have a clearer picture", Brian replied, showing his own reluctance.

Asklepios, Aegean Sea, Sunday, July 27

"You got to be kidding me, son", Walter "L.J." Jackson roared with laughter and shook his head.

"No, I am not. As I told you, it wasn't my bloody fault." Rowan timidly tried to defend himself.

"It wasn't your fault? Let me see if I get this straight. You buy this girl as a gift for your psychopathic Saudi friend, and during her first visit on shore she just walks out of the casino with another whore and no one noticed a thing? And above all that they both know about you and Tarek?" Despite the seriousness of the situation, L.J. had a hard time not to laugh out loud again. While he looked at Rowan with amusement, Jonathan Brown didn't show any reaction, but the look in his eyes spoke volumes.

"I told you that I have the situation under control. I have..." Rowan continued to defend himself, but the heavy Texan cut him off.

"Do you now? Please explain to us what makes you think that?" L.J.'s voice had taken a dangerous tone. The British playboy didn't like the way L.J. spoke to him, but he knew the Texan was much calmer than Sir Samuel Cunningham would be when he would tell him. Rowan took a moment before he continued.

"I know the name of the escort, and I gave all her information including a picture of her and Elena to our local contact. It took him a while, but eventually he found the address."

"And what happened next?" L.J. asked, his patience growing thin.

"Prince Tarek had his men already in place, so I gave them the information and let them handle it. That way nothing will come back to us." Rowan explained with confidence in his resolution to the matter. He was confident that this would satisfy both L.J and Jonathan.

"*You!*" L.J. corrected him.

"Excuse me?" Rowan didn't know what L.J. was getting at.

"If something will come back, it will come back to *you*, not *us*." L.J. clarified.

"Bloody hell. Nothing will come back."

"Okay! So what did they do?"

"They went in Friday night", Rowan started and checked his cell phone.

"And?"

"I'm just waiting for a confirmation."

"Still waiting? Why the hell don't you call your contact?" L.J. barked at him.

Rowan bit his tongue, but did as he was told. He turned his back to the two Americans as he spoke to his contact. Without saying a word, he ended the call only a few moments later. Rowan was obviously uncomfortable and looked at the horizon, avoiding eye contact with L.J. and Jonathan.

"And?" L.J. gestured after a moment of silence. "Let me guess. They blew it?"

Rowan swallowed and shifted nervously in his chair.

"I don't know details, but they encountered some problems."

"Define *problems!*" L.J. demanded. He had to try very hard to stay calm.

"Like I said, I don't know details. All they told me was that they had to abandon their mission, and that one of them got stabbed in the leg." Rowan explained, trying to lay some blame on Tarek's bodyguards.

"So one of those idiots got himself stabbed in the leg by a whore. Are you kidding me? How the hell did that happen?"

"I told you, I don't know details! They didn't tell me!" Rowan insisted.

"What happened to the women? Where are their bodies? They did kill them, right?" L.J. was afraid to ask, but he needed clarification, even though he had a feeling he knew the answer to that.

"No, they did not. They both got away", Rowan admitted with defeat.

"Excuse me? Come again? Did you just say they both got away? Alive?" L.J. couldn't help but laugh, and he briefly exchanged a look with Jonathan, whose expression had yet to change.

"Yes, that's what they told me."

"Well, this keeps getting better and better", the Texan commented with a laugh and sat back in his chair. Nobody spoke for the next couple minutes. L.J. had a hard time digesting what the young British playboy had just told him. "What do you plan to tell Samuel about this?" he finally asked, this time in a much calmer voice.

"Samuel?" Rowan almost chuckled, but the situation was too serious for that. "I will talk to him later. He knows that I can take care of things."

L.J. leaned forward. "Rowan! Tarek's guys are idiots. Period! They screwed up. *You* screwed up! Make no mistake about this. *You* have to fix this. Do you have any idea what can happen to the project, to *us*, if they go to the police and tell them everything?"

"They won't go to the police, they are..."

"Rowan. You are an idiot!" L.J. cut him off again. "Listen to me. Even the most stupid police officer will listen to them once they mention human trafficking and an international black market for human organs. In case you haven't noticed, what we are doing here is illegal. All of it! So you better get your shit straight and clean this mess up." L.J. hissed. "Do you know where the women are?"

"Not yet. Our man in London is working on it. He should find them soon. Once we know where they are, we will clean up."

"You are using the words *should* and *will* way too often, boy! That does not make me feel comfortable."

"I told you that I have it..."

"Shut up! I will tell you what you will do! You will find those women. Once you do, you silence them. Forever! Get rid of them and make sure that you do this sooner rather than later. And if I were you, I would already be on my way to that helicopter. Do I make myself clear?" L.J. snarled at Rowan. The Briton knew that the conversation was over, and quite frankly, he had heard enough insults. Without another word, Rowan rose from his chair and left. L.J. and Jonathan were seething as they watched him disappear from their sight.

The Texan shook his head in disbelief. "I knew that it was a huge mistake to bring that idiot in." He threw his napkin on the table and looked at Jonathan. The American had not said a single word, but he didn't have to. Before he continued, L.J. looked around to make sure that they were still alone.

"We might have to get rid of all the girls and the donors. Wait until the situation is clear and we know what is going on and then go from there. What do you think?" the Texan asked his friend.

Jonathan Brown thought for a few minutes, but finally slowly nodded.

"You are right. We can't take the risk", he said, this time in his John Wayne animated voice.

"The hospital itself is legit, so there are no issues there. It won't be the end of the project. Just a minor delay. We can't take the risk, my friend."

"No, we cannot." Jonathan clearly had some issues with the decision, but knew that it was best.

"There is plenty supply of young women and homeless people. We can restart the project within twenty-four hours. It won't be an issue. The infection is already working, and the first deliveries have arrived. Even if someone inspects Asklepios, they can't find anything." L.J. shared his thoughts, looking at his long time friend.

"What about Rowan?" Jonathan wanted to know.

"I don't think we can get rid of him. Cunningham will never agree to it. But I might have an idea!" L.J. noted and stared at the horizon.

"Tarek?"

"Him I do not trust. He can be a loose cannon, and we do not have any control over him. Problem is that he is a Saudi prince. We can't just waltz in and kill him. Let me think on that one."

"What about her?" Jonathan wanted to know. He knew what the answer would be, but he had to hear it from his friend.

"Your friend Natascha? I'm afraid she has to go. She draws way too much attention. You know that, Jonathan." L.J. explained calmly and watched his friend. Jonathan didn't say anything, his eyes just wandered to the horizon.

"She still has to pay for what she did to me! She has to suffer the same way I do!" Jonathan insisted.

"Let me talk to the doctors. Maybe we can kill more than one bird with one stone!"

EuroSecCorporation, London, Sunday, July 27

"Okay, ladies and gentlemen, where are we at?" It was just after midnight when Brian called his employees back into the conference room. A quick look around showed him some exhausted faces, but he knew that his crew would keep going until he ordered them to stop. "Shira, what did you find out about Rowan?" the former admiral wanted to know, as the Israeli added another empty cardboard box from a local delivery service to a growing stack in the corner. Still chewing on her late night snack, she wiped her hands on her jeans and walked back to the table to gather her notes.

"First of all, I want to mention that Alba helped us a lot. She knows Rowan personally and helped us profile him. But let's start from the beginning. Rowan Dean Harrison, thirty-four years old, only son of Lady Amelia and the late Sir James Harrison and heir to the Harrison business empire. Junior studied business and politics at Oxford, but several generous monetary donations might have helped him to graduate. Destined to take over the family business, he became more involved in the daily business operations even at a young age." Shira went on for another twenty minutes, mentioning all the different business ventures Rowan was involved in, as well as all the charities that he officially supported. She continued listing several mansions he owned, his party life, and finally finished with EuroSec officially assessing him at low risk when he was a client.

"Interesting. Do we know where he is at the moment?" Klaus wanted to know.

"Last time I met him was last Wednesday in Monte Carlo. That was the twenty-third." Alba answered. "It is difficult to reach Rowan if you are not a close friend of him. He only has one cell phone which he picks up himself. Even on his business phone, he does not accept calls without caller ID. Any calls to his office will be answered by his secretary."

"Hm, okay. We only have the number for his business cell phone. Do you have his private cell number?"

"Yes, I do. To get him to pick up his phone, we called him from my old cell phone. We called him from outside one of the clubs, in case he traces it. That way it looks like I was looking for him. Our plan was to tell him that I wanted to meet with him, but we didn't get through. His cell phone is turned off. We will keep trying."

"You think it's going to work?"

"Not sure, but he definitely wants to get his hands on me."

"True enough. Anything else?" Brian wanted to know and looked at Ariel.

"Not for the moment. We are running a couple ideas to set up a fake business meeting with him, hopefully for tomorrow, but we are just getting started."

"Okay, not sure if we can get an official appointment on such a short notice, but might be worth a try. In the meantime, let's see if there are any other places he might be hanging out."

"I can write down a list of the clubs that he usually visits on a weekend. There are only a few, but it might help."

"It certainly will. Ariel, once we are done here you can take a couple guys, split them up and see if he shows up somewhere. Entrance to the clubs might be a different story altogether. Shira?" Brian looked at his trusted senior female employee.

"We will go", Shira reassured her boss as she spoke for the women.

"I will come with you. I might be able to help." Alba insisted.

"That's your call, Miss Casillas", Brian said before Klaus continued.

"Miss Casillas, what can you tell us about Rowan as a person?" Klaus asked. After all, if anyone in this room would know anything about Rowan, it would be the beautiful Spaniard. Alba thought for a few moments and made a face. She was about to break the unwritten rule about her business, but she didn't care. After hearing from Elena about Rowan's actions, the decision felt easy.

"Well, I don't know where to begin", she said. "Rowan became my client a little over a year ago. I was on a sports gala with another client when we met. He is friends with several music stars and athletes, mostly soccer players and race car drivers. During the gala he asked for my contact. I did my usual research on him, but couldn't find anything unusual. Since then, I escorted him at least twice a month to some charities or parties, but sometimes he wanted to see me two or three times a week in private. Believe it or not, he is highly intelligent and has a brilliant mind, but he also likes to party. His lifestyle was the reason he struggled at the university. I accompanied him to everything from receptions with the Royal family to some shady drug parties. He loves hard liquor and occasionally does drugs, mostly cocaine. When we were together, he never had any violent tendencies or outbursts or any unusual requests, but he can be a real insensitive jerk when he is drunk." Alba went on and told everyone which of his many cars was his most favourite and why, as well as which mansion he preferred to stay during the week. She could also give them an insight on his daily routine and that he suffered from extreme arachnophobia. "Trust me, he is so afraid of spiders that he once paid me a thousand pounds just to get a bottle of wine from the cellar", she elaborated. Alba thought for a few more moments, but couldn't think of anything else that was worth mentioning.

"That was certainly very helpful, Miss Casillas. Thank you very much."

"Oh, wait! There is one more thing!" Alba quickly interrupted Klaus. "Rowan Harrison is extremely well connected. He has some very important friends in high places. Not only with the police. Lawyers, attorneys, even judges."

"That is certainly interesting", Brian said and exchanged a quick look with Klaus. His gut had been right. Sitting beside Alba, Shira suddenly cursed herself in Hebrew, causing all the other Israeli's to laugh out loud. Everybody else just looked at each other, wondering what Shira had just called herself.

"There is something you want to add, Shira?" Brian carefully asked, not certain what her reaction would be.

"I am so stupid! Rowan! The abbot! That gala back then. How could I forget?" she went on, followed by more Hebrew curses.

"In English, please?"

"Back at the gala, Natascha filled in for Talia on the protection detail for Rowan. It was that evening when Rowan talked to that bishop. He said that his family had made a donation to the church. It was the same bishop that this reporter, Kyle McRae talked to. Kyle is the reporter Natascha tried to find. Turns out that the bishop is the abbot from Whitmore Abbey. It all fits together now", Shira hurried to the white board and drew a schematic with all the names and connections on the board. "Rowan Harrison knows the abbot of Whitmore Abbey. I stood right beside them when they talked!" Everyone watched patiently as Shira connected individual names on the white board with arrows.

"Well, I think that this is more than just a coincidence. Nick!"

"Yes?"

"Natascha must have mentioned something to you about that reporter. Start a new timeline with those names. Start at the gala. I want to see the connections. Check her laptop. Miss Casillas, can you please help him fit Rowan in there as best as possible?"

"Si!"

"Perfect! Now we are getting somewhere. Shira, you and Ole-Einar were on that assignment as well, if I remember correctly. I want you both to help Nick with the timeline before you get back to your original task, understood? Okay. Ariel, do you think you can run Whitmore Abbey through the Mossad?"

"I can try, but you have to understand that the Mossad is an intelligence agency. It is not Wikipedia. If something or someone does not pose a threat to Israel and its people, they will have no intelligence on it at all. Besides, we do not work there anymore. All we can do is call in favours, if you know what I mean", Ariel tried to convince them not to expect too much.

"Understood, just make sure you get all the details!" Brian replied unimpressed, before his eyes locked on Jack MacDonald. "Jack, is there anything you could find out about that hospital?"

"Well, I am not going to say that my mother in law is fat, but she is sustainable", the former British SAS Team Leader started dryly as he rose from his chair. Scratching his chin, he looked at only one sheet of paper with not too much information on it. "We had not much time to come up with anything, truth be told. We first tried basic internet searches, but we were swamped with so much information that it would take days for a task force to filter that material. So we looked on the dark web", Jack explained and paused for a second.

"You better not have used one of our bloody computers for that", Brian growled at him.

"No...well...yes...but no, not directly!" Jack struggled with a nervous chuckle.

"You don't sound very convincing!" Brian's voice dropped to a snarled hiss.

"Talia was able to get us a non-traceable connection, at least so she said", Jack finally continued, his scepticism clear in his voice as he looked at the young Israeli next to him.

"It will work, trust me!" Talia replied on the defensive. The annoyance in her tone made it clear that she had had that particular argument with Jack before.

"Anyway, we had more luck on the dark web. We didn't find anything in human trafficking that would help us, but we found some chatrooms where they talked about how the rich and wealthy can jump up a few spots on a list for organ transplantation. We only found one place so far. It is called *Asklepios*. That could be it."

"Details!" Brian demanded.

"I was afraid you'd ask that. According to the chatrooms, *Asklepios* is the hospital of choice for the rich and famous for basically everything. Annual retreat to a health resort, severe trauma cases, reconstructive surgery, convalescent care, burn unit, palliative care..."

"Organ transplantation?"

"Yes, definitely organ transplantation. They seem to be specialised in that. Like I said, not many details yet, but if you want to jump a couple spots on the list and have the money to spare, this seems to be the place."

"Interesting. Any word where all those organs are coming from?"

"Not yet", Jack shook his head, "but we'll keep digging. The majority of the patients are not there for organ transplantations, and it looks like most of the business is legit. I don't think that those who are scheduled for organ transplantation care where the organs come from. I think they're happy to pay and get to live another day."

"Hm, you might have a point there. Location?"

"That's a good one. *Asklepios* is Greek. In ancient Greek mythology, it is the name for the God of medicine. Considering our resources and time, we hit a wall there rather quickly. If I was to bet, I would look somewhere in the Aegean Sea. There are hundreds of little islands that can house such a facility. With the financial crisis in Greece, I can see no reason why an investment group with deep pockets and the right connections couldn't get their hands on one of those islands. The climate would be perfect, and the logistics would also be manageable. Down there, shuttle boats run twenty-four seven to connect the islands. We'll stay late and see if we can find something else. Talia signed in to one of the chatrooms and-"

"She did what?" Brian barked and stared at the Israeli.

"It's safe! It's not the first time I'm doing this", Talia reassured with all eyes resting on her. The expression on Brian's face made it clear that he was anything but convinced.

"Carry on", he growled in Jack's direction.

"Like I said, our cyber terrorist here signed in to one of the chat rooms and asked some question. Not much has happened yet, but according to the timelines we expect some answers within the next six to eight hours."

"You are using a profile?"

"Yes, we do. It should work for now."

"Great. Anything else for now?"

"No, not really. Lots of information, but we don't know what is credible or not. It'll take some time, but we're working on it."

"Okay, Gunnar, any ideas why Natascha is using our cyber terrorist's name and why it seems to work?"

"Well", the former instructor of the Norwegian Navy Special Operations Commando began and got out of his chair. "You asked for both reasonable as well as unreasonable theories, and you also know that I am much better at blowing stuff up than at this, so don't expect too much. We mostly speculated, but we came up with a few interesting theories. Elena confirmed that Rowan had definitely seen Natascha inside this hospital. When he came to pick her up, they held Elena in a different room that also had a control station with several monitors to check on their prisoners. It was on one of those monitors that Rowan had clearly identified Natascha. Elena recalls that Rowan told the physicians that he *knew* her. He also seemed to be very surprised to see Natascha there. To Elena's knowledge, Rowan has not seen Natascha in person, and we don't know if Natascha was aware that Rowan was even there."

"But the point is that Rowan knows", Brian summed up.

"Yes, sir, that is the point. As far as her using Talia's name, we can only speculate. Fact is, that at least a certain number of people inside that facility have to know about Natascha's real name and identity. We believe that they are part of the group who are in charge of her abduction. We also learned from Elena that the same people are part of the medical staff who are involved in the black market for illegal organ transplantation." The Norwegian went on with his report using Elena's first hand observation to run them through a typical day inside the hospital. "So, based on what we know, we can say that most of the medical staff knows her real identity, but that the other prisoners only know her as Talia. It is safe to assume that the medical staff and the prisoners do not talk to each other. As for the *why* she is doing this, we can also only speculate, but Nick, Shira and Talia agree that she simply doesn't trust anyone, and that she is most likely planning to escape. The fact that she is using a different identity also shows us that she is mentally stable and still somewhat in control over her situation", Gunnar finished. Everybody took a few moments to allow his words to sink in.

"Klaus?" Brian looked at his friend as he finished some notes.

"I thought about that myself", the former German general concluded. "I have to agree with Gunnar, but I will have a closer look at the notes."

"Yeah, probably won't hurt", Brian mentioned and looked at his own notes. "Okay, I think that will do it for today. We are quite a bit further ahead now than we were this morning. New information has to come from reliable sources, which we can only contact in the morning. By then we will also hear back from Sean. Maybe he heard something from his old friends at Scotland Yard. I suggest that we all go-"

"My apology for interrupting you, Brian, but I have some very interesting news", Sean MacLeod burst into the conference room. "You were finished, weren't you?" he reassured himself with a quick glance at Brian.

"I am obviously finished now", the former admiral muttered, but Sean already turned to address the whole group.

"I spent all day at the Yard, but they only made slow progress. So I visited a couple old friends and checked if someone reported the incident with Tarek's bodyguards, but also drew a blank there. Miss Casillas, you said that neither Rowan nor Prince Tarek know where you live, correct?"

"Si!"

"And you have not used your cell phone or credit cards since you left the casino in Monte Carlo, correct?"

"Si! Except for calling him outside the club to try to find him."

"Rowan also doesn't know what kind of car you drive and therefore cannot know the licence plate, is that also correct?"

"Si!"

"So, with all that, I was wondering how Tarek's bodyguards knew so quickly where to find you and Elena. I kept thinking about who knew that Elena was with you in the first place. Your website does not contain any information or any clues about where you live, especially since you work as an independent. So I dug a little bit deeper. It turns out that there is a BOLO out for you." Sean paused for a second to let the words sink in.

"*Bolo?*" Alba asked with a quizzical brow.

"*Being On Look Out*. Basically means that if a police officer sees you, they have to report it. But anyway, according to the police surveillance system, you ran a traffic light Friday night. Facial recognition software automatically compared and matched your face from the traffic surveillance system to the open BOLO. With that, they had your licence plate."

"And my name and address..." Alba finished with a worrisome and defeated tone. She knew that Rowan was well connected, but it reassured her in her decision not to trust the authorities in this.

"Do we know who issued the BOLO and why?" Brian wanted to know.

"As for the *why*, I was told that it is in connection with human trafficking. As for the *who*, I also got an answer, and you're not going to like it."

- 24 -

Asklepios, Aegean Sea, Sunday, July 27

"Damn!" Natascha cursed as another coughing fit shook her body. Her cough had started earlier that night. At first, she had not thought too much about it, but now it kept her awake, and despite being so exhausted she could barely keep her eyes open. With every coughing fit it felt like the next one was worse than the first. She tried to sit up from her bunk, but had to crouch as another cough shook her violently.

"Are you okay?" Jake asked. His thoughts raced as he recalled Natascha's story about what she had done on B-Level today. The possibility that there had been something wrong with her biohazard suit crossed his mind. Neither he nor Natascha had an idea about what exactly was going on down at B-Level, but it was clearly life-threatening.

"No, Jake, I'm not. I feel like I'm burning up", Natascha gasped with panic as another fit of coughs overwhelmed her.

"Shit!" Jake didn't know what to do. He wasn't even certain if there was anything that he *could* do. His eyes searched the room, but it was done more so out of habit. There was nothing in it to begin with, let alone anything that he could use to help Natascha. Suddenly he had an idea and got off the bunk.

One level above, Kurt Morrison just finished his round. Even now, in the middle of the night, he looked like the poster boy for an advertising campaign for the military academy. His uniform was spotless and ironed, his hair still cut to military standard. The twenty-eight year old security guard from Iowa took one more look at the myriad of stars and the moon before opening the door and walking inside. After one tour in the Middle East with the Forces, he had gladly accepted this job. Being single and almost broke, he had applied to every security company he could find on the internet, but certain comments in his personnel file didn't allow his second career to take off.

With the bills for child support from a previous relationship still coming on a regular basis, he was more than happy when this company approached him with an offer. Not hesitating for a minute, he jumped at the opportunity, even if it was not quite as adventurous as he had hoped for. On the plus side, the cheques kept coming on time, the weather was always sunny and warm, he could keep in shape by using one of the several gyms, and his co-workers weren't too bad either. *Especially the red haired Irish devil,* he grinned walking towards the control room, thinking about Melissa, who was on duty with him for the night.

He didn't care that they were short staffed tonight, a direct result from Natascha's attack on both Lamar and Kevin. Thinking about the attack, he shook his head and snickered. *Those idiots don't know how to fight. I would have choked that bitch out,* he thought, but he had to admit that he was glad he did not have to deal with that. Being the only guard also meant that he and Melissa were alone. They were seeing each other for a couple of weeks now, but it was the first time they were alone on-duty together. Their superiors left them alone, which was another added bonus.

Kurt pulled the door to the control room open.

"Hi! How is it looking outside?" Melissa asked, happy that her lover was back. Kurt didn't answer right away. He unclipped his duty belt and slung it over a chair.

"Take a guess", he complained. The only thing he was missing was some action. Since he had started a couple of months ago, there had not been a single incident.

"Look on the bright side", Melissa tried to cheer him up and smiled.

"What bright side?"

"The less that is going on, the more time you can spend with me", the Irish winked at him and reached for a deck of cards. She always knew how to cheer Kurt up.

"Yes, Ma'am", Kurt laughed with an impish grin. "What are we playing for?" he asked reaching for a sheet of paper and a pen.

"Loser is on top?" Melissa suggested with a devilish grin.

"Loser is on top, all right Ma'am", Kurt laughed in anticipation. As far as he was concerned, there wouldn't be a loser in this game. They only interrupted their game to glance at the monitors now and then, but they would notice if something unusual would happen since they were motion controlled.

It was just two in the morning by the time they finished their third round. One of the monitors indicated unusual activity. Both Melissa and Kurt watched instantly as they saw Jake waving frantically at the camera.

"What the hell does Jake want?" Melissa asked and studied the live footage and turned the volume up.

"Hey!" They could hear Jake yelling at the camera in the ceiling as he waved his arm. "Hey! We need help! Talia is sick. She is burning up!"

"Bloody hell. What is wrong with that bloody cunt now?" Melissa cursed and used the controls to zoom in. "She is so getting on my nerves, and no one is allowed to touch her!" she kept complaining as she carefully watched Natascha shaking under another coughing fit.

"You think she could be-" Kurt started, obviously concerned, but Melissa cut him off.

"No, there is no way. She was only with them this morning, besides, they followed protocol."

"Something is wrong with her", Kurt mentioned as Natascha curled up on the bunk, coughing so hard that the veins in her neck were bulging and her face red from the affliction.

"Serves her right if you ask me. She is getting treated like a princess anyway", Melissa hissed as she got out of her chair.

"I have to come with you", Kurt insisted and clipped his duty belt back on.

"Why, are you afraid I can't handle that cunt's ass? Need I remind you that I kicked her fat ass more than once?" the Irish went on as she led their way out of the control room. "I am not as stupid as Lamar and Kevin. If that bitch so much as winks at me, I'm going to shock her senseless", Melissa promised and checked the charge on her taser. Satisfied to see a full battery indicator, she hoped Natascha would give her a reason to use it again.

"Just gimme a reason. *Any* reason would be fine", the redheaded nurse whispered as they approached the door to Natascha's and Jake's cell. She quickly peeked through the lens in the door and was satisfied to see Jake tending to Natascha. She was even more satisfied to see that Natascha was still curled up on the bed.

"Stupid bitch!" Melissa cursed and watched as Kurt opened the door.

"What the bloody hell is wrong with you now?" Melissa demanded to know. The annoyance and hatred towards Natascha was clear in her voice. "Hey, I'm talking to you!" the Irish repeated as Natascha remained silent.

"Can't you see that she is sick?" Jake hectically answered for her. "That coughing started earlier this evening, but it got worse. Natascha can barely breathe. You need to help her!" Jake pleaded, but Melissa didn't seem to be concerned.

"Oh, really? And who can guarantee me that she's not faking this?"

"Please!...Help me!" Natascha begged, her breath labouring, another cough shaking her as she sat up.

"Shut up! I did not ask you", Melissa snarled at her, but Natascha didn't care. Her back slumped against the wall for support, or otherwise she would have collapsed to the bed again. Her eyes almost closed, she could do nothing but wait and hope that Melissa would help her. *Yeah, what are the chances of that?* She thought, her breathing rattling.

Melissa kept watching for a few moments. She couldn't decide whether Natascha was trying to trick her or not, but she really seemed to be in bad shape. It wasn't that she cared for her well-being, it was quite the opposite. She knew the trouble she would be in if something would happen to Natascha if she ignored this. It had been made very clear to the medical staff that Natascha had to be in almost perfect physical condition for whatever Jonathan Brown had planned for her, and Melissa was well aware of that.

"Okay, fine. Let's have a look", the Irish nurse eventually stated with disgust and holstered her stun gun. She took her little pencil flashlight and stepped closer to Natascha once she had her gloves and a mouth barrier on. "Open your eyes!" Melissa ordered. Natascha slowly obliged and sat straight as Melissa bent forward to examine her. A split second later, Natascha grabbed Melissa's opposite wrist. Before Melissa realised what was happening, Natascha pulled her towards herself as hard as she could. With her free hand Natascha reached for the back of Melissa's head, making sure the Irish couldn't turn away, her face hitting the steel wall with full force. The Irish didn't even have enough time to shriek as blood gushed from a large gash on her forehead and from her nose and mouth.

"Shit!" Kurt yelled and reached for his baton, but before he could wield it Natascha had already secured Melissa's taser and aimed it at Kurt. The pinching pain of the two wire probes hitting his chest was nothing compared to the pain that followed immediately. The pain was so excruciating that Kurt couldn't even scream. He just fell to the ground, his head hitting hard against the wall and the edge of the bed. It was only when Natascha was convinced that he was unconscious that she released the trigger.

Next she shot up from the bed and closed the door to her cell. She had no time to lose. She unclipped Kurt's duty belt, wielded the baton and hurriedly destroyed the cameras in the ceiling and in the bathroom.

"Jesus!" Jake jumped. Her actions had taken him by complete surprise. Natascha didn't say anything. Taking the handcuffs she fed one side through the steel bed frame before snapping them around Kurt's wrist.

"Towel!" Natascha called to Jake and pointed to the bathroom. Jake retrieved the item and Natascha forced it into Kurt's mouth.

"Okay, as for you", Natascha finally said as she paid closer attention to Melissa, but the nurse was still fighting consciousness. "Oh, you're still awake? I'm sorry, my bad", Natascha coldly said and pulled Melissa's head back by her hair to thrust it against the floor. It wasn't hard, just enough for the nurse to finally pass out. Natascha checked Kurt's duty belt and found another pair of flex cuffs. She used them to tie Melissa's hands and ankles together before gagging her as well.

Jake watched as Natascha quickly checked the key cards, a two-way radio and a set of keys. A smile appeared on Natascha's face as she checked Kurt's stun gun. It was a different model, requiring direct personal contact, which was essential further down her plan. She adjusted the duty belt and put it on, her eyes resting on Jake as he took a closer look at Melissa and Kurt.

"What are we going to do now?" Jake turned around to face Natascha. The pain he felt as she kicked him in the groin as hard as she could was so intense that he immediately collapsed to the floor, gasping for air. Natascha immediately followed through and kneeled on his throat while securing his hand in a very painful wrist lock.

"How the hell do you know my name?" She asked him calmly, but her voice didn't leave any doubt about her intentions as she applied more pressure on his throat and wrist. Jake could barely breathe, the pain overwhelming his senses.

"I...they..." he started gurgling, but Natascha did not ease the pressure.

"How the hell do you know my name?" She asked again, applying even more pressure. "You are one of them, right? They sent you to spy on me, right? Sending in a guy with almost the same story as mine, right? You even let them beat you to make sure you appeal to my protective instincts, right? That explains why you didn't try to help me when they came for me. That explains why you just stood there and watched two minutes ago, right?" Jake couldn't speak, but Natascha knew that she was right. His eyes showed nothing but hatred for her as she increased the pressure on his throat. It was only a few seconds later that Jake passed out.

Natascha checked Kurt's belt she had around her waist for any more flex cuffs, then tactfully removed the shoelaces out of Kurt's combat boots and used them to tie Jake to the steel frame. She removed Kurt's socks to gag Jake and tore a piece of the blanket to keep it in place. Satisfied with her work, Natascha quickly stood up and looked around. She estimated that less than three minutes had passed since Kurt and Melissa had set foot into her cell, but so far no one seemed to have noticed anything.

When they had escorted her through the control room earlier that evening, her eyes glanced at the duty roster for the night shift, and she had noticed that only Melissa and Kurt would be on duty. Her plan to lure them both into her cell and leaving the monitors uncontrolled worked. With the easy part of her plan over, she took Kurt's wrist watch and glanced at her prisoners. Melissa slowly regained consciousness.

"Oh, seriously?" Natascha sighed before she hit Melissa's head on the floor again, knocking the nurse back unconscious. "Okay, I got no time to lose", Natascha told herself and slowly opened the door to her cell. A quick glance showed her that the corridor was free. Natascha turned to her right and stopped under the next camera.

"That better be working", she muttered as she smashed the camera with the baton like she had done the others. She carefully looked around, but no one seemed to have noticed anything yet. Since this camera was not protected like the one in her cell, she only had to poke around for a few seconds before the cables hang loose. If she remembered right, she had overheard one technician in the control room complaining about how old the closed-circuit system was.

"Now or never", Natascha encouraged herself and held Kurt's stun gun at the electrical wires. She closed her eyes and turned her head to the side as she pressed the trigger. Sparks flew immediately as twenty-thousand additional volts shot through the wiring causing severe damage to the closed-circuit surveillance system and instantly turning all the cameras off.

"Ouch, ouch, ouch", Natascha cursed and shook her hand where some sparks had burned her skin. Satisfied, she looked at her work and quickly moved on. It only took her a few seconds before she reached Kyle McRae's cell. A quick look through the lens showed him sleeping in his bed. Finding the right key from Kurt's key ring took a little longer than she had expected, but she finally stepped inside.

"Kyle! Wake up!" She hissed, and he started awake with a frantic kick. A smile crossed his face when he recognised her and he quickly rose to his feet. He closed his cell door behind them before following Natascha down the corridor.

"Where is Jake?" Kyle whispered as they rounded another corner.

"He's currently reconsidering his family planning. He's tied to the bed with Melissa and Kurt."

"He is *what?*"

"He's one of them. They placed him in my cell to spy on me." Natascha explained as they stopped in front of Lawrence's and Charles' cell. Like before, a quick peek through the lens showed her that they were both sleeping.

"Let me do the honours", Kyle said and took the keys from Natascha while she secured the corridor. So far her plan was working, but she knew that this was still the easy part.

"Where is Jake?" Lawrence whispered as they moved down the corridor together.

"Reconsidering his life choices", Natascha calmly replied. "He is one of them. Had to take him out too."

"May I ask who else you had to take out?" Charles was both curious and impressed.

"Melissa and I think his name is Kurt."

"Oh, I bet you're not going to lose any sleep over her", Lawrence commented dryly as they stopped in front of the double door.

"No, not really. Okay, here we are", Natascha said as she retrieved the magnetic key card from Kurt's belt. "Might as well give it a try", Natascha whispered and held the magnetic key card against the card reader. They could all hear the single *beep*, but the little LED indicator remained red. "Okay, time for plan B." The disappointment was clear in Natascha's voice. Their last option had to work. She took Kurt's stun gun and was satisfied that it showed a green indicator light.

Asking for some room, Natascha used the baton to smash a light in the ceiling. Satisfied, she removed most of the glass before pressing the stun gun up against the wiring, pulling the trigger. The additional twenty-thousand volt in the system had the desired effect. Although the circuit breakers did their job, the high voltage caused several of the old wires to melt. The smoke from the melted wire set the smoke and fire detectors off, sounding the alarm, while the emergency lights slowly came to life.

"Come on!" Natascha nervously hissed between clinched teeth as they all stared at the door. With no one in the control room, the emergency program took over, the red LED indicator turned green, and Natascha didn't waste any time and opened the door. Her plan was working.

"Quick! Let's go", she ushered them through the door. Natascha knew they had to move fast while the fire alarm was still ringing,. They ran down the next corridor towards the stairs. To their relief, the door remained unlocked during the alarm.

Lawrence pointed to the emergency sign on the wall, and the group followed the stairs up. None of them had been here before.

"We have to hurry! The moment they turn the alarm off, the doors will lock!" Natascha reminded them and took the lead again. Lawrence and Charles were already out of breath, but she had to run ahead to open the next door.

As she had feared, the obnoxious alarm silenced.

"Shit!" Natascha cursed, but she noticed that the emergency lights were still on. Maybe they were lucky. She took a quick look at her surroundings while waiting for her friends.

"What the hell?" Natascha had no idea what to make of what she saw at the end of the corridor. Before she could take another look, Lawrence and Charles finally caught up to her, with Kyle bringing up the rear.

"We are getting too old for this", Charles complained and panted. Natascha quickly looked around and pulled a fire extinguisher from the wall. If not for anything else, it would make a great weapon. They could already hear voices as they slowly walked down the corridor. Contrary to the aisles they had seen on the lower levels, this corridor here was at least twice as wide, with a beautiful white marble floor. The walls were also not bare steel like below but covered by an expensive carpet and several paintings.

It didn't take them long before they approached the double-winged glass door at the end of the corridor. Natascha tried to hide the fire extinguisher behind her back as they looked through the door. At least three or four dozen people walked tiredly inside what looked like a large hall.

"What is this place?" Lawrence asked with wonder. "This looks more like a mall than a hospital."

They could all see several seating areas in the centre of the hall, nicely decorated with live palm trees and luxury fountains. It took Natascha a few seconds before she focussed on the people again. She was confused. They were all dressed in morning robes, and the expressions on their faces clearly showed that they had no idea what to do or where to go after being rudely awakened by the fire alarm.

"What the hell?" Natascha repeated, still not sure what to make of this. A quick glance at her friends only showed her that they were as lost for words as she was.

"I think those are the regular patients. Look, there are some nurses now. Never seen them before", Charles commented as several nurses mixed with the patients, helping them to get outside. Natascha looked them over again and agreed, none of them looked familiar. So far it looked like they were all following the protocol.

"Excuse me, please!" a heavy accent voiced from behind them, interrupting their concentration. All four startled. Natascha instinctively brought the fire extinguisher up as she spun around, ready to use it, but as fast as she had brought it up, she let it sink again.

"I don't think you will be needing that, my dear. The personnel around here is very well trained. I am sure this is just a false alarm", the older gentleman said with a confident smile. Natascha estimated that the man standing in front of her in his morning robe was at least seventy years old.

"I'm sorry", Natascha mumbled her apology. Not sure what to think, the gentleman just stared at them as he reached for the door.

"Do you mind?" he asked Natascha, who was still blocking his way.

"I'm sorry, I'm just..." Natascha kept mumbling, but she took a step aside and watched as the gentleman opened the door. Her surprise amplified as he held the door open for them, gesturing them to come through. Natascha and her friends briefly glanced at each other and shrugged their shoulders before they followed the gentleman through the door.

"You got to be kidding me!" Natascha stammered as she looked around. Their small group quickly moved along the wall, following the crowd of patients being ushered by the nurses to the outside. The reality started to sink in the moment they stepped through the door. It took them less than a second to realise that they were not on an island.

"This is a ship. This is a goddamn cruise ship. Not again. I am on another fucking ship!"

***EuroSecCorporation*, London, Sunday, July 27**

"Well, at least he doesn't look like crap anymore", Brian whispered to Klaus. They both looked at Nick, who sat with Elena acquiring as much information from her as possible.

"Yes, let's hope it will stay that way", Klaus answered and sat in his usual chair. It was just after nine o'clock, and a quick scan over the different tables showed him several empty cups of coffee, indicating that his employees must have had an early start after a short night. Brian allowed them to finish whatever they were doing before he wished them a good morning.

"Ariel, any news on Rowan?" he finally started.

"No. Once we were done last night we split up and visited four different clubs that he usually hangs out during the weekend. The guys couldn't get in, but Shira and the ladies had no problems. Turns out that he was nowhere to be found."

"Where are they anyway?" Brian asked. He had noticed the absence of the female personnel.

"After our meeting yesterday I took Elena home and stayed with her. The last text message I received from my sister was at zero four hundred this morning, telling me that they were done for the night. I told them to get some shuteye, but I think they will be here around noon. She knows that I will call them should we need them sooner."

"Where is Alba now? She is not at your place by herself, is she?" Brian's voice reflected the concern for the Spanish woman.

"No, she crammed in at Shira's place."

"Okay. Makes sense. Jack, what can you tell me about *Asklepios*?"

"Haven't had much time since midnight, but I tried to find the island on the internet. I didn't get any results and checked the dark web. We received several replies to our original message, and it turns out that *Asklepios* is not an island, but a ship."

"Come again?" Brian asked with a frown.

"Yes, *Asklepios* is a ship. She is just over one-hundred-eighty metres long and registered with thirty-five thousand tons. Used to be a midsize cruise ship over a decade ago, serving mostly the Mediterranean and Black Sea. Got sold to an investment holding group eight years ago and underwent major reconstruction for two years. They turned her into a modern hospital ship. We didn't find details, but it seems like the upper decks and her amenities remained in place. Her lower decks were all turned into medical facilities which rival the most modern hospitals in the Western world. We don't have confirmed information about crew size, number of patients, blue-prints or any of that yet."

"Understood. Okay, let's get serious, who owns it, what flag are they flying and where the bloody hell is she?"

"First, we don't know. As I said, the owners are an investment holding group. We are still looking into it. I expect to find a bunch of shell companies to be honest, so let's not expect too much. Second, we don't know where she is registered yet, but again, we will look into it. Third, all we could find out so far is that she is anchored somewhere in the Aegean Sea." Jack finished and sorted his notes.

"On this, we might actually be able to get some information", Ariel took the initiative, just as Brian's eyes locked on him.

"I will make a couple calls to some old friends. I would be surprised if our Navy wouldn't be able to give us some coordinates", the retired admiral added and glanced at Klaus, but the former German general had nothing to add.

"Nick, how are you doing?"

"Hanging in there, Boss. My wife is still alive, that keeps me going."

"How is your daughter, Nick?"

"With her grandparents. Doing fine."

"Glad to hear that. What can you tell us about this reporter, Whitmore Abbey and the gala?" Brian wanted to know. Nick got up and drew a new timeline on the whiteboard, including all the information he could gather about it in the short time. He also explained the incident on the gala between Kyle McRae and the bishop and didn't forget to mention Natascha retrieving the torn notes from the waste basket.

"Bloody hell, that can be a hornet's nest", Brian commented once Nick was finished.

"Yes, Brian, this is interesting, and I am certain that it is not a coincidence, but I still can't see the connection between this and Natascha's abduction." Klaus shook his head and went over a paper with some additional notes. "Nobody knew that Natascha even took the bone fragments. She didn't tell anyone, and she couldn't find that reporter. It doesn't fit."

"You're right, Klaus. It doesn't. Not if we're talking about that paedophile ring. The authorities shut down complete investigations that had substantial evidence. So far, this is nothing. Unless...." Brian started to think.

"Unless she found something completely different. Something significant, without even realising it."

"Could be, but the only connection we have is Rowan Harrison, who, according to Elena Romanov, had no intention to help Natascha. Why? Is it because there is a connection to Whitmore Abbey or is it just because he is a criminal?"

"Damned if I know. We need Rowan. He knows the answer."

"Agreed. And someone has to call Mark again at the institute in Germany. Maybe he was able to find something out about those bone fragments. Shira has his number?"

"Yes. I'll tell her to get him on the phone tomorrow."

"Okay, let's make some phone calls. Keep digging, guys. We'll meet again at thirteen hundred. Gunnar, I want you to set up a schedule for surveillance for all the places Rowan can show up, starting tonight. Check the duty roster to see who is available. Any questions?"

Asklepios, Aegean Sea, Sunday, July 27

Natascha slowly woke up. She had no idea what had happened after they had set foot on the deck, but a stinging pain in her neck where the tranquilliser had hit her gave her an idea. Realising that her futile attempt to escape or signal for help had ended rather quickly, she found herself in a treatment room on B-Deck. She tried to move her arms and soon noticed she was restrained to a bed. She could hear Dr Sheridan Evans talking, and her eyes soon focussed on Jonathan Brown.

"I must admit that I am quite impressed. Honestly, the injuries that you inflicted on my staff are remarkable." Dr Sheridan Evans' eyes were still glued to her clipboard as she spoke. Jonathan's gaze soon met Natascha's, but he showed no reaction. Walter Leroy Jackson stood behind him, his anger seething behind his quivering lip as he watched Natascha.

"First you injure Kevin and Lamar and now this." Dr Evans continued, still reading the notes on her clipboard as she continued. "One security guard with a severe laceration, electrical burns and a grade three concussion. I'm sure you're disappointed to hear that Melissa is still alive. However, she is also suffering a grade three concussion, a broken nose and also has a severe laceration." Dr Sheridan Evans briefly looked at Natascha as she flipped her page, but Natascha's eyes were locked on Jonathan Brown. "Those two will be unable to work for quite some time, but Melissa is begging me to grant her permission to kill you."

"No!" Jonathan Brown cut in. He was so agitated that his voice was nothing more than a rattling sound. "No one touches her but me!" he insisted. The speech computer clearly had technical issues translating the signals.

"Don't worry, we know the arrangements. I just want to let her know that there are quite a few unhappy people out there at the moment. Melissa can't wait to see you again", Dr Evans said with a scowl.

"Whatever, she had it coming. How's Jake doing?" Natascha shot back and shifted her gaze towards the physician. Dr Evans looked at her clipboard again.

"I'm going to spare you the medical details aside from his strangulation marks, but Dr Edwards is still trying to get his testicles out."

"Good! Tell him that I'll shove them down his throat the next time I see him!" Natascha spat coldly.

"Jesus!" L.J. couldn't help but shiver.

"I'm afraid that won't be happening. I don't believe you'll see either one of them again. The same for your friends."

"What about them? What did you do with them?"

"You have to know that there are certain consequences for not abiding the rules. In this case your friends did not only foolishly follow you, but they also supported you. Those actions have consequences. Severe consequences."

"They didn't do anything. You can leave them alone", Natascha argued, but she knew that this wouldn't change the fate of her three friends. They had all been marked for death long time ago.

"I'm afraid that's not an option. They are in isolation right now. Their organs will be harvested in the next few days. They will finally do good then", Dr Evans explained with authority on her way to a medical cabinet. Natascha felt like a failure, wondering if they would have made it if she had tried harder. She felt guilty, despite the fact that they were all destined to this end anyway.

"You seem to be lost for words", Dr Evans commented as she took an IV from the cabinet. Natascha shook her head, her memory taking her back to Kyle, Lawrence and Charles. *All they ever wanted to do was some good!* Natascha thought, but kept it to herself. She would not give them the pleasure of being too emotional, but it felt harder than she was willing to admit.

"How does it make you feel, knowing they will die because of you?" Jonathan Brown finally accused her. He knew perfectly well how to torture her with just words. Although Natascha silently shook her head in denial, he was satisfied to see tears strike her face. Natascha knew that she was innocent, but she somehow still felt responsible for dragging them into this. Jonathan's words cut like a hot knife through her. A new wave of guilt overcame her as she thought about the two British veterans and the reporter. The emotional pain she felt was overwhelming, only the sharp pain of a needle injected into her arm brought her back to reality.

"What the hell?" Natascha looked at her arm, where Dr Evans just prepared the IV.

"Oh, I'm sorry I wasn't careful enough!" Dr Evans laughed before she went back to the medicine cabinet. Natascha followed the physician with her eyes, but the realisation slowly started to sink in as she watched the physician.

"What is this?" Natascha's voice was nothing but a whisper. She felt fear flooding her senses as she saw the small flask and a syringe in Dr Evans hands.

"Let me put it this way: it will help you with the cough. You will no longer have to simulate it", the doctor explained coldly. As the panic started to rise in Natascha, Dr Evans slowly turned towards her. The echo of her footsteps felt like a countdown as she approached her. She had no idea what serum was in the flask, but she knew that it would seal her fate.

"No!" Natascha wanted to scream, but her broken voice was barely audible. Tears ran freely down her cheeks. There was nothing she could do but watch as Dr Evans drew up the syringe from the flask. She flicked it a couple times to release any air bubbles before connecting the syringe to the IV.

"No! Please!" Natascha cried, but she knew that her pleas were futile.

"It is ready", Dr Evans ignored her and nodded towards Jonathan Brown who steered his wheelchair beside Natascha's bed. His eyes locked on hers, and she could see the satisfaction in his eyes.

"They will make you pay for this", Natascha hissed at Jonathan. He reached for the syringe and slowly pushed the liquid through the IV into Natascha's body.

- *25* -

***EuroSecCorporation*, London, Sunday, July 27**

"Bloody hell, he has to be somewhere!" Jack MacDonald, the former British SAS Team Leader complained and tossed his cell phone on the table after receiving another negative report. For several hours, EuroSec had all the known residences of Rowan Harrison under surveillance, but so far they had not been able to locate him. "Does he have reason to believe that someone is after him?" Jack asked a general question and looked around.

"We can't say for sure, but we also don't know how many other places he uses to hang out. We just have to stay focussed and keep looking." Klaus answered, trying to keep the motivation going. Their focus was interrupted as Shira led the small group of women into the conference room.

"What if he is out of the country?" Jack returned. It was a very polite way to express his concern that Rowan could panic and start cleaning up his tracks.

"One more reason to find him fast", Brian stated with finality. He didn't want Nick to get more worried than he already was, if that was even possible.

"What are they talking about?" Alba whispered to Shira.

"We're still trying to find Rowan. Maybe he's not in London anymore, but we have no way to know for sure", the Israeli answered before she turned towards Ariel. "What about the sayanim? We should be able to use them, or am I wrong?" Shira asked her brother.

"I had the same idea. I went to the embassy this morning and forwarded all the information we have."

"You want me to call him?" Shira asked, this time in Hebrew. With *him* she referred to General Rashid, who was not only the director of the Israeli Mossad, but also their father.

"Should I call General Rashid myself? Might not hurt", Brian mentioned and stepped beside them, as if he had read Shira's mind. During the events on the *Northern Explorer*, General Rashid had proved himself to Brian and Klaus not only as a trusted ally, but also as a great friend.

"It definitely won't hurt, but I'll call him first. He will be home today anyway", Shira answered with a smile and went to set up a Skype call to her family in Tel Aviv.

"And there is nothing we can do, but wait", Brian growled as he looked around. There was nothing he hated more than sitting around waiting for answers.

"What was the name of the company in Monaco that we worked with during the Formula One Grand Prix? Some of their blokes were British. They seemed to be okay. Maybe we can contact and ask them to keep their eyes and ears open? Maybe they will see something?" Jack threw in as he entertained a new thought.

"It's a long shot, but I can see if I can find the information somewhere", Brian growled. He was not totally convinced that this would be the breakthrough they needed, but it was better than nothing.

"I think I found him", Alba enthusiastically announced and found herself to be the centre of all attention as the conference room fell silent.

"Come again?" Brian carefully asked. The retired admiral wasn't sure if he should trust his ears.

"I think I found him!" Alba repeated and held her cell phone up. She started to feel uncomfortable with all eyes locked on her. "Couple weeks ago he mentioned something about a fundraiser event starting next week, which he wanted me to accompany him to. I totally forgot about it, but I thought that with the current situation he might not go there and cancel his commitment. Since the organiser is a close friend of his, he will most likely tell him. So I called his friend", the Spaniard simply explained.

"And what did you tell him?" Ariel wanted to know. He was concerned that Alba might have said something that could spook Rowan.

"I told him nothing. I just asked him about the fundraiser and that I tried to contact Rowan because of it. He told me that Rowan called him last night to cancel, but that pig also told him that he will be in Monaco this week." Alba shrugged her shoulders. Based on the expressions on everyone's face, she wasn't even sure if what she had just told them was helpful or not. They simply stared at her. "What? Did I do something wrong?" she asked after a few seconds of silence.

"No, quite the opposite", Brian finally broke the silence and smiled at her. Sometimes the solution was so simple. "Ariel, see if you can find the information from the security company in Monaco. It's in our files somewhere. Try to find out the contact from the employees. I'll make a call to their office and ask for their help. Jack?"

"I'll call a couple friends at the SAS. Maybe with a little bit luck we can find some former lads down there. After all, Monaco is the place for the rich and famous."

Brian sat at his usual spot at the table, right beside the phone, waiting for Ariel to bring him the information. A quick look around showed him and Klaus that almost everyone was on the phone again, including Alba. For some reason Brian believed that she might be on to something, but since she spoke in French, he didn't understand everything she said. His thoughts were interrupted when Ariel handed him a small folder about their detail in Monaco.

"I just called the casino and Rowan checked in to the hotel last night. He has his usual suite booked for the next five days." Alba shared her information the moment she ended the call. Once again the conference room was silent as all eyes rested on her. "I just told them that I had to leave due to a medical emergency, and that I wanted to know if they kept my personal belongings. I also told them that I am supposed to meet with Rowan down there and asked if he had already checked in."

"And they just told you that?" Ariel couldn't hide his surprise.

"Why shouldn't they? They know me." Alba Casillas explained with a shrug.

"So Rowan is in Monaco right now?"

"No", the Spaniard shook her head. "He checked in last night, but he left this morning and told them that he will be back on Tuesday."

Asklepios, Aegean Sea, Monday, July 28

"Bloody hell! You can't be serious!" Rowan cursed as he nervously paced Jonathan's cabin. First they had summoned him like a dog, but now they expected him to put himself at great risk.

"Let's not forget who is responsible for this mess. Those two whores walked out from right underneath your nose while you were drunk, or did I get that wrong?" Walter asked the young Briton to refresh his memory. His silence was answer enough.

"Do you have the slightest clue how much you screwed up?" Walter Leroy Jackson asked calmly from his chair. The Texan didn't even bother to raise his voice. He didn't even give Rowan the courtesy to look at him. "Our whole operation has to shut down because of your mistake. That woman directly links you to this ship and our operation. We are losing millions of dollars, so forgive me if this causes a minor inconvenience to you."

"*Minor inconvenience?*" Rowan scowled. He wanted to say something, but he bit his tongue. As much as he hated to admit it, but the Texan had a valid point. "You're asking me to take her back? Do you know how many people are looking for her right now in England?" Rowan almost lost it.

"For starters, I am not *asking* you to take her back, I am *telling* you. That's a huge difference. Besides, I am not telling you to take her back to London. Christ, that would be three women pointing their fingers at you. I want you to give her to your psychopathic friend, the Saudi Prince."

"Why? What is he supposed to do with her?"

"Nothing. All he has to do is keep her safe for a week or two until this is all over. As long as he doesn't touch her. I somehow believe that he's the right guy for the job." It was the first time that L.J. glanced at Rowan.

"Yes, but why him? Why do I have to drag her back all the way to Europe? Why don't you just bloody shoot her right here and now and toss her overboard? Why take the bloody risk? If you want to see her dead, why don't you just get it over with?"

"We have our reasons, trust me", L.J. stated calmly, looking at Jonathan.

"And what might those reasons be?" Rowan wanted to know. He became more agitated by the minute.

"I would have told you if you would need to know. Your latest track record is anything but impressive, so don't even start to argue with me."

Rowan shook his head in disbelief. He still paced the room, and he very much wanted to argue with the Texan, but he knew that he would lose that argument. He also knew that L.J. would not waste a second to insult Rowan again by rubbing his failure in. Rowan certainly did not need another reminder that he had not only screwed up once, but twice. Considering that, he could call himself lucky to be still alive. It took him a couple minutes to calm down. He knew what he had to do. He had to prove that he still had control. That he was able to clean up this mess. This could very well be his last chance.

"Okay. I think I can meet with Prince Tarek tonight. Luckily she's not his type, so I think I can persuade him not to touch her."

"It's very important that she doesn't even get a scratch. I'm the only one to touch her", the metallic voice of Jonathan Brown's speech computer said. Rowan looked at the American. It was the first time that he spoke during this conversation. The expression on his face, as far as Rowan could read it, showed him how serious the American was.

"Don't worry. He owes me a favour." Rowan promised, not entirely sure what this was about. Whatever the reasons were, it seemed to be very important to Jonathan, and Rowan certainly didn't want to disappoint him again. "I have one question about the transport. I heard that she kicked some butt, can we sedate her enough so that she won't make any trouble?"

"Yes, I already arranged everything with Dr Evans." L.J. mentioned and looked at his expensive golden Rolex. "They're prepping her as we speak. You can pick her up in about thirty minutes."

"Okay", Rowan replied and turned around. He was determined to get it over with and headed for the door.

"Oh, Rowan!" L.J.'s voice kept him back.

"What?"

"Don't screw this one up as well. My patience is running very thin with you." Rowan didn't bother to answer. He just walked out and had to control himself not to slam the door. He already looked very much like a fool.

"Bloody bastard!" Rowan cursed the heavy Texan through clinched teeth on his way to the elevator. One of the regular guards used his key card to grant Rowan access to the lower decks where Dr Evans waited for him in one of the examination rooms.

"Good afternoon. I assume you are here to pick up our special guest?" Dr Evans asked.

"Yes, how is she doing?"

"She is heavily sedated. Took four guys to hold her still long enough for me to give her the needle. She is feisty", Dr Evans noted, not without a hint of admiration in her voice.

"Blimey, she is one crazy bitch", Rowan commented, more to himself, as he walked closer to the gurney.

"I wouldn't get too close. Four of our people are still in sick bay because of her. She has enough anaesthetics in her system to keep a horse calm, but I would still be cautious. She fooled us more than once."

"How much longer?" Rowan asked.

"She will be asleep within the next five minutes. She is safe to transport then." Rowan just nodded and took another step closer to Natascha. For some reason, Natascha slowly turned her head towards him and even opened her eyes, but only seconds later, her head fell to the side.

"Rowan, there is something else!" Dr Sheridan Evans whispered after she convinced herself that no one could hear them.

"What is it, Sheridan?"

"Do you know that the Americans made me inject Natascha the bug?"

"They did what?" Rowan asked surprised.

"Yes", Dr Evans whispered and shyly looked around before she continued. "They had me set the IV and Jonathan pushed the bug in himself. I don't know what their history is, but they really hate each other. They didn't tell you?"

"Bloody hell! No, they did not!" Rowan cursed and immediately paced the room. "So that is why they don't want Tarek to touch her. Once she is infectious she will kill everyone on Tarek's ship. Those bastards crossed me. They're hoping that I will infect myself too!" Rowan stated as he connected the dots.

"She will be infectious in a few days, but yes, if she is confined to a ship, the mortality rate will be one hundred percent", Dr Evans explained.

"What about me?" Rowan's concern was evident in his voice.

"I explained it to you before, Rowan. You're totally safe. They don't know how the bug works."

"Those bloody bastards!" Rowan shook his head as he saw L.J.'s face in his mind. He looked at Dr Evans and couldn't help but hug her. "Thank you! I really owe you one!"

"No, you don't. Remember, if it wasn't for you and your father, I wouldn't even be here. You gave me this great opportunity. I owe you."

"Talking about my father, is it ready?" Rowan's voice sounded serious as he changed the subject.

"Yes, it is. Just give me a second", Dr Evans answered and walked to a freezer. She entered her PIN code and swiped the magnetic key card before she could open the door. She took out a little shock proof box, closed the door again and put it on the table.

Rowan walked over beside her and anxiously watched as she opened the box.

"This is it. You remember what I told you about it?"

"Yes, I do!" Rowan answered. He was fascinated by the little flask which was securely protected in the little box.

"My father...how long?"

"Once it is injected, the bug will start mutating for about ninety-six hours. He will be infectious after that. Very infectious."

"Good!" Rowan commented with a smile, his eyes sparkling with anticipation.

"Rowan, I know that your father only has a few months to live anyway, but are you sure you want to do this? He will not survive this." Dr Evans reminded him.

"Bloody hell! Yes, I'm sure! He made it clear that they all deserve to die!"

West of Al-Hasakah, Syria, Tuesday, July 29

"Here, you must drink!" Monique tried to encourage the teenage girl as she supported her head. The young woman barely had enough energy to hold the cup, but managed a few sips. Monique smiled and wiped the teenager's face before getting up again. Her eyes wandered over all the sick people inside the large tent. Monique had restlessly cared for them for the last three days, only getting a few hours of sleep herself. The lack of sleep took its toll, and Monique had to yawn. Not far from her she saw Moonif Nasser. He was the elder who had taken her from Nizar's tent to help with the sick. Moonif only spoke little English, but it was obvious to Monique that she was under his protection for the moment.

Almost every day, she witnessed a heated argument between Moonif and Nizar, which always left the younger of the two warriors even more furious than he had been before. Monique's attention shifted from Moonif, who was just tending to a young

Taliban warrior, back to the many sick in front of her. Not only did her former training as a paramedic prove to be helpful, it also quickly showed everybody that she knew what she was doing, but Monique couldn't help but shake her head in frustration. Her own situation aside, she couldn't figure out how to help these people. Three days ago, when she first saw the large tent, there were around thirty people sick. Now she counted close to seventy people in serious condition. Men, women, and children. To make matters worse, the only medical supplies in the camp were nothing more but outdated standard first aid kits, nothing that could help treat a lethal disease.

The young French picked up the canister with drinking water and walked over to Amber. Her condition was getting worse with every hour that passed by, blood running from her nose and mouth. Monique took a towel and wiped Amber's forehead, but the young woman didn't show any reaction. Her pulse was so weak that Monique could barely feel it. It was clear to her that Amber would not survive another hour. A tear ran down Monique's face as she held the young women's hand. Monique had no idea how much time passed, but it didn't take long before she felt Amber's hand losing strength. Monique cried as she checked for Amber's pulse one last time, but she couldn't find it.

"Goodbye, my friend!" Monique sobbed with more tears running down her face. She closed Amber's lifeless eyes and pulled her blanket over her head. That was all she could do for her. It wouldn't take long before some men would come in to collect her dead body. Her corpse would then be disrespectfully thrown on the back of the large truck with all the other corpses, before being dumped in a mass grave at night. Monique had known Amber for only a couple of days, but to think of what would happen to her still made her cry.

Her thoughts were interrupted as several pick-up trucks pulled up inside the cavern. Monique noticed the surprise on Moonif's face. The tribal elder got up and left the tent, his escort of heavily armed warriors following in tow. The young French could hear a heated argument outside the tent, and she was curious enough to risk a peek. No one stopped her as she slipped through the tent flap. She counted six pickup trucks. They all had a machine gun mounted on the bed, and additional steel plates were used for extra protection, especially where the windows had been. She could see a trail of bullet holes. The vehicles were covered with them.

Monique watched as some of the desert warriors left their vehicles. They looked battered and tired. Most of them had suffered minor injuries, their robes and clothes covered with blood, most likely their own. Moonif followed their leader to one of the truck's cargo bed and quickly looked for Monique. The moment he saw her, he gestured for her to come over. Monique hesitated for a second, but eventually walked over. She could hear the moans before she even saw the men. Those warriors had not been as lucky as their Taliban brothers. Several men suffered from severe traumatic wounds, mostly caused by high calibre gun shots and grenade fragments. After what these people had done to her and the other young women, Monique couldn't care less about their fate. But she knew that helping them would not only keep her alive for now, it would also increase her value to Moonif and stop everyone from raping her. The smell of blood and burnt flesh engulfed her senses as she took another step towards the injured warrior, but his brother quickly stuck his arm out to block

Monique from touching him. He was obviously appalled that a woman was supposed to treat his brother, which he made clear to Moonif with another tirade.

Fine with me, asshole! Monique thought and managed a concerned look. Her gaze wandered over the body of the injured men in front of her. Her eyes stopped on the piece of fabric his brother kept pressing on the upper leg. The fabric was soaked with bright red blood, which was still seeping out from the large open wound caused by a grenade fragment. *His artery is totally gone.* Monique noticed and had a hard time not to smile. Even if his brother would let her help him, he had zero chance of survival in this camp. Her eyes wandered to the other casualties. One of them was already dead, and another warrior would be right beside him soon, his head injuries were too severe. Monique walked over to the last truck. The person there had a belly wound, but she couldn't see how severe it was. *I hope he dies painfully!* Monique wished and turned around. Moonif raised his voice to end the argument and pointed to the large first aid tent. The new arrivals helped each other, some of them carrying those who couldn't walk on their own. Monique waited for a few moments, but finally followed them.

"No!" Monique shouted, as two men dragged Amber's lifeless body out of the tent to make more space, but they didn't even look at her. Monique quickly looked around, her eyes meeting Moonif's, who simply shook his head. Reluctantly Monique nodded and obeyed. She knew that her survival would depend on him. Not certain what to do, she went back to her previous routine.

It didn't take her long to notice that the new arrivals refused to be treated by women. There was something else Monique noticed. One of the warriors looked different from the others. Because of his full beard it had taken her a while, but it was obvious that he was not from the region. *You are European!* Monique realised and kept watching the guy. She estimated him to be in his mid-twenties. He was limping, but so far he had not received or wanted any treatment. *Clearly some medical training!* Monique thought as the young man walked from one injured person to the next, trying to help them as best as he could. After two hours he eventually walked out of the tent with one of his friends to stretch his legs and get some air. Monique couldn't resist and followed them out. She found them sitting on the hood of one of the trucks, listening to their leader who had another argument with Moonif. Monique couldn't understand what they argued about, but she noticed that the one guy translated for the European.

"Moonif says that many people fell ill. Many dying."

"The bloody disease is everywhere. Does he know what is causing it?" the European asked. *Ah, you are British!* Monique recognised the accent.

"Don't know why. Maybe the water, maybe the food."

"Bollocks. This is not caused by the water or the food. This is something else."

"Don't know. Moonif concerned."

"Bet he is. What about the slaves? Can we at least get some slaves?" Monique winced at the comment and her eyes grew wide. *What did you expect, you idiot! He is one of them!* She tried to tell herself.

"Hey, Sami!" the European's friend yelled to get his leader's attention, before he continued in Arab. *He is asking him about the slaves. About me!* Monique realised.

Her body tensed, and she took another step back into the shadow of the tent. Moonif answered and gestured wildly.

"Moonif said that many slaves dead or sick. Only few still healthy. Those who healthy have to help with the sick. Said that he expects more slaves tomorrow or day after. Then we can have them, but not now."

Twenty-four hours! I got twenty-four hours to get out of here! Monique thought and almost started to panic. She knew that she would not be able to survive another night like the first one after the auction. *I have to get out of here! I must get out of here! I need a plan.* She told herself and ducked back inside the tent. She knew that she needed to have at least some kind of a plan. *How do I get out of here?* She kept asking herself as she continued with her routine.

She covered her face even more once she saw the British mercenary and his friend return. The last thing she wanted to do was to attract their attention. *How can I get out of here?* Her eyes wandered over all the people in the tent, and she suddenly knew the answer.

That might actually work, she convinced herself, after she had thought about her plan for an hour. She was so focussed that she didn't even notice the mild headache and the tickling sensation in her throat that made her cough.

- *26* -

Casino de Monte Carlo, **Monte Carlo, Monaco, Tuesday, July 29**

Bloody hell! Rowan thought and stared at his empty glass. It had not been his first drink of the day, and as far as he was concerned, it would definitely not be the last one either. He didn't know how many more of these expensive cocktails he would need to forget the last twenty-four hours, but he was determined to find out.

Last night had been a rude awakening for him. He had never trusted those damn Yankees in the first place, but he had no other choice but to team up with them. Working with a lethal disease was best done on a ship somewhere on the open sea, and not in the middle of London. Under different circumstances he would have not chosen this road, but his father's condition left him no choice but to cooperate with these Cowboys. The only reason they were in business together was their mutual interest. *Well, at least some of it is mutual!* Rowan thought with a snicker. Personally he couldn't care less about them, and L.J. had made it very clear that their dislike was mutual.

The young British playboy emptied his glass and checked his reflection in the mirror over the bar. *You knew what you were getting in to. There is no way out now. Bloody betrayal, that's what this is.* Rowan tried to concentrate. Once he was able to shove his personal feelings aside, he realised that his original plan had not been jeopardised. He didn't care about the Taliban or ISIS or whatever terror was going on in the Middle East. He had his own agenda, and as far as he was concerned, he was taking on a terror organisation of global proportions.

His plan was nothing short of lunacy, but so far no one suspected anything. Rowan had to admit that he owed Dr Sheridan Evans for warning him. His thoughts circled back to Natascha. Her fate was sealed. Thinking about the young woman, he had to shake his head. Something was different about her. Rowan thought for a moment and concluded that it was because of the one night at the gala, where she had worked to protect him. He had really liked her that evening. Handing her over to his psychopathic friend made him as guilty as anyone else. Rowan was actually confident that the Saudi prince would follow his instructions not to touch her. Not that it would matter at all, she was carrying the bug. Rowan knew that this was L.J.'s plan to use Natascha not only to get rid of him, but also the Saudi Prince, and any connection between him and *Asklepios*.

As upset as he was about their betrayal, he could not stop thinking about Natascha. *Her blood is on your hands, mate!* He lectured himself as he stared at his reflection in the mirror behind the bar. *She is just collateral damage. It happens every day in a war,* Rowan tried to convince himself. *And we are at war! You are at war!* He knew that his only way out of this would be feet first and in a coffin. *If nothing else, that damn cowboy will make sure of that,* Rowan reminded himself of the consequences, looking at his reflection in the mirror again.

The young waitress caught Rowan's eyes and smiled. Rowan just showed her his empty glass, prompting her to pour him another drink immediately. He returned her smile and watched her charging the drink to his suite. Her hips were full, and she carried herself light on her feet. She made her uniform look irresistible, the way the fabric contoured to her shape. He bit his lip with thought. *Why not?* He encouraged himself, wondering why he had not thought of it before. He needed to get out of his head, and alcohol was not working.

It was a Tuesday evening, which was a slow night even for the casino in Monte Carlo. Rowan turned around and took a few moments to let his gaze drift over the floor. He found what he was looking for at one of the Black Jack tables. An older gentleman, Rowan estimated him to be around sixty, was handing out chips to two much younger women. *They are definitely not his daughters*, Rowan grinned as he kept watching the little group. His suspicion was confirmed when one of the young ladies brushed a kiss on the older gentleman's cheek. Rowan didn't know what she expected, but the guy's face didn't even flinch. Instead, he just handed the exotic woman another handful of high value chips. Judging by the expression on the escort's face, that was exactly what she had expected.

The playboy turned around to check his reflection in the mirror one last time. He finished his drink, took two fresh mints and adjusted his tie, before he casually walked over to the Black Jack table. The closer he came, the more he liked what he saw. *You have expensive taste, mate!* Rowan made a mental comment as he looked at the two women. Both were obviously south of thirty, their lustrous exotic looks clearly reminding Rowan of his former escort, Saphir.

He admired the black-haired beauty, the way her hair flowed over the contours of her collarbone and the fitted bodice of her full-length black dress. He felt a twinge of excitement as he examined her sophistication, how the dress accentuated the curves of her body. Her breasts were mysteriously concealed behind the straight neckline, with only the full-length slit revealing the soft skin of her leg, offering a peek at what beauty laid underneath. Rowan licked his lips before turning his attention to the blonde, who wore a much shorter blue dress, showing more skin than the first. He didn't mind. Her skin radiated under the plunging neckline.

He watched as she turned to politely laugh at whatever disinteresting conversation was happening, and he swallowed hard as he savoured the view of her firm, long legs as she gingerly shifted her weight from one leg to the other. She turned slowly, the curve of her breast visible from the side, presenting a trail that every man instantly desired to follow. Rowan cleared his throat and kept watching them from a distance when the blonde bombshell met his voracious gaze and seductively winked at him. Even for an experienced playboy like himself, the lust in her eyes at that moment couldn't stop the shiver from descending his spine. Casually, Rowan lifted his glass to toast the stunning twenty-five year old, who returned his pleasantry with an alluring gesture.

The Briton reflected upon tonight's events so far. He agreed that the evening had a negatively rough start for him, but he had just befriended a drop-dead gorgeous blonde on the plus side. A smile brightened his face as he contemplated the sexual pleasures that would await him later. There was no way that the older gentleman would take both escorts with him. Rowan didn't want to lose any more time and approached the Black Jack table. He always had a stack of chips in his pocket and placed them on the table in plain sight, announcing his presence.

"And to whom do I owe the pleasure?" he asked and looked at the little group. The older gentleman with the dark sunglasses just briefly glanced at him with disinterest, solely offering a nod without introducing himself.

"You can call me Mandy", the young blonde smiled at him. The other beauty still looked like she was surgically attached to the gentleman's arm. Rowan had made his intentions clear, and he knew that Mandy would not break the unwritten rule and show him any more attention so long as she was with her client. Rowan was familiar with the rules of her profession and entered the game, not without admiring Mandy's superbly formed backside.

The two women took their turns betting on their hands, their laughter fuelled by vintage champagne. As much fun as they had, it became quite clear to Rowan that they didn't know much about Black Jack. After five rounds he revised his earlier statement, and he was now convinced that they had absolutely no idea whatsoever. By now he had also learned that the beautiful black-haired woman answered to Viola. Laughing gushingly, both ladies played Black Jack as thoughtfully as a bucket full of concrete and as subtle as a category five hurricane. It took them only little over eight minutes to burn five thousand Euros.

For the first time, Rowan noticed that the gentleman showed a reaction as he winced when he saw the last of his chips disappear. Focussed to control the damage, he finally reached for the emergency brakes by sliding his arm around Viola's perfectly formed waist before leading her away from the table, leaving Mandy with Rowan.

"Well, that didn't take long", the gentleman growled, barely audible, as Viola threw a quick glance back at the table, still giggling. Not only had Talia enjoyed playing Black Jack for the first time in her life, she had also totally forgotten that she had just burned a fair chunk of Admiral Whittaker's hard earned personal cash.

Just two hundred metres east of the casino, inside Port Hercule on board of the motor yacht *Cloud Dancer*, Shira's eyes were glued on the screen.

"Okay, contact is made!" the young Israeli confirmed and looked up from her laptop. Jack MacDonald and Gunnar Eriksson from Operation Control, as well as her brother were standing right behind her with Nick. The rest of Team A was either inside the casino to keep an eye on Noah and Rowan, or unpacking the many bags of gear they had carried on board. They had also brought Alba not only for her language skills, but also for her familiarity with the location.

Shira looked through one of the large panoramic windows, spotting the casino's silhouette westwards, as if she could see Noah and Rowan from here. Thinking about the logistics a couple of days ago, luck had favoured them as Ole-Einar and Rolf remembered one of their clients, a very wealthy client by the name of Iain Walker. And not only was Iain very rich, he was also the proud owner of the forty-five metre long *Cloud Dancer*, which was conveniently securely fastened to the dock inside Port Hercule. Coincidentally, the forty-two year old owner was currently occupied in Hollywood, shooting his latest action movie. Nevertheless, when Ole-Einar and Rolf contacted him, he stood by his word. The promise he had given to them a couple of months ago inside a London bar had been heavily influenced by several factors. One was the overwhelming success of his then latest movie at the box office during the opening week. Other factors included the undivided attention of a young starlet and the effect of several bottles of ridiculously expensive champagne, which he had shared with Ole-Einar and Rolf that evening after their assignment was over. At the end of the night, he had invited them to stay on his yacht whenever they wanted to. After convincing Iain that they would spend a couple of days with some girls in Monte Carlo, all that was left to do for Ole-Einar and Rolf was to pick up the keys at the harbour master. It turned out that they had hit a home run with the *Cloud Dancer*. Not only did the yacht accommodate all the staff, it also provided them with much needed privacy. They figured that it could have been problematic to explain all the high tech surveillance gear to the room service, if they would have had to rent several hotel rooms at the casino or any other hotel. Since the arrangement included that the *Cloud Dancer* was not to leave the dock, they were getting away without the crew. The only problem they had was that the owner was under the impression that only Ole-Einar and Rolf were using his multi-million dollar toy in the presence of their female companions. For some reason, they had both failed to mention that a total of fifteen people would turn this floating man cave into a mobile ops centre.

While Noah, who had introduced herself to Rowan as Mandy, continued to seduce the British heir, Ariel announced that retired Admiral Brian Whittaker and Talia were already walking down the dock. Usually the retired admiral felt much more comfortable around ships than inside a casino, but the fact that the young Israeli had just lost five thousand Euros of his own money somehow dampened his spirit. Talia on the other hand was dealing with some issues of her own. The combination of drinking almost a complete bottle of champagne in such a short time and walking in high heels on a hot night after hours in an air conditioned casino proved to be a serious challenge for her. She supposed it helped with their cover that she had to cling to Brian's arm, when in actuality she was struggling to stay upright.

The retired admiral had to admit that the twenty-four year old Israeli looked absolutely stunning in her dress, but he also entertained the thought of rendering little to no assistance should she indeed stumble towards the harbour water. Unaware of the admiral's intentions, Talia was lucky that such an event would have caused unnecessary and unwanted attention.

"My lady", Brian eventually said and stepped aside to let Talia walk first over the gangway to the *Cloud Dancer*.

"Thank you...sir", Talia stammered and concentrated on walking the narrow gangway with high heels.

"You know you can take those off", Brian offered his professional advice as the Israeli inched over the gangway.

"That's okay...sir...I can manage", Talia replied, her voice tense from her concentration. "I'm almost-" the young woman continued, but she lost her balance and tumbled head first on *Cloud Dancer*'s deck. Luckily for her, the young Israeli was able to change the direction a little bit and landed on the white cushioned seats first, from where she slid under the table.

"All aboard", retired admiral Whittaker noted dryly. A steady flow of Hebrew curses coming from underneath the table reassured him that Talia was fine. "I'm going to change into something more comfortable", he quickly announced as he entered the state room.

"Where is Talia?" Ariel wanted to know.

"Drunk as a sailor underneath the aft deck table", Brian commented humourlessly with a wave of his hand. Shira and the others quickly glanced at each other before their eyes scanned the aft deck, where Talia just crawled out from underneath the table.

"Oh my God! I hate those shoes", the young woman cursed as she stumbled inside the state room.

"I hope you didn't get any blood on those cushions!" Rolf immediately said, clearly showing his priorities as he hastened outside to double check. The Israeli remained silent and rolled her eyes at his lack of care for her wellbeing. Talia slowly stepped over to Shira, who now turned her attention back to the computer screen and the radio. None of them were so foolish to attempt to sneak in a video camera inside one of the most secure casinos in the world. Not only did they have signal jammers, but if they would get caught, they would face serious legal consequences. Instead, they relied on simple eye contact between their team members, and it was not until outside the casino that they radioed back to Shira.

"According to our guys they're still at the bar inside the casino", Shira updated her friend.

"Good. I need some water. I think I'm drunk", she slurred and thankfully took the bottle of water Alba handed her. "I think the admiral hates me", she started and emptied half the bottle. "I don't know why. I think the mission was a success, but he didn't talk to me at all on the way back."

"How did you like playing Black Jack?" Ariel asked, trying to give her a hint.

"Oh, that was so much fun! Did you ever play?" Talia was much more excited now.

"A couple of times", Ariel replied, while Shira bit her lip to prevent a fit of laughter.

"This was the first time I played Black Jack. I really liked it." Talia explained joyfully and drank more water.

"From all we heard that was kind of obvious. I think you set a new record."

"What do you mean? It wasn't my money", Talia replied, but the expression on her face suddenly darkened as the realisation set in. "Oh my God! Are you saying...?" The Israeli finally put the pieces together and emptied the bottle of water, trying to sober up as quickly as possible.

"Yes, it was my money", Brian calmly said, standing right behind her. The twenty-four year old couldn't help but spurt the water in her mouth all over the place.

"Oh my God! I am so sorry, sir! I didn't know. I mean, I..." Talia started, but didn't know what to say to improve her situation. "I'll go and change", she finally muttered and headed for one of the cabins, "and then I will quietly kill myself", she added in a much calmer voice.

"Just make sure you don't get any blood on the carpet or the furniture!" Rolf called after her, which earned him a very rude hand gesture and a string of Hebrew death threats.

"My apologies, Boss. I thought she would at least understand the basics of the game." Ariel tried to offer at least a little bit of solace, but the expression on Brian's face clearly showed him that he was not very successful with it.

"I can guarantee you that neither Talia nor Noah understand the very concept of Black Jack. They accomplished what they were supposed to do, so let's focus on that. Anything new from the casino, Shira?"

"No. According to our guys they're still at the bar."

"Is everything else in place?" Brian wanted to know. Spending a couple of hours in the casino waiting for Rowan had kept him out of the loop.

"Everything is ready."

"Perfect. Ole-Einar and Gunnar", the retired admiral turned around.

"Yes, sir?"

"I want a full status report on this ship."

"Ahem, what do mean, sir?" Ole-Einar hesitantly asked. He had to promise the owner that *Cloud Dancer* would not get a single scratch, and the tone in Brian's voice sent a shiver down the Norwegian's back.

"I mean that I want a full status report on this ship. Water tanks, diesel tanks, auxiliary fuel for the generators, equipment, power, batteries. Didn't they teach you anything at the Norwegian Navy Special Operations Commando?"

"Well, they did, sir, but...you know...it sounds like you plan to move this ship. One of the conditions that Iain gave us was not to move the ship. He was very specific about that."

"I did not say that I want to move the ship. I said that I want a status report on it. Should we have to move fast for whatever reason, I do not want to be caught with our pants down for not knowing how much diesel we got, and in what general state she is", the admiral explained.

"But we do not have the crew-" Ole-Einar stopped as the retired admiral cut him off.

"Son, my last command was on a British battle cruiser. Over half of the people on this ship have served in a Navy. Do you really think I need a crew? If I were you I would get that status report", Brian stared him down, his voice taking a dangerous tone. Although no longer in the Navy, he was not used to his orders being questioned.

"Getting that status report now, sir", Ole-Einar quickly confirmed and disappeared downstairs, praying that this was not a bad idea. Brian shook his head and turned towards Shira.

"Anything new from Klaus while I was gone? Do we have a connection?"

"We do have a Skype connection with London, but Klaus has not contacted us yet. Our status report is not due for another hour."

"Very well. Now, what do we got here?" Brian asked and stepped closer to the ship's controls.

EuroSecCorporation, **London, Tuesday, July 29**
Klaus sat behind his desk and leaned back in his comfortable leather chair. He stared at the ceiling, his mind spinning. A quick glance at his watch showed him that it was

already late in the night, but he and his wife were not ready to call it a day yet. For a few moments he watched Brigitte through the open door. Seeing her sitting behind the desk she shared with Natascha prompted Klaus' thoughts to drift away even further.

It was now the second time that Natascha was in serious trouble. Klaus exhaled sharply, wondering if Natascha was even still alive, and if they would ever see her again. He was usually the last person to let any situation reveal any emotional response, but he found the last couple of days to be overwhelmingly stressful. His eyes wandered to a picture of Natascha, Nick, and their daughter Shira-Sarah. Just before the majority of their people had left for Monaco, Shira had placed the picture on Klaus' desk as a grim reminder of what was at stake. It was not that Klaus needed it, but he didn't dare move it or turn it away. It was then that he realised that he had stared at it quite often. His eyes were still glued to the picture as he shook his head, wondering what the outcome for the young family would be. He tried to find some distraction and turned the TV on. The news channel covered the usual British topics before turning to the latest international news. The retired general's interest grew when a news anchor reported about the ongoing conflict in Syria.

"Will it ever stop?" he wondered out loud, the video footage showing what appeared to be dozens of dead bodies. He turned the volume up.

"...as well as several other officials from different voluntary health and medical organisations report that at least over two hundred members of the international terror organisation fell victim to a yet unknown disease. A spokesperson called the deaths an extraordinary event and a public health risk. Although the virus has not yet been identified, there is a serious concern of the virulence of this virus becoming a national and even potentially an international pandemic. The spokesperson confirmed that the casualties are mostly amongst members of the terror organisation, and that the virus seems to be spreading rapidly between them. According to the health organisations, the real number of casualties is believed to be much higher. Since the current situation in Syria makes proper treatment of the infected people impossible, health organisations are calling for an immediate stop of all military actions. While there has been no official statement from engaged nations, the Vatican has already commented on the recent events, calling them-"

Klaus' attention was interrupted as his phone rang. Pressing the mute button on the remote, he quickly glanced at Brigitte. His wife just shrugged her shoulders, indicating that the call had not gone through the switchboard first but directly to Klaus' line. Looking at the display he noticed the blocked ID, but the retired general picked up the receiver before it rang again.

"One moment, sir. Establishing a secure line and passing you through", a young male voice notified him before Klaus had the chance to say a word. He took the moment and turned the TV off. His mood immediately brightened when he recognised General Rashid's voice. The director of the Israeli Mossad sounded almost enthusiastic, despite the time of the day.

"Shalom, my friend. Do you have any news?" the Israeli asked.

"I'm afraid not. We found Rowan in Monte Carlo at one of the casinos, and our team is making contact with him as we speak."

"How do you plan to execute this mission?"

"We did a psychological profile on him. One of our assets used to be his escort for well over a year. She shared some very valuable information with us. Our plan is to get him under our control by the end of the night. Based on our intel, we expect he will jump with both feet into a honey trap. Once we have him, we will go from there."

"Sounds like a black op to me."

"Never said it was legal."

"It might be better if I don't know any more details", General Rashid laughed before he continued. "On another note, I do have some information for you. It took a while, but we finally got something. Not certain about the accuracy of the reports, all the info came from our sayanim. Considering the nature of the situation, I did not have the time or means to verify the information yet, but there is little reason to doubt it."

"Okay, what do you got?" Klaus asked, collecting a pen and paper, ready to take notes.

"We checked out Rowan Harrison. A few things you might already know, but I'll just give you what we got. He's the only son to Lady Amelia Harrison and the late Sir James Harrison from the Harrison business empire. After his father passed away, he took charge of most branches of their business empire. He has started several new business relationships since taking control."

"Hm, that's interesting", Klaus commented as he scribbled some notes. He didn't know how it would fit in, but he knew any information could be valuable.

"We might be able to get some more information about whom he is doing business with."

"It certainly won't hurt. As you know, our resources are extremely limited. The disadvantages of a private company."

"I understand. Shira has mentioned an abbey?"

"Yes, Whitmore Abbey."

"She said that our friend Brian is trying to find out if your Explosive Ordnance Disposal Unit worked on a bomb there. Is that correct?"

"That is correct. He made some calls first thing Monday morning, but he hasn't heard anything back."

"It might be a coincidence, but I find it interesting that Rowan Harrison donated lots of money to Whitmore Abbey through his companies."

"Hm, you know what I think about coincidences", Klaus noted sarcastically. "Do we know how much?"

"We are talking millions of pounds. Official donations. Didn't even try to hide it."

"There is certainly something going on there, but I have to focus on finding Natascha for now. Were you able to find something out about *Asklepios*?" Klaus wanted to know.

"Nothing that you don't already know. The real owners are hiding behind shell companies hidden inside shell companies. That will take us a while. We should have a confirmed position on *Asklepios* within the next twenty-four hours. We have satellite images of all the cruise ships in the Aegean Sea and are just going through the data. You'd be surprised how many ships we're talking about."

"Hm, that many?"

"Yes. Like I said, I should have some confirmed data for you sometime tomorrow. It is safe to say that it will be outside any territorial waters. Any idea what you're going to do then?"

"Time is an issue. You know as well as I do that the official ways have zero chance of success within the time window that we have. We have a few ideas, but we need to talk to Rowan first. We have technically no intel on the hospital ship itself." Klaus answered. He and Brian had discussed the legal complications of this matter in great detail. The more they discussed it, the more frustrated they became.

"You do know that I cannot officially offer you any assistance, but if you need a favour..." General Rashid offered without getting too specific.

"Understood. We might need someone to break us out of jail, so I might take you up on that." Klaus joked, but for some reason his voice didn't reflect it.

"Let's hope it does not have to come to that. Shalom, my friend."

"Shalom! We are in your debt, again." Klaus replied, but the line was already dead. He put the phone down and went over his notes again. He spent the next couple of minutes sorting the information and adding some additional thoughts before turning his attention to his computer again.

"Okay, time to call the guys", he murmured as he established the Skype connection.

On board the private yacht *Cloud Dancer*, Port Hercule, Monaco, Tuesday, July 29

"Klaus is calling us on the video link", Shira announced loudly to get everyone's attention on the bridge. Brian immediately lowered the user manual for the multi-functional screen he was reading and stepped behind her.

"Silencio!" the retired British admiral called as Nick, Jack MacDonald, and Gunnar Eriksson joined him.

"Talk to me Klaus! What's the news?" Brian came straight to the point. They listened carefully for the next few minutes as Klaus filled them in. "That is certainly interesting, but as you already said, it does not help us right now."

"No, it doesn't, but for some weird reason some of the information is making me nervous. I'll certainly dig a little bit deeper. On the plus side, we should have a confirmed position on *Asklepios* within the next twenty-four hours."

"Understood!"

"What's new on your end?"

"Well, we're all in position. Noah is still with Rowan in the casino. We should see some movement there soon. We don't know how long it will take to get the information we need, but the guys are getting creative." Brian explained with a low voice. Klaus was silent. They didn't know what it would take to make Rowan speak, but they were prepared to find out.

"How is the ship?" Klaus finally asked, glad to change the subject.

"She's not bad", Brian told him and looked around. "Little bit cramped with all of us on board, but other than that she is a beauty."

"Sounds good to me. I will call it a day here. We will talk again in the morning unless something goes south."

"Affirmative. Have a good night." Brian said and ended the conversation, his attention turning to the casino in the distance. His lip twitched as he thought about what Klaus had just told him.

"Ahem, Boss?" Ole-Einar interrupted him.

"Yes? What is it?" Brian answered calmly and turned around to face the Norwegian.

"I got the status report on *Cloud Dancer*", the Norwegian reported, his eyes nervously glancing over the user manuals that were laid out in front of the retired admiral. Ole-Einar didn't have to be a genius to realise that Brian would not hesitate to use Iain's ship should they have to. The Norwegian just hoped that it wouldn't come to that.

"Good! How do we look?" Brian wanted to know and picked up the user manual again.

"All the tanks are at least ninety percent full, except for the waste water, which is empty. From what we can see, she is fully operational."

"You mentioned something about an air compressor earlier?"

"Yes, that's correct. Iain is a passionate diver. There is an air compressor and several scuba tanks on board. There are also a few large industrial K-bottles with oxygen and helium to mix breathing gas."

"Hm, interesting. Any diving gear?"

"Surprisingly, yes. Looks like six complete sets of gear, even rebreathers and scooters."

"Okay. I think I'll just have a quick look for myself. Shira, you call me once Noah and Rowan leave the casino. Is everyone in position?"

"Yes, everyone is still in position."

"Perfect. Nick, Gunnar, Jack, you come with me." Brian nodded and went one deck below.

"I can't believe we're doing this!" Ole-Einar stated nervously as he stowed the user manuals back in their drawers.

"Relax! We're just operating from his ship, we're not driving it." Shira replied.

"Yeah? Then why is he so interested in how to operate it?" Ole-Einar hissed nervously. He was concerned that the retired admiral would hear him.

"For heaven's sake, Ole. He is an admiral. This is a ship. Duh! Make the connection!"

"You better be right!" Ole-Einar muttered closing the drawer as Rolf stepped into the bridge.

"Oh good! I'm going to pee before the action starts", Shira sighed with relief at his arrival. The Israeli got out of the captain's chair and hastened downstairs. Rolf stepped beside his friend and exhaled sharply.

"I hope this wasn't a bad idea", he shared the same concerns as the Norwegian. Before Ole-Einar could say anything, their attention was drawn to the beeping sound of one of the monitors beside the satellite telephone.

"What the hell is that?" Ole-Einar asked curiously and looked at the screen.

"Shit! That's Iain! That's a video call!" Rolf noticed with disbelief.

"We have to answer it before he sends the harbour master looking for us."

"Damn!" Rolf cursed and looked around quickly. At least there was no one else on the bridge. He pressed a blinking button and immediately saw Iain's face on the large screen. The little video insert on the top of the screen showed them that Iain saw the whole bridge in a live view.

"Hi Iain! How are you doing?" Ole-Einar asked nervously, trying to block the camera as much as he could with his body.

"Hi brother! I'm doing great! How are you two holding up? I just want to check in to see if my baby is still afloat?"

"Oh, no worries here buddy. She's amazing. We can't believe you let us stay on your ship!"

"Ah, come on. It's not like you brought a whole gang on the ship, right?"

"Ha, oh my God, can you imagine?" Ole-Einar laughed nervously.

"Hey, who is the old dude?" Iain wanted to know.

"Old dude?" Ole-Einar wondered and turned around to see that Brian had just entered the bridge again. Luckily it was just Brian and no one else. "Oh! Him!" Ole-Einar chuckled with realisation and walked over to put an arm around Brian's shoulder. "This is just my old man! Say hello, pops!" Ole-Einar encouraged in such a loud voice as if Brian was deaf.

"Hello, sir!" Brian played along and waved to the camera.

"This is the gentleman who owns the ship, pops. The famous actor I told you about!" Ole-Einar continued, almost yelling and praying that no one else would come up to the bridge.

"Nice ship that you have, sir! I used to be in the navy and I begged my son to show me the ship. I promise I didn't touch anything! I have seen all your movies, too! I am a big fan!" Brian laughed at the camera, pretending to sound older than he was while hiding the radar system user manual behind his back.

"No worries. She's probably different from what you're used to, isn't she?" Iain boasted proudly.

"Yes, indeed she is", Brian continued to laugh and glanced around the bridge again with admiration. His smile froze suddenly as he saw Shira and Talia walking in, "Oh dear Lord!"

Shira and Talia were alarmed by his surprise and stopped dead in their tracks.

"Wow, those are the girls you brought?" Iain laughed as he noticed them on the camera.

"Ahem, yes, those are the girls!" Ole-Einar quickly played along, hoping that he still sounded somewhat convincing.

"Well, I'll leave you kids alone now and get back to my hotel. Beautiful ship that you have here, thank you!" Brian laughed, giving Shira and Talia a second to come up with a plan. The retired admiral quickly waved at the camera and retreated one deck below to make sure that no one else would walk upstairs.

"Come on, baby. Don't be shy!" Ole-Einar invited Shira and Talia and held his arm out. The two women quickly played along, and, despite their sweat pants and T-shirt apparel, put their most seductive smile on. Shira snuggled against Ole-Einar, who put his arm around her back and slapped her on her butt. Shira couldn't help but shriek with surprise, and she just smiled at the huge Norwegian, even when his hand started to rub her bum. He knew he would pay for this later.

"Nice, man, nice!" Iain laughed.

"So, how is Hollywood? How's the movie going?" Rolf tried to change the subject. He was more of a gentleman as he and Talia just embraced each other.

"Ah, it went well until last week. My supporting actor got injured. Nothing big, but enough to put the whole production on hold for three weeks. We continued shooting scenes without him, but that ended yesterday."

"So, what are you doing now?" Ole-Einar nervously asked, his hand unintentionally grabbing Shira's bum, his fingers squeezing her buttocks. The young Israeli straightened, equally nervous about Iain as Ole-Einar was, but still played along.

"Our plane just touched down thirty minutes ago. I'll be through customs in about ten minutes and should be in Monaco soon. Don't start the party without me!" Iain laughed and waved his cell phone around to show them the airport.

"Wow, that is....that is..." Ole-Einar stammered and was lost for words. His grip on Shira's butt strengthened to the point that she had to bite her lip.

"That is amazing!" Shira quickly managed through her clinched teeth. "I am such a huge fan of you, and I cannot wait to meet you! When exactly will you be here?" the Israeli innocently asked. It took all her willpower to ignore the pain from Ole-Einar's fingers digging into her gluteus muscle.

"Like I said, we just touched down in Nice."

"Oh, Nice?...Wow...that is...that is so close. That is really close, isn't it?" Shira laughed nervously, glancing to Ole-Einar.

"Little less than thirty klicks, if I remember right. I should be there within one hour, I think."

"One hour!" Shira's voice burst as Ole-Einar's fingers dug even deeper in the muscle of her buttock. "One hour! Wow, that is...so soon!"

"Like I said, don't start the party without me. Listen, I'm at customs now. See you soon!" Iain promised and ended the call.

"We are so screwed!" Ole-Einar surmised. They all stared at the now black monitor. Brian, Nick and Ariel walked over, closely followed by Gunnar and Jack.

"Iain will be here within the hour", the Norwegian explained, but he knew that they had listened in. He eased his grip on Shira's bum and absentmindedly started to rub it again. "What are we going to do now?" Ole-Einar asked, but no one had an answer. It would take at least three hours to take all their gear off the ship, and they were still in the middle of an operation.

"First of all, you're going to take your hand off my ass or I'll kill you! Hand off ass!" Shira demanded in a threateningly low voice.

"What?" Ole-Einar asked, still rubbing her bum. He was lost in thoughts.

"I said hand off ass. Off ass now", Shira hissed, staring up at him.

"Oh, you mean...never mind, I'm sorry!" Ole-Einar finally realised and let her go.

"You're an animal!" Shira cursed and rubbed her buttock to ease the pain. Despite the seriousness of their situation they couldn't help but snicker.

"Well, there's not much we can do now. Once he gets here, we simply have to tell him what's going on and hope for the best. Rolf, Ole, you both know him. What are the chances that he'll play along?" Brian shrugged with curiosity.

"I don't know. He thinks that he's an adventurer and all that, but the fact remains that we lied to his face about what we are doing with his ship. I don't know how he will react to that. I think it's a fifty-fifty between him being totally enthusiastic about all this, or him calling the cops the moment he sets foot on his ship." Ole-Einar shared his concern.

"I think he's right, Boss", Rolf added. "We are pushing it pretty far. Let's not forget that what's about to happen is not..." Rolf didn't have to finish the sentence.

"Can I say something?" Alba interrupted them. No one had noticed the Spaniard had joined them. "I looked him up on his website. All of his movies are about his character saving some beautiful woman at the end. No offence, but isn't this exactly what we are doing here?"

"This is not a movie, Alba."

"Not for us, but it might be for him. He's been playing that role for over fifteen years, it is the way he thinks, it's his way of living. There's a reason that he hasn't settled down yet. Agreed, he won't like the fact that we literally stole his multi-million dollar yacht, but have you even looked around in here? Everything here screams adventure. I'm confident he will help us. He will realise that this could be his only chance in real life to show the world that he can really do this stuff. All we have to do is to keep him out of the direct line of fire. Last time I checked, you guys were pretty good at that. I checked his Facebook page and googled him. His taste in women is pretty straight forward. Young and beautiful", Alba explained and looked at the other women on the bridge. "I think we got that covered. Let me talk to him, he'll be fine."

"I think she has a point!" Ariel supported Alba, although he had to admit that he wasn't exactly sure how far the Spaniard would go to convince Iain. Judging by the expression on Brian Whittaker's face, that seemed to be his concern as well, but he was still weighing their options.

"You think you can...*talk* him into this?" Brian asked, trying to make his point that he didn't expect anything else from her.

"I am certain, yes. He will be very upset in the beginning, but eventually he will help us. Judging by his character he might even start swinging at Ole-Einar and Rolf to prove his point", Alba added hesitantly and shyly smiled at the two.

"Come again?" Ole-Einar asked in disbelief.

"It's in his movies. It's his trademark. He punches everyone who betrays him. So there is a realistic chance that he punches you, too." Alba explained with a wave of her hand. Ole-Einar and Rolf looked at each other. They both knew that Iain Walker's experience was solely based on staged and well choreographed fights.

"You will not hit him back, am I clear about that?" Brian ordered as if he had read their minds.

"Well, we wouldn't knock him out, but are you telling us to just lie down and take it from him?"

"Yes, that is exactly what I am telling you. You have a problem with that?" Brian growled.

"No, I don't have a problem with that", Ole-Einar hesitated through clinched teeth.

"Great, now that that is sorted, let's see where we are. Iain will be here within the hour. We have no reason to believe that we can stall him, so we have to make sure that Rowan is already under our control by the time Iain arrives. Shira, can you give the team the message to speed things up?"

"Of course", Shira replied and took the radio.

"Okay. Ariel, Gunnar. What about the cabin where we are planning to keep him? Is it ready?"

"Yes, it is. We decided on a storage unit just beside the engine room. Just enough room for what we want to do, and it is almost sound proof. Alba, Talia and Shira were inside screaming from the top of their lungs, but with the generators running, we couldn't hear any of them inside or outside the ship. It will work."

"Perfect. Nick?"

"Yes, sir?" Nick immediately replied. He knew that he had to follow Brian's orders down to the letter as a condition to come along.

"You do not move from my side. Am I clear about that, son?"

"Yes, sir, crystal clear." Nick reluctantly promised. He knew that the former admiral was right. If he would get his hands on Rowan, there was a realistic chance that he would beat him to death before he could reveal crucial information about how to free Natascha.

"Perfect. Talia? You're ready?" the retired admiral asked in his fatherly voice now and turned around to face the Israeli.

"Yes, sir, I am ready. Not all that comfortable, but ready", the twenty-four year old admitted and looked down at her morning robe. A quick shower and some more water had helped her to sober up.

"Okay, let's see it!" Ole-Einar quickly added in anticipation, eying her up.

"Lick me!" Talia hissed back and threw him a killing glance.

"It's *bite me*, not *lick me,* Talia", Shira quickly corrected her friend. "You might give the guys the wrong idea", the Israeli added. The threatening look she threw at her male team members made it clear that she wouldn't tolerate any comments on this. Satisfied that they kept their thoughts to themselves, she turned her attention to Talia again.

"Don't worry, you'll be fine", she tried to reassure her friend with a smile before she picked up the radio again.

Shira listened to their report. "Okay, they're on the move. It's show time. Let's go!" she announced.

***Casino de Monte Carlo*, Monte Carlo, Monaco, Tuesday, July 29**
Even at her young age of twenty-five years, Noah had faced her fair share of challenges. The young Israeli had never thought she would ever meet a challenge she would rather run away from like this one. The problem was not Rowan, who expressed his fair share of compliments on how beautiful she looked, but rather the large bottle of expensive Krug champagne standing right in front of them. She was not used to drinking regularly to begin with, and she had totally underestimated the effect the champagne would have on her. She assessed her situation for the tenth time in as

many minutes and came to the same conclusion that Talia had already drawn earlier that evening: she was totally drunk. To make matters worse, a quick look at Rowan revealed that he didn't seem to notice the champagne at all. Noah knew that she would have to act sooner rather than later, otherwise she would be the one getting carried away instead of the British heir.

"I think we should go now", Noah finally looked him in his eyes and whispered as seductively as her intoxicated state would allow.

"I think that's a great idea, my love", Rowan replied, his eyes sparkling in anticipation as he got the waiter's attention. While Rowan signed the tab to his usual suite, Noah quickly made eye-contact with one of her teammates before she rose to her feet.

"Allow me", Rowan offered his arm. All seriousness aside, Noah gladly accepted the help as she cursed her high heels and her drunken stupor.

"No, I have to go to my place first!" Noah quickly whispered as Rowan headed for the elevators.

"Your place? Why do you have to go to your place? I have the suite booked", he contested, the disappointment clear in his voice.

Good point! Why do I have to go there? Noah asked herself as she desperately tried to remember the cover story she had worked out earlier.

"Remember my friend? She'll be there waiting for us!" Noah seductively whispered in his ear when she finally remembered. He looked her over and a wicked grin crossed his lips. She glanced down to her hand in his arm, then back to his eyes, giving her a moment to collect her thoughts and charge her seduction. "It's not far, we are staying on one of the yachts in the marina", she smiled enticingly, directing Rowan towards the exit.

The Briton couldn't believe his luck and a brief frown crossed his brow for a second before he succumbed to her siren call. Rowan was usually not the guy who would indulge in a late evening stroll along the marina, but the thoughts of the sexual pleasures awaiting him was motivation enough. Why have one if he could enjoy two?

"So, which one is it?" he finally asked a couple of minutes later as they walked past the medium size yachts towards the larger ships.

"That one over there", Noah pointed at the *Cloud Dancer* when they were about fifty metres away. She was glad that she had refused taking a limousine as the fresh air helped to clear her head.

"The *Cloud Dancer*", Rowan slowed his stroll to admire the sleek silhouette of the forty-five metre yacht. "Does the old gentleman own the yacht?" Rowan asked curiously as he referred to their meeting at the Black Jack table.

"No, he is staying at the casino. We know the owner of the yacht, and he's letting us use it when we're around", Noah lied. "We have her all to ourselves. Just you, me, Viola, and the rest of the night. You think you can handle us?" Noah whispered mesmerisingly as she led him by the hand over the gangway.

"Hell, I will die trying", Rowan laughed and followed her over the aft deck to the large sliding doors and inside the main state room. He had already forgotten the worries that bothered him earlier that night.

"Blimey!" Rowan exhaled as his eyes rested on Talia. The twenty-four year old leaned lasciviously against the bar, the tight bikini showing more than it was hiding. He looked over her as he had earlier, catching his lip between his teeth as the mystery of the beauty underneath her dress was finally revealed. Her firm breasts and pert bum were so inviting that he salivated instantly.

"Ah, Viola, it is such a pleasure to meet you again", Rowan quickly refocussed and took another step towards her, while Noah closed the door behind him.

"The pleasure is all mine", Talia hissed seductively. Before Rowan could say anything else, he felt the sudden sharp pain of a needle stab into his thigh.

"What the hell-" he started and spun around, but he immediately felt the anaesthetic's effect as it locked all his muscles. He wanted to announce his protest, but Talia's hand quickly covered his mouth from behind, and he was only able to produce a gurgling sound. His eyes widened and he watched as Noah carefully placed the syringe back on the table. The room started to spin in front of his eyes and he tried to balance himself, attempting to escape, but his body didn't obey him anymore. It only took a few seconds before he sank to his knees, his eyes still locked on Noah.

"Good night, lover boy", Noah commented dryly as he fell unconsciously to his side, "time for some answers."

- 27 -

West of Al-Hasakah, Syria, Wednesday, July 30
It was just after midnight, and for the first time in many hours, Monique sat down and took some time for herself. She took a bite from some bread and closed her eyes as she chewed. The fact that there was almost no light in the tent at this time played to her advantage. Sitting in one of the dark corners, it was practically impossible to see her. She took her time with the little bit of bread that she was brave enough to eat. One of the older women had given it to her, and Monique called herself lucky once she noticed that it was fresh. After she finished her slice, she checked for her tea. It was still too hot to drink, but she made sure to boil all the water for at least ten minutes before consuming any of it. Monique wasn't even sure if it would make a difference any more or not, but she was determined not to take any unnecessary risks.

Blowing some air on the tea to cool it down, the young French looked around, her eyes wandering over the countless bodies of the sick or wounded. Only a handful of lights were operational. They covered some areas with a dark yellow glimmer, but certainly not to a level that would have deemed satisfying for a medical facility. A movement at the tent flap caught her attention. The gust of cold, fresh air from the desert night was not the reason Monique felt a cold shiver descending her spine. She immediately recognised Nazir Algafari, the man who had bought her not too long ago. As he looked around, Monique quickly covered her face again to blend in with the canvas behind her. Nazir's eyes wandered over all the sick people until he found the British mercenary, who had not left the side of his dying friend for hours. The Briton first didn't understand what Nizar wanted, but eventually someone translated for him. Monique tilted her head a little bit to eavesdrop on their conversation.

"Nazir has slave. Beautiful slave. Young slave. Nazir knows that you asked for slave. Nazir wants to sell you slave."

Monique's jaw dropped once she realised that they were talking about her. Her memories of the horrors of her first night flared up again. It took her a moment before she calmed down enough to understand what they were talking about.

"Okay, tell him that I pay what he is asking, but I want to have a look at the new slaves first, understood?"

Nazir listened and quickly shook his friend's hand. Monique knew that she had just been sold again.

The hell I am! The young French thought, determined to put her plan into action as soon as the opportunity would present itself.

It turned out that luck was on her side. She only had to wait twenty more minutes before four men came into the tent performing their grim routine of removing the dead bodies. Monique got up to help them. Although she was a woman, the warriors respected the decision of their elder Moonif Nasser, who had somehow realised that Monique had the highest medical training of all of them.

The men waited patiently for her to assess each one for vital signs and signal them whether a person was still alive or not. *We might as well take all of them!*

Monique thought a couple of minutes later as she barely felt a pulse on one of the infected people. Even those who were only wounded didn't stand a chance of survival being in the same space as the diseased. Monique still had no idea what they were dealing with, but she knew that the hygienic conditions at this camp were the perfect breeding ground for whatever bug was causing all this havoc. She choked once she reached the body of a young child. She took the blanket and covered the little girl as a swell of tears overwhelmed her. She took a quick look around and reassured herself that the four Taliban were still busy carrying corpses out to the truck.

"I'm sorry, but you're my ticket out of here", Monique whispered her apology and held the little girl's hand. She had died earlier that evening, but Monique didn't say anything.

Without another word she swiftly picked up the little corpse and walked towards the open tent flap. The cold air from the desert hit her face and dried her tears. Looking around, she found the four men at the truck, ready to go back inside the tent to continue their grim routine. Monique shook her head, signalling them that she was carrying the last victim. They just stared at her. One of the men tried to take the body of the dead child, but Monique held the child closer to her and turned away. She had seen them throwing the bodies on the truck, and she would not allow them to do the same with the body of this little girl. The man who tried to take the child looked to the others with confusion, but they just shrugged before turning away to their other duties.

Monique climbed onto the truck where she carefully laid the young girl to rest. Her heart was racing as she quickly glanced around to make sure that no one paid any attention to her. She quickly lay down and pulled a blanket over her own body, blending in perfectly with all the other dead bodies.

She could feel her heart pounding in her throat for what felt like hours before she heard the old truck's engine roar to life just minutes later. Monique couldn't help but smile as the truck passed all the check points without getting searched. Even twenty minutes into their journey, Monique didn't dare to lift the blanket to take a look around. She managed five more minutes before she stuck her head out to take a deep breath. She inhaled the fresh air under the open sky, which was no comparison to the stalled stench inside the tent. The stars shone so bright that she was able to see relatively well once her eyes adjusted. She risked raising her head to see where they were going, but they were on the outskirts of the desert, and it was impossible to recognise any features in the landscape. *Okay, so far so good!* Monique told herself and lay back down again, thinking about what her next move would be. In all honesty, she had never thought about making it this far, realising that she lacked an actual plan how to escape the truck. Monique knew though she would rather die trying than to go back to that hellhole.

The engine's sound changed as the truck started to climb into the mountains again. Monique risked another glance and noticed the large boulders and rock formations beside the road. They would provide her with the perfect hiding spot. She kept looking ahead and decided that this could be her best chance. The truck could stop any moment, and then it would be much more difficult to escape.

Monique took her blanket and crawled over the dead bodies to the back of the truck. She carefully climbed over the wooden boards of the tailgate and looked at the ground. Luckily for her, the truck was not moving that fast as its old frame shook and moaned under the tension of the climb of the steep desert road. She was thankful that her jump would not seriously injure her as much as it would at a higher speed.

Monique risked another peek ahead and saw her chance. There was a sharp curve in the road and a large boulder right beside the street. She waited a few more seconds and knew she had to jump at the right angle and the right moment to not be seen in the side mirrors. She felt anticipation helplessly rising deep within her, and she bit her tongue to prevent her from screaming as she leapt from the truck.

She felt a singe of pain burn through her body as she made contact with the rough terrain, landing harder than she had anticipated. She clenched her teeth from the pain and knew she had to focus not to be seen. She immediately lay as flat as she could on the road without moving. With her adrenaline pumping, she struggled against the urge to get up and run. She waited still, her breath heaving as she listened to the sound of the truck disappearing in the distance. Carefully, she risked lifting her head again. A quick look around confirmed that she was alone. She could not see any lights or hear any sounds to suggest that there was anyone around in any direction. She quickly got up to her feet and ran behind one of the large boulders for cover.

She felt some muscle pain from her landing, but aside from that and a few scratches, she was relieved she was not injured. She leaned her back against the boulder and looked to the sky, trying to calm her fast and shaky breath. *You made it! You really made it!* She smiled exhaustedly before looking around again. She had no idea where she was or what direction to go, but she knew that being stranded in the desert alone was better than where she had been.

Monique looked up the road where the truck had disappeared, then looked back in the other direction before picking up her blanket she had used to cover the dead girl. Earlier that evening she had managed to hide a water bottle and some bread in it. She took the water bottle, opened it and enjoyed a couple sips. Satisfied, she closed the bottle and picked up the blanket again. It was only now that she realised that her headache had gotten worse, same with the irritation in her throat. Monique cleared her throat and pushed the thought aside. With another glance at her surroundings, she turned around and started running. Her legs were shaking and she felt heavy as she kicked through the sand, away from the road, out into the desert.

On board the private yacht *Cloud Dancer*, Port Hercule, Monaco, Wednesday, July 30

Rowan had barely touched the floor when Ole-Einar and Rolf rushed into the state room. While they quickly handcuffed the Briton with a pair of zip-ties, Shira handed Talia back her morning robe. Rolf couldn't refrain from whistling at the sight.

"I got to know, what does the tattoo mean?" he asked as he shamelessly stared at the artwork on Talia's hip.

"It's Hebrew and means 'so one may walk in peace.' You will lose a precious part of your body if you keep staring at my butt!" Talia hissed as she tightly closed the morning robe around her.

"Speaking of such violence, let's bring this piece of shit below deck", Ole-Einar said and effortlessly picked Rowan up just to let him drop on the floor again. "Sorry, mate, my mistake", the Norwegian apologised playfully before picking him up for good this time.

Just as he and Rolf started to carry him below deck, Shira yelled at them,

"Quickly! Iain is walking down the quay. He will be here in about twenty seconds. Alba! Come up! Showtime!"

"Shit, this is going down south fast!" Ole-Einar complained as he and Rolf rushed Rowan downstairs. "Why is everybody getting to enjoy Talia in a tight bikini but us? That's not fair!" Rolf complained from the staircase just as Talia removed her morning robe again. His attention got distracted when Alba pressed herself past them, also wearing nothing but a tight bikini.

"Oh dear Lord! That's just not fair! Why are you doing this?" Rolf complained, dropping Rowan's leg with protest.

"Because you're all perverts and pigs."

"No disagreement there, but we should still be there with you just in case!" Rolf refused to give up without a fight, but Shira did not have any of it.

"Shush now! He's on the gangway!" their friend warned before she closed the door behind them just in time. When she turned around again, Iain had already slid the large door leading to the aft deck open. The surprise was evident on his face once he saw Shira, Alba, and Talia. He paused for a moment to recover.

"Good evening, ladies", he said, his eyes resting on the two half-naked women. "And who might you be?" Iain looked at Alba.

"I'm a surprise", the Spaniard laughed and walked over to the couch. "Come here, sit with me, please", she whispered lasciviously.

"Well, I don't mind if I do. It is *my* ship after all", Iain laughed and joined Alba on the soft leather couch. He couldn't care less where Rolf and Ole-Einar were, and he wished he would have checked his breath before he stepped on the yacht. He knew the guys were going to have a good time here, though he didn't expect to see such beauty awaiting him. He slipped his arm around Alba's shoulder and felt intrigued by the encounter.

He looked her over and could feel her soft skin under his fingertips. He went to open his mouth to speak when Alba started, "Iain, I'm afraid we need to talk", the Spaniard continued, the seriousness in her voice cloaked in her best smile.

"Talk?" Iain's confusion was evident. That was the last thing he had on his mind. He could not believe what he had just heard. "You want to talk?" He just wanted to make sure that he had heard her right the first time.

"Yes, Iain. Unfortunately we have to talk", Shira confirmed from behind and sat beside him on the couch.

Brian, Nick and the rest of their crew patiently waited one deck below. They were all trying to listen to what was happening above, turning their attention to the ceiling or to the staircase as if they could see what was happening.

"I don't hear any shouting and screaming yet", Brian whispered encouragingly. As a precaution he had placed Ariel and Gunnar closest to the door, just in case they had to rush upstairs.

"Rowan is securely tied up in the storage unit. Olaf and Jack are with him", Rolf whispered to Brian when he and Ole-Einar joined them.

"How is it going?" the Norwegian wanted to know, staring at the ceiling.

"So far so good. No screaming or loud voices. I only hear the ladies talking", Brian filled them in.

"I think Alba does most of the talking", Ariel commented. He stood closest to the door and had the best vantage on eavesdropping on them.

"Let's hope she knows what the bloody hell she's doing", Brian said tensely. They could not remember if they had ever seen the former admiral so tense. Brian certainly didn't like it not to be in control.

"She will be fine. Shira is with her. She will make sure that the facts are all accurate", Ariel tried to reassure his boss.

"What the hell is taking them so long?" Ole-Einar asked after another ten minutes of uncertainty had passed by. As if Shira had heard him, they could all hear her voice now.

"Ole! Rolf! Can you please come up? Nick! Brian, you too."

"You two go first", the former admiral insisted and pushed Rolf and Ole-Einar in front of him. "If he starts swinging, he might as well hit those who deserve it."

"What kind of logic is that?" Rolf tried to complain, but readily followed the steps upstairs. When they opened the door, their eyes immediately fell on Shira, Talia, and Alba, who stood at the bar watching Iain. The movie star nervously paced the state room, but at least he seemed to have himself under control. He looked up once he noticed the four men.

"Nick! I want you to meet Iain Walker", Shira calmly introduced them.

"Dude. I'm so sorry about your wife! I read about what happened to both of you a couple of years ago and now this. Man, I'm so sorry!" Iain's voice shook with heartfelt concern as he walked to Nick and clapped him on the shoulder while shaking hands.

"Thank you! I really appreciate it", Nick replied. He was definitely surprised by Iain's reaction. He had no idea what the ladies had told him, but it must have worked.

"No problem, man. Anything you need! Anything I can do to help!" Iain offered and turned towards Brian.

"Iain, I want you to meet retired Admiral Brian Whittaker."

"Ah, the Navy guy. Nice touch, *pops*."

"My sincere apologies. I wish we would have met under different circumstances. I trust that my employee has explained the situation."

"Yes, me too." Iain answered bitterly, but still shook the admiral's hand before turning towards Ole-Einar and Rolf. No introductions were needed here as Iain slowly walked over towards them.

"I should knock you out for lying to me, dude, but Shira told me that you might punch back", Iain said and looked up to the huge Norwegian, who was at least ten centimetres taller than him.

"If we weren't so pressed for time I would even let you. My apology. I was convinced that lying to you was the fastest and safest way to get what we needed. It was my idea, and I am sorry for that." Ole-Einar apologised.

"So you thought that I'm just a stupid money bag that can be taken advantage of?”

“No, that is-” Ole-Einar started, but Brian Whittaker cut him off.

“I don’t want to be rude, and I totally understand that we are on your ship, Mr Walker, but we’re still pressed for time here, I am afraid.”

“Understood. I just want to make sure that everybody knows that I don’t like being taken advantage of and lied to. I am not an idiot or a pushover.”

“You made that very clear, Iain, and I can assure you that we are all aware of that.” Shira tried to reassure him.

“Yeah, right. That’s why you greeted me with the half naked women”, Iain voiced his frustration. He turned around and paced the state room again. “Not that I don’t mind the female touch, but all you had to do was ask.”

“So will you help us?” Shira asked after a few seconds, which felt like an eternity.

“Of course I will help you! How can I not help you?” Iain shouted and walked to the bar to pour himself a drink.

“I hope you don’t mind?” he asked and looked around.

“By all means, this is your ship”, Shira answered with a smile.

“Bloody right it is.” Iain agreed, taking a quick sip of his drink. “So what’s next? Shira said that you have that scumbag already on board?”

“Yes, that’s correct. We used the aft storage room, right beside the engine room.”

“That should work”, Iain emptied his drink and nodded. “Okay! Let’s go! Let’s see if we can get some information out of that asshole!” Everyone was totally caught off guard as Iain slammed his glass down on the expensive teak bar and started walking towards the staircase. Shira stepped in front of him in protest.

“Well, unfortunately we can’t let you do that, Iain. It’s for your own protection”, Shira tried to talk some sense into him.

“What do you mean? We have questions! He has answers!” Iain pointed with confidence.

“I really like the way you think, son, but it’s not that simple.” Brian started to explain. “Don’t forget that what we are doing here is highly illegal. It would be best for you if you were not on the ship at all.”

“Bloody hell no! This is my ship and I can do whatever I want to do on it.”

“We are still in the territorial waters of Monaco, and therefore we are subject to the law and all the criminal consequences that come with it.” Brian continued.

“Screw them! We cast the lines and drive the *Cloud Dancer* into international waters before we start grilling his balls.”

The team took a pause and looked at the retired admiral with surprise.

“That’s not such a bad idea, Boss”, Ole-Einar commented dryly.

“The idea is good, and I certainly cannot tell you to leave your own ship.”

“Damn right you can’t!”

“But it is in your interest to be as little involved in this as possible. Trust me, the criminal consequences could be severe.” Brian seemed to have hit a nerve with Iain. The movie star just stood there for a few moments and finally nodded. This added twist was something he had never read in any movie script before.

“Okay, that makes sense. As long as nobody treats me like an idiot.”

"Promised! Are you ready to meet the rest of our team?" Brian asked.

"Sure, why not. Bring them all up!" Iain muttered with resignation and sat down on the couch again. "I really wish we would have met under different circumstances", he smiled at Alba while the state room filled with the remaining team members.

"Iain, I want you to meet Ariel, Gunnar and Noah. Two more of our team, Olaf and Jack, are guarding our prisoner at the moment." Shira introduced them as they walked through the door and came over to shake Iain's hand.

"Wow, that just looked like one of those Disney cartoons when all those little mice come dancing onto the stage", Iain laughed and sat back in his comfortable couch. "So, what's next?"

"We'll go and ask Rowan some questions. I suggest that you stay up here for the next hour or so", Shira winked at him.

"I'll stay with you", Alba quickly offered her companionship before Iain could protest. "But I will go and dress first", she quickly added and winked at him before leaving with Talia.

Ole-Einar followed Brian and Ariel down to the aft storage room. At the bottom of the stairs the retired admiral turned around and blocked the way.

"Okay gentlemen. I appreciate that you came with me this far, but I have to insist that I talk to Rowan alone. We can't forget that what we are doing here is highly illegal, and-" Brian started, but for the first time he could remember, Ariel not only cut him off, but also gently shoved him to the side.

"With all due respect, sir, this is not my first rodeo. I agreed on keeping Nick out of this for obvious reasons, but that asshole knows where Natascha is, and I am not wasting another second." Ariel simply said and walked by him, his eyes already focussed on the other end of the corridor.

"What he said", Ole-Einar simply shrugged and squeezed his large frame past the retired admiral.

"No respect any more these days", Brian mumbled bringing up the rear. They reacted exactly as he had predicted it.

"Don't tell us you expected anything else", Ole-Einar commented drily.

"Not really, I just thought that I should state that for the bloody record."

"Noted." Ariel arrived at the aft storage room and knocked at the door. Olaf Magnusson opened and the let the three in.

"How is he doing?" Brian wanted to know as he stepped right in front of the British playboy, who was now tied to a chair.

"Just waking up, sir. Took him a little bit longer than it should have." Olaf commented and raised an eyebrow.

"Very well then. Olaf, you and Jack can leave. We will take it from here."

"Very well, sir. We will be outside if you need us."

"Appreciate it. Oh, one more thing", Brian said and turned around to look at them.

"Someone should tell Iain to turn on the auxiliary generators as well, just for the additional noise." Olaf and Jack exchanged a quick look before they nodded. Brian waited until they closed the door before turning towards Rowan again. Rowan slowly opened his eyes and swallowed a couple of times. He looked at the three people standing right in front of him, but his brain struggled to register what had happened. It took him a while before he noticed that his arms and legs were tied to the chair he was sitting on.

"What the-" he started as he finally began to recognise Ole-Einar and Ariel.

"Rowan Harrison, I am going to make this very short and very clear", Brian explained coldly and pointedly. "You are involved in human trafficking and illegal organ trafficking. You are involved in the illegal activities taking place on board the hospital ship *Asklepios*, which is currently in the Aegean Sea. You are also involved in the disappearance of Natascha Rehfeld, and you do know exactly where she is. I give you thirty seconds to tell us where she is, otherwise you will experience such pain that you wish you were dead."

"What?" Rowan responded with confusion, but he had understood enough to realise that he was in serious trouble. "So this is going to be the good cop-bad cop routine?" he laughed as he looked from Ole-Einar to Ariel. Without saying a word, the retired admiral punched Rowan in the face. Rowan's head tilted back and his mouth fell open.

"Bloody hell, that hurts. I am not used to that", Brian cursed and shook his hand as he turned away.

"Ahem, Boss, I think you knocked him out", Ole-Einar noticed, unable to hide the surprise in his voice.

"What?" Brian asked and spun around, but Rowan's head was still tilted back. "That can't be. I didn't hit him that hard", Brian almost apologised and took a closer look, but Rowan was out cold. "This is bloody marvellous. The guy is a wimp. How are we going to get an answer if he passes out the moment we ask him a question?" Brian asked.

"Good point", Ariel commented and also leaned forward to take a closer look. "I might be able to mix something, but it will take some time, and I am not certain if it will work on him."

"I don't think we have another choice", Brian agreed.

"Well, at least he didn't scream." Ole-Einar's comment was interrupted by some frantic knocks on the door. The Norwegian opened to let Shira in.

"Is he not awake yet?" Shira sounded surprised as her eyes fell on Rowan. It was only now that she noticed the little trickle of blood coming from his nose. "Did you knock him out?" Shira asked in an accusing tone and looked at Ole-Einar.

"No, it wasn't me", the huge Norwegian raised his hands as if he was offended by the Israeli's accusation. Shira's gaze immediately wandered to her brother, who also lifted his hands in an innocent gesture.

"It was actually me", Brian admitted and rubbed his knuckles.

"You, sir?" Shira was totally stunned, her gaze shifting to Rowan again. "No disrespect, sir, but how...?"

"Beats me. I didn't hit him that hard." Brian remained apologetic.

"But you enjoyed it?" Shira asked smiling.

"Can't say that I didn't", Brian smiled back.

"Did he say anything?"

"Never made it that far. We're just discussing what to do about this."

"It is safe to say that he is not saying anything at the moment. He has to wake up first." Shira explained and tilted Rowan's head to the other side.

"He shouldn't be out much longer. Shira, do you mind keeping an eye on him? We will go up and discuss what we are going to do next." Brian said and opened the door, not without throwing another look at Rowan.

"Sure, no problem. Maybe he will talk to me." Shira commented. The retired admiral froze for a second, not certain what to make of Shira's impish grin. With Ariel and Ole-Einar already on their way, Brian just shook his head before he followed them.

"Talia", he recognised the youngest of his employees, who squeezed against the wall to let Brian pass.

"Sir", the young Israeli smiled back, shyly holding her hands behind her back. The retired admiral did not notice the small cardboard box Talia was hiding behind her back, but for some reason and despite the heat under deck, he felt a chill running down his spine.

***Shadow of the Orient*, Mediterranean Sea, south of Monaco, Wednesday, July 30**
Natascha slowly opened her eyes. It took her a while to fully wake up, but she didn't dare to move. Someone had dimmed the lights in the ceiling, yet they still hurt her eyes. She closed them again and just lay on her stomach, trying to piece together what had happened to her. She didn't know what Dr Evans had given her or for how many hours or days she had been out cold, but she knew that it had been a long time. She tried to swallow, but her throat was so dry that it almost hurt. Natascha still didn't dare to move and concentrated on her body first. She didn't feel any abnormal pain, which she found positive. A mild headache bothered her, but Natascha blamed the drugs and dehydration for that. Considering the circumstances, she was satisfied to feel relatively okay and slowly opened her eyes a bit to risk a peek. Once her eyes adjusted to the light, she gladly recognised that she was lying on a comfortable king-size bed instead of the small bunk in her old cell.

Well, at least that is an improvement; Natascha tried to comfort herself and closed her eyes again for a second before she sat up. It was only now that she noticed that she was not tied up, although her wrists and ankles still showed marks from the zip ties they had used during her transport. Once she sat upright, she opened her eyes again and massaged her wrists.

"Wow! Definitely an improvement!" she commented and looked around. Natascha's eyes first recognised the carpet, and although she wasn't an expert on such things, she could see that it was expensive. Her eyes wandered around the room, noticing the exorbitant furniture along the walls. Everything seemed to be handmade of exotic wood, decorated in an oriental theme. The walls were covered with a satin-like material.

"Oh, you got to be kidding me. Not another damn ship!" Natascha cursed as she finally noticed the window. She estimated the cabin to be at least five by eight metres, but it was evident that she was alone in it. Opposite to her bed was even a tiny kitchen with a bar. She couldn't help but frown as she recognised the bowl with fresh fruits on the table and a full-size fridge in the corner.

"There has to be a catch somewhere", Natascha thought and absentmindedly scratched where Dr Evans had injected her. She looked at her skin, but saw nothing but a little red dot. Dr Evans had given her such a high dose of anaesthetics that her memory of the last couple days was erased. The last thing she remembered was being in the same room with Jonathan Brown, his friend and Dr Evans, but even her failed attempt to escape *Asklepios* was nothing more than a blur, and she wondered if it was a dream.

"Okay, don't think about that. It will come back", Natascha tried to reassure herself. By now she had been drugged so many times that she knew the memory would come back eventually. "Where the hell is Nick?" she asked herself as she slowly rose to her feet. But not knowing if her friends were even looking for her didn't improve her mood either.

"Of course they are looking for me. I can feel it!" Natascha convinced herself. "Wow, not good", she whispered and had to close her eyes as a wave of nausea came over her. It took her a few seconds before she could walk over to the fridge. It didn't even surprise her that it was fully stocked with oriental food and all kinds of different juices. Natascha picked some fruits and a pitcher with orange juice and sat at the table. She took her time but almost drank the whole pitcher. She couldn't remember anything feeling as good as the cold liquid running down her throat. With her headache almost gone, Natascha took her time eating as much fruit as she could. She could not remember the last time she had a healthy meal.

With her hunger and thirst satisfied, Natascha decided to take a closer look at her surroundings and headed straight for the window. Natascha had no idea what time it was, but it was definitely night. All she could see on the horizon was the odd light, but she had no idea if they were from other ships or the shore. Judging by her position above the water and the fact that she didn't hear the engines or felt any vibrations, she figured she had to be on a larger yacht. She reassured herself by having another look at her state room sized cabin. Taking another bite from an apple, she already started working on a plan.

"Well, that would have been too easy", Natascha commented as she tried the window, only to find it locked. Turning around, she started walking along the wall, checking behind every curtain and each expensive rug hanging from the wall. Next on her list were the side stands and dressers, but she didn't find anything useful in them. It was only now that she noticed a clock on the nightstand.

"Okay, now I know what time it is." Natascha even took the time to check under the bed, but even there the carpet was spotless. "This place is cleaner than mine", she mumbled and got up on her feet again. Next on her exploration was the bathroom. She entered the room and went to look for a light switch when, to her surprise, the room illuminated and the ventilator turned on the moment she stepped through the door.

"Wow!" Natascha marvelled at the space. The whole bathroom was made of extravagant marble with jade inserts. Her eyes fell on the large whirlpool in the corner, which she decided to examine first. From there she took a closer look at the shower.

"Would be about time", she whispered sniffing at herself. She wasn't sure if she should risk taking a shower or not, but decided to follow that thought later.

"What do we got here?" Natascha wondered and opened a cupboard underneath the sink. "Ha! Jackpot", she laughed as her eyes fell on several cleaning agents. "There must be something here to make a bomb with", she muttered and took inventory. "Better than nothing", she finally noted with satisfaction and closed the door again before walking back into the large room. It was only now that she noticed a dress on the bed. It was almost the same colour as the sheets, and she only realised now that someone must have covered her with the sheets after they had dropped her here. She figured that at one point she must have briefly woken up and pushed the sheets away, covering the dress. She picked it up to have a closer look at it.

"Yeah, I don't think so", she commented dryly and threw it back on the bed. Her eyes fell on the bathroom door again, from where they wandered to the other door. Just by the room's layout, she knew that this door was either guarded or locked, but she figured that no one had noticed that she was awake yet. At least she had not found any hidden cameras or microphones, though she also admitted to herself that she was far from being an expert on finding those. Considering her options, Natascha was torn between taking a shower and opening the second door.

"You have no idea what happens once you open that door. Might as well smell good when you do it", she finally opted for the shower and headed to the bathroom again. Disappointment hit her once she noticed that she couldn't lock the door from the inside. She decided to take the risk and just a minute later she enjoyed the warm water on her skin. Her eyes fell on the vast selection of overpriced toiletries, and she shamelessly used much more than she usually would. As revitalising as the shower was, she got out of it after just a few minutes and picked one of the many towels to dry off.

"Yuck!" she made a face as she picked up her old clothes again. Just as she was dressed, she heard the door to her cabin open. Her attention darted at the sound and she saw two bodyguards entering, followed by a man in a white tunic with a keffiyeh and agal. Natascha did not recognise him, but she knew she should not trust those dark, threatening eyes. Prince Tarek smiled devilishly as he glided towards her.

- *28* -

On board the private yacht *Cloud Dancer*, Port Hercule, Monaco, Wednesday, July 30

"Any other ideas?" Brian asked and looked around his team, awaiting an answer.

"Maybe Ariel has something he can mix. It is just too stupid that we didn't think about it sooner", Gunnar Eriksson commented.

"As far as I remember, he has to mix it just before you use it, and it is not without a certain risk either", the retired admiral explained and stared at the carpet as if it could give him an answer.

"I don't give a damn about the risk. If he doesn't tell us where my wife is, I will go down and beat it out of him", Nick complained, pacing the state room. Understandably, his agitation had reached a level that kept him at the edge of losing self-control.

"I hear you, son, I hear you, but trust me, you won't get far by beating him", Brian noted and glanced absentmindedly at his knuckles.

"Maybe not, but I would certainly feel better." Nick snapped back. There was no point in arguing with Nick now. The admiral knew that the former member of the German GSG 9 was right and just made a face as their attention was drawn to heavy footsteps on the stairs.

"Sir, you should come quickly. I don't know what Shira and Talia are doing to him, but Rowan is squealing like a pig. I tried to check, but they locked the door from the inside", an exhausted Ole-Einar shouted. As if they had just waited for the signal, they all jumped up and started to the stairs.

"Someone go and find Ariel", Brian shouted as he rushed down the stairs first, Nick close on his heels. "I should have seen that coming", the retired admiral complained. "Shira and Talia were both all so innocent when we left. I should have known that they were up to something. And how the bloody hell did she sober up so quickly?" Brian pulled the last door open and almost tripped in his step when he saw Shira and Talia standing giggling in front of the aft storage room.

"What is going on here?" Brian demanded to know, approaching them so cautiously as if he was navigating a destroyer through a mine field. It was only now that they could hear Rowan screaming from the top of his lungs, even over the loud noise of the ship's diesel engines and generators. Hearing his agony, the retired admiral was not even sure if he really wanted to know.

"We are interrogating Rowan." Shira simply explained and couldn't help but laugh at Rowan's new wave of frantic screams.

"How? What are you doing to him? Who is in there?" Brian demanded to know and pointed at the door.

"We brought in an expert", Shira smiled and exchanged a quick look with Talia, who couldn't hold back another fit of laughter.

"An expert? I thought I made it clear that we would handle this ourselves?" Brian raised his voice, unable to hide his concern.

"Oh, no worries, he is very reliable. Walter won't talk", Shira laughed. Talia was laughing so hard that tears ran down her face.

"*Walter*? Who the bloody hell is Walter?" Brian demanded to know and looked at Nick, but he just shrugged and shook his head.

"Yes, Walter", Talia answered enthusiastically and opened the door.

"Dear Lord in heaven", Brian exclaimed as he and Nick took a retreating step back at the unexpected sight. Their eyes fell on a gigantic goliath bird-eater tarantula. Its species being one of the largest spiders on Earth, Walter had no problem holding on comfortably, sitting exactly where Talia had put him minutes ago; on top of Rowan's head. Four of his legs had found a comfortable footing in Rowan's face, while the remaining four legs rested securely on his ears and the back of his head. The louder Rowan screamed, the firmer Walter held on. The Briton could not see everybody staring at him, his arachnophobia currently making him experience the ninth circle of his personal inner hell. His frantic screams were so loud that Shira's ears started to hurt.

"Stop screaming or he'll bite you in your face! Don't forget that he's one of the deadliest spiders in the world. One bite from him and his venom will dissolve all your tissue. It will take days before you die, but the agonising pain of the flesh falling off your skull will make you beg for a fast and merciful death." Shira yelled over Rowan's frantic screams, but the British playboy was hyperventilating now. The Israeli closed the door again to leave Rowan alone with his worst nightmare, before turning her attention to the admiral again.

"Walter?" Brian wasn't too certain if what he had just witnessed was really happening.

"Yes, Walter", Shira laughed and looked at Talia.

"He's actually my pet. He's totally harmless, but Rowan doesn't know that", the young Israeli explained.

"Alba told us about Rowan's arachnophobia, so we thought it couldn't hurt to bring Walter along", Shira added and looked at the door again. The muffled sound of Rowan's screams was still clearly audible.

"That monster has a name?" Ole-Einar asked. His passion for Walter was not nearly on the same level as Talia's.

"Of course it has a name", Talia hissed back feeling insulted.

"Is it working?" Brian cautiously asked.

"We haven't asked him any questions yet. We just went in and told him what a horrible death he will suffer should he get bitten. Then we sat Walter on his head and left", Shira explained and looked at Talia.

"We should probably get back in there. I don't want him to hurt Walter", Talia said. The concern for her beloved pet started to grow.

"You let her keep a giant tarantula in your house?" Brian asked with sudden realisation and looked at Nick.

"In all honesty, I didn't know that anything was in that terrarium", Nick said to his defence.

"He is nocturnal. And sometimes she lets him out of the terrarium", Shira explained and disappeared with Talia through the door before Nick had a chance to fully process the information. With images of his young daughter petting a gigantic tarantula fresh in his mind, the two Israeli closed the door behind them and turned towards Rowan.

Still screaming from the top of his lungs, the young Briton looked at the two women, not certain what new horrors were waiting for him. To keep their bluff and Rowan's horror alive, Talia donned a pair of heavy rubber gloves before she carefully picked up her pet again. She could have sworn that Walter, if he could, would have sighed with relief for finally getting off that uncomfortable place. It still took Rowan a couple more minutes to calm down. His eyes were glued on the cardboard box where Talia had securely placed Walter.

"Hey!" Shira snapped her fingers right in front of his eyes to get his attention. Still panting, Rowan eventually looked at the young Israeli. His face was still as red as the fire extinguisher beside the door. Shira opened a bottle of water in front of him, inserted a straw and took a sip before she offered it to him.

"Here! Drink something!" She told him and watched as he emptied half the bottle.

"So, here is the situation. We know that Natascha is on *Asklepios* and that you are in over your ears in an illegal trafficking ring for young women and human organs, so do not play any games with us. Understood?"

"Yes..." Rowan asked and nodded, still gasping for air.

"Natascha! Where exactly is she and where is *Asklepios*?" Shira wanted to know, but Rowan frantically shook his head. "Talia! Get the spider out again!" the Israeli immediately said.

"NO!" Rowan yelled, his eyes focussed on Talia who donned the gloves again as she turned towards the cardboard box. "Natascha is no longer on *Asklepios*! I swear!"

"What do you mean?" Shira asked. Talia brought the cardboard box closer to Rowan, her hand at the cover.

"WHAT I SAID! She is no longer on *Asklepios*."

"Is she still alive?" Shira shouted and grabbed Rowan's head.

"Yes...yes...yes! She is still alive. I swear."

"Where the hell is she?" Shira yelled, but Rowan had to swallow. Whatever time it took for him to come up with an answer, it was too long for Shira. She just nodded at Talia, and the young Israeli immediately opened the box and reached in to take a petrified Walter out again. Poor Walter had absolutely no interest in getting close to that obnoxious human being again and made that very clear by raising his front legs in a threatening display. His legs now only centimetres away from Rowan's face, the Briton feared for his life again.

"She is on another ship!"

"Where?" Walter feared as much for his life as Rowan did, and his legs were almost touching Rowan's face. The arachnid was determined to not get eaten by the human with the large open mouth right in front of him and spread his fangs, ready to fight.

"Right here in Monte Carlo. My friend's ship." Rowan's voice broke off, and his body stiffened as the next panic attack started to overcome him.

"What's the name of the ship?" Four of Walter's legs now touched Rowan's face.

"*Shad-*" Rowan started, but he passed out before he could relay the information.

"What a wimp!" Shira noted as Talia set Walter back in his box where he immediately retreated in a corner, glad to have not been eaten.

"Can we wake him up again?" Talia asked and watched Shira slapping Rowan's face. His face tilted to the other side from the force.

"He is out cold again. That might take a while. Let's tell the others what we know." Shira suggested and already opened the door, where an expecting crowd waited for them.

"And?" Brian asked impatiently.

"He is out cold again, but we could confirm that Natascha is still alive-" a sigh of relief went through the crowd, "but no longer on *Asklepios*."

"Where is she?" Nick demanded immediately, searching them for the answer.

"He said that she is right here in Monte Carlo on a friend's ship. We asked him for a name, but he only said *Shad* before he passed out."

"*Shad?* Strange name for a ship. Let's get our girl back. Rolf, you keep an eye on that wimp. Make sure that he stays where he is. Nick, you're with me!" Brian added as everybody rushed upstairs.

Following Brian's request to stay behind, Alba had been kind enough to fill Iain in on some details. As she had predicted, the action movie star calmed down significantly after his initial anger had subsided.

"I really hope that I can help find her", he shook his head and swirled the orange juice in his hands.

"I am very confident. They are really good at what they do."

"I know, they worked for me before, but I guess you already know that", Iain smiled at the beautiful Spanish woman. Their conversation was cut short when the whole gang appeared in the state room again.

"Any luck?" Iain asked, rising to his feet.

"Yes! She is no longer on that damn hospital ship, but she is now on a ship here in Monte Carlo. He must have dropped her off last night when he arrived. He passed out again before he could tell us the full name of the ship, but it is something with *Shad*. Does that ring a bell?" Brian asked Iain. The movie star made a face, stood up and took a look outside at some of the other yachts.

"Not really. I am here quite often, but I don't pay any attention to the other ships that much. I could go and ask the harbour master. They know me."

"Good idea. Go! Talia, Jack, you both go with him! Ariel! Over here!" Brian ordered and turned on the multi-function display. Iain was so excited to be part of the action that he didn't object. Instead, he showed his famous boyish grin as he followed Talia and Jack outside.

"Come on, come on, come on!" the retired admiral nervously tapped the top of the screen as the GPS and navigational charts came alive. "Okay, here is what we do. Until we hear back from the harbour master, I want you to spread out and look for any large yacht that comes close to that bloody name. Shira and Ole-Einar, you two cover Quai Rainier III. Go! Gunnar and Noah, you check out Quai Antoine!" Brian showed the locations on the monitor as his team members started rushing off the yacht.

"Ariel and Olaf, you check out Quai Louis II." The retired admiral didn't have to say anything else. By the time he looked up only Nick and Alba were with him. "Nick! I have seen some paper charts here somewhere. Find them and put stickers with our teams on the respective locations. I want to move fast once we have identified the ship. Alba!"

"Yes, sir?" the Spaniard answered, automatically falling in the habit of addressing Brian as sir.

"You do not have to call me sir. Do you remember Rowan mentioning a ship with that name? Anything that comes close to it?" Alba stared outside the window but finally shook her head.

"I'm sorry, but I don't remember that name at all", she sourly admitted.

"It is either *Shade* or *Shadow of the Orient*", Nick suddenly shouted.

"How do you know that? Are you sure?" Brian was clearly surprised.

"I remember Rowan telling me and Ole-Einar during that gala about it. He was totally drunk, but that's the name he used. He said it is a party boat and that he could get us in."

"Finalmente!" Alba cursed and closed her eyes.

"That doesn't sound good", Brian commented as the Spaniard shook her head over her own stupidity.

"Nick is right. *Shadow of the Orient* is the name of his friend's yacht, but there is more."

"Okay, just hold on a second! First we have to figure out where she is", Brian instructed and issued a group call over the two-way cell-phone to inform them of the new development

"The *Shadow of the Orient* is a much larger yacht than this, almost twice the size, but there is more!" Alba explained and shook her head in horror.

"What is it?" Brian and Nick asked in unison.

"It is Tarek. He owns the *Shadow of the Orient*", Alba almost spit the name out as she thought of the person who had almost killed her.

"Wait a second! Are you telling me that Rowan handed my wife over to that perverted monster?" Nick cried aloud, his face reflecting the horror he felt inside.

"Si!"

"We deal with that later, Nick!" Brian instructed before he forwarded the information. When he turned around seconds later, Nick was gone. All he could hear were his footsteps on the stairs leading below deck.

"Bollocks!" Brian cursed and ran after him, leaving a dumbfounded Alba behind.

Less than a hundred metres away, Shira and Ole-Einar exchanged a look as they listened to Brian over the cellphone.

"Dammit! That's not good. Let's hope she's still somewhere close", Shira hissed and looked around, but Ole-Einar already started running down the pier. They would have to run all around the harbour to get to Quai Rainier III, which would take them at least several minutes.

"You're not coming?" Ole-Einar shouted as he looked back.

"Come this way! I got an idea!" Shira shouted back and started to run westwards. It only took them a little over a minute before they stopped at the end of the Quai.

Panting, Shira stared over the water to the other side of the port, where Quai Rainier III was located. Her instincts were right. Most of the large vessel were either docked right at Quai Rainier III, or anchored outside.

"Can you read any of the names, Ole?" Shira asked and walked up and down the edge of the pier to get a better look at the names of the ships that were little over one hundred metres away. Although it was almost one o'clock in the morning, Port Hercule was brightly lit by hundreds of flood lights, giving almost daylight conditions.

"Some of them, but nothing that comes close to what we are looking for", the huge Norwegian shook his head in frustration. "Come on, give us a break!"

"I don't think she's still here. With her size, we should easily see her", Shira summarised and radioed the other teams, only to hear the disappointment in their voice that they had not been successful either.

"Maybe they left earlier today?" Ole-Einar wondered out loud and scanned the horizon.

"Wouldn't the harbour master know about that, or?" Shira wanted to know.

"Hm...not necessarily. They technically have to notify them, but that doesn't mean that they are actually doing it. I assume that a Saudi prince has a standing tab and pretty good credit card. Chances are slim that they even bother contacting him when he is leaving."

"Is there a way to find out?" Shira asked impatiently, her eyes now focussed on several dots on the horizon.

"There might be! The *Cloud Dancer* might be able to pick her up on the radar. Let's get back to the yacht!" Ole-Einar shouted and already started sprinting eastwards towards their yacht while Shira shared the information over the cellphone.

Brian was unaware of what was going on outside. Rushing downstairs he had totally forgotten his cell phone on the bridge.

"I hope he doesn't do anything stupid", the retired admiral muttered as he opened the door to the corridor leading to the aft storage cabin. His hopes that Rolf would have stopped Nick didn't materialise either. Nick's friend and colleague still stood guard at the storage cabin, but the door was now open. Even from the distance, Brian could easily hear the fight.

"What about following a direct order these days?" the retired admiral snarled at Rolf as he got closer and squeezed past the former German Kampfschwimmer.

"I did. You ordered me to keep an eye on the asshole and make sure he doesn't go anywhere. He is still there", Rolf shrugged his shoulder and pushed the door open to make some room for his boss.

"Smart ass!" Brian hissed back and turned his attention to Nick before he could beat Rowan to death. Although Nick had untied Rowan first, the outcome was still the same. Holding Rowan with his left hand, Nick pressed the Briton tight against the steel wall, delivering strikes to his face with his right elbow. Rowan's face was already poorly swollen, blood running from several open gushes and a broken nose.

"What...the...fuck...have...you...done...to...my...wife?" Nick screamed from the top his lungs, each word followed by another elbow strike. All the frustration, his fear for Natascha, the uncertainty, the sleepless nights, all his nightmares, he put everything in those strikes. "Where...the...hell...is...she?" He screamed again, but Rowan was already unconscious, unable to answer. It didn't matter to Nick, he wasn't finished with Rowan yet.

"That's enough, Nick!" Brian's calm voice stopped him, before he could deliver another strike. Nick felt the gentle touch of Brian's hand on his shoulder, but his eyes remained locked on Rowan. Instead of punching him, Nick grabbed Rowan with both hands and tossed him to the ground, where the playboy rolled on his stomach and moaned.

"It's okay, son. Go upstairs and clean yourself up", Brian suggested and padded Nick on his shoulder. "You got blood all over you", he added with a smile as Nick finally turned around and looked down at the retired admiral.

"If...I promise you...I will kill him!" Nick promised with a fire burning deep in his eyes. He turned on his heel and kicked the chair into the corner before he left the storage room.

"Yeah, go figure", Brian sighed once he heard Nick's footsteps fading in the corridor. He waited a couple more moments to make sure that Rowan was not seriously injured, but a broken jaw and broken nose seemed to be the worst of his injuries. The Briton slowly rolled around, covering his face in his hands.

"If you have something to say that could help us to get her back, now would be a good moment", Brian whispered coldly, but Rowan didn't show any reaction. "Next time, I won't stop him", the retired admiral calmly added before he left the storage cabin.

"I'm sorry, sir. If it does make a difference, I would have stopped him soon enough", Rolf apologised in a low voice. The retired admiral knew that Nick's friend was sincere.

"No need to be sorry!" Brian commented and closed the door to the storage cabin behind him.

"Sir?" Rolf wasn't sure if he had heard him correctly.

"It was my fault. You were right. I should have been more specific with my instructions. You just followed my orders. You didn't do anything wrong", Brian winked at him and slowly walked down the corridor towards the stairs. "Don't go in there by yourself. Who knows what he is up to? I will send someone down shortly and you can fix him up and tie him to the chair again."

"Send Nick", Rolf laughed, but the retired admiral didn't respond to that. He was already wondering what his people would have found out. He entered the bridge almost at the same time as Ole-Einar.

"Talk to me!" Brian barked at the Norwegian and walked to pick up his radio.

"Doesn't look like the *Shadow* is still in the port, but there are several large yachts at the horizon. Not sure if they signed out with the harbour master, but maybe the radar can pick something up."

"Good thinking!" Brian complimented and immediately went to the multi-functional screen to activate the radar. "We might need to..." he started and looked at the other yachts right beside him, blocking his radar. "Ole, if the *Shadow* is no longer in port, then there is no reason for us to be here either. Did we hear anything from the harbour master yet?"

"No, sir, but they are talking to them as we speak."

"Okay, good." Brian commented and prepared to start the engines.

"Where is Nick?" Ole-Einar sounded concerned as he looked around. It was only now that he noticed his friend's absence. His eyes rested on Alba, but the Spaniard just looked at Brian instead.

"I assume he is in his cabin. He has to clean himself up." Brian noted dryly and briefly glanced at Shira, who just arrived.

"Why is he cleaning himself up?" Ole-Einar asked curiously.

"Because he was covered in blood", the retired admiral kept explaining as he pressed another row of buttons.

"Sir?"

"He got his hands on Rowan."

Shira and Ole-Einar exchanged a concerned look.

"How the hell did that happen?" the Israeli inquired.

"Ah, I don't know", Brian shrugged his shoulders. "Didn't pay attention for a second and he was gone. Nick gave him a decent beating, that's all."

"But how-" Shira started, but Brian cut her off. "Once Nick heard that Natascha is with that psychopath, he ran downstairs and beat Rowan to a pulp, which I personally totally understand. Do you have a problem with that, Shira?" Brian asked and raised his voice, his eyes now resting on the Israeli.

"No, sir, I do not", the Israeli apologetically smiled. She couldn't blame Nick or the admiral for what had happened. She knew that Brian had a soft spot for Natascha, especially after the fiasco in the North-West Passage. Besides, Shira would have done the same thing. The signal tone from their cell phones announced an incoming group call.

"Yes, Whittaker here. What is the news?"

"So we have been at the harbour master and according to him, the *Shadow of the Orient* was at anchor outside the bay, but left late this afternoon."

"Bollocks!" Brian cursed and looked at the open sea. "Did they file a plan or did they say if they will be back?"

"They were heading south, down the Italian coast line. There is a chance they are setting course for the Suez Canal."

"Of course they are heading south. We are in Monaco", the retired admiral mumbled. "Okay, everybody come back to the yacht now. We got to go to plan B." Brian Whittaker ordered. Just couple of hundred metres away, Iain Walker started running down the Qaui with his famous, big boyish grin. He had no idea what plan B meant for his multi-million dollar yacht, but he could not contain his excitement.

West of Al-Hasakah, Syria, Wednesday, July 30
Monique had no idea how long she had been running for, or how far she had gotten

away. Her fear of what would happen to her if recaptured had fuelled her battered body for the last couple of hours. The young French didn't even know where she was running, as long as it was away from her capturers and their camp. Looking at the sun rising in the East, she stopped for a moment, trying to catch her breath. By now the rasping feeling in her throat had become a constant pain, and her headaches had also gotten worse.

Must be the dehydration, Monique thought and took her water bottle. She knew better, but still refused to believe that she was infected. She shook the water bottle and realised that she was down to the last few sips. She decided to save it for later in the day, when the sun would burn mercilessly onto the desert sand. The first warming rays of sunlight started touching her, but her body refused to warm up. It was only now that she noticed how much she was shivering. She first blamed it on the adrenaline from her escape, but she couldn't deny that she was freezing. She looked up to the sun, convinced that she would warm up soon.

Five more minutes, then I got to go again, she told herself and stared at a mountain range in the distance. Monique knew that by now her escape must have been noticed, but she had no idea if they would even bother chasing after her or not. As far as she was concerned, the desert warriors had a much bigger problem at their hands than her escape. No matter what, Monique was determined not to take the risk, and the little mountain range in the distance could provide her with the much needed cover to hide during the day. Although she was freezing now, she would not risk running in the heat of the day, unexposed and easy to be spotted over long distances. Not that she considered what she was doing as running, she thought as she continued her trot. By now she was so weak that it was nothing more than a walk, but she kept pushing herself to move on.

Her eyes were set at the mountain range as she continued her journey, her feet kicking little stones and swirling up the dust as she moved forward. After two more hours she stopped again and drank the rest of her water. The hot wind was blowing in her face, accelerating her dehydration. Looking back, she was satisfied not to see any followers. Her hands were shaking so bad that it was difficult for her to take the bread out of the pocket in the blanket. She ate the little bit that was left, her gaze wandering up to the mountain range again. A feeling of disappointment came over her as she noticed that she had barely covered any distance in the last couple hours. It was now late in the morning, and the sun burned down without any mercy, but she was still freezing and shivering, which only fuelled her frustration. Monique tried to take a couple deep breaths, but the pain in her throat made that difficult. She had to cough. With each cough, her headache also seemed to get worse. Just as she opened her eyes again, she noticed the sun reflecting on something in the near distance, between her and the mountain range. People!

Shit! They are coming for me! Monique had a hard time not to panic and looked around. She was under no illusion that she could run away from anyone in her current condition, but with a little bit of luck, she should be able to hide. There were enough large boulders around her that could provide some cover. Monique burst into tears when she looked up again, but there was no mistake. The people were much closer than she had previously thought. Even over the distance she counted at least five or six. The young woman had no idea why she was doing it, as they had probably already seen her, but she immediately dropped down to the ground and crawled to a nearby boulder for some cover. There was even a little space between the boulder and the ground for her to crawl into. Certainly not enough to hide her completely, but it was better than nothing. Rubbing her blanket and what had been given to her as a burka in the dirt to better blend in, she risked one last peek around the large rock and her heart missed a beat. The group was definitely coming towards her. They must have seen her.

The young French didn't waste another second and squeezed in underneath the large rock. Monique even kept her eyes closed as she waited for what would happen next. At first the warm sand felt comfortable, and it helped her to stop shivering, but now she was freezing uncontrollably again.

Oh my God, please let them go by! Monique prayed and fought hard to remain still. She had no idea where the people were, but she knew they had to be somewhere close by now. Monique decided to stay in this position until the middle of the night just to be safe. She concentrated on her breathing, trying hard not to cough. The minutes slowly past by, but Monique had lost her sense of time. Her head was hidden underneath her dirty blanket that still smelled like that old tent, but she still didn't dare to risk a glance. Instead she concentrated on listening to her surroundings, trying to identify footsteps or some chatter maybe, but there was nothing. It seemed eerily silent, and she felt that maybe they had passed by already. Then suddenly, unexpectedly, she heard the burst of a male voice yelling in Arab. Her blood froze instantaneously. She didn't understand what the guy said, but it didn't matter. They had found her.

- *29* -

***Shadow of the Orient*, Mediterranean Sea, south of Monaco, Wednesday, July 30**
After a couple hours of sleep Natascha restlessly paced through her luxurious cabin. Her mind was spinning around the warning Prince Tarek had told her a few hours ago. No one had touched her, but Prince Tarek had given her a very graphic speech about what would happen to her should she dare to leave her cabin or try to signal for help. It was clear to her that, excluding the accommodations, her situation had not improved at all, but Natascha was now more determined than ever to not go down without a fight.

During the morning, some of Prince Tarek's men had covered the cabin's window from the outside, making it impossible for her to see what was going on outside or to use the light as an SOS signal. Natascha noticed that they didn't lock her cabin door when they left, but she decided it would be smart to heed his warning for now.

"You can bet that it is a trap to test you", she told herself as she threw a hateful glance at the door. She was convinced that one of Prince Tarek's goons stood guard on the other side. As soon as they had left her, Natascha found something that she could use as a wedge to block the door from the inside. It wouldn't stop anyone from coming in, but it would definitely slow them down.

"Okay, we got sunny-boy and at least two goons", Natascha recapitulated as she tried to figure out how many adversaries she was dealing with. She considered the size of the yacht and the size of the crew it would take to run it, but the more she thought about it, the more discouraged she got.

"Damn, that's not going to work", she concluded and made a face, still pacing her cabin as she started to work on another plan. A quick look at the alarm clock told her that it was almost noon, which explained why she felt hungry again. Just as she walked over to the fridge, someone knocked at the door. Natascha frowned. From all the things she expected, someone actually knocking at the door certainly was not one of them.

"Okay, that's weird", Natascha commented and quickly walked over to remove the wedge before she opened the door. She was further surprised when she saw two young Arabian women, each carrying a tray with food, enter her cabin. Natascha was literally lost for words when the two women, both dressed in traditional hijabs, just walked in and placed the trays on the table.

"Okay, hm, thank you, I guess", Natascha tried to be polite. Her intuition told her that the two women didn't like her very much. The hateful look they threw at her only confirmed her theory. With the door still open, Natascha immediately took the chance to risk a peek, but one of Tarek's goons blocked her instantly. He didn't say anything, but his sheer presence was enough for Natascha to back off.

"I was just wondering if it's possible to get some fresh air. Someone has blocked my window", she smiled at him, but the guy didn't even flinch a muscle in his face. Natascha had no idea that this was the same guy who Shira had stabbed in the leg days earlier in Alba's condo. She had also no idea that Prince Tarek had briefed everyone from the captain to the kitchen-staff about what Natascha had done to several guards on *Asklepios,* and that they were allowed to use any force necessary to stop her should she try to escape. To have him guarding her cabin was Prince Tarek's idea of adding insult to injury to his former bodyguard for getting stabbed not only by a woman, but by an Israeli.

"I'll take that as a no", Natascha concluded and retreated back into her cabin, where she watched how the two women arranged the food on the table, and how they completely ignored her.

"Thank you!" Natascha smiled at them, but they avoided making eye contact with her as they left the cabin. Natascha waited to hear if they would lock the door this time, but was satisfied when they didn't. Even with the guard blocking her sight immediately, she had still had enough time to see that there was no fancy card reader or any other electromagnetic lock built into her door. She carefully placed the wedge under the door again before she walked to the table.

"Okay, what do we got here?" she wondered and started to pick up the covers from the different plates. Natascha raised her eyebrows at the sight of the delicious looking chicken. She smelled some spices she didn't know, and despite her situation she did not have the feeling that they had drugged her food. After all, Prince Tarek himself had explained to her why she was on his ship. Not that she trusted him, but he simply had no reason to lie to her on that matter. Natascha continued uncovering the remaining plates, satisfied to find a meal which would have cost her a fortune at any restaurant.

"Well, you always wanted to try the culinary arts of the Middle-East, might as well do it now", she told herself and sat down. She took her time eating, but her mind was already working on another escape plan. Natascha checked the trays again just to confirm that they had not provided her with any silverware.

"That would have been too much to ask, I guess", she complained and picked up the other chicken leg. She broke it apart and continued eating.

"Might as well go caveman style", she smiled and nibbled the meat off the bones. Natascha weighed her options and decided to wait a couple more hours until nightfall. She assumed that the skeleton staff would be on duty then, which could make things much easier for her. All she could accomplish until then was to get a couple hours of rest. Before she lay down in the comfortable bed, she positioned both trays with all the plates and bowls right against the door. If someone would attempt to come in while she was sleeping, she would at least wake up. Satisfied with her improvised alarm system Natascha lay down and dimmed the lights by simply clapping her hands.

"Ah, one day you will be rich, too", she told herself and closed her eyes. Her body had not had any sleep rhythm at all during the last several days. Besides, her mind kept spinning about her next attempt to escape, which didn't help either. Lying in bed she noticed her headache coming back. It didn't bother her too much yet, but she hoped that it would be gone by the time she would wake up later.

"So much for exotic spices", Natascha complained as she felt a rasping pain in her throat.

West of Al-Hasakah, Syria, Wednesday, July 30
It took Monique all her willpower not to scream. *Maybe they are talking to each other*, she hoped, but she knew better. The men repeated the command in Arab, but even now Monique could hear the clear accent in his voice. She still didn't dare to move, not willing to accept certain defeat.

"Hey, show me your hands or I'll shoot", a male voice commanded now in English. For a moment Monique was totally petrified, images of the British mercenary in the camp flashing up in her mind, but she finally obeyed and stuck both hands out from underneath her blanket.

"Don't shoot!" she begged and started to crawl out from her hiding spot.

"Freeze or I'll shoot! Don't move!" the same voice commanded again. The tone in his voice made it clear that he would not hesitate to kill her. "Don't move!" he repeated, and Monique could hear at least two people walking around her, but still in a safe distance. One of them kneeled down, concentrating on her hands.

"I do not see any wires, Captain", the person kneeling beside her commented and got up again. They increased the distance before ordering her to come out further.

Monique obeyed, but still had no idea who these people were and what they wanted.

"Stay on your knees! Put the blanket down slowly!" Monique did as she was told. The soldiers positioned themselves in a way that Monique had to look into the sun to see them. She blinked and covered her eyes, but still had a hard time recognising them.

"Please! You got to help me! They want to kill me!" Monique begged. For reasons unknown to her, she trusted these people.

"Just don't move, Ma'am, we just want to make sure you are not going to blow us all up."

"What?" Monique heard him, but she had no idea what he was talking about. Before she could ask him again, one of the soldiers came over and searched her.

"No wires or any signs of an IED, Captain", the soldier reported with a sigh of relief and took a few steps back without lowering his weapon.

"Who are you and what the bloody hell are you doing here?" the commanding officer asked her over the barrel of his assault rifle. Monique quickly looked around before she told them about her escape.

"Blimey! You are far away from home. Can you stand?"

"I think so, yes!"

"Ay-up, you can stand up slowly. Weapons down." Monique couldn't help but smile and slowly got back to her feet. Immediately a wave of nausea came over her, together with a pounding headache and the pain in her throat. She closed her eyes and had to hold on to the boulder to not fall down to the ground again.

"You okay, Ma'am?" the soldier asked.

"I don't think so. I...I believe that I'm sick", Monique shook her head and leaned against the rock. She wiped her forehead and shook her head. Blinded by a bright red light, she had to close her eyes. "Ouch, what was that?" she wanted to know. Instead of answering her, the soldier whispered in his radio.

"Serge, stand down. Subject is friendly, scene is secure."

"Roger that. I told you she is a friendly. That's five quid, Captain", another voice answered over the radio. The sniper and his spotter were over one kilometre away, covering their comrades from their nest on the high ground in the mountain range.

"Which I will gladly pay, mate. Keep an eye out there for us, will you?"

"Roger that."

"Ma'am, my name is Callum Finlay, I am a captain of the British SAS."

"You are what?" Monique asked. She had never heard of the SAS before.

"The good guys, Ma'am. We are the good guys. We are searching for that camp you escaped from. I have a feeling you can help us find it." Captain Finlay explained, but Monique didn't care. All she had heard was him saying *the good guys.* For the first time in weeks she sighed with relief and sank down to the ground again.

"Ma'am? Are you okay?" Alistair Brooks asked and kneeled beside her. "I'm a medic. Let me see if there is something we can do for you."

"Make it quick, Doc. We have to get back to cover", Captain Finlay reminded him and nervously looked around. "Serge, how is it looking?" he asked his sniper over the radio again.

"All green. You are good", Sergeant Fergus MacRory informed him from behind his laser sights.

"Don't touch me!" Monique shook her head as Major Brooks wanted to check her vitals. The Major exchanged a quick look with his captain.

"I just want to help you. This is hostile territory and we have to get back to some cover. We have to move fast", the British doctor explained to her, but Monique just shook her head, tears running down her cheeks.

"You can't touch me. I don't know what it is, but I am sick. I'm dying. They are all dying", Monique cried. Even Major Finlay, who had seen his share of conflicts, stood there with his mouth open, as he and his perplexed team listened to Monique's story.

On board the private yacht *Cloud Dancer*, south of Monaco, Wednesday, July 30

"When they told me you were in the navy, they didn't mention anything that you had been in command of a battle cruiser", Iain commented dryly as he sat beside Brian on the bridge. He brought a cup of tea for the retired admiral and an energy drink for himself.

"Cheers", Brian smiled and took the tea. He used the spoon to swirl the slice of lemon in it as his eyes scanned the horizon. It was now just after noon, and their radar had picked up the *Shadow of the Orient* just a few hours earlier. According to his calculations it would take them until later in the night before they would be in a position to execute their plan. Brian double checked their position to the *Shadow of the Orient* and was satisfied that his plotted course was still correct. With nothing else to do but wait everybody else had gone to their cabins to find some sleep. Executing their plan of action would require their total concentration.

"Yes, I have been on ships most of my active career", the retired admiral said and shared some of his experience with the movie star as he leaned back in the captain's chair. He still felt guilty for literally highjacking his multi-million dollar yacht, but it turned out that Alba had been right. Iain obviously started to enjoy his shot at this real life adventure without having the slightest idea about the possible consequences of these actions. He and Brian spent the next hour sharing some stories before their subject shifted to the yacht's technical details. Iain still couldn't believe how fast the retired admiral had moved his beloved *Cloud Dancer* out of the harbour last night.

"Man, this is the first time I am on my yacht without the original crew to run it", Iain shook his head. "I should do this more often", he laughed.

"Oh, by all means, you might as well take the command. After all, she is your ship", Brian laughed and stood up to switch places with Iain. The forty-two year old movie star laughed like a little child in a candy store as he took his seat in the captain's chair, checking all the instruments.

"Anything I have to watch out for?" he wanted to know.

"Not really, she is running on auto pilot at the moment. We just have to pass the *Shadow* well on starboard at some point before night fall. But she is going pretty fast, so we have to stay on this course for a couple more hours", Brian explained and leaned back.

While Brian introduced Iain to the navigational system of his own yacht, Nick lay awake in his bunk below deck. He had not left his cabin since he had given Rowan a beating. Following Brian's advice, he had taken a long shower not only to clean himself up, but also to calm down. By the time he was finished, the *Cloud Dancer* was already moving and Shira had visited his cabin to update him on the latest development. Surprisingly, Nick had managed to get a couple of hours of sleep. He knew what was at stake. Now, hours later, Ole-Einar and Rolf, with whom he shared the cabin, had just left when Shira knocked at the door. She didn't even wait for him to say anything and just opened the door. Nick knew that either Ole-Einar or Rolf must have asked her to check on him. He didn't mind it, they both only wanted what was best for him, and Nick preferred talking to Shira over anyone else. She had always been there for him, and Natascha was like a sister to her.

"Are you awake?" the Israeli asked as she peeked into the cabin.

"Sure, come in", Nick invited her and made some room on his bed. Shira made herself comfortable right beside him and closed her eyes for a few moments to relax.

"I fixed up Rowan. You broke his nose. He is also missing a tooth or two", Shira tiredly informed Nick.

"Yeah, well, he still has a heartbeat. I'm not losing any sleep over him. Tell me something I care about."

"We are gaining on the *Shadow*. Tonight is the night, Nick. Are you ready?"

"Not the first time I'm chasing after my wife, held hostage on a ship, isn't it?" Nick mocked, thinking back to the events that had happened in the North-West-Passage a couple of years ago.

"True, but this time you're not coming back from the dead, and we'll all be there right from the beginning", Shira tried to comfort him.

"Yes, but we have no idea what we are up against", Nick sourly stated. Shira knew that he had a valid point, but there was nothing they could do about it.

"We do have the element of surprise. We definitely have the advantage", the

Israeli noted, her eyes still closed.

"I only hope that-" Nick started, but he had to choke. He instinctively held Shira's hand. A tear ran down his face as he thought of Natascha. They were so close to her, yet so far away.

"Don't even go there, Nick. She is still alive. I know it!"

"How can you know? It has been too long!" Nick sobbed.

"I can feel it, Nick." Shira stated in a tone that left no room for doubt. Nick couldn't share her level of confidence and shook his head. Neither of them spoke for the next few minutes and before long, Nick could hear Shira's faint snoring beside him. For some reason, her presence gave him enough hope that he also dozed off again. It was not until late in the afternoon when a gentle knock at the cabin door woke them both up.

"Sorry, but the admiral wants us on the bridge in thirty minutes", Talia smiled at them.

"Thanks!" Shira yawned and stretched. "What is it?" she asked Nick, who made a face once the young Israeli left.

"It's Talia. She..." Nick started but just shook his head. He didn't know how to explain it. For some reason it felt wrong to him.

"You mean she reminds you of Natascha?" Shira helped him.

"Yes, she does a lot. It is not that I...it is just difficult...now...Every time I see her I see Natascha, it is just...." Nick stuttered. He had no idea how to explain it.

"I know. The girls were making fun of their resemblances since day one. She does indeed look like a younger sister of her", Shira laughed. "Don't feel bad about it. Talia knows how you feel", Shira tried to reassure him.

"She knows? How does she know?"

"Nick, just because she is the youngest does not mean that she's stupid", Shira yawned again and rose from the bed. "Okay, I'll go to my cabin and get a shower. Let's make sure we can get a bite to eat before the action starts", the Israeli said as another yawn parted her lips.

Within twenty minutes everybody sat in the large state room, having some snacks. Brian looked into everyone's eyes before he started.

"Ladies, Gentlemen. We passed the *Shadow of the Orient* about one hour ago, and if she stays on her course, we will be in position just after midnight", the retired admiral paused for a second to let the information set in. "Before I get into the details, I have to stress it again that what we are about to do is nothing less than an act of-" Brian continued, but from all his employees, it was Talia who cut him off.

"Sir, you are wasting time. We all know what we are doing here and what is about to happen. Let's leave the peace talks to someone else and let us get our sister back."

For most in the state room it was the first time that they saw Brian Whittaker lost for words. It took the retired admiral a couple of seconds to recover. The expression on everyone's face made it clear that they all agreed with the young Israeli.

"Okay then", he finally smiled. "Klaus was able to get some blue prints of the *Shadow of the Orient*. Before that son of a bitch bought the yacht couple of years ago, she was available for charter. We have no idea if she has been rebuilt on the inside or not, but at least we will have an idea. Ariel, Gunnar, Jack and I already came up with a plan. Gunnar and Jack, you have Team One with Nick, Noah and Rolf. Our two Vikings are team two. Ariel and Shira, you are team three. Any questions so far?" Brian briskly asked before he spent the next hour explaining the details of their upcoming rescue attempt.

"Oh, there is one more thing", he said just as everyone got up to prepare themselves. They all froze and looked at him. "Gunnar, Jack", Brian addressed his two senior team leaders while he still studied the blue prints of the *Shadow of the Orient*.

"Yes?" Jack MacDonald, former British SAS Team Leader and Gunnar Eriksson, former instructor of the Norwegian Navy Special Operations Commando exchanged a glance. Brian finally looked at them.

"Just in case this whole bloody operation goes south, I need you to do something for me."

Asklepios, Aegean Sea, Thursday, July 31

Dr Sheridan Evans knocked at L.J.'s cabin. She found it challenging to find the right balance between just waking Mr Jackson up and scaring him to death. A quick look at her watch showed that it was almost one in the morning. The physician leaned closer to the door to listen, but all she could hear was Mr Jackson's snoring. Sheridan made a face and knocked again, this time a little bit louder, but with the same result. Even when she knocked at the door again, all she got back in return was some more snoring.

"Screw this", Dr Evans mumbled and opened the door. She turned on the dimmer just enough to not wake the heavy Texan up abruptly. Instead, she carefully walked over to his bedside.

"Mr Jackson!" Dr Sheridan Evans whispered, but L.J. was still sleeping soundly. "Mr Jackson", she repeated, this time a little bit louder. She gently touched his shoulder. The Texan finally woke up, mumbling something before he recognised where he was and what had just happened.

"Dear Lord in heaven", he kept stuttering and looked at the watch on the nightstand. "This better be good. What happened?" he demanded to know as he sat up.

"Mr Gates sent me to get you. He received a code alpha message about ten minutes ago", Dr Evans quickly filled him in. That was all that it took to fully wake him up.

"Shit! Code alpha?" Leroy Jackson hoped that Dr Evans was wrong, but she had no reason to lie to him. "Damn! When did he receive the message? Ten minutes ago you said?" he asked while putting his morning robe over his pyjamas. He didn't even bother to change into his day clothes.

"That's about right, yes." Dr Evans confirmed and checked her watch again.

"Shit!" L.J. cursed and slipped into his slippers. "Any details?" he wanted to know as he followed the physician through the corridor. He could see that she shook her head.

"Mr Gates received the message on his private terminal in his cabin. I am just following his request to personally get you", Dr Evans shrugged without even looking back.

"Ah, yes, right", he simply said, but L.J. was so lost in his thoughts that he didn't hear her mild complaint about being used as a courier. Neither of them spoke again until they both stood in front of Mr Gates' cabin. Dr Evans gently knocked before she entered.

"I present Mr Jackson, as requested", the physician commented with disinterest in the task, but neither of the men cared or recognised it. She just shook her head again and left.

"Code alpha? What happened?" Leroy Jackson asked the second Dr Evans had closed the door.

"Sit", Jonathan Brown said with heavy breathing and looked at one of the chairs. L.J. knew his friend long enough to know that his was not a suggestion, but rather an order based on the severity of their situation. The Texan sat down and looked at his friend. Jonathan's face was all sweaty, and a quick glance at the monitors showed an elevated heart beat of almost one hundred and ten. Even the oxygen flow from the assisted breathing machine was much higher than normal. Whatever had happened, it must have been very serious to make Jonathan so nervous.

"Rowan! He is missing." Jonathan finally said, and even the voice computer couldn't mask the concern in his voice. L.J. took a few moments to digest the information. In his personal perfect world, he would be more than happy to get rid of that useless playboy, but his disappearance raised several questions, which, if answered truthfully, could jeopardise their whole operation. The Texan thought about all the different reasons why Rowan could be missing, but he somehow felt that there was more to it.

"I assume that he's not curing his hangover somewhere, right? What do we know?" he eventually asked, his eyes resting on Jonathan.

"Nothing for sure yet, our sources are still trying to figure out what exactly happened", Jonathan shook his head before he continued. "He didn't check in for an important appointment yesterday. His office couldn't reach him and his cell phone cannot be located." Jonathan paused for a moment to allow his breathing to get under control again. "He has last been seen leaving the casino in Monte Carlo with an unknown young woman", Jonathan sourly said, the anger dropping his voice almost to a hiss. L.J. shook his head. Although it was far from unusual for Rowan to pick up some random dates, something suddenly felt very wrong.

"How certain are we that she's not just another whore?" the Texan hoped for the impossible and leaned back, closing his eyes. He knew the answer already, but he wanted to hear it from Jonathan.

"Pretty certain. Rowan usually never leaves the casino with one of his dates. His suite has literally not been touched."

"Still, he could have just taken her somewhere else..." L.J. tried to find a reasonable explanation. He knew that Rowan would jump with both feet into a honey trap.

"His father called in the code alpha", Jonathan destroyed the little hope that Leroy had.

"Shit!" the Texan cursed and closed his eyes. "What about Natascha? Do we know if he delivered her to his friend?" L.J. inquired, but Jonathan didn't answer right away. The mentioning of his nemesis caused all his hatred to flare up again, which also increased both his heart rate and his breathing.

"Yes, he had securely delivered her without problems. He confirmed that late Tuesday night. There were no problems."

"Where is she now?"

"It seems that Tarek sticks to the agreement. His yacht has left Monaco and is heading towards the Suez Canal."

"Okay, at least we are rid of her." L.J. exhaled. It was certainly not what Jonathan wanted to hear, but they had to cut their losses. As much as he sympathised with his friend, Jonathan's private vendetta could not get in the way of their real operation.

"You think it was a professional job?" L.J. wanted to know.

"Yes, so does his father. They are well connected with the law enforcement in London, and they seem to think that it looks like that."

"Okay, prove it to me."

"Local law enforcement checked the hotel video surveillance. No one recognised the women Rowan left with. Usually his company is well known there. All the video surveillance outside the casino was interrupted just long enough for them to disappear."

"Oh dear Lord in heaven", Leroy Jackson sighed.

"He won't help us now. From what I know, Rowan's father is using his influence to get the British authorities involved."

"You think it could be someone looking for Natascha?"

"Could be, but how would they know?"

"True enough. That leaves the whore that walked out right from underneath his nose in Monaco. She must have told someone."

"Maybe, but why wouldn't they officially arrest Rowan and let Tarek sail away? No, whoever is after him is on a mission." Jonathan said. Even with the speech computer, the resignation was quite obvious in his voice.

"You think we should pull the plug?"

"The remaining women have to be shipped off immediately. We already know how devastating the disease is working. I don't think we have another choice." Jonathan decided. Neither of them spoke for the next couple of minutes as they processed the information again.

"Okay, let's do it", L.J. shook finally shook his head and waved his hands with resignation.

- *30* -

On board of *Shadow of the Orient*, Gulf of Hammamet, east of Tunis, Thursday, July 31

Hilal cursed as one of the red warning lights on the large instrument panel started flashing. His night shift had started just like any other night shift: without a problem, but now his attention focussed on the visual alarm. He put the magazine aside and rose from the captain's chair. At thirty-two years of age, Hilal could look back at an impressive career with the Royal Saudi Arabian Navy, where he had served his country for over a decade. He was proud of his achievements, especially at his young age, and everyone was certain that he was destined to receive his own command sooner rather than later. His career plans were put on hold when Prince Tarek turned to the Navy to pick his crew for his latest toy. Whether Hilal did or did not like the new assignment didn't matter, he knew that when someone like Prince Tarek requested his service, he'd better like it, and that's what he did. Right now, Hilal was more concerned about the visual alarm than his future career. The flashing light had already gotten the attention of another crew member, who also stepped closer to the instruments to take a look and to await orders. For now, Nabil just stood there silently as Hilal checked the different digital gauges and monitors.

"Hm, that is strange", the thirty-two year-old naval officer commented as he read the information on one of the monitors.

"What is it?" Nabil wanted to know.

"We got a vibration alarm at the starboard propeller. Nothing serious, but we have to check it out."

"What could it be? Mechanical failure?"

"No, most likely a fishing net or a drifting rope", Hilal explained and zoomed in on the radar to check if they had missed the contact of a radar reflector installed on a fishing net. All he could see was a party boat some distance away to their starboard side.

"But how can that happen? I thought the propellers were protected against such things?"

"They are, Nabil, they are, but that doesn't mean that it works all the time", Hilal explained to him as he stopped all engines. The *Shadow of the Orient* was now drifting in the sea.

"Shall I get the divers ready?" Nabil anticipated.

"Not for now. Let's go outside and have a look first, maybe we can see what caused the problem." Hilal turned towards the door and put on his cover before he left the bridge. Although he was assigned to the *Shadow of the Orient*, he was still officially a member of the Royal Saudi Arabian Navy and proudly wore their uniform.

The warm air of the Mediterranean Sea blew in his face as he stepped out into the night. A quick glance at his watch showed him that it was just after one in the morning. Heavy clouds covered the sky. His eyes scanned the horizon and the sea as he walked aft, but he couldn't see anything in this darkness. Convinced that this would only be a minor mishap, he finally leaned over the railing to see what was causing the vibration. Without looking up, Hilal took the powerful search light Nabil eagerly handed him. The naval officer closely inspected the water surface, hoping to see any indication of what could have caused this incident, but it didn't matter from which side he looked, he couldn't see anything.

"Hm, that is strange, can't see a damn thing", he finally mentioned more to himself as he turned the search light off again.

"No rope?" Nabil wanted to know.

"Not that I can see", Hilal admitted as he walked back to the bridge.

"What are we doing now? Should we reconsider sending the divers?"

"No, I hope that won't be necessary. I will run the starboard propeller in reverse. It sometimes frees it up. If that doesn't work, then we'll get the divers ready", Hilal explained as Nabil closed the door behind them. The young crew member eagerly watched as Hilal turned the starboard propeller shaft into reverse and let it run for a few moments. They could both feel the vibration running through the yacht.

"Shit, that's not good", Hilal cursed as he stopped the engine again. It was only a second later that he was already on his way back aft again, this time he carried the search light himself. The result was the same, no matter how hard he tried, he couldn't see anything. His options were limited. Technically he could make way with just one propeller, but they would lose a significant amount of time. If he would send in the divers now, they would be able to make up the lost time later and keep to their schedule.

"Okay, Nabil, let's get two divers ready. Lower the diving platform and make sure the dive ladder is secure. I will be back at the bridge and see what else I can do. Let me know once the divers are ready."

"Sure", Nabil nodded and turned around.

"Oh, Nabil, one more thing!"

"Yes?"

"Don't make too much noise. I don't want his Highness to wake up, understood?"

"Absolutely!"

As Nabil hurried below deck, Hilal closed the door behind him and took another look at the controls. The red light was still flashing, but everything else seemed to be in order. Hilal shook his head, he still had no idea how this could have happened. He debated with himself whether he should wake up his captain, but decided against it and just made an entry in the ships log book. It was only twenty minutes later when Nabil contacted him over the radio.

"Yes, Nabil, what is it?"

"The divers are ready and waiting for your order."

"Okay, I'm on my way", Hilal replied and made sure that the engines were in neutral. Satisfied that there was no risk for his divers, Hilal took his cover and joined Nibal at the aft diving platform. By now several flood lights illuminated the stern and the water surface below them. Hilal watched as Sameh and Alim performed their final buddy check on their scuba units.

"All safe back here?" Hilal wanted to know.

"Yes, we can't see anything from here either. They are ready to go in."

"Okay, let's go", Hilal nodded and waved at the divers. Together they watched them jump into the water, where they popped back to the surface for a few seconds before finally descending towards the propeller. Hilal had utmost confidence in his crew. Besides, this was merely nothing but a routine exercise for them. He and Nibal both stared at the bubbles emerging along the hull, the only sign that divers were actually down there. Less than a minute later and the first diver came back to the surface. He slowly swam to the platform. The naval officer walked over to the diver and crouched down beside him.

"What is it?"

"It looks like we caught a rope. There is actually quite a bit of it."

"Can you unwind it?"

"I'm afraid we have to cut it. It is melted together."

"Aw, dammit", Hilal cursed. "How long will it take?"

"Sameh is already cutting. I think we should be done within the hour."

Hilal didn't like the answer, but he knew that the divers were working as fast as possible. He looked at his expensive watch. If the divers could free the prop, then this whole incident would not cost him more than two hours. They could easily catch up during the next twenty-four hours.

"Okay, go back and help him. Once you are done I want you to take a look at the rudder and the other propeller. Check on the line cutters, I want to know how we managed to pick up the rope", Hilal instructed. The diver just tapped his head to signal that he had understood and immediately descended again. Hilal rose to his feet and shook his head. He knew that each propeller shaft had a line cutter installed. They were specifically designed to cut any rope before it could entangle itself around the propeller.

"You stay here, Nibal. Let me know once the divers are out of the water again. We have to make up for some lost time. I will be on the bridge."

"Yes, Hilal, I will let you know." Nabil waved with his radio and looked back to the surface. Just as Hilal started walking back, Alim surfaced.

"Hilal! Wait!" Nabil shouted after him. The young naval officer turned around and came back.

"What is it?" he asked and looked at the diver.

"There is something strange with this rope", Alim explained and handed a short piece of rope to Nabil. "It has a steel cable in it. I have never seen that before. The cable is thin and the rope is still light enough to float, but we are having a hard time cutting it. This will take a couple of hours and we do need some wire cutters."

Hilal silently examined the piece of rope. He could clearly see where the line cutters had done their job, but he also knew that they were no match for a stainless steel cable like this. Something didn't look right to him and he picked the individual strings apart.

"What is the problem?" Nabil wanted to know after he handed the diver a set of wire cutters.

"I don't know, Nabil, but this doesn't look right. It looks like a brand new rope to me. If it is floating debris, it would have been in the water for quite some time. It would have lost its colour, and there would be some algae on it, but look at it!" he said and turned the rope in his hands. "This looks like it's brand new." Hilal shook his head. "I have to inform the captain about this. I will be on the bridge. Keep me informed", Hilal finally stated and rushed back. His eyes scanned the horizon, but he still couldn't see anything that would explain why this rope was around his propeller.

During his career at the Navy he had learned that he could always trust on his instincts, and something told him that this party boat might have something to do with it. A quick look on the radar would tell him exactly where they were. He remembered that they had followed them since Monaco before they passed them earlier. He silently shook his head again and shut the door to the bridge behind him. His eyes immediately caught several more red warning lights.

"What the hell?"

Natascha had no idea what was happening on the bridge or with the propellers. She woke up to a pounding headache, and the rasping pain in her throat made her cough.

"Great! That's the last thing I need now", she complained and stared at the ceiling. A quick glance at the alarm clock showed her that it was quarter after two in the morning. She had set the alarm for two thirty, but was pleased that it didn't go off. Natascha allowed herself a couple more minutes before she reached over to cancel the alarm. But even that little movement was enough to cause her some nausea.

"This is awesome!" Despite the situation, her sarcasm was one of the things that helped her to deal with all this. "I think I'm running a fever", she said and wiped the sweat from her forehead. It took her a couple more minutes before she found enough energy to sit up. A new wave of nausea caused her to close her eyes. The headache also intensified.

"Shit, that is not going to work!" Natascha tried to focus and finally managed to boil herself a cup of tea. Sitting at the table, she slowly sipped the tea and could feel the relief in her throat, but her headache remained the same. It took her a couple more moments before she was awake enough to reassess her situation and the plan she had come up with. Thinking about her daughter gave her the strength she needed as she slowly walked to the bathroom.

"Okay, let's make Shira proud, I know you are in here somewhere", Natascha mumbled and dug into the cabinet with all the different cleaning agents again. It took her only a few seconds before she found what she was looking for.

"Well, it's not a gun, but better than nothing", she commented on her way back. She had not turned the lights on for several reasons. For one, she didn't want to lose her night vision and second, she didn't know if the guard outside her door would notice the light or not. The last thing she needed was him to be suspicious. She knew that she had to surprise him, should her plan work. Slowly, she walked to the door. Just as she reached for the handle, another wave of nausea came over her, forcing her to close her eyes and to take a couple of deep breaths.

"Come on, you have given birth to your daughter, you can do this!" With the new encouragement she reached for the handle and slowly opened the door.

Hilal stared at the main computer monitor and shook his head. "How the hell can the engines overheat?" he wondered aloud, but there was no one with him on the bridge who could answer that question for him.

He ran the diagnostic software, but everything else was normal. This didn't make any sense to him, but he knew he had to act fast. The temperature of the two main engines was dangerously high, and if he wouldn't turn them off immediately, he would seriously risk permanent damage. It took the auxiliary generators only a few seconds to kick in, but Hilal nervously followed their start-up on the monitor. The moment they were running smoothly, he turned the main engines off. He had absolutely no idea what was going on, but he knew he had to wake the captain. It would be his decision then whether to wake Prince Tarek or not, but either way, Hilal needed something that he could tell them.

"Nabil! Are you there?" he shouted in the radio.

"Yes! We are still working at the propellers. What can I do for you?"

"I need to know how much longer, and I need a diver to check out the cooling water intakes. For some reason our main engines are overheating."

"Overheating? But how?"

"I don't know yet, that's why I need a diver to check the cooling water intakes. Maybe we picked up more debris that blocked the intakes. The main engines are turned off and we are running on the generators, so there is no suction on the intakes. Just make sure that the diver checks it right away, understood?"

"Yes!" Nabil answered and turned towards the platform. He kneeled down and used a hammer to tap the diving ladder three times. With the sound travelling in water so much faster than in air, he knew that the divers would hear it. Nabil didn't have to wait long before Alim surfaced at the ladder.

"How much longer?" Nabil wanted to know.

"It will take a while. We are almost half way done, but we have to change tanks soon."

"Okay, I want you to take Sameh and check the cooling water intakes before you both come out. For some reason our engines are overheating, and Hilal thinks that we might have picked up more debris. Understood?"

"Yes, we will check that out immediately", Alim answered and disappeared underneath the surface not a second later. Nabil waved at him and picked up his radio to call Hilal.

"Yes, Nabil, what is it?"

"They are almost halfway done with the rope. I told them to check the cold water cooling intakes. I should have some news for you in a few minutes."

"Okay, keep me informed."

"Sure", Nabil answered and looked at the fading stream of bubbles. He knew that the divers were on their way along the hull now. While Nabil kept staring at the surface, just a couple of metres below him Sameh and Alim came upon the stern thruster. They immediately stopped and looked at each other. There was no mistake, their dive lights clearly illuminated a fender that had been stuffed into the thruster and then inflated. It was the fastest and most accurate way of rendering a thruster useless without damaging it. They both looked at each other again, not sure if they could believe their eyes. It was clear to them that this was nothing that the *Shadow of the Orient* could have picked up by accident. The only explanation was divers who manually sabotaged the *Shadow of the Orient* with the wire cable before using the fenders to render her unmanoeuvrable.

Their masks could not hide the suspicion in their faces as they kept swimming along the hull towards the cooling water intakes. They shone their lights at the hull and into the open sea. They were not sure whether they wanted to catch who had done this or not. While Sameh kept watching the blue water around them, Alim let his light shine over the main engine's cooling water intake. Just as they expected, another fender blocked the intake completely, not allowing any cooling water to reach the engine. Both Sameh and Alim signalled each other to get back to the platform. There was no point in checking the other intakes or thrusters, and they both wanted to have back-up under water before they would attempt to remove the fenders or finish their work on the propellers. They kept looking around nervously, but they never saw them coming.

Using their powerful scooters, two divers appeared out of nowhere and attacked them from behind. By the time Sameh and Alim noticed them it was already too late. Sameh felt the sharp pain in his throat and wondered where the green cloud in front of him was coming from. Already struggling with death, he didn't realise that it was his own blood. In a last effort he tried to turn around to face his attacker, but the other diver had Sameh's scuba tank tight between his knees, preventing him to turn. With every heartbeat, another cloud of blood left his body and Sameh felt that his end was near. His body became motionless and everything went dark. The last thing Sameh saw was his friend Alim sharing the same fate.

The two divers with their rebreathers seemed to be unimpressed and waited for the death struggle to be over. It didn't take long before they dragged Sameh's and Alim's lifeless bodies with them and away from the *Shadow of the Orient*. They let all the air out of the Saudis buoyancy compensators and watched as the two bodies sank into the abyss. Without losing another second they turned around and scootered back to the *Shadow of the Orient*. The next stage of their plan was about to begin.

Hilal shook his head and glanced at his watch. A curse left his lips as his eyes scanned the monitors again. The only positive thing for the moment was the absence of any new alarms. His only hope was for some good news from the divers before he would wake up the captain. Just as he looked at his watch again for the second time in as many minutes, the lights on the bridge were turned off.

"What the hell is going on now?" he wondered out loud. The only light now came from the monitors and gauges, which helped him to find his way to the panel with the main light switches right beside the door.

"Leave it!" an unfamiliar voice ordered in a dangerously calm tone. Hilal froze for a second. His eyes caught the laser dot just to the left of his head on the wall before it disappeared. He knew that the dot was now projected on the back of his head. The recognisable sound of a gun being cocked made the intruder's intentions clear.

"Do not move until I say so. This is not about you. Do what I say and you will live. Try to resist and you will die, it will not effect the outcome of tonight's mission, understood?" the male voice calmly explained. Hilal didn't know what to think, but for some reason he was convinced that this intruder knew very well what he was doing. For now, Hilal decided to take the option that would let him live and simply nodded. His navy experience allowed him to stay relatively calm.

"It would be foolish to shoot me, the guards would be here within seconds", Hilal tried to win some time, thinking about how he could alert the others.

"I am fully aware of that", The voice replied calmly. Hilal's body tensed as he felt the cold steel of a combat knife at his throat. He had no idea from where the second person had sneaked up on him like that.

"Put your left arm behind your back slowly, please." Hilal was left with nothing else to do but to obey. His mouth dried as he first placed his left and then his right arm behind his back. Without taking the pressure from the knife, the second intruder managed to close the flex cuffs around his wrists. With his hands securely tied behind his back, Hilal was relieved to feel the pressure from the knife on his throat easing up. The Saudi took the chance to swallow and took a deep breath, but that was all he could do before he was gagged. For a moment he was puzzled as he thought to have smelled a perfume. Before he could think more about it, the second intruder already placed a blindfold over his head.

"You will now slowly walk backwards until you reach the wall", the male voice ordered again. With the knife already cutting into his skin again, Hilal carefully shuffled towards the wall, where he was told to sit down. Thirty seconds later and his legs were tied as well. Unable to move, call for help, or even see anything, Hilal was out of options. Not having seen even a glimpse of the intruders was a clear indication to him that he was dealing with professionals. The woman closely watched Hilal, as her partner slowly walked over to the control desk. The lights inside the bridge were still out, but they didn't seem to need it. The switches were all illuminated. He rearranged his combat mask slightly as he studied the labels. It took him a few seconds before he found the right one. A smile appeared on his lips as he pressed the button. Satisfied, he turned around and looked at Hilal again.

"Okay my friend, let's talk!" Ariel finally said and looked at his sister, who returned his smile underneath her mask.

Nabil's eyes scanned the water, but he couldn't see any bubbles. *Maybe they found something at the intakes and are fixing it already*, he told himself. That would be the best case scenario and would allow them to be underway again before dawn. Nabil paced the aft deck, his eyes restlessly scanning the water and the total darkness surrounding them. His attention turned to his left when he thought he heard something, and his flashlight followed at the approximate direction of the sound when it happened again. The light cut through the darkness, but it did not reveal anything. Nabil made a face and clipped the flashlight back on his belt. With both hands on the railing, he leaned over to have a look along the yacht's sleek hull when all of a sudden the search lights were turned off.

"Ah, come on, seriously?" Nabil complained. It was so dark that he could barely see a couple metres. He was reaching for his own flashlight when he saw the familiar glow of the divers' underwater lights surfacing at the ladder.

"Of course they are coming back now", the Saudi muttered as he turned his flashlight back on again. He rushed over to the edge of the platform, but the first thing to break the surface were the powerful LED dive lights. Instinctively Nabil closed his eyes and raised his free hand as the powerful spot light shone right in his face. Nabil heard the faint pop of a speargun, followed by a sudden pain in the centre of his chest. His eyes widened as he looked down, his flashlight slipping out of his hand as he fell into the water. The two divers caught Nabil's lifeless body as he fell towards them, eliminating most of the splashing noise once he hit the water. Without saying a word, one of the divers took his own weight belt off and tied it around Nabil. A second later and the next body was on its way to the bottom of the Mediterranean Sea.

The two divers finally popped their heads out of the water and carefully scanned the deck and diver platform, but they couldn't see anyone. Ole-Einar and Olaf finally closed the loops of their closed circuit rebreathers and removed their masks.

"Okay, talk to us, how do we look?" Ole-Einar whispered in a little radio.

"Both night vision and infrared show all clear. You are good to go. We will be there in twenty seconds." Jack MacDonald answered. The two Norwegians briefly looked at each other. While Olaf started to take his gear off in the water, Ole-Einar covered for him.

"Ay up, mates", they heard Jack MacDonald's voice whispering behind them. The Briton leaned over the side of *Cloud Dancer*'s zodiac and reached for the platform. Rolf, Gunnar, and Nick stored their oars in the RIB. The two powerful outboard engines were in the water, but not running. With the centre console painted dark grey and all lights and radar reflectors removed, it was extremely difficult to spot the seven metre long zodiac in the water.

"Status update!" Jack required.

"Two Saudi divers plus one guard are down in Davy Jones' locker. One propeller is still down and we blocked the rudder. Cooling water intake as well as all thrusters are blocked. This ship goes nowhere. How are Ariel and Shira?"

"So far so good. Both are on the bridge and they have the first mate under their control." Jack whispered and looked around. By now, Gunnar, Nick, Rolf, and Noah were already on the platform and securing the aft deck, while Ole-Einar and Olaf were busy stowing their rebreathers into the zodiac. Jack waited for them to finish before he assembled their group. There was no more talking now. One quick look was all that they needed. They donned their night vision goggles and waited in silence. Before long the radio crackled and they heard the crucial information they needed. All eyes rested on Noah, who translated the Hebrew dialect into English.

"Okay, that's it. Let's get our girl back", Jack whispered. Olaf stayed behind to secure the yacht's aft deck and diving platform, the rest of them simply disappeared into the darkness of the night.

Back on the bridge Ariel took his time to open a file on his smart phone while he silently watched the Saudi. He glanced at Shira, who was occupied with the monitors.

"How much longer?" Ariel whispered. As before, he and his sister were using their native Hebrew dialect, making it impossible for Hilal to understand them.

"If they have a surveillance system, I should have...ah, here it is." Shira answered and looked at a brightly lit corridor. The surveillance camera only showed one cabin door and one guard, who sat on his chair.

"Sure that's it?" Ariel wanted confirmation.

"No, but it is the only camera that shows a cabin door, the rest are all installed either in the engine room or in the stern section. It has to be it."

"One guard?"

"Not sure", Shira shook her head and studied the image. "There is only one guard visible and only one chair, but the angle of the camera is tight. There might be others."

"Well, we will find out", Ariel commented dryly and moved towards Hilal.

Hilal noticed the attacker kneeling right beside him, and he was nervous what would happen next. His breathing increased, and he cursed himself for flinching when Ariel just touched his shoulder.

"I will ask you a couple of simple questions, to which you can either nod or shake your head. Should you try to scream or do anything else stupid, I will be forced to silence you permanently. Do you understand me?" Ariel whispered. Hilal waited for a second, but he slowly nodded as he felt the cold steel of Ariel's combat knife on his throat again.

"Perfect! So here is the first question: Do you know why we are here?" Hilal cursed the day that damn British playboy had brought this woman on board. He knew back then that she was different. They were used to Prince Tarek's extravagant parties, but the moment that British playboy had dropped her off, he knew that this woman was trouble.

He was still cursing Rowan in his mind when he felt more pressure of the cold steel on his throat. Reluctantly and very carefully, he nodded again. Although he obeyed so far, his mind kept spinning to find a way to alert the guards. Nabil would surely come and check on him if he wouldn't answer any of his calls. Thinking about Nabil, he just realised that he had not called in yet. That posed another problem, and Hilal started to think about another way out. What if he could send them in the wrong direction? Towards the guards? His pride and loyalty made it difficult to surrender like this. His career, and maybe even his life, would be over if Prince Tarek would find out how easily he had been captured and given up the information. But that would also require him to survive this ordeal first. Ariel's voice interrupted his thoughts again.

"Is she still alive?" Ariel had just asked the most crucial question of all. It was the only time that his voice reflected any emotion. His eyes met Shira's as they waited for what seemed to be an eternity. They were both holding their breath, afraid of the answer, but Hilal finally nodded. Like Shira, Ariel closed his eyes for a moment and they both exhaled deeply in their relief. Shira immediately forwarded the information over the radio to Talia.

"I am looking at the yacht's blueprints at the moment. I have to know on which deck she is and you will tell me. Is she on E-Deck?" Ariel whispered, but Hilal didn't show any reaction.

"Very well, if you insist", Ariel simply commented. At first Hilal was surprised to feel the pressure from the knife on his throat disappear, but only seconds later he felt a sharp pain in his wrist where Ariel had cut him.

"Remain calm", Ariel ordered him, the knife now back on Hilal's throat. "I just nicked your main artery at your wrist. Not much, and very easy to fix, but if I do not tend to it, you will be dead within the next few minutes. As you can imagine, I will only fix you once I get what I want. So, the longer you stall me, or try to trap me, the lower your chances of survival." Ariel gave Hilal a couple seconds to understand what he had just told him. Hilal's breathing was heavy, and he franticly searched for a solution, but he could not think of any. For the first time he had to think about his beautiful wife and his two little children. How proud she had been when he had told her about his new assignment, the memories of that day flashing right in front of him.

"Do you really want to die for nothing?" Ariel calmly asked. He had noticed the conflict Hilal was faced with. Finally, thinking about his family again, the Saudi shook his head.

"I knew you wouldn't throw your life away. I guess you owe me", Ariel smiled and looked at Shira, who simply shook her head. She had just lost five pounds over the bet she had had with her brother, but was too occupied with the electronics to retort.

"So, where is she? D-Deck?" Ariel started again, but Hilal shook his head.

"C-Deck?" This time Hilal nodded in resignation.

"Port side?"

Hilal shook his head.

"Bow section?"

Hilal nodded.

"Guards?"

Hilal paused, unsure how to respond.

"I believe you lost about half a litre of blood by now. It's really messy over here." Ariel updated him on his condition, and asked again, "Guards?"

Hilal hesitated, and then finally nodded. He already felt drowsy and tried to calm his breathing and heartbeat down.

"How many? One?"

Hilal nodded again.

"Are you sure? Remember, the longer it will take me, the lower your chances of survival", Ariel reminded him.

Hilal just nodded.

"Very well. Lie down and try to keep calm. It will increase your chances of survival." Ariel helped Hilal to lie down, but he didn't tend to his wound. As he looked up, Shira was already on the little radio.

"C-Deck, starboard side, bow section, one guard", was all she said.

"And now we wait!" Ariel smiled while Shira kept her eyes on the image from the surveillance camera.

"Oh shit!" Shira hissed and contacted Talia on the *Cloud Dancer.* Her eyes widened as she watched the door to Natascha's cabin slowly open.

On board the private yacht *Cloud Dancer*, Gulf of Hammamet, east of Tunis, Thursday, July 31

Of all the people on the bridge, Brian seemed to be the most relaxed. His eyes were glued to the radar screen, not leaving the little dot marking the *Shadow of the Orient* out of his sight. Only now and then he turned around, took the binoculars and walked aft to see if he could make out some movement on Prince Tarek's yacht. The former admiral had ordered all lights, including their position lights, to be turned off on the *Cloud Dancer*. The only illumination came from an emergency light, but it was nothing more than a red glimmer.

"Come on, guys, you have done this before. Clean infiltration, rescue and extraction", the retired admiral murmured as he watched through the binoculars, but as before, he couldn't see any indication about what was going on there at the moment.

"Seeing anything?" Iain whispered as he walked over to him.

"No, all the same. Here, have a look", Brian answered and handed him the binoculars while he walked back to the bridge. His eyes fell on Rowan, who had his hands tied behind his back to a table leg that was bolted to the floor. They all agreed that it would be easier to keep an eye on him on the bridge, rather than having him locked up without direct supervision. Even though he was tied to the table, Talia kept a sharp eye on him. Brian had insisted for her to stay behind to translate the Hebrew radio messages.

"Anything new?" the retired admiral asked as he came closer.

"Negative, sir. They have her location and are moving in."

"Hm", Brian nodded. His attention was drawn to the stairs as Alba came up. Initially she wanted to stay in one of the cabins, mostly because she was too disgusted by Rowan's presence, but her anxiety got the best of her.

"Are they back yet?" the Spaniard nervously asked, completely ignoring Rowan.

"We are good, Miss Casillas, but we are not that good", Brian tried to smile.

"How much are they paying you?" Rowan laughed once he saw her. Alba threw him a hateful look and started a tirade mixed with Spanish curses. Rowan tried to laugh at her, but winced when a sharp pain shot through his face. Nick's beating had certainly taken its toll on him.

"If you don't shut up, I'll personally blindfold and gag you", Brian reminded him.

"Right. And what are you going to do next? In case you have forgotten, you can't just make me disappear." Rowan mocked. Brian didn't answer. He knew that Rowan had a valid point. What they had done could hardly be called a legal arrest. The retired admiral had to admit that this part of their plan needed some significant improvement.

"You are involved in human and organ trafficking. Only God knows what else you have done. We're not talking about some unpaid parking tickets here."

"God? Oh, I don't think he has anything to do with this. Well, some might think different", Rowan snickered. Brian and Talia exchanged a puzzled look. They had no idea what the British playboy was talking about.

"I do have some unpaid parking tickets, I might add." Rowan half snickered,

"No seriously, what is your plan? To just hand me over to the authorities? Based on what? The word of a whore?" Rowan ranted and spit at Alba's direction.

"There is more than one witness. Natascha is still alive. The British authorities believed her when a whole government accused her. Trust me, they will believe her this time, too." Brian stated with finality and walked out aft again to take another look with the binoculars. Rowan's silence showed him that he must have hit a nerve. A quick glance from the corner of his eyes revealed that Rowan was getting nervous now. Rowan's eyes wandered over the floor as if he could find the answer to his problems there. He had heard about Natascha's ordeal a couple of years back, and Brian was right. She was not a random homeless girl without credibility. She had a voice the authorities would listen to. Not only that, but she had seen him on *Asklepios* when he had picked her up. *What if she remembers anything from the conversation I had with Sheridan*? Rowan wondered. For some reason he heard L.J.'s voice in his head, when he had cautioned him that even the most stupid cop would listen if someone would talk about what was happening on *Asklepios*. It was only now that Rowan realised that this could end very badly for him.

"But you are right, Rowan, I have to admit that", Brian continued as he came back in. Rowan's struggle did not go unnoticed with him, and he decided to push the Briton a little bit further. "You see, I'm looking at the bigger picture here. Your friends, and whatever perverted thing you are running on that hospital ship, will be over soon. Trust me on that one", Brian promised, although he was uncertain how any of that would happen, but he didn't have to tell Rowan that. "I'm caught in a predicament here. My first priority is to get Natascha back. My best people are taking care of that as we speak. My second priority is to shut you guys down, which will also be achieved. Unfortunately, and I have to admit that, we are not operating one hundred percent legally here, if you know what I mean."

Rowan just laughed, but had to grimace as the pain shot through his mouth.

"If I turn you in, and trust me, I would really love to see you being brought to justice, it would draw a lot of unwanted attention towards us and my company. That is something I have to consider for the future. It could cause some legal trouble, and quite frankly, I can do without that. At the moment, I am considering to simply hand you over to your friend over there. I'm sure he would love to talk to you after he finds out who put us on his trail." Brian calmly stated and nodded towards the *Shadow of the Orient*.

"What do you mean?" Rowan whispered fearfully. That was something he had not considered.

"I mean, it's simple. At the moment, there are a couple of my best men over there, taking him and his crew apart as we speak, to rescue Natascha. I'm sure that your psychopathic buddy will be able to add two and two together when it comes to who had blown the whistle on him. So, what will stop me from simply throwing you in the water before we leave? It is up to you which direction you swim, but realistically, his ship will be the only option. Can you imagine his surprise when he is fishing you out of the water? What a coincidence that would be!" Brian thought aloud, marvelling at the idea. Rowan threw a nervous glance at Alba.

"Si! I told them all about that perverted pig!" she hissed at him. Rowan swallowed hard. He knew that Prince Tarek had a tendency to react with extreme violence, but he considered themselves friends. Friends? No, they were just mere business partners, who partied together a couple of times a year after another shady business deal. The lump in Rowan's throat grew larger. He once witnessed what Prince Tarek had done to someone who had betrayed him. Rowan knew that whatever the British authorities would do to him, whatever prison they would throw him into, nothing could be as bad as what Prince Tarek would do to him after tonight.

"I want a deal!" Rowan finally whispered. Now it was Brian's turn to be surprised.

"Excuse me? You want what?" the retired admiral asked and turned around to face him.

"You heard me right! I want a deal. I will tell you what I know, but in exchange you make sure that Tarek does not get his hands on me."

"Not sure if there is anything else that we need to know. We already know where Natascha is. And quite frankly, should she have even as much as a scratch, Prince Tarek will be like the Easter Bunny compared to what Nick and the other lads are going to do to you." Brian calmly explained. Rowan's mind kept spinning. He needed to buy some time to get as far away from Prince Tarek as possible. And hopefully he would be in custody before they would realise how sick Natascha really was.

"I admit it. There is an illegal trafficking ring for young women and human organs on *Asklepios*. I will testify to it, okay?" Rowan pleaded. He tried to remain calm, but he felt the panic rise inside him.

"I told you before that we are aware of that. There are witnesses for it. Tell me something I don't know!" Brian demanded. He curiously watched as Rowan grew more nervous by the second.

"There is something else going on. It is big. Really big! Much bigger than you can even imagine. And you have no idea who is involved in it", Rowan hastily confessed, shaking his head.

"Okay, slow down for a second here. Let's start from the beginning. How big is it?" Brian figured that Rowan picked the worst possible time for a confession, but this could be their only chance to get this information.

"First I want your word that we have a deal!" Rowan shook his head and demonstratively pressed his lips together, showing that he wouldn't say another word. Brian thought for a moment. Legally he was in no position to bargain or grant a deal, but if lives were at stake, he couldn't care less.

"Okay, here is the deal. You tell us what you know, and I make sure that Tarek does not get his hands on you." Brian promised calmly. Rowan took a couple moments to think about it. He bit his lip hard enough that he started bleeding, but he didn't even notice it. Too many scenarios were playing out in his mind right now. Worst case scenario was that either Tarek or the Americans would get their hands on him. That would be game over right there. Best case scenario, he would spend the rest of his life in prison, most likely in solitary confinement. *I will not survive that! I can't go to prison!* He just realised that he was out of options. *Remember what you told yourself back in the casino? That you sold your soul to the devil? That the only way out of this is feet first? Well, mate, the time has come to pay the piper.*

Rowan decided on the only available option for him and finally nodded, "Okay, I will tell you what I know."

"Very well", Brian nodded and looked at Talia. The young Israeli nodded and picked up her cell phone. She walked over to Rowan to set up her phone to record his confession. For a brief second she turned her back towards him. That was the moment Rowan had waited for.

- *31* -

On board of *Shadow of the Orient*, Gulf of Hammamet, east of Tunis, Friday, August 1

Natascha was determined to escape. Hiding behind the door, she held her breath and simply waited. If she was lucky, her guard would come in to check on her. If not, he would call for back-up first, and her attempt to escape was over before she would even make it out of her cabin.

It is now or never! She thought and held on to her weapon with determination. Another wave of nausea surprised her and rushed through her body just as she tightened her grip. She had to fight hard not to throw up. *Not now!* She kept telling herself and opened her eyes again, slowly opening the door. Luckily for her, Kamal chose option one. He noticed immediately when the cabin door opened. For some reason his hatred for Natascha was only matched by the shame of his personal failure in Alba's apartment, when a women less than half his size had stabbed him. To add insult to injury, she had done with his own knife. A sharp pain shot through his leg as he rose to his feet, reminding him of that shameful incident. He flinched, but that was the only emotion he showed. He would not alert the others. He would not lose the little bit of respect the others had for him. With a swift movement he took his knife out and carefully glanced into the cabin. It was too dark for him to see anything, but he wasn't foolish. Prince Tarek's warning was still fresh in his mind. Kamal knew that this woman had severely injured several other men, and he didn't plan to simply walk into her dark cabin. He slowly took the first step, his eyes still having difficulty to adjust to the darkness.

"Lights on", he said in Arab, but nothing happened. Kamal frowned as he remembered that Prince Tarek had changed the command to Natascha's language. His hatred for this woman grew even bigger and, reaching for the light switch, he took the next step. That was as far as Natascha let him come. Determined that this was her only chance, she stepped right in front of him from behind the door. Kamal's eyes widened with surprise, but before he could react, Natascha pressed the lever on the fire extinguisher and sprayed Kamal in his face. In a futile attempt to protect himself he closed his eyes and raised his hands against her attack, but it was already too late. Holding his breath, he tried to grab the extinguisher from her hands, but the sharp pain shot through his groin as Natascha kicked him as hard as she could. Kamal stumbled forward, his hands still reaching out, but Natascha put all her strength into hitting his chin with the little fire extinguisher she had found in the bathroom. Kamal's head flew back, but he was still standing. Another kick into his groin and Tarek's bodyguard finally sank to his knees, but he was still conscious. Natascha didn't take the chance and hit him again with the fire extinguisher; this time on the back of his head, blood streaming from the large gash caused by the impact.

"Take that, you asshole!" she exhaled as he finally sank to the floor. She quickly kneeled down and picked up his knife when the next wave of nausea overcame her. It took her a couple moments before she could open her eyes, but she had to cough when she took a deep breath. Natascha had barely any strength left and sank to her hands.

"Shit, this is not good", she groaned and closed her eyes again. *You have to get up! You have to get off this ship! Now! Before anyone else notices what is going on!* She told herself and found some new motivation. Natascha managed to pull herself together and straightened up. Out of the corner of her eyes she caught some movement. Kamal started to move again.

"Come on, seriously?" Natascha expressed her exasperation and picked up the fire extinguisher, ready to hit him again. Just as she turned to deliver the blow, a hand covered her mouth from behind. Natascha started with surprise and the hand gripped tighter around her as she realised that her escape was over.

On board the private yacht *Cloud Dancer*, Gulf of Hammamet, east of Tunis, Friday, August 1
Using the element of surprise to his advantage, Rowan jumped up and attacked Talia from behind. A second later and he wrapped the rope they had tied him with around her neck. His actions caught everyone off guard. Alba screamed, and Brian rushed towards Rowan, but he already used Talia as a shield in front of him. For him, the young Israeli was his ticket out of this. Unfortunately for him, Talia didn't play along and heel-stomped Rowan on his foot, painfully breaking several small bones. Rowan screamed and loosened his grip for a second, which was enough for Talia to reach back over her head. She dug both thumbs into Rowan's eyes and pushed as hard she could. Rowan's scream reached another pitch as they both stumbled backwards and down the stairs, just before Brian could reach them.

"Bollocks!" Brian yelled and rushed after them, with Iain close on his heels. By the time they caught up, it was already over. Talia just rose to her feet and massaged her throat.

"It's okay, sir", she coughed. "I just need a second, I'm fine", she tried to reassure the retired admiral. All their eyes fell on Rowan, who had yet to move.

"Careful!" Brian warned Talia as she bent over to check on him.

"That's okay, sir. I think I heard his neck break when we fell. I was on top of him all the way down. It doesn't take that much", the young Israeli explained and checked Rowan's pulse. Rowan's head fell in an awkward angle to the side, his eyes still wide open, staring at the wall.

"No, sir, he is gone. I'm sorry", Talia apologised as Brian stepped over Rowan's lifeless body.

"Stop apologising", Brian insisted and embraced her for a moment. He had no idea why he did it, but he couldn't help it. It was the second time in as many minutes that Talia was totally caught by surprise. Not certain what to do, she just stood there, taking her time to recover from the attack. Brian let go of her a couple seconds later.

"Thank you, sir, I'm already feeling much better", she smiled at him politely, not sure what else to say.

"Well..." Brian started, but he also had a hard time finding an explanation. He decided that it would be best to just give a smile. "Okay, so how the bloody hell was he able to free himself?" Brian asked and turned towards Rowan's body.

"Must have been able to somehow untie the knot", Talia shrugged and made a face as she bent over Rowan again to double check on his condition.

"Is he...dead?" Iain finally managed to whisper. Brian and Talia looked at him. The expression on his face told them everything they needed to know. Iain's illusion was shattered. He just realised that this was not a well choreographed fight performed by stunt doubles. Standing on the first step, the actor's eyes were glued on Rowan's lifeless body. Iain could not move.

"Yes, son, he is dead", Brian nodded calmly, clapping Iain on his shoulder.

"It...It all happened so fast! There was nothing I could do! I am...I am..." Iain stuttered in disbelief. To him, all this seemed to be wrong. He was used to being the hero who came to the rescue, but this had happened all so fast and was over before he could even react. He walked down the last step, still shaking his head.

"I'm sorry that this happened on your yacht, son", Brian apologised and patted him on the shoulder. He wanted to give Iain the few moments he obviously needed to deal with the situation. Talia threw a last glance on Rowan before she followed Brian, but Iain stopped her.

"Are you okay? Did he...I mean...you did..." Iain started, but he couldn't find the right words and just stared at her.

"Yes, Iain, I'm fine. Really! Thank you", Talia smiled back, patting his shoulder just like Brian did.

"But how can you..." Iain shook his head. He simply couldn't understand why Talia remained so calm when he was about to freak out. In his movies it was always the other way around. Talia just smiled at him.

"I appreciate your concern, but I really am fine. If you excuse me, I have to get upstairs. They are calling us on the radio", Talia smiled again and squeezed by the actor. Iain watched as they left the scene like it was nothing, until his eyes rested on Alba, who only dared to take a peek from around the corner. Compared to Talia, the Spaniard was the complete opposite. She couldn't hold her tears back and started shaking uncontrollably. Slowly, she made her way down the stairs and absentmindedly took the hand Iain offered her. She stopped beside Rowan's lifeless body. His empty eyes stared at a point on the wall, still reflecting the fear he had felt during the last moment of his life. The longer Alba stared at him, the more she was surprised how little sympathy she felt for the British playboy. After listening to Elena's story, all her sympathy for Rowan had simply disappeared. She just shook her head and silently turned around, allowing Iain to escort her back up to the bridge. Caring for a beautiful woman, the actor was now definitely back in his element. He helped Alba to the couch and poured her an orange juice.

"Here, drink that." Alba just nodded and thankfully took the glass. It was only now that Iain realised how focussed Brian and Talia were over the radio. For some reason he did not believe that it had anything to do with Rowan's death.

"I will take care of the body. I will cover him up, if that is okay?" he wanted to know, but Brian and Talia were so focussed, that they didn't even recognise what he had said. Iain didn't understand what Shira was telling them over the radio, but the tone in her voice was a clear indication that something was going horribly wrong on board the *Shadow of the Orient*.

On board of *Shadow of the Orient*, Gulf of Hammamet, east of Tunis, Friday, August 1

Natascha struggled to turn around. She tried to turn the fire extinguisher in her hands to spray her attacker, but a second person swiftly disarmed her of her weapon without inflicting any pain.

"Shh! It's okay, angel", a familiar voice whispered in her ears. His embrace tightening around her with reassurance. "It's us, Natascha. We are with you now. It's Nick, okay? I'm here. I got you", he tried to calm her down and kissed her. He didn't dare to look at her. Tears ran from his closed eyes, realising that he was finally holding his wife in his arms again.

"It will be all good now!" He promised. Nick never noticed before how good her hair smelled. What only lasted seconds seemed to have been an eternity, but he finally felt how all the tension fell from Natascha. She relaxed completely in his arms, her body shaking under her tears. Nick slowly opened his eyes, realisation hitting him that they had found her and that she was alive. He removed his hand from her mouth.

He silently helped her up to her feet and almost lost his balance when Natascha wrapped her arms around him, burying her face into his shoulder. Tears were streaming uncontrollably from her eyes, but she didn't even try to contain them.

Nick took a deep breath and watched as Ole-Einar and Rolf gagged and tied Kamal up. The powder from the fire extinguisher was still in the air and irritating their eyes and throats, but neither of them seemed to care. Nick had his arms wrapped around her so tight that she could barely breathe, but for Natascha it was the best feeling in the world.

"Okay, lads, we got to go", Jack MacDonald whispered. It was a miracle that none of the crew had noticed anything yet, and Jack certainly didn't plan to push their luck any further. Ole-Einar kneeled beside Kamal again, whose face reflected the hatred he felt towards the intruders. Without a comment, the Viking punched him in the face. This time he was knocked out cold.

"Now, Nick!" Jack rushed when Nick and Natascha didn't move. Everyone else was already in position and waiting for them.

"What the hell took you so long? I had to do most of the work myself!" Natascha finally managed, but her laugh turned into a cough again. This time she was so euphoric that it didn't bother her.

"Sorry, we had to find the ship first this time. What the hell is it with you and ships?" Nick whispered back, his relief evident in his voice. Natascha could only see his eyes, but she knew that he was smiling at her underneath the face mask.

"Guys, we have no time for that. We have to get out of here now!" Jack interrupted them and eventually grabbed Nick's shoulder. Nick finally nodded and fell in line just behind Ole-Einar and Rolf, who were leading them back to the aft deck. Jack carefully closed the door to Natascha's cabin again, while Gunnar and Noah made sure that no one would attack them from behind.

"Yes!" Shira had a hard time to conceal her excitement when the monitor showed her friends moving out again with a seemingly unwounded Natascha. Noah confirmed to her over the radio that they were on their way back to the platform, ready to leave the ship.

"Confirming, angel has been rescued. Retreating now, one more hostile down, angel moving on her own", Shira quickly informed Talia on the *Cloud Dancer*. Shira's eyes were still glued to the monitor of the surveillance camera, showing her friends moving out. Ariel finally took care of Hilal's cut. By now the Saudi was barely moving, he had already lost a significant amount of blood. Ariel took a little pouch with a trauma pack from his belt and opened it. His mind was as focussed on his task as Shira's was now set on the electric wiring underneath the control desk. She was almost finished and just started screwing the covers back on the desk, but they never saw the guard coming. They only noticed him when he opened the door to the bridge. All three looked at each other in total surprise. While Shira and Ariel were caught completely off guard, twenty-six year old Hamit was equally surprised. He simply wanted to check in with his friend and wondered why the lights on the bridge were out. His eyes wandered from Shira to Ariel, and from him to Hilal. It took him less than a second to realise what was going on.

Yelling at Ariel and Shira in Arab, he raised his pistol. Shira's reaction was a sheer reflex. She managed to get hold of his hand wielding the gun and instinctively hit him repeatedly in his throat with her other hand. With his windpipe crushed, Hamit was unable to breathe. A gasping sound was all he could manage as he sank to his knees, the surprise and horror clearly reflecting in his eyes. Shira tried to take the pistol from him, but Hamit's fingers were clenched around it tightly in his last dying moment. Devoted to warn his friends and His Highness, he did the only thing he was able to do and pulled the trigger.

They were not moving very fast, but Natascha still had a hard time to keep up. The fight with Kamal had expelled the little bit of energy she had to begin with.

"Nick! I can't..." she stammered and clung to him. Without losing stride, he swept her off her feet and carried her.

"Just tuck your head in", he whispered calmly as they came around a corner. Natascha simply nodded and closed her eyes. She felt so sick that she had a hard time staying conscious.

"All clear!" Rolf whispered and held the door open that led to the aft deck. Ole-Einar took point and secured the aft deck before Nick squeezed through the door, Natascha still in his arms. Natascha opened her eyes again. It was the first time that she inhaled some fresh air. She remained silent and allowed Nick to hand her over to Olaf, who was already waiting in the RIB.

"Quickly, we got no-" Olaf welcomed them, but he was cut off by the unmistaken sound of a shot being fired.

On board the private yacht *Cloud Dancer*, Gulf of Hammamet, east of Tunis, Friday, August 1

"Did you hear that?" Brian asked the obvious and rushed outside.

"Yes", Talia confirmed and held up her radio. The retired admiral and the young Israeli scanned the darkness, but all they could see were the position lights of the *Shadow of the Orient* a couple of hundred metres away.

"Only one shot, right?" Brian asked for confirmation.

"That's what I heard, sir", Talia nodded before she turned towards Iain and Alba, who slowly came over to join them. "It would be best for you to stay inside for now. We really don't know what is going on over there, and depending on what they are shooting with, we can very well be in range", the young Israeli explained to Iain and Alba before she looked at the sliding door again. She knew that she was technically in no position to tell Iain what to do on his own yacht, but he had no idea about the danger he was in.

"She is right, son", Brian whispered from beside her. It seemed as if he would have read Talia's mind. The retired admiral didn't bother to turn around, but the sound of the sliding door told him what he needed to know.

"Thank you, sir", Talia smiled at her boss and scanned the horizon again, but her attention was drawn to the radio, hearing Noah's voice.

"She says that there was a gun shot", Talia translated the obvious and made a face.

"Oh, really? What else is new?" Brian replied sarcastically. He knew that Noah would have given them more information if she had any. "Technically that leaves Shira and Ariel", Brian mumbled, his eyes still fixed in the binoculars. Talia didn't even bother to call Shira. They knew that she would give a status update the moment she would find the time for it. Talia stared at the radio, desperately waiting to hear from her friends again, but it was Jack MacDonald's voice they heard next.

"Ay up, skipper. Better start those engines and get out of there. This is going south. We will catch up."

Not a second later and they could see most of the lights on the *Shadow of the Orient* being turned on.

"Bollocks! Time to get out of here! Get on your position", the retired admiral cursed and rushed back into the bridge.

On board of *Shadow of the Orient*, Gulf of Hammamet, east of Tunis, Friday, August 1

Ariel and Shira just stared at each other. It felt like an eternity, but after a few seconds their eyes fell on Hamit's dead body.

"Are you okay?" Ariel asked, concerned.

"Yes", Shira nodded quickly. The bullet had hit the back wall of the bridge without causing too much damage. They both looked at each other. They knew they had to get out of there quickly. Before Shira could react, Ariel was already on his feet and rushing towards the door. Shira didn't bother with the remaining screws and followed her brother outside. If at all, they would only have seconds to make their escape. Going into this mission, they had absolutely no information on how many guards and what kind of weapons they would possibly have to deal with.

Given Prince Tarek's history, they all had a good idea that it wouldn't be a walk in the park. Ariel quickly scanned to both sides before he started running aft, closely followed by his sister. They didn't even bother with the noise they made, they knew that the shot must have woken up everyone on board.

"Start the engines, we are coming. We got surprised by a guard on the bridge, but we are fine. We will jump!" Shira shouted in the radio, but she already heard voices behind her. She risked a quick peek, the lights on the bridge and several other sections coming back to life. It would only be a matter of seconds before someone would shoot at them.

"Quick Ariel, they're coming!" she yelled, but they were already at the end of the walkway. Without losing stride they both lunged over the railing. They were still in the air when they heard the alarm being sounded. A quick glance and Shira saw the surprise on the faces of her friends, who were already in the RIB and waiting for them, the powerful twin three hundred horsepower outboard engines idling. It felt like she was in slow motion in this moment when suddenly the warm waters of the Southern Mediterranean Sea closed over her. The impact had been much harder then she had hoped for, and all the air was pressed out of her lungs. Shira fought against the urge to inhale, she knew that the RIB had to be somewhere to her right. Keeping her eyes closed, she swam a couple strokes under water and suddenly felt a pair of strong hands grabbing her arms. A second later and Ole-Einar pulled her over the side and threw her into the RIB, where she fell on her brother.

"Go! Go! Go!" the Norwegian yelled, his eyes falling on several guards rushing on the aft deck. "Shit!" he quickly added once he noticed their weapons.

Up on the bridge, Prince Tarek rushed through the door, closely followed by two of his bodyguards.

"What is going on?" he demanded to know and rose his voice above the alarm as he tied his morning robe. His eyes fell from Captain Djamal, who had literally arrived seconds before him, to Hilal, still lying on the floor, gagged, tied up and blindfolded.

"Intruders on the aft deck, your Highness", Captain Djamal reported as he freed Hilal. "They came for the woman", he continued before he checked the vitals on Hamit. Captain Djamal knew immediately that there was nothing else that could be done for his man and looked back at the Prince, slowly shaking his head.

"That bitch!" Prince Tarek cursed and followed several heavily armed guards to the aft section.

"There they are!" Tarek yelled the obvious and pointed at the RIB, which was less than twenty metres away. "Kill them!" he ordered as his men raised their AK 47's. A second later the air was filled with the distinctive sound of fully automatic weapons.

"Cover!" Ole-Einar yelled not a second too soon. Projectiles were flying dangerously close over their heads as they threw themselves on the RIB's floor. Olaf crouched behind the steering column, desperately trying to keep the accelerating RIB in a straight line while he held on with one hand on the wheel and the other to a support bar. Several projectiles hit the steel plate they had installed in an angle as a make shift cover and ricocheted off into the sky.

"Shit!" he cursed and ducked down even lower. He didn't dare to look back, his main concern was to get them out of range fast. Another round of projectiles ricocheted off the other steel plate they had used to cover the outboard engines.

"Stay down!" the Norwegian yelled as the next round of projectiles flew dangerously close over their heads. More shots were fired. This time some of the projectiles penetrated the steel plate covering the engines. Once through, the plastic cover of the outboard engine was no match for the projectiles. A fraction of a second later, and one of the three hundred horsepower outboard engines was nothing more than dead weight, producing nothing but black smoke.

"Dammit!" Olaf cursed and looked back for a second.

"You keep driving! Just get us out of here!" Ole-Einar yelled at his friend. There was nothing they could do at the moment except to get as much distance between themselves and the *Shadow of the Orient*.

"Don't shoot back! The flash of your muzzle fire will give away our position!" Jack MacDonald ordered. Ole-Einar reluctantly followed his order, but his good intentions were futile when the familiar sound of flares being shot reached them. Within a few seconds they were right on top of them.

"Great! We look like a Christmas tree!" Olaf yelled and glanced up.

"Just keep driving! We are almost out of range!" Jack yelled back.

"Can I shoot them now?" Ole-Einar asked, wielding his gun again, cursing the flares as they created almost daylight conditions.

"You're never gonna hit them", Jack yelled. Ole-Einar glanced back, using the already damaged outboard engine for cover.

"I know, but I am not entering the halls of Valhalla without shooting back", Ole-Einar laughed and emptied the magazine of his Sig Sauer. He knew that it would be impossible for him to hit anyone on the *Shadow of the Orient* with his pistol over that distance, but maybe it would make their enemies take cover. The flares had all died off, but it didn't stop the Arabs from shooting.

"When you get there, you can say hi to my ancestors. I'm not ready to go there yet", Olaf complained.

"Has anyone sabotaged their RIB?" Ole-Einar wanted to know as he saw what looked like a very fast RIB being launched.

"Yes, that thing won't move an inch", Olaf shouted back.

"What about the two jet skis?"

"The what?" Olaf quickly looked back. The look in his face was answer enough.

"The two jet skis. You know, the ones with the bad guys on it."

"Dammit! They must have kept them somewhere else", Olaf cursed.

"Shit!" the Norwegian cursed and ducked as another round of projectiles penetrated the tubes of the RIB. Holes as big as a fist allowed the air to escape rapidly.

"We need some help here!" Jack yelled into his radio, just as the jet skis started to come at them, closing the distance at an alarming rate.

Prince Tarek was in such a rage that his face was nothing but a grimace.

"Kill them!" he kept yelling and watched as the flares lit up the night.

"They are almost out of range!" Captain Djamal stated the obvious, but Tarek did not react. He watched as the two jet skis, each carrying a pilot and a shooter, revved up and shot forward into the darkness. Prince Tarek's eyes fell on the crew of the RIB. They had all taken their positions, but when the pilot tried to start the engines, nothing happened.

"What's wrong?" Tarek yelled at the pilot. Instead of answering, the pilot quickly opened the covers to the engines, only to find all the wiring cut. He cursed and gestured to Prince Tarek to see for himself. Their RIB was dead in the water. The Saudi prince cursed and turned around to look at three other guards who carried a large case to the aft platform. He finally smiled when they opened the cover.

"They are as good as dead!"

On board the private yacht *Cloud Dancer*, Gulf of Hammamet, east of Tunis, Friday, August 1

Talia tried to concentrate, but the ship's movement didn't allow her to take the shot. Lying on the top roof of the bridge looking aft, she took a couple deep breaths. The young woman had the target clear in her sights, but every time she wanted to pull the trigger, the *Cloud Dancer* gently rolled in another wave. Not much, but even the slightest movement caused her to lose sight of her target. She took her finger off the trigger and searched for her target again.

"How is it looking up there?" Brian yelled through the open window from the bridge. He wondered why she had not shot yet.

"It is impossible. Too much movement. We have to stop."

"Are we out of their range?" Brian wanted to know.

"For the moment we are, but I do not know what else they got, so I want to finish this and get out of here!" the young Israeli shouted back. Brian eased up on the throttle and put the *Cloud Dancer* into neutral.

Up on the roof, Talia took another deep breath and refocussed. She looked through the scope and immediately picked up the RIB with her friends. She noticed that it was dangerously low in the water and smoke coming from one of the outboard engines. It would take them only a few more seconds to be out of range, and they should reach the *Cloud Dancer* within the next minute. Her focus shifted from the RIB towards her first target. She adjusted her rifle for a few millimetres to get it centred in her sights. The invisible range finding laser projected a green dot inside her sights, showing her exactly where the projectile would hit. *That would be in perfect conditions, not from a ship that is gently rolling in the waves*, Talia thought. She held her breath and pulled the trigger. Her face grimaced when she noticed that she had missed. She quickly reloaded the next bullet into the chamber and aimed again. Holding her breath and squeezing the trigger came natural to her. The suspension system in the rifle's stock absorbed most of the recoil. Another miss. Talia cursed and loaded another bullet. Same procedure. Aim, breathe, shoot. Around five hundred metres away, one of the jet skis' pilots got hit in the chest before he even heard the shot. The .338 Lapua Magnum projectile killed him and the shooter sitting behind him instantly. Talia only took a second to confirm her hit before she adjusted her IWI DAN long range sniper rifle. It didn't take her long to pick up the second jet ski. The muzzle fire gave it up almost instantly. Talia adjusted her sights, the green laser dot resting on the centre of the human shape of what could only be the pilot. She took a couple deep breaths and squeezed the trigger. Another miss. Talia cursed and reloaded. She simply kept aiming for centre mass and pulled the trigger again. The high velocity projectile hit its target slightly off centre, but the outcome was the same. Both the driver and the shooter were killed almost instantly.

"Threat eliminated", she finally radioed, scanning the area through her sights. She aimed at the RIB with her friends, which was now limping towards the *Cloud Dancer*. The second outboard engine had been hit as well and was only idling. The range finder in her sights informed her that they were less than one hundred metres away. A little adjustment showed her the *Shadow of the Orient*, now over eight hundred metres away. Talia sighed her relief. Her friends were well out of range of the AK 47's Prince Tarek's men were using.

With the *Cloud Dancer* gently rolling in the waves, the *Shadow of the Orient* kept rocking in and out of her sights. Talia aimed at the huge radar dome on top of Prince Tarek's yacht. *Why not?* The Israeli thought and took a couple deep breaths. The radar dome was a much bigger target than the jet ski pilots, but it was over twice the distance. At least the *Cloud Dancer* was no longer rolling in the waves any more. Talia squeezed the trigger, but as she expected, the projectile didn't find its target. Another shot. The white plastic cover of the radar dome showed a fist size hole not a second later.

"Yes!" Talia shouted as she saw the damage through her scope. She quickly adjusted her rifle and aimed at the second dome. It took her three more shots before the *Shadow of the Orient* was without any radar. Satisfied with her marksmanship, she focussed on the shooters again, but her attention shifted to her friends, who just tied their RIB to the *Cloud Dancer*.

"Okay, let's move quickly!" Brian greeted them and took the line Rolf had tossed him. "How is she doing?" the former admiral wanted to know and looked at Natascha. It was only when Nick finally got up that Brian could catch a glimpse of her. As expected, Nick had shielded his wife, but now he struggled to lift her up.

"She will be fine, but she is very exhausted. I will check her out once we are inside", Ariel informed his boss as he helped Nick.

"You go up, I'll give you a hand", Ole-Einar quickly stepped in. Without losing another second, Nick and Rolf climbed on board the *Cloud Dancer*.

"Careful now", Ole-Einar urged and easily lifted Natascha over his head. Together with Rolf, Nick grabbed her and moments later she was resting in his arms. Natascha had just enough strength to hold on around his neck and to manage a smile.

"Thanks guys", she whispered, but Nick was already on his way inside. Iain slid the door open for him and let them pass before he stepped outside on the aft deck. His jaw dropped when he saw what was left of his once precious RIB.

"Sorry, mate, they were shooting at us." Ole-Einar said as he climbed on the aft deck, leaving a speechless Iain staring at the remains of the RIB.

"Look at the bright side: It still floats", Olaf showed his sympathy as he also climbed out of the RIB. Brian took the moment to fill everyone in about what had happened to Rowan.

"Shit! Seriously?" Ole-Einar didn't want to believe it. His concern for Talia sent a nauseating feeling through his stomach. "Hey, Talia, you all right?" he shouted and looked at the young Israeli, who still monitored the *Shadow of the Orient* through her sights.

"Thanks, big guy, but I'm fine", she answered, without taking her eyes off her target.

"Okay, let's get out of here. Get that RIB back on board and-" Brian Whittaker started, but the sound of Talia firing several shots cut him off.

"Guys! They got a RPG. Incoming in about one minute!" Talia shouted while inserting another magazine into her rifle.

"They got what?" Iain was totally stunned, but no one paid any attention to him. Brian immediately took control and started barking orders.

On board of *Shadow of the Orient*, Gulf of Hammamet, east of Tunis, Friday, August 1

"I want them all dead!" Prince Tarek spat. He had no idea about the fate of the four guards on the jet skis, but he didn't care about them. His only desire was to kill the intruders. Impatiently he watched as two of his men readied the grenade launcher.

"Keep shooting!" he shouted at his other guards who had lowered their weapons. No one was foolish enough to tell him that the enemy was out of range. Firing their own weapons, they did not notice the .338 projectiles hitting the walls behind them until one of the guards got hit in the chest. Instead of taking cover, Prince Tarek just stared into the distance, where the *Cloud Dancer* had to be somewhere.

"What is taking you so long?" he yelled at the two guards.

They didn't reply as they shouldered the deadly weapon with the heat-seeking grenade. It took the guard only a second to find the heat-signature produced by *Cloud Dancer*'s twin diesel engines. The weapon locked in. A little movement of his finger, and the heat-seeking missile arched into the air, rapidly gaining speed and altitude. Everybody watched its trail of fire with anticipation as the missile followed its projected path into its target. Only seconds after being fired, the missile rapidly lost altitude, closing in on the *Cloud Dancer*. The yacht was nothing more than a sitting duck, impossible for the missile to miss.

"Yes!" Prince Tarek shouted as he saw the huge fireball on the horizon where, just seconds before, the *Cloud Dancer* had been. They kept watching the fireball in silence, until there was only a faint orange glimmer.

- *32* -

On board the private yacht *Cloud Dancer*, Gulf of Hammamet, east of Tunis, Friday, August 1

"Holy Shit! I can't believe that actually worked!" Ole-Einar marvelled and shook his head at the sight of the little pieces of floating debris about fifty metres away, which was all that was left from the RIB.

"Yeah, that was a close one", Rolf agreed, also staring at some last pieces of the RIB that were still burning.

"It's amazing what you can do with some tracer ammunition, an oxygen tank and some cans of gasoline", Gunnar explained and fist pumped Jack MacDonald beside him.

"Hey! Talia! Nice shooting!" Ole-Einar laughed and looked at the young Israeli, who still observed the *Shadow of the Orient* through the sights on her long range sniper rifle.

"Thanks, but that was actually the easiest shot tonight", she replied and exchanged the magazine holding the tracer rounds with the magazine of her preferred bullets.

"How does it look over there?" Brian wanted to know.

"They all returned inside. Looks like we are safe now", Talia reported with satisfaction.

"Very well, let's hope it stays like that. It won't work twice", the retired admiral sighed with relief that it had worked the first time.

"No, it won't, we don't have another RIB", Ole-Einar snickered. The rest of them followed suit. "I think we all owe you our life, sir. With all due respect, but that was some clever thinking", Ole-Einar chirped at the retired admiral.

"The key is to anticipate. Plan for the worst, hope for the best. It was one of the scenarios that came to my mind while planning this. That's the reason we had all those cans and the oxygen already stored here on deck. The solution was simple. Just create a heat signature greater than the one of this yacht. By simply putting an oxygen tank with its valve open and a couple cans of gasoline in the RIB, all we had to do was to put it into motion and let it go. The rest was up to Talia and her tracer rounds. Bottom line, this was nothing more than a poor man's missile defence system." Brian explained with a shrug.

"Poor man my ass!" Iain complained. His eyes were still fixed at the last remaining burning pieces of rubber left from his several hundred thousand dollar RIB.

"Do you know how expensive that was?"

"Yes, and I'm sorry, son, but we really didn't have any other choice."

"What if the engine stalled? Or what if it didn't catch fire?" Iain whined, still waiting for some sort of justification for what had just happened.

"Then we would all be dead by now", Ole-Einar patted him on the shoulder and walked inside.

"Same if they shoot a second heat seeking missile, just for good measure. We should really get out of their range while they can't move", Brian smiled and gestured Iain to get inside again.

On board of *Shadow of the Orient*, Gulf of Hammamet, east of Tunis, Friday, August 1

Convinced that his enemies were dead, Prince Tarek stood on the bridge and stared at the control desk. Two electricians were currently checking out the damage Shira had caused to the electronics. Their worried looks said it all.

"Damage report!" Prince Tarek barked at them after a few minutes. As far as he was concerned, they had wasted more than enough time.

"Your Highness, many of the cables and connections were ripped out. The actual damage is minimal. It will take some time, but we should be able to fix this in a matter of hours."

"What exactly is damaged?"

"The radar, one GPS unit, two radios, the auto pilot and several control wires for alarms."

"Work as fast as you can. We are still operational, yes?"

"No, we're not", Hilal commented from the back. It was only now that Prince Tarek paid attention to him.

"Why not?" he angrily snapped.

"Whoever did this knew how to render the *Shadow of the Orient* unmanoeuvrable." Hilal explained and straightened up a little bit. He was still too weak to stand and sat against the wall for support. A medic tended to his wound and fixed an IV.

"How so?"

"They fed a floating rope with a stainless steel core into our propellers. I noticed some vibrations and had to send two divers in. The main engines were overheating. I assume that they sabotaged the cooling water intakes, so I had to turn the main engines off and switch to the auxiliary generators. I'm not sure, but I wouldn't be surprised if they sabotaged the thrusters as well."

"Why wasn't I informed about this?" Captain Djamal wanted to know.

"We had it under control until-" Hilal continued, but Prince Tarek cut him off.

"Silence! Are you telling me that we are sitting dead in the water?" Prince Tarek wanted to know.

"I'm afraid so", Hilal answered. The prince exchanged a quick glance with Captain Djamal before he turned towards the electricians.

"Is this true? We can't go anywhere?"

"Your Highness, all the wiring for the alarm systems are still damaged. I would not risk running the yacht without checking underwater first." This was clearly not the answer the prince wanted to hear.

"Out of my way!" he ordered and stepped closer to the control desk. Captain Djamal exchanged a concerned look with the electricians, but Prince Tarek didn't care. Pushing a row of buttons, he felt the vibration when the main engines started again, but all the monitors remained dark. He activated the bow thrusters and moved the joystick, but the *Shadow of the Orient* didn't move. Usually her bow would slowly move sideways, but the only thing they heard was the unusual sound the electric motor made deep inside the hull. Prince Tarek cursed and pounded on the buttons to turn the two diesels off again. Frustrated, he turned towards Djamal.

"Find out where those two divers are and send everyone in who can swim. We have no time to lose."

"Right away, your Highness", Captain Djamal bowed before he repeated the orders over his radio. Tarek took a couple steps towards Hilal.

"What happened next? Why are you injured?" he wanted to know.

"I was supervising the activities at the aft deck. When I got back to the bridge, several silent alarms indicated that the main engines were overheating. I initiated the process to shut them down when the lights went out. That's when two assassins ambushed me", Hilal continued and swallowed. He knew that the next part of his story would provoke the ire of Prince Tarek.

"And?"

"There was a man and a woman, they-"

"A woman? A woman did this to you?" Tarek barked and pointed at Hilal's injury. With his free hand, the prince took a revolver out of the pocket of his morning robe. Hilal didn't answer and closed his eyes. A shiver ran down his spine. He took a couple of deep breaths before he continued shamefully.

"Your Highness, they were professionals. They forced me to tell them where we kept our prisoner while they sabotaged the control desk. I could hear them."

"And you told them that?" Prince Tarek's voice was nothing but a dangerous snarl now.

"I had no choice. They-" Hilal started, but Prince Tarek refused to let him finish and shot him. He had heard enough. Again, his men had disgracefully failed him. Hilal's body slumped lifelessly into the wall, his eyes still open as if he couldn't understand that he was dead now.

"Get them out of here", Prince Tarek finally gestured at Hilal's and Hamit's dead bodies. While some crew members executed the grim task, Captain Djamal received word over the radio that they had found a ship boarding ladder attached to the bow section.

"Of course, they were all concentrated on the aft deck", Prince Tarek commented before he turned towards the electricians again. "Is the surveillance video still working?"

"Yes, Your Highness, the surveillance cameras operate on a closed loop. You can see the footage on this monitor over here", one of them explained and activated the menu on the display. Prince Tarek stepped over and spent the next couple minutes watching how Kamal slowly entered Natascha's cabin, just to be sprayed with the fire extinguisher. The prince shook his head. "He didn't even call for back-up. Djamal, you are with me." With the captain close on his heels, the Saudi prince rushed through his yacht towards Natascha's cabin. Kamal owed him an explanation. By now, two guards had untied Kamal, who was slowly gaining consciousness again.

"Leave us!" Prince Tarek hissed to the guards. His eyes, full of disgust, rested on Kamal. "So, this is the second time that you were beaten down by a woman", Prince Tarek started. Kamal didn't answer. There was nothing left to say. He knew that he had failed again and that he had only moments to live. But death didn't frighten him.

What was worse for him was that he would never get his pride back. "A woman less than half your size", Prince Tarek continued and paced around in the cabin, kicking the now empty fire extinguisher, "was able to trick you, and worse still, she was also able to overpower you." Kamal refused to show a reaction. He simply stared to the ground, knowing that Prince Tarek would not give him another chance.

"This is the second time you have failed me. I gave you a second chance, yet you continued to disappoint me. I will not make the same mistake again!" Prince Tarek stated determinedly and wielded his gun.

On board the private yacht *Cloud Dancer*, Gulf of Hammamet, east of Tunis, Friday, August 1

Brian Whittaker's attention was locked on the radar screen. He noticed with satisfaction that the dot marking the *Shadow of the Orient* had not moved at all. Only a few more seconds and they would be out of reach of any hand held weapon system he could think of. The retired admiral kept running the *Cloud Dancer* at full speed for another couple minutes before he finally eased up on the throttle and set the auto pilot for a northerly course closer to shore. With the *Cloud Dancer* speeding ahead and all systems operating flawlessly, he finally turned around. His eyes met Shira's.

"Where is she?" he wanted to know.

Shira smiled back and looked at her friend who sat with Nick in front of the large monitor at the other end of the state room. By now, half to the guys stood behind them, showing their support. Brian slowly walked over. He wanted to say something, but it was only now that he realised that Natascha was crying. A quick glance at the live video conference on the monitor showed the image of Natascha's parents with her daughter, who was fast asleep in her bed. With tears streaming down her face, Natascha rested her head on Nick's shoulder as he had gently placed his arm around hers.

"I never expected to see her again", she whispered, her eyes still glued on her daughter.

"Welcome home, Natascha", Brian welcomed her and gently placed his hand on her shoulder. Natascha finally looked up at her friends, who had all gone above and beyond again to rescue her.

"Thank you! All of you!" Natascha cried and stood up before she started to hug every one of them to thank them personally.

"What is it with you and ships?" Ole-Einar wanted to know, just as he let her go.

"Hey, I don't know. Last thing I remember I was jogging in the park", Natascha laughed with relief that she was still alive and turned towards Rolf.

"Yeah, about that. What happened to not jogging alone?" he questioned seriously.

"I know. I just...I don't know...I wasn't thinking. It won't happen again", Natascha promised and frowned as she saw Iain.

"We haven't had the pleasure yet. Allow me to introduce myself. Iain Walker, owner of this ship. I'm the guy your friends stole this beautiful yacht from before they shanghaied me into this rescue mission and blew up my RIB. Welcome onboard the *Cloud Dancer*", he introduced himself with his famous boyish grin.

"You are Iain Walker!" Natascha stammered, now that she recognised him.

"Yes, the one and only", he laughed back.

"This is *your* ship?"

"Yes, it is. The one that your friends stole from me", he explained repeatedly with a grin. Natascha threw a puzzled look at Nick, but he just shrugged his shoulders and made a face.

"Sort of a long story", her husband explained, "but he has a point."

"They stole my ship!" Iain insisted.

"You volunteered!" Rolf defended their actions. Natascha looked at Brian. She couldn't imagine that they had actually stolen a multi-million dollar yacht to rescue her, but the retired admiral just smiled.

"Just as Nick said. It is a long story. And he has a point."

"Well, someone has to tell me that story once I'm awake", Natascha explained. She was certain that it was an entertaining story, but at the moment all she wanted was a hot shower and some sleep. She would worry about the rest later.

"How are you doing?" Brian exhaled.

"I think I'm okay. I have been drugged so many times the last couple days that I don't remember everything. There are only bits and pieces here and there." Natascha started and summarised what had happened to her. For reasons unknown to her, she didn't mention Jonathan Brown to anyone. She wasn't sure if they would believe her or not. Even worse, she didn't even know if she could believe her memory or not. Everything was still a blur. She did, however, mention Brian's brother to him.

"I'm sorry, sir", Natascha finished. Another tear ran down her face. "He and Charles risked their lives to help me. Maybe they are still alive. We have to find them. We have to help them!"

"It's okay, Natascha. We will find them. We know about *Asklepios*. You go and have a nice warm shower. If you want, Ariel can check you out", Brian suggested. Natascha knew that Ariel had training as a combat medic, a fact which had saved Shira's life back when she had caught a bullet for Natascha on board the *Northern Explorer*.

"I don't think that's necessary. I am just full of drugs at the moment", Natascha said and had to cough. Her last couple hours were so euphoric that she had totally forgotten about her illness. "And I'm getting a cold", she added, still not remembering the injection Jonathan Brown had given her.

"Go get some rest", Brian told her. Natascha nodded and waited for Nick to show her the way, when her eyes fell on Alba.

"Oh. Okay, I didn't expect to see you here." Natascha was confused and stopped.

"Hi!" Alba smiled. "Nice to have you back", she warmheartedly welcomed Natascha.

"Miss Casillas was a crucial part in helping us find you. Without her, we wouldn't be here now", Brian Whittaker explained.

"Ah, it was nothing", Alba waved him off, while Natascha's eyes widened with surprise. She didn't know what to say, and it took her a couple seconds before she thanked her as well, before she and Nick finally retreated to a cabin.

"So, I'm gone for a couple of days and you bring *her* along?" Natascha tried to tease Nick on their way down to their cabin, but he certainly wasn't in the mood.

"Believe it or not, but she is the reason we found you."

"I did say thank you to her", Natascha defended herself, but Nick just glanced at her and opened the cabin door.

"Oh, yeah, this is exactly what I need now!" Natascha said as her eyes fell on the shower in the nearby bathroom. It wasn't a minute later when the warm water hit her skin. This time she could finally relax. She didn't know for how long she stood there, but eventually the warm water was getting cold. She turned off the tap and took the towel Nick had prepared for her.

"I threw your clothes in the laundry. Shira brought something for you", Nick said and pointed at a few items on the chair.

"You sure you're okay?" Nick asked as he noticed some bruises on her body.

"Yes, Nick, I'm fine. Nothing to worry about", Natascha tried to calm her husband down. She only knew too well that Nick wouldn't let her sleep until she would have told him everything. All that mattered to her at the moment was that she was safe. She knew she needed to let that sink in first before she was able to tell them anything about her abduction.

"Ariel could check you out. It wouldn't hurt!"

"Yeah, maybe in his dreams! Not going to happen. I'm fine", Natascha stated with finality as she crawled into the bed. She had to cough again. A shiver ran down her back. "Damn cold", she complained, her eyes already closed. "You coming?" She asked Nick, who was lying beside her a moment later. Natascha spooned as close as she could into him. "I can't believe you brought her along", Natascha joked again, dead tired.

"Not funny, angel."

"Ah come on, it is a little bit funny." Natascha whispered, but Nick just kissed her on the back of her head before he pulled her in even closer.

"Nick?" Natascha whispered after a few moments.

"Yes, what is it?"

"This is the second time you came to rescue me."

"I know, I'm getting too old for this."

"I think you're the one."

"Thanks, I love you, too", Nick laughed.

"I love you, Nick. I really do", was all Natascha managed to say, but the end of her words were already trailing off as she fell asleep.

- *33* -

Natascha's former Marine Biology Institute, Germany, Friday, August 1
Mark put his second cup of coffee down and picked up his cell phone again. He lost track of how many times he had checked his device to see if there was a message or missed call from Shira. He stared at the empty display for a few moments and frustratedly placed it back on his desk. For some reason he trusted her to update him as soon as there was any progress in their quest of rescuing Natascha. He thought he had resolved those feelings for Natascha, but evidently they were still strong. Over the last couple of days he had come to the conclusion that his feelings were amplified by his concerns for her, but nevertheless, he found it impossible to concentrate. A whistling sound from his cell phone announced another message. He reached for it so fast that he almost spilled his coffee.

"Shit!" he cursed, once he noticed that it was only a message from a friend, asking him if he wanted to join him for lunch. Mark looked at his watch. It was only eleven in the morning and, like the last couple of days, he wasn't even hungry. Sitting in his lab and waiting for Shira to contact him with an update felt really nerve-racking. What was even worse was the fact that there was simply nothing he could do to help. He was so frustrated that he had instructed his students to rerun and finish the DNA tests on the bone fragments Natascha had sent him. He knew that it wouldn't make a difference, but at least it gave him the feeling that he actually did something to help her. Mark kept staring at the wall, still lost in his thoughts. He didn't register any of the conversations that his lab-students had. He startled when someone tapped him on the shoulder.

"Jesus, Nicole. What is it?" Mark took a deep breath.

"I'm sorry", Nicole apologised and made a face. After all, she had tried several times unsuccessfully to get his attention. "Just wanted to let you know that the DNA sampling for the blood you found in the tooth-" Nicole explained, but the sudden sound of the alarm cut her off.

"What the-" Mark cursed and jumped up as the rest of his students literally froze. All eyes rested on the machine generating the audible alarm. The penetrating ringing was supported by a flashing red light as the machine locked down. None of the students dared to move. Everyone waited for Mark to take the initiative. They had practised this many times before, and they all knew that they were completely safe, but they also just learned the hard way that no drill could efficiently prepare them for the real scenario. Another sound mixed with the alarm when the phone started to ring. Mark knew he had to answer it, but he was still unable to move.

"Are you getting this?" Nicole stuttered.

"Yeah, I'm getting this", Mark said and picked up the receiver. "Yes, Mark here...I don't know yet, I am on my way to check it out...No, it was a sample I was testing for someone else...Of course we are secure. The alarm triggered the safety protocol and the sample is locked in...Yes, give me one minute and I will call you back." Mark put the receiver down and walked over to the mass spectrometric detector. He first made sure that the unit was secure before he turned the audible alarm off. "Okay, what did you find that made you so nervous?" he asked the machine and searched for some detailed information on the touch screen.

"Holy shit!" he cursed, his hands instinctively retreating from the machine as if it had burned them.

EuroSecCorporation, London, Friday, August 1

Klaus steered his black Audi Q7 in his private parking spot in front of the *EuroSec* building. A quick glance on the digital clock showed him that it was almost noon.

"Aw, I'm getting too old for this", he yawned and stretched as best as he could behind the steering wheel. Like the rest of his employees, he had stayed most of the night in the conference room patiently waiting for Brian to update everyone on their rescue mission's outcome. After they had finally received word, he could feel the tension in the room lift and the stress fall off his shoulders. The former general thought about the events of last night, happy about the outcome when he entered the building. With a smile on his face he took the stairs and cheerfully greeted his employees on his way to his office. The news about the successful mission had spread like wildfire.

"Good morning, Tamar, how are things?" he looked at the young Israeli, who had made herself comfortable behind Natascha's desk.

"Good morning, sir. Things are much better than twenty-four hours ago", she replied and got ready to get up.

"No need to get up. My wife won't be here today. After last night I told her to take the day off. Any news from the gang?"

"No, sir, nothing new since you left. Just a message from the admiral that they are awake and waiting for you to contact them for a video conference."

"Okay, I can do that over the secure line. Anything else?"

"The private line rang a couple times and I took the liberty answering it."

"Appreciate it", Klaus answered and poured himself a cup of coffee. "Did General Rashid call?"

"No, sir, no calls from Israel. You want me to contact him?"

"No, that won't be necessary. I will call the general right after the video conference with Brian. I guess we owe him that much. Was there anything else that needs my immediate attention?" he asked and added some sugar and milk.

"I left some notes on your desk. There were two calls that stood out. One was from a..." Tamar stopped and searched for her notes, "Colonel Harris. He is with the Regimental Head Quarters of Royal Engineers?" Tamar said and made a face, not sure if what she had marked down made any sense.

"Yes, that's British Army. He is most likely from the bomb disposal unit. I will call him back right away. What was the other call?"

"The second call was from a Colonel Thompson. He wanted to talk to the retired admiral personally. He didn't say anything else." Tamar finished and shrugged.

"Colonel Thompson?" Klaus repeated Tand frowned. Stirring his coffee with a spoon, he tried to remember if he had heard the name before. "Hm, Thompson...the name does ring a bell, but I cannot place him at the moment. Colonel Thompson...And he didn't say anything?"

"No, sir, unfortunately not. He sounded very secretive, but somehow it seemed to be important."

"Hm, okay. I will call him back. His number is on my desk?"

"Yes, sir. He gave me a number to call back. It is not the same as on the caller ID, but I placed it on your desk."

"The plot thickens!" Klaus joked with a smile and walked with his cup of coffee into his office. Taking a sip, he sat down and skimmed through the notes, but there was nothing in there that got him too excited. The former general checked the caller ID on his phone and called the Regimental Head Quarters Royal Engineers. His call was almost answered immediately.

"Good Morning. Klaus Schwartze from EuroSecCorporation returning a call from Colonel Harris, please."

"One moment, please."

Klaus took another sip of his coffee while he listened to some music on the phone. It took a few moments, but Colonel Harris finally picked up.

"Harris here. Brian, is that you, you old dog?"

"I'm afraid the old dog is out in the yard playing, this is Klaus Schwartze", the former general replied with a brief laugh.

"Oh, I'm terribly sorry. My adjutant just told me that EuroSec is calling. I expected Brian. How can I help you?"

"I have the same question. I am just returning your call. Brian won't be back until Monday. Is there a message I can relay to him?"

"Ah, yes. There is. He called me a couple of days ago and inquired if our guys from the Explosive Ordnance Disposal Unit were in Whitmore Abbey. I checked the reports and made some calls, but we have never been there. To the best of our knowledge a nearby mine got hit couple times during the big war, but there are no reports of unexploded bombs up there. Is there anything we missed?"

"No, sir. I believe your records are correct. That was the answer we were looking for. I assume that Brian filled you in?"

"No, he actually didn't. You know him. That cunning old fox gets more secretive the older he gets. Tell him that he owes me a bottle of port for this. And tell him that I won't settle for the cheap stuff this time."

"I will make sure he gets the message", Klaus laughed. "Thank you very much, Colonel. That was very helpful. I will make sure Brian gets back to you."

"Cheers. Goodbye."

Klaus just made a quick note before he picked up the receiver again. This time he dialled the number Tamar had written down.

"That is definitely not a government number", Klaus mumbled as he waited for the call to be connected.

"Who is this?" a male voice harshly greeted him over static noise.

"Returning your call from zero nine fifty-five", Klaus stated. Something told him that it would be wise not to use his real name.

"You operating a secure line?" the unknown voice wanted to know. Klaus didn't answer and just hung up. He glanced at the number on the note again before he looked up.

"Tamar!"

"Yes, sir?" the young Israeli entered his office.

"I need a secure, non-traceable line, please. For Colonel Thompson."

"Right away, sir." Tamar smiled and took the note out of Klaus' hand. It took her only a couple of seconds to establish the encrypted connection.

"Okay, sir, you can pick up."

"Thank you, Tamar", Klaus said and listened to the static again.

"Who is this?" the male voice harshly greeted him again.

"Retired General Klaus Schwartze, EuroSecCorporation, calling from a secure line."

"Good morning, sir. Colonel Thompson here. Regimental Head Quarters British SAS. How are you doing, sir?"

"Ah yes", Klaus remembered. He and Brian had met with Colonel Edward Thompson several times during the last couple of years on business. "What can I do for you, Ed?"

"The question is what can I do for you? You're in the office?"

"Yes, I am. It is a secure location." Klaus replied and started to look out of the window to the parking lot.

"I will be there in thirty minutes." Thompson said. The connection was dead not a second later.

"Now the plot really thickens", Klaus muttered and walked over to Tamar to inform her. "What do we know about him?" he wanted to know. Tamar shrugged and opened a file on the computer.

"Colonel Edward Thompson..." she started and skipped through his official bio. "Spent most of his career in the SAS. Says here that he served with a Lawrence Whittaker!" Tamar frowned and looked at Klaus.

"Yes, Brian's brother. One of the homeless guys who disappeared. What else do we have on him?"

"We did some exercises and clinics together with one of his units, and Brian visited some trade shows with him. Last meeting with him was in April this year."

"I remember that. He is a very close friend of Brian and considered trustworthy. Will be interesting to hear what he has to say, if he is coming out all the way to talk to us."

"Does he know what is going on?"

"Yes, he does. He served together with Brian's brother in the SAS. A battle cruiser under Brian's command served them several times as a mobile command unit. He and Brian go back a long way. Brian informed him about Lawrence's disappearance and how he is involved in this case. So he does know about Natascha as well."

"Does he know that we found her?"

"I don't think so. If he does know, it would have come from Brian. I think he is equally concerned about Lawrence and Charles. Well, I think we will find out soon."

"I should probably go and get a cup of Earl Grey ready then."

"Earl Grey?" Klaus was puzzled.

"Yes, it says in the file that he loves a cup of Earl Grey and whole wheat cookies", Tamar explained. Klaus shrugged his shoulders and checked his watch on his way back to the office. He had enough time to establish a secure connection with Brian.

"Good afternoon, skipper." Klaus greeted his friend once he saw his face on the monitor.

"Ay up", Brian murmured in the microphone and picked up his cup of coffee. It was clear that he was still very tired. Shira, Ariel, Jack and Gunnar also stepped closer to the monitor.

"Where are you guys now?" Klaus wanted to know.

"Halfway up the Italian coast. If everything goes smooth, we should make landfall within the next twelve hours", the retired admiral answered and took another sip of his coffee.

"Perfect. I'll make sure someone is waiting there for you. We had a couple calls here this morning. Colonel Harris from the Regimental Head Quarters Royal Army Engineers called and informed us that their guys from the Explosive Ordnance Disposal Unit have never been at Whitmore Abbey."

"No surprise there", Brian growled. "Just confirms our theory that a private outfit had their hands in it. What else did Harris say?" Brian wanted to know.

"He called you a couple names and told me to remind you that this information costs you a bottle of port. He made me promise to tell you to make sure not to buy the cheap stuff this time."

"Blimey, this is public information. He acts as if I asked him for the alarm codes for Buckingham palace. I will get him his booze. He is one step away from being the chief engineer on the red nose express. Who was the other call?"

"Colonel Edward Thompson, head honcho of the SAS."

"Ah, Ed. Did he have something for us or was he just checking in?"

"He actually has something for us. Called the office early and left a note for me to call him back on a secure line. Once I did, he insisted to meet me at a secure location within thirty minutes. He should be here any minute. Do you want to wait for him before we start?"

"We might as well. I kept him in the loop, sort of. I owe him that much."

"It's your call. I believe that's him right there", Klaus commented and looked at Tamar, who answered the door.

"Make sure you got some Earl Grey and some cookies for him. He loves his damn cookies."

"Yeah, we got that covered", Klaus reassured his friend and stood up to greet Colonel Edward Thompson.

"Hi, Ed. Nice to see you again", Klaus welcomed the Colonel and shook his hand.

"Klaus, it's a pleasure", Edward replied. He didn't wear his uniform, but he didn't have to. His whole appearance and posture literally screamed that he was military. He quickly glanced around before he sat down, just as Tamar brought him a cup of tea and a plate with whole wheat cookies.

"Cheers! I see that Brian still keeps notes on his friends. That old fox knows all the tricks."

"You do know that the old fox can hear you?" Brian growled at him from the large monitor.

"Ah, Brian, there you are. How are you doing?"

"Good, Ed. How are you?"

"Could be better, could be worse. This is a secure location?" the Colonel wanted to know and took another look around.

"Bloody hell it is. Would be in jail long time ago if it wasn't, wouldn't I?" Brian almost sounded insulted.

"Sure you would. Rightfully so, I suppose. But please, do not let me stop you", Colonel Thompson finally said and leaned back. Klaus nodded his agreement and concentrated on the screen.

"Okay! How is our sleeping beauty?" Klaus wanted to know. Brian shook his head and took another sip of his coffee before he finally answered.

"She is shaken, but not stirred. Slept until about one hour ago. She came up, thanked everyone again and we were able to talk to her a little bit before she lay down again. She has so many anaesthetic drugs in her system that it will take her a while before everything is washed out. She already remembers more than she did last night, but the last thing she remembers is her attempt to escape from *Asklepios*. She has no idea how she got on board the *Shadow of the Orient*."

"Ariel?"

"As Brian said, her memory will come back, but it will take a couple more hours, maybe even days. Other than that, she is totally fine, considering the circumstances."

"Did you examine her?"

"No! Two reasons! I'm an emergency combat medic, but she definitely does not need any trauma first aid."

"And the other reason?" Klaus wanted to know after Ariel didn't reveal more.

"I'm going to spare you her exact words, but it had something to do with a rusty knife and my testicles, should I dare start examining her." Ariel grimaced. Shira had to bite her lip.

"Okay, so what could she tell us? What about Lawrence and Charles?" Klaus wanted to know and leaned forward for his cup of coffee.

"Well, so far most of our theory is right. *Asklepios* is indeed a former cruise ship turned into a hospital ship. She was also locked-up in one cabin with poor Elena, before Harrison took her off the ship. Natascha also confirmed that this reporter, what is his name?" Brian wondered and looked at Shira.

"Kyle McRae."

"Yeah, that this Kyle McRae is also on the ship. Last time she saw Charles and Lawrence they were still alive. As a fact, they even tried to escape together, but she can't remember what happened next. They seem to abduct young women from all over Europe to support their human trafficking ring. She also mentioned several homeless people, who are snatched for their organs."

"Jesus", Klaus shook his head.

"It gets better. She remembers helping out in one section of the ship that looks like a quarantine station. Bio-hazard suits, air-locks, negative pressure, the whole nine yards. According to her, there are several women on that station who were all in bad shape."

"Hm, to what end?" Klaus wondered. A horrible suspicion started to form in his mind.

"Got no idea, to be honest. Maybe she remembers more when she wakes up. She is totally exhausted."

"Maybe I can help here", Colonel Edward Thompson mentioned calmly, much to Klaus' and Brian's surprise. "I trust you still follow the world news?" the Colonel continued.

"We try to keep up with what's going on around us, yes." Klaus shrugged.

"What do you know about female slaves amongst ISIS rebels in Syria?" Colonel Thompson asked. His eyes focussed as he had another sip of his tea.

"To my knowledge they exist, unfortunately. I spoke to a couple guys from back in the day. Seems to be difficult to locate them. Makes a rescue mission impossible."

"Correct. There are several mobile camps, but they never stay at the same spot for more than a couple of days. They found a way to stay invisible to our satellites. Not sure how they are pulling that off, but they are pretty good at it."

"Insider information about satellite fly-by time?"

"Most certainly, but still. Anyway, I have a couple of my boys down there in the field. West of Al-Hasakah, it's a place in the middle of nowhere and still a strong hold of ISIS rebels. Their mission is to find and trail those camps. We are hoping that we can rescue some of the women."

"Continue", Klaus urged him.

"Two days ago, our lads were on patrol when they found a woman in the middle of the desert. They approached her. Turned out that she is a twenty-one year old French nurse, who quit her job to travel and have some fun. She told us that she and her Swedish friend, I think Freja is her name, were abducted and drugged by a couple guys in Paris. She was then smuggled to a medical facility, which she believed was a large ship. Does this ring a bell?"

"*Asklepios.*" Klaus answered.

"She didn't know the name of the ship. She couldn't remember how long she had been there, but she was convinced to have recognised one Rowan Harrison, who apparently was there to *buy* a woman", Colonel Thompson explained. He sipped from his tea and took another cookie to let the news sink in.

"Yes, we made that connection as well", Klaus confirmed and quickly filled the Colonel in on how they had met Elena and what she had told them.

"Bloody hell, that is quite the coincidence", Colonel Thompson admitted. Now it was his turn to shake his head before he continued. "Anyway, this Monique told us that she had been drugged. Once she woke up, she found herself together with other women on the back of an old truck in the middle of the desert. They delivered them to one of those mobile rebel camps, where she was auctioned off to the highest bidder." Thompson took another sip from his tea and watched Klaus and Brian shaking their heads in disgust.

"There were couple more European women there as slaves, mostly drifters from the street."

"Takes a while before someone is missing them", Klaus murmured.

"Exactly. I spare you the details what happened to her there, but she told us that the rebels started dying at an alarming rate from some sort of disease. For some reason the tribal elder recognised that she seemed to have some medical training and put her in charge of the sick. One night she took the chance to escape on a truck full of dead bodies on their way to a mass grave and started running. That's when the lads found her."

"How is she doing now?"

"Unfortunately she didn't make it. We couldn't save her. She was too sick."

"Was she able to tell you where the camp is?"

"Not really, but she was helpful."

"What about the disease?"

"Not sure yet. I'm waiting for a detailed report from our medic."

"Did she say anything about Natascha or Lawrence and Charles?"

"No, she never mentioned the names, but when I received the report, I immediately made the connection to your situation. Glad to hear that you got her back!"

"Yeah, it was quite an ordeal, to be honest. We got lucky on this one", Brian admitted. His mind was spinning. "So let me see if I got this straight", he finally continued. "Rowan was involved with a group operating a hospital ship for the wealthy. But in reality, they run a trafficking operation for humans and illegally harvested organs?"

"That's what it looks like", Klaus confirmed.

"And in addition to that, they sell women as slaves to ISIS rebels in terrorist strong holds?" Brian summarised, but it didn't make sense to him.

"Correct, but to what end?" Klaus wanted to know. He had the same thought. "It is known that women down there are sold for just a few dollars or in exchange for some goods. Why go through all the trouble? There is no money in it", the former general analysed.

"Exactly. Unless it is not about the human trafficking, but about something else. What if they have something to do with the disease?"

"That would make sense. There is currently a huge outbreak in Syria. ISIS rebels are dropping like flies. No aid organisation is going into that region", Klaus continued their thought.

"Bloody hell. They infect some of the women with a lethal virus and it spreads like wildfire. That is one way to fight terrorism", Brian noted with sarcasm.

"We have to find that ship", Klaus shook his head and looked at Colonel Thompson.

"Not only that", Brian added. "We also have to find what bloody virus they use and where the bloody hell they are getting it from." If they were right, then the whole scenario reached a dimension where Klaus and Brian were not even bystanders anymore.

"I can help with the ship", Ed Thompson calmly reassured Klaus. "Our Navy found it relatively quickly."

"You found her? What are you going to do?"

"Yes, we found the ship, and with Monique's statement we had enough information to believe that British citizens and a former member of our unit are on board that ship and currently being held there against their will. And that there is a realistic threat against Great Britain in form of a potential biological weapon, which can also be traced back to *Asklepios*." Colonel Thompson calmly explained. It took Klaus and Brian a couple of seconds before they understood the magnitude of the statement.

"Are you trying to tell me...that you...." Klaus started, but he was lost for words.

"Yes, that's why I'm here to tell you. I just got back. The operation started yesterday morning. I wanted to tell you that your girl was not there, but you already know that. We also got Charles and Lawrence. They are in bad shape but will survive. Same for that reporter." Colonel Thompson nodded and toasted with his tea. Klaus and Brian stared at each other over the monitor.

"Thank God!" Brian stammered and, thinking about his brother, couldn't hold a tear back. Shira placed her hand on his shoulder. Klaus was still processing the information, but he had to smile watching his friend like that.

"When we entered *Asklepios*, we noticed that one level housed several labs. I'm not talking about a normal medical lab, I'm talking about a high end, top of the line, biochemical research facility. Pretty much fits the description of what your girl mentioned. Once they noticed we were coming, they initiated their emergency protocol, which destroyed absolutely everything in there. The place was sterile when we finally accessed it, but we are interrogating two physicians. They will break soon enough."

"What about the other physicians?" Brian wanted to know.

"Not sure yet. They are all in on the human trafficking and illegal organ trade, but it looks like only a few selected people even know about the virus. It will take weeks just to find that out."

"So we are still drawing blanks when it comes to the virus!" Klaus stated frustratedly.

"Sir! You have a call!" Tamar interrupted them. Klaus didn't even notice she entered the office.

"What?" he asked her when he finally looked at her.

"You should take that call, sir. It is Mark from Germany. Natascha's contact from the institute. He insists that it is urgent." Tamar explained with serious tone. Klaus knew that she would have never interrupted them if it was not important. He picked up the phone.

"Yes, Klaus Schwartze here. What is it, Mark?"

"I ran the DNA. I found some blood in the root canal in one of those jawbones. It was enough to run the DNA on it!" Mark was talking so fast his words were almost blending into the next.

"Let me guess. You found a virus." Klaus interrupted the scientist.

"No, sir. Not a virus, but I found a bacteria!"

"A bacteria? What bacteria did you find?"

"*Yersinia pestis.* Also known as *Y.pestis.*"

"*Y.pestis?*" Klaus repeated. His face turned as white as a sheet of paper. "Yes, *Y.pestis.* Better known as pneumonic plague."

- 34 -

On board the private yacht *Cloud Dancer*, Mediterranean Sea, south of Monaco, Friday, August 1

The only noise came from the twin diesel engines humming deep inside the hull of the *Cloud Dancer*. Mark's words were horrifying, but they had no reason to doubt him.

"Well, I guess we found the bacteria they were using and the connection to *Whitmore Abbey* after all", Brian finally broke the silence. "Mark, are you still there?" the retired admiral wanted to know.

"Yes, I am", Mark answered in a serious tone.

"Are you...I mean...you are safe, right?" Brian first wanted to make sure.

"Yes, we are safe. We always follow protocol here. We were all a little scared when the alarm went off. We didn't expect it, to be honest."

"Okay. Y.pestis. The pneumonic plague. No disrespect, but you are certain about this?"

"Yes, there is no doubt", Mark explained. "To be quite honest, it all makes sense", he added with an apologetic tone.

"Okay. Prove it to me!" Brian encouraged.

"Natascha sent me three bone fragments. When I first examined them, I noticed that they were from three different people. A child about ten years of age, a female adult in her mid twenties, and a male adult over thirty years old. Natascha wanted to know how old those fragments are, and if I could date them to a certain time period. The bones from the child and the male adult were around three hundred fifty years old, and..."

"Wait a second, did you just say three hundred and fifty years?" Brian interrupted him. He wanted to make sure that he had understood him correctly. "After all that time, how are there any bones intact?"

"According to Natascha–" Mark had to swallow at her name before he continued. "According to Natascha, those fragments were sealed in the mud with no oxygen. The bone fragment from the adult woman is about six hundred fifty to six hundred sixty years old. She found that one deeper in the mud."

"So that definitely rules out any connection to the paedophile ring." Klaus stated.

"Exactly. I told Inspector Conolly that days ago", Mark explained. This was news to Klaus and Brian and they exchanged a look. "Anyway, this time I checked the DNA on them and found the bacteria. It all makes sense now. The cavern Natascha found was part of the crypt. The woman most likely died in the outbreak of the plague in thirteen-hundred-fifty-two and was buried there. The man and the child can definitely be linked to the second outbreak of the pneumonic plague in sixteen hundred-sixty-seven. Natascha found a century old crypt with victims of the pneumonic plague which had been sealed off."

"And that's how they got the bacteria", Klaus recapitulated before everyone was lost in their own thoughts again.

"Can I ask something?" Mark finally broke the silence.

"Of course. What is it?" Klaus wanted to know.

"Natascha. Is she...are there any news?" Mark carefully asked.

"Yes! There is! We rescued her a couple of hours ago. You are technically the first person to know."

"Oh my God, that is great! Where is she?"

"I'm sorry, we can't share that information yet, but she is safe. I will make sure she will contact you when it's the right time."

"I would appreciate it! Thank you!"

"Just wait a second", Klaus stopped Mark from ending the call. "Since we have you on the phone we might as well ask you. The pneumonic plague. What can you tell us about it?"

"Hm, for starters, it is a highly contagious bacterial disease, characterised by fever, delirium, and infection of the lungs. The pneumonic plague infects the respiratory system. It spreads rapidly and can be transmitted directly from human to human. There is an old saying describing the victims as having breakfast with their family and supper with their ancestors."

"Oh my God!" Brian was shocked. Colonel Thompson immediately made a call to forward the information.

"What are the signs and symptoms?" Klaus asked in a calm voice. His face was pale.

"If I remember correctly from what I have read about it, it usually starts with some coughing. Fever, headache, weakness, and rapidly developing pneumonia with shortness of breath, chest pain, and coughing up blood will follow soon after. After that–" Mark tried to continue, but Shira had heard enough. His words had sent a shiver down her spine, and she couldn't help but think of Natascha. She and Ariel spun around and rushed down the stairs.

"Oh, here you are", Nick stopped them at the bottom of the stairs. "I was just looking for you", Nick said and looked at Ariel. "Natascha got a fever this morning and she started coughing again. She must have caught something on the ship. I was wondering if you have some antibiotics, maybe? She isn't feeling that well."

"Where is she?" Shira asked him and the look in her eyes made Nick tremble with worry.

"She is trying to sleep. Why? What is going on?" Nick exchanged a glance between Ariel and Shira, desperately searching for answers. He noticed they had taken another step back from him. Shira exchanged a glance with her brother before telling Nick what they had learned.

"The *plague*? Are you fucking kidding me? You're trying to tell me that Natascha has the plague?" Nick scoffed incredulously.

"We don't know, Nick, but there is a possibility." Nick turned around with disgust at such a suggestion, and Shira grabbed his arm with frustration, before quickly retracting her hand to her side. "Listen to me! We're on a ship and we have to take some precautions. We can't take the risk, Nick! We simply can't!" Shira tried to explain, but she could see that Nick's anger was swelling, his shoulders tightened back and he inhaled sharply. Shira knew he was one step away from losing it. He stepped away from her and paced the space, shaking his head with despair. "Nick! Listen! Brian is already on the horn trying to figure something out, okay? We'll help her, but until we know for sure, we have to quarantine her as best as we can, okay?"

Nick choked back tears and quickly nodded his compliance.

"Nick, you have been with her the most since we got her back. How are you feeling?" Ariel asked, keeping his distance. The fact that Nick had spent the last couple of hours with his wife was serious cause for concern for Ariel.

"I'm not leaving her alone now!" Nick whispered and shook his head.

"You might not have to. I think I got an idea", Shira tried to comfort him.

Brian Whittaker pressed a button on the satellite phone to end the call and checked his watch. Less than thirty minutes ago Mark's phone call had changed everything. Since then he had been on the satellite phone desperately trying to find a solution. He knew that Klaus was doing the same from his office. He had an idea, called his friends and used up all his favours, but he wasn't sure if that would be enough. The retired admiral leaned back in the captain's chair and rubbed his temples.

"Okay, let's see how they're doing", he finally commented, more to himself and got out of the captain's chair. Most of his employees were still asleep and unaware to the new development. They had decided that it would make more sense to isolate Natascha first.

The retired admiral walked lightly on his feet trying not to wake anyone up as he made his way downstairs. As expected, Ariel and Shira were outside Nick's and Natascha's cabin. Ariel turned his attention to the retired admiral when he heard him approaching.

"How are we doing?" Brian asked softly, examining their work.

"We do what we can", Ariel mumbled from underneath his clinical face mask. Like Shira, he also wore latex gloves as she taped the door air tight. Shira smoothed the tape over a note she attached to the door reminding everyone not to open it.

"Where is Nick?" Brian was afraid to ask and stared at the door. He knew the answer, but he needed confirmation.

"He's in there with her. There was no way to talk him out of it. Besides, he has already been with her since last night", Ariel explained knowing there was no need for him to say more. The consequences Nick was about to face were only too clear to them.

"Their cabin shares the bathroom with the cabin right beside it", Ariel continued and gestured down the aisle. "So Nick went in through the other cabin where he dressed into a drysuit. That's as close to a bio hazard suit as we are going to get on this ship. We'll use the bathroom as a lock. Once inside, he will use wet towels to seal the door. The other door and the air vents he will seal with tape. The air condition is shut off as well. It should work."

"Okay. How certain are we about her condition?" Brian whispered, afraid that someone could hear them. Ariel shrugged and shook his head.

"There's no point for me to examine her. Nick said that she developed a fever and that she started coughing again. It could be just an infection, but considering what we know we simply can't take the risk."

"Anything we can do for her?" Brian wanted to know. There was almost a sense of resignation in his voice, but after all that she had been through he refused to give up now. Ariel looked at him. His stare was answer enough.

"I gave Nick some antibiotics for her and something to get the fever down. It will certainly not hurt."

Brian took another step closer to the door, but Shira stepped in front of him.

"Sorry, Brian, but you really shouldn't take the risk without protection."

"How can I talk to him?"

Shira took one last look at the door before returning her attention to the retired admiral's desperate eyes, "He has a laptop in there. We have a video and audio feed with them."

On the other side of the door, Natascha lay in her bed, her eyes resting on Nick. Shortly after her rescue she had forgotten all about her illness, convinced that a hot shower and Nick's presence was all she needed. But for the last few hours her condition had gotten worse. Rapidly! Covered by two blankets she was still shivering. Another coughing fit shook her just as Nick was done taking her temperature.

"I got you, angel", he whispered softly as he wiped her forehead. It took Natascha a few seconds before she had herself under control again.

"How high is it?" she asked under her stertorous breath.

"Forty point six degrees Celsius", Nick swallowed and held the digital thermostat in front of the camera lens of their laptop. His wife was literally burning up. Natascha glanced at the computer. It seemed to her that everyone was staring at her through the digital camera.

"Have they never seen someone dying before?" she asked in a broken voice.

"You're not going to die! I won't allow it!" Nick shot back, but he knew that his support was futile.

"Liar", Natascha tried to smile, but her face grimaced underneath her surgical mask when she had to cough again. Nick reached for the drink that was sitting on the nightstand. He felt the latex gloves pull against the tape that was bound around his wrists at the seals of his drysuit. He would have been in there regardless of all of this precaution, but he agreed to Shira's conditional demands. He offered her something to drink, which she gladly took.

"Nick?"

"Yes, what can I do for you?"

"I remember!"

"What do you remember?" Nick anxiously asked. He wanted to know every piece of information that could help his wife.

"Back on the ship. There was a doctor. A woman. Evans is her name. I think she injected me with something. Could have been this plague. Rowan Harrison was there with her. She gave him the bacteria for his father. They are planning something bad." Natascha squeezed the words through her laboured breath. She did not have the energy or the will to yet talk about her arch enemy, Jonathan Brown.

"Anything else you can remember?" Nick wanted to know, but Natascha only shook her head. Nick checked the laptop. Shira took some notes and Ariel was already on the satellite phone to update Klaus and Colonel Thompson. Natascha took another glance at the screen, but she couldn't bare the sight of her friends. All the sorrow and their deep concern they felt for Natascha reflected in their faces. She looked back down and closed her eyes again. Tears silently ran down her cheeks.

"Nick!" she finally whispered.

"Yes?"

"Why are you doing this?" Natascha choked.

"I'm here to help you, I will–" he started, but his wife interrupted him.

"No, Nick, why are doing this? You shouldn't be here, you should be outside and–" Natascha cried, but Nick didn't let her finish and stroked her hair.

"I'm right here where I belong, angel. Right beside you. I just got you back, I'm not going to leave you. Not now, nor ever, do you hear that?" Nick whispered. Natascha had her eyes closed and cried.

"But what if you get sick? You have to stay healthy...you have to be there for our daughter when I am....when I am gone!" Natascha sobbed, shaken by another cough. This time it took her almost thirty-seconds before she could breathe normally again.

"You're not going anywhere. We're not in medieval times anymore. This is the twenty-first century and you're a healthy young woman. You're going to pull through this, do you hear me?" Nick told her. He had no idea where he had the strength to remain at least somewhat positive, but Natascha only shook her head weakly. The thought that she wouldn't see her daughter again worked her into another fit of coughing. Tears were now streaming uncontrollably down her face as she whispered her daughter's name and how much she loved her.

"Can you please turn the camera off? I don't want them to–" Natascha managed after a while, but her voice broke with another cough. Nick supported her back and, as before, gave her a towel to cough into after he had removed her mask. Each of her coughing fits seemed to be more severe than the previous. With her whole body shaking and her eyes closed, Nick supported his wife to lay back and pulled a new mask over her face. He looked at the towel, the blood she had just coughed up clearly visible. Nick gently wiped the blood from around Natascha's nose and showed the blood stained towel to the camera, before he placed it into a ziplock bag. Eventually he granted Natascha her wish and turned the video signal off.

"Jesus Christ", Brian exhaled sharply as the monitor went black. He didn't know what else to say. As far as he was concerned, there was nothing else to say. He slowly turned around, noticing that most of his people were crying as well. Shira had her face buried into Rolf's shoulder and Talia cried uncontrollably into Ole-Einar's chest. The tall Norwegian could do nothing more than just hold her as tears were running down his own face. Seconds turned into minutes, as they listened in silence to the audio feed of Natascha coughing uncontrollably.

"Is there anything we can do?" Gunnar whispered what had been asked many times before. Ariel just shook his head, the image of the blood stained towel still clear in his mind. He had to swallow before he could say anything.

"She can breathe the oxygen from the diving emergency kit, which will help. I gave Nick antibiotics for her. They might be able to slow the infection down, but she needs different antibiotics and she needs them fast", he whispered despondently.

"Okay, I think we can all agree that we're not helping her by standing here. I want everyone outside on the top deck. No need for us to take a greater risk than absolutely necessary. Prepare the deck for the helicopter and stand by. They shouldn't take much longer. We should all wear gloves and face masks from now on. Let's go", Brian finally took the lead again. "Nick got clear instructions for the transport?" the retired admiral asked Ariel as everyone retreated outside.

"Yes, he knows what to do."

"Jesus, why the hell is he doing this?" Brian asked, but he immediately shook his head. "Never mind, stupid question." Being alone with the retired admiral, Ariel took a seat in the second captain's chair. They could both hear how Nick tried to comfort Natascha. Brian turned around to make sure that no one else was with them.

"What is the risk of him getting infected?" he asked and looked at the Israeli.

"It depends. The further the infection, the more infectious she is. He is wearing a dry suit, latex gloves, and a surgical face mask, but...", Ariel couldn't finish and just shook his head.

"Do you think that–" Brian started, but he was interrupted by the military helicopter contacting them over the radio.

"Yes, this is *Cloud Dancer*, go ahead." Brian answered. The helicopter pilot confirmed their position and wind direction, before he gave final instructions for their approach.

"Roger that. Will turn to course zero-zero-five and holding her steady at two knots over ground."

"We do have a visual. Roger and out!" Brian leaned forward and looked north. He could see the rapidly approaching Chinook helicopter in the distance. The characteristic noise of its tandem rotor soon echoed through the air louder as it neared.

"It's a Medical Emergency Response Team. How did you get them here so fast?" Ariel wondered and watched the helicopter.

"They are part of the Joint Expeditionary Force of the Royal British Navy. I knew that they are in the area and gave it a try. Had to use up all my favours for this one", the retired admiral admitted. The MERT Chinook helicopters were nothing less than an emergency hospital with two rotors.

"Okay, let's do this!" Brian got a little bit of enthusiasm back as he leaned forward to adjust the course of the *Cloud Dancer*. Ariel was already outside to instruct his team members, but they all knew what to do. With the Chinook helicopter hovering just twenty metres over the *Cloud Dancer*, they all watched as six medics rappelled down from its side doors the moment the helicopter was grounded.

"Major William McCoy, sir. Pleasure to see you again, sir. Where is she?" the young man yelled over the deafening sound of the twin rotors.

"Thanks for coming out, Bill. I owe you big time for this. This is Ariel Rashid. He will bring you up to speed. I will be at the helm to make sure that your rotors don't push us too far off course. This is not exactly a battle cruiser", Brian yelled back and wanted to turn around, but Major McCoy got hold of his arm.

"Negative, sir. If she really is infected with Y.pestis, then we do not have a choice but to follow protocol."

"How long before we know if she really has...?" Brian started, but he couldn't manage to say *plague*.

"Test takes seventy-two hours to be certain. Anything else is just guessing."

"What about us?" Brian waved his hand around to the rest of his team.

"This is Captain Kent Wallace! He is in charge from now on!" Major McCoy pointed at another member of the MERT. Brian glanced at him. He estimated Captain Wallace, who was built like a brick wall, to be in his mid-thirties.

"It's a pleasure, sir." Captain Wallace grinned as boyishly as Iain Walker as he tipped his helmet.

"Thanks for coming, son. What do you need us to do?" Brian asked pointedly. While the remaining soldiers of the medical unit dressed into their bio hazard suits, Brian and the rest of his team listened carefully to Captain Wallace's instructions.

EuroSecCorporation, London, Monday, August 4

"Yes, that is unfortunately all she remembered", Klaus answered General Rashid over the video conference and took another sip of his coffee before he continued. "Lady Amelia Harrison and Sir James Harrison ran a business empire, but other than that, they are quite ordinary. After Sir James' death, their son took over most parts of their business. Lady Amelia spends most of her time running her charity. The late Sir James Harrison made himself known as a philanthropist until he passed away. We can't find anything about them, not even anything as insignificant as an unpaid parking ticket let alone a scandal. If they were up to something, he is doing a damn good job of hiding it."

"No disrespect, but the question has to be asked about how reliable Natascha's statement is."

"I agree, but I know her. Even in her condition she wouldn't make a statement like that unless she is absolutely certain. Besides, why would she make it up?"

"I understand you, Klaus, and both Ariel and Shira always spoke very highly of her, but in her condition..." General Rashid didn't finish the sentence. Klaus couldn't blame him for not believing her. The head of the Mossad didn't know Natascha as well as he did.

"Maybe I can get one of my men to dig a little deeper into the family tree of our deceased friend Rowan Harrison. Who knows what, or who, will fall out if we start shaking it", the Israeli finally promised. Considering the magnitude of the case, he gave Natascha the benefit of a doubt. "Talking about her condition, is there anything new from Colonel Thompson?"

"No, unfortunately not. When he informed us last Friday it was more out of courtesy towards Brian because of his brother. Since then we have been kept out of the loop. The disadvantages of being a private contractor. I am certain he will give us some information eventually, but for now we are just sitting in the dark. Anything on your side?"

"No, my friend, unfortunately not. We received several reports, but nothing confirmed yet. I haven't even heard from my children yet", the general stated frustratedly. Klaus nodded.

"I am sure Brian will contact us when he gets the chance. Unfortunately I have to let you go. Conolly from Scotland Yard is here to see me. I will keep you posted."

"Thank you. Shalom, my friend." General Rashid replied and ended the video call. Klaus took a few moments before he walked into the conference room to meet chief inspector William Conolly.

"Good morning, Bill. What can I do for you?" Klaus smiled and shook his hand. Being Conolly's superior during his time at Scotland Yard before joining *EuroSecCorporation*, Sean took the liberty to sit in. Besides, he was still the official liaison between them and Scotland Yard.

"Good morning, Klaus. Actually I have a few questions that I hope you might be able to help me with. Good morning, Sean", William recognised his old colleague before he sat down. He watched as Klaus personally prepared some tea. He thanked him, but he didn't touch it.

"Okay, how can I help you?"

"It is about Rowan Harrison", Inspector Conolly stated briskly. His hopes of Klaus or Sean showing a reaction were shattered right away. Just as he expected, neither of them even flinched a muscle.

"Yes? What about him?" Klaus asked in return and leaned back in his chair.

"We are looking for him. He is missing since last Wednesday."

"He is missing? How can we help?" Sean asked from Conolly's left side. The chief inspector looked into Sean's eyes, but he knew that he couldn't intimidate his former superior.

"Well, since you're offering your help, you might as well tell me what you know." Sean stated and opened the manila folder he placed on the table. Without a word, he presented several pictures, all showing how Noah, disguised as Mandy, seduced Rowan at the casino in Monte Carlo, and sorted them on the table. "It seems to me that Rowan was with one of your employees the last time he has been seen. Is that correct?" Conolly wanted to know. Klaus didn't even bother to lean forward. Instead he instructed Tamar over the intercom to bring in Rowan's file. It was only a couple of seconds before she entered the room.

"That is correct. This is a picture of Noah Cohen, who does indeed work for us", Klaus confirmed freely from Bill's right.

"We were on a company retreat with a client in Monaco last Wednesday. Famous movie star. He invited us to stay on his yacht." Sean added without skipping a beat.

"Our people arrived there early. Two of our employees, Noah Cohen and Talia Levi, had never been in the Monte Carlo casino before, and since they had a couple hours to spare, Brian invited them", Klaus continued from the other side, before Sean took over.

"They met Rowan Harrison in the casino, who also knows our client, but meeting Rowan was a sheer coincidence."

"Rowan spotted Brian and the two ladies at one of the tables and he came over."

"As you can see here in his file", Klaus continued from the other side and spread some sheets over the table for Conolly to see. "Rowan is our client since this spring. He just wanted to chat." Klaus explained without showing any emotions. The chief inspector stared at him and placed the last still picture taken from the surveillance video on the table. It indeed showed Rowan together with Brian Whittaker and Noah and Talia at the Black Jack table.

"Rowan has a–" Sean started and allowed William to look at him, before he continued, "Let's say, a *soft spot* for beautiful women. During that evening he invited Noah for a drink at the bar. She was off the clock. They had a couple of drinks and then they left together." Sean explained and pointed at the different pictures, as if he was reading a bed time story to a child.

"After they left", Klaus took over, forcing William to look at him again. The chief inspector felt as if he was watching a tennis game, "they both went back to our client's yacht. It turned out that our client had invited him all along."

"They arrived just minutes before our client. Once everyone was aboard, we left the harbour heading out to the Mediterranean."

"Yes, I got that so far. What did you say was the name of the yacht?" William asked and looked down as he took his pen out.

"I didn't, but the name of the yacht is *Cloud Dancer*."

"Yes, right. *Cloud Dancer,* that's what the harbour master confirmed. Don't you find it strange that they left without the official crew?" William asked curiously. He wasn't quite ready to admit defeat yet.

"A crew for what?" Sean asked with a raised brow.

"To run the yacht."

"Are you serious? Every one of our employees on that yacht has a background with a naval Special Forces unit, and you have a retired admiral from a former battle cruiser at the helm. You do not honestly believe that Brian would let anyone else run a yacht like that?"

"Okay, so where did they go from there?"

"They cruised down the Italian coast and rendezvoused with another yacht off the coast of Tunis on Friday. Another one of Rowan's friend. They used the zodiac from the *Shadow of the Orient* for the transfer. Once he was in the zodiac, we steered back north."

"So you left him in the middle of the Mediterranean Sea in a little rubber boat?"

"No, we watched him make a fifty metre transfer in a seven metre long RIB with twin engines. Once he arrived at the other yacht, he waved at us and off they went. For any further information about his whereabouts, you have to contact the *Shadow of the Orient,* I'm afraid." Klaus was not willing to offer any more information. The former general calculated that there was a low risk of the *Shadow of the Orient* answering to anyone.

"Look, Bill", Sean tried to get back in the good book. "I will write you a report with everything we know about Rowan Harrison. When we worked for him and where. Maybe there is something in there that can help you find him again, but we never had any reason to believe that there is anyone out there trying to hurt him."

"Thank you, Sean, I would really appreciate that", Conolly admitted through his teeth and made some notes before he got up. "Let me know if he contacts you, okay?"

"Sure, we will. Goodbye, Bill", Klaus said and shook Conolly's hand. He and Sean watched after him until the main door closed behind him.

"We winged that pretty good", Sean commented dryly as they watched Conolly walk out into the parking lot.

"Yeah, considering that we didn't know what he wanted. Do you think that he knows about Natascha already?"

"I haven't heard anything at Scotland Yard indicating that they already know about *Asklepios*. Not sure why, but I'm certain it will only be a matter of hours before MI5 will brief them. I will meet an old friend of mine today and try to find out what the bloody hell is going on there. We have to come up with something to tell Conolly."

"I'm working on it", Klaus calmly said as they both watched Conolly exit the parking lot.

On board the British frigate *HMS Montrose*, Duke class, Monday, August 4
If someone would ask Brian to describe the last seventy-two hours, *frustrating* might be topping his list. Quarantined at *HMS Montrose*'s medical station, he and his team had spent the last couple of days doing nothing else but sleeping, staring into the blue UV-lights, playing cards, and running the medical staff crazy. On the plus side, none of them showed any signs or symptoms of the plague. On the down side, they had been tested so many times that they all felt like pin cushions.

Brian insisted for the medical staff to keep him personally in the loop about Natascha's condition. Granting his wish, they were told that Natascha's condition was critical, and that they were waiting for her test results to reveal further details. She was kept in single isolation at a different station, same as Nick, who was deemed at a higher risk. Resting on his bunk, the retired admiral opened his eyes and immediately rose to his feet once he noticed chief medical officer, Dr Crawford, entering their isolation station. It took a few seconds in the air lock to equalise the air pressure before the sliding door finally opened.

"Hi Doc, what's the word?" Brian greeted him. The fact that Dr Crawford entered the room this time without a surgical mask and gloves was encouraging news. Dr Crawford, a stocky built physician originally from Manchester, briefly smiled at the retired admiral and shook his hand.

"You and your team tested negative, including Nick", he informed them, but Brian immediately noticed the serious expression on his face.

"And Natascha?" he asked as he buttoned his shirt. They all got closer, eager to hear what Dr Crawford had to say. Dr Crawford slowly shook his head before he confirmed their worst nightmare.

"I'm afraid she is not that lucky. She is fighting a serious bacterial infection and–"

"Doc! What is it?"

"As you suspected, it is the pneumonic plague. She's in an advanced state", Dr Crawford calmly explained with a sad expression. They didn't need any more explanation.

"Has Nick been told?" Brian swallowed. Dr Crawford just nodded. "Where is he?" Brian barked, already on his way to the air lock which was now permanently open.

The rest of his team followed right on his heels determined to locate Nick immediately. The moment they stepped out of the isolation station and through the door they saw Nick. At least what was left of him. They stopped mid stride at the sight of their broken friend, leaning against the window he was looking through, shaking uncontrollably by the news he had just received. Brian slowly walked up, not certain how to comfort Nick. All he could manage was to place his hand on his shoulder, before he also looked through the window into the isolation station.

"Jesus Christ", he whispered once his eyes fell on Natascha lying helplessly in her bed with several IVs running into her arms. She was so weak her eyes were closed. One physician in protective gear, Dr Pit, was with her, switching an empty IV bottle for a full one. A quick glance on the monitors indicated a dangerously low blood pressure and a weak pulse. A nasal tube supplied her with additional oxygen.

"We're doing everything for her that is medically possible. All we can do now is wait", Dr Crawford offered little solace as he stepped beside them.

"What will happen to her?" Nick asked in a broken voice, his eyes locked on his wife. Dr Crawford looked at him, not sure how much truth he could handle now, but Brian nodded at him.

"The pneumonic plague is a bacterial infection, attacking the respiratory system. Your wife already shows advanced symptoms like fever and...", Dr Crawford paused, trying to find a gentle way to explain it, but he wasn't sure if that was possible.

"She was coughing up blood last Friday when you evacuated us", Nick sobbed.

"Yes, that's correct, four days ago", Dr Crawford confirmed and looked at Natascha's face. Even through the window, they could clearly see the bloodstained skin around her mouth and nose. Dr Pit carefully cleaned her face, but she didn't show any reaction.

"What will happen next?" Nick insisted through gritted teeth.

Dr Crawford looked at the ceiling for a moment, and he knew that there was no sense in creating false hope. He took a few moments before he answered.

"Unfortunately, in most cases, the infection will progress rather quickly. Once the patient becomes unconscious, the pneumonia will ultimately lead to respiratory failure."

"Most cases?" Brian frowned incredulously. "Doc, we're not in medieval times anymore."

"No, we're certainly not."

Brian's eyes fell on Natascha again.

"What is the mortality rate?" the retired admiral asked in a low voice. "I mean, back then", he quickly added.

Dr Crawford didn't answer right away, but there was no way in sugar coating the truth. "Back then?" Dr Crawford bit his lip for a moment with consideration. "At least ninety percent."

"Jesus! But today it's different, right? She's a young and healthy woman. Her diet cannot be compared to what they ate couple hundred years ago, right? Bloody hell, you have antibiotics today, they must be helping her somehow?"

"Her general condition is certainly in her favour, and she's getting the right antibiotics now..." Dr Crawford explained with a sad expression and shook his head.

"But what?"

"It's very important that the antibiotics are administered as early as possible. She arrived here at an advanced state." Dr Crawford's answer didn't leave much room for any hope.

"So, does that mean there is nothing you can do for her?" Brian read between the lines, searching the doctor for answers.

"We're doing everything medically possible, I can guarantee you that, but she lost consciousness a couple of hours ago. I'm really sorry." Dr Crawford felt as if he had just confirmed her death sentence.

They could feel the tension descend upon the room, as Brian glanced at the rest of his team. Shira and Talia leaned against the wall for support, before descending down the wall in unison, their faces buried beneath their hands.

"I want to be with her", Nick eventually whispered over the sobbing that surrounded him.

"Of course. Come with me, we have to take some precautions", Dr Crawford softly spoke and placed his arm around Nick's shoulder. Ariel took Nick's spot beside Brian, and together with the retired admiral they watched as Dr Crawford led Nick through the next door. Ariel's eyes fell on Natascha, the very sight of her pierced him deep with sorrow. His mind was spinning. He knew there was nothing they could have done differently, yet he couldn't stop thinking about what he knew. They all stood there for hours, in silence, just watching Nick desperately holding Natascha's hand in his own, tears burning streaks down his face as he caressed her hand helplessly.

"There's some food in the galley for you guys." Colonel Edward Thompson's rasping voice stirred them from their lethargy as he approached them.

"Bloody hell, what are you doing here?" Brian couldn't hide his surprise.

"I was in the area and thought to stop by", Colonel Thompson lied and shrugged. "How does it look?" he wanted to know as he stood beside Brian.

"Not that good, Ed", Brian admitted with a lump in his throat. "She fell unconscious couple hours ago. Doc said that's not good."

"Bloody hell, she's still alive, isn't she? So stop talking like that. As long as she's breathing there is still hope. This might be a ship, but it's still one of the best medical facilities in the world", Colonel Thompson barked, making it clear why he was with the Regimental Head Quarters of the SAS.

"You're right, Ed", Brian nodded, feigning positivity. "It's just..." he trailed when he couldn't find the words. It was only when the retired admiral turned around that he noticed most of his team members heading for the galley. He knew they would be gone for only a moment before returning with haste. He glanced from Shira, to Ariel, and finally rested his eyes on Talia, neither of them having moved. Shira wiped her hand across her cheek, batting a tear aside as Talia heaved a sigh.

Colonel Thompson carefully turned around and checked the corridor to make sure that they were alone.

"There's something you should know", the Colonel started, but demonstratively looked at the Israeli's first before he revealed more information. Brian glared at him for a moment, then nodded with encouragement to continue.

"Remember I told you that we're interrogating two doctors from that ship?"

"Yes, of course I do. Are you telling me that they're here?" Brian wanted to know. Now it was Colonel Thompson's turn to be surprised. "Why else would you be here other than to get a detailed debriefing and the potential transport of terrorists?"

Brian shared his suspicion. "I didn't retire that long ago", he added and almost sounded insulted, but Colonel Thompson just shrugged again.

"That's true. The two doctors are indeed on board the *Montrose* as we speak."

"And?"

"Walk with me", Ed Thompson whispered and turned around. His head barely moved, but it was enough for Ariel to see that he gestured him to come along too. They didn't speak as they walked down the corridor. They turned for the staircase and took two flights of stairs down, following Colonel Ed Thompson into another corridor.

"I was thinking, and there is something that didn't make any bloody sense", Colonel Thompson whispered as he guided them deeper into the ship. "They kidnap young women from the streets to sell them into slavery to some ISIS groups in Syria, correct?" Colonel Thompson pointed out what they already knew. "They also got hands on that bloody bacteria, thanks to this Rowan Harrison", He spat the name with such distaste that it took him a moment before he continued. "They infect some poor women with the bloody bacteria and, after a couple of days, they ship them out and sell them to terrorists. Once in their camp, the towel heads all drop like flies and are off to meet their maker, less the seventy-two virgins."

"Okay?"

"What is puzzling me is this", Ed turned around and blocked his friend. He paused his thoughts as two seamen passed by them. "Your girl up there is in pretty good physical condition –"

"She might not–" Brian interrupted him.

"Rubbish! Shut up and listen, Brian. Your girl up there is in pretty good physical condition, yet she is barely hanging in there. On the other side, you have those women that they snatched from the streets. Drug addicts, drifters, you name it. Women who are in much worst shape to begin with than your girl. Yet they manage to hang on long enough to be transported in a stinky boat to shore, then thrown in the back of an old truck, travelling hundreds of kilometres through the dessert before they reach their destination." Ed let the words sink in for a moment. Just by the expression on Brian's face he knew that his friend had not thought about that before. "Let's move", Ed whispered and turned around. "Makes me think about what the doctors have to say about it."

"Do you think the bacteria has been altered?" Brian finally asked, drumming his finger on the crook of his elbow.

"Do I look like a bloody biochemist to you? I don't know. We have to ask the bloody doctors for that. By the way, your brother and his friend are staying in this cabin. I believe they're being released from sick bay today. I assume they told you?"

"Blimey! They didn't!" Brian exalted and looked through the open cabin door as if he had never seen the inside of a cabin before. An orderly was just preparing it.

"Did you ask?" Ed asked in return.

"No, I didn't", Brian mumbled and looked down. Colonel Thompson spun around and stared his friend down.

"Listen to me! I want to be perfectly clear on this: before you or Lawrence leave this ship, you blokes better talk to each other, you got that? I will lock you both into a bloody cell if I have to." Thompson threatened him, instinctively puffing his chest as he ordered him. Brian felt a sense of dread and nodded his defeat. He knew Ed was right.

"Great! I knew you would be reasonable. Now let's keep moving", Ed turned around and led them down another level. A guard stood at attention once he saw the Colonel. Thompson saluted him and the guard let them pass without questions. They walked through the door and turned into another corridor. At its end four members of the SAS guarded two cells. They all straightened up at the sight of their commanding officer. Colonel Thompson stopped and turned around to face Brian and Ariel.

"Listen, we could only ask them basic questions, our hands are still tied by some stupid laws and regulations. They're out of quarantine, and we have orders to bring them to London later this evening where specialists will talk to them. If anyone knows anything about how to help your girl, it would be them", the Colonel pointed with purpose. Ariel curiously watched as Ed Thompson closed the door behind him. Brian's eyes narrowed with focus.

"Surveillance?" the retired admiral wanted to know.

"There are a couple of video cameras in the cabin, but you know how old these frigates are. Look at the wiring. All the video footage is going over those cables there." Colonel Thompson answered and pointed at a cable harness along the ceiling.

"Yeah, bloody electronics fail all the time. Must be the salt in the air", Brian commented dryly. Brian and Colonel Thompson simultaneously turned towards Ariel and looked at him.

"Boys, why don't you come over here", Ed Thompson shouted down the corridor. "I want you to meet an old friend of mine, retired Admiral Brian Whittaker." And with that, Colonel Thompson reached up and ripped the video cables out of the socket, killing the surveillance footage to the bridge immediately.

"Look at how old they are! Very fragile!" Brian marvelled and pulled them down even further to take a closer look as the Colonel called in to report that everything was okay. He made a point in stating that they would fix it and not need a technician to help them. Ariel slowly started walking down the corridor, his eyes fixed on the two cabin doors. The SAS unit met him halfway.

"The bloke is on your left, the woman to your right", one of them mentioned as they walked past the Israeli. Without a hesitation in his step, Ariel bumped into one of them and took his combat knife.

"I will be needing that back once you're done", the SAS member commented before they met with Colonel Thompson and Brian.

"Bloody hell!" Colonel Thompson hissed as he watched Ariel. "Oh, I forgot to ask you. You're still hiring, right? I might be out of a job soon." Ed cleared his throat. He was focussed on Ariel as the Israeli closed the door to Dr Evans' cabin behind him. The steel door muffled her scream to a murmur.

It was unbeknownst to Nick what was happening a couple decks below, and it was unlikely that he would have cared anyway. He had spent the last couple hours at the only place where he wanted to be, right beside Natascha, tightly holding her hand. A quick glance at the monitor showed him that his wife had a high fever, yet her hand felt cold. Nick winced when he noticed the blood trickling from her nose.

"I got you, angel", he whispered and carefully cleaned her face before stroking her hair. "Remember when we went to Italy with pumpkin?" Nick asked and started telling her about their last little trip. He had lost all sense for time, only listening to the shallow gurgling breath, indicating the liquid building up in her lungs. He almost shrieked when Dr Pit patted him on the shoulder.

"I'm sorry to interrupt you, but the admiral wants to talk to you", he apologised and gestured to the window. Nick looked up and turned around. He was surprised to see Brian and Talia waving at him from the other side of the window. Still holding Natascha's hand he wanted to wave them away, nothing was more important than this moment, right here. He sighed and turned back to his wife, setting her hand back to her bed before he approached the air-lock. Only a few minutes later, he joined Dr Crawford, Brian, and Talia.

"We have some news that will help Natascha", Brian could barely contain his enthusiasm. "You have to come with me", the retired admiral insisted and started walking. "Now, it really doesn't matter how we got this information, the important part is that we have it, understood?" Neither Nick nor the doctor answered as they followed Brian a couple of decks below, until they finally entered the corridor leading to the prisoners.

"Hi. How are you doing?" one of the SAS unit members greeted them. Nick just looked at them. The soldiers simply stood there, taking turns examining some old video cable. Colonel Ed Thompson waited at the end of the corridor. He just nodded at them before he opened the door.

"What is going on here?" Dr Crawford barked the moment he walked into the cell. His eyes rested on Dr Evans, who was blindfolded and restrained to a chair. She sobbed, but seemed to be otherwise unharmed. It was obvious that she was in distress. Ariel stood behind her and Shira joined his side.

"We are speeding up the interrogation process a little bit, Doc", Brian calmly explained. "Don't worry, she is fine", he added with comfort before he turned to face Dr Evans.

"Dr Evans!" Brian addressed her, this time in his military voice. The physician startled. "Can you please tell Dr Crawford here what you have just told my two friends a couple of minutes ago?" Brian encouraged her, but Dr Evans just lowered her head and kept sobbing. Shira walked up to her from behind and gently flicked her fingers against her ears. Dr Evans flinched at the touch. Shira bent down and whispered something in her ear. Neither Brian nor anyone else understood what the Israeli had just told her, but Dr Evans nodded hectically and took a couple of deep breaths.

"The...the bacteria is altered", she started and had to swallow before she continued.

"How?" Shira softly prodded her, standing right behind her.

"They gave us the Yersinia Pestis bacteria...but not before they altered it. They...they had to build in a...an insurance policy...in case it gets out of control."

"What did they do? What is the insurance policy?" Shira whispered.

"Tetanus..." Dr Evans sobbed.

"Tetanus?" Dr Crawford replied, puzzled.

"Yes...Tetanus. Both bacterias are combined..."

"Dear Lord in heaven!" Dr Crawford exhaled.

"The insurance policy is in the vaccination, isn't it?" Brian interrogated, and Dr Evans nodded. "Most people in the first world countries are vaccinated against Tetanus, but the ISIS rebels are not", Brian filled in the blanks, "So they all die from the pneumonic plague if they are not vaccinated against Tetanus?" Another nod as Dr Evans confirmed Brian's theory.

"What about those who are vaccinated? What happens to them?" Brian wanted to know. Ariel stepped closer to Nick, ready to hold him back if necessary. Dr Evans swallowed hard, but didn't answer until Shira flicked her ears again.

"They can get infected", Dr Evans started and shook her head.

"I'm gonna kill you!" Nick yelled and charged the physician. Dr Evans instinctively cringed at the flurry of movement. Still blindfolded, she could only hear as Ariel grappled Nick and struggled to keep him at bay.

"A little bit more information, Doc", Brian prompted with a whisper. He bent down a little before he continued. "I'm not sure how long he can hold him back. His strength might have something to do with his wife dying just a couple metres from here. You were scared of those two–" Brian stopped for a second to glance at Shira and Ariel, "but don't be fooled, they are like the Easter Bunny in comparison." Brian informed her and she returned her focus to Brian as he continued. "So, what happens to them?"

"They get infected, but that's not all."

"What else?"

"They will develop the same symptoms as the pneumonic plague, but...the disease is highly infectious...spreads over the airways...the bug is altered to work faster...much faster...but the Tetanus vaccination will eventually kill the infection after a few days...however..." Dr Evans choked.

"What do you mean by *however*?" Brian hissed.

"However...she...they injected the bacteria directly into her blood stream...it is too much for her immune system to handle...the damage is done!" Dr Evans' voice quivered. Brian's face was but a hairbreadth away from hers.

"She is young...healthy...with a balanced nutrition...she can survive..." Dr Evans stammered barely inaudible. Brian quickly looked at Dr Crawford, but the physician already opened the door and was on his way out. "For your own sake, you better be right about this!" Brian hissed at her. Ariel let Nick go.

"Okay, okay! I'm fine!" Nick promised and threw his arms in the air. Ariel took a step back to give his friend some space. Just as the Israeli looked at Colonel Thompson, Nick pushed him hard in the back and stripped the combat knife from him. In a quick flurry of motions, Nick rammed the knife all the way down to the handle into Dr Evan's thigh.

"That's for infecting my wife with the plague!" Nick hissed over her blood-curling scream before he let go of the handle and left.

- *35* -

British Military Intelligence, Section 5, London, Thursday, August 7
The silence lingered like a dark cloud over Brian and Klaus. So did the accusations from the British MI5, who had swiftly taken over the investigation the moment someone mentioned the word *terrorist*. Klaus and Brian felt justified in their actions, but they wouldn't be too surprised if MI5 would reopen the London Tower just for them. Intelligence Manager Gregor Powell had made his point very clear in his opening statement.

Earlier that day Brian had laughed at Klaus' sarcastic joke about having a lawyer on speed dial, but now he considered it a rookie mistake for not having done so. Brian exhaled deeply and his eyes fell on Colonel Thompson, who looked incredibly concerned. If the allegations would stick, then the SAS officer was pretty far up the creek without a paddle himself, and finding a new job would be the least of his issues.

They sat in a conference room, but they might as well have put them into an interrogation cell. Brian watched Intelligence Manager Powell arrange his notes before he checked his watch. He quickly glanced at Klaus, but his friend had not flinched a muscle since Powell's opening statement. Brian knew that Klaus' analytical mind was probably spinning out of control, so he decided to look at Colonel Edward Thompson. But Ed sat there as if he was carved out of stone himself. *Damn SAS training*, Brian thought, failing to read any emotion on Ed's face other than the concerned one he presented.

With not many options left, Brian decided to keep a close eye on Powell. The retired admiral estimated him to be in his mid to late fifties. Even in his tailored suit, he looked rather ordinary, lacking the aura of authority that Klaus or Ed commanded in their presence. Powell adjusted his glasses again, and Brian noticed that he did this at least once a minute. He knew those brown eyes didn't miss a thing. *The perfect spook!* Brian concluded. He wasn't foolish enough to let Powell's appearance cloud his judgement. The silence was interrupted when the door opened.

"I suppose that's the firing squad", Brian whispered and looked up. "Oh bloody hell, this keeps getting better and better", Brian muttered through clinched teeth as he saw an agent escorting Chief Inspector William Conolly into the conference room.

Conolly was so surprised that he was literally lost for words. Brian smiled at him.

"Chief Inspector Conolly! Thank you for coming on such a short notice. I'm Intelligence Manager Gregor Powell." Powell greeted him and shook his hand.

"But of course. Anything I can do to help. It's a pleasure to meet you." William replied and took the last remaining seat.

"I trust you know Mr Whittaker and Mr Schwartze from *EuroSecCorporation?*"

"I do. Brian, Klaus!" William greeted them, but Brian just kept his polite smile. Klaus remained motionless as he was.

"I also want you to meet Colonel Edward Thompson, Regimental Headquarters SAS", Powell continued, gesturing to Ed. "Chief Inspector, I have asked you to join us today because both our agency and MI6 are currently investigating a situation that poses a potential biological terrorist threat against Great Britain and other nations. During our investigation we came upon some information that falls into your jurisdiction. Does the name Natascha Rehfeld mean anything to you?" Gregor Powell asked. Conolly quickly glanced at Klaus and Brian, but only Brian looked back at him.

"Yes, it actually does. I'm currently running an investigation into her disappearance. All the evidence indicates that she has been kidnapped."

"Can you please tell me what you know?" the intelligence manager requested. Conolly straightened up and spent the next thirty minutes outlining exactly what he knew.

"Are you aware of Miss Rehfeld's past and the former accusations against her?" Gregor Powell continued.

"*False accusations!*" Brian interrupted him with heat. "Let's not forget that she is innocent and that she even received a written apology from the president of the United States."

"Of course. My apologies. Mr Conolly, are you aware of those false accusations and the events that led to them?"

"Of course I am. I was part of the investigation back then as well", he admitted freely.

"Very well. Chief Inspector Conolly, do you have any idea about Miss Rehfeld's current location?"

"Here we go", Brian mumbled, but the intelligence manager ignored his comment.

"No, sir, I don't", Conolly frowned, his eyes now resting on Brian and Klaus, certain he was missing something.

"Well, I officially inform you that Natascha Rehfeld had indeed been kidnapped by a group of mostly unknown people, who not only ran a human trafficking ring, but also planned to initiate a biological terrorist attack, possibly on British soil. She had been held hostage on a large ship before she was transferred to a private yacht called the *Shadow of the Orient*. The yacht is registered to a Saudi prince by the name of Tarek bin Mohammed." Brian closed his eyes, grimaced, and looked at the ceiling.

Conolly's jaw dropped, then raised and lowered as if it was swinging broken when he struggled to find words. "How do you know that?" he finally asked in disbelief.

"It might come to you as a surprise to hear that last week some employees of *EuroSecCorporation,* under the direct order of Brian Whittaker and Klaus Schwartze–"

"They actually volunteered!" Brian corrected, but he couldn't impress the intelligence manager.

"–under the direct order of Brian Whittaker and Klaus Schwartze stole a yacht, the *Cloud Dancer*–"

"We borrowed it." Brian corrected him again, raising his hand. "The guy has it back."

"–in the harbour of Monte Carlo. They then kidnapped its owner, one Iain

Walker, before–”

“He volunteered also! The bloke is a customer of ours!”

“–before they followed the *Shadow of the Orient* through the Mediterranean Sea all the way down to Tunis, where they finally ambushed the prince and freed Natascha Rehfeld.” Gregor Powell ignored Brian’s comments and kept his focus on Conolly as he provided him the sequence of events.

“But how...” Conolly finally mouthed, and then restarted with a new beat, “No, I didn’t know about that. So you have her back? How is she?” It was little relief for Brian to realise that Conolly was more concerned about Natascha’s well-being than the actual case.

“I’m afraid to say that she was exposed to the nasty bacteria the terrorists planned to use in their attack. Unfortunately she’s comatose. As for the events on how they got her back, all that happened last Friday.” Powell added impassively.

“Blimey, that is horrible news. I’m glad that you found her, but...wait second! *Last Friday* you said?” Conolly looked at Powell.

“Yes, I’m afraid. Last Friday. They didn’t contact you?”

“No, they didn’t.”

“And you had absolutely no knowledge about this operation?”

“Bloody hell no! Of course not! That is highly illegal!” Conolly stated the obvious.

“We were in international waters”, Brian complained half-heartedly.

“Why the hell didn’t you tell me?” Conolly asked his friends.

“I wish I could. The last couple of days were dark times”, Brian sarcastically commented, but Conolly had no way of knowing that he was referring to the outbreak of the plague in the 14th and 17th century.

“Chief Inspector Conolly”, Powell continued to break the awkward silence that had fallen over them. “Does the name Rowan Harrison mean anything to you?”

“Bloody hell! You kidnapped him, too?” Conolly angrily looked at Brian, but all of a sudden the retired admiral admired the lights under the ceiling.

“Chief Inspector, please. Does the name mean anything do you?” Intelligence Manager Powell repeated.

“Yes, it does”, Conolly answered and shook his head before he made eye contact again. “I’m currently investigating the disappearance of Mr Harrison as well.”

“Can you please tell me how far you are in your investigations?”

“Sure”, William replied and filled Powell in.

“Would you be surprised to hear that Mr Harrison might be connected to the human trafficking ring and the terrorist threat against the crown?” Conolly was clearly shocked by Powell’s question and made a face.

“The bloke is certainly shady. He lives the life of a playboy in the fast lane. There might be one or two mud puddles that he has his foot in, but human trafficking? Terrorism? I don’t know. Nothing in our files indicates any such connections. Can I ask where that information is coming from, or is that classified?”

“The information came from Miss Rehfeld shortly after her rescue. She accused him being part of the cell. According to her, she personally witnessed him talking to one of the major terrorists we currently have in custody.”

"Those are strong accusations. Her proof?"

"Her own eye witness account." Powell finished. Conolly raised an eye brow.

"There's also a former acquaintance of Mr Harrison, a Spanish national by the name of Alba Casillas–" Brian flinched when Powell revealed her name, but the intelligence manager didn't care, "who used to accompany Mr Harrison to certain events. She also stated that he and this Saudi prince are well known to each other."

"Are you saying that a member of the Royal Saudi family is connected to human trafficking and a suspected terrorist plot against the British crown?" Conolly couldn't even believe the words that were coming out of his mouth.

"We're not sure yet, to be honest. But the fact that Miss Rehfeld was rescued from Prince Tarek's yacht cannot be ignored, especially since there is a connection between Mr Harrison and Prince Tarek."

"Understood. Given the circumstances, I believe that it's fair to ask if Mr Rowan Harrison has been found yet?" Conolly asked and accusingly looked at Brian and Klaus.

"I certainly sympathise with you", Intelligence Manager Powell remarked with a hint of sarcasm. Brian just growled and made a face before Powell continued. "Unfortunately we are not aware of Mr Harrison's current location. Miss Casillas contacted Mr Whittaker's company several days ago. There was an eighteen year-old woman by the name of Elena Romanov with her. Miss Romanov claimed that she had been the victim of the human trafficking ring. She stated that she had been held prisoner at the very ship that is currently the focus of our investigation. Miss Romanov also claimed that she had not only seen Natascha Rehfeld, but she had actually shared her cell with her during that time. Did anyone from Mr Whittaker's company inform you about that?"

"You do know that he also owns fifty percent of the company?" Brian wondered and nodded towards Klaus, but the former German general still didn't move.

"No, they did not inform me about that", Chief Inspector Conolly admitted coldly. The disappointment was clear in his voice.

"That's what I thought", Powell nodded. "According to Mr Whittaker, it was none other than Rowan Harrison who bought Elena Romanov from the human trafficking ring to present her as a gift to Prince Tarek bin Muhammed. When Prince Tarek and Rowan Harrison met in Monaco, Alba Casillas was there to accompany Rowan Harrison. That's when she met Elena Romanov. Miss Casillas did not only help her to escape, she also introduced her to *EuroSecCorporation*." Powell drank some water to allow the words to sink in. "Knowing that Rowan Harrison was the key to finding Natascha, Mr Whittaker and his company used their resources and contacts to track Mr Harrison down in Monaco."

"Where they kidnapped him", Conolly surmised where the story was going.

"We didn't kidnap that cheeky bugger. He volunteered. Check the bloody video footage from the harbour master."

"Confronted with the possible charges against him, and in the face of certain torture–"

"Torture? Wait a second! What the bloody hell are you talking about?" Brian protested and straightened in his chair.

"Four of your Israeli employees are currently hiding inside the Israeli embassy. They were with you on that yacht, and at least two of them have a shady past", Powell informed Brian. The retired admiral just made a face.

"They had a difficult childhood", Brian mumbled.

"Either way, Mr Harrison informed them that Natascha Rehfeld was at that point on board the *Shadow of the Orient*. We believe that they rendezvoused in international waters to exchange prisoners." Intelligence Manager Powell closed.

"Well, I must admit, it certainly sounded different when Klaus told me the story", Conolly admitted and shook his head. He and Powell carefully watched for any reaction, but Klaus had yet to move. Brian grimaced and shifted in his seat, certain he would be led to the gallows if this were another time. "So, does MI5 want me to close the book on those investigations?" Conolly finally asked after a couple moments.

"No, not yet", Intelligence Manager Powell answered and leaned back in his chair. "I'm asking you for two things. One, I want you to tell Mr Whittaker and Mr Schwartze about the possible legal consequences of their actions. Two, I need you to interview Alba Casillas and Elena Romanov. Mr Whittaker here confirmed that they are in one of their safe houses."

"Wait a second! What are you talking about? That was not part of the deal!" Brian growled threateningly as he leaned forward. Even Klaus threw a perplexed glance at the intelligence manager.

"Mr Whittaker, I know about the service you have done for her Majesty, but make no mistake! You overplayed your hand in this one." Powell stated thoughtfully before he continued. "I do believe that it's time for you to cut your bloody losses. So far everything has been very civilised, but you and Mr Schwartze are facing some very serious charges. If I were you, I would start cooperating by giving Chief Inspector Conolly the chance to talk to these two women. They might have crucial information that can help us prevent a terrorist attack. Do you really want to obstruct such an investigation? You should consider yourself fortunate that we have not yet charged you with treason!" Powell coldly added, throwing a quick, accusing glance at Colonel Edward Thompson. "I believe it's in your best interest that it stays that way."

Brian thought for a few moments. He flinched when his cell phone rang. "It's from one of my men at the hospital where Natascha is", he explained after a quick glance on the display. His voice was shaking. He didn't expect a phone call from there.

The device was still ringing.

"You can answer it", Powell offered, knowing the importance of the call.

"Yes? Whittaker here!" Brian answered through the lump in his throat. "Nick! Slow down! What happened?"

Klaus straightened up in his seat, watching in horror as Brian closed his eyes. The retired admiral twisted his lips in a futile attempt to keep his composure.

"I'm so sorry Nick!" he finally managed, confirming what Klaus feared. "You stay with her, son. We will take care of the arrangements. We will be there as soon as possible, do you hear me?" Brian promised with a shaking voice, but Nick had already hung up. The retired admiral stared at his cell phone, not knowing what to say. Klaus put a hand on his shoulder, his face reflecting the sorrow he felt.

"Natascha...she...her lung", Brian started, but the words refused to form. He just managed to shake his head and wiped a tear from his face.

"Jesus!" SAS Colonel Edward Thompson said. "I'm really sorry to hear that, Brian. My condolences, Klaus", he offered.

"I want to offer my condolences, too", Chief Inspector Conolly added.

"I'm really sorry for your loss, Mr Whittaker, I really am, but please let us not lose focus on the matter at hand. Miss Romanov and Miss Casillas are now the only witnesses in this case who can link Rowan Harrison and Prince Tarek to this organisation. The faster Chief Inspector Conolly can talk to them, the better our chances of finding those bastards who are behind this", Powell reminded them of the gravity of this situation.

"I'm going to interview them, Brian, not interrogate them. You know me. I'm a friend!" Conolly added with reassurance. Brian's eyes still stared at his cell phone, and Conolly was uncertain if Brian had even heard them at all. What Brian had feared all along had happened. The expression on his face was a clear indication that he didn't care anymore. Reluctantly he glanced over to his friend. Klaus slowly nodded.

"My late brother in law, Gordon Ramshaw, had an estate outside London. My wife is the sole beneficiary. The main house is now used as a women's shelter, but we are using the guest house as one of our safe houses." Brian stated calmly, with defeat. "You will find both women there."

Gordon Ramshaw's former residence, east of London, Friday, August 8
The leaves on the perfectly trimmed shrubs in the large park swayed gently in the mild breeze coming up from the river. Dark clouds covered the sky, refusing any light from the moon or the stars to shine to the ground. A quick glance at his watch showed the man that it was almost two o'clock in the morning. For hours he and his team had watched the guesthouse from their stakeout, but so far they had only seen two guards. Luck seemed to favour them. The last time they had seen them was about three hours ago on their last foot patrol around the house. Shortly after that, all but one light was turned off.

The assassin in the dark grey jumpsuit picked up his binoculars and studied the window again. The flickering light told him that whoever was in that room had most likely the TV running. Slowly he put the binoculars down and unlocked his cell phone. With such short notice he didn't want to take a risk and looked at the pictures from the two marks again. Alba Casillas and Elena Romanov.

An incoming signal caught his attention. The other team was ready to move. The assassin glanced at his partner. Even though they were only one metre apart, he could barely see him, just enough to see that he nodded. The assassin typed a reply and stowed the cell phone in his pocket before getting up. Without making a single sound, they covered the distance to the guest house precisely as planned. Two minutes later and the phone cables transmitting the alarm were cut. They tactically advanced around the corner to meet the other team at the main entrance. A quick glance and they knew that everything was going according to plan. It took them less than thirty seconds before they sneaked through the door.

So far the two women upstairs had not noticed anything. Drowning their grief of

Natascha's death in several bottles of cheap wine and some TV shows, it was not likely that the stealth of four well trained assassins would catch their attention. Undetected by anyone, the intruders reached the top of the stairs. A few seconds later and they had found cover to the left and right of the door. Only their leader took the chance and peeked inside the room.

The only light came from the television screen, but it was all he needed. He couldn't help but smile once he confirmed both targets. Even better, there was no sign of anyone else in the room. His eyes caught a movement, and he quickly noticed that it was only the curtains swaying in front of the open window. The younger of the two women, the one with the blonde hair, reached for the last slice of pizza before she stared at the TV again. This was the moment he had waited for. With both women in the same room and not paying attention, the assassins swiftly moved in, their combat knives at the ready. They had already picked their individual victims. Only three more steps, yet the women were still oblivious to the mortal danger.

The leader raised his knife hand, but that was his last moment before the projectile hit him in the head. The lights were turned on before his lifeless body even touched the floor. The eyes of the remaining assassins grew wide at the sight of their dead friend and the green laser dot now dancing from face to face, blinding them as it rhythmically jumped from each target.

"Ay-up, lads. Don't you fucking move", Rolf calmly ordered from the door, the laser on his SigSauer projecting a red dot on the back of the head of the intruder furthest left. He swiftly took a couple of steps to make room for Olaf and Ole-Einar. "Drop the knives or I'm going to blow your brains out", Rolf added. The tone in his voice didn't leave any room for doubt. To make matters worse, the women were also aiming their guns at them. Surprisingly, neither of them looked tipsy, and the barrels of their guns were dangerously steady. The assassins had yet to move, but it dawned on them that they had no choice. So far the only movement came from Noah, who, disguised as Elena Romanov, still nibbled at the pizza slice in one hand, while holding her SigSauer in the other. Her eyes, however, were locked on the assassin who wanted to cut her throat a mere thirty seconds ago. The green laser dot from Ariel's rifle focussed on the assassins' eyes, a clear reminder that they were out of options. "Last warning, drop your knives or die!" Rolf repeated his order

"Maybe they don't speak English?" Shira wondered, still sitting in the comfortable lazy-boy chair, in which she had pretended to be Alba Casillas. She got up and repeated the order in Arab, but with no result.

"Oh, they understand, they're just stubborn", Noah added and, finished with her late night snack, licked her fingers. She also got up.

"Don't even think about it!" Shira warned the assassin right in front of her. She noticed his eyes dancing nervously from one woman to the other, but it was too late. Determined to fulfil his mission, the attacker lunged forward, his serrated combat knife coming dangerously close to Shira's face. The Israeli fired and jumped back, desperately trying to get out of the direction of the attack. At such a short distance she couldn't miss. The 9mm projectile from her SigSauer ended the attacker's life instantly, but the danger was far from over. With the lazy-boy chair in her back, Shira had nowhere to go. Still in a forward motion, the assassin's lifeless body fell against her, pushing her off balance. Noah moved in to help Shira, and with the sudden change of positions Ariel, Rolf, Olaf, and Ole-Einar no longer had a clear line of fire any more.

The remaining two attackers noticed this and immediately used the confusion to their advantage, attacking the women in front of them. This time they wanted to take them as a hostage, a bargaining chip for their way out. Instead of slashing Noah with the knife, the attacker grabbed her hair. With her eyes on Shira, Noah was caught off guard and didn't react fast enough. She screamed as the assassin jarred her head back by a fistful of her hair. Just as the attacker pulled her in, Rolf was already over him. With his left hand he grabbed the attacker's knife hand, his fingers locking like vice grips around the wrist. Rolf used his forward motion to bend the attackers arm back. In the same motion he punched the attacker in the face repeatedly with his right hand, bludgeoning him with the butt of his gun. Every blow ripped open a new gash on his face, blood quickly covering his face as Rolf drove the attacker back against the wall. Three more blows followed, the cold steel of the SigSauer breaking through the skin on the assassin's face, destroying his jaw and teeth to the point that he was unrecognisable. It was only when the intruder sank lifelessly to the floor that Rolf finally released him. He did not have to be a physician to determine that this attacker would never harm anyone again.

Shira grunted and stumbled to regain her balance as she stepped over the assassin that had fallen into her. Just as she tried to get up, the last attacker grabbed her by the throat and pushed her backwards. The Israeli tripped over the assassin she had shot just seconds ago and pulled her attacker down with her. They both hit the ground hard. Her attacker released his grip for a second, allowing Shira to catch her breath and control his knife hand. Before she could do anything else, Ole-Einar came to her rescue. The huge Norwegian got hold of the assassin by the back of his head and his chin. The assassin squirmed and instinctively grabbed the Norwegian's wrist with desperation as Ole-Einar lifted him up above his head, snapping his neck before he tossed the lifeless body away like a rag doll. The fight had only lasted mere seconds, but it had drained them all.

"Status report!" Ariel's voice crackled over the radio.

"Four threats eliminated", Rolf replied and looked around. Ole-Einar and Olaf confirmed the deaths of the attackers. "Shira?"

"I'm okay, dammit!" the Israeli cursed.

"Noah?"

"Lost a couple hairs, but that should be it."

Scotland Yard, London, Friday, August 8

Brian Whittaker didn't slow down as he marched through the entrance hall of Scotland Yard. The expression on his face let everyone from the janitor up to high ranking officers know to clear a path for the retired admiral. In his wake were Intelligence Manager Gregor Powell from MI5, his friend Sean MacLeod, and Ole-Einar. They had not planned for the Viking to come along, but after last night's events they were short on volunteers to tell him that. A quick flick from Powell's badge allowed them to pass the security check point without getting stopped.

"You sure he is in his bloody office?" Brian asked as the elevator door closed behind them.

"According to our audio surveillance, yes, he is." Powell confirmed. Brian frowned for a second at the thought of MI5 running surveillance inside Scotland Yard.

"I appreciate you letting me come along on this, Greg", Brian admitted in a calm voice, his eyes fixed on the illuminated buttons on the elevator.

"Didn't have much choice, did I? I knew you had connections, but Jesus Christ, I got my marching orders on this one from the highest place possible."

"Sorry for that, but time was of an essence. Besides, you are getting the credit for taking them down", the retired admiral apologised sourly.

"Never mind, mate. Just promise me that you keep the Viking under control. He looks like he's going on a raid", Powell nervously replied, shyly looking back over his shoulder at Ole-Einar, who towered over them.

"You hear that, big guy? You behave!" Brian ordered. His directive was as genuinely ignored as it was given. "There, I told him", Brian nodded towards Powell.

"You got to be bloody kidding me", Gregor Powell exhaled sharply, just as the typical sound of a gong indicated that they had reached the designated floor.

"Excuse me", Ole-Einar snarled the moment the doors opened and pushed through Whittaker and Powell, turning right.

"I'm sorry, what did you say? I couldn't hear you!" Brian innocently looked at Gregor as they tried to catch up with the Norseman. Sean followed them with a big grin on his face.

"Excuse me! Do you have an appointment?" William Conolly's secretary asked and rose from behind her desk.

"He is expecting us", Brian reassured her with a raise of his hand, taking quick strides to keep up with Ole-Einar. Gregor Powell chose the more official option and showed his badge.

"Bloody hell!" he yelled as Ole-Einar kicked the door to Conolly's private office in. His kick ripped the door from its hinges, causing it to fly into the office where it landed with a loud bang against Conolly's desk.

"Jesus!" the chief inspector yelled and jumped up, toppling his chair. Before he could adequately assess the scene in front of him, Ole-Einar had already shoved the remains of the door out of his way and reached over the table to grab Conolly by his collar.

"What the–?" was all the chief inspector could manage before the Viking lifted him over the table and slammed him on the floor. Conolly's scream matched the sound of the alarm that resounded through the building.

"William Conolly! You are hereby under arrest!" Powell yelled against the alarm and added a whole list of crimes as Ole-Einar put some handcuffs on Conolly. With the chief inspector safely secured on the floor with a huge Viking on his back, Powell spent several minutes convincing the armed guards to lower their weapons and understand the legitimacy of their arrest. It took him a couple more minutes and some phone calls to convince Conolly's supervisor that this was indeed a legal arrest and, looking at the door, not an act of terrorism.

"You can send the invoice for the repairs to my office. I insist!" Brian offered

Conolly's superior, handing him a business card as they escorted their former friend to the elevator.

"I thought you promised me you would keep him under control", Powell complained to Brian the moment the elevator doors shut.

"I did! You should see him when he's pissed, this was nothing." Brian stated innocently and gestured with his arms.

"For Christ sake! What were you thinking?" Powell barked suddenly, directly to Ole-Einar this time.

"How my ancestors must have felt?" the Norwegian calmly replied, referring to the Viking's raids on England a couple centuries ago. The intelligence manager just shook his head and turned around again.

"Smart ass!" Powell whispered. Brian and Sean couldn't help the grin on their faces.

It was almost one hour later before Intelligence Manager Powell finally closed the door to the interrogation room behind him. He took a seat at the table next to Brian. Opposite to them sat William Conolly. He massaged his wrists. The handcuffs had left some nasty red streams. The cup of coffee was untouched. Gregor Powell tossed a folder onto the table and exhaled sharply, his eyes examining Conolly.

"Terrorism and treason, Mr Conolly. Doesn't get much worse than that." Powell calmly started, reminding Conolly about the severity of the charges. The former chief inspector flinched a little, but that was his only reaction.

"I want a lawyer", he calmly replied.

"Not going to happen", Powell shook his head. "Not with those charges." Neither of them spoke for the next few minutes.

"Why are you here?" Conolly finally looked at Brian.

"Brian's company used to do the odd job for us. Years ago." Powell's statement seemed to be news to Conolly, who dubiously shook his head.

"Not a reason to be here", he rightfully remarked.

"Okay, let's try this. His company is currently working this job for us", Powell explained.

"Let me guess", Conolly started and looked at his former friend. "MI5 and MI6 are taking the credit for this one and in return they will give you a get-out-of-jail-free-card for the bloody raid you ran in Monaco and the Mediterranean. Am I right?"

"Something like that, yes", Brian freely admitted, holding eye contact.

"Bloody hell, that's what I thought. So the whole meeting yesterday was a set up?"

"No, mate. It was just to confirm what we already suspected. You're dirty."

"What makes you think that?" Conolly wanted to know. Brian reached for the folder and took a picture from a traffic camera as well as the BOLO out. He glanced at them for a second before he placed them in front of Conolly.

"July twenty-fifth! The day Alba Casillas contacted us for help. She and Elena Romanov had just arrived in London from Monte Carlo the evening before. By that time, Rowan Harrison and Prince Tarek had already contacted you to look for them. You immediately initiated a directive to every police officer to be on the lookout for

Miss Casillas as a person of interest connected to a human trafficking ring. Bloody hell, Bill, she was helping an innocent woman get away from a monster, and you put a BOLO out for human trafficking? Are you mental?" Brian exclaimed hotly, his words clipped. "Ariel and Shira escorted her to her condo. Poor woman was so frightened that she ran a red traffic light. Since the BOLO on her was for human trafficking, her picture from the traffic camera raised a red flag the moment she ran that damn light. Guess what? Not even one hour later, two goons from Prince Tarek's private army show up at her place, ready to slice'n dice. If it wouldn't have been for Ariel and Shira, you would have even more blood on your hands, mate."

"How are you going to prove this?" Conolly scoffed at their story.

"We downloaded the data from the cell tower your burn phone connected to, Mr Conolly." Intelligence Manager Powell explained dryly.

"Listen, mate. I don't know what you're getting out of this", Brian continued and leaned forward, "but why the hell did you send a professional wet team after the girls last night? Don't you think they've been through enough?" Brian snarled.

"Why do you–" Conolly started, but Brian slammed his hand on the table to shut him up.

"Christ sake! Don't start that shit. The guest house was a set-up and you're the only one who knew about it, so don't give me that bull!" Brian shouted and abruptly stood up, toppling his chair.

"Brian!" Powell tried to calm him down, reaching for his arm, but the retired admiral turned away and leaned on the table.

"By God! I swear to you! I already lost one person, I'm not going to lose another one. If anything happens to those two women, I will unleash my people at you. I will reveal every single bloody detail about you. No matter what hole they're going to throw you in–"

"Brian! That's enough!"

"My men will get to you, and by God they will make you suffer. Do you bloody hear me?"

"Are you threatening me?" Conolly returned, sounding more nervous than he wanted to.

"No, it's not a threat, mate! It's a bloody promise!" Brian finished and left the interrogation room.

- 36 -

EuroSecCorporation, **London, Wednesday, August 13**

"So, how was it?" the blonde woman thoughtfully asked from behind her desk as most members of *EuroSecCorporation* walked back in.

"I hate funerals", Brian admitted with a polite smile and walked to his office.

"Yeah, not much fun at all. Most people cried. No one laughed", Klaus complained, close on Brian's heels.

"I told you, people like me", the young lady apologetically shrugged. "Sorry, I meant *liked me*. I'm not used to being dead", she shuddered and looked at Nick. "How did I look?"

"Not too bad. I got to hold you during the whole ceremony. At least you weren't that heavy", he commented and placed an urn on her desk.

"I love you, too. You could be a little bit more sympathetic. After all, this was my funeral", Natascha complained and couldn't help but cough. She still struggled with the aftermaths of the infection.

"Don't be harsh on him", Ariel commented nonchalantly as he walked by. "He did cry."

"Aww, that's so cute", Natascha teased.

"You better be nice, I already buried you once", Nick threatened his wife and kissed her on the top of her head.

"Should I be concerned how much you enjoy kissing a blonde?" Natascha wanted to know and threw a piercing glance at Nick, who let her dyed hair run through his fingers. He just shrugged with a knowing smile before he went to the washroom, humming a melody that could resemble a song from a famous Columbian singer.

"And stop calling me Shakira!" Natascha yelled after him, but her raised voice immediately set her into a fit of coughing.

"You okay?" Shira and Talia walked by and wanted to know.

"Yes, considering that I was on my death bed last week I'm fine", Natascha complained and straightened up before she looked at her friends again. "Damn! Having the plague really does take a toll on you. I just have to take it slow for a couple more weeks, I guess. No need to be worried."

"It's good to have you back here at the office. Must have gotten boring at the safe house", Talia smiled, seeing that her spirits were unyielding.

"Want to have a tea?" Shira invited her friend.

"Sure, why not?" Natascha got up and slowly followed the two Israelis into the break room.

"It's alive. The zombie apocalypse is here!" Rolf theatrically yelled from the couch.

"Zombies feed on brains, so you're totally safe. Get up or I'll bite you anyway", Natascha threatened and made her way to the couch.

"You haven't been infectious for days, remember?" Rolf kept teasing and slowly sat up.

"True. But I'm so full of antibiotics that three people get healthy every time I sneeze. Now get up or I'll cough at you and you can never use a sick day in your life again."

"I'm getting up! I'm getting up!" Rolf hurried and left the couch to Natascha.

"Ah, that feels good. I'm still so damn tired", she complained and lay down.

"That will pass. Here's your tea", Shira encouraged her and placed a cup in front of her.

"Thanks, sis", Natascha said and rolled onto her side, carefully watching her friend.

"What is it?" Shira wanted to know and squeezed onto the couch. She knew that something was bothering her friend.

"I don't know about this whole faking my death thing." Natascha shook her head. "It feels weird."

"I don't know. I never died before, but I bet it feels weird." Shira laughed.

"Who knows that I'm alive?"

"Besides us, only your parents and one guy from MI5. I told my father, but don't worry about him. He knows more important secrets", Shira smiled.

"I bet he does." Natascha answered, but her mind was trailing off again. "At the funeral, did you see–" Natascha started, but she didn't finish her question.

"Yes, they were all there. Your friends from the aquarium, Erika, Andreas, Mario and...", Shira hesitated for a second, making sure that Nick wasn't there. "...and Mark", she finally whispered. Natascha looked up at her friend.

"They were there? They came all the way from Germany?" Natascha couldn't deny that she was touched. "How...how did they–"

"What do you expect? They were very emotional, Natascha." Shira explained calmly. Natascha swallowed.

"And Mark?"

"Yes, he too. He must still be thinking a lot about you", the Israeli guessed.

"I feel bad for them. Is there no way to tell them?" Natascha wanted to know.

"Natascha, you know that we can't do this. Not until we know who's exactly behind this. We're certain that Conolly told everyone that you're dead. We should keep it that way until we know you are safe."

Natascha's mouth twisted at the thought, but she knew that Shira was right. Her mood brightened when Talia brought her daughter into the break room. Shira-Sarah laughed and jumped onto the couch. Natascha joined her laughter and immediately started to tickle her daughter. Shira couldn't help but smile.

"Don't forget the meeting in about thirty minutes. That's if you feel up for it." Shira reminded her.

"I'll manage, no worries. Thank you!" Natascha laughed and spent some quality time with her daughter until Nick picked her up.

"You ready to go?" he asked after kissing them.

"I'm coming. I will be right back, pumpkin. You stay with aunt Talia, will you?" Nick and Natascha walked down towards Brian's office.

"Can you sing *Hips don't*–" Rolf commented at her sight in the hallway, but

Natascha threateningly pointed her finger at him and cut him off.

"One more word escapes your throat and I'm going to rip your tongue out!" she warned him bluntly. It took her a couple more moments before she finally sat down in the conference room. Besides her and Nick, she saw Brian, Klaus, the members of Operation Control as well as Intelligence Manager Gregor Powell.

"A miracle!" Klaus welcomed her.

"Yeah, just let me figure out how to turn water into wine and we can take this show on the road." Natascha smiled back and took a couple deep breaths.

"How are you feeling, Natascha?" Brian wanted to know and gave her a warm smile.

"Still exhausted, but I'm feeling better with every day. Thank you! But for the record, I want to state that I really don't like the idea of faking my death. It hurts my friends a lot."

"We totally understand that, but until we know for sure who is behind this, we have no other choice. Which brings me to the purpose of this meeting. I want you to meet Intelligence Manager Gregor Powell from MI5."

"Miss Rehfeld!"

Natascha just nodded. She didn't even try to hide her scepticism towards strangers, especially after Conolly's betrayal.

"The events you were involved in", Brian started carefully, "pose a potential terrorist threat on a global scale. Therefore Ariel and Shira are also here to relay and share information with their own government."

"Ah, global terrorism. Here I go again", Natascha commented and made a face.

"Natascha", Brian continued without skipping a beat. "We have a theory on how you fit into this. It all started with that letter that this reporter Kyle McRae handed over to Abbot Hetley during that gala event. The abbot tore the letter up and you retrieved it, is that correct?"

"Yes, I picked it out of the garbage bin. I didn't steal it from a priest, as my beloved husband accused me", Natascha explained and winked at Nick, who just made a face. "It's hard to believe, but it really was a coincidence that I dove in Whitmore Abbey just a short time later. Up there, my dive buddy Mario and I discovered a connection from an old, flooded mine to the catacombs inside the abbey. Inside the catacombs I found several human bones. The fact that this very part of the catacombs was sealed off from the abbey by a brick wall made me believe that I found evidence supporting Kyle's research. You know, the whole child abuse thing", Natascha added and looked at Powell. "I also made the mistake to confront the abbot in the nearby village, informing him that I have proof linking his abbey to the child abuse scandal. Before we left, I arranged the remains to be sent to an old friend of mine in Germany and asked him to carbon date them. Not long after that and I got snatched in the park while I was on a run."

"It's safe to say that Abbot Hetley informed Rowan Harrison shortly after the confrontation." Brian interjected, continuing his explanation. "Harrison donated millions to the abbey. We believe that those donations were payment to grant them access to the catacombs and the remains of the plague victims. Since Kyle McRae was also on *Asklepios*, we believe that they indeed eliminated every known threat against them. Knowing that you posed a risk to their operation, they kidnapped and brought you to that ship. They injected you with the bacteria and this Harrison bloke handed you over to Prince Tarek. For all we know, he's the one who supplied the muscle in the attempt to kill Alba and Elena. We think that the organisation tried to cover up their tracks. If you would have been infectious on his yacht, there would have been no survivors."

"Yeah, I seem to have that effect", Natascha forlornly whispered. "Did you find out how exactly they planned to use the bacteria?"

"Dr Evans told us that the insurance policy to stop the infection is in the Tetanus vaccination. They separated the abducted women into two groups."

"Group A and B", Natascha commented.

"Right. One group was for women without the Tetanus vaccination. If they did not qualify for organ donors", Powell paused and took a deep breath, "they were shipped off and sold as slaves right away. The other group was for women with the Tetanus vaccination. They injected them the altered Y.Pestis bacteria. After that, they isolated and monitored them until the Tetanus vaccination killed the infection. Once stable, they injected them again and shipped them out to be sold as slaves as well. A couple days later, after arriving at their final destination, they would be highly infectious, but with much weaker symptoms for themselves."

"Holy shit, how sick are those bastards?" Natascha shook her head in disbelief.

"It is fundamental biological warfare", Powell explained. "Usually the infection spreads by air, but they injected you the bacteria directly into the blood stream. It explains why you had such..." the intelligence manager stopped and searched for the right words.

"Why I almost died", Natascha finished his sentence.

"Yes, that's correct. Luckily you have the right vaccination and Ariel gave you some antibiotics, which slowed the infection down until you were in professional medical care. You never received the second injection. Consider yourself lucky."

"Yeah, right", Natascha remarked sarcastically. "What else did the doctor say? What about the other doctor? What was his name? Edwards?"

"Correct. We haven't cracked him yet. So far he just confirmed what we already know. Dr Evans is also not as cooperative as she was earlier. Her medical treatment interferes heavily with our interrogation. Must have something to do with the huge stab wound in her thigh." Powell explained and accusingly looked at Nick.

"Stab wound?" Natascha questioned and followed Powell's accusatory glare to her husband. This was news to her. "What did you do?"

"A tragic accident", Brian explained with indifference. "Dr Evans was kept under guard of the SAS on board the *HMS Montrose*. When we came to talk to her, we noticed that one of the guards had lost his combat knife. Luckily Nick found it and was kind enough to bring it back to him. Unfortunately he stumbled and the knife grazed Dr Evan's thigh."

"Very tragic", Klaus added with confirmation.

"The knife had to be surgically removed", Powell objected with frustration and massaged his temples.

"The floor was very slippery", Brian insisted with an upturned palm.

"Very tragic indeed", Klaus repeated.

"Bloody hell, will you two please stop it? I'm not buying any of this", Powell reminded them.

"You stabbed that damn bitch in the leg? For me?" Natascha marvelled. A smile appeared on her face.

"You heard them, it was an accident", Nick winked at her.

"Aww, that is so sweet. Thanks! That means I don't have to hunt her down and kill her", Natascha said warmheartedly. Intelligence Manager Powell pretended not to hear any of this and shook his head. Natascha finally changed the subject. "What about Rowan Harrison's father? Any idea what's going on with him?"

"No disrespect, but how certain are you about what you have heard that day?" Powell politely asked.

Natascha exhaled and shook her head. "Don't know. As certain as someone can be with a shit load of drugs in their system, I guess. Why?"

"His father, Sir James Harrison, died a couple of years ago", Brian explained.

Natascha shook her head. "Hm, I'm thinking about it a lot, but I'm convinced that Rowan picked up the bacteria for his father. That bitch told him that it will mutate for ninety-six hours before he would be infectious. She seemed to be very concerned. She said something about his father dying within the next year, but wanted to make sure that they knew what they were about to do. If I remember it correctly, Rowan simply said something like 'they all deserve to die.' I'll never forget that. Shortly after that my lights went out. I remember more details now, so if I can think of anything else I will certainly let you know."

"I really appreciate it. We have to be realistic here. From a medical standpoint there's a chance that your memory is not that accurate, but I have no reason not to believe you. Maybe Rowan wanted to finish what his father started? Unfortunately we cannot interrogate Rowan Harrison anymore, so every piece of information is crucial." Powell remarked with an accusing glance at Brian.

"Another tragic accident. He put his hands on one of my employees", Brian defended himself.

"Very unfortunate indeed", Klaus nodded.

"Here we go again with those bloody accidents", Powell mumbled, already working on his statement for the inquiry he eventually would have to face. "Do you even realise how many tragic accidents your men were involved in so far?" Powell shook his head with resignation. "We looked a little closer at the Harrison business group. Especially at Rowan's activities since he took over. He started a business relationship with Sir Samuel Cunningham, who is another business tycoon." Powell started a slide show on his laptop. Everybody stared at the images of Sir Cunningham, which were now projected onto the wall. Powell took his time to let the images sink in before he continued. "Cunningham is one of the global leaders in the pharmaceutical industry, and he has a whole portfolio on various smaller businesses. The man runs an empire. When we looked at him, we discovered that he lately invested heavily in his pharmaceutical programs. He upgraded his already well-equipped laboratories with the latest technology. We're not exactly sure what they're working on at the moment, but a couple of years ago he hired some of the world's leading biochemists. If I were a betting man, I would think they're working on something in the line of vaccination. Sir Cunningham is suffering from poliomyelitis since early childhood. He has always been a strong advocate and forerunner of vaccinations in this field. These days he relies heavily on walking aids, and on some days even the wheelchair."

"Certainly the type of person you need if you want to create a bloody bug", Brian summarised. "I assume you're looking into him?"

"No, once we got a hot lead we usually don't follow it anymore." Powell answered sarcastically. "Of course we're looking into it!"

"Since we're all here", Natascha continued after a few moments of silence. "Is there any news about Kyle, or any of the others?"

"Since none of them were infected with the bacteria, they're all healing up."

"I want to meet up with them once this is all over", Natascha demanded sternly.

"I understand. As soon as you are amongst the living again." Brian promised.

"What about that damn ship? Any news about the infected women?"

"Unfortunately not. We assume that they're somewhere in Syria by now. It looks like only a few members of the medical personnel were involved in the biological attack. Most of them were there for their normal patients. They're all guilty when it comes to the illegal trafficking of human organs, but it will take years to prove which patient knew what. To make matters worse, the medical files all use aliases. At this point, we don't even know who was on the ship." Powell finished. He didn't even try to hide his disappointment. Natascha felt a lump rising in her throat.

"If there are no more questions, we should talk about Whitmore Abbey", Brian continued and leaned back.

"Very well", Powell acknowledged and removed his glasses. "We know that the *Y.pestis* came from the catacombs of Whitmore Abbey, but we do have a problem. We–"

"Don't tell me that this damn abbot gets away with this!" Natascha cut him off, anger dropping her voice to a snarled hiss. Brian and Klaus exchanged an amused glance. They knew that Natascha wouldn't like this part of the conversation, but they didn't expect Natascha to interrupt, much less question, an intelligence manager from MI5.

"It's not my intention to let them get away with it. If we're talking about a biological terrorist attack, our actions will not stop in front of the walls of Whitmore Abbey. I can assure you that."

"Too bad that the children back then were only victims of paedophiles and not a terrorist cell", Natascha added coldly.

"Ahem, Natascha, can we please focus on the issue at hand for now? Thank you", Brian politely reminded her. Natascha shifted in her seat.

An awkward silence descended over the table for a couple of moments before Powell continued.

"We need to prove that the *Y.pestis* indeed came from Whitmore Abbey."

"Prove?" Natascha frowned. "What do you mean? I picked those fragments up there myself. I gave them to Erika who then sent them to Mark." She stopped and noticed the serious expression on all the faces staring at her. "Okay, I must admit, there might be a few links missing in the chain of evidence, but back then that was all

I could do.”

“We know that, but our problem remains. We need more bone fragments from the catacombs. Once we have them, we can test the DNA of the bacteria in the bones against the DNA of the bacteria you got injected with.”

“Okay?” Natascha shrugged. “So you are...what? MI5? Why don’t you get a warrant and send James Bond in?”

“Well, for one, James works for MI6, not MI5. Furthermore, being MI5, we do indeed have the means to shortcut getting a warrant without raising too much interest. But we all know how well connected Whitmore Abbey is, and we currently don’t know who is involved in this. The last thing we need is someone tipping Whitmore Abbey off before the ink is dry on the warrant.”

“So you’re asking me to go back diving there and collect more bones?” Natascha couldn’t even hide her surprise. “In case you didn’t notice, I got the plague.”

“Natascha!” Brian gently intervened and tried his best smile.

“What?”

“This isn’t about you. This isn’t about you at all. You just don’t give anyone else a chance to say anything. No one is asking you for another dive there. We’re officially working for MI5, and we will go in there and collect some evidence for them. All we need is you telling us how we get to the catacombs”, Brian explained in his fatherly tone.

“Oh! Okay...That is, hm, different then.” Natascha finally relaxed.

“Unfortunately”, he continued carefully, “we cannot simply sneak into the abbey and start tearing down a brick wall. I mean, we could do it, but by the time we get the test results back everyone will be gone. So our boys have to go in underwater. Same route you took. In and out. That’s the reason MI5 asked us to help them out.”

“Then you need me up there. The lines are still in the mine leading to the catacombs, but you need me topside in case something goes wrong. Wait! Who is diving?” Natascha’s bewildered glance darkened as she noticed everyone looking at Nick.

“Oh no! Not a chance!” She barked once she realised.

“And Ole-Einar–” Nick carefully explained, but Natascha cut him off.

“You? Deep cave penetration?”

“Not much different from–” Nick started to defend himself, but Klaus quickly interjected.

“Nick! Natascha! You might want to discuss this somewhere else. We are finished here!” He said sternly. Somehow he felt that Nick mentioning him diving for nuclear warheads inside the wreck of a Russian submarine back in the North West Passage would raise some unpleasant questions with their guest from MI5. Nick and Natascha exchanged a look and left the conference room. Natascha’s displeasure of Nick volunteering for this mission without talking to her first was evident. After everything that she had been through, the risk of losing everything and just getting it back, for Nick to just risk throwing it all away again. No, she couldn’t have it.

Intelligence Manager Powell waited until they were gone, before he turned to Brian and Klaus. “You’re sure she wasn’t infected with rabies?”

Natascha paced Shira's small office the moment she entered. She turned back on her heel towards her husband after he had closed the door. "Why you?"

"It will be Ole-Einar, Olaf, Rolf and me. You said it yourself, it's a shallow environment and the lines are already there."

"Didn't we agree the other day that we're going to lay low until all of this is over? Just to increase the chances of our daughter growing up with both parents?"

"Yes, we did. And I still think that way, but–"

"There are no *buts* in this, Nick. I don't want you to dive in there. We're not talking about the main mine shaft, this side tunnel is a natural formation, much smaller."

"The Russian submarine I had to penetrate wasn't any bigger, besides, it was much deeper and we had zero visibility."

"Yes, but no one is forcing you to dive here."

"Listen, all we have to do there is one dive. We let Ole-Einar and Olaf do the actual diving and Rolf and I are the standby divers. Come on, if you were in my position, you would be all over this. And you wouldn't take no for an answer." Nick reasoned. Natascha stared blankly at him for a few seconds.

Her eyes narrowed when she spoke, "You know me that good, don't you?"

"You kidding me? I remember very well when you asked for permission."

"So you're going to take your clothes off and try to distract me so that I don't say no?" Natascha probed, trying to look innocent. Nick's eyes turned into little slits.

"I knew you did that on purpose back then. I knew it!"

"Whatever works", Natascha shrugged, spinning a pen on Shira's desk.

"Stay on topic. We have a deal?"

"Oh, you noticed that I tried to stall you."

"Yes, I did. Do we have a deal or do I really have to take my shirt off first? Don't forget that what we're doing will help to put those behind bars who deserve it."

"Aw, now you are playing the noble card, that's not fair. I'm still debating, maybe you should take your shirt off to distract me. Might help me make up my mind." Natascha teased him. She watched in amusement as Nick pulled the shirt over his head.

Nick held his arms out to display his chest, and after a moment of silence he looked at the lights. "This is Shira's office. The lighting in here is terrible. It's not quite as romantic as our bedroom, so take that into consideration." Nick explained in a serious expression and threw his shirt at his wife to break Natascha's silence.

"I think I wasn't wearing anything that evening", Natascha stated and gestured at Nick's pants. The shock was evident on his face, but before he could protest, the door opened and Shira walked in.

"Oh, you're begging for permission to go to that mine, yes?" She curiously asked and occupied her chair behind her desk, anxiously watching her friends.

"This is kind of a special moment. I just want to see how far he will go."

"In that case, just pretend I'm not here", their Israeli friend grinned and leaned back hopefully, her eyes resting on Nick.

"So, where were we? Right, you're trying to distract me further!" Natascha said with a devious smile as she faced Nick again. Nick looked back between the two of them, but Natascha pointed at his pants again to remind him where he had left off.

"Sorry to disappoint you, Shira, but Natascha and I will continue this discussion at home. Not that there is anything to discuss!" Nick stated firmly.

"You're such a party pooper. I'm fine with you being up there as a safety diver, but under one condition!"

"You want to see the plans of the mine, not deeper than twenty metres and four hundred metres maximum penetration, just to be fair?"

"Ha, ha, ha, you are so funny. The condition is that I'm coming up there with you guys as the dive supervisor. I can help if something goes wrong and you know that." Natascha demanded. The tone in her voice made it clear that this was not up for debate.

"Natascha, this has to happen rather fast, and I'm not sure if you're fit enough for this..."

"I hate to agree with him, but he might have a point", Shira commented from behind her desk.

"Shush, I let you see my husband without a shirt in your office, you owe me."

"True, but I expected more than just that", the Israeli theatrically gestured at Nick. "Besides, I see more of these guys when I accidentally walk into the shower."

"You do that on purpose?" Nick wondered out loud. Shira just threw him a knowing glance and smiled.

"Come on, Nick, seriously? You can hear the showers through the door. Of course we're doing this on purpose." Natascha explained.

"*We?*"

"Oh, I mean them. Not me. I would never do something like that!" Natascha tried to defend herself and bit her lip.

"We will talk about that at home", Nick said with authority.

"Okay, if you insist. So we are good?" Natascha hesitated.

"Yes, we are good."

"See, that wasn't too bad", she finished and brushed a kiss on Nick's cheek before she left. Nick stared at the door. Shira started to shake her head in amusement.

"Wait a second. She caved way too fast. I wasn't done discussing her coming along as a supervisor."

"Don't blame her! You said that you were good when she asked you", Shira laughed.

"You were in on this! This whole shower thing got me distracted. You two are working together."

"You think?" Shira finally laughed. "You guys are so predictable. But you should maybe put your shirt back on before you get into trouble."

"Trouble? What kind of trouble?" Nick doubted easily. Not a second later and the door to the office opened again. Ariel walked in and his feet planted firmly at the sight.

"What are you doing half naked in front of my sister?"

EuroSecCorporation, London, Friday, August 15

"And you made it through *that*?" Ole-Einar wondered as they watched

Natascha's underwater video on the screen.

"It's not as tight as it looks", Natascha quickly explained, but she threw a concerned glance at Nick anyway. "This is where the old cribbing came down. From the water edge to there is one-hundred-and-twenty metres."

"Back it up a little bit, I want to see that again", the tall Norwegian asked. He was seriously concerned if he could squeeze himself through those timbers. "I might have to take my gear off to get through that", he muttered, more to himself as he made a note. Natascha just made a face. She didn't like the risks associated with such a task, but she knew that above everyone Ole-Einar was especially well trained.

"If you follow the line", she continued once Ole-Einar paid attention again, "you will come to the entrance of the side tunnel, which is right here", She pointed on the screen. "This is one-hundred-thirty-eight metres from the water edge. I tied the line into the main line. Once you enter the side tunnel, it gets a little bit tighter. Don't forget that this is a natural formation." They kept watching the video footage, immediately noticing the different environment. "One-hundred-and-eight metres from the entrance to the side tunnel is the old well. Most of the wooden shaft is now on the bottom there. Be careful, there are some old nails sticking out of the wood. Mario actually managed to puncture his breathing loop in this." Natascha warned her friends. Ole-Einar cursed in Norwegian and scribbled a couple more notes. "If you have to take your gear off to pass through the old cribbing in the main shaft, you will have to take if off here as well. There is definitely less room here", Natascha explained and watched herself on the screen squeezing through the timber. "Once you're through, it is another seventy-two metres to the catacombs. The depth at the well is around sixteen metres, and from there it gradually gets shallower all the way to the catacombs."

"Piece of cake, as long as you don't screw it up", Ole-Einar stated and looked at Olaf. "The only way I fit through that is if I take my gear off underwater."

"I will be fine", Olaf commented and looked at his own notes.

"So you're sure we don't need a permit for this? It took my father quite a while to get one", Natascha changed the subject. "Right, we're not even there", she quickly added as she noticed the looks everyone threw at her. "That also answers the question about the keys for the gate."

"This is sort of a secret military operation, not a scientific expedition, Natascha." Ole-Einar calmly reminded her.

"You remember when you broke into the abbey's catacombs? Above water?" Nick reminded her with a smile.

"Oh, like that!" Natascha made a face. She felt betrayed.

"Yes, just like that."

"According to Mario, you infiltrated into enemy territory in plain sight during broad daylight. This should be like a vacation for you." Ole-Einar winked at her.

"You didn't have to put it like that. Makes it sound much worse than what it actually was", Natascha defended herself half-heartedly.

"Ah, don't sell yourself short, you're an experienced criminal and outlaw", Rolf added as he stood up.

"Will you please stop it? My daughter is here somewhere. Don't want her to hear such things." Natascha laughed, but she quickly became serious again. The thought of leaving her daughter with Shira and Talia for the next two days made her feel nervous. The team left the room, leaving her and Nick behind.

"Having second thoughts?" Nick asked her once they were alone.

"I don't know what to think, to be honest", she admitted and sat down again. "I mean, I know that she'll be totally fine with Shira and Talia, but does she understand that we're gone for just two days?"

"Look Natascha, you don't have to come up there with us. Believe it or not, we are completely capable of executing this task without you. You know that."

"Yes, I know, it is just...I don't know. It seems that this is the only way for me to sort of..." Natascha searched for the right words.

"To sort of get back at them?" Nick helped her out. He knew his wife perfectly. Natascha looked at him, lost in thoughts.

"Yeah, I guess you can put it that way. All this time when I was gone, I was either drugged out of my mind or completely helpless. I just couldn't do anything."

"Come on, you know that's not true. You sent three people to the hospital and you managed to free some of your friends and escape."

"Right, and how far did we get?"

"That's not the point, angel. You had no way of knowing that you were on a ship. The point is that you fought back. Successfully, I might add!"

"I still ended up with the plague, remember?" Natascha's tone soured. She certainly didn't agree with her partner.

"Look, I'm not going to have another argument with you about this. We discussed this before. If you want to come along as a dive supervisor, that's fine. I completely understand that. If you want to stay home with our daughter, that's also fine."

"Argh, I just don't know. What if she thinks that I'm not coming back again?"

"For one, we can actually call her whenever we want or whenever she wants to talk to us, and two, she handled that whole situation remarkably well. Shira, Talia, your parents, they all–"

"Yeah, I know", Natascha cut him off suddenly. She dropped the pen she had used as a pointer on the table. "Maybe she doesn't need me anymore."

Her words caught him off guard and he stood there dumbly and watched as she closed the door behind her on her way out. He calmly cleaned the table and sat down. It took him a moment to calm his beating heart. Several minutes went by before the door opened again. Nick looked up. He hoped for Natascha to come back and was disappointed to see Shira.

"Still the same problem, I assume?" She asked. Nick sighed with frustration. He was well aware that Shira knew about their struggle.

"It's not getting better at all. She snaps from one second to the other", he explained and sadly shook his head.

"It will come, don't worry. She needs some time. This is the second time that this happened to her, and–"

"I know, Shira, I don't have to hear it again!" He interrupted her before he apologised.

"Don't worry", Shira smiled, "I totally understand."

"Did you see her?"

"I did. She went down to the daycare. Give her some space." Shira advised. Nick just sat there and shook his head.

Storming down the stairs, Natascha cooled down a little bit, but not enough to go back and apologise.

"Dammit!" She cursed and stopped just before the door leading to the ground level. "This can't go on like this. I'm not going to be on the run for the rest of my life", she promised herself and picked up her cell phone. It took her only a few seconds to write the text message. Natascha exhaled sharply as she impatiently waited for the answer. The minute it took before the typical sound of her cell phone alerted her to the incoming message felt like an eternity.

"About time", she complained as she read it. It took her only a few moments to send her reply. Satisfied, she finally eased up a little bit, but still didn't open the door to the ground floor. Instead she leaned back against the wall, closed her eyes and tried to calm the rage that was still burning inside her. As so many times before during the last couple of days, her mind started spinning, and she had a hard time to control herself. She longed to be able to do something, to seek revenge, to protect her daughter, and her marriage.

"What is it?" The soft male voice interrupted her thoughts. She slowly opened her eyes and looked at her friend. She had not heard him coming, but she knew that she had not paid any attention at all to begin with.

"Sorry for bothering you like this", Natascha calmly apologised and held her cell phone up.

"Are you okay?" His question carried the concern he felt for her.

"Yes...No...Maybe...Hell, I don't know", Natascha stammered in defeat and threw her arms up.

"You still feel that rage in you?" Natascha was surprised how well he knew her.

"Yes, I do", she freely admitted. A wave of guilt came over her as she thought about Nick. "We have to talk. There is something I have to get off my chest."

"Hm, okay. Does Nick–"

"No, he doesn't", Natascha quickly interrupted and shook her head. "I know it sounds stupid, but I can't talk to him about this."

"Okay, now I'm curious", her friend stepped closer.

"It's about something that happened on *Asklepios*", Natascha admitted and paced the little room they had, staring at the walls. "Actually, it's not about *something* so much as it is about *someone*. I have to know the truth and I need you to do me a favour. And Nick can't know any of this", Natascha said resolutely. Her friend just looked at her, but finally he nodded.

- *37* -

Outside of London, Great Britain, Saturday, August 16
The rain pounded mercilessly against the mausoleum's white marble. The man sitting inside didn't care about the cold summer weather. Even when the strong gusts drove the rain directly against the walls, the lone visitor could barely hear it. This mausoleum was his refuge. It was built for an eternity, and no weather could ever bother him here. He didn't know how many hours he had spent here since his wife passed away last year, but he didn't care. It was the only place where his servants weren't allowed to follow him. His instructions in that matter were resolute, and, as always, they were respectfully waiting outside. As the many times before when visiting this place, he had lost all feeling for time, sitting there and staring at the pictures of the only two people he had ever cared about in his life. His wife's picture was embedded in the marble headstone. It was an artistic masterpiece, at which he stared at almost every day. A bouquet of white lilies, his deceased wife's favourite flowers, was carefully sculpted out of the head stone as well. His eyes, hidden behind the dark sunglasses, were glued to her picture. Slowly, his gaze wandered to the second picture on the massive marble plate. It was only recently that he had put it there. Looking at his son's image, another sharp pain pierced his heart.

I couldn't even bury him! He had to swallow. He knew that his relationship with him had never been the typical father-son relationship, but despite everything, he had loved his son like only a father could. His passing only convinced him in his plan. The quivering lips were the only signs of emotions that he ever showed. Even now, with no one else present who could have seen him, he kept his authoritarian posture. Waves of guilt flooded him. He knew that he could have helped his wife, but she had kept her illness from him until it was too late. He didn't know why she had never told him, but he would never forgive himself. She probably did not want him to worry, but that was little solace, if any. Her demise had been a motivating factor in his last actions. Without her, there was nothing left in this world for him. Too much of him had died that day.

His last wish was simple: *Revenge!* It was the only thought crossing his mind at the moment. *Revenge! On all those responsible for my suffering. My whole life I've been suffering because of them. Decades, filled with nothing but pain! That ends now! My revenge will be of biblical proportions, and there is nothing they can do about this!* A satisfying smile briefly appeared in his face, steadying his quivering lip. It quickly disappeared as the alarm on his cell phone interrupted his thoughts. It took him a while until he managed to get the device out of his blazer pocket. He grimaced at the pain it caused him, but he eventually turned it off.

Time to go! He slowly got up and leaned forward to kiss the top plate of the sarcophagus. His left hand rested on the cold marble while he slowly removed a sealed envelope from his blazer's inside pocket. He carefully placed it in plain sight, but his eyes remained glued on the pictures of his loved ones.

"Not much longer now, Love, and we will be united again", he whispered and had to cough. It took him a few seconds to recover, and it wasn't until then that he noticed the little bit of blood coming out of his nose. He carefully took his satin handkerchief out and cleaned his face. He stared at it for a moment, noticing that the blood covered his initials: *SAC*. Seconds passed by as he glanced at them. For a moment it was like he was lost in thoughts, but he did not remember any of the thoughts he had. He shook his head and quickly recovered, returning the handkerchief to his pocket. With a faint smile he looked at his wife's picture for one last time. The last minute had cost him more energy than he dared to admit, but he was not ignorant of the losing battle his body was fighting at the moment. At his age and condition, there was only one possible outcome.

"Soon, my Love, very soon!" he repeated his vow one last time. He never even looked back, his eyes now focussed on his two servants who patiently opened the doors of his Bentley Bentayga.

Whitmore Abbey, Western England, Great Britain, Saturday, August 16
"Great, some shitty weather is the last thing we need on our vacation", Natascha commented as the first rain drops landed on their windshield. She leaned forward and looked at the dark grey sky above. "Yep, that's going to be a wet weekend", she exhaled. Nick just took a quick peek at the clouds and nodded. He paid more attention to the road as he steered their RV out of Whitmore.

They left the last houses of the little village behind them and Nick's eyes followed the only road leading towards the abbey. It was impossible not to notice the bright red pop-up tent at the side of the road. As soon as they got closer, Nick and Natascha saw the person sitting behind the desk slowly getting up. Trying to stay out of the rain, the man slowly waved them down.

"It's a trap! He's trying to rob us! Run him! Run him over!" Natascha hissed, but Nick only shook his head. Unable to hear Natascha, the monk waving them down simply smiled as Nick slowed the large RV. Looking ahead they could see that other RV's were already parked outside the abbey's massive walls.

"Is this the only way to the mine?"

"Yes, as far as I know. It's on the other side of this hill. You can only see the top part of the abbey's wall from there. I don't think they can see the mine at all, unless they're crawling on top of their walls. Do we have to register with him?" Natascha wondered, looking at the monk.

"Stay down, guys", Nick suggested with a quick glance into the rear view mirror. Ole-Einar, Rolf and Olaf crouched down on the floor in the back, making sure that they couldn't be seen.

"We're not running an innocent monk over, Natascha", Nick calmly explained as he applied the parking brake. "Now try to be nice to him, will you?" he pleaded to his wife in the same tone he asked his daughter not to make a mess out of her room. Natascha made a face, but Nick already pressed the button to lower the window before she could comment.

"Peace be with you! So nice to see a young couple finding their way to us. You are staying for the night?"

"Yes, we will. Can we park over there? We have some issues with our generator and I don't want to bother anyone." Nick asked and gestured to the other side of the hill where the mine was.

"Yes, there is plenty of space", the monk answered and wrote down the licence plate. He handed them a bag with some information material. "I am afraid that the reception dinner tonight is already completely booked, but there are still some open spots for some of the seminars", he enthusiastically added. Nick smiled through the sudden pain he felt in his thigh. The monk could not see how Natascha's fingernails dug into him. "You also might want to come to the mass early, spaces might be limited tonight." Natascha winced at the words as Nick took the bag from the monk and handed it to her.

"We will make sure to be there in time. My wife doesn't want to miss this. Thank you very much!" Nick said and closed the window just in time before Natascha complained about the plastic bag. She took the program leaflet out of the bag and threw a killing glance at her husband, who slowly set the RV into motion.

"You want to hear what your wife is going to tell you?" Natascha finally broke her silence.

"Relax, sweet-cheeks, I'm not dragging you into any seminars or have them perform an exorcism on you, although..." Nick trailed off.

"Don't even go there", Natascha laughed.

"As you wish! We'll just take a walk in the gardens. Whoever is watching this RV will see nothing else but a young couple spending some quality time during their vacation", Nick suggested. Natascha looked appalled.

"I want a divorce!" She firmly demanded. "If dragging me through an abbey in this weather is your idea of some quality time for our vacation, then I want a divorce right here and now."

"You do know that you will be undercover, right? You are just *pretending* that you are on some quality time together." Ole-Einar tried to explain from behind.

"Silence in the spare seats. I'm not concerned about the *quality time together* with my husband, it is the location that gives me the creeps. An *abbey*", Natascha shuddered.

"Relax, we can just pretend to have a good time together. If that doesn't work, maybe I let you do some grave robbing, or have you pick a couple locks, or let you break into the catacombs again." Nick tried to cheer her up, but Natascha slapped his shoulder.

"If you didn't know any better, you would think she has to go to the dentist", Ole-Einar muttered from the rear. Natascha threw him a killing glance over the mirror.

"See it as your second honeymoon", the Norwegian suggested with a big grin.

"Oh, no, we are not going to do *that* in there."

"Ah, come on, angel, don't be shy", Nick laughed.

"Oh, that's not it. I told you that this place gives me the creeps. I couldn't get into the mood." Natascha laughed and pointed to the right. "Okay, keep going this way."

"Oh great! This is absolutely marvellous", Natascha commented theatrically after looking at some of the other visitors. Nick slowly steered the RV.

"What is it?" Rolf asked from the back, just as Nick started laughing.

"Look at them. They are all old people!" Natascha complained and pointed out of the window. Rolf and the two Norwegians walked to the front and looked for themselves.

"And? You don't like old people? What's the problem?" Ole-Einar asked.

"I don't mind old people, but I can only imagine what they will think about me if they see four guys and me living in one RV." Natascha complained shyly and hid her face behind her hands.

"You know", Ole-Einar shrugged and started to smile, "there are actually movies–"

"Shush!" Natascha interrupted him and raised her hand. "Not one more word! Sharing an RV with you guys is already bad enough."

"Hey, we had to spend several days in quarantine together because of you. That was much worse." Ole-Einar reminded her.

"Yeah, the girls told me all about it. According to them, you have seemed to enjoyed it." Natascha looked out the RV again and started a new beat, "Now get down. Since only Nick and I are supposed to be in here, we should make sure that no one sees you." With her friends sitting on the floor again, Natascha looked ahead as they came to the other side of the hill. "Do you see the gate over there?"

"Hm, will we even fit through?" Nick wondered as he steered the RV closer to the gate.

"We had no problems with the Sprinter from the institute. How much wider is this?" Natascha wondered.

"Could get tight." Nick noticed as he drove by the gate. He kept going and parked the RV out of sight from the abbey.

"You guys should probably stay on the floor until we know what's going on", Natascha suggested and climbed out of her seat to get to the back of the RV.

"I totally agree", the Norwegian said, making himself comfortable on the floor as Natascha carefully balanced over them. "You should make some coffee!" He added with a serious expression as he pointed at the coffee machine. Natascha just looked at him as she closed the curtains, preventing anyone from looking inside.

"Please?" Ole-Einar added, but Natascha's only reaction was a very rude hand gesture as she started to boil some water. The big grin on the Norwegian's face faded once he realised that Natascha only made coffee for herself and Nick. Totally ignoring her friends, Natascha balanced back to her passenger seat and handed Nick the other cup.

"So, what are we going to do next?" she wondered and took a sip.

"I guess we wait. Look at all the people. There is even another bus coming." Nick gestured down the road as the wipers cleaned the windshield again. The rain drops were falling harder now.

"You think they can see us?"

"Not sure. They can only catch a glimpse of the RV, but we couldn't see the gate from the road."

"What's the distance to the gate?" Rolf asked from behind.

"Around forty metres", Natascha estimated.

"That's more like sixty, sweet-cheeks", Nick commented.

"You wish! That explains a lot of things", Natascha sarcastically shot back. The guys in the back chuckled. "Back then we practised with the reels at that gate, and I'm telling you that this is not more than forty-five metres." Natascha explained.

"Okay. How far from behind the gate? Is that the entrance right there?"

"Yes, it is. Not more than fifty metres. The gate has a normal key and then there are steel doors at the actual mine. Both use the same kind of key."

"That won't be a problem", Rolf noted. "There is no need to try to squeeze this rig through there. I guess our best bet is to assemble the gear in here, get ready and see what happens. Are we all cool with that?"

"Sure, I don't know if it makes sense to wait until dark. If they cannot see us from the abbey, then we might as well go."

"Okay, so that is settled. Let's get the gear together then. Natascha, if you would, please..." Ole-Einar stated seriously and pointed at the door. Natascha watched him through the rear view mirror. Her eyes narrowed.

"What do you want now?" she hissed, fixing him with a cold glare.

"Some of our gear is in the storage compartments. Since we cannot access it from the inside and we are not supposed to be seen outside, well, someone has to get it for us."

"And what possesses you to believe that I am that someone?" Natascha calmly asked back and took another sip of her coffee.

"Well, I assume that Nick will be busy planning your romantic abbey tour, so naturally that leaves you, but–" the Norwegian started, but Natascha simply cut him off by raising her hand. Her cell phone just announced an incoming face-time call from Shira. With his wife on the phone and the rain drops falling even harder, Nick stepped outside and quickly got the bags with the diving gear. It took him a couple minutes, but he finally closed the door behind him again. It was only now that Natascha ended the call.

"Shira said that everything is fine. The pumpkin said hi", she smiled before she looked at all the gear and her wet husband. "Oh, you're already done? My bad. A shame I couldn't help", she joked with an impish grin.

"I'm seriously considering dragging you into the mass tonight for that", Nick replied through clenched teeth.

It was a couple of hours later in the afternoon when Natascha's worst fears seemed to materialise as Nick took her for a little walk.

"And this is a good idea because?" Natascha asked for the fifth time in as many minutes. Holding her hand, Nick was lucky enough that he didn't have to drag his wife up to the abbey, but the closer they got, the more reluctant Natascha became.

"I told you before. If someone is watching us, I want them to see that we are indeed walking up to the abbey. Besides, I want to figure out if they can see us from up here", Nick explained as they got closer to the main entrance gate. They both stopped. Natascha was surprised how many people she noticed inside the courtyard. She could only imagine how many more were roaming in the garden and all the buildings. She couldn't help it, but a shiver ran down her spine as her mind drifted back to the fate of all the children who had suffered behind these large, centuries old gates. With Natascha's mind trailing in the past, Nick used the moment to see if he could spot their RV or any other part of the mine. He was satisfied when he noticed that his wife had been right before. There was no way that they could be seen from the abbey. He quickly told Natascha.

"I told you so", she said, still absentminded. Nick noticed how she felt and placed an arm around her. He didn't have to ask, he knew exactly what bothered her. Her feelings reflected on him, and he had to admit that he didn't feel all that comfortable either.

"Let's go, angel. There is no reason for us to walk through these gates", he whispered and brushed a kiss on her cheek. Natascha swallowed hard and nodded. Just as they started walking back, they noticed a black Bentley Bentayga slowly making its way up the road. Nick and Natascha stepped aside to make some room for the large SUV. They tried to catch a glimpse through the windows, but their design did not allow them to see anything. Nick looked after the SUV, but quickly turned around to catch up to Natascha, who was already on her way back down to the RV.

The man in the back seat didn't pay any attention to them. He was used to people staring at his rare SUV, but he didn't care. To him, all the people who made room for his SUV were nothing more than bystanders. Worst case scenario, they would become innocent casualties in a war that wasn't their own, but even that didn't matter to him. He knew that he wouldn't live much longer. The medications in his body miraculously kept him going despite the losing battle he fought against the bacteria. Not a sound disturbed the peaceful atmosphere inside the Bentley as it drove through the gates. The old man slowly looked ahead. A satisfied smile appeared on his face once he noticed the many cars with the diplomatic licence plates to the Holy See.

They are all here, he thought, just as his driver stopped the Bentley.

Nick's and Natascha's house, just outside London, Saturday, August 16
"Is the turnip sleeping yet?" Talia wanted to know as she walked into the kitchen. Her hair was still wet from the shower she had just taken. Wrapped in nothing else but a large towel, the young Israeli steered directly to the fridge, looking for her bowl of fruits.

"It's still a pumpkin, Talia, but yes, she's finally sleeping", Shira reminded her with correction. Her eyes were glued to her laptop.

"Ah, damn, I don't know why I always mix those two up. Did anything happen?" Focussed on her fruit salad, Talia turned to the window and looked outside. Her back was still turned towards Shira.

"Not much. Nick called. They're about to start the diving operation and told us that they will not have any cell service inside the mine."

"Hm, how is Natascha doing?" Talia took another spoonful as she watched a couple of birds on their little lawn.

"Seems to be fine. The guys sent me a message that they're picking on her, and that she's slowly getting her wits back."

"You think she's fine?" Talia didn't sound too convinced.

"She told Nick to run over a monk with the RV and wanted to divorce him for taking her on a walk to the abbey", Shira calmly explained, still staring at the monitor as she tried to organise and copy some files to a data stick.

"She is definitely getting better then. Is your brother coming today?" Talia asked hopefully, shoving another spoonful of fruit salad into her mouth. But she frustratedly shook her head before Shira answered her. "Gosh, I can't believe he fell for that escort." Disappointed with the lack of attention she had received from Ariel, she stabbed a grape in her fruit salad with more force than it was necessary.

"He didn't fall for her. He just finds her attractive. My brother is not immune to beautiful women. Besides, you know as well as I do that he hasn't seen her since we got out of quarantine."

"He seems to be immune to me", she muttered. "Is she still with that movie star? What's his name, Iain?" Talia frustratedly wanted to know and watched a neighbour driving away. With his car gone, it was only now that she recognised Ariel's motorcycle parked at the side of the street. Her eyes widened and her whole body froze.

"Yes, Iain is his name", Ariel commented from the door. Talia had been so focussed on her fruit salad, that she had not noticed him. "Once his yacht was disinfected, they both sailed off into the sunset. And no, I have not heard from her since", he added with his typical grin. Talia's eyes grew even wider as she blushed another shade of red.

"You didn't tell me that he's here!" Talia hissed at Shira, trying to ignore Ariel.

"Why would I? Ariel arrived while you took your shower. He was with his godchild." Shira defended herself.

"Still, you could have warned me!"

"I didn't know you were going on a rant", Shira defended herself without taking her eyes from the laptop. Ariel couldn't help but smile while Talia failed at her futile attempt to ignore him.

"You do realise that I'm standing right here, do you?" he laughed and sat beside his sister.

"Did you hear...I mean, did you...?" Talia stammered. She usually felt butterflies in her stomach when seeing Ariel, but for some reason they all seemed to have died suddenly from embarrassment. Since no hole opened up in the ground that could have swallowed her, she clung to her towel to avoid the most embarrassing scenario possible. Her face was now almost the same colour as the strawberry in her fruit salad. Ariel just winked at her.

"Stop torturing her!" Shira hissed at her brother and punched him on his arm. "Talia, maybe you want to get some clothes on?" she added after giving the young Israeli a once over.

"Oh, yes, right", Talia said, wrapping the towel tighter around her. "Maybe I will wake up soon and this was all just a bad dream", she muttered on her way out. Shira shook her head and continued to organise the files. It took Talia only a few moments before she came back.

"Okay, so what do you got here?" she wanted to know and joined them at the table.

"Intelligence Manager Powell gave us a laptop with some information about

Cunningham. They are short on people and he asked us to go through it." Ariel explained.

"Really? I didn't expect that from him. He trusts us a lot."

"Time is of an essence, I assume. Anyway, we should have a look at what we can find. Is there any structure in these files, Shira?"

His sister shook her head. "I don't know yet. Most of it looks like personal notes on certain business deals, but this one here can be promising." Shira pointed at an icon on her laptop.

"What is it?"

"Seems to be digitalised images from handwritten notes. Looks very personal to me. Let me see if I can..." Shira started and stared at the computer screen. All three focussed on the images now.

"What is this?" Talia asked and pointed at a certain image. "Is that a DNA test?"

"Looks like it. There is a second one here as well." Shira discovered the other image. "It is not a DNA test, it says here that it is a paternity test."

"I thought the Cunningham's didn't have children", Ariel mentioned.

"They didn't. The question is, why a DNA test if it is their child? Maybe Cunningham had a child with someone else?"

"That would be interesting. Maybe we should send the image to MI5. They can run the DNA database against it." Ariel suggested and looked for his cell phone.

"Wait! Go back one image. I think I saw something about Whitmore Abbey!" Talia shouted. Shira scrolled back. They slowly tensed up as their eyes widened.

"Oh my God! Can this even be?" Talia voiced her disbelief. Shira was completely speechless and could do nothing more than shake her head. Ariel's response was much like his sister's, and he was already on his cell phone.

"Brian? We need an emergency meeting within the hour. Klaus, you, and Powell."

- *38* -

***EuroSecCorporation*, London, Saturday, August 16**

"Cunningham was an orphan at Whitmore Abbey. And here I thought I have seen it all. Okay, let me see if I get this straight", Brian started as he paced the conference room. The former admiral still had a hard time believing what he had just heard. He paused at the window and looked over the parking lot. "You copied those files from the laptop Greg gave us, correct? And in those files were some personal notes that most likely no one else has seen before, correct?"

"Yes", Shira confirmed matter of factly. "They represent sort of a timeline of events in his life. Some look like old diary entries that he commented on decades later. Others are just medical notes. It will take a while to check everything out."

"Greg?" Brian glanced at the large monitor. Intelligence Manager Gregor Powell nodded.

"That is correct, Brian. We didn't have the chance to check it all out yet, but with the recent development I have our best people working on it as a priority. I appreciate the prompt heads up."

"No worries, I still owe you for not dragging us to the gallows for treason and piracy. Okay, Shira, you interrupt me if I get something wrong. Cunningham grew up as an orphan in Whitmore Abbey and was adopted at the age of three, correct?"

"Correct, we were able to confirm that", Gregor Powell stated.

"But Cunningham insisted all the time that his mother was also at Whitmore Abbey, correct?"

"Yes, we are trying to find out who the bloody hell she was, but I would not hold my breath", Gregor admitted.

"So, his adopting parents were so religious that he never received any vaccination. Shortly after being adopted, he suffered from polio, which eventually marked him for life."

"Unfortunately."

"Once of age, he left his adoptive parents and changed his name legally to Cunningham. Do we have any knowledge of his biological mother's name?"

"No, we do not. There are simply no records left and there is absolutely no way in finding that out any more. Cunningham spent decades on finding his biological mother without success."

"Hm, okay. So he first got himself a different name and a double PhD in biochemistry and medicine at Edinburgh to go with it. The guy married his sweetheart and they were together for forty years before she died of cancer last year."

"Yes."

"During his career in the pharmaceutical industry he funded several campaigns against Whitmore Abbey and also hired some private investigators, but nothing substantial ever materialised." The scepticism in his voice reflected in his facial expression.

"Unfortunately that is also correct."

"That doesn't make sense to me", Brian admitted and returned to his chair before he continued. "I can see why Cunningham spends millions in hiring private investigators. The guy wanted to find his biological mother. What I don't understand is, why did he finance several campaigns to bring Whitmore Abbey to justice, yet he works with them to create a super bug? Why?"

"Don't really know. Maybe his priorities changed over the decades. Going against Whitmore Abbey was more of a private vendetta for him. Going against extremist terrorist groups is an operation on a global scale. Could be the reason he put his differences aside", Powell shared his thoughts.

"Not sure if I agree with you. If I would have to profile him based on what we know, then there is no way that he would work with them. His whole life he blamed them for his misery, and most likely rightfully so. His feelings against them are rooted very deep. I'm not buying it. I think he is up to something else." Klaus shook his head. He sounded convincing. Brian looked at his friend for a few moments, considering what he had just said.

"According to our knowledge, Cunningham and his wife never had any children, correct?" Brian continued.

"Correct", Shira and Gregor Powell answered simultaneously.

"Still, Cunningham did a DNA test to confirm that he had a child. He accepted the fact and set up a trust fund."

"Yes."

"Do we have any idea who that child might be?" Brian looked at Powell.

"We might, mate. I'm just getting a notification here", the intelligence manager answered and picked up his phone. All eyes rested on him until he finished the call. "Well, that was certainly interesting. We ran the DNA. Turns out we got a hit in the missing person database."

"And? Anyone we know?" Brian wanted to know.

"Oh yes, you know the bloke! You're not going to believe it."

Whitmore Abbey, Western England, Great Britain, Saturday, August 16
The twisted maze of wooden timber was slowly coming into view as Olaf and Ole-Einar closed in on the old well. With Ole-Einar in the lead, they both released the trigger on their scooters and stopped. Following their dive plan, they stowed their scooters in a safe position where they could easily find them on their way back. Ole-Einar turned towards the well and they took their time to check for any hazards. Natascha's report of Mario rupturing a hose and suffering catastrophic equipment failure was a grim reminder how fast things could go wrong inside an overhead environment.

Not taking his hand off the cave line Natascha had laid earlier in the summer, his eyes followed the thin white line through the timber as far as his underwater light would shine. *Not tight my ass!* The Norwegian thought and shook his head at the sight. Maybe Natascha and Mario had been able to get through the structure comfortably, but he and Olaf would really have to squeeze through it. A quick look back confirmed that his friend had come to the same conclusion. Ole-Einar glanced at his dive computer. They were right on schedule, but they had to come up with a plan quickly, otherwise Nick and Rolf would start searching for them. With a little flick of his fins, Ole-Einar closed the distance to the old wooden beams and took a closer look. There was no way he could fit through it with his gear on. *I should have paid more attention to the video,* he cursed himself and studied the beams one by one. He was not concerned about taking his gear off and pushing it in front of him to get through, it was something he had done dozens of times before. His concern was about the visibility. Hovering motionlessly in the water like they were right now stirred up minimal sediment, but that would change once they would remove their rebreathers. They would literally be blind while squeezing through the collapsed timber structure, and he wanted to make sure that there was not a nail in their passage. He knew that he could deal with an equipment failure similar to Mario's, after all they had planned for that. His bigger concern was to puncture or maybe even rupture their drysuits on a protruding nail. With a water temperature just above the freezing mark, they would face a life-threatening situation.

Ole-Einar took a breath. He could not spend another moment worrying about all that without taking any sort of action. As expected, a sediment cloud stirred up as he took off his rebreather, disturbing the visibility. He knew this would get worse as Olaf started to take his unit off as well. It took them only a few moments, but the visibility was now reduced to nothing. Their powerful lights were unable to penetrate the dark brown sediment cloud. With his rebreather ready in front of him, it didn't take long before Olaf squeezed his calf, signalling him that he was also ready. Ole-Einar let Natascha's cave line run through his fingers as he carefully moved forward. He knew that he had to be close to the first beam when he hit his head on it. He cursed, adjusted himself and slowly squeezed underneath it. The Norwegian did not take his hands off the cave line and visualised Natascha's path through the maze. *She must be mental, but she has some balls,* he cursed and slowly inched forward. He counted the beams they passed, knowing that they should be free any moment now.

Ole-Einar slowed down even more, this was the part he could not see before he had taken the gear off. He knew this was the area where Mario had punctured his hose. It was another tight passage he had to squeeze through. *I have no idea how she made it through here,* he wondered. *Maybe it has something to do with her being half my size,* he answered as he used his hands to pull himself forward. It was not a second later that he noticed the ice cold water rushing into his damaged dry suit.

EuroSecCorporation, London, Saturday, August 16

"Rowan Harrison? The son of Sir Archibald Cunningham? You got to be kidding me." Brian couldn't hide his surprise about this revelation.

"Not if the DNA tests in his personal files are correct", Powell confirmed. "The first one is from thirty-five years ago. The second one is from twenty years ago, I believe."

"Two tests?" Brian questioned the logic. "Could there be a second child?"

"No, both tests are from identical DNA. The second test was most likely because of a much higher accuracy due to advancements in technology. I bet he did the bloody tests himself."

"Okay, so he is his son. Why didn't anyone know?"

"Because of the money. Cunningham and the Harrison's knew each other. He and Miss Harrison had a fling and junior came into this world. Safe to say that money was talking to make sure that there was no scandal."

"I agree. After her Majesty awarded him the knighthood, a lot of doors opened and he made excellent contacts. That would have never happened with a bastard child." Klaus added.

"Makes sense", Brian nodded.

"Since both families came from money, junior could grow up with his mother. I assume he contacted Rowan once he was of age and mature enough to avoid a scandal. It would have been easy for him to prove that he is his father. I assume that they started doing business together not long after that."

"Blimey, I didn't see that one coming", the retired admiral nodded and poured himself another cup of coffee. "Okay, what else do we have?"

"Wait a second! Something isn't right", Shira interrupted her boss. She had her eyes closed and tried to remember what Natascha had told her. "Do you remember what Natascha mentioned about Rowan? What he said about his father, when he picked Natascha up to deliver her to that Saudi Prince?" The Israeli searched her laptop for her notes. "She was convinced that Rowan's father was up to something, and it had something to do with the bacteria that this Dr Evans gave to Rowan, correct?"

"I believe so", Ariel confirmed her suspicion. They gave Shira the few seconds she needed to pull up her notes.

"There it is. According to Natascha's memory, Rowan picked up the bacteria for his father. Dr Evans also mentioned that Rowan's father would die within the next year, and if they were certain about what they were about to do. According to this, Rowan simply answered that *they all deserve to die*. It all makes sense now! Since Sir James Harrison passed away years ago, we thought that this was a dead end, especially with Rowan's–" Shira stopped for a second to search for the right word.

"Disappearance!" Ariel helped her with a smile. Powell rolled his eyes.

"Yes, that's what I'm looking for. Thank you. Especially with Rowan's disappearance."

"So Cunningham is going to infect himself with the bacteria? At his age and condition? To what end? Even if he has the Tetanus vaccination, he won't survive it."

"No, but he can still infect others. And he most likely doesn't care about dying himself", Shira confirmed with a quick glance at her notes.

"But who is he going to infect?" Powell wanted to know. "He has to know that the bacteria is not lethal amongst people with Tetanus vaccination."

"It all fits together. He knows that he is dying anyway within the next twelve months, and he has already lost his wife and his only son. There is nothing for him worth living for anymore. All he has left is his revenge on those he always blamed for his misery."

"His adoptive parents refused him any medical treatment, but they are certainly dead by now."

"Yes, that's correct. But why did they refuse it? They refused it because of their highly religious beliefs. This is not about them. He grew up in Whitmore Abbey and was adopted most likely against the will of his biological mother. It all started there. And I think that is where he wants to end it. Take a look at the clerics, mostly old people with a weakened immune system. Hard to believe they can recover from the plague, no matter what vaccination they received decades ago." Klaus shared his theory. It took only a few seconds for his words to sink in.

"Bloody hell, are you telling me that he is going after Whitmore Abbey?" Brian wanted to know.

"Aren't they hosting the international Bishop's conference? The place will be packed with older clerics from all over Europe and even the Vatican."

"Blimey, he is going to kill them all", Brian concluded and looked at Gregor.

"Give me a second here, I just want to check where he is", the intelligence manager said and worked the computer. It only took him a few seconds. "Here we go. The bloke has expensive taste. Several Bentleys are registered to his name, as well as a private helicopter. One moment, just checking the GPS locators on them...the helicopter is still at his residence, and there are only two cars missing. A black Bentley Bentayga and a Jaguar...and they currently are...bollocks. He is already at Whitmore Abbey."

Whitmore Abbey, Western England, Great Britain, Saturday, August 16
"Damn! This is cold!" Ole-Einar cursed through clinched teeth as he broke through the surface inside the catacombs. By the time he was through the debris field, his drysuit was almost flooded. Even his thick thinsulate dive underwear could no longer keep him warm. The Norwegian didn't bother to waste any more time trying to put his rebreather back on. He knew that it was only a short distance to the catacombs and had simply pushed on as fast as he could. Standing in hip deep water, he shivered so severely that he had difficulty unclipping the inflator hose from his drysuit. Finally free from the rebreather, he secured the unit and tried to get warm again. He quickly glanced behind him, the faint glimmer of Olaf's dive light telling him that his friend would be there soon.

"Come on! Hurry up", Ole-Einar muttered and waited patiently for Olaf to break the surface.

"You okay?" Olaf whispered after he had closed his breathing loop. Ole-Einar shook his head.

"I'm totally flooded."

"Yeah, I saw the air coming out of your suit when you took off", Olaf shone his light on Ole-Einar's shoulder. "I can see the hole. Pretty big. There is no way you can make it back in this suit, mate."

"No kidding", Ole-Einar shivered. "Okay, what are the alternatives. We can either bust through this wall", Ole-Einar nodded towards the brick wall, "and walk out of here, or you go back and bring me my spare suit and some dry undergarment. I can start digging around while you're gone."

"Agreed. Can't bust through the wall. Would compromise the mission. I better get back right away before they start looking for us."

"Yeah, that debris field was much tighter than it looked in the video. What the hell was she thinking?"

"Don't forget that Natascha is half our size, but I know what you mean", Olaf said and put his mask back on.

"If we tell Nick how tight that is, he's going to take her to the wood shed to give her some spanking."

"Ah, well, you know Natascha. She would probably enjoy that."

"Probably would. Okay mate, don't get stuck. If no one comes back within two hours, I will go through the wall."

"Agreed. Have a nice day! Don't go anywhere!" Olaf teased his friend.

"Smart ass!" Ole-Einar muttered, but his friend was already gone.

EuroSecCorporation, London, Saturday, August 16

"I might have an idea", Klaus whispered to Brian as they watched Powell over the monitor. The intelligence manager was still barking orders over his phone.

"I don't like it", Brian shook his head.

"What? My idea? You don't even know what it is." Klaus was appalled.

"No need, I won't like it", Brian insisted and gestured at the monitor where Powell just ended his phone call.

"I got people on their way to cover Cunningham's residence. Also sending some agents to Whitmore, but it will take some time. I don't want to ask the locals to help us, but we might have no choice", the intelligence manager stated. "Unless..." he slowly added, looking hopefully at Brian and Klaus.

"No!" Brian firmly stated.

"Yes, I had the same idea", Klaus stated at the same time.

"Klaus, I don't want to put Natascha in such a situation. She's not trained for it, and I think we can all agree that she has been through enough", Brian explained his hesitation.

"Agreed, but we also have four former members of special forces up there, who are more than capable of dealing with this situation. Not only are they most likely the most skilled people in that area, we also know that their vaccination is up to date. Don't forget that we are talking about a potential biological attack on British soil. Our guys know what they are up against, the locals don't. You really want to take that risk?"

"Our guys don't have weapons."

"Weapons? For what? They have to arrest an old guy sitting in a wheelchair."

"What about his detail? I highly doubt he's travelling by himself. There's at least a driver with him."

"We have to take that risk."

"I will see what we can find out about that", Powell reached for his phone.

"I still don't like Natascha being in the middle of it."

"It actually might help her", Shira added. "She struggled the last couple of weeks, feeling helpless that she couldn't do anything."

Brian looked at Shira. He still wasn't convinced that this was a good idea, but Klaus had a point.

"Okay, send them the details, but I want to make sure Natascha stays out of it."

Whitmore Abbey, Western England, Great Britain, Saturday, August 16

"Passing the thirty minute mark now", Nick commented with a quick glance at his watch. His breath condensed in the cold air inside the mine. A little LED light fastened to a beam provided just enough light for them to see, but they didn't want anyone on the outside to get suspicious.

"So glad you're here. I have no idea what I would do without you", Natascha sarcastically commented as she marked the time down on her clipboard.

"I know, what *would* you do without me?" Nick returned easily.

"Die from the plague and kill everyone around me?" she commented more coldly than necessary. Nick immediately regretted his question. The last thing he wanted to do was to bring that up again. "I'm sorry, Nick. That was stupid from me", Natascha apologised and quickly placed a hand on his thigh. Nick looked at her and felt how sincere she was. He held her hand.

"Your hand is cold. Do you want me to get you another jacket?" Nick tactfully changed the subject and turned to her.

"I have a better idea", she answered sweetly and snuggled against her husband, resting her head against his shoulder. "Once we're home I'm going to let you do that perverted thing you always wanted to try", she promised him in a calm whisper.

"It is not a perversion, it's a fetish. And you're the one who wants to try it, remember?" Nick laughed wrapping his arms around her.

"Oh, do I?" Natascha pulled away from him and refocussed her attention on the clipboard in her hand, feigning innocence.

"Yes, you do", Nick confirmed and kissed Natascha's cheeks. "I love you more than ever", he whispered in her ear, pulling her in closely again. "I am so glad you're feeling better."

"Yes, I actually feel much better today."

A dancing light behind them announced Rolf's return and the end of their little private moment.

"How are they doing? Anything happening?" their friend's deep voice cut through the darkness. He stared at the cave line which was tied to a wooden beam outside the water. The ray of light from his strong LED headlight danced over the seemingly dark water. No ripple disturbed its surface. There was absolutely no indication that their two Vikings were diving here.

"They are just past the thirty minute mark. If they're really as fast as you say, they should be inside the catacombs any minute now. All depends if they have to take the gear off getting through the cribbing and the old well", Natascha explained easily.

"Okay, that would add another ten to fifteen minutes, assuming that they don't have any issues with the scooters." Rolf mumbled, still staring at the dark surface.

"How does it look outside?" Natascha wanted to know.

"Still pissing rain, but no soul in sight. I'd say we're safe, but I will go back to the entrance just to make sure." He turned around to face them. "Oh, did I ruin a romantic moment?" he bluntly asked with an impish grin.

"Not more than usual", Natascha explained and snuggled against her husband again.

"Then my mission here is complete. Let me know if you need me", Rolf said and disappeared into the darkness.

Natascha shook her head with a laugh. "For some reason you just have to like him."

"Yeah, tell me about it", Nick agreed and pulled Natascha closer to him.

"Gosh, I would have really loved to have seen Ole-Einar storming into Conolly's office", Natascha chuckled at the very thought.

"Hm, he didn't like the hit on Shira and Noah."

"He made that quite obvious, I would say."

"Yes, he did. Can't say that I blame him. If I could–"

"No, Nick, don't go there, please. Not now. I just want to be here with you. I know this is not the romantic scene they write about in novels, but let's not ruin this moment, okay?" Natascha implored and quickly kissed Nick. He caressed her face and just smiled.

"Okay, that's one hour now. They should be coming back soon", Nick eventually commented after another glance at his watch.

"Let's hope that the scooters didn't die on them."

"Why would they?" Nick shared his optimism. A bouncing light from the mine entrance announced Rolf's return.

"Okay folks, I'm coming, just a fair warning", he bellowed from a distance, determined to give them a moment to ensure they were decent. "Any sign of them yet?"

"No, not yet", Nick shook his head. He didn't bother to get up. They had another thirty minutes before they would start to gear up to go after their friends.

"You think they had any issues?" Rolf asked with a lilt of concern in his voice.

"Don't know. It's not that bad down there. The main mine shaft is really large, and even the side tunnel isn't that bad. Mario and I had no problems whatsoever."

"Besides rupturing a breathing loop on a rebreather", Nick reminded her.

"Yeah, well, besides that."

"And losing daddy's ROV", he continued flatly.

"I thought we would never talk about that again?" Natascha made a dramatic face.

"Just saying", Nick concluded and rose to his feet with attention, excitement in his voice, "I think they're coming!"

They could indeed see a strong LED underwater light glow brighter as Olaf came closer to the surface.

"Perfect! That means we can get out of here and nail that son of a bitch", Natascha said and also stood up.

"What is it with your wife and the church?" Rolf looked at Nick.

"I'm not touching that. You have to ask her yourself", Nick defended himself with a grin.

"What happened?" Natascha wanted to know and looked at Olaf the second he broke the surface. It was clear that he was by himself.

"Ole-Einar's fine, but he's inside the catacombs. He ruptured his drysuit going through the beams from the old well", Olaf explained and couldn't help to throw a stern look at Natascha. "I have to get his spare suit and some undergarment. There is no way he can make it back like this. His suit totally flooded. He's freezing his balls off."

"Didn't you guys pay any attention to your buoyancy?" Natascha shook her head and made a comment on her clipboard.

"Not much to pay attention to if you have to take your gear off and literally pull yourself through with your hands", Olaf defended his friend. "We couldn't see anything from all that sediment!"

"Well, we didn't have to–" Natascha started, but she quickly realised that this wouldn't get them anywhere. "Never mind, I will go and get his gear. Rolf, can I use your watertight zip bag?" she asked and turned around to walk to the mine entrance.

"Sure, no problem. I believe it's on your bed", her friend said.

"My bed? Why is–" Natascha wondered, but then realised she would rather not know. "Argh! Never mind! Boys! They think they can dive...if they would lose some weight they would fit through wide open spaces", she ranted, making sure her friends could hear her. She knew that Ole-Einar would be fine. Cold, but fine. Though she still did not see the point in hiding her frustration. Just as she stepped outside into the rain, her cell phone started vibrating.

"Okay, okay", Natascha muttered, but waited until she was inside the RV before she took her phone out of her pocket. While she threw Ole-Einar's spare suit and undergarment on the bed, she quickly looked at the screen. Natascha frowned once she realised that she had missed several calls from Brian and received at least a dozen messages from Shira. A cold shiver ran down her spine. Natascha knew that something was wrong and opened the text messages.

"Oh shit!"

Back in the mine, Nick and Rolf checked Olaf's gear for any damage, but couldn't see anything that would give them any cause for concern.

"Did you find any bones?" Nick wanted to know and double checked the pressure gauges on Olaf's gear.

"No. I didn't bother looking and turned around right away, but Ole-Einar wants to dig while I'm gone. I'm pretty sure he will find something. Let's hope it's enough to find some DNA."

"Yeah, let's hope." Nick said, but his voice lacked enthusiasm.

"How's she doing? She seems to be getting her wits back", Olaf looked at Nick, and his friend just shook his head.

"Don't ask me. I honestly don't know. She's recovering physically, don't get me wrong, but I don't know if she will ever be the same", Nick whispered after a quick glance to the mine entrance. He paused for a moment before he continued. "What is taking her so long?"

"No idea. Maybe you can go and give her a hand. And while you're there, make sure to bring some dry socks and glove liners back with you as well. Mine are in the front pocket of my dive bag if you can't find any other."

"Yeah, might as well have a look", Nick agreed and started towards the exit.

The rain was still pouring down as he ran the short distance to their RV. It felt like it took him longer than usual to get back to the RV, but he finally opened the door, sealing it behind him.

"Hey angel, how are you doing?" Nick spun around, but he quickly realised that Natascha wasn't inside.

"Natascha?" he asked and took a second to double check the space. He could see his and Rolf's cell phones in the middle of the table. It was not where he remembered to have put his device, but Nick ignored it and checked the little bathroom instead. It was empty. There was no sign of her. Nick walked over to their bed and found Ole-Einar's spare drysuit and undergarment. "Hm, that's weird", Nick thought and looked around again, but there was no sign of a struggle. He quickly checked outside the RV, but he still couldn't find her. "She should have her phone on", he commented absentmindedly and finally picked up his own. A quick glance at the screen and he could see that it was swamped with notifications. A light frown furrowed his brow. They were all identical.

Turnip is fine. Call ASAP. Level 1 for Whitmore. Nick made a face. He knew that Level 1 stood for an immediate risk for life. Looking around, he pressed the speed dial for Shira's phone. His friend picked up after the first ring.

"Hey Shira, just got your messages. We don't have cell reception inside the mine. What's going on?" Nick wanted to know, scanning through the windows to see if he could spot Natascha.

"You already got him?" Shira sounded puzzled.

"Got who?" Nick frowned as he straightened up. Shira cursed in Hebrew.

"Nick, where is Natascha? Her cell phone is turned off."

"I don't know. I've been looking for her myself. I was just about to call her when I saw your messages", Nick quickly defended himself. "Do you have any idea where she might be? And who is it we are supposed to have?" Nick wondered. His back tightened as Shira briefed him on the latest developments. He put his cell phone on the table, turned the speaker on and stripped out of his drysuit.

"Are you sure about that?" Nick wanted to know as he changed into something more comfortable.

"Yes, we are. Our intel shows that Cunningham is already there. He's driving a black Bentley Bentayga, and its GPS shows that he's already at the abbey."

"I think I saw a black Bentayga arriving a few hours ago when Natascha and I went for a walk", Nick explained as he wrote a note for Rolf.

"A few hours? Then we don't have any more time to lose! Get Rolf and go after Cunningham", Brian entered the conversation. He knew that his hopes for Natascha to stay out of this were already shattered.

"No argument there, sir, but first I have to find Natascha. Knowing her, she most likely went up to the abbey to check if she can find the car. Shira, what did she say when she called you?" Nick demanded to know and was already out the door. He started running towards the abbey.

"She said she's going to tell you. Powell is trying to trace her cell phone, but it's still turned off. Where are you now?"

"I'm almost at the abbey. I have to find her first before I can get Rolf and the others. Listen Shira, I assume that Rolf will be looking for me in the RV anytime soon. I left a note for him right with his cell phone. Tell him to get Olaf and to meet me at the abbey. Ole-Einar will have to wait in the catacombs. He will manage. Okay. I'm at the abbey now", Nick panted and stopped at the wooden gates to catch his breath. He carefully peeked around the wall, but didn't see anyone. The heavy rain had driven almost everybody inside.

"Shira, I need some directions for the parking lot inside the abbey. I don't think that Cunningham parked outside with the other visitors. The Bentayga I saw earlier today drove right through the gates, but I don't see any cars like that from here."

"You have to stay to your right. The parking lot is behind the main cathedral. Right beside some maintenance buildings. Just follow the road."

Nick stayed close to the walls, determined to keep out of sight as best as he could. Nick followed the driveway all the way to the other end of the abbey grounds to get to the parking lot. It took him almost ten minutes before he was finally close enough to recognise the vehicles. The black luxury SUV was parked with several cars from the Vatican just beside the maintenance building.

"I got a visual on the Bentayga, but not on Natascha or anyone else." Nick reported and rhymed off the licence plate to Shira.

"That's a positive on the licence plate. Can you see if anyone is in the vehicle?" Shira directed him.

"On a Bentayga? I don't think you can look through the windows, but I will check." Nick slowly approached the vehicle. His eyes caught another visitor information board and the schedule.

"According to the schedule, the mass will start in about one hour. We should probably make sure that Cunningham doesn't get there."

"Affirmative."

"Well, it's pissing rain here. Safe to say that they're all inside. I'm moving in on the Bentayga. If she's not there, I will check out the cathedral." Nick commented and walked to an arcade to his left.

"Agreed." Shira confirmed, beginning a new beat, "Nick, what is the battery status on your cell?"

"About sixty percent left."

"Okay. I'll send you a picture of Cunningham, just so you know whom to look for."

"Do we know who is with him?"

"Powell is taking care of that as we speak. As soon as we know, you will know. Give me a second here. Rolf is calling."

"Okay. I'll keep looking."

Sixty metres away and out of Nick's sight, Natascha hid behind one of the massive stone pillars that supported the arcade leading to the main building's doors. The heavy rain pounded on the metal roof above her as her eyes scanned the vehicles from the Vatican. She didn't consider herself very knowledgeable when it came to identifying cars and SUV's, but she remembered Nick staring at a large black SUV passing them on their way back from the abbey.

"I think that one there is it", Natascha commented to herself as she tried to read the little decal on the massive SUV. She didn't dare to get any closer, although it didn't look like anyone was in it. Natascha tried to turn her cell phone on again, but her battery was so low that it didn't let her.

"Damn!" she cursed, knowing that Nick and the others would be frantically searching for her by now. "I better get back down there", she murmured with a last look at her phone. She was so focussed on her thoughts that she jumped at the sudden touch of a hand on her shoulder. Her first reaction was to scream, but a second hand covered her mouth immediately.

- *39* -

***EuroSecCorporation*, London, Saturday, August 16**

"I told you this is a bad idea", Brian shouted and looked at Klaus. The retired admiral could no longer sit in his chair and paced the conference room.

"They will be fine, just give them time." Klaus tried to calm his friend, but he had to admit, he had never thought of Natascha running off the reservation like that.

"What the hell is she thinking? And why is her cell phone turned off? Bloody hell!" Brian shouted. It was little solace to Klaus that his friend shared his concern, but the former general couldn't help the uneasy feeling that was building up inside him.

"Maybe her battery died", he tried to offer the best case scenario.

"Yeah, maybe. Or maybe someone from Cunningham's detail recognised her and got to her before Nick could? Any updates from them yet, Greg?" Brian yelled at the video conference monitor.

"Just getting something now, mate. Took us a while to find out who is working for him and in what position. According to our latest info, there is a four man team providing Cunningham's security. Victor Dalton is the team leader, then there are Robert Black, Wayne Shea, and Paul Ferguson."

"Do those names ring any bells?" Brian asked his people.

"That Dalton bloke sounds familiar. Victor is his first name?" Jack Connory from Operation Control asked.

"Yes, Victor Dalton. I should have his record here any second."

"I remember a Victor Dalton from the SAS. Not in my unit, but he had a reputation. Had lots of potential, but eventually they had to let him go. Developed some anger management issues, I guess."

"Yes, you're right", Powell confirmed and displayed Dalton's service record on the monitor. "Couple tours in Iraq and Afghanistan. Dishonourable discharge for use of excessive and unnecessary force. His whole unit reported him."

"Great, the guy is a psycho and he knows what he's doing. That's the last thing we need. What about the other blokes?" Brian barked.

"All three of them are former S014, that's the Royalty Protection Group. They left the force four years ago and started working for Cunningham almost immediately after that. I hate to say it, but your boys are up against some serious muscle." Powell commented with discontent.

"No kidding", Brian commented as he mulled over the new information. "I don't like it. I don't like it at all! Shira! Give me an update!"

"Rolf just told Olaf and is already on his way to the abbey. Olaf will catch up with him as soon as he is out of his drysuit. We should be able to trace their cell phones?" Shira asked and looked at Powell, her own cell phone glued to her ear.

"Yes, that shouldn't be a problem."

"Put it on the screen." Brian barked. "Where is Nick?"

"Trying to call him now but he's not picking up. Something is wrong."

Whitmore Abbey, Western England, Great Britain, Saturday, August 16

"Nick! Are you out of your mind?" Natascha gasped as Nick released his hand from her mouth.

"Sorry, but I could ask you the same. I called you, but you were so focussed that you didn't hear me in the rain. What the hell do you think you're doing, and why is your cell phone turned off?" Nick demanded to know with an unfamiliar tone in his voice.

"Sorry, I know that it's stupid–"

"Damn right it's stupid. Do you have any idea how worried we all are? How worried I am?" Nick harshly interrupted her. It was only now when she saw the concern in Nick's face that she realised what she had done.

"You're right, it was stupid", she apologetically shook her head. "I just wanted to take a quick look to see where the car is. I thought I could save some time so that you and the guys could start searching for Cunningham right away once Olaf and Ole-Einar are back. I know it was stupid." Natascha kept shaking her head. Nick knew that she was sincere.

"For heaven's sake Natascha, you can't just run away like that. Why is your cell phone turned off? We are desperately trying to reach you."

"I was just about to call you, but my battery died. I can't even turn the damn thing on", she explained and held her unit up. "Maybe you should call them and tell them that you found me."

"I would advise against that", a cold voice with British accent ordered them. Nick and Natascha spun around. They had no idea how the two men had managed to sneak up on them like this, but it didn't matter. The guns they were pointing at them left no room for any doubt that they meant business.

"Move and she will die", Victor Dalton threatened Nick. He had no reason not to believe him. "Your cell phones, toss them over", Victor ordered. Natascha briefly looked at Nick, but he just nodded. With two professionals pointing guns at them, there was nothing else they could do.

"You're not going to shoot us here in the middle of the abbey, are you?" Natascha asked with disbelief, even though she noticed that there was no one else around.

"Don't!" Nick whispered his objections. He was not quite as optimistic as his wife.

"You want to bet your life on it, Miss Rehfeld?" Victor's cold voice did not carry any emotion. "The cell phones, please. I will not ask for them again."

Natascha glanced at Nick and he nodded again with encouragement. He looked back to their assailants, wondering who they were and how they could possibly know Natascha, or that she was still alive.

"Facial recognition software", Victor answered their unspoken question as they slid their cell phones across the pavement. "There was a time when your face was in every database of pretty much every agency in this world. Being in the top ten wanted terrorists has that effect on the popularity level of your mug. I got curious when you showed so much interest in our vehicle." Victor neither took his eyes nor his gun off them while Robert Black smashed the phones with his gun. He threw the remains into a waste bin.

"Now, shall we, please?" Victor waved his gun at the door leading to the maintenance building. Nick and Natascha looked at each other and hesitated. If they could just stall them a little bit longer, it could be enough time for Rolf to come to their rescue.

"What do you want?" Natascha asked suddenly.

"For now I want you to go through that door, please", Dalton politely instructed. "Now! I won't say it again", he added with a cutting tone.

"But I don't–" Natascha started, but Victor had heard enough. With an annoying look he nodded at Robert, who shot Nick point blank without a moment of hesitation.

EuroSecCorporation, London, Saturday, August 16

"Where the bloody hell are they?" Brian barked hotly. "And where are Rolf and Olaf?"

"Rolf is almost at the abbey. Should be with Nick within a few minutes. Olaf is leaving the RV now." Shira updated with a look on the monitor.

"Not good enough. I have a bad feeling about this. Tell them to hurry up", Brian ordered and shook his head. He didn't like the development of this situation, especially since he had no control over it. Brian continued to pace the conference room as Klaus worked on another problem.

"Greg, can I ask you something?" the retired general looked at the monitor.

"Kind of busy here, what is it?" Intelligence Manager Powell announced from behind his computer.

"I just had a thought. Let's assume the worst case scenario–"

"You're a bloody ray of sunshine", Brian interrupted him.

"I'm realistic here. So let's assume that Cunningham is indeed infectious with the pneumonic plague. What are our guys suppose to do with him? What is their risk of getting infected themselves? I know they are vaccinated, but so was Natascha."

"Yeah, I was afraid you would ask that", Powell answered flatly. "Our guys are currently grilling the balls of the physicians. As soon as we know, you will."

Whitmore Abbey, Western England, Great Britain, Saturday, August 16

"Talk to me Shira. Where are they? I don't have a visual", Rolf panted as he looked at the parked vehicles from the same corner Nick had a couple of minutes ago.

"Nick should be to your left. About sixty metres. Do you see anything?"

"Negative. Is there a chance that he's inside?" Rolf ran over the parking lot, looking in every direction. He didn't like this at all, and he could feel a disconcerting feeling rising deep within him.

"No, I don't think we can pick up the signals through those walls, but it doesn't look like he's inside. You should see him. He's about ten metres in front of you." Shira advised. Rolf shook his head and spun around scanning all directions, but there was no sign of either of them.

"They're not here, Shira. I don't see anything. Are you certain?"

"Yes, five metres. Straight ahead."

Rolf noticed the waste bin and rushed over. "Give me a second here", he told

Shira as he ripped the cover off the bin. "Oh, shit. This is not good, Shira, not good at all. I just found both their cell phones. Someone smashed them and threw them in a garbage bin."

For a moment Shira closed her eyes, hoping that Rolf was mistaken, but she knew better. What she didn't know was that it was about to get worse. Much worse.

"Shira, we have a problem here. I just found blood. On the ground. On the wall. There is blood everywhere", Rolf's broken voice reported over the cell phone.

"What the hell is wrong with you?" Natascha yelled at Victor as she supported Nick.

"You raise your voice again and the next bullet will go in his liver and not in his arm", Victor calmly warned, still pointing his gun at Nick. Natascha looked at her husband, but Nick grimaced under the pain. It was not until they were through the door that Victor allowed Natascha to briefly check on her husband.

"It's a through and through", Natascha quickly determined after looking at the exit wound. "The bleeding stopped, you will be fine", she tried to encourage Nick, but the pain in his right arm burned so strong that he could barely hear her.

"Son of a bitch!" he cursed and bent over, desperately looking for a position that would alleviate some of the pain.

"Keep moving, we don't have all day", Victor ordered and waved his gun encouragingly. Nick and Natascha knew that he wasn't bluffing. A new wave of pain shot through Nick's body as he briefly leaned with his wounded arm against the stone wall, but eventually he started to walk. Robert Black led the way, making sure that the corridors were all clear. Just as they came around another corner, Nick tumbled against the wall again. He clenched his teeth as a new wave of pain shot through his arm.

"He needs a break!" Natascha demanded and placed her arm around his shoulder.

"No he doesn't. I didn't shoot him in the leg. Now keep moving."

"You do know that you're going to die, too? Right?" Natascha started as they moved on. "If your boss has the plague, there is no way you two are not infected, you know that?"

"Shut up. One more word and he's dead", Victor said. Natascha bit her lip. It was not the reaction she had hoped for. Reluctantly she kept going. It wasn't long before she came to a familiar area of the abbey.

"Wait!" Victor ordered and watched as Robert checked the area. It took him only a few seconds before he signalled to his boss that it was all clear.

"Keep moving", the former SAS operative ordered and pushed Nick in the back. "I guess you know where to go from here?" he suggestively smiled at Natascha.

"Yeah, the catacombs."

"About time you are here!" Rolf commented as Olaf's run slowed to a walk. He quickly filled him in.

"Shit! That's not good", the Norwegian said. Looking at the two broken cell phones, he didn't have to be a genius to figure out whose blood it was they were looking at. As he looked around, his eyes fell on a tiny metallic object on the ground.

"I think I found something", he said and quickly picked up an empty shell casing. He looked at it closely. "Calibre twenty-two", he explained before he sniffed the casing. "Recently fired. I think we found what they shot with."

Rolf turned to him with surprise and a sense of hope in his voice. "A calibre twenty-two?"

EuroSecCorporation, London, Saturday, August 16

"A twenty-two?" Shira wanted to be sure.

"Yes, a twenty-two. Could have been much worse. Although, we don't know the extent of the injury, but it looks like only one shot. We can't find any other shell casings, and I think we wasted enough time. They have to be somewhere inside. There is only one door nearby and we will take it." Rolf informed and focussed on the door with determination. "Listen Shira, I don't think we'll have cell reception once we're inside, but we will get back to you as soon as we find them."

"Understood, just make sure that–" Shira started, but Intelligence Manager Powell interrupted her.

"NO! We don't have any more time. Rolf, can you hear me?" Powell shouted over video transmission.

"Yes, sir. We can hear you."

"Listen to me! Forget about them. Cunningham is more important. I need you to go to the main cathedral and find Cunningham."

"What?" Brian couldn't believe what he had just heard.

"Yes, Brian, you heard me right. Go after Cunningham! Rolf, do you copy?"

"Just wait a second here. They are my people out there, and currently two of them are missing. At least one of them with a gunshot wound, as far as we know. We are unarmed and up against an equal number of well-trained and armed opponents. The bloody hell! You know as well as I do what the procedure is on this." Brian barked his objection.

"Yes, Brian. And generally I would agree with you, but not under these circumstances. We cannot risk the life of hundreds of people to look for two of your guys. Your guys are professionals, they know what to do."

"Bloody hell she does! She is not even–"

"I'm sorry Brian, but we do not have a choice." Powell interrupted Brian again, then turned his attention back to the team. "Rolf do you copy?"

"Sorry, sir, can you come again? You're breaking up, we can't hear you", they heard Rolf's voice over the cell phone. A second later it was turned off.

"Damn technology", Klaus muttered dryly. Despite the seriousness of the situation, Shira had a difficult time keeping a straight face and hid her smile behind her hand.

- 40 -

Whitmore Abbey, Western England, Great Britain, Saturday, August 16

"We are so getting fired for this", Rolf surmised with a worried glance at the cell phone before he slipped it into his pocket.

"Let's worry about that after we find them, okay?" Olaf suggested and moved towards the door. Satisfied that it wasn't locked, he carefully turned the handle and pulled it open. A quick peek inside revealed that the small corridor right behind it was empty.

"All clear", he whispered and quickly stepped inside, immediately making room for Rolf. "I somehow feel naked doing this without a gun", Olaf commented as Rolf quietly closed the door behind them.

"If it makes you feel better, I brought my dive knife", Rolf tried to cheer him up.

"So did I, and no, it doesn't. What was that about bringing a knife to a gun fight?" Olaf slowly moved forward. They were lucky that there was enough ambient light in this area that they could see everything.

"What is that on the wall over there? Looks kind of wet", Rolf pointed at a darker spot. "It's blood!" he determined once he had a closer look at it. They were both relieved that they didn't find any more blood on the floor.

"Okay, so whoever got shot can still walk. That's a good sign", Rolf whispered and they started to follow the corridor around a bend.

It didn't take them long before they reached a T-Section. They carefully looked in both directions, but didn't see anyone. Without saying a word, Olaf pointed at another blood smear on one of the walls a couple of metres away. They carefully rushed over to examine the evidence.

"Looks like the bleeding has stopped", Rolf commented on the absence of any blood on the floor. "Whoever was shot leaned against the wall", Rolf concluded and stood right beside the blood stain with speculation. "Look at the height. Given the amount of blood and the height of this smear, I would say that Nick got shot in the shoulder or in the arm."

"Not only that", Olaf said and pointed at another faint blood stain further down the wall. "I bet that Natascha is supporting him and they are using every chance they get to mark the walls."

"Natascha is leaving us a trail with her husband's blood!" Rolf exclaimed with a grin on his face, and turned to Olaf with surprise. "She's been paying attention in class."

Olaf returned the smile and looked back down the corridor. "Thank God for Shira's patience."

Natascha carefully watched Robert as he opened the door leading to the stairs to the catacombs. Natascha's eyes fell on one of the door locks she had picked what felt like a lifetime ago.

"Here, rest!" Natascha tried to encourage Nick and gently pushed him against the wall.

"Ouch!" Nick grimaced as his wounded arm touched the wall again.

"Sorry!" Natascha apologised while she smeared some more of his blood against the wall. Not much, just enough for Rolf and Olaf to notice.

Once they were through this door it wouldn't matter anymore. There was only one direction from there. "Don't worry, Nick, we will get out of this. We always do, do you hear me?" Nick couldn't answer behind his grimace of pain.

A familiar sound alerted Natascha that the lock was open. Robert pushed the heavy wooden door open and they waited for Natascha and Nick to take the lead.

"Careful, those steps are slippery", Natascha warned Nick and supported him as best as she could.

The two tactical flashlights their capturers shone provided them with enough light as the descended the century old stone steps. It didn't take them long before they stood in front of the second solid wooden door separating them from the catacomb.

"Wait!" Victor ordered, shining his light in their faces.

"Put your hands behind your back", Robert barked and looked at Natascha. She hesitated for a second, but knew that there was no point in resisting him. Reluctantly she allowed Robert to tape her wrists.

"You, too", Victor ordered and pointed his gun at Nick.

"Wait! He's shot–" Natascha started, but quickly fell silent as the gun pointed at her now. Nick groaned as Robert taped his wrists together behind his back. Satisfied that their prisoners couldn't move their arms any more, Robert finally unlocked the door.

"Well, here we are," Victor smiled and waved his gun towards the door, "in you go."

Natascha and Nick slowly stepped into the cavern-like catacomb. Natascha immediately noticed that the water level had subsided. Other than a few puddles at the brick wall, the ground was dry.

"Stop right there", came the next order, this time from Robert. He quickly searched them and took their watches and a set of keys, but didn't find anything else. Looking at Victor he simply shrugged and threw the items in front of the door.

"Don't go anywhere", Victor said and locked the door from the outside.

"Great!" Natascha muttered in the pitch black darkness.

Not far from them, Olaf and Rolf reached the door leading to the stone steps.

"There is another one", Rolf noticed and pointed at the blood stain.

"Okay, let's do this!" Olaf tried to offer some encouragement, but his voice didn't reflect it. They both knew that the odds were against them. Just as his hand reached the handle, they heard the door opening behind them. They both spun around, but Paul Ferguson already pointed his gun at them.

"Hello, chaps. Going for a stroll, are we?" the former bodyguard asked. He closed the door without taking his eyes or gun off Rolf and Olaf. They slowly raised their hands. They knew that they had no chance at this distance. Just as they thought it couldn't get any worse, the door leading to the steps behind them opened.

"Well, what do we got here?" Victor exclaimed, raising his gun to the ready.

"Against the wall!" Robert ordered. Olaf and Rolf didn't hesitate. They knew that they were dealing with professionals who were in a supreme tactical position and also armed. With Victor and Paul covering him, Robert quickly searched their latest prisoners.

"Bringing a knife to a gun fight, are we? How bloody stupid is that?" Robert scoffed as he removed their knives from their possession. "Arms behind your back", he ordered. A few seconds later and Rolf and Olaf had their wrists taped together.

"Bring them to the others. Paul and I will go back to the dinner", Victor ordered as he turned around.

"Okay, gents, let's go", Robert pointed his gun at the door leading to the catacombs.

"Nick? How are you doing?" Natascha whispered into the darkness. "You think Rolf and Olaf will find the trail we left them?"

"They better, otherwise we're in trouble", Nick groaned from a corner.

"Not yet", Natascha commented hopefully, and twisted her hands "They didn't find the little tool in my pants."

"That's inviting such inappropriate comments right now", Nick tried to laugh, but another burst of pain shot through him.

"Ha, serves you right. You guys are all the same", Natascha scoffed, fidgeting at her waistband. "How is the arm? Still hurting?"

"Angel, the guy shot me at point blank range. It hurts like hell, but I will manage. It's not as bad as I wanted them to believe, I just wanted to win some time. Sorry if I got you worried", Nick groaned.

"No problem, I figured that. Otherwise you'd be kind of a wimp. You know, being former special forces and all that."

"You're watching too many movies. Can I not get a little bit of sympathy for getting shot?" Nick groaned with a laugh.

"Honey, I gave natural birth to our daughter. Don't tell me about pain. You got my sympathies, but you have to suck it up if we want to get out of here", Natascha stated nonchalantly.

"And you're spending way too much time with Shira", Nick tried to laugh again.

"Would you prefer I be helplessly sitting here crying? Been there and done that. Didn't work."

"No, I like you better this way. Kinda scary, but–"

"Yes! I got it!" Natascha triumphed. "Sorry that I interrupted you. What were you saying?" she apologised.

"That you're a good wife", Nick whispered.

"Sorry, I couldn't hear you."

"I said that you are a good wife."

"Still can't hear you. What was that?" Natascha teased with a chuckle, but before Nick could say anything they heard the familiar sound of the key in the door lock.

"Shit, I'm not ready yet", Natascha tightly whispered.

"Don't do anything stupid", Nick warned her as Robert pulled the door open.

"Ay up, gents. We got some more visitors", the former bodyguard announced and made room for Olaf and Rolf.

"You got caught? You let yourself get caught?" Natascha gasped as her friends walked in.

"Sorry, it didn't quite go as planned", Rolf hissed through gritted teeth. "Nick! How are you doing?" he wanted to know as the shine from Robert's flashlight fell on his friend, but Nick only shook his head. His face was nothing but a grimace again.

"Enough of the chit-chat. Sit down!" Robert ordered and pushed Rolf so hard that he fell.

"Asshole", Rolf cursed and rolled on his back. Olaf didn't need any encouragement. With a satisfied grin, Robert waved his flashlight over his prisoners. The light shone on Natascha. She closed her eyes and didn't see the expression change on Robert's face.

"Why not?" Robert laughed and took a step closer to Natascha. "You! Stand up!" he ordered her, not without pointing his gun.

"No argument, pal, but if you touch her, I will kill you", Nick threatened the former bodyguard.

Robert just laughed at him.

"It's okay, Nick. Don't worry", Natascha whispered as she first rolled on her knees before she got up, her hands still behind her back. "You won't hurt me, right?" Natascha hesitantly asked, her voice breaking, feigning the fear she felt.

"And what makes you think that?" Robert laughed and stuck his gun in his waist band as he stepped right in front of the frightened woman.

"Because I got my hands free", Natascha coldly answered as she attacked Robert.

Victor Dalton had no idea what was going on inside the catacombs as he and Paul walked back towards the dining room.

"I want you to go back and cover the parking lot, in case someone else comes looking for them. I will be in the dining hall with Wayne", the former SAS operative said as they neared a cross section to another corridor. Paul just nodded and turned left, while Victor kept going straight.

He followed the next corridor to his right, which led him to an entrance hall. It was only here that he saw some visitors. His eyes quickly scanned them as he kept going, but he didn't see anything concerning. He directed his steps towards a staircase to his right and ignored the *no trespassing* sign. Victor took the steps with purpose, his eyes already searching the area in front of him. At the top of the stairs he turned left and could already hear the many voices from the private dining hall. He walked around the last bend and stopped right behind the open door.

"Anything happening?" he whispered at Wayne.

"No, they just finished a couple minutes ago. The abbot thanked Cunningham for his generous donation."

"How is he holding up?"

"Hard to tell from here, to be honest", Wayne shrugged. "I saw him wiping his face a few times. I assume he coughed up some blood, but I don't think the others have noticed anything yet. He is fading fast.”

“Did he give his speech yet?”

“He was too weak for that. He only thanked them for the invitation and that he wants to shake everyone's hand”, Wayne said with a raised eyebrow.

Victor nodded knowingly. “And so it begins!”

Natascha's movement came from her hip. Robert's nose shattered under all the weight Natascha had thrown behind her open palm strike, excruciating pain shooting immediately through his face. A scream escaped his throat, but Natascha didn't stop as she tried to dig her fingers into his eyes. Instinctively Robert dropped his flashlight and raised his arms to protect his face. Natascha anticipated his move and had already pulled her hands back, only to punch Robert in his throat, but his arms were too tight and she didn't hit him right.

“You damn bitch!” Robert yelled, his face full of blood, but Natascha wasn't intimidated and tried to kick him in the groin as hard as she could. Unfortunately for her, Robert's training took over and he was able to turn sideways at the last moment. Natascha connected with his hip, not nearly the effect she had hoped for.

“Could need some help here!” Natascha yelled, realising that Robert was far from being finished. Not only that, he also still had the gun. Natascha didn't hear what her friends were shouting at her as they tried to get up. She did the only logical thing and kept charging. She aimed for Robert's face, but the former bodyguard easily blocked her arm, only to get kicked against the knee. Natascha scraped her foot down his shin, causing him to scream in pain again.

“Some help here now!” Natascha shouted even louder, desperately looking at the brick wall, while she dodged one of Robert's fists. She was able to hit him again in the face, but Robert grabbed her and pushed her away. Natascha didn't lose her balance, but it was enough for Robert to get hold of his gun. He stepped backwards until his back was against the brick wall, increasing the distance away from Natascha, making it impossible for her to keep attacking him.

“Bloody hell! Enough of this!” He yelled, clearly embarrassed by getting his ass kicked by a woman. The wide beam from the flashlight on the ground was enough for him to see her. He raised his gun. Natascha didn't stand a chance. Just as he was about to pull the trigger, he felt the wall behind him shift with a groan.

“Jesus!” Natascha shrieked and jumped back as Ole-Einar burst through the wall, right there where Robert stood. The former bodyguard didn't stand a chance, getting buried under the bricks and a huge Viking. The gun slipped from his hand and landed not far from Rolf. Robert struggled against the pain that had enveloped him. Bricks scattered around him and a Viking landed on top of him.

Ole-Einar quickly looked around, satisfied to see that his friends were okay. Underneath him, Robert moaned and tried to get up, but Ole-Einar didn't move and pushed Robert's head into the ground.

“Bad guy!” Natascha panted and simply pointed at Robert. That was all that Ole-Einar had to hear. The last thing Robert saw was the huge right fist that hit him on the side of the head a fraction of a second later, knocking him out cold.

“Jesus, Ole, that was close. Thanks!” Natascha tried to catch her breath. With the adrenaline gone, she felt her body shaking with release.

"Oh, never mind, my pleasure. I would have helped you sooner, but I could barely hear you on the other side of the wall." Ole-Einar dryly commented. He found the roll of tape on Robert's belt and turned the former bodyguard into a human cocoon.

"Yeah, I knew you were still there, so I wasn't too concerned. At least someone I can rely on. Had to do most of it myself." Natascha stabbed at her friends as she worked on freeing them. "You guys are getting old."

"For the record, we wouldn't be in this misery if you didn't run off the reservation", Rolf defended himself and massaged his wrists.

"There is that, sorry guys", Natascha apologetically admitted.

"I don't want to be nosy, but would someone please explain to me why you're all locked up here in this hole, while I froze my ass off waiting for you?" Ole-Einar demanded to know, and his eyes rested on Olaf.

Since Natascha felt responsible for them being in this situation, she quickly updated her friend on the sequence of events. Ole-Einar listened carefully and was relieved to finally get out of his flooded dry suit.

Natascha eventually tended to Nick's wound again.

"How are you holding up?"

"It's not too bad as long as I don't have to move my arm. Not sure if I'm much of a help here, but I can bring you back to the RV."

"Yeah, not a bad idea. We should have a first aid kit in there", Natascha said with another look at the wound.

"We should go now before they start missing this scumbag", Rolf suggested and checked Robert's gun.

"Careful, it's loaded", Nick tried to joke as he threw a hateful glance at Robert. The former bodyguard just woke up, but Natascha was already upon him.

"That's for shooting my husband, asshole!" She said and punched him on his already broken nose. Even with his mouth taped shut, everyone could hear the muffled scream as Robert flinched.

"That's my girl", Nick smiled proudly as Natascha walked back to him.

"And one day I will even learn to cook", she smiled back before they left the catacomb.

With the tactical flashlight in one hand and Robert's gun in the other, Rolf quickly led the little group up the stairs. He pointed at the door and whispered for Olaf to check it.

"Damn, that scumbag must have the key", Olaf whispered as he found the door locked. "Ole and I can go back down and get it."

"Wait, let me give it a try", Natascha suggested and started to unbuckle her belt.

"Oh, yeah!" Ole-Einar whistled.

"You're all the damn same!" Natascha rolled her eyes and fitted her lock picking tool together. "Seems like I got to do everything myself these days", she mumbled and kneeled beside the door. She stared at the lock trying to remember how it worked when Ole-Einar's foot flew by just a few centimetres from her head. She shrieked as the door flew open with a deafening sound, Rolf immediately advancing through it, the gun at a ready.

"All clear", he quickly announced. Ole-Einar grabbed the still shocked Natascha by her elbow, urging her to her feet. "We're kind of in a hurry."

"Or we can just kick the door in and scare the crap out of me", Natascha whispered and put her belt back on.

"Does anyone know where we go from here?" Rolf asked as they slowly made their way towards the next door.

"Let's make a phone call first, I think there are a number of worried people in the conference room by now." Ole-Einar suggested.

"Great idea. Anyone still have a cell phone?" Rolf asked back. They looked at each other.

"Okay, Plan B then", Ole-Einar continued. "Nick, you and Natascha go back to the RV. My cell phone should be there somewhere. Call Brian and tell them that we are after Cunningham."

"Can I ask something?" Rolf interrupted his friend. "What are we going to do with him? Are we going to arrest him, or do you plan to storm into the mass and execute him in front of hundreds of people? His body will still be infectious, and I'm not even talking about any body fluids we might spill."

"Assuming we can get passed his three remaining bodyguards..."

"We have to quarantine him somewhere." Rolf explained. "And everyone he was in contact with," he added.

"We can lock them all up in the catacombs?" Natascha suggested with a shrug.

"Natascha, you're not going to lock dozens of the Vatican's highest clerics in the catacombs."

"Why not?" Natascha retorted with heat.

"She has a point there, Rolf. We can't be picky about this. But what about Cunningham? He's in a wheelchair, isn't he? Kinda difficult getting down to the catacombs."

"Well, one big push and he–"

"Natascha! Will you stop it!"

"Listen Ole", Natascha stepped up with purpose. "I just got over that damn plague, and I can guarantee you that it was not a walk in the park. Not for me and certainly not for my family. So if locking up an already dead man in the catacombs means that other people don't have to experience what I did, I will gladly drag him down there myself. And don't even get me started on the poor girls on the ship."

Ole-Einar didn't say anything. He knew that Natascha was right.

"Okay, let's talk about the bodyguards. We have to assume that there are still three of them left, right?"

"Yes, as far as we know."

"Okay, so they are most likely all armed and we got what? A twenty-two with how many rounds?" Ole-Einar watched as Rolf emptied the magazine to check.

"Six", Rolf replied and made a face.

"Six rounds for three guys? That should work, or?" Natascha naively asked.

"Sure, if they don't move and not shoot back", Rolf tried to explain.

"Who is your best shot here?" Natascha looked around.

"Believe it or not, but leftie here has the score to beat", Ole-Einar said and nodded at Nick. Natascha looked at her husband. She was obviously impressed and had not known that detail about him.

"I'm not just a pretty face", Nick smiled at her through his grimace.

"You're certainly not", Ole-Einar confirmed. "Let's stay on the topic here. If we can separate Cunningham and his wolves from the rest, we might have a chance, otherwise this can get ugly."

"I don't want to be a coward, but what are the risks of him infecting us?" Rolf wanted to know. It was a concern that was clearly heavy on everyone's mind. They all looked at each other.

"Oh, for heaven's sake. I will go if I have to!" Natascha finally determined.

"You? Are you out of your mind? Definitely not!" Nick's protest stood out from the others.

"Listen to me!" Natascha tried to calm them down. "We can safely assume that he has infected himself with the same bacteria that they infected me with, right?"

"Yes, the pneumonic plague", Rolf reminded everyone.

"So I'm already over it. I got anti-bodies. I can't get infected again." Natascha stated with confidence. Their silence was deafening as she looked at each of them, "Right?" She added after no one said anything. This time she didn't sound nearly as confident as she did a moment ago.

"I don't know, Natascha. We're not talking about the measles here. I think once is enough. Remember what we said about not pushing it any more? I think we both pushed it pretty far this time." Nick tried to reason with her.

"What if Natascha is right?" Ole-Einar countered, but their discussion got cut short by the ringing of the huge cathedral bells, indicating them that the mass was about to start.

"Doesn't matter anymore. We're running out of time. Let's go to the cathedral."

"I should come!" Natascha insisted.

"Under one condition. You and I are staying back. No argument!" Nick stated with finality. Natascha quickly nodded and they finally moved forward.

They followed a corridor leading from the chapel to the main cathedral. The singing from the choir reached them, and it was only moments later that they could see the altar and the front rows. It didn't seem like anyone had noticed them yet.

"Anyone's eyes on Cunningham?" Ole-Einar nervously asked. He had yet to see an image of him.

"Front row, far right", Rolf helped him out.

"That's the abbot up there. The one who is waving his hands like crazy", Natascha whispered in his ear.

"He is not waving! He is giving his blessing!" Rolf explained with a deep sigh. "And why are you here? Get back!" He hissed at her, pointing away.

"Oh, right, sorry", Natascha apologised and sneaked back.

"Any eyes on the bodyguards?" Rolf wanted to know.

"I think I see two of them", Olaf reported.

"Would help if we knew what the third one looks like", Nick said what everyone was thinking.

"Let's think logically. The bloke is SAS, right?"

"Yes."

"So he most likely sent his man down to the catacombs to check on the scumbag who is rolled up down there."

"Shouldn't we have seen him then?"

"Who knows which way he took."

"Doesn't matter. We have to get the people out of here. How can we do that?"

"What about a fire?" Natascha suggested hopefully.

"Natascha! You're not going to burn a century old abbey down! What is it with you and the church?" Rolf remarked.

"Okay, what about the fire alarm then? There is one over there", Natascha pointed over her shoulder at the corner behind them.

"No one is going to pull that fire alarm!" A cold voice ordered from behind them. Natascha could hear the team around her seemingly sigh in unison. "If anyone moves, she dies", Paul whispered and emerged from that very corner.

A few steps and he pressed the muzzle of his gun against the back of Natascha's head. She carefully raised her hands. "Move back–" Paul continued, but Natascha took her chance. She quickly spun around, her right hand finding Paul's gun, blocking the hammer with her grip as she pivoted just out of the line of fire. Her left hand already landed a crushing blow against Paul's throat, crushing it on impact.

He gurgled against the strike.

"Oh dear God!" Nick gasped his surprise and came to Natascha's help.

With one hand still securing Paul's gun, she repeatedly kept kneeing him in the groin while punching him in the throat with her other hand. Before any of the other guys could help her, Natascha had already swept his feet away from underneath him. Paul landed hard on the floor, still gasping for air while Natascha did not loose control over his gun hand. A devastating knee strike to Paul's head knocked him out instantly. Natascha secured his gun and planted her feet, catching her breath.

"May I please pull the fire alarm now?" She asked through her gasp.

"You're spending too much time with Shira, my love. Way too much", Nick insisted and kneeled on Paul's back. "There! I got him now!" He smiled at his wife. Natascha rolled her eyes and handed the gun to Olaf.

"Here, will that be enough now?"

"That just might do the trick", Olaf commented and checked the gun. To Olaf's surprise, the skirmish did not seem to have alarmed anyone in the main cathedral.

"You might as well pull that fire alarm. Seems like you're doing most of the work anyway", Ole-Einar shrugged. Natascha stayed close to the wall as she sneaked back. She didn't waste any time and pulled the alarm as soon as she reached it. The deafening sound of the fire alarm immediately filled the cathedral. Natascha moved back and they eagerly watched as the crowd scrambled to their feet with confusion.

"What the hell are they waiting for?" Natascha wanted to know. So far everyone was just standing there and looking at each other. The clerics were motionless and looked dumbly at each other. Victor and Wayne seemed suspicious.

"They think this is a false alarm", Ole-Einar noticed.

"Hey, angel!" Nick alerted his wife and tossed her a zippo he had taken from

Paul.

"Sweet!" Natascha smiled and walked to a heavy tapestry.

"Natascha! You are not burning the abbey down!" Ole-Einar shot in a harsh whisper.

"I'm not going to burn the abbey down, I'm just creating some smoke. Look around, this is the only flammable material in this stone corridor. Besides, this is such a heavy material, it will barely burn. All we need is for one person to see the smoke or smell the fire. The moment they move, we will put the fire back out. Nothing can happen", Natascha explained as she put the zippo to the fabric.

"It's going to be so much fun watching you when you explain this to the boss", Rolf laughed at Nick, who kept searching Paul.

"Why me?" Nick found Rolf's and Olaf's cell phones in one of Paul's cargo pockets.

"You're the one who married her, buddy." Rolf explained as the fabric finally caught some fire. Against Natascha's predictions, it only took seconds for the century old fabric to be fully engulfed in flames.

"Oops!" She managed as the flames already licked up the four metre high ceiling. As predicted, the smoke drifted towards the cathedral. The visitors just stood there, frozen on the spot as they watched the heavy smoke rolling in. Finally a woman screamed. It seemed as if that was the signal everyone was waiting for. All of a sudden everybody started screaming, and people started to run with a panic towards the large exit doors. Abbot Hetley tried to calm the people from the altar, but even using his microphone, his voice was no match for the fire alarm and the screams.

"Get back! Behind the corner!" Ole-Einar yelled as one of Cunningham's bodyguards ran towards them. "We can use him as bait!" The Norwegian pointed at Paul. Nick used his left hand to pull him away just as the burning remains of the curtain came down.

Now safe from the fire, Nick let the still unconscious body drop to the ground and moved quickly behind the corner. The thick smoke had prevented them from being seen. Rolf peeked around the corner, carefully watching how Wayne slowly made his way past the curtain, his gun elevated, ready. He finally spotted Paul. Rolf waited until Wayne kneeled down to check on his colleague.

"Don't move!" He shouted as he and Olaf stormed around the corner. Wayne hesitated for a moment, weighing his odds. "Don't even think about it, pal." Rolf warned him. Wayne quickly determined that Rolf and Olaf knew what they were doing. Reluctantly he slid his gun over.

"On the ground! Face away from us! Hands behind your back!" Rolf slowly advanced forward until he could place his foot onto Wayne's gun. He shuffled backwards and kicked it towards Ole-Einar, who quickly checked the gun as he picked it up.

"All safe!" Olaf said once he had used some of the tape to secure Wayne.

"Let's finish this!" Ole-Einar advanced forward with Rolf. "Nick, you and Natascha pull these scumbags behind the corner and stay with them. Olaf, we go three-man formation. The smoke is lifting. First target is Cunningham's goon."

"Roger that", Olaf confirmed and took formation. They quickly advanced through the corridor until they had a better view of the cathedral. There were only a few visitors left, but most of the clerics had gathered around the altar and Cunningham. So far none of the clerics noticed them, but the former SAS operative had already spotted them.

Victor opened fire immediately.

- *41* -

***EuroSecCorporation*, London, Saturday, August 16**
"Talk to me, Shira! I need to know where they are!" Brian barked and paced the conference room much faster as he had earlier.

"Can you please sit down? I'm getting dizzy just watching you. I'm trying to concentrate!" Klaus tried to calm his friend.

"Sorry, but I can't sit still any more. Shira!" Brian yelled at his Israeli operative.

"I appreciate the confidence you have in me, Boss, but you do know that there is absolutely nothing I can do until they are outside again and have their cell phones turned on", Shira defended herself.

"I know. My apology for yelling at you", Brian softly apologised before he turned to the monitor showing the video conference. "Greg!" Brian barked from the top of his lungs again. "Any news?"

"Polite as always, aren't we. Not much news, but I got some choppers with our specialists on the way to contain the scene. ETA is ten minutes. Local law enforcement is going up there right now to make sure no one leaves the premises. First cars should be at the abbey any second."

"Can you get direct intel?" Brian wanted to know.

"Of course. I have a standing line with the officer in charge. They just pulled up at the abbey. Give me a second here...he says that people are panicking." Brian exchanged a worried look with Klaus.

"Damn, that's not good", Brian brushed his hand through his hair. His eyes fell back on the monitor.

"Hold on. He just spoke to some people and according to them the abbey is on fire." MI5 Intelligence Manager Powell stated.

"On fire? The abbey?" Brian repeated with surprise. He looked at Klaus, who seemed to be as shocked about this revelation as the former admiral.

"Yes. There is smoke coming from of the cathedral. They're having a hard time keeping the people from leaving the abbey grounds."

"Bloody hell, that's the last thing we need. Where are our people? And why is the abbey on fire, Shira?" Brian barked, demanding answers.

"Don't look at me. How am I supposed to know?" Shira defended herself again and tried to call Rolf's and Olaf's cell phone again.

"Oh dear God, that is not good. Not good at all", Powell said from the monitor. "What is it?"

"The officer in charge just reported that he had heard multiple gun shots coming from the abbey."

"Dammit!" Brian cursed, knowing that none of his people had guns.

Whitmore Abbey, Western England, Great Britain, Saturday, August 16
Victor fired three shots at Ole-Einar, but they went wide. The panicked screams from the visitors mixed with the fire alarm as Victor pushed Cunningham out of his

wheelchair. As far as he was concerned, his mission here was over. He knew that Cunningham was as good as dead, and he needed the confusion for his escape. With the keys for Cunningham's SUV still in his pocket, he quickly blended in with the fleeing crowd, rushing for the nearest exit.

"Olaf, Rolf! You stay with Cunningham! Nobody touches him!" Ole-Einar yelled and charged after the former SAS operative. The Norwegian towered most of the people, yet he had a hard time spotting Victor in the crowd. "He is heading for the car! He is getting away!" Ole-Einar shouted over the screams of the people once he reached the door.

"What happened? You guys okay?" Natascha shouted at Rolf from her secure position.

"Yes, we're fine. Cunningham is down. Victor is going for the car." Rolf shouted back and gave her the thumbs up.

"I don't think so!" Natascha said to herself and checked the items Nick had taken from Wayne and Paul.

"What are you looking for?" Nick wanted to know. He was still kneeling on their captives.

"This!" Natascha smiled, holding up a set of car keys as she dashed back to her feet.

"For heaven's sake, be careful!" Nick helplessly shouted after her, but Natascha was already on her way. She sprinted through the abbey, taking the shorter route to the parking lot. Her steps echoed from the centuries old stone wall as she ran down the corridors. It took her a couple of minutes, but she finally reached the door leading to the parking lot. She recognised Nick's blood on the wall, reminding her how quickly their situation could change.

"Okay girl, you can do this!" She encouraged herself and opened the door just wide enough to take a peek. She spotted Victor in the distance, and he was already at the black Bentley Bentayga.

"Hell no!" Natascha cursed and slipped through the door. Not far away, the Bentayga's six hundred horsepower W12 engine came to life.

"Come on! Where are you?" Natascha impatiently hissed through her teeth and pressed the button on her key fob. A smile crossed her face as the doors of a black Jaguar opened just in front of her.

"Where the hell are you?" She complained, this time looking for Ole-Einar, as she slipped behind the steering wheel. The supercharged V8 engine started the moment she touched the button.

"Come on! Come on! Come on!" She nervously looked around for Ole-Einar, waiting for the gear shifter to rise from the centre console, but her friend was nowhere to be seen. Further down the parking lot, Victor already shifted the Bentayga into forward. The 6.0 litre engine catapulted the luxury SUV forward, the automatic traction control offering perfect acceleration as he shot through the parking lot. The former SAS operative didn't even see the Jaguar until it was too late.

"This is a bad idea!" Natascha sighed, bracing herself for impact as she shot backwards out of the parking spot. The black Jaguar hit the Bentayga directly on the right quarter panel. Natascha screamed as the much smaller luxury sedan whirled around by the impact, a myriad of deploying airbags cushioning her into position. The Jaguar came to a sudden stop as it hit the car parked beside it, but the 2.5 ton heavy Bentayga was still on its course of destruction. Victor lost control over the vehicle and, not wearing a seat belt, was at the mercy of physics as the Bentayga broke to the left, where it smashed into three parked cars before coming to a standstill.

Inside the wrangled mess of the Jaguar, Natascha released her seat belt and pushed the deflating airbags out of her way as she turned around to see where the Bentayga was, and if her plan had worked.

"Oops!" Natascha mouthed at the sight of the destruction she had caused.

"Bitch!" Victor cursed. The airbags had done their job, but the former SAS operative was still groggy from the impact. He waited for the airbags to deflate, but could not open the door as it was smashed into place. He slowly crawled over to the passenger seat and picked his gun up from the floor. "Dammit!" he cursed, noticing that both doors on the passenger side had solid contact with a tangled mess of steel that once represented two Lancias from the Vatican fleet. "I'm going to kill that bitch!" Victor promised himself and crawled to the back seat, eager to get out.

"Okay, Ole, now would be a great time to show up!" Natascha anticipated and left the Jaguar. She looked around, but there was still no sign of her tall Norwegian friend. "Time for Plan B", she decided and headed towards the door again, but Victor had already spotted her.

Natascha heard his scream and instinctively dove to the ground just before the first shots were fired. Her breath was heavy as she impacted the ground, and she counted three shots, but none of them were even close to her. Natascha waited for a couple of seconds, but nothing happened.

"Natascha! Are you all right?" She eventually heard Ole-Einar's familiar voice.

"Yes! I'm fine! Did you shoot him?"

"Yes! I got him. You're safe." Ole-Einar said, kneeling beside Victor. "Don't come any closer, I double tapped him in the head", her Norwegian friend warned her. Natascha stayed back, grateful that Ole-Einar's upper body blocked the sight of the bloody corpse.

"What the hell are you even doing here?"

"It seemed to be a good idea at the time, but now that you mention it", Natascha said weakly and looked around. At least six cars were significantly damaged. "But the main thing is that we got him, right?"

"Yes, you got that one right. Now get back to the others. The police are already here. I will take care of this. If you get stopped by the police, just identify yourself."

"Okay", Natascha nodded and turned around. She slowly walked back to the door. Her active role in Victor's death weighed heavier on her shoulders than she dared to admit. With her hand on the door handle, she turned around to Ole-Einar.

"Ole?"

"Yes?"

"Thanks!" Natascha smiled at him.

Her Norwegian friend smiled back. "Any time, Natascha. You can be proud of yourself today. You kicked some ass!"

Natascha nodded and opened the door. It didn't take her long before she was back to Nick. He was still busy keeping their prisoners on the ground. The police had not made it to them.

"Jesus, what happened?" Nick asked her and got up. It was only now that Natascha looked down at herself. Her jeans and sweater were full of mud from diving to the ground just a few minutes ago.

"I'm okay, don't worry. We got him", she smiled and hugged Nick.

"Ole-Einar okay?"

"Yes, he is fine. He had to shoot him", Natascha commented, and she suddenly felt sick to her stomach at the thought.

"It's okay, angel. It's either them or us, you know that." Nick tried to comfort her with a kiss.

"I know. I will be fine. Just give me a few minutes." Natascha smiled and looked down the corridor where Rolf and Olaf struggled to control the scene. "I better go and see if I can help them. You okay here?" She wanted to know and looked at their two prisoners.

"Yes, I will manage. You go ahead. Clearly looks like they can use another person."

"Love you!" Natascha kissed him again and hurried down the corridor towards the altar. Nick was right. Rolf and Olaf had a hard time trying to keep the clerics away from Sir Cunningham. The industrialist was still on the floor, but to Natascha it looked like no one had touched him.

"Thank God you are here! This is crazy. How is Ole?" Rolf wanted to know. He was clearly relieved to see Natascha.

"Ole is fine. The bad guy not so much. He had to shoot him", Natascha managed and swallowed. Rolf and Olaf only nodded. Natascha took another step towards Sir Cunningham. He was still alive, but he was in bad condition. Natascha didn't really want to, but for reasons unknown to her, she kneeled beside the old man. The industrialist managed to roll on his back. Blood trickled from his nose and mouth, his shallow breaths rattling. Despite the pitiful sight, Natascha knew better and kept a safe distance.

"Are you a doctor? Aren't you going to help him?" One of the clerics asked her, puzzled that she was not helping him.

Natascha ignored the priest and stared at Cunningham, "Sir Cunningham! Hey! Can you hear me?" Natascha shouted. The dying man finally looked at her.

"Sir Cunningham! I have to know! Did you infect yourself with the pestis bacteria?" Natascha looked for a reaction. A murmur went through the clerics as they took a step back. They were certainly nervous about what they had just heard.

"Sir Cunningham! Did you infect yourself with the pestis? Yes or no?" Natascha pushed. She fought the urge to grab him by the collar, but maintained her safe distance.

Sir Cunningham started to smile and nodded before he looked at Abbot Hetley. He collected his remaining strength. A cough shook his battered body, and it took him a few moments before he finally managed to control himself.

"You may not know about me", he started with a weak voice. Each word cost him a lot of energy, but Sir Cunningham eventually continued, his eyes fixed on the abbot. "Maybe even your predecessor won't remember me...but I will never forget him...I will never forget what he had done to me and my mother." Sir Cunningham had to cough. It took him almost a minute before he had himself under control again. More bloody froth ran from his mouth. "You know what my last memory is of my mother?" Another cough shook his body. This time it took him much longer to recover. He closed his eyes and swallowed. "You know what my *only* memory is of my mother?" Sir Cunningham took his time before he continued. "The only memory I have of my mother is being ripped out of the arms of a crying woman." Sir Cunningham swallowed to let his words sink in. "Being ripped away from her, just to get handed over to two strangers who ruined my life." Sir Samuel Archibald Cunningham's voice grew soft.

All the anger and hatred he had stored for decades were finally out in the open. Natascha could see a wave of relaxation going through his body. Tears came to her eyes listening to Sir Cunningham, but she resisted the urge of helping him. "Two strangers, who I was told were my parents... Two strangers, who ruined my life with their beliefs." Sir Cunningham coughed up more blood. His breathing became more laboured. Natascha could hear the liquid in his lungs with every breath he took, but Sir Cunningham managed to go on. "Two strangers, who were not my parents...who had the only thing my mother never had." Sir Cunningham had to take a break. "Money!" He finally managed, his eyes still on Hetley. "Your people sold me to someone else because my mother had no money...How dare you?...For decades...I tried to find her...I couldn't...Because of you!" Sir Cunningham stared at the abbot. It took him the little strength he had left, but he had to get these words off his chest. "This is my revenge... On you...On all of you!" His voice broke as he let his eyes wander over the other clerics for the first time. "She is right", he continued eventually and managed to smile at Natascha. "I got the plague...Remember earlier?" Sir Cunningham smiled and looked up. He knew he only had a few moments left. His eyes fell on Natascha again. "I never knew my father...I never met my mother again...All I have is the memory of her name." Sir Cunningham whispered finally, his mother's name rolling off his tongue in his last breath, "Cathy."

"He has the plague?" One of the clerics voiced his disbelief and quickly crossed himself as he took another step back. Many of the others followed.

"You remember earlier today? After the evening supper?"

"We all shook hands with him. We greeted him with the brotherly kiss of the church", another dignitary said shockingly, as he too crossed himself.

"It's the plague! We are all infected! We are all going to die!" Abbot Hetley finally spoke. He almost panicked.

"Yeah, well, karma is a bitch, isn't it", Natascha dryly commented and rose to her feet. The abbot was so shocked about the comment that he was left speechless. For the first time he took a closer look at Natascha. He suddenly flinched as he finally recognised her.

"Yes, that's right. It's me again. You are finished! One way or another!" Natascha started, but she was cut short by the police officers who stormed the cathedral. Rolf managed to stop them and, thanks to a phone call with Gregor Powell, convinced them that they were the good guys.

"There is an infectious body behind the altar and we got three more people in our custody. Nick is over there with two of them, while the third person is in the catacombs. Ole-Einar here will guide you", Rolf explained. By now, the specialists wearing biological Haz-Mat suits arrived and finally took over the scene. It took a few more minutes before Rolf was permitted to leave the cathedral with Nick, Natascha, and Olaf. The moment they got closer to the door, his cell phone finally rang.

"Yes, Rolf here", Rolf answered. He listened only for a second before his face turned into a painful grimace. He lowered the device and gestured it to Nick, "Here, for you."

"For me?" Nick wondered, but, against his better judgment, he took the phone. "Hello? Nick here."

"Whittaker here! If I were you, I would not pass me on to someone else. Am I clear on that?" Nick heard the snarling growl of the former admiral.

"Crystal clear, sir. What can I do for you?"

"For starters, you can tell me what the bloody hell is going on. The last sit rep I received was Rolf telling me about you and the missus gone missing, your cell phones smashed, and a lot of blood on the ground by a twenty-two. Since everyone kept ignoring me for the better part of the last hour, I just thought I might call and see if anyone can tell me what the bloody hell is going on up there!"

- *42* -

***EuroSecCorporation*, London, Wednesday, August 20**
Gregor Powell sat at the conference table. The cup of tea in front of him was as untouched as the plate of cookies Brian had personally served him. Both the former admiral and Klaus threw a pitiful look at the intelligence manager, who had buried his face behind his hands halfway through the briefing.

"I'm so going to get fired over this", Powell murmured and massaged his temples once Brian finished.

"It is actually not as bad as it sounds", Brain apologetically countered.

"Not as bad at it sounds? Are you bloody serious?" Powell argued, his face still hidden behind his hands. "Please interrupt if I get this wrong, but your part-time secretary ran off the reservation–"

"She is not part of the senior staff, and I told you that it was a bad idea", Brian excused her.

"–closely followed by her husband."

"He cares a lot for her."

"They get caught and the husband gets shot. Natascha then left a trail by smearing century-old walls–"

"We are talking about a stone wall, not a bloody painting."

"–in the historic parts of the abbey with her husband's blood."

"She didn't have a marker, and it wasn't that much blood."

"While she and her husband got thrown into the catacombs, your other two specialists managed to get caught."

"They were actually outgunned."

"Cunningham's goon locked them up in the catacombs as well, and when he wanted to get friendly with Natascha, she managed to beat him up–"

"She had no choice!"

"–with the help of that huge Viking, who not only destroyed an office at Scotland Yard, but also burst through a wall of a historic grave site."

"What was she supposed to do?"

"After they escaped, your young lady then set fire to a two-hundred-and-fifty year old antiquity, which had once been donated by the Royal family to the arch-bishop–"

"In her defence, she didn't know that it was *that* expensive."

"–but not before she beat up another one of Cunningham's goons."

"Again, she had no choice. Our team was short staffed due to Nick's gunshot wound."

"After that, the visitors scurried in a sudden panic to flee the burning abbey–"

"Be realistic. It was just an old curtain."

"–and she ran to the parking lot–"

"That was some fast thinking on her part!"

"–where she used Cunningham's Jaguar to stop a Bentley Bentayga–"

"Yes, that Victor bloke was about to get away."

"–which also belonged to Cunningham, but not without destroying a total of six cars."

"Collateral damage. You should know that. Besides, she did stop him, didn't she?" Brian persistently defended Natascha. Powell still had his face buried behind his hands. Brian and Klaus watched as he sorted some papers. He finally found the information he was looking for.

"True, but we usually don't face such charges. In this case they're talking about her specifically."

"And? She was fighting a bloody terrorist attack on British soil. You're not going to stick any of that on her, are you?"

"No, of course not, but do you have any idea how much bloody paperwork I got with this? You already made me pay to replace that damn zodiac which you had turned into a bloody missile-defence-system."

"Bloody hell, Greg. These are peanuts compared to your other operations."

"That's true, but my other operations usually do not make the front page of the London Times. Do you have any idea how much time it took to come up with a decent story?"

"Isn't that why they pay you the big bucks?"

"Not nearly enough, mate."

"Well, I think it will get worse", Brian suddenly smiled.

"How so?" Powell lowered the documents he held. "How could this possibly get worse?" It looked as if Powell was almost crying now.

"Someone has to tell Natascha that MI5 let the abbot get away. And that *someone* is certainly not going to be me." As if Brian's statement was the clue, they all heard the typical rhythm of Ariel knocking at the door. "Enter, if you are one of us", the retired admiral barked. The Israeli opened the door. Shira, Nick, Natascha and the rest of the Whitmore team followed.

"Natascha! Great to see you. Here, sit down!" Brian enthusiastically said and offered Natascha one of the comfortable chairs. "How was the quarantine?" Brian smiled. Natascha just threw him a glance that said it all. "Oh, that good?" The former admiral tried to joke.

"What could be better than being locked up for three days and having the medical staff going crazy every time I sneezed?" At least Natascha had her sarcasm back.

"I'm sorry, but it was a precaution we had to take. An outbreak of the pneumonic plague could be life threatening." Gregor Powell tried to be diplomatic.

"Oh really? No kidding! Tell me more about it!" Natascha looked at him incredulously.

"Natascha, you remember MI5 Intelligence Manager Gregor Powell, right?" Brian tried to ease the situation.

"Of course I do."

"Well, Mrs. Rehfeld. You certainly have my sympathy for what has happened to you, and I don't want to take up any more of your time than absolutely necessary. But since you had an active part in this mission, we just have to do a quick debriefing."

Powell opened his folder and took a sip of his tea. He sorted through some papers again and took a cookie, but for some reason he still felt nervous.

"I am not sure if they told you, but our interrogation specialists successfully interrogated Dr Evans while you were in isolation. According to her, Sir Cunningham was not yet infectious at the time of his visit at Whitmore Abbey and during his last moments. The bacteria they found in Sir Cunningham had the same DNA as the one we found in your blood. Based on the current information we have about the bacteria, our specialists confirmed that as well."

"So there was no risk for the visitors?" Natascha hopefully asked.

"No, Natascha. Fortunately there was not." Powell smiled at her. That was the easy part. He took another sip of his tea as he braced for the hard part. "There is something else you should know. I'm not sure how familiar you are with such operations", Powell started.

"Well, unfortunately I'm getting used to it by now, but at least this time nobody declared me a terrorist." Natascha sourly commented.

"Again, I'm sorry. Since you will hear about this anyway, we all came to the conclusion that it is best to tell you right away. I just want you to know that something like this is normal, but I can assure you that nothing can happen to you." Powell carefully explained, hopefully looking at Brian and Klaus.

"What will I hear? Is someone pressing charges against me? Let me guess! Whitmore Abbey charges me for ruining the cars?" Natascha's voice became cold.

"No, they are not, but Cunningham's lawyers are pressing charges for grand theft auto and ruining the Jaguar and the Bentayga. They want over a quarter million pounds. The Vatican is looking for another hundred thousand pounds for demolishing the other four cars." Powell explained and fixed his tie. "Whitmore Abbey is pressing charges for arson, grave robbery, disturbing the peace, and disturbing a grave site."

Natascha released a sigh, her frustration evident. Her throat was too dry for anything else. Looking for help, her eyes fell on Nick, but it was Shira who broke the silence.

"I am actually proud of you. You still left some tracks and evidence, but you didn't make the top ten of the most wanted terrorists this time. You are getting better at this undercover work", her Israeli friend told her with a smile.

"Well, we weren't planning to go back there anyway, were we?" Nick tried to cheer his wife up.

"Not really. They can really do that? Am I in trouble?" Natascha nervously asked. Somehow this news sounded like something she wouldn't be able to get out of.

"Of course not. It is just their way of showing how bloody pissed they are. MI5 will settle the bill, isn't that right, Greg?" Brian reassured and looked at his friend expectantly.

"I will have to spend hours in front of hearings", Gregor nodded before Brian continued. "Fact is that you played a deciding factor in preventing a biological terrorist attack on British soil. That sort of trumps the charges", Brian winked at her joyfully.

"Why is it always me?" Natascha asked innocently.

"Well, don't be too harsh on yourself. I think you had some bad influences in the last couple of years", Brian tried to comfort her. His eyes rested accusingly on Shira.

"What did I do? Why are you looking at me?" Shira defended herself, confused. Natascha winked at her.

"So, what about the bone fragments Ole-Einar found. Any luck with them?" Natascha changed the subject.

"Yes. The DNA of the bacteria matches. So that proves beyond a doubt that they got the *Y.pestis* from Whitmore Abbey." Powell shifted uncomfortably in his chair.

"Oh, that's great news", Natascha relaxed. "So you are going to nail that son of a bitch?"

"Excuse me?" Powell asked.

"I mean the abbot. You have him in custody, don't you?"

"No. We do not have him in custody." Powell confessed, bracing for the explosion that Natascha was about to hit him with.

"What do you mean?" Natascha asked, letting anger drop her voice to a snarled hiss. She slowly straightened up in her chair. Shira had to bite her lip.

"Once Abbot Hetley learned that Cunningham had infected himself with a lethal bacteria to kill them all, he used the confusion to...make himself unavailable for the arrest."

"Do you mind me asking how he managed to escape?"

"He simply took one of the remaining cars from the Vatican and left."

"Just like that? And no one stopped him?"

"The vehicle fleet of the Vatican is under the protection of diplomatic immunity, unfortunately. The local law enforcement officers didn't know better and let him leave."

"Please tell me that he's kidding me", Natascha looked at Brian.

"Unfortunately not, Natascha", Brian apologised. "Augustinus Hetley is currently inside the Vatican and under the protection of diplomatic immunity."

"Ha!" Natascha couldn't help but laugh. "You are joking. You are just messing with me, right?" Natascha laughed again, certain this could not be the truth.

"No, we are not. But I can assure you that we *will* get him. One way or another. There is no question that he is involved in this", Powell guaranteed her.

Natascha drummed her fingers on the table with thought, "I really hope you're right. I would hate to see him get away."

- *43* -

London Aquarium, London, England, Thursday, September 11

"Hey Kyle! It is so nice seeing you again", Natascha laughed at the sight of her visitor. Kyle McRae opened his arms and pulled Natascha in for a hug.

"Ah, it is so good to see you. I never thought I would see you again", the reporter laughed as he let her go.

"Yes, those were some crazy times. Let's go and get a decent cup of coffee. My treat." Natascha invited him and led the way. "So, how is it going? When is your article going to come out?"

"Forget the article", Kyle laughed. "Thanks to you I got so much material that I'm actually writing a book."

"A book? Oh my God, that is awesome. I bet you will not have any issues finding a publisher."

"I got several publishing houses showing interest in it. There is just so much information. People should know about it. Maybe they can solve some of the mysteries now."

"Yeah, maybe." Natascha laughed as she assumed a seat at a table. She shifted into it and began, "So, can I ask you about your own family research?"

"You mean Cunningham? That is something else, let me tell you that." They both ordered their coffee before Kyle continued. "After my grandmother Cathy Sheppard fled from Whitmore Abbey that night, she gave birth to her and Gordon Ferguson's son. That son was none other than the late Sir Samuel Archibald Cunningham."

"Oh my God. What are the odds? I only thought about it when he mentioned your grandmother's name in the abbey, but I didn't think that he meant *your* grandmother. Talking about her was the last thing he did before he passed away."

"Well, I'm certainly glad you mentioned it. There was never any contact between him and our family. However, DNA tests show that we are directly related. Cathy Sheppard gave birth to my mother in fifty-nine, but unfortunately died only a couple years later. And there were simply no records of Cunningham."

"But how can that be?"

"The abbey changed his name and forged a birth certificate before his adoption."

"Go figure. What about Gordon Ferguson?" Natascha wanted to know.

"Nothing. Unfortunately there are no records whatsoever. Plenty of people with the same name, but no connection. I'm afraid he will always remain a mystery."

"I'm sorry to hear that. I hope that you can find some closure." Natascha tried to offer some comfort. She smiled as the waitress brought their coffee. "Thanks, Nancy."

"Yeah, kind of an avalanche of information. But enough of me. How are you holding up?"

"Me? I'm doing fine, I guess." Natascha shrugged as she rotated her coffee cup in her hand. "I'm back to my normal health and I should be able to go diving again soon. Other than that, I'm taking it very easy, and I'm catching up on the time I missed with my daughter.”

“Yes, those were some tough days. Too bad I’m not allowed to write about that.” Kyle didn’t even try to hide his disappointment.

“Give it some time. Let them do their job. I’m sure it will still make a good story in a year or two.” Natascha tried to explain.

“You do know that I’m a reporter, right? Do you have any idea how difficult this is going to be?” Kyle laughed.

“I can imagine, but believe me, it is much safer for you this way. They are still looking for some of the scumbags.” Natascha’s mood shifted as she thought about Jonathan Brown.

“You’re right. I should be careful with my research. That’s how those bastards got me the first time.” Kyle finally agreed. “Listen, there is something I meant to ask you”, he said after he tried his coffee.

“Fire away.”

“With all the information you gave me, I think it is only fair that I mention you in the book. Would that be all right?” Kyle’s offer caught Natascha by surprise. She placed her own cup down, almost spilling some of her coffee.

“Wow, that is quite an honour. I don’t know what to say”, Natascha truthfully said and took a couple of moments to think about it. She couldn’t help but play with her new watch. Shira had insisted that she used one of those fitness gadgets with a real time GPS tracker. It had driven her friend mad not knowing where she had been at Whitmore Abbey. Natascha refused it initially, and it was only after Shira had threatened to wipe the floor with her in the combat room before she obliged. A useful tool, but for Natascha it was also a grim reminder that a certain someone was still out there looking for her. Natascha took another sip of coffee before she finally answered. “I really appreciate the offer, Kyle, but I think I have to decline. I would be rather happy if you do not mention me or my name in it at all.”

“Are you sure about that?” Kyle wondered.

“Yes, I am.” Natascha laughed. Now it was Kyle’s turn to be perplexed.

Natascha’s eyes fell on another couple walking into the cafeteria. They were casually dressed, but they seemed out of place.

“Well, my offer stands. Let me know if you change your mind”, Kyle smiled at her and rose from his seat.

The other couple just ordered some croissants and coffee.

“I appreciate it. We will definitely stay in touch.” Natascha said as they hugged again. She waited until Kyle was gone and placed some money on the table. She then took the empty cups and brought them to the counter, before she walked over to the couple.

“Hi Ariel. Talia! What are you two doing here?” Natascha wondered with an inquisitive grin.

“We need to talk”, her Israeli friend smiled.

***EuroSecCorporation*, London, Monday, September 15**
Natascha parked at her usual spot and hurried through the rain. She quickly slipped through the door, having so much momentum that she almost bumped into Lawrence.

"Hi, Lawrence", Natascha cheerfully greeted Brian's brother, who now shared his duties as maintenance worker with Charles MacLean.

"Oh, hi, good to see you. Still raining out there?" Lawrence asked and glanced out to the parking lot.

"Just the usual, it is not too bad." Natascha answered on her way to the daycare.

"As long as you don't go running in the park", Lawrence reminded her sternly.

"No, I promise." Natascha smiled sweetly and slipped through the door, relieved to find out that her daughter was taking her nap.

After exchanging the latest gossip, she made her way up the stairs, checking her cell phone for a message from Nick. Recovered from his injury and back on full duty, he had volunteered on short notice to fill in on a multi-day assignment. He was only gone since last Thursday, but Natascha missed him already, especially since they wanted to spend more time together around their daughter. To make matters worse, he was not expected to be back for another couple of days. Natascha made a face, seeing that Nick had not messaged her yet. She knew how difficult it was for him to reach her, but she was still disappointed. She just sent him a quick note and opened the door.

"Hi", she smiled at some of her friends before she made herself comfortable behind her desk. A quick glance at the clock showed her that she was just a few minutes early for her one o'clock start. The next thirty minutes were spent with a cup of tea and sorting through the incoming e-mails.

"Oh come on, don't get on my nerves." Natascha sipped from her cup, deleting another e-mail with unrealistic demands. She got distracted when Shira stormed from her office.

"Hey Shira. How–" Natascha started, but Shira cut her off.

"Since when did you know?" Shira briskly asked her. "Why didn't you tell me?" Her friend demanded to know. Shira's voice was nothing more than a hiss. She didn't even give Natascha the time to answer. Natascha couldn't remember the last time she had seen her best friend being so upset. It was quite obvious that Shira had figured out what Natascha had been hiding from her.

"You know why. I don't want to drag you into this. I almost got you killed once." Natascha truthfully answered. Shira just looked into her eyes, trying to figure out if she should believe her or not. Natascha held the stare.

"We have to tell Brian and Klaus." Shira decided, shaking her head.

"Why?" Natascha questioned immediately. "It is none of their business."

"None of their business?" Shira scoffed. She couldn't believe what she had just heard. "Do you have any idea how much they have risked for you?"

"Yes, I actually do", Natascha muttered bitterly. Shira had a point.

"You owe them that much, Natascha, and you know that." Shira continued, but Natascha just looked out of the window. A tear materialised in her eye.

"Does Nick know?" Shira asked softly. After all, she knew how much this troubled her friend. Natascha just shook her head. Shira said something in Hebrew.

"Oh dear God, Natascha." Natascha shrugged at the words. Shira was so stunned that she couldn't say anything else.

"How did you find out?" Natascha wanted to know, blowing her nose.

"He is my brother, Natascha. We share the same contacts. And he dragged Talia into this.”

“Talia? What did she do?” Now it was Natascha’s turn to look surprised.

“I’d rather not say”, Shira defended her friend as the elevator door opened. Klaus and Brian came back from lunch.

“Natascha, is everything okay? Did something happen?” Brian immediately asked, noticing the tears on her cheek. Natascha looked at Shira, but her friend remained silent, giving her the chance to explain herself.

“I’m fine, but there is something we have to talk about. In private.” Natascha finally started.

“Hm, okay. Just let me check my schedule”, Brian offered casually. He was already on his way to his office.

“No, Brian. We need to talk now.” Natascha said sternly. Brian stopped mid stride. It was the first time Natascha had taken the offer to call him by his first name, and he knew that she would have not done it if it wasn’t important. He exchanged a quick look with Klaus before he gestured to his office.

“So, what can I help you with?” Brian curiously looked at Natascha after sitting down.

“It is about my brother”, Shira started instead.

“What about Ariel? Is he in trouble?” Klaus wanted to know. His instincts told him that something big was about to happen.

“Last Thursday he and Talia took this week off. Talia stayed at his place, and I have not seen her since. This morning I had something to discuss with him. I waited until noon and checked in on him, but he is gone. He disappeared.” Shira added.

“How do you know that he disappeared? Is it not possible that they are just on a short vacation?” Brian asked. He didn’t quite share Shira’s concern for her brother just yet.

“No, I checked the embassy to see if he is there. I was told that he activated one of his old identities. He also got one for Talia. That means they are gone.”

“Since this morning?” Klaus wanted to know from Shira, but it was Natascha who answered.

“Actually he and Talia are gone since Thursday. They left together that afternoon. They stopped at the aquarium to tell me.” Natascha whispered. Shira’s jaw dropped. This was obviously news to her. Klaus and Brian exchanged a nervous look. The former general straightened up in his chair.

“Since Thursday? You knew this?” Shira almost yelled. Klaus raised his hand.

“From the beginning”, the former general ordered. “Shira, what do you know?”

Shira stared at Natascha who simply nodded.

“Do you remember when Gregor Powell gave us that laptop with the information about Sir Cunningham?” the Israeli finally started.

“Yes.”

“Well, apparently Ariel had Talia install a sleeper software in it before they gave it back.”

“In English, please.”

“The software allowed him to log into the laptop and bypass MI5’s firewall to hack into their database with Powell’s security clearance.” Shira exhaled sharply with a stern look at Natascha.

"He better didn't do that from this building", Brian growled at her. It was only now that the possible legal consequences of Ariel's actions slowly dawned on Natascha. The word *espionage* came to her mind. She had the scary feeling that her next meeting with the intelligence manager of MI5 would not be as pleasant as their previous ones.

"I honestly don't know what access he used, but I'm certain it wasn't from here", Shira tried to reassure Brian, but it was little comfort.

"This keeps getting better and better", Brian growled and looked at Klaus.

"Do you know what your brother was after?" Klaus inquired, his eyes trying to read the young Israeli woman.

"I asked Ariel for a favour. It is my fault. He is trying to help me", Natascha whispered instead. Brian and Klaus just stared at her. The look on their faces reflected the seriousness of the situation. Slowly, Natascha continued. "Ariel used Powell's computer to access the information MI5 has on *Asklepios.*"

"Dear Lord! Natascha, do you even have the slightest–" Brian growled, but Klaus just raised his hand.

"Please, Brian, that will not help us. Natascha, continue, please."

"Ariel found out that MI5 interrogated one of the guards from *Asklepios.* An American by the name of Kurt Morrison."

"And?"

"He is the guard I tasered when I tried to escape."

"The one you tied up in your cell?" Brian wanted to clarify.

"Yes, that's the one. He didn't know too much about what was really going on, but his girlfriend did. She was one of the nurses who was deeply involved in everything that was going on."

"You met her?"

"Oh yeah, I met her. Melissa O'Brian. I still owe that red-haired bitch a beating", Natascha growled her disgust for her favourite nurse. She straightened herself up before she continued. "She didn't miss an opportunity to hit or insult me. It turns out that her older brother used to be a reporter. He fell victim to ISIS rebels during an assignment in Syria. Melissa went berserk on the internet about it and even used the dark web looking for opportunities to get back at them. I assume that's how the people behind *Asklepios* found her." Natascha paused for a moment to let the information sink in. "Anyway, when the British Navy stormed *Asklepios,* she was missing, besides one Victor Gates and another couple. The couple were Walter Leroy Jackson and his wife Samantha."

"Are those their real names? I thought they only used aliases in their files, and that it would take months to identify them." Brian wanted to know.

"I don't know if Ariel found out himself or if MI5 did, but Ariel discovered that Samantha Jackson was in desperate need for a new kidney, and that she couldn't get one in the States. He could track their passports from the States to Greece and Turkey a couple of times. Turned out those dates matched with their presence on the ship according to the patient files with their alias. I saw a fat guy in his late fifties or early sixties. Always wearing this stupid cowboy hat. Ariel showed me a picture and it was

Jackson." Natascha's face reflected the hatred she felt for this man. Brian and Klaus exchanged a quick look, giving her the time she needed before she could continue.

"Jackson is an American oil tycoon. I had no idea, but Ariel found out that he used to be one of Jonathan Brown's closest business partners before Brown switched to politics." Natascha revealed casually, but for everybody else it was surprising news. Klaus straightened up even more.

"Are you sure about that?" He hesitantly asked.

"Oh yeah, I'm sure about it. Back on the ship, Jackson was always with another patient. One Victor Gates." Natascha almost spit the name. "Gates was confined to the wheelchair permanently. Severe burn wounds. In desperate need of a new lung and some other organs." Natascha kept staring at a blank spot on the table. Brian and Klaus exchanged another glance. They did not miss the lack of sympathy Natascha expressed for this guy. "That bastard even survived an execution style gunshot wound to the head, before his damn hunting cabin collapsed on him during the fire. Somehow he crawled out of it."

Shira's jaw fell open. Brian showed the same reaction, and even Klaus couldn't hide the surprise of this revelation. By now they all knew who Natascha was talking about.

"Ariel assumes that Jackson pulled some strings back then to get Brown out of the country and to have the whole mess covered up. When I didn't keep my mouth shut towards that abbot about the bones I found while diving, Hetley panicked. Ariel found out that Sir Cunningham visited Whitmore Abbey shortly later, and he thinks that Hetley told Cunningham about me and the risk I posed to their operation, should that damn bacteria ever be traced back to them. Once I was on the ship, I used Talia's name, but Jackson knew who I really was. You want to know what he did next?" Natascha asked, for the first time looking up and into their faces.

"He gave me as a present to that monster. So he could torture me to brighten up his day. That's what he did!" Someone could have heard a pin drop in the office. They were too shocked to say anything, so Natascha continued. "I knew that my time was running out, so I tried to escape before they could hurt me, but I got caught. This was at the same time you guys snatched Rowan. They started to panic and jumped ship. Jackson just wanted to kill me right away, but Jonathan insisted that I suffer. While I was on a stretcher, Dr Evans prepared an IV with the plague bacteria. Jonathan injected it himself into my arm. Jackson just stood there and watched. My lights went out and when I woke up I was on the *Shadow.*" Natascha finished. The hatred in her face had made room for sadness. She straightened up. "Nick doesn't know about any of this, and I want to keep it like that. He has suffered enough because of me."

"That's why you confided to Ariel. Because he visited Jonathan back then", Shira concluded.

"Yes, I mean we all suspected it was him, right?" Natascha grimaced shyly.

"Why didn't you tell me?" Shira wanted to know.

"I told you before. You almost got killed once because of me. So did Nick. You have both suffered enough because of me. You all have! Especially my daughter!" Natascha firmly stated.

"So what is this favour you asked Ariel for?" Brian asked. He had a pretty good idea what it was, but he wanted to hear it from Natascha.

"You want him to kill them, right?" Shira said. She sounded upset. "You knew that he would feel guilty once you told him. You knew that he couldn't say no!" Shira accused her best friend and stood up. Brian and Klaus were just bystanders now. Natascha slowly looked up. Her eyes locked with Shira's.

"So what?" Natascha asked coldly. "I'm tired of running. Besides, I don't want him to kill them."

"Oh, you don't? And why do I not believe that?"

"I just want him to find them."

"For what? You want to press charges?" Shira refused to believe her.

"No! So that I can kill them myself." Natascha threatened. The room fell silent. Shira was lost for words. This was not the Natascha they knew. "You know the mess I was in after getting over the plague, Shira. You know how helpless and frustrated I felt because I couldn't do anything."

"Looking at Whitmore Abbey, someone could disagree", Shira said.

"It is not about them, Shira. It is about *him*!" Natascha stood up and started pacing Brian's office. "I can't keep living like this. He is half dead and sitting in a wheelchair, yet he still managed to get his hands on me. He infected me with the plague, for Christ sake!" Natascha unravelled her frustrations and found herself standing at the window overlooking the parking lot. "Last time my best friend got shot, and we all thought you were gone. This time it was Nick. We had to fake my own death." Natascha shook her head. "I thought I could manage it, but thinking that he can get his hands on my daughter-" Natascha's voice broke. She didn't dare to continue. "You and Ariel trained me the last couple of years. I think I changed. I did things at Whitmore Abbey I never thought I would ever be able to do, but as long as he is still alive, we will always have to look over our shoulder and innocent people will get hurt. The world is better off without that bastard."

"No argument there", Shira agreed. "But what on Earth makes you think that you can kill him? What do you think is going to happen? That my brother gives you a call once he finds him? That he sits back, waiting for you to show up in whatever part of the world that might be?"

"I...I don't know yet", Natascha stammered. She had to agree that this part of her revenge needed some fine tuning.

"What if they are in the States? Please don't tell me that you think you could *actually* cross that border. You have no idea what will happen to you should you ever set foot on American soil."

"I know that I can't go there. I–"

"And what about your family? You want me to babysit your daughter, sitting on the couch, watching a movie with your husband, while you are out there plotting your revenge?"

"No, but I know that I–"

"No, Natascha. You don't know. And you are hoping that Ariel will do the dirty work for you. What happened in the Arctic was self-defence, don't you ever get that wrong. Just because you took some self-defence lessons does not mean you are a trained assassin. That's not you! And trust me, you definitely do not want to be like that!" Shira stormed out of the office, leaving a stunned Natascha behind.

Brian frowned and threw a doubtful look at Klaus. The former general had yet to show any emotion.

"What a mess", Brian finally shook his head, this time looking at Natascha. "How much time you think we got before Powell finds out?" The former admiral wondered and walked over to the window. His mind was spinning.

"Based on what I have just heard, I believe that Ariel found something important on Thursday. Knowing Powell, I'd say he is already assembling the firing squad. Couple of hours max." Klaus confirmed what Brian feared.

"That's what I thought. How the bloody hell are we going to get out of this one?" Brian's eyes scanned the parking lot, as if the answer to his problem would present itself there.

"We can't. Not out of this one." Klaus destroyed any hopes his friend might have had.

"You are such a damn realist." Brian growled.

"I might have an idea or two", Klaus shrugged.

"Any of them good?"

"Not really. I need more time."

Natascha had followed their conversation without taking part in it. Shira's words weighed too heavy on her conscience. Her friend was right, and Natascha felt stupid for letting her hatred cloud her judgment like that. Not only the risk she had put her friends in, but the dooming legal consequences for Brian and Klaus were too overwhelming.

"Is it okay if I go?" She finally broke the silence that was hanging over them.

"Yes, Natascha, you can go", Brian whispered. The disappointment in his voice made Natascha flinch. She slowly walked to the door and pulled it open.

"I will be either at my desk or in the gym", she whispered, but Brian just nodded. "I don't know if it means anything, but I am sorry." She finally apologised.

"I know, Natascha, I know. Unfortunately that won't help us." Brian said without even looking at her.

"Let us know if you are going to leave the building, okay?" Klaus told her. Natascha had to swallow. She was too ashamed to look at Klaus and stared at the floor instead. "And don't call Nick yet. Let me see first what I can do."

Natascha simply nodded and left the office.

"Don't tell me that you really think we can get out of this one?" Brian turned towards Klaus once Natascha had left.

"I don't", Klaus shook his head.

"Shall we call him?"

"No, let him come to us. Let me do the talking", Klaus suggested. Brian didn't seem to be convinced. He made a face and sat down again, desperately looking for a solution.

Somewhere in the Swiss Alps, Monday, September 15

"Are we there yet?" Talia exhaled and straightened up to catch her breath. The thirty pounds backpack took its toll after hours of hiking through dense forest in the alpine mountain regions.

"Almost. How did you make it through boot camp?" Ariel smiled at her, but he showed little mercy and pushed on.

"All I'm saying is that we could slow down a little bit to take in the landscape. This forest is actually quite beautiful." Talia explained and took a deep breath, inhaling the clean air. She sat down the backpack and took her water bottle from a side pocket. "Ah, that feels good", she commented after a few sips. "Want some?" She asked and showed Ariel the bottle.

"Why not?" Ariel caught the bottle. He also looked around, admiring the view over the mountain lake in the distance. The weather forecast predicted heavy rainfall later that day, and the first clouds were already rolling in. While most tourists didn't like the forecast, it was perfect for Ariel's and Talia's mission. Ariel almost emptied the bottle and tossed it back to Talia. The young Israeli stowed it back into her backpack.

"Oh, you almost came off", she commented and retied her hiking boots to the backpack. Before they had left the main hiking trail about twenty kilometres ago, they had switched to special shoes with a flat, soft sole, which made it much more difficult to track. They also changed from their regular hiking clothes into camouflage wear, making them more or less invisible to the untrained eye. Since then they had played every trick in the book of an assassination sniper, utilising mountain ranges, deer paths and brooks to their advantage.

"This is it?" Talia asked, this time more serious after hiking for another twenty minutes. They had just crossed the mountain ridge.

"Yes, that is it." Ariel confirmed. The couple looked over a beautiful valley.

A couple hundred metres below, a brook divided the two hillsides before flowing into a picturesque mountain lake in the distance. The old spruce and juniper trees looked like a dark green sea and gave the scenery a majestic touch. There was really no better place for the private clinic, towering atop of the opposite hillside overlooking the mountain lake and endless forest.

"Oh, this is so beautiful." Talia marvelled at the sight. "You are sure this is a hospital?"

"Yes, this is the place. Let's do this." Ariel said and they both removed their backpacks. They carefully unfolded a camouflaged tarp on the ground. No one spoke for the next couple of minutes. It took Ariel only a few moments to assemble his sniper rifle while Talia scanned the area with her range finding scope. Ariel unfolded the bipod and mounted the laser scope on his rifle.

"Well, not exactly what I had in mind when you promised me a romantic picnic in a wooded mountain area", Talia said after a while and laid down beside Ariel.

"Don't worry, love, it will get better." Ariel responded easily, then began a new beat, "Okay, tell me what you see." Ariel tested her. He placed a few different bullets beside his rifle, not sure yet which one to use.

"Okay. Let's see", Talia started and looked through her range finder. "Only one road to the hospital, at least eight kilometres long, leading down to the village by the lake. Only way in and out with a motorised vehicle." Talia reported, and then mumbled, "I guess that explains why we are not doing a drive-by shooting."

"This is not the Middle-East. They would have the road blocked long before we get on the main street. What else?"

"Okay, we are located to the south of the hospital, so even if someone is looking in this direction, they will be looking at the sun. None of our gear can reflect the sun if it is at our backs. No risk of enemy sniper fire, so that is going to be easy. The hillside will echo the shot, but it will also be more difficult for them to determine where it came from. According to the flags on the castle, there is a slight wind from the East, you might have to adjust for that."

"Good. Now take the range finder down." Ariel smiled at her. "Distance to target?"

Talia smiled back. She liked it when Ariel tested her. She looked back at the hospital. "Okay, I'd say four-hundred-twenty metres to the main entrance", she finally noted.

"No, that's at least four-hundred-sixty", Ariel whispered.

"Want to bet?" Talia pushed him.

"Sure. Loser pays for dinner?"

"Fine with me!" Talia agreed and handed him her scope. "Here, see for yourself why I finished top of my class at sniper training." The confidence in her voice could not be missed.

"Four-hundred-and-eighteen metres", Ariel admitted with amazement. "I am impressed." Ariel selected a bullet based on their assessment.

"No, take this one", Talia shook her head and pointed at a different one. "Your altitude drop is only fifty metres, and you have the wind at the hospital. This one here is faster."

"Technically you are correct, my love, but this is my rifle, my scope, and that's the bullet I'm comfortable with."

"You're the one taking the shot", Talia shrugged and picked up her scope again. "And you're so old school", she mumbled afterwards, teasingly.

"I heard that." Ariel informed her and started to polish the projectile.

"So do we know where he is?" She wanted to know a minute later.

"Yes, we do. Brown has the private suite on the forth flour, southwest corner."

"Okay, got it. Four-hundred-and-twelve metres to the balcony."

"Anyone on it?" Ariel asked as he chambered the round into his rifle.

"No, not on the balcony, but I can see some movement behind the glass. The balcony door is open. You are not planning to shoot through the window, or? We don't know how thick it is, and I do not have a clear identification."

"No, not going through the window. With this weather, he will come to the balcony sooner or later."

"Will he be alone?"

"Jackson is not here. The only person with him is Melissa O'Brian. We are not going after her unless she gets in our way."

"She is the red-head, isn't she?"

"Yes."

"Okay, I got a visual on her, but I can't see what she's doing."

"Affirmative", Ariel commented and adjusted his scope to the balcony.

"Our first picnic and I end up being a spotter for you. What is wrong with this world?" Talia complained as she continued to look through the scope.

"Oh, come on. You don't find this romantic?" Ariel toyed.

"No, not really, to be honest. Tell me again, why are we doing this? Please tell me that it's not because of Natascha."

"It is not because of Natascha. Well, maybe a tiny little bit. You will be surprised to know that this is not the first time I'm trying to kill him."

"Oh, so *that's* why you are so tense. Now I understand. It's about your pride." Talia determined with a little more bitterness than necessary. Ariel threw her a disapproving glance.

"Okay, if not pride, what is the other reason?"

"I get the chance to take out a guy who infected innocent young women with the plague, before he sold them as slaves. Is that a good enough reason for you?"

"Yes, I can live with that, even if he can't. So what's the rush? He's clearly not going anywhere in the condition that he's in."

"I want to shoot him before the Brits get a chance to mess this up."

"You think they will shoot him?" Talia sounded surprised.

"No, not really. I think that they will try something stupid, like poisoning him."

"In a place like that? That will take weeks just for the infiltration." Talia objected.

"And that's why I love you!" Ariel smiled. He leaned over to give her a quick kiss.

"That's the only reason?" Talia sounded disappointed. Ariel just laughed.

"No, there are a couple more."

Talia admired him for a moment, the look in his eyes melting her. She bit her lip before she snapped out of her reverie. "Let's get this over with!" Talia enthusiastically said and picked up her cell phone. She pressed the speed dial button and let it ring four times before she ended the call. She had just signalled that they were ready and in position. Thirty seconds later, her phone rang in return. They both looked with anticipation at the screen. It rang once, twice, three times, and even a fourth time, but then the call ended.

"Great, Nick is in position. Now we wait!" Ariel answered and made himself comfortable again behind his rifle.

Roughly six-hundred metres from the Israeli sniper nest, and more or less twelve hundred kilometres from where Natascha thought he would be, Nick laid his cell phone down. So far he had spent the better part of the day approaching the hospital from the opposite mountain ridge. Just like his friends, the trees protected his own position from being discovered. With a clear line of fire to the park-like garden on the back side, the hospital was now covered from both sides. Should Jonathan Brown decide to go to the park instead of the balcony, he would still be in the crosshairs. The worst case scenario would be if Jonathan Brown would not come out at all, forcing Nick to penetrate the hospital grounds through the park. Undetected from the surveillance cameras and guards at the main entrance, he would simply pull the fire alarm and set off a smoke grenade, forcing his wife's arch nemesis into the open. With his mind set, Nick opened a picture of Natascha and his daughter on his cell phone.

"Sorry I lied to you, angel", Nick whispered before he started scanning the patients in the park through the scope.

Watching a football game in his suite, Jonathan Brown had no idea about the deadly web that was spun around him. His favoured team was up fourteen points, with only two minutes to go, and that was all that mattered to him at the moment. Melissa was in her nearby room. Her worries after fleeing *Asklepios* were eased by now. Accepting her new position at Jonathan Brown's side, she realised rather quickly that there wasn't much that money couldn't buy. A new life and identity certainly were no problem. At first, she had been overwhelmed by this facility, which was so nicely nestled inside the Swiss Alps, but now she felt like it was her home. The only thing she missed from *Asklepios* was her fling. She had no idea what had happened to Kurt, but knowing him, she wouldn't be surprised to hear that he got killed trying to fight off some special forces. Melissa sorrowfully shook her head thinking back at her time with him. She waved her memories aside when she heard Jonathan asking for her.

"Yes, I'm coming", Melissa replied and appeared just a few seconds later from her room.

"What is the weather like?" Jonathan asked over his speech computer in his John Wayne voice. The Irish nurse walked out on the balcony and looked at the sky.

"It's cloudy. I think it will start raining within the next hour. You want to go outside for a bit?" Melissa tried to encourage him.

"What time is it?"

"Almost three thirty. You should really go outside. They are calling for rain for most of the week."

"I was thinking about it. Can you please help me?" Jonathan asked.

"Of course", Melissa smiled at Jonathan, ignoring the frustration in his voice. It took them about half an hour to get ready, but Jonathan finally steered his wheelchair away from the bed.

"Just wait a second, please. I have to connect the oxygen tank", Melissa slowed him down. Only a few moments later, Jonathan enjoyed the clean mountain air. His eyes wandered along the trees on the hill side before they rested on the mountain lake in the distance. He didn't know why, but the water always did something magical for him.

"This is so beautiful", Melissa spoke what both were thinking. Jonathan just nodded and exhaled deeply. Up in the hillside and under the protection of the trees, Jonathan's face was clearly visible through the scope. The laser dot, only visible inside the scope adjusted itself after measuring the distance, showing the shooter exactly where the projectile would hit. Only a small adjustment was needed to compensate for the wind before the index finger found the trigger. Less than three pounds trigger weight was now all that stood between life and death.

***EuroSecCorporation*, London, Monday, September 15**
Natascha first thought that she would feel better after confessing to Klaus and Brian, but the guilt she felt after learning about the possible consequences of her selfish

vendetta weighed heavily on her mind. On top of that, the damage she had done to her friendship with Shira weighed even more. She had absolutely no idea how to fix that. With her mind spinning, she kept staring at her computer for almost half an hour, but she didn't even recognise what she was looking at.

"I can't work like that", she cursed and changed into her gym clothes. Determined to blow off some steam, she walked to the combat room and was glad to find it empty. Natascha picked a playlist from her cell phone and inserted her ear buds. For a moment she contemplated her cell phone, debating with herself whether to call Nick or not, but she finally decided against it. There was no need to lose the little bit of trust Klaus and Brian had left in her. With the music playing, she started to work the bag. It took her a couple of minutes before she finally slowed down. She kept throwing a couple more punches and kicks sporadically, before she stopped to pick up her towel. Natascha cursed. She thought unleashing her frustration on the bag would help alleviate her thoughts. But even as she was wiping the sweat from her face, she caught herself still thinking about the mess she was in and how she could possibly explain that to Nick. Frustrated that she couldn't even imagine a positive outcome, she threw the towel to the ground and turned around.

"Oh my God!" Natascha shrieked when she finally saw Shira at the door. Her friend apologetically raised her arms and stepped closer. Natascha stopped the music.

"I'm sorry, I didn't want to startle you, but you didn't hear me with your music on." Shira began her apology.

"No, problem. Shira...I don't know what to–" Natascha started, but Shira cut her off.

"I want to apologise, Natascha."

"You? Apologise for what?" Natascha didn't understand. That was the last thing she expected.

"Listen to me!" Shira told her and took her by the arm. Natascha let Shira drag her to the window. "We do not have much time, Powell and his men are already on their way. They will be here shortly." Shira explained with a stern voice.

"How do you know that?" Natascha was puzzled.

"It doesn't matter. Listen! There is something you have to know."

"What?"

"I'm sorry that I yelled at you in front of them, but I had no choice. Do you understand?"

"No, I do not", Natascha admitted, but she felt that Shira was sincere.

"I saw Klaus and Brian coming back from their lunch, so I knew that they would be passing your desk shortly after. I'm sorry Brian saw you crying, but that was the only way he would talk to us right away."

"So...you're telling me that you knew all along?" Natascha didn't know whether she should feel bad about this or not.

"In all fairness, Ariel tried to hide it, but given the fact that I'm still sharing a place with his new girlfriend, who also happens to be my protégé, and that I am good at what I'm doing, yes, I figured it out. He also admitted it when I asked him."

"So, why didn't you tell me? Why didn't *he* tell me?"

"Isn't that obvious?" Now it was Shira who was puzzled.

"No, not really." Natascha made a face.

"To protect you!"

"To protect me? From what?"

"Brian, Klaus, MI5, everyone." Shira started and nervously looked outside the window to see if Powell was already in the parking lot. Satisfied that this was not yet the case, she looked at Natascha again. "It is better if Brian and Klaus think that you did this out of revenge and for your family. They can understand that. I think they actually respect that, and they will do all they can to keep you clear from any legal consequences."

"But I–"

"Natascha, listen to me. We're not talking about hacking a computer, we are talking about espionage within the British Military Intelligence. They are taking that very seriously, and it is much better to have Brian and Klaus on your side. You understand that?" Natascha nodded. She had to swallow. The severity of the consequences overwhelmed her again. "The best thing that can happen for you, is–" Shira started, but her eyes fell on the three black Jaguars entering their parking lot at a significant speed. Two of them drove to the front entry, the third one drove around to cover the rear fire escape. Shira cursed in Hebrew.

"What are we going to do now?" Natascha panicked as several men exited the vehicles. Shira grabbed her by her arm again and spun her around.

"Listen! There is no more time. Do you forgive me?"

"What?"

"Do you forgive me?"

"Yes, of course I do, why–"

"Do you trust me?" Shira cut her off, her eyes scanning the door.

"Shira, what is this about?" Natascha didn't really understand.

"Do you trust me?" Shira repeated. Natascha finally relaxed.

"Of course I trust you, Shira."

Shira looked Natascha deep in her eyes. "Then let me handle this, okay?"

Gregor Powell took the stairs with determination, casually glancing at the laptop under his left hand. Brian personally waited for him at the top of the stairs. He had obviously seen the cars as well.

"Good afternoon, Greg. We have been waiting for you. Why don't you come in?"

"Brian!" Powell acknowledged his friend with an icy tone and walked through the door. To Brian's surprise, the MI5 agent was by himself.

"No firing squad?" Brian murmured and looked down the staircase. Powell didn't comment on it. He briskly walked towards Brian's office.

"Klaus!" He simply greeted the former general before he sat down.

"Gregor." Klaus nodded. Brian closed the door behind him.

"You might want to get Shira and Natascha before we start. I assume Ariel and Talia are currently missing or not available?"

Brian couldn't help but flinch at Powell's demand. He was way too informed for Brian's liking. The former admiral just nodded and found the two women moments later in the combat room.

"The inquisition has started. He demands your presence", Brian told them. Natascha and Shira exchanged a quick look. Panic rose inside Natascha as she followed Brian back to his office.

"Don't say anything!" Shira whispered a stern warning to her friend. They were both surprised to see that Powell was by himself. Natascha's stomach churned at the sight of the familiar laptop the intelligence manager placed on the table. The atmosphere in the office could be described as icy at best.

"This is a secure room?" Powell wanted to know and looked at Brian and Klaus.

"Yes, it is." Brian replied.

"Very well. I guess you all know why I'm here, right?" Powell asked and checked for a file on his computer.

"We might have an idea", Brian growled. Powell threw him a disapproving look before he started a video on his laptop. He turned the device so that everyone could see the screen.

"This video was taken from a security camera at a private hospital in the Swiss Alps about one hour ago." Powell explained. They silently watched the footage of a camera showing a door leading to a park-like garden. For several seconds they only saw a few people moving along. Underneath the table, Shira took Natascha's hand and held it firmly. The video footage showed several people suddenly looking at an exploding fireball further down in the park. Powell noticed how Natascha flinched at the explosion and stopped the footage.

"At four twenty-five local time, something that you would describe as *another tragic accident* occurred inside the recreational garden of this private clinic. What looks like a horrible accident was in our opinion a well executed assassination", Powell started and continued to play the footage. The next sequence showed an enhanced image in slow motion. It was difficult to see, but they could all make out a person in a wheel-chair, as well as a second person right beside him. The following seconds showed a sudden movement from the standing person, before they disappeared in an explosion.

"It is safe to say that those two didn't survive the attack. In fact, they are still looking for some of their remains, but luckily there was no one else injured." Powell commented and looked at Natascha. He knew that Klaus, Brian and Shira wouldn't show any reaction at all.

"Any idea what happened?" Klaus inquired.

"Not really, I can only guess. Several patients claimed to have heard something like a shot just a second before the explosion. That would explain why they all looked at the poor guy in the wheelchair. My theory is that someone–" Powell threw an accusing look at both women, "–executed him with a long range rifle. Second shot was a tracer round into the oxygen tank attached to the wheelchair. The explosion covered the actual echo of the second shot." Powell theorised and looked at their faces. "Am I getting close so far?" he asked. No one said anything. They just looked at him in return, except for Natascha. Her eyes were glued to the monitor. Somehow she didn't feel sorry, her familiar feeling of hatred started to swell up from deep inside her. It didn't go unnoticed to Powell. "I see you are wondering if that was *him*." He commented and started another video file. "Or should I say *hoping*?" Shira squeezed Natascha's hand, signalling her to remain silent. "This footage here is from five minutes before the explosion. See who is driving his wheelchair through the doors, followed by his personal nurse?" Natascha tried not to show any emotion, but couldn't help twist her mouth at the clear and enhanced footage of Jonathan Brown and Melissa O'Brian. Even the small oxygen tank on the side of the wheelchair was clearly recognisable. Natascha started shaking. She didn't know why, but she was so relieved that tears started running down her face.

"Yes, it was him. And Melissa O'Brian", Powell confirmed as he scrutinised Natascha's face. To everyone's surprise, Powell closed the laptop and got up. "So, off the record, I want to thank you for doing our job, but I would appreciate it if you let us handle this in the future."

Klaus frowned. Like everyone else in the room he felt like he was missing something.

"Yes, that is it." Powell noticed. "Oh, I assume you're wondering about the espionage. No, we are not pressing charges. Fact is, we consider Jonathan Brown to be a terrorist. Infecting young women with the plague to use them in his biological warfare against ISIS? Doesn't look good in our books. Not to mention the illegal organ trade and that he helped Cunningham bringing the bacteria back on British soil." The intelligence manager casually explained. "Like I said, thank you for doing our job."

"Come again?" Brian couldn't hide his surprise. "Are you telling me that you used my people, my company, to do your dirty work?"

Powell smiled knowingly and tucked his laptop under his arm before exiting the room, leaving everyone else stunned. It took a while before the reality sank in.

Shira shook her head. "Damn, he played us", she laughed, overwhelmed by the relief she felt. She had expected much worse.

"Bloody hell, did he ever", Brian commented and watched from the window as the three cars left again.

"Can someone please tell me what is going on?" Natascha finally asked. She realised she was lacking some finesse in the world of spooks.

"Greg knows our company. He knows that we employ a former Mossad assassination team", Brian started and threw a quick glance at Shira.

"I grew up in a bad neighbourhood", Shira smiled coldly, but Brian ignored her.

"We had to strike a deal with him over Rowan Harrison's disappearance. Once he learned how far we went for getting you back, he must have realised that he could let us do the dirty work for him."

"He handed Ariel a laptop with sensitive information about Cunningham", Klaus continued. "Powell knows about Ariel's past, and that he would not be able to resist using that laptop to gain access to MI5's database. It is safe to say that they let him only find the information relevant to locating Jonathan Brown. He knew how fierce you were about your revenge. He realised that during the two debriefings we had."

"Nick always says that my temper will get me in trouble", Natascha apologised.

"Yes, it is quite uncommon that someone cuts an intelligence manager from MI5 off, but you did it a couple of times", Brian added. "Anyway, he let Ariel find all the information he needed to get to Jonathan Brown. After that, all he had to do was sit back and let him finish the job for them.”

"I didn’t see that one coming", Klaus admitted and shook his head.

"And the best thing is that Natascha had nothing to do with the laptop." Shira laughed. Brian looked at her.

"Yeah, nice touch to keep her out of this", the former admiral growled. "Now get out", he added. Natascha still tried to process what had just happened, but Shira just pulled her up and led her out.

"Natascha!" Brian stopped her at the door. "Never disappoint me like this again! If you have an issue, you come to us. You don’t go behind our back. Understood?" Brian barked. Natascha nodded and followed Shira out. Brian sat down behind his desk again, looking at Klaus.

"They played us like a bloody fiddle", he finally determined.

"That they did", Klaus admittedly nodded. "But better to get played than getting charged with espionage. They did it right in front of us."

"They all did! Natascha did it, our former assassins did it, Powell did it. Bloody hell, I wouldn’t be surprised if the mail man is playing us. I’m really thinking I’m getting too old for this."

Nick’s and Natascha’s house, just outside London, Monday, September 15
Natascha carefully closed the door to her daughter’s bedroom. Shira-Sarah had a hard time going to sleep, most likely because of how nervous Natascha had been all day.

"Finally!" Natascha exhaled and walked back into the living room. Shira smiled at her from the couch and opened another wine bottle. Natascha lounged beside her, still shaking her head after reflecting on today’s events.

"God! I still can’t believe that this is all over now. I was kind of careless." Natascha took the bottle. It was only now that she realised she had forgotten to bring the glasses again. She just shrugged and, as with the first one, drank from the bottle.

"Kind of careless?" Shira laughed and took the bottle back. Natascha made a face. "You almost got everyone from Operation Control arrested for espionage. Careless is not the word I would be using."

"Ah, come on, it wasn’t *that* bad", Natascha tried to laugh. The fact that her best friend was sitting beside her on the couch laughing was such a relief. The bottle of wine she was taking a couple more generous swigs from certainly contributed to this feeling.

"You tried to burn down a historic abbey, caused half a million in damage to Cunningham’s and the Vatican’s fleet, and you talked us into espionage. It’s a miracle they didn’t burn us at the stake."

"Well, if you put it like that", Natascha admitted with a chuckle and handed the bottle back to her friend. By now it was already half empty. "Thank you Shira! For everything! Without you, this all would have ended differently." She added as seriously as she could. Her Israeli friend just waved her off and read the label on the bottle again.

"Never mind. I just couldn’t keep watching how you tore yourself up any more." Shira took a couple generous gulps.

"Yeah, but still. I owe you. Big time. Again, I might add."

"And one day I will collect, but today is not that day. Today we celebrate!" Shira proclaimed, taking another sip. The bottle was almost empty. She handed it back to Natascha.

"I don't know what I'm going to tell Nick", Natascha shook her head. This time it was her turn to read the label. Something she felt she should have done before. "Oh, this is strong hooch", Natascha slandered the wine, already noticing its effect. It didn't keep her from taking another sip. "I mean, he basically lied to me. He went behind my back to work with you guys", Natascha stated and floored the bottle. Shira was already at their little liquor cabinet.

"What is this?" The Israeli asked and held up a bottle of Bailey's.

"That?" Natascha took a closer look. Not being used to drinking any amount of alcohol at all, she was already tipsy. "Oh, that is good stuff. We got it as a present. Bring it over", Natascha demanded and placed the empty wine bottle on the end table. "Where was I?" She restarted, watching how Shira opened the bottle. The Israeli first took a sniff. Satisfied, she took a sip before handing the bottle to Natascha. "Right!" Her best friend continued, finally remembering what she wanted to say. "Nick! He went behind my back. And he didn't go alone either. He worked with Ariel and Talia." Natascha complained and also took a generous sip. She closed her eyes and kept the Irish whiskey cream in her mouth, handing the bottle back to Shira.

"He went as much behind your back as you did behind his." Shira defended him and took the next sip. She also noticed the effects of the alcohol by now. "If anything, you should be thankful!"

Another sip.

Natascha looked at her and demanded the bottle.

"Yeah, I am. Can't really complain about him, can I?" Natascha made a face with the next gulp. She read the label. "Wow, this stuff is strong. Maybe we should use glasses", Natascha contemplated, but decided that it was already too late for that and took another swig instead.

"No, you cannot complain about him. Look at what he did for you", Shira lectured and took the bottle from her, allowing herself another generous drink. "When he comes home, you should–" Shira frowned and looked at her watch. "When is he getting home?" The liquor had already its affect on Shira, who couldn't even remember when she had had the last alcoholic beverage.

"How the hell should I know? They have their cell phones turned off. You're the spook! Gimme that!" Natascha complained and took possession of the bottle for a couple more sips.

"Right, given the success of the mission, Nick would leave Switzerland through the German border. From there he would take the next flight to London from Munich. It shouldn't be much longer."

"Oh my God! How is he going to get the rifle on the plane?" Natascha suddenly seriously wondered. Her mind was clearly clouded by now. She handed the bottle back to her friend.

"No problem", Shira waved her off, taking another sip. "Standard procedure for Ariel and Talia would be to retreat to the embassy in Bern. The weapons will be shipped as diplomatic parcels."

"Oh, I see", Natascha said. It all seemed to make sense to her now.

"So, do you know what you're going to tell him?" Shira still wanted to know, taking another sip before she handed the now almost empty bottle back to Natascha.

"Oh, yes! I do! When he comes home, I will tell him that I know that he collabo-... collaba-...worked behind my back, and that I forgive him, and that he is the best husband in the world. And then he and I will go to the bedroom...and then we will...well, you know what we will do." Natascha said and floored the Bailey's bottle as well.

"That's what you're going to tell him?" Shira laughed at her. "Where do you get your motivational speeches from? A fortune cookie?" The Israeli guffawed, but before Natascha could even answer, they heard the door opening.

"That better be him, because I'm too drunk to kick someone's ass!" Natascha commented and looked at the door. Shira kept laughing.

"What did I miss?" Nick chuckled at the sight of the empty bottles and the intoxicated women. Natascha had to concentrate, but she finally managed to stand up as Shira used the opportunity to make herself comfortable on the couch.

"I hope you missed me!" Natascha greeted him with a kiss.

"Of course I did, angel!" Nick embraced her.

"Tell him, Natascha!" Shira demanded from the couch. She was almost done building her nest with all the pillows.

"Okay! I will!" Natascha looked at her friend and shook her head at the sight. "Nick! There is something I have to tell you!" She concentrated, looking into Nick's eyes.

"Yes, angel, what is it?" Nick had a hard time staying serious at their sight.

"I know what you have done, and I just want you to know that..." Natascha started, but totally forgot what she wanted to say. She helplessly looked at Shira, who was now comfortably curled up on the couch, ready to fall asleep. The Israeli looked at her in anticipation.

"Ah, what the heck", Natascha turned back to Nick. "All you need to know is that I love you more than ever!" She eventually managed and kissed him passionately.

"See, that wasn't too bad!" Shira commented and closed her eyes.